Anne Mather

Anne Mather was first published by Mills & Boon in 1969. Now, with over one hundred novels to her name, she has established herself as a writer of great international acclaim—her books are loved by romance readers everywhere.

Anne Mather began writing when she was a child, progressing through torrid teenage romances to the kind of adult romances she likes to read. She's married, with two grown-up children, and she lives in the north-east of England where she was born. Apart from writing, Anne enjoys reading, driving, and travelling to different places to find settings for new novels. She considers herself very lucky to do something that she not only enjoys but also gets paid for!

Also by Anne Mather

STRANGE INTIMACY
BRITTLE BONDAGE
RAW SILK
TREACHEROUS LONGINGS
A WOMAN OF PASSION
RELATIVE SINS

Anne Mather

RICH AS SIN
SNOWFIRE
TIDEWATER SEDUCTION

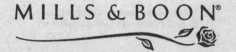

MILLS & BOON®

MILLS & BOON and MILLS & BOON with the Rose Device are registered trademarks of the publisher.
Harlequin Mills & Boon Limited,
Eton House, 18-24 Paradise Road, Richmond, Surrey, TW9 1SR

RICH AS SIN, SNOWFIRE and TIDEWATER SEDUCTION were first published in separate, single volumes in 1992, 1993 and 1992 respectively by Mills & Boon Limited.

RICH AS SIN © Anne Mather 1992
SNOWFIRE © Anne Mather 1993
TIDEWATER SEDUCTION © Anne Mather 1992

ISBN 0 263 80054 7

62-9608

Printed and bound in Great Britain
by BPC Paperbacks Limited, Aylesbury

RICH AS SIN

CHAPTER ONE

IT WAS the thumping in his head that woke him. That, and the sour taste in his mouth, which was an unpleasant reminder of the amount of alcohol he had consumed the night before. But what the hell? No one really cared whether he went to bed sober, or drank himself into a senseless stupor. He was unattached: a free agent. No longer the brunt of any woman's dissatisfactions. He could please himself what he did; how he lived. And if the knowledge didn't exactly please him, then tough! Given enough time, he'd get used to it.

Or would he? Rolling over in the tumbled bed, Matthew cast a bleary eye at the clock on the nearby table. God! he grunted ruefully. It was after twelve o'clock! No wonder his head was thumping. As he hadn't eaten a thing since noon the previous day, he was probably starving as well as dehydrating.

Still, he defended himself, as he hauled himself into an upright position and sat for a moment, waiting for the sledgehammer in his skull to slow its pace, he had been working until after midnight. The new program he was devising was probably going to outsell all his other programs, and he shouldn't be too hard on himself if he used alcohol as a stimulant. The fact that he hadn't needed that kind of stimulation until Melissa walked out on him was something he preferred not to remember. Time would deal with Melissa as it had dealt with everything else. And at least he had his work to alleviate his misery.

Pushing himself to his feet, he paused again before lurching across the expensive shag-pile carpet to the bathroom. After attending to his most immediate needs, he leaned on the porcelain basin and viewed his stubbled features without enthusiasm. His eyes were bloodshot;

there was a distinctly unhealthy tinge of greyness in his skin; and, to cap it all, it was two days since he had shaved, so that he resembled nothing so much as a derelict, one of those homeless vagrants who wandered around the country looking for hand-outs.

Which was probably unfair to them, reflected Matthew drily, rubbing a hand over his bristling jawline. At least they had a reason for looking the way they did. He had a decent home, and an occupation, and, because of his maternal grandfather's business acumen, more money than he knew what to do with. No reason at all to behave like an alcoholic, and certainly no reason to look like one.

Grimacing, he turned away from the mirror and stepped into the shower stall. Deliberately ignoring the temperature control, he allowed a stream of cold water to cascade down on to his shuddering body. God! For a moment, the iciness of it almost stopped his breath. But then, squeezing shower gel on to his hands, he began to lather himself fiercely, abrading his protesting flesh, as the water pummelled his head and shoulders.

He felt marginally better when he stepped out of the marble-tiled stall, and wrapped a huge cream bath-sheet about him. His head was still throbbing, but the dragging feeling of lethargy had dissipated somewhat. He didn't feel good, and he knew better than to believe that he would improve as the day wore on. But at least he was awake and active. And the computer keyboard would take care of the rest.

His razor beckoned, and with a sigh of resignation he picked it up. He wouldn't suit a beard, anyway, he consoled himself, as he concentrated on not turning his face into a mess of bloody cuts. Which wasn't easy, when his hand tended to shake at the most inopportune moments. God, he should have had a drink before he started this. It was amazing how a shot of Scotch could stabilise his senses.

He managed to finish the job without creating too much havoc, and dropped the towel on to the cold tiles of the bathroom floor. Then, after another ironic grimace at his appearance, he walked back into the bedroom, wrinkling his nose at the sour smell of alcohol that hit him. Indifferent to the fact that he was naked, and the temperature outside somewhere in the low forties, Matthew unlatched the windows to his balcony and threw them open. Then, after withstanding the blast of cold air that hit him with what he considered was admirable fortitude, he groped for his denims and pulled them on.

He was rummaging in his closet for a clean polo shirt when there was a knock at the bedroom door. Turning, he surveyed the closed door for fully fifteen seconds without answering, and then, stifling his impatience, he called, 'Yeah? What do you want?'

The door opened, just a crack, and a man's bald head appeared. 'Oh,' he said, when he saw Matthew. 'You're up, sir. Will you be wanting some breakfast?'

Matthew's mouth compressed. 'At half-past twelve, Jeeves? I don't think so. I'll just have a sandwich. I want to get to work.'

The door widened to admit the intruder, a huge, giant of a man, whose massive shoulders and straining paunch were constrained beneath navy blue worsted and spotless white linen. The uniform of a gentleman's gentleman sat oddly on such a big man's shoulders, but Matthew knew better than to suggest an alternative. The other man was proud of his appearance.

'Are you going to the office, sir?' he enquired, his sharp eyes taking in the open balcony doors and the untidy state of the bedroom. 'And I wish you wouldn't call me Jeeves, Mr Putnam. I don't like it, and you know it.'

Matthew gave the man a resigned look, and then, having no luck in finding a clean shirt, he reached for the sweatshirt he had discarded the night before. 'No, I don't plan to go into the office today,' he was beginning, when the manservant snatched the sweatshirt out of his hands. 'For God's sake, Victor, what the hell do you think you're doing?'

'Well, judging by your appearance, I'd guess you'd just had a shower, sir,' declared Victor mildly, 'and I'm

sure you didn't intend to wear this rather—odorous—
item. You have a whole drawer full of clean shirts in the
closet behind you. Just tell me what you want, and I'll
get it out for you.'

'I can dress myself, thank you—Creighton,' drawled
Matthew, with rather less patience. 'Why don't you get
out of here until I'm finished? Go and make some coffee
or something. I don't need a nursemaid.'

'Did I say you did?' Victor rolled the offending
sweatshirt into a ball, and stood his ground. 'But, as it
happens, you look as if you need someone's assistance.
Your mother isn't going to like this. She's not going to
like it at all.'

'My mother?' Matthew paused in the act of choosing
a shirt from the drawer Victor had indicated, and turned
to look at him again. 'What does my mother have to do
with anything?'

'Have you forgotten? You're meeting her for lunch in
a little over half an hour.'

'Oh, God!' Matthew slammed the drawer with his hip,
and pulled a black polo shirt over his head. The sombre
colour only accentuated the pallor of his olive skin, and
Victor's tongue clicked his disapproval. But Matthew was
indifferent to anyone's feelings but his own at that
moment, and the prospect of eating lunch with his
mother and enduring her condemnation of his lifestyle
was enough to make him wish he'd stayed in bed.

'A sandwich, you said, sir,' murmured Victor, evidently deciding it would be politic to give his employer
a breathing space, and Matthew cast him a brooding
look.

'Nothing to eat,' he snarled, the jaw he had shaved
so inexpertly clenched aggressively. 'Just fetch me a beer,
and no arguments. Oh, and call me a cab. With a bit of
luck there won't be any available.'

Victor paused in the doorway, his broad features
showing his dismay. 'I can drive you, Mr Putnam,' he
protested, but his employer's face was adamant.

'I said I'll take a cab,' Matthew retorted. 'Just do it,
Victor. And hurry up with that beer!'

Three-quarters of an hour later, Matthew stepped out of the minicab and bent to shove a five-pound note into the driver's hand. 'Thanks,' he said, without meaning it, waving away the change the man would have given him. Then, with a tight smile at the doorman's proffered greeting, he vaulted up the steps and through the swing glass doors into the Ritz's elegant foyer.

The dining-room was at the far end of the hallway, but guests took pre-luncheon drinks in the gilded splendour of the Palm Court. It was there Matthew knew he would find his mother, delicately sipping the Perrier water which was all she allowed herself in the middle of the day. Caroline Putnam—née Apollonius—guarded her appearance with almost as much reverence as her son disregarded his, and it was her proud boast that her wedding dress fitted her as well today as it had done more than thirty years ago.

Of course, the fact that the marriage she had worn the wedding dress for had lasted a considerably shorter time she considered of little consequence. She had married Joseph Putnam when she was only eighteen, much against her parents' wishes, and had soon come to realise her father had been right all along. A penniless Englishman, of good stock but little business acumen, Joseph Putnam had lingered only long enough to sire their only offspring, before taking off on a round-the-world yacht-race that had ended in disaster off the Cape of Good Hope. Of course, Caroline had been suitably grief-stricken when the news was delivered, but no one could deny she had been relieved. It had saved her the publicity—and the expense—of a messy divorce, and Aristotle Apollonius—who preferred the sobriquet of Apollo, for obvious reasons—had been more than willing to take his errant daughter, and her small son, back to Greece.

But, from Matthew's point of view, it had not been an entirely satisfactory solution. Despite the fact that 'Apollo' had had only one child, Caroline, and that therefore Matthew was the only heir to the enormous shipping fortune he had amassed, the boy grew up with a regrettable dislike of his grandfather's use of his money. The politics of power didn't interest Matthew; he saw no merit in controlling people's lives for purely personal gain. And, because his father had left sufficient funds for him to be educated in England, at the same schools he himself had attended, where a spartan regime went hand in hand with a distinct need for self-preservation, he had acquired a cynical aversion towards wealth in all its forms. It was a constant bone of contention between Matthew and the other members of his family, and the fact that he had made his home in England was no small contribution to the continuing discord.

Which was why Matthew was not looking forward to this particular lunch with his mother. Ever since the split with Melissa she had been trying, so far unsuccessfully, to persuade him to come back to Athens. Despite the fact that he had now formed his own company, specialising in computer software, and had no interest in taking his place on the board of the Apollonius Shipping Corporation, Caroline persisted in pursuing her goal.

The trouble was, Matthew was very much afraid that sooner or later she might succeed. He might be able to evade the issue so long as his grandfather was alive, but Apollo was over seventy years old. In ten years, twenty at the most, he was going to die, and then what excuse would he have for avoiding his responsibilities? Whether he liked it or not, hundreds—*thousands*—of people relied on the Apollonius Shipping Corporation for their livelihoods, and there was no way he could sit back and let his grandfather's relatives jealously tear to shreds what he had achieved.

The head waiter recognised him as he climbed the steps into the brightly lit atrium. It might be a dismal early April day outside, but the Palm Court of the London Ritz was as cheerfully brilliant as ever.

'Good morning, Mr Putnam,' the man said, his eyes moving from Matthew to the elegantly dressed woman at a corner table. 'Your mother is waiting for you.'

'Yes, thanks.' Matthew bestowed another brief smile, and started across the room. 'Oh—bring me a Scotch and soda, will you? I see my mother's already on the soft stuff.'

The waiter smiled, and moved away, and Matthew continued on to where his mother was seated on a striped couch. 'Mama,' he greeted her formally, bending to brush his lips against hers. 'Sorry I'm late.'

Caroline Putnam viewed her son with reproof mingled with reluctant pride. Tall, like his father, and dark, like his maternal forebears, Matthew attracted attention wherever he went. Particularly female attention, Caroline admitted, somewhat irritably. Not surprisingly, he had the lean good looks that had attracted her to Joseph Putnam in the first place, but the weaknesses she had not initially recognised in his father had been more than compensated for by her own father's genes. Matthew might not want to accept it, but he was far more like his grandfather than he would admit. He was arrogant, and stubborn, and absurdly independent. He made arbitrary decisions, and expected other people to abide by them. And, allied to that, he had the hooded eyes and muscled strength of a predator: an irresistible combination of sensuality and brute strength.

But he was letting himself go, thought Caroline tersely, viewing the slight thickening of his midriff that swelled above his belt. And jeans, and a leather jerkin! To have lunch with his mother! It was all that bitch Melissa's fault. Announcing she had fallen in love with someone else! Probably because Matthew had been in no hurry to take her to the altar.

'I should have thought you'd have had plenty of time to arrange your schedule so you wouldn't be late,' she remarked now, the attractive accent she still retained taking a little of the sharpness out of her tone. 'I know you haven't been into the office. I called earlier, and Robert told me you were not there.'

'No.' Matthew's response was hardly satisfactory. 'So—when did you arrive?'

'Here—or in England?' Caroline enquired in a clipped voice, jewelled fingers toying with the triple string of cultured pearls that encircled her slender throat, and Matthew's mouth took on a lazy slant.

'In England,' he replied, humouring her. 'I imagine you're occupying your usual suite upstairs.'

'Yes, and you might have taken the trouble to arrive in time to escort me down,' retorted his mother, the dark eyes she had passed on to her son flashing angrily. 'Honestly, Matt, I think you go out of your way to humiliate me! Leaving me sitting here alone! What if some undesirable lout had approached me?'

'The Ritz doesn't admit undesirable louts,' remarked Matthew mildly, nodding his thanks as his Scotch and soda was delivered to the table. 'You could sit here all day and no one would trouble you. But—I admit I should have phoned. As I said before, I'm sorry.'

Caroline sniffed, but her expression had softened somewhat, and although she observed the enthusiasm with which her son swallowed half his drink her reaction was more resigned than censorious.

'Oh, well,' she said, taking a sip of the iced spa water in her glass, 'you're here now, and that's what really matters. For myself, I arrived last evening, and went straight off to that charity gala at the Albert Hall. Your Uncle Henry escorted me. Aunt Celia is still indisposed.'

Matthew nodded. His uncle's wife had never enjoyed the best of health, although he privately believed that her many illnesses were self-induced. It was commonly known that Henry Putnam was inclined to enjoy the company of the opposite sex rather too well, and poor Aunt Celia had paid the price of being too trusting. Nevertheless, from his mother's point of view, the situation could not have been more convenient. She had a ready escort, whenever she needed one, without the complications that an unfettered relationship might have created for someone in her position.

'You, I imagine, were combing the less salubrious nightspots of the city,' she added, as Matthew's summoning of the waiter for a second drink reactivated her impatience. 'Matt, don't you think you're behaving rather foolishly? For heaven's sake, if you were so besotted with the girl, why didn't you marry her, instead of just—sleeping with her?'

Matthew's mouth flattened. 'You know what I think about marriage,' he answered, after issuing further instructions to the waiter. 'Just leave it, will you, Mama? I'll go to hell my own way, if you don't mind. Now—tell me why you wanted to see me. Or was it just to voice your disapproval—yet again?'

'Of course not.'

Caroline uncrossed her silk-clad legs and then recrossed them again in the other direction. Watching her, Matthew had no difficulty in understanding why his father's brother was so willing to squire her around. At forty-eight, Caroline looked ten years younger, and Matthew was quite prepared to believe that anyone here today who didn't know them would automatically assume he was her lover, not her son.

'You know it's your grandfather's birthday at the end of the month, don't you?' she went on now, and Matthew's dark brow ascended in disbelief.

'So it is,' he agreed, after a moment's thought. 'I'd forgotten. How old is the old devil? Seventy-one?'

'He's seventy-two, actually,' declared Caroline flatly. 'If you remember, you couldn't come to his seventy-first birthday because it clashed with—with Melissa's parents' anniversary ball or something. In any event,' she hurried on, not wanting to linger over unwelcome memories, 'we'd like you to join the family for the celebrations. Apollo's inviting everyone, and it will look rather odd if you're not there.'

Matthew regarded his mother tolerantly over the rim of his glass. 'As it did last year, you mean?'

'No.' Caroline sighed. 'Last year wasn't so important to him!' she exclaimed irritably. And then, as if regretting her candour, she added, 'Never mind about last year. Will you come?'

Matthew frowned. 'What's so special about this year?'

'Well—he's a year older, for one thing...'

'And?'

'And—and—he's not been well,' admitted his mother reluctantly. 'You know how he's always had trouble with his chest. I think it's been a little more troublesome than usual, and it's made him aware of his own mortality.'

Matthew's mouth turned down. 'If he stopped smoking those damned cigars, he might give his respiration system a chance. How many does he get through in a day? Fifteen? Twenty?'

'Oh, not as many as that, surely!' Caroline looked appalled. 'In any case, Apollo would say that if he couldn't live his life the way he wanted to live it, there wouldn't be much point in going on.'

'Hmm.' Matthew could see the subject upset her, and decided to desist. 'Well, I don't know about this birthday bash. You know family parties aren't my style.'

Caroline snorted. 'The way I hear it, social gatherings of any kind aren't your style! You've become a hermit, Matt. A recluse. You don't go anywhere—except into the office occasionally—you don't see anyone——'

'And where've you got all this information from?' enquired Matthew wearily. 'No, don't tell me. I can guess. The admirable Victor!'

'I—may have had the few odd words with your major-domo when I called——'

'I'll bet!'

'—but you know Victor cares about you, too. He wouldn't tell me anything if he didn't think it was in your best interests.'

'Really?'

'Yes, really.' His mother gave a resigned sigh. 'Matt, I don't want to interfere——'

'Then don't.'

'—but I care about you as well. And—and I do wish you'd get this—this infatuation for Melissa Mainwaring out of your system.'

'Right.' Matthew lifted a hand to summon the waiter again. 'Shall we look at the menu?

Caroline opened her mouth to make a protest, and then closed it again. What was the use? she asked herself impotently, feeling all the pangs of frustrated mother-love as her son turned to speak to the restaurant manager. Matthew was such an attractive man; he had everything to live for. Yet he was allowing a spoilt little bitch, who hadn't got an intelligent thought in her empty little head, to tear his life to pieces.

An hour later, as she was enjoying her second cup of coffee, Caroline risked broaching the subject again. As they ate—and she had noticed Matthew had only picked at his food—the conversation had ranged from the previous night's gala to the preparations for the forthcoming birthday celebrations. It had been the kind of conversation she could have had with anyone. Certainly not the intimate tête-à-tête she had hoped to achieve. Which was why she decided to bring Melissa's name back into the proceedings. Like a wound that was festering, her son's infatuation with the woman wouldn't heal until it had been thoroughly aired.

'And—when are Melissa and her prince planning to get married?' she enquired tensely. 'They are going to get married, aren't they? I'm sure I read something about it in last week's tabloids.'

Matthew replaced the cup he had been holding back in its saucer. He should have known better than to imagine his mother would leave well alone. And, of course, she was right. There had been a report that Brigadier Alfred Mainwaring's daughter was going to marry the prince of some unpronounceable Eastern European country. The nuptials were planned to take place in June, and no doubt Caroline knew that as well as he did.

'Soon,' he remarked now, meeting his mother's innocent gaze with cool deliberation. 'Why? Do you think you'll get an invitation? How would they describe you? Oh, yes. The mother of the best man!'

Caroline's lips tightened. 'Joke if you like, but you are—or rather you would be, if you'd stop feeling sorry for yourself. I never thought a son of mine could behave so mindlessly! Perhaps you are your father's son, after all.'

Matthew's mouth twisted, and with an exclamation of disgust his mother thrust back her chair and got to her feet. 'I'm going to my room,' she declared angrily, and then, conscious of the stir she was creating, she put a steadying hand on the edge of the table. 'Come and see me tomorrow,' she added in an undertone, as if regretting her hasty announcement. 'And think about your grandfather's birthday. Needless to say, he expects you to be there.'

Matthew did think about what his mother had said, as he walked back to his apartment. The luxurious penthouse he had bought with his own money occupied the top floor of a tall block of apartments in Culver Mews in Knightsbridge, and although he knew Victor wouldn't approve Matthew enjoyed the unaccustomed exercise. It reminded him it was too long since he had been to the gym, and that Victor's obsession with his personal protection meant he had too few opportunities to walk anywhere. And, although it was a cold day, with a threat of rain in the air, the daffodils were out in the park, and the early cherry blossom was already appearing on the trees.

It reminded him of what Greece was like at this time of the year, and most particularly Delphus, the island where his grandfather had his home. The sprawling villa where he had spent the early years of his childhood did hold some happy memories for him, and it would be good to see Yannis again, and Nicos, and all the aunts and cousins he remembered from his youth.

But it wasn't just the idea of obeying his finer instincts, and pleasing his mother for once, that occupied his thoughts as he strode past Hyde Park Corner. It was what his mother had said about Melissa that stuck in his mind. And, although thinking of her with Georgio Ivanov still tore his gut, he was unwillingly aware that she had a point. He should have married her when he had the chance. Goodness knew, she had been eager enough to take the plunge. It had been the one sour note in their relationship, that he had been so unwilling to make their association legal. A lack of commitment was how she had put it, on those increasingly frequent occasions when she had accused him of not loving her enough.

Matthew pushed his hands deeper into the pockets of his leather jacket. *Love*! His lips twisted. He doubted Melissa knew the meaning of the word. No one who professed to love someone as much as she had always professed to love him could have fallen out of love so quickly. And he was cynically aware that Melissa's 'love' was more probably available to the highest bidder. Oh, he might have been her first choice, both sexually and financially, but Ivanov was offering marriage, and that all-important ring on her finger.

For himself, he had never felt any urgency to seek that legitimising scrap of paper. What they had had—or rather, what he had thought they had had—was far more binding than a contract that could just as easily be broken. But he was becoming aware that what Melissa had wanted from him was more than his undying devotion. She had wanted security, the kind of security she could only get if he signed on the dotted line.

So, why should he be so surprised? he asked himself now. His parents' marriage had fallen apart as much because his father was unambitious as through any character weakness on his part. He had long since learned how convenient his father's sudden death had proved to be, for, although his mother might sometimes sentimentalise about his passing, she was not her father's daughter for nothing. All his life, the great god Mammon had ruled his family's actions. And he had been a fool to think that Melissa was any different from the rest.

Victor was waiting when the lift doors slid back at the twenty-second floor. As Matthew stepped on to the hushed luxury of the Chinese rug that virtually filled the panelled foyer, the man came to meet him in obvious disapproval.

'You walked,' he declared, brushing drops of rain from the soft fabric of the jacket his employer slung off, with an impatient finger.

'I walked,' agreed Matthew, heading for the inner
hallway that led to his study. 'Rob didn't call, did he?
He knew I was having lunch with my mother.'

'Mr Prescott didn't call, no,' Victor assured him
tersely, and then, with a change of tone, he added, 'But
you do have some mail. The lunchtime delivery came
while you were out.' He adopted an expectant expression. 'Would you like to see it?'

Matthew paused, with his hand against the panels of
his private sanctum. 'Now, what's that supposed to
mean?' he enquired shortly. 'You know I always glance
through the afternoon mail at dinnertime. It's probably
only bills, in any case.' He hesitated. 'Or do you know
something I don't?'

A trace of colour invaded Victor's bullish features.
'Now, how would I——?'

'Victor!'

The man sighed. 'Well—there appears to be a letter
from Miss Mainwaring,' he admitted nervously. 'I
thought you might wish to see it. As—as——'

'As I appear to be drowning in self-pity, right?'
suggested Matthew, tamping down the unwilling thought
that Melissa might have come to her senses.

'No, sir!' Victor was indignant. 'I just thought——'

'Where is it?'

Matthew couldn't stand the suspense any longer. Even
though his common sense told him that if Melissa wanted
to come back, she would hardly write him a letter telling
him so, he needed the proof. Damn her, he swore savagely. What could she want now?

Victor riffled through the small pile of business letters
and advertising material occupying a silver tray placed
on a polished, semi-circular hall table. The letter, with
its unmistakable scent of rose petals, was at the bottom,
and although he was impatient Matthew didn't miss the
significance.

'Can I get you some tea, sir?' Victor enquired, as his
employer slid his thumb beneath the seal, but Matthew
shook his head.

'Nothing, thanks,' he said, heading back towards his study. 'I'll let you know when I'm hungry.'

Victor looked disappointed, but Matthew couldn't help it. He had no idea why Melissa might be writing to him, and the last thing he needed was Victor peering metaphorically over his shoulder. To emphasise this point, he went into the study and closed the door, before withdrawing the letter from its envelope. Then, noticing that his hands were shaking, he uttered another bitter oath.

Indifferent to the somewhat austere familiarity of his surroundings, Matthew rested his shoulder-blades against the door as he scanned the hand-written missive. Melissa's handwriting had never been particularly legible, and in his present agitated state it was difficult to read the scrawling words. But patience eventually won out over stress, and he was able to translate the gist of the message.

Amazingly, it was an invitation. Melissa was writing to ask if he would come to a party she and her fiancé were giving, to celebrate their engagement. Apparently, although the announcement had already been made formally at the dinner her parents had given in their honour, this party was to be a much less formal affair, for close friends and acquaintances.

The air rushed out of Matthew's lungs in a harsh whoosh. For a few moments, he stared at the letter in his hand, as if expecting it to self-destruct in his fingers. And then, tossing it savagely on to his desk, he bent forward to grip the scarred mahogany with clenched fists. My God, he thought disbelievingly, Melissa actually thought he might attend her engagement party! The idea was ludicrous! And insensitive to the point of cruelty.

It took him several minutes, during which time he wished he had asked Victor to fetch him a bottle of Scotch, to recover his composure. He should have known the letter was not going to be good news. Melissa wanted her revenge, and by God, she was determined to get it.

An expletive burst from his lips, and he straightened abruptly, his jaw clenching as he examined how it made him feel. For the first time since she had walked out on him, he felt a healthy sense of resentment. She was deliberately turning the knife in the wound. And she obviously expected him to refuse.

Poor Georgio, Matthew thought grimly. He doubted he knew Melissa had invited her ex-lover to their engagement party. What an irony! But what exactly was Melissa's game?

Of course, it was possible she wanted him back. Matthew's stomach muscles tightened at the thought. But not on the old terms, he acknowledged, with strengthening cynicism. She had made that plain enough when he'd implored her to stay.

So what was she trying to do? Play one lover off against another? He gave a bitter smile. It might be amusing to find out. There had always been a latent sense of masochism in their relationship.

CHAPTER TWO

'BUT why are you doing this?' Paul Webster regarded his fiancée with impatient eyes. 'I thought the café was doing well enough. Why do you need to supplement your income by acting as someone's skivvy?'

'It's not like that.' Samantha Maxwell endeavoured to keep her temper. 'But you have to understand that this is a new departure. And one which, if it's successful, could prove really exciting.'

Paul snorted. 'Exciting? Working every hour God sends!'

'Not *every* hour,' replied Samantha reasonably. 'Just an odd evening here and there. And it's not as if you're going to miss seeing me. You have to visit your clients, and I'll visit mine.'

'Well, I think you're crazy!'

'Yes, I know.' Samantha pushed a strand of toffee-coloured hair behind her ear and tried to concentrate on the shopping list in front of her. But it wasn't easy with Paul baulking her at every turn, persisting in regarding her job as a secondary occupation.

'I mean,' he went on, as if sensing he was pushing her too hard and attempting to be persuasive, 'it's not as if you're a trained chef, or anything. You're an English graduate, Sam. You could be a teacher. Instead of which, you're playing at housewife in someone else's kitchen.'

Samantha's nostrils flared as she looked up. 'I am not playing at housewife,' she retorted sharply. 'And, whether you like it or not, I enjoy what I do. You can't seem to understand that getting this branch of the business going is a real adventure. And it could be just the beginning of a whole new career.'

'Making other people's meals!'

'Catering—for people who don't have the time, or the inclination, to do it themselves.'

'As I said, playing housewife in other people's kitchens.'

'If you want to put it that way.' Samantha was growing tired of the argument. She looked reflectively around the empty café, with its Austrian blinds and gingham tablecloths. 'I'd have thought you'd be glad I was making such a success of the business. After all, it was your idea that I open this place.'

'Yes. Because you didn't know what you wanted to do, when you left university, and the lease was available. If you hadn't voiced some crazy notion of starting a sandwich-round, I doubt if I'd have suggested it.'

'But you did,' Samantha reminded him, straightening a silver condiment set, and adjusting a fan of scarlet napkins. 'And I'm very grateful to you. It's what I've always wanted to do. Only—well, Mum and Dad were keen that I went to university, and they'd worked so hard to send me there, I couldn't disappoint them. I'm not sorry I went. It taught me a lot. Not least, what my priorities are, and what I hope to achieve.'

'Success in business!' Paul shook his head. 'And all this time I thought you wanted to marry me.'

'I do.' Samantha turned to him then, her honey-pale features taut with worry. 'But it's not the only objective in my life. I need a career, Paul. I really do.'

Paul sighed. 'And you think branching out into personal catering is the answer?'

'I don't know. I haven't done enough of it yet to find out. But meeting Jenny like that was a godsend. And the contacts I made at her dinner party are priceless!'

'But they're all in the West End! I don't like the idea of you driving all that way home in the dark!'

'Oh, Paul!' Samantha tilted her head to one side, and then, abandoning her defensive stance, she crossed to where he was sitting, and perched on his lap. 'You don't have to worry about my safety. I'm a perfectly good driver, and in any case the nights are getting lighter.'

'And what happens when the winter comes again?' persisted Paul, though he had softened sufficiently to nuzzle her neck with his lips. 'Still, we'll be married by then, won't we? You'll have more than your hands full looking after me.'

'Mmm.'

Samantha's response was doubtful, but Paul was too busy nibbling her ear to notice. Nevertheless, when his hand moved to the buttoned fastening of her shirt, she stopped him. It wasn't that she didn't love Paul; she did. But, unlike him, she couldn't switch moods so completely. And she didn't share his willingness to use sex to mend their differences.

'Hey——'

Her protective grip on the lapels of her shirt brought a grunt of protest, but Samantha slid lightly off his knee, and adopted a rueful smile.

'Do you realise what time it is?' she exclaimed, running a nervous palm down the seam of her neat black skirt. 'I've got to call at the wholesaler's before I go home, and if I don't hurry they'll be closed before I get there.'

Paul regarded her dourly for a moment and then, as if controlling his impatience, he rose obediently to his feet. He was a tall man, solid and handsome, in a blond, Nordic sort of way. He liked outdoor activities, and played rugby regularly, which accounted for his rather stolid appearance. He liked to think he was very fit, though Samantha knew he sank rather too many beers in the clubhouse after the match to be in really good shape. Nevertheless, he was kind, and fairly even-tempered, and extremely loyal. And Samantha had known him for over six years, ever since they first got to know one another at the local sixth-form college.

'You know,' he said now, taking a strand of her hair between his thumb and forefinger, and smoothing out its curl, and Samantha's heart sank. 'I must be the only man in Northfleet whose girlfriend is still a virgin. Whose *fiancée* is still a virgin,' he corrected himself heavily. 'Am I going to have to wait until our wedding night, Sam? Is that why you won't let me touch you?'

Samantha suppressed an inward groan, and reached for her jacket, which had been lying over the back of a nearby chair. 'I do let you touch me,' she protested, wishing Paul hadn't chosen this minute to start another conversation about their relationship. 'But we've only been engaged for a little over a month. Give me time. Let me get used to the idea.'

Paul's mouth tightened. 'I could say that you shouldn't have to "get used" to the idea,' he retorted, with rather more heat. 'For God's sake, Sam, it's almost the twenty-first century! As you're so fond of reminding me, women want to be equal with men!'

'Intellectually equal, not sexually,' she countered, pushing her arms into the sleeves of her jacket. Her nail caught on the lining as she did so, and she emitted a sharp gasp of frustration. 'Not now, Paul, please. I'm simply not in the mood.'

'Sometimes I wonder if you ever will be,' he muttered, and although she had only heard the tone of his mumbled protest Samantha swung round.

'What?'

'Forget it.' Paul wound his club scarf around his neck and headed towards the door. 'So—when is this party supposed to be? And who did you say it was for?'

Samantha checked that all the lights were out and that the alarm was set, and followed him outside. 'It's an engagement party,' she answered, locking the door behind them. 'It's next Tuesday, at a house in Eyton Gate. I dealt with someone called Lederer, but I think he was just a secretary or something.'

'Eyton Gate, eh?' Paul pulled a wry face, as they crossed the pavement to where his car was waiting. 'You're really hitting the big time, aren't you?'

'I hope so.' Samantha endeavoured to sustain the feeling of excitement she had felt when she'd taken the call. 'So—I'll see you tomorrow, yes?'

'If my mother's cooking isn't too simple for you,' remarked Paul caustically, swinging open the car door, and Samantha sighed.

'Will you stop this?' she exclaimed. 'Can't you at least find it in your heart to be pleased that I'm making some progress? I don't want to be a waitress all my life.'

'I don't want you to be a waitress all your life either,' he retorted, levering his bulk behind the wheel of the sporty little Mazda. Then, with a shrug, he reached out and grabbed her hand. 'OK. I guess I am pleased for you, really. Just don't get too high-powered, will you? Or you may decide you don't want to marry a hard-working estate agent, after all.'

'Since when are estate agents hard-working?' queried Samantha, her smile mirroring her relief. 'OK, I promise I won't. Now, I must go, or the wholesaler's really will be closed.'

Paul nodded, and Samantha waited until he had driven away before crossing the road to where her own Mini van was parked. Although the back of the van was fitted with shelves to transport the food she prepared at home, she reflected that she would have to get a small transit if she planned to expand into catering in a big way. It was all very well using the Mini when all she did was ride back and forth from home, with an occasional trip to the Cash and Carry. But travelling the fifty or so miles from this small Essex town to London and back was going to put a definite strain on her capabilities. Particularly as sometimes she might have to take Debbie with her.

Her mother had a meal waiting when she finally got home. Although she worked with food all day, Samantha seldom ate anything at the café. Besides, the little restaurant closed at five-thirty, and by the time Samantha and her assistant, Debbie Donaldson, had scoured all the equipment, cleaned the dining-room and spread fresh cloths on the tables, she was quite happy to let someone wait on her for a change.

'You look tired,' said Mrs Maxwell frankly, setting a plate of home-made steak and kidney pie in front of her daughter, and Samantha's lips twisted.

'Do I?' she said. 'Thank you. That's all I wanted to hear.'

'Well, you do,' declared her mother, seating herself across from her daughter and viewing the smudges beneath the younger woman's eyes with some concern. 'What have you been doing until this time? Your father and your sister had their meal over an hour ago. Don't blame me if yours is dried up. It's been in the oven since half-past six.'

Samantha smiled. 'It's fine,' she said, unenthusiastically forking a mouthful of limp pastry into her mouth. 'And you know I had to go to the wholesaler's. I told you that this morning.'

'Until this time?'

'Well—I was late leaving.' Samantha moistened her lips. 'Paul came round just after we closed.'

'Ah.' Mrs Maxwell didn't sound surprised. 'And what did he have to say?'

Samantha grimaced. 'Can't you guess?'

'He's not happy about you doing these private dinner parties, is he? And quite honestly, I don't blame him.'

'Oh, Mum!'

'Don't "Oh, Mum" me. You know how we feel about it. Your Dad and I, that is. I wish you'd never met that Jennifer Gregory again. She's unsettled you, and I can't forgive her for that.'

'Mum, I met Jenny at university, remember? And it was your and Dad's idea that I go there. And her name's Spellman now, not Gregory. And whatever you say, I think she's provided me with a marvellous opportunity.'

'To cook for someone else. To be a servant, in someone else's home.'

'No!' Samantha gasped. 'You're beginning to sound like Paul. It's not like that. I just do the catering, that's all. It's what I do, Mum. What do you think running a café is all about?'

'The café's yours—or you pay the lease, anyway, thanks to that insurance your grandmother left you.'

'And I'll still be running the café, as well as providing a catering service for anyone who can afford me.'

'Hmm.' Mrs Maxwell didn't sound impressed. 'And do they know—these friends of Jenny's, I mean—that you're not a professional caterer?'

'I *am* a professional caterer.'

'I don't think a night school diploma is the same as real professional experience,' persisted her mother. 'They probably think you've worked in some top London restaurant. I wonder what they'd say if they saw the Honey Pot?'

'I don't particularly care,' exclaimed Samantha, pushing her barely touched plate aside. 'But thanks for your support. It's what I really needed. Now, if you don't mind, I'll go and take a shower.'

Mrs Maxwell sighed. 'I'm sorry,' she said, as her daughter got up from the table. 'Perhaps I was a little harsh. But I worry about you, Sam, I do honestly. Don't you think you have enough on, running the café practically single-handed, without taking on more work, to add to the burden?'

Samantha hesitated. 'It doesn't occur to you that I'm going to be paid far more for the catering than I'll ever earn in the café, does it? I don't want to give up the café. I want to improve it. And, if I'm successful, I may be able to afford a full-time cook to work in the kitchen. That way, we could expand the menu, both for the café and the catering service.'

Her mother frowned. 'Well, what does Paul say?'

'Paul just wants me to go on running the café until we get married. Then—who knows? I don't think he envisages me continuing with my career much beyond the first year.'

Mrs Maxwell sighed. 'Well, that doesn't sound unreasonable to me. And, after all, until you met Jennifer Greg—Spellman again, you seemed happy enough doing what you were doing. Then she tells you she's giving a dinner party, and that her caterers have let her down at the last minute, and before we know it you're dashing off to London, and getting these big ideas.'

'Mum, the dinner party was a huge success! Everyone said so. And, believe it or not, good caterers are worth their weight in gold to these people. Times are changing. The days when people could afford to employ a full-time cook are long-gone. Besides, people don't want to do that kind of work nowadays; not for someone else, anyway,' she added hastily. 'That's why people like me are in such demand. We come in, we cook the meal, and we go away again. And it's much more intimate than taking your guests to a restaurant.'

Mrs Maxwell shook her head. 'All the same, I don't think even you imagined what would happen?'

'The phone calls, you mean?' Samantha gave a rueful smile. 'No, I didn't. But isn't it exciting? I could probably work *every* night of the week, if I wanted.'

'But you're not going to?' Her mother looked alarmed.

'No, I've told you.' Samantha paused. 'To begin with, I'm only going to take on one, maybe two nights' work in any week. Then, we'll see how it goes. At the moment, all I want to think about is next Tuesday's engagement party.'

'In Mayfair.'

'Well, it's Belgravia, actually,' said Samantha evenly. 'But yes. It's in the West End. Apparently the female half of the happy couple is a friend of Jenny's. And they're having the party at her fiancé's house.'

Mrs Maxwell shook her head. 'Well, you watch out, Sam. These people aren't like us, you know, and you being an attractive girl and everything—just watch your step.'

Samantha smiled. 'Yes, Mum.'

'Well, you can laugh. But it's true. Some people think money can buy anything.'

Samantha's expression softened. 'I know,' she said, recognising her mother's very real fears on her behalf. 'But I am twenty-four, you know. I know what I'm doing.'

After popping her head round the living-room door to offer a belated greeting to her father and her younger sister Penny, Samantha trudged up the stairs to her room. She was tired. She freely admitted it. But it was more a mental tiredness, born of the arguments she had had with both Paul and her mother, than any physical weakness on her part. It was so hard to make them understand how she felt about this latest development in her career. When she left university, it was true, she had no serious plans for her future. Oh, she had always liked messing about in the kitchen, and trying new recipes on the family, but she had just regarded that as a hobby, until her father had put the idea of starting a sandwich-round into her head.

As the manager of a jeweller's in the High Street, Mr Maxwell had got into the habit of going into the local pub for a sandwich at lunchtime, but, as he said, he didn't always want the beer that went with it. He had encouraged Samantha when she had put forward her idea of using her car to deliver home-made sandwiches all over town, and Paul's offer of the lease on what had previously been a rather sleazy café had just been an extension of that. She had still provided sandwiches, but her clients had had to come to her for them, and pretty soon she had branched out into quiches, and salads, and home-made cakes and scones. The Honey Pot had taken off, and during the past two years it had gone from strength to strength. She even employed a full-time assistant now, and her account books were beginning to show a healthy profit. But this latest development was something else, and it was hard to be enthusiastic when everyone else thought she was getting out of her depth.

Standing in the shower, she avoided looking at her reflection in the walls of the Perspex stall. She was half afraid of what she might see in the dark-fringed depths of her eyes, eyes that could change from green to grey, according to her mood. Was she being too ambitious? she wondered, scooping gel from the bottle and lathering her damp hair. Was that what Paul was afraid of? She had never thought of herself as being so, but she couldn't deny she was excited. She would have to think of a name for the new service, she thought, determinedly putting all negative thoughts aside. Not the Honey Pot again. That belonged to the café. So how about 'Honey Homemaker', just to keep the connection?

*　　*　　*

The buffet looked perfect, even if Samantha had had a few small set-backs at the beginning. Finding that one of the smoked salmon mousses had lost its shape on the journey had been a minor disaster, but happily she had prepared more than she needed, and that obstacle had been overcome.

Then Miss Mainwaring, her employer's fiancée, had thrown a paddy because there was no caviare. A buffet wasn't a buffet without caviare, she had exclaimed, and it had taken a great deal of effort on her fiancé's behalf to persuade her that it really wasn't important.

He had been nice, Samantha reflected, as she gathered her belongings together, preparatory to leaving. A prince, moreover, although his title wasn't one she was familiar with. But then, she wasn't familiar with these people at all, she acknowledged ruefully. A fact that had been made clear to her by Melissa Mainwaring's biting tongue.

All the same, it had been an edifying experience, and she had learned one or two salutory lessons. She had discovered, for instance, that it was far harder to organise a buffet than it was to arrange a formal sit-down dinner. And luck had played a part in saving her from ruining this unique opportunity. It hadn't occurred to her, until she was unloading the pizza, that it was no use providing hot food when you couldn't be assured the guests would eat to order. But thankfully her pizzas tasted just as good cold as hot, and instead of offering them in slices, as she had originally intended, she cut the juicy wedges into bite-sized squares, easily handled on the end of a cocktail spear.

Happily, the rest of the food offered no problems. Her tarts and quiches looked appetisingly rich against the backcloth of finely embossed damask. And Samantha threaded strands of asparagus fern between the plates of meats and salads, adding scarlet rosebuds to enhance the luscious trifles. When she left the tables to go downstairs and pack up, there was already a satisfying group of guests admiring her efforts. She just hoped everything tasted as good as it looked. One other difference between the buffet and a formal dinner was that she didn't stay around long enough to find out.

Which was a pity, because she'd enjoyed working in this kitchen. With its quarry-tiled floor, and solid mahogany fittings, it reminded her of pictures she had seen of Victorian kitchens. However, no Victorian kitchen had ever had its standards of cleanliness, or provided such a wealth of gadgets to make cooking here a pleasure.

Upstairs had been impressive, too. Dividing doors had been rolled back to create a huge reception area, and although Samantha had only had a glimpse of the linen-hung walls and high carved ceilings as she and the waiters, hired for the occasion, carried the food up from the kitchen, it had been enough. Evidently, whatever else he was, Prince Georgio was not a member of some impoverished aristocracy. On the contrary, he must be extremely rich—and Miss Mainwaring probably knew it.

An unkind conclusion, Samantha reproved herself severely, as she packed plates and dishes back into the cold-boxes she had brought them in. Afer all, she knew nothing about Melissa Mainwaring, except that she was a friend of Jenny's, and she was fond of caviare. And if she, Samantha, wanted to make a success of this business, she had to try and get on with everybody. Even spoilt little rich girls who enjoyed making scenes!

She was so intent on what she was doing, so absorbed with her thoughts, that when she turned and saw the man leaning against the tall freezer she started violently. She had thought she was alone, all the waiters hired for the evening busy circulating the champagne upstairs. But in the next instant she realised that this man was no waiter, and in the same breath she saw the half-open door behind him.

Until then, she hadn't noticed the rear entry. The house, one of a row of terraced Georgian properties, had been designed to provide living accommodation on its three upper floors. The lower ground floor, where Samantha was now, was entered by means of area steps at the front of the house, and it had never occurred to her that there might be a back entrance on this level. Or that it might be unlocked.

Her mouth drying, she looked at the man with anxious eyes. Who was he? she wondered. A servant? A *thief*? He didn't look entirely English, and although he wasn't heavily built, like Paul, there was a muscular hardness to his lean body. She supposed he was about six feet; again, not as tall as Paul, but more powerfully masculine. His dark hair needed cutting, and there was a film of stubble on his chin. It added to the air of toughness and alienation that exuded from him, an aura that was strengthened by the fact that he was dressed totally in black.

Swallowing, Samantha decided she had no choice but to bluff it out. There was no way she could get round the table and make it to either of the other two doors without him catching her. Something told her he would move just as swiftly as the predator he resembled, but perhaps he would leave her alone if he thought she was no threat to him.

'I—er—the party's not down here,' she said, stifling an exclamation as her shaking hands clattered two quiche plates together. God! She was trying not to do anything to agitate him. At this rate, he'd soon guess that she was scared rigid.

But, 'I know,' he remarked, in a laconic voice, making no move to budge from his lounging position. 'I'm sorry if I startled you,' he added. 'I assumed everyone would be upstairs. I imagine Ivanov's guests have arrived by now, haven't they?'

Samantha blinked. *Ivanov's* guests! So he knew whose house it was, then. Did that make it better or worse? She was too shocked to make a decision.

And his voice disturbed her. It had a low gravelly edge that scraped across her nerves. Yet it was a cultivated voice, as well. Hoarse, but not the broad London accent she would have expected.

He moved then and, in spite of herself, she flinched. She didn't quite know what she expected him to do, but when her eyes alighted on the knife she had used to cut the pizza lying on the table beside her, her fingers flexed automatically.

'I guess you're wondering what I'm doing here,' he began, his lips twisting half sardonically, and Samantha took a choking breath. His upper lip was quite thin, she noticed inconsequently, but the lower one was full and sensual. The mark of a sensitive nature, she wondered wildly, or simply an indication of brute strength?

'I—it's nothing to do with me,' she said, aware that her voice had risen half an octave. She edged one of the cold-boxes forward so that it hid the knife from his view. Then, as her fingers closed around the handle, 'Is—is Mr Ivanov expecting you?'

A faint smile touched his mouth. His lips parted to reveal even white teeth, and his tongue appeared to dampen a corner in a decidedly amused gesture. '*Mr* Ivanov?' he echoed, as Samantha's scattered senses registered the powerful attraction of that smile. 'I gather you don't know him very well.'

Samantha's lips tightened. Did he mean because she hadn't addressed him as *Prince* Ivanov? Or simply because she had said *Mr* Ivanov?

'I—don't,' she declared, realising he hadn't answered her question. Her fingers took a firmer hold on the knife. 'Wh-why don't you go up and see him?'

It was a calculated risk she was taking. She had no idea what he might do when confronted with a roomful of Prince Georgio's guests, but at least it would give her a chance to call the police. And there was no point in trying to be a hero—a *heroine*—when he was so much taller and stronger than she was. She might find the courage to use the knife to defend herself, but she couldn't see herself using it to stop him from invading the party. Indeed, the very idea of sinking its cruel blade into his yielding flesh was enough to bring her out in a cold sweat.

'Yes,' he said now, pushing his hands into the pockets of his leather jacket, 'why don't I do that?' But then, dispelling the feeling of relief that his words had kindled, his heavy lids narrowed the penetration of eyes so dark, they seemed as black as his outfit. 'So what are you doing down here?'

'Me?' It was almost a squeak, and Samantha cleared her throat before continuing. 'I——' It was still too high, and she consciously tried to lower her tone. 'I—I'm just the ca-caterer.'

'The caterer?' he echoed, half disbelievingly, and she realised that in her hip-length sweater and black leggings she didn't look like anyone's idea of a waitress. But she had changed out of the neat white blouse and short black skirt she had worn to set out the buffet tables. In here, five minutes ago, she remembered, in horror. God! She should be grateful he hadn't surprised her in her bra and panties!

'I—yes, the caterer,' she confirmed, the memory of what could have happened giving her a momentary respite. 'That—that's what I'm doing. Packing up my things.'

His frown was thoughtful, drawing his straight black brows together. He had nice eyebrows, she thought, dark and vital, like his hair, and his nose was straight and well-formed, between bones that accentuated the hollows of his cheeks. Altogether, it was a disturbingly attractive face, she acknowledged, and then inwardly flayed herself for thinking so. For pity's sake, the man was an intruder, or worse! How could she find him attractive? She must be losing her mind!

He moved again, approaching the table this time, and all thoughts of his appearance fled. All her old fears flooded back in full measure, and when he put out a hand to examine the nearest cold-box her nerve snapped. Snatching up the knife, she positioned it against her midriff, holding it with both hands, the handle towards her stomach, the blade pointing viciously outwards.

'Don't touch anything!' she cried, unable to hold down her panic any longer. 'Get—get away from the table. Or—or I'll use this. Believe me, I know how.'

His expression was ludicrous. If she hadn't known better, she might almost have believed he was as shocked as she was. He stared at her as if she had really lost her senses, and his hands came out of his pockets to perform a soothing gesture.

'Hey,' he said, 'calm down——'

'Keep away from me!' Samantha was shaking like a leaf, and her hold on the knife was desperate. Her palms were sweating with the knowledge that she had really burned her boats now. She had shown him she didn't trust him, and there was no turning back.

'Please,' he protested, 'put the knife down. You're making a terrible mistake——'

'You made the mistake in coming here,' she retorted, glancing behind her, measuring the distance to the stairs. 'If—if you have any sense you'll get out of here. If you're still here when I get back, the police will—ouch!'

Her words were brought to an abrupt halt when he lunged forward and grabbed her arm. Taking advantage of her momentary lapse in concentration, he grasped her wrist and twisted sharply. The knife fell to the floor with a loud clatter, and before she could turn away he jerked her hard against him.

Her first crazy thought was that she had been right: his body was much harder and tougher than Paul's. And the second was that he was no gentleman. A gentleman wouldn't twist her arm up behind her back until it felt as if it might break, or hold her as if there was some danger of her laying a karate chop across the back of his neck. The only kind of chops she knew about were lamb, and pork, and if it weren't so serious she could almost find it funny.

A sob escaped her, but it was as much a suppression of the hysterical laughter that was bubbling inside her as an expression of pain. Nevertheless, he heard it, and his hold on her arm eased ever so slightly, as he drew back to look down at her.

'Are you crazy, or what?' he demanded, and she was relieved to see he looked no more menacing than he had done a few moments ago. But he had been drinking. She could smell it on his breath.

'You—you ask me that!' she got out, trying to free
her other arm that was imprisoned by her side. 'After—
after breaking in here!'

'Are you kidding?' He blinked now, and she thought
what absurdly long eyelashes he had, for a man. But she
was making far too many personal observations about
him, and she determinedly schooled her thoughts along
with her expression. 'I didn't break in,' he added impatiently. 'Believe it or not, I have an invitation!'

'You do?' Samantha wasn't sure whether she should
believe him or not, but as he was holding the upper
hand—in more ways than one, she acknowledged painfully—what choice did she have?

'Yes.' He let go of the arm he had been punishing,
and transferred his hold to her waist. 'Can I trust you
not to pull another stunt like that, if I let you go?'

Samantha's lips trembled, but a smile was tugging at
the corners of her mouth. 'I—I think so,' she said, becoming conscious of the underlying intimacy of their
situation. Whether he realised it or not, she was acutely
aware of his lean hips inclined towards hers, and the
muscled thigh that was threatening to part her legs. 'Are
you going to? Let me go, I mean,' she appended, as the
ambiguity of her words brought an embarrassed wave
of colour to her cheeks.

Amazingly, the ebony eyes darkened. Samantha
wouldn't have believed they could, and it wasn't so much
an increasing definition of colour as a deepening of
quality, a softening, that gave the pupils a curious
lightness.

'Do you want me to?' he asked, and there was a distinctly husky timbre to his hoarse voice now that caused
a feathering of flesh all over her body. Dear heaven, he
was sexy, she thought, her senses racing out of control.
It wasn't exactly what he was saying, it was the way he
was saying it, and her tongue appeared to wet her lips
in unknowing invitation.

'I——' she began, knowing how she ought to answer
him, but hesitating none the less. And then a voice that

she remembered rather too well broke over them in shrill accusation.

'Matt! Matt, is that you? In God's name, what are you doing down here?'

Melissa Mainwaring came down the stairs as she spoke, her short-skirted dress of crisp blue taffeta rustling as she did so. It also slipped enticingly off one white shoulder, drawing attention to the pearly quality of her skin, and the ripe, rounded shape it concealed.

The man stiffened. There was no other way to describe the sudden freezing of his body. With unhurried but nevertheless decisive movements, he released Samantha and stepped back, his expression twisting oddly in the harsh track of a spotlight. It gave her the opportunity to try and gather her own composure, though the expression in Melissa's eyes as she looked at her was not encouraging.

She had reached the bottom of the stairs now, and her high heels rang noisily against the copper-coloured tiles. But, her attention was all on the man beside Samantha now and, although she clearly hadn't liked their earlier closeness, his subsequent withdrawal had mollified her somewhat.

'You came,' she said, her expression changing to one of extreme satisfaction. 'I hoped you would.'

'Did you?'

His response was scarcely enthusiastic, though Samantha sensed that he was holding his real emotions in check. There was a distinct tenseness in the way he held himself, in the way he spoke. Something was going on here, something she knew nothing about, and she wished, with all her heart, that she could escape before his control snapped.

'Yes.' The woman's gaze switched to the girl beside him, and Samantha thought how ironic it was that she and Melissa should have had that altercation earlier. It made the present situation so much more awkward, and she just wanted to pick up her boxes and leave. 'I see Miss Maxwell let you in.'

'I let myself in,' the man contradicted her, but Melissa was not appeased.

'But you know one another,' she probed, crossing her arms across her midriff, and massaging her elbows with delicate hands.

'No.' The man—*Matt*?—shifted his weight from one foot to the other, pushing his hands into the pockets of his leather jacket. 'Miss—Maxwell?' He looked briefly at Samantha, and she quickly bent her head. 'Miss Maxwell thought I was an intruder.'

Melissa frowned. 'Is this true?' she asked, and Samantha sighed.

'Yes.'

'It was my fault for coming in the back way,' declared Matt sardonically. He bent to pick up the knife that still lay glinting on the floor, but although he glanced at Samantha as he did so he made no mention of it. 'So— I believe congratulations are in order. You finally got someone to take the bait.'

If Samantha was shocked by his words, Melissa was more so. 'You—bastard!' she choked, and the look she cast in the other woman's direction was eloquent of the fury she felt at Samantha's being a witness to her humiliation. There would be no useful contacts from this dinner party, not if Melissa had anything to do with it, Samantha thought ruefully. But at the same time she felt a small sense of satisfaction that whatever was going on here, the man—Matt? Matthew?—was apparently quite capable of holding his own.

'I—if you'll excuse me,' she murmured, deciding not to push her luck. It was one thing to be an unwilling witness; it was quite another to become a participant in their quarrel.

Melissa took a deep breath. 'Where are you going?'

Samantha moistened her lips. 'I'm leaving.'

'Like hell you are!' Melissa shot Matthew a crippling glare. 'People haven't even started eating yet. It'll be hours before the tables can be cleared. Go to the bathroom, or somewhere. Mr Putnam and I only need a few moments' privacy.'

'No.' Samantha thrust the last of her belongings into the boxes, and fastened the safety clips. Right now, she didn't particularly care if she smashed all her dishes. She just wanted to get out of there, for more reasons than she cared to consider. 'I—your—that is, the prince knows I only—prepare the food. I don't clean up afterwards.'

'Why not?' Melissa's undoubtedly striking features were less than appealing at this moment. 'You're just a waitress, aren't you? That's what you're doing here.'

'No,' said Samantha again, snatching up her jacket, and grabbing hold of two of the cold-boxes. 'I just—deliver the food, that's all.' It was easier than trying to explain. 'And now, as I say, I must be going. It—it's getting late, and I've got a long way to drive.'

Melissa looked as if she would have liked to try and stop her by force, but, instead, she contented herself with a sarcastic sneer. 'Well, you can tell your employer we weren't very impressed with the service,' she declared spitefully. 'Oh, and mention the caviare, won't you? You have heard of caviare, I assume?'

Samantha gritted her teeth, intensely aware of the man standing listening to the proceedings, with a faintly mocking expression on his dark face. 'I'll remember,' she said tightly, bumping the boxes against the cupboards as she struggled to the door. Just a few more yards, she thought, wondering how she could turn the handle without wasting time putting her boxes down, and then the man intervened.

'Allow me,' he said, reaching past her to pull open the door, and she gave him a grateful smile. 'Drive carefully,' he added, as she hurriedly ascended the steps, but any response she might have made died on her lips. As she glanced behind her, Melissa came to grasp his arm, and drag him back into the kitchen. Samantha's last glimpse was of the two of them standing very close together, and of Melissa's scarlet-tipped fingers spread against his chest.

CHAPTER THREE

THE HONEY POT was hectic, and Samantha was busy microwaving dozens of the individual earthenware dishes of her home-made lasagne when she saw him.

It was odd, that sudden awareness, but she noticed him the moment he entered the café. Afterwards, she told herself it was the stir his leather-clad appearance caused among the bank clerks, shop assistants, and other office workers, who made up the bulk of the lunchtime crowd. But, whatever it was, she knew an unfamiliar sense of panic, as he threaded his way between the tables.

Debbie Donaldson, her assistant, whose job it was to serve the customers and clear the tables, intercepted him before he could reach the refrigerated cabinets, where delicious plates of sandwiches and salads were on display.

'A table for one?' she enquired, her wide blue eyes assessing, taking in his dark attractive features and leanly muscled frame.

'What?' His eyes had been on Samantha, who was hurriedly preparing another of the pre-cooked pasta dishes for the microwave, and trying to pretend she hadn't seen him. 'Oh——' He expelled his breath on an impatient sigh, and glanced briefly round the small restaurant. 'Yes. Why not?' His gaze narrowed to enclose only Debbie. 'Can you fit me in?'

'I'm sure I can.'

Debbie's lips parted to reveal a provocative tongue, and Samantha, unwillingly aware of how impressionable the eighteen-year-old was, felt a surge of raw frustration. What was he doing here? she wondered, stifling a curse as she burned her thumb on a hot dish. He was a long way from Eyton Gate and Belgravia. How on earth had he found her? And who the hell was he anyway?

A surreptitious glance across the room informed her that Debbie had seated him at a small table in the bow window. It was one of the only two tables left vacant in the café, and was usually reserved for Mr Harris, the manager of the local building society. But Debbie wasn't looking her way, so Samantha couldn't signal that that table was unavailable. Debbie's attention was firmly fixed on her customer—as was the attention of most of the females present.

Not that she could blame them, Samantha admitted ruefully, trying to concentrate on what she was doing. He was clean-shaven this morning, and the hooded eyes and stark uncompromising features possessed a potent sensuality. Two sausages, one cannelloni, and two egg and cress sandwiches, she recited silently, struggling to remember the orders. But his presence disturbed her, reminding her as it did of that evening two nights ago, when he had invaded Prince Georgio's kitchen.

She had tried to put the memory of that evening out of her mind. She didn't want to think about her emotions at that time. She had told herself it was natural not to want to dwell on the scare he had given her. But the truth was, her fears had been superseded by the way he had made her feel when he'd disarmed her.

Disarmed her in more ways than one, she thought drily, trying to make light of it. And who would want to remember the things Melissa Mainwaring had said to her? No, the whole evening had been a disaster. She was actually having second thoughts about continuing that particular side of the business.

'He says he wants to speak to you.'

Debbie's vaguely resentful voice rang in her ear, and Samantha stopped spreading the egg and cress mixture on the bread and looked at her assistant.

'Who?' she asked, keeping her back firmly to the tables, and Debbie gave her a disbelieving look.

'Who do you think?' she exclaimed. 'The joker sitting over there by the window. The one doing an imitation of Mel Gibson.'

Samantha blinked, really confused this time. 'Mel Gibson?' she echoed.

'Mad Max?' suggested Debbie shortly, in the tone of one explaining table manners to a five-year-old. 'And don't pretend you didn't see him come in. You and half the female population of Northfleet!'

Samantha expelled her breath, and laid one slice of bread over the other. 'Well—what does he want?' she asked, praying he hadn't told Debbie of their earlier encounter. But the younger girl only shrugged.

'I don't know. He just said he wanted to speak to you. Do you know him? Is he a friend of Paul's?'

'Hardly.' The word was out before Samantha could prevent it, but she covered herself by adding swiftly, 'I ask you: does he look like a friend of Paul's?'

Debbie cast a glance over her shoulder. 'Well, no,' she admitted. 'I can't honestly see Paul buying leather gear, let alone getting into it.' She turned back to look at her employer. 'So what do you think he wants? Protection money?'

Samantha's amused gasp had a trace of hysteria in it. 'Protection money!' she echoed disparagingly. My God! Debbie had some imagination. She sobered abruptly. But perhaps it wasn't so far-fetched. Maybe she did need protection. From him!

'Well, are you going to go and see what he wants, or aren't you?' Debbie demanded, resentful that her idea had been dismissed so wholeheartedly. 'I suppose he could have a message or something. You know, one of those express delivery services. It's obvious he's come on a motorbike.'

'Is it?'

Now Samantha permitted herself another brief glance in his direction. To her relief, he was looking out of the window and didn't see her. But her own reaction to his lounging figure was no less disruptive because of that.

'I'd say so,' Debbie declared now, edging Samantha aside, and taking over the slicing of the sandwich. 'Go on. You'd better see what he wants. I get the feeling he's not going to go away until he's spoken to you.'

Samantha expelled her breath unevenly, and looked down at her bibbed apron. Her immediate impulse was to take it off, but of course she didn't. So far as she knew, he was here to have lunch just like any other of her customers. He had asked her to serve him because he felt that their previous encounter entitled him to trade on their acquaintance. And besides, she could imagine Debbie's reaction if she attempted to smarten herself up to speak to him. He had already caused enough of a stir by coming here. Paul was bound to hear about it anyway, so why exacerbate an already awkward situation?

In consequence, she felt a certain amount of trepidation as she made her way towards him. The smiles she cast at her regular customers were unusually tight, and the words she did exchange were short and to the point. It wasn't that she never served the customers. On the contrary, sometimes she and Debbie were both practically run off their feet, particularly at weekends. But this was different, and she knew it. And with Debbie's eyes upon her, it was difficult to behave naturally.

He half got out of his seat, as she approached the table, but then, as if realising it wasn't the done thing, he subsided again. With his arm hooked across the back of his chair, and his ankle resting easily across his knee, he lazily resumed his lounging position.

'You'll forgive me for not getting up,' he said, as she reached the table, and Samantha came to an unwilling halt.

'What can I get you?' she asked, carefully ignoring his attempt to be familiar. 'The menu's on the table.'

'So it is.' His eyes flicked carelessly over the plastic clip that held the printed card. 'What would you recommend?' He glanced about him. 'The lasagne appears to be popular.'

Samantha thrust her fists into the pouchlike pocket of her apron. 'What do you want?' she demanded, and they both knew she was not talking about the menu now. 'I'm very busy.'

'So I see.' His dark eyes assessed her flushed cheeks, and the wisps of moist hair that clung to her forehead. 'How long have you been running this place?'

'Two years—if that's any concern of yours.' Samantha's nervousness was giving way to indignation. 'Look, I don't know why you've come here, but I wish you hadn't. Now, if you want to eat, OK. Otherwise, I'm going to have to ask you to vacate this table.'

Humour tugged at the corners of his lips, but he reached obediently for the menu. 'I'll have—a toasted cheese sandwich,' he said, after a moment. 'Oh—and a beer, too. If you have one.'

Samantha was fairly sure he knew they didn't have a licence to serve alcohol, and her nails dug into her palms. 'That'll have to be a fruit juice,' she informed him, resenting the fact that she had no excuse not to serve him. And, remembering he had been drinking the last time she spoke to him, she added tautly, 'Perhaps you'd be better off at the pub!'

'No. I'll stay here,' he responded, setting the menu back on the table. 'Thanks.'

Samantha hesitated, and then, realising she had no further reason to linger, she turned and stamped back into the kitchen. But her normally even-tempered mood was shattered, and Debbie eyed her warily as she slapped two slices of bread under the grill.

'What did he say?' she asked, after a moment, curiosity getting the better of her, and Samantha cast her a scowling glance.

'Nothing,' she replied at last, realising she was going the right way to arouse the girl's suspicions. 'He wants a toasted cheese sandwich and a glass of orange juice. You can take it to him.'

'Me?' Debbie looked surprised, and Samantha couldn't blame her. 'So why did he ask for you to serve him?'

'Who knows?' Samantha flipped the bread over, and reached for the cheese. 'Go and see if any tables need clearing. As you've commandeered Mr Harris's table, you'll have to find somewhere else to put him when he comes in.'

Debbie pressed her lips together. 'Are you sure you're all right, Sam?' she persisted, evidently feeling some responsibility for what had happened, and not happy with the result. 'You look—sort of upset.'

'Don't be silly, Debbie.' Samantha managed a faint smile, as she covered the bread with cheese, and returned it to the grill. 'I'm just annoyed because there was no earthly reason why you couldn't have—have taken his order, that's all. Now, hurry up. This is almost ready.'

For the next half-hour, Samantha managed to keep herself too busy to pay any attention to her unwelcome visitor. There were meals to heat and serve, extra salads to be made, and plenty of dirty plates to load into the dishwasher. If Debbie thought she was less talkative than usual, she didn't say anything. Besides, she was busy too, and it wasn't until the café had practically cleared that Samantha noticed that *he* was still there.

It didn't really surprise her. She guessed Debbie would have said something if he had departed. But seeing him still seated at the table, apparently engrossed in a newspaper someone must have left behind, still infuriated her, and she wished she had the strength to throw him out.

'Go and tell him we're getting ready to close,' she murmured to Debbie, but the younger girl firmly shook her head.

'You know we don't close until half-past five,' she said. 'If you want to lie about it, you do it. He wasn't too pleased when I brought his sandwich, so don't expect me to do your dirty work.'

Samantha grimaced. 'I'm only asking you to fib a little. He doesn't know anything about this place.'

'How do you know that?'

Debbie was looking at her with that curious look again, and Samantha expelled a frustrated sigh. 'I don't—*know*—not for sure. But you haven't seen him round here before, have you? It's obvious he's not going to know what our hours are.'

'They're written on the door,' retorted Debbie flatly, and Samantha acknowledged that she had forgotten that.

'OK,' she said, giving in. 'I'll go and see if he's finished.'

He looked up as she reached the table, and, seeing who it was, he folded the newspaper and put it aside. 'Very nice,' he said, and for a moment she was so nervous, she didn't know what he was talking about. 'The sandwich,' he prompted, noticing her blank expression. 'As good as any I've tasted. You had the consistency of the cheese just right.'

Samantha allowed all the air to escape from her lungs, and then took a steadying breath. 'So,' she said, 'is that all? Would you like your bill?'

'What I'd like is for you to sit down with me,' he replied evenly, no trace of humour in his expression now. 'You've been running yourself ragged for the last hour, at least. Don't you think you deserve a break?'

'I'll have a break when all the customers have gone,' she told him crisply, wishing she had taken the time to go to the bathroom before marching over here. Her brown hair was coming loose from the single braid she had plaited that morning, and she was sure her face was streaked with sweat. It shouldn't matter how she looked as far as he was concerned, but it did. She couldn't help remembering Melissa Mainwaring's pale, exquisite face, and her long, elegant hand on his sleeve.

He shrugged then, and stood up, immediately putting her at even more of a disadvantage. In her low-heeled shoes, she was little more than five and a half feet, and she had to tilt her head to look up at him.

'What time do you close?' he asked, and Samantha, who had expected him to ask how much he owed her, took a step backwards.

'I—half-past five,' she said, recognising that there was no point in lying about it. 'Um—that'll be two pounds twenty. One-fifty for the sandwich, and seventy pence for the juice.'

She hated asking him for the money. She would have much preferred to say it was on the house. But Debbie would want to know why she hadn't charged him, and it was too complicated to go into details.

'What?' He frowned. And then, realising what she was saying, he pulled a five pound note from the pocket of his leather trousers. 'Here.' He handed it over. 'Now, will you have a drink with me, *after* you close?'

Samantha was staggered. 'Why?'

He shrugged. 'Why not?'

'I can't.' Samantha shook her head.

'Why can't you?'

Samantha swallowed, and glanced behind her to make sure Debbie wasn't eavesdropping on their conversation. Then, lifting her left hand, she showed him the diamond solitaire Paul had given her. 'I don't think my fiancé would approve.'

He expelled his breath then, and there was a distinct note of sarcasm in his harsh voice as he said, 'I'm only asking you to have a drink with me. I'm not planning on taking you to bed.'

Samantha's cheeks flamed. 'You wouldn't get the chance!' she retorted hotly, despising the shiver of excitement that ran through her at his words. Had Melissa Mainwaring been to bed with him? she wondered. Was that why he had treated her with such a lack of respect?

'Perhaps not.' He was disturbingly equivocal about her denial. 'So—will you join me for a drink? Anywhere you like. You know the area better than I do.'

An image of sitting in some smoky bar, with him beside her on an intimate banquette, flashed into her mind. She could already feel the hard strength of his thigh, as it brushed against hers, and smell the heady warmth of his breath, as it cooled her hot temple . . .

With an effort, she thrust those thoughts aside, and struggled to appear indifferent. 'I can't,' she said again, smoothing the note he had given her between fingers that were slightly damp. 'I—er—I'll get your change.'

But when she closed the till he was gone. She was left with the two pounds eighty pence in her hand, feeling rather like a cheap tart who hadn't given satisfaction. It didn't help when Debbie came and looked over her shoulder either. 'Some tip,' she remarked, continuing on her way to clear the table. But Samantha felt like taking his money and throwing it into the street.

The afternoon dragged. Once the lunchtime rush was over, they were never very busy, catering mainly for young mothers with toddlers, or older women wanting a break in the middle of their shopping.

Debbie left at twenty-five past. Her bus was at twenty-five to six, and Samantha generally let her go in time to catch it. Otherwise, she felt obliged to drop the girl off on her way home, and that entailed a detour.

Samantha was seeing Paul that evening, so she worked fairly speedily after the 'Closed' sign had been put in place. They were going to the new multiplex cinema to see a film Paul had told her about. He was picking her up from home at a quarter-past seven. Which should give her time to have a shower, and hopefully dispel the feelings of ambivalance that had hung about her all afternoon.

She left the café at twenty to six, setting the safety alarm, and locking the door behind her. It was a cool evening, with drops of rain in the air, and she hoped it would warm up for Easter, which was only a couple of weeks away. Although some sturdy cherry trees were attempting to come into blossom, the east wind was deterring all but the hardiest growth. It was one of the chilliest springs Samantha could remember, and she wrapped her raincoat closely about her as she made a dash for her van.

The van coughed, but it started at the second attempt, and she patted the wheel approvingly. The little Mini had never let her down yet, but there was no denying she needed a larger vehicle.

And yet, she argued frowningly, waiting for a break in the traffic so that she could pull away, if she wasn't going to continue with her outside catering, was there a lot of point? The Mini was quite capable of running her around town, and she seldom went any distance in the ordinary way unless she was with Paul.

Unwillingly, the reasons why she was having second thoughts about the catering brought *that* man's face to mind. She hadn't forgotten what had happened at lunchtime. On the contrary, she was having the greatest difficulty keeping thoughts of him at bay. The trouble was, no matter how she might deny it to herself, she had been curious as to why he had taken the trouble to come and find her. And, although the idea that he might have some personal interest in her was too far-fetched to contemplate, she felt a quiver of excitement whenever she thought of him.

'Get real, Sam!' she chided herself angrily, as she braked for the lights at Park Terrace. What possible interest could someone like him have in an ordinary female like herself? She wasn't chic; she wasn't elegant; she wasn't even particularly good-looking. The only advantages she possessed were that she had fairly long legs for a girl of her height, and that she was blessedly slim. Having said that, her breasts had always been a little too heavy, and her fine toffee hair had to be permed to give it any body. At present, it was in that crimped state of being neither straight nor curly, and for working she dragged it ruthlessly into a tight braid. Not exactly what he was used to, she was sure, even if he couldn't compete with the rich Prince Georgio.

She had guessed that that was why he hadn't arrived at the party like all the other guests. It was obvious he and Melissa Mainwaring knew one another rather better than her wealthy fiancé was aware. But she guessed Miss Mainwaring would always have an eye to the main chance. And she had chosen security, instead of...what? *Love*? Samantha's nose wrinkled. Lust, more like, she essayed scornfully, not liking where her musings were taking her. But she couldn't prevent the image of the pair of them on a bed together from invading her troubled thoughts, and the knowledge of how that made her feel was like a bitter taste in her mouth.

In consequence, she spent the evening trying to make it up to Paul. Not that he was aware of what she was doing. He just thought she was more affectionate than usual. Which made for a rather difficult scene, when it was time to say goodnight. He naturally assumed she would welcome his advances, and she was hot, and dispirited, when she eventually let herself into the house. Why couldn't she be like other girls? she wondered, wearily, as she tugged a brush through her tumbled hair. Of course, most of the girls she had gone to school with were married by now, so they didn't have this problem. Nevertheless, she remembered how they used to talk before they got a ring on their finger. And her reactions to Paul bore little resemblance to their eager confidences.

The phone rang soon after she got into work the next morning. And when she picked it up a voice she didn't recognise said, 'Miss Maxwell, please.'

'This is Miss Maxwell,' she replied, automatically reaching for her notebook. Her doubts of the evening before had been dispelled somewhat by the unexpected arrival of the sun, and she swiftly decided that if this was another catering assignment she would do it.

'I understand you operate an independent catering service,' the unfamiliar male voice continued, and Samantha dropped into the chair beside her desk. The tiny office was really just a storeroom, off the main serving area, but it did provide a little privacy, when the café was busy.

'That's right,' she said now. 'I have catered for a couple of dinner parties recently. What did you have in mind? Buffet catering is fairly standard, but more formal menus can be to your choice, of course.'

'Of course.' The man was silent for a moment, and Samantha wondered if he was having second thoughts. But then, he added, 'Perhaps it would be best if we could meet and discuss the arrangements. It is rather an important occasion, and I wouldn't like there to be any hitches.'

Samantha frowned. 'Would this dinner party be in London?' she asked, mentally cataloguing her plans for the rest of the week. Apart from being tied up during the day with the café, her evenings were reasonably flexible. As long as Paul didn't take offence if she had to cancel any of his arrangements.

'It's—er—it's a boardroom lunch actually,' said the man, after another moment's hesitation. 'Does that present any problems?'

'A lunch!' Samantha was dismayed. It hadn't occurred to her to consider that she might be invited to cater for a lunch. This was when she needed another assistant, she thought unhappily. There was no way Debbie could cope with the café single-handedly.

'It is in London,' added the man, as if to fill the void Samantha's procrastination had created. 'The company's J.P. Software International. The offices are just off the north side of Regent Street. You'd be catering for—approximately thirty people.'

'Yes.'

Samantha's brain was working madly. Despite what she had thought the night before, the idea of finding a lunchtime clientele was appealing. It had so many advantages. Not least, leaving her evenings free for other things. But, if she turned this down, she might not be asked again. She wondered how he had got her name. She really would have to get some cards printed.

'Well, Mr—er—er——?'

'Burgess,' supplied the man, after another of those infinitesimal pauses, but Samantha scarcely noticed.

'Well, Mr Burgess,' she said, 'I have to tell you, my previous experience has all been in evening engagements.'

All? She grimaced, and shifted the phone to her other ear. Two dinner parties didn't actually justify the word 'all'. But so what? She had to start somewhere.

'Does this mean you're not equipped to take on any afternoon appointments?' he queried, and Samantha sighed.

'Not exactly, no. But——'

'I suggest you come and talk it over with our PR department,' declared the man, overriding her objections. 'I'm sure we can work something out.'

Can we? For a moment, Samantha was half afraid she had said those words aloud, but there was no response from Mr Burgess, so she concluded, with some relief, that she hadn't. All the same, she didn't see how it could be done—unless her mother could be persuaded to help her.

'How—er—how did you get this number?' she asked, to give herself time to consider, and the man sucked in his breath.

'I—why, from a friend who attended a reception recently in Eyton Gate,' he replied swiftly, and, although Samantha was too absorbed to notice any inflexion in his voice, any connection with that occasion was enough to give her pause.

'Do you mind telling me who it was who gave you my number?' she enquired, realising it was hardly her business, but needing to know just the same.

'Um—no.' The man hesitated again, but Samantha was too anxious to hear what he had to say to notice. 'A chap by the name of Matthew Putnam,' he said offhandedly. And then, 'Does it matter? Is he a friend of yours, or something?'

CHAPTER FOUR

'THAT was a clever touch, Victor,' remarked Matthew, as his manservant put down the phone. His lips twisted admiringly. 'Implying that I might have some ulterior motive for recommending her was masterly. She was so busy denying any connection between us, she hardly noticed what she was agreeing to.'

'Well, I don't like it, Mr Putnam,' replied the older man tersely. 'For heaven's sake, why would you want to get involved with some second-rate waitress from Northfleet?'

Matthew's mouth tightened, and he swung the feet he had had propped on the edge of his desk, while Victor made the call to Samantha Maxwell, to the floor. 'She's not second-rate, and she's not a waitress,' he declared, his eyes cold as they surveyed the other man. 'And I'll— get involved, as you put it—with who I like. You may not think so, but you're not my keeper! Now, get out of here.'

'Yes, sir.'

Victor went, but Matthew could tell by the stiffness of the man's shoulders that he hadn't heard the last of it. He knew Victor too well, and Victor knew him. They'd been together too many years now for any minor contretemps to come between them. But, nevertheless, he was getting too familiar where Matthew's personal life was concerned. And, although he had never really liked Melissa, he had resigned himself to the fact that their relationship might become permanent.

But it hadn't, thought Matthew grimly, remembering the night of the engagement party with some distaste. And he had been fool enough to go there. If he'd had any sense he'd have stayed away, instead of believing he could beat Melissa at her own game.

53

Yet, to a point, he had, he conceded broodingly, re-membering how outraged she'd been at finding him with the Maxwell girl. Melissa hadn't liked seeing him with another woman, however innocent that encounter had been.

But, after the girl had gone, it hadn't been so easy to play it cool. Melissa had got the wrong idea about him being there, in spite of the unconventional means of his arrival. And perhaps she had hoped he had had a change of heart. Whatever, she had certainly not acted like a woman who was engaged to another man. And he was only human, however degenerate that might make him feel.

He was glad now he had been the one to suggest they ought to go upstairs to the party. Playing games was one thing; deliberately seducing another man's fiancée was another. Which was probably why Melissa had made such a big thing of going to Ivanov, and hanging on his arm for the rest of the evening. She had wanted to make him squirm, and to a certain extent she had succeeded.

But he hadn't let her have it all her own way. Partly to provoke Melissa, and partly to relieve his own frus-tration, he had made a play for Briony Clarke, the second most attractive woman at the party—and one of Melissa's closest friends.

The irony was, Briony had fallen for it, hook, line and sinker. And, when she did, Matthew had discovered it wasn't as much fun hurting people as he had thought. In consequence, he had stalked out long before the party was over, uncaring what interpretation Melissa might put on his actions.

But, curiously enough, it hadn't been Melissa or Briony who had occupied his thoughts when he eventually got to bed. He had found himself thinking about the Maxwell girl, and remembering how terrified she had been, confronting him with a knife. God! A short laugh escaped him. She had really thought he was an intruder. But, designer stubble and all, he probably hadn't looked particularly civilised.

Nevertheless, it had been a novelty, being regarded as someone outside the law. Despite the fact that he had always fought for his independence, there had never been a time when he had actually broken the law. Oh, he had done things when he was a student that his mother and his grandfather would not have approved of, but they had had no criminal intent. Consequently, to be treated as a possible burglar or worse had had a singular appeal. Not that he wished to repeat it. The experience had been rather too real for comfort. But the girl—what was it her waitress had called her? Sam? Samantha—she had had definite possibilities.

Which was why he had made it his business to find out who, and what, she was. It hadn't been difficult. Ivanov's secretary had been quite flattered that Matthew had been so impressed with the buffet that he wanted the number of the caterer. Lederer knew nothing of his previous association with Melissa, and even less about Samantha Maxwell.

In truth, Matthew didn't know what he intended when he drove down to Northfleet, a couple of days later. Maybe Victor had a point. Maybe it was the fact that she came from a different background from his that had excited his interest. Certainly she was nothing like the women he was used to dealing with. It wasn't just that she worked for her living. Many of the women he knew ran galleries, or boutiques, or were involved in public relations and modelling. One or two of them even owned their own businesses, though nothing quite so physical as running a café. No, it was more to do with her attitude; with the kind of defensive stance she had adopted towards him. She didn't seem to like him, which was also a novelty, for, although he had never seen any great attraction in his appearance, the fact remained that most women seemed to find him presentable.

Even so, it was hard to justify what he was doing now, even to himself. He didn't honestly know why he was doing it. Just because she had turned him down, he had engineered this totally trumped-up charade And why? So she would accept an invitation to see him again Only

she didn't think she was seeing him. Her appointment
was supposedly with Andy Lucas, his public relations
manager.

His jaw hardening, Matthew pulled the computer
keyboard towards him and punched in the code for the
current system he was working on. But even when the
complicated program unfolded on the screen he found
no escape in the data it provided. His mind was still active
with thoughts of the upcoming meeting with Samantha
Maxwell, and despite his impatience he was tempted to
cancel it.

Still in two minds, he switched off the computer and
left his study. He had decided to go into the office after
all, and he would think about what he was going to do
about the Maxwell girl later. It wasn't that important,
for Pete's sake! She was only a blasted waitress! She
ought to be flattered he was taking an interest in her!

But, as he changed out of the sweat-suit he had worn
to the gym earlier, he knew he was being less than fair.
He might never have been involved with a woman like
her before, but, conversely, he had never treated any
woman differently from another. He wasn't a snob, and
he certainly didn't consider himself better than anyone
else because of his background. Which was why trying
to find excuses for what he was doing this time was
proving so difficult. What did he want from her?
Companionship? *Sex*? For pity's sake, could he be that
desperate?

And yet, as he pulled on navy blue trousers and rum-
maged through a pile of silk shirts for one he liked, he
was uncomfortably aware of the hardening in his groin
when he recalled how good her breasts had felt,
cushioned against his chest. She had had rather full
breasts, he remembered, and long, long legs. Her face
hadn't been particularly striking; her cheeks had been
too round, and her mouth too big. But it had been a
sexy mouth, particularly when she had been frightened,
and her lower lip had jutted forwards. And she had
beautiful green eyes, long, and slightly slanted, and
fringed by dark lashes, which must surely be cosmetic.

His lips twisted. For someone who denied a serious interest in the girl, he certainly remembered a lot about her. Remembered, too, a distinct unwillingness to let her go, even when Melissa had come down the stairs and found them. But that had probably been because he knew how sucked Melissa would feel, seeing them together. That was probably why he was pursuing the connection. Because he knew how infuriated Melissa would be.

His friend and managing director Robert Prescott was deep in a discussion about computer viruses with their sales manager Martin Ryan when Matthew arrived at the office. J.P. Software International occupied the top two floors of a high-rise in Cumberland Place, with Matthew's office, and the boardroom, and the offices of his senior management team, on the upper level. Now, Matthew came to rest his shoulder against the frame of Robert's door, acknowledging his second-in-command's raised eyebrows with a grimace of his own.

'I know,' he said. 'You didn't expect to see me. Well, I thought it was time I came to see what you were doing.'

Robert grinned, their relationship one of long standing, and of mutual respect. 'I'm glad to see you're still alive,' he remarked, as Martin Ryan got up from the desk and made some comment about having things to do. He waited until the door had closed behind the other man before adding drily, 'According to your mother, you're drinking yourself to death!'

'Mmm.' Matthew flung himself into the chair across from his friend and pulled a face. 'My mother exaggerates,' he declared, leaning forward to pluck a brochure advertising some sophisticated hardware from Robert's desk. 'What's this stuff like?' he queried, flicking through its pages. 'I hear these new lap-tops weigh less than six pounds.'

Robert regarded him tolerantly. 'So I hear,' he conceded, prepared to wait until Matthew chose to tell him why he had really come into the office. It wasn't just to exchange gossip. Matthew wasn't like that.

'Of course, they're still working on the screens.'

'Yes.'

'And I guess only the most expensive of them have anything like the capability of a desktop.'

'Yes.'

Matthew looked up, aware of the monosyllabic answers he was receiving, and the reason for them. He gave a rueful grin. 'I'm so glad you agree.'

Robert shrugged. 'What's not to agree? We get a dozen of those pamphlets dropped through our door every day. They all claim to have made a breakthrough in computer technology. Some of them have. Most of them haven't. They've just adapted someone else's idea.'

Matthew tossed the brochure back on to the desk. 'So speaks the complete cynic.'

'You get cynical in this business,' retorted Robert, his hand hovering over the button on his intercom. 'Can I interest you in some coffee?'

Matthew shrugged. 'Why not? What's a little caffeine between friends?'

Robert spoke to his secretary, and then lay back in his chair, steepling his fingers. 'So,' he said, curiosity getting the better of him, 'did you finish the program? Is that what we owe the honour of this visit to?'

Matthew arched one dark brow. 'Don't be facetious, Rob. It doesn't suit you. Until recently, I spent as much time in this office as you did.'

'Yeah.' Robert had to acknowledge that this was true. 'I guess you must have decided to take your mother's advice for once.'

'My mother's advice is to leave the running of this place to you, and go and live in Athens,' retorted Matthew grimly. 'What's your opinion of that?'

Robert frowned. 'You know what my opinion is. I'm an administrator, Matt. You're the brains around here.'

'I'd dispute that,' said Matthew flatly, breaking off as a knock sounded at the door. He waited until Robert's secretary had set the tray containing their cups of coffee on the desk and left the room before continuing, 'But what will happen when my grandfather retires is anybody's guess.'

Robert grimaced. 'Well, let's hope that day is a long way off,' he declared firmly. 'Now——' He handed one of the cups to his friend. 'Sugar but no cream, is that right?'

'Thanks.' Matthew took the cup, and gave a cursory glance at its contents. 'Black as hell's kettle. Just as I like it.'

Robert's lips twitched. 'OK.' He paused. 'So why did you decide to come in today? Is there a problem?'

'You might say that.' Matthew swallowed a mouthful of the coffee, and scowled as it scalded his throat. 'Damn! This is hot as hell, too! What's Judy trying to do? Burn my tongue out?'

'Hardly.' Robert was cautious as he sipped from his own cup. 'She was probably hoping you'd like it hot! Or that's the rumour anyway.'

'Ha, ha!' Matthew regarded his friend without rancour. 'But, as it happens, I do have a problem. A slight one, anyway. And—well, I want your help.'

Robert put down his cup. 'Go on.'

Matthew sighed. 'It's not that easy.'

'Why?' Robert looked wary. 'Is it personal?'

Matthew took a breath. 'Yes.'

Robert looked resigned. 'Don't tell me: you've seen Melissa.'

'I have seen Melissa.' Matthew's expression hardened. 'But that's not why I'm here.'

'No?'

'No.' Matthew was sardonic. 'As a matter of fact, it's someone else.'

'Another woman?' Robert looked staggered now.

'Yes.' Matthew half wished he hadn't started this. 'I met her at Melissa's engagement party.'

'*You* went to Melissa's engagement party?'

'I was invited,' agreed Matthew flatly. 'So what? We're still civilised human beings, aren't we?'

Robert shook his head. 'You tell me!'

'What's that supposed to mean?'

'Well, you haven't been particularly civil since Melissa walked out, have you?' he protested, reacting to Matthew's angry response.

'Maybe not.' Matthew took a moment to acknowledge the truth of that. 'Anyway, I'm going to have to live with it, aren't I? One way or the other.'

'So what's your problem?' Robert was curious. 'Who is this girl, anyway? Do I know her?'

'Unlikely.' Matthew's mouth flattened. 'Her name's Maxwell. Samantha Maxwell.'

'Does she live in London?'

'No.' Matthew shook his head. 'She lives in a little town in Essex. She's just a nice girl from a very ordinary background.'

'You're kidding!'

'No, I'm not.' Matthew was trying his best not to let Robert rile him in this. 'Anyway, who she is isn't important. What she does is.'

'Come again.'

Matthew changed tack. 'Do you remember telling me about this proposed meeting we're having with Koysaki?'

'I should do. I arranged it.'

'That's right.' Matthew paused. 'Well, I wondered if it might be a good idea to throw a lunch for them here. In the boardroom. I know you were talking about taking them out for dinner, but it occurred to me that a working lunch might suit all of us better.'

Robert blinked. 'OK. If you say so.' He lifted his shoulders. 'Forgive me, but what does this have to do with your new girlfriend?'

'She's not my new girlfriend,' declared Matthew drily. 'I don't even think she likes me. But——' he expelled his breath '—she's a professional caterer. And, I've preempted your approval, and asked her if she could give us a quote.'

'For the Koysaki lunch?'

'Yep.'

Robert shook his head. 'Are you telling me this is the only way you can see her again?'

'Something like that.'

'Does she know who you are?'

'No.'

'Then tell her.'

'No.' Matthew got up from his chair, and paced over to the window. 'If you knew her, you wouldn't even suggest it. Besides which, she's engaged.'

'God, Matt!' Robert finished his coffee, and thrust his cup aside. 'What is all this about? I don't believe you're that desperate to see this girl again! And, at the risk of getting my head bitten off, what about Melissa?'

'What about Melissa?' Matthew pushed his hands into his trouser pockets. 'I must say, for someone who professes to care about me, you certainly like turning the knife.'

'Don't be stupid!' Robert pushed back his chair, and got to his feet. 'It's just that—well, a week ago you weren't even returning my calls. Now, you've come up with this idea of getting some girl to arrange a lunch for the Japanese. Do I take it she was the caterer at Melissa's party?'

'It was Ivanov's party, actually,' said Matthew, splitting hairs. 'But yes. She did organise it. And it was pretty good, too. I think you'll be impressed.'

Robert looked nonplussed. 'I can't believe this, you know. Is she a raving beauty, or what?'

'No.' Matthew had to be honest. 'As I say, she's fairly ordinary, really. She has nice eyes, and nice——' he shunned the word *breasts* and added '—legs. She—intrigues me.'

'Because she turned you down, probably,' remarked Robert drily. 'Honestly, Matt, are you sure you know what you're doing?'

'No.' Matthew gave a rueful grin, and Robert couldn't help responding. 'But Melissa's going to be mad as hell when she finds out!'

Matthew's personal assistant paused in her boss's doorway and gave her employer a puzzled look. 'I say what?'

'You just tell her that Mr Burgess isn't here, but that his second-in-command will see her. OK?'

Mrs Mackay sighed. 'But who is Mr Burgess, Mr Putnam?' Her stalwart Scottish nature rebelled at the deception. 'What if she asks me that?'

'She won't.' Matthew tipped his chair back on its rear castors. 'Just do it, Mary, there's a good girl. Oh—and bring me the Koysaki file.'

Mrs Mackay returned a few moments later with the requested item, but her homely face still wore a look of disapproval. However, having worked for Matthew for the past eight years, she was reluctantly prepared to do as he asked. In every other way, he was a considerate employer, and she never stopped thanking her lucky stars that, at the age of forty-two, she had landed such a plum position. Oh, she knew why. It was common knowledge in the office that Matthew had grown tired of younger, more glamorous PAs, whose prime objective had been to marry the boss. Nevertheless, she considered herself extremely fortunate to enjoy his confidence, even if, in this instance, he had chosen not to be absolutely frank.

The door closed behind her, and Matthew flipped open the Koysaki file. The Japanese company, whose representatives were flying to England at the end of the week, were looking for a software company through which they could channel their own product into Europe. It was a deal that interested Matthew greatly, offering as it did the opportunities for a similar expansion of J.P. Software into Japan. And, although he usually left all the talking to Robert, this was one occasion when he wouldn't mind sitting in on their discussions.

But, in spite of his interest in the project, Matthew found he couldn't concentrate. Instead, he closed the file again, and tapped his fingernails against the cardboard folder. What if she didn't come? he thought tautly, remembering how offhand she had been when he'd seen her. What if she'd discovered that Victor had nothing to do with J.P. Software International? Or—conversely—that Matthew Putnam had? It would be just his bad luck if she'd chosen to check out her client. And, in spite of her indifference, he didn't think she'd forgotten his name.

The buzzer on his desk sounded, and he started at the sound. Damn, he thought, he was as edgy as a roadrunner. Thank God Mrs Mackay couldn't see him.

'Yes,' he said, finding his voice, and depressing the receiver. 'What is it?'

'Miss Maxwell is here, Mr—er——' Matthew winced as she stuttered over the omission. 'Um—shall I send her in?'

'If you would.' Matthew took a deep breath and rose to his feet, no longer so convinced that this was a good idea.

Mrs Mackay opened the door. 'Miss Maxwell, sir,' she said, carefully avoiding a repeat of her earlier hesitation. She ushered the younger woman forward. 'Would you like some coffee?'

'Why not?'

Matthew said the words without giving them a great deal of thought. His attention was all on the newcomer, his eyes narrowing over slightly windswept curls and a pale grey suit whose skirt ended a couple of inches above her knee. She looked the same, but different, a harassed efficiency giving way to nervous anticipation.

That is, until she saw him; until she recognised that she had been tricked. Then, she glanced round at the departing Mrs Mackay with a distinct air of uncertainty, her hitherto pale features deepening with attractive colour. And she was attractive, Matthew admitted reluctantly. More attractive than he had been prepared to acknowledge. Those wide green eyes possessed a timeless beauty, although at present their expression was anything but remote.

'You,' she said, in an accusing tone, as the door closed behind Mrs Mackay. 'You're not Mr Burgess!'

Matthew forwent the idea of offering her his hand, and gestured to the chair at the other side of the desk. 'Did anyone say I was?' he queried, arching one dark brow. 'Allow me to introduce myself: I'm Matthew Putnam.'

'I know that.' Her lips tightened.

'Very well. Won't you sit down?' he suggested. 'The coffee won't be long.'

'I don't want any coffee,' she retorted tensely, gripping the leather portfolio she had brought with her, with both hands. Her tongue appeared to wet lips that were a delicious shade of copper, and Matthew found his eyes following its provocative progress. 'Just tell me why you've brought me here. And wasted a whole morning of my time!'

Matthew felt a twinge of anger. Just who the hell did she think she was? he wondered hotly. As far as she knew, she had been brought here to discuss a business proposition. What had he said to give her the impression that anything had changed?

'I suggest you sit down—and cool down,' he advised, keeping his own tone as unemotional as he could manage. 'Or is this the usual way you conduct business? I have to tell you, I've not come across these confrontational tactics before.'

She took a few deep breaths, and the sides of her jacket parted and came together invitingly. She was wearing a cream blouse under her jacket, and the lacy jabot at its neck fluttered accordingly. Her shoulders were back, and the rounded curve of her breasts swelled against the soft material. Matthew felt his own unwilling response to her undoubted femininity, and subsided into his chair. To hell with being polite, he decided grimly. Self-respect was more important just at present.

But, as if his words had aroused some doubt in her mind, too, Miss Maxwell chose that moment to inch forward, and brace her hips on the edge of the chair opposite. Matthew wouldn't have said she was sitting exactly, although she had drawn her knees tightly together. Nevertheless, she was not looking down at him, as she would have been otherwise, and her grip on the portfolio was less tense.

Her eyes flickered up, met his, and flickered away again. Eyes that had hazel flecks in them now, turning the green to grey. He watched as she cast a surreptitious glance about the room, before returning her attention to the portfolio.

'I—do I take it there really is a business lunch to cater for?' she asked at last, and Matthew knew a momentary sense of self-contempt. It was so easy to manipulate her, he thought disgustedly, tempted to lay bare the whole charade. But on the heels of this thought came the memory of how Melissa had treated him, and he consoled himself with the knowledge that she could have refused the invitation.

'Naturally, there's a lunch,' he said now, managing to sound convincingly put out. 'As—as my colleague said over the phone, it's for approximately twenty-five to thirty people. Our guests are Japanese, actually. So perhaps you could include some ethnic food as well.'

'Japanese?' Her eyes widened as they turned to his, and Matthew had the crazy thought that he might drown in their depths. His fingers itched to touch the long silky lashes that curled back against her lids, and smooth the curve of her temple, where it disappeared into the streaky mass of hair. 'I'm afraid I know nothing about Japanese food.'

'No?'

Matthew held her gaze deliberately, and saw the moment when panic entered her eyes. For seconds longer, she allowed him to mesmerise her, as a snake would hypnotise a rabbit. Then Mrs Mackay knocked at the door, and the compelling mood was broken.

'Just put the tray over there,' Matthew ordered, making space for it on his desk, his tone betraying just a trace of the irritation he was feeling. But Mrs Mackay noticed it, and her face assumed a matching expression.

'Can I get you anything else, Mr Putnam?' she enquired, and Matthew could hear the increased Scottish twang in her tone, which denoted her disapproval.

'No, thanks,' he said, impatient for her to leave them alone, and she took the hint.

'Well, I'll just be outside, if you want me,' she added, as a parting shot, and Matthew guessed that was as much for Miss Maxwell's benefit as his own.

With the door closed, he decided to take advantage
of the opportunity the coffee afforded. 'Won't you join
me?' he requested of her now bent head and, although
she was clearly unwilling, discretion fought with valour,
and won.

'Thank you,' she said, though he noticed she didn't
trust herself to meet his gaze again. 'Um—milk, and no
sugar.'

'It's cream,' he said wryly, and she pulled a rueful
face.

'Another nail in the diet,' she quipped, giving the first
indication that she was beginning to trust him. She took
the cup he handed her, but avoided touching his hand.
'Thanks.' She sipped, and looked around her. 'This is
a beautiful office.'

'I'm glad you like it.' Matthew poured himself a cup
of coffee, but made no attempt to drink it. Instead, he
lay back in his chair and said, 'So—who's minding the
café today?'

It was a mistake. She stiffened at once, and he knew
she was remembering his invasion of her space. But what
the hell; for all she knew he had been down there,
checking out the place. Not for any *personal* reasons.

'Is it important?' she asked now, and once again those
cool eyes were turned on him. Evidently, anger provided
a defence behind which she could shelter. But he wasn't
daunted by such a puerile display.

'Not at all,' he countered, pushing himself forward,
and resting his elbows on the desk. 'Are you usually this
touchy with would-be clients?'

A deepening trace of warm colour entered her neck,
just below the jawline, and spread rapidly upwards. 'I'm
sorry,' she said tightly, setting her cup back on the tray
with a betraying clatter. 'As a matter of fact, this whole—
catering—thing is a new departure for me, and I'm not
at all sure I want to continue with it.' She gathered up
the leather case that had been resting on her knees,
holding it in front of her like a would-be shield, and got
to her feet. 'I—appreciate your confidence, but I don't
think I'm the person to—to—accommodate you in this

matter. I don't have the experience, and—and I certainly don't feel it would be—appropriate for me to—to waste your time and mine in—in continuing with this discussion.' She sidestepped the chair, and began to retreat towards the door. 'I'm sure you'll find—someone else——'

Her excuses ended abruptly as Matthew left his chair and came after her. Impatience marred his lean dark features as he strode past her, successfully blocking her exit and bringing her to a standstill.

'You *appreciate*, that you can't *accommodate*, and it wouldn't be *appropriate*,' he mocked harshly, realising that if he wasn't careful she was going to walk out of here without leaving him even the flimsiest of excuses for seeing her again. His lips twisted. 'What's the matter, Miss Maxwell? Are you afraid of me?'

'No!'

The denial was swift enough, but hardly convincing. Her hands were white-knuckled as they gripped the portfolio. But, although he was sure she would have liked to keep a healthy distance between them, courage, or simply grim determination, kept her where she was.

'No?' he echoed scornfully, giving up all hope of handling this calmly. The scent of her body was drifting to his nostrils, a mixture of skin cream, and cologne, and a definite trace of nervous arousal. Whatever she said, he did disturb her, and the urge to touch her was growing out of control.

'Will you get out of my way?' she asked tensely, evidently still believing she could handle the situation. And he supposed she could, if she chose to cry for help, and Mrs Mackay came rushing to the rescue.

'Will you tell me why you've changed your mind about organising the lunch?' he countered, and, unable to prevent himself, he put out a hand and tucked a silky coil of hair behind her ear. Her head jerked away from his fingers, but she didn't dash his hand away. And, acting purely on impulse, he allowed the tips of his fingers to trail away down her neck to the collarless jacket of her suit.

'I should have thought that was obvious,' she declared now, rushing into speech, as if it was the only way she could cope with his advances. 'You don't want my professional services, Mr Putnam. You just want to play sexual games! Well, I'm sorry, but I'm not interested in your offer, whatever it is. So step out of the way, and let me go.'

Matthew's jaw hardened. Until she spoke, he had thought he might have let her go, unchallenged. He knew she was engaged. She had displayed her ring proudly. And, despite his suspicions, he had been having second thoughts about his intentions. He had actually felt a twinge of remorse for setting her up this way. She was a decent girl, after all, and if he needed a scapegoat there were plenty of other women around. Women who had nothing to lose.

But his finer feelings foundered on the sharp edge of her contempt. It was one thing for him to think about letting her off the hook, and quite another for her to believe she could force the issue. For God's sake, didn't she know better than to throw her indifference in his face? Didn't she know how irresistible it was to prove her wrong?

His eyes moved over her, noticing that for all her brave outburst she was breathing rather fast. The lace jabot fairly quivered as she fought to calm herself, and he guessed that only her grip on the portfolio prevented her from making some nervous gesture.

She was biting her lips, too, a sure sign that she was agitated. The lower lip was red and sore from being drawn between her teeth, and her tongue came to soothe it, before it was attacked again.

'Don't you ever play games, Sam?' he asked softly, and saw the start she gave at his casual use of her name. Perhaps she'd assumed he didn't know it. After all, she hadn't heard his conversation with her waitress.

'I—can I leave?' she demanded, instead of answering him. Her voice had risen slightly, and he guessed that she was anxious. Anxious, and a little apprehensive, he guessed shrewdly. What would she do if he said no?

'Why don't you just sit down and we'll talk about it?' he said, tracing the edge of her jacket with his thumb and forefinger. Even now, her vulnerability pricked his conscience. But, when the backs of his fingers brushed the curve of her breast, the feeling was electric. Warm skin, lightly covered by the fine fabric of her blouse, swelled against his hand, and the need to feel their fullness overpowered him.

But before his fingers could explore those tantalising peaks, she had dashed his hand away and darted for the door. Only an instinctive lunge on his part prevented her from snatching the door open, and his palm slammed into the panel, right beside her head.

She spun round against the door, her eyes showing her dismay. No, not dismay; that was too mild a term. She looked shocked; astounded; desperate to escape, and—hunted. Yes, that was the word. She looked like a cornered animal. And, in spite of his intentions, Matthew knew a moment's regret.

'Are you mad?' she choked, as his other hand came to rest on the other side of her head, effectively imprisoning her against the door. 'I—I'll scream!'

'Go ahead,' he said recklessly, the feminine scent of her body enveloping him once more. The more she fought him, the more aroused she became, and he didn't believe she would call for help and humiliate herself so completely.

But he was wrong. He apprehended the fact just a split second before she opened her mouth. And, although it wasn't the way he had intended to play it, there was only one way to silence her. With a muffled oath, he cut the scream off at its source, his mouth fastening over hers with bruising insistence.

She resisted, of course. The leather portfolio went flying, and she used both hands to try and force him away. Her balled fists slammed into his stomach, making him catch his breath. But it was when her knee attempted to connect with the most vulnerable part of his body that he reacted more forcefully, lowering his weight against her, and pinning her against the door.

Her jaw sagged, stunned by the crushing pressure of his heavy frame. He was robbing her of breath, he knew, but it was the only way to control her, and his hand left the door to curl about her throat. He stroked the taut skin, caressing and soothing, and when he felt her strength ebbing he slid his tongue between her teeth.

She bit it, but not hard, and beneath his insistence the tenor of the kiss changed. Her mouth softened under his, her lips opening of their own free will, to admit his searching invasion. Her hands, stilled by his brutal subjugation, now clutched the lapels of his jacket, as if needing a lifeline, and her legs parted helplessly when he wedged his thigh between.

She was so soft, so submissive; silk, and lace, and sweetness, tongue and lips yielding to the mastery of his. She was trembling; he could feel it; but fire leapt between them as he continued to possess her mouth. His body was responding; getting heavier; hardening; making him wish he could take her there, hard against the door. Or maybe on the floor; his senses reeled at the prospect. Lifting her legs, wrapping them around him, plunging deep into her hot, damp core...

He should have realised it had been too easy. Her sudden weakness; her submission. He should have suspected there was more to it than sex.

But the truth was, he was too bemused by his own arousal to give any thought to what she might be thinking, might be feeling. He was seduced by the idea of what it would be like, undressing her, making love with her, showing her how perfectly they could fit together. He felt so sure of her response that he was foolish enough to ease away from her, so that he could separate her blouse from the waistband of her skirt. He wanted to slide his hands underneath the filmy fabric. The prospect of touching her soft skin tantalised him, and the button-hard nipples were just aching for his caress.

Or so he had fondly imagined. But, once again, he should have known better than to think he could anticipate anything she might do. She must have just been waiting for some show of weakness on his part, and when he drew away from her she took her chance.

Afterwards, Matthew realised, she had only succeeded because he'd let her. If he had been on his guard, she would never have been able to push him off balance. But he wasn't, and she did, and he was still reeling against a potted palm when she fled out of the door. He heard Mrs Mackay utter a startled cry as a waste-paper bin was overturned, but the slamming of the outer door revealed she hadn't faltered. Which left him with the ignominious task of explaining to his assistant why Miss Maxwell had left in such a hurry and tamping down his own frustration at the inept way he had handled the situation.

CHAPTER FIVE

'BUT I don't understand. Why haven't you reported it to the police?'

'Because I haven't.' Samantha's head was aching, and she wished her mother would stop looking at her as if *she* had done something dreadful. 'It's only a leather portfolio, Mum. Nothing to get steamed up about.'

'I shouldn't have to remind you that your dad and I bought you that portfolio,' retorted her mother shortly. 'And you say you dropped it on the Tube, and you haven't even mentioned it to the authorities!'

Samantha took off her suit jacket, and draped it over a chair. 'I've told you: I didn't realise it was missing until I was walking up from the station.' She glanced round the café, which was empty except for a couple of teenagers, sitting at the table in the window. 'Anyway, thanks for covering for me. Has it been busy?'

'It was busy at lunchtime.' Mrs Maxwell was offhand. 'I must say, I thought you'd have been back before this. It's nearly five!'

'I know. I'm sorry.' Samantha had prepared herself for this while she was tramping round the streets of London. 'But you know what it's like. The buses are all full, and you can't get a taxi.'

'For three hours!' Mrs Maxwell wasn't convinced. 'I expected you back about two o'clock. Three, at the latest. What on earth have you been doing all this time? Did you arrange the booking?'

'Well—no.' Samantha knew there was no point in pretending otherwise. Her mother would find out soon enough. 'I—they wanted an ethnic meal. Japanese food; sushi, stuff like that. I couldn't do it.'

Mrs Maxwell stared at her. 'And didn't they tell you that when they arranged the interview?'

'Obviously not.' But Samantha could feel the colour invading her cheeks as she spoke. God, how she hated all this subterfuge! She was no good at lying. No good at anything, except getting herself into trouble.

Her mother sniffed. 'And it took you six hours to find that out?'

'The journey took the better part of three hours,' protested Samantha, able to be honest about that, at least. 'You know what the traffic is like in town. That's why I didn't take the car.'

'Even so...'

'Well——' Samantha licked her lips, and discovered they were still bare of lipstick. Damn, she should have found time to renew her make-up. But she had been walking around in a daze ever since she left Matthew Putnam's office. And it had taken her some time to find out where she was. 'I had to wait,' she offered feebly. 'And then we had coffee, and talked about—about other things.'

'What other things?'

'This and that.' Samantha shrugged, and jabbed a button on the till, pretending to be examining the takings. 'Just—just the usual sort of things, Mum. How cold it's been. How pretty the blossom is in the park. What sort of summer we're going to have.'

'Huh.' Her mother still sounded sceptical. 'It seems to me you've just been wasting your time. And mine, too, I might add. Well, I hope this isn't going to happen too often.'

'It won't.' Samantha closed the till with a snap that brought Debbie out of the small office, ostensibly to see what was going on. But Samantha didn't doubt she had heard everything that had been said. There was no privacy in the café.

Mrs Maxwell arched her sandy brows now. 'No?'

'No,' said Samantha, giving Debbie a look that revealed she knew exactly what the girl had been doing. 'I've decided not to continue with the outside catering. As you said, Mum, I don't have the experience, or the expertise.'

Her mother looked surprised. 'But—I thought—don't you already have some bookings?'

'I have one,' agreed Samantha heavily, realising she was going to have to take some aspirin. Her head was really thumping now. 'A formal dinner on Saturday night. It was someone who attended Jenny's dinner party, and got my number from her. But after that I'm not accepting any more bookings. It's too—time-consuming. And I don't think I want the responsibility.'

Paul was delighted when he found out, and Mrs Maxwell couldn't wait to tell him. When he called round at the house later that evening, he had hardly got his coat off before she had spilled the news. Samantha, still nursing her headache, was in no mood to cope with his instant jubilation. She shouldn't have made that announcement, she thought wearily. She should have just stopped accepting bookings, and let them find out for themselves. Instead, she had to listen to Paul and her mother congratulating each other on knowing better all along. And pretend that she was happy, when what she really felt was sick.

Still, the combined effects of their delight and her headache did give her an excuse to say little in her own defence. And it also enabled her to refuse Paul's invitation to go for a drink at the pub, without arousing any animosity. She wanted to be alone with him, she told herself. Of course she did. But right now she felt too ashamed of what had happened earlier in the day to enjoy Paul's unalloyed affection. She felt as if she had betrayed him, and herself, and it would take some time to reconcile her actions.

The trouble was, she couldn't get what had happened out of her mind. Which wasn't surprising, really, she decided firmly. After all, women often required counselling after suffering an attempted rape. Only it hadn't been an attempted rape, she amended ruefully. An assault? Yes, definitely an assault. But she hadn't been in any real danger. Not of losing her virginity, or anything catastrophic like that. Dear God, if he had suspected she was still a virgin, he probably wouldn't have touched her with a barge-pole. That he hadn't was probably her bad luck.

Probably?

Her nails curled into her palms. That was the trouble. She was too ambivalent about the whole affair. And it was her response to what he had done that disturbed her most. Oh, she had consoled herself with the knowledge that, as soon as he had given her half a chance, she had been out of there. She had flown out of that office as if half the demons in hell had been at her heels. Goodness knew what his secretary must have thought. Overturning the waste-bin like that, and not even stopping to say sorry. So much for her role as a female executive. When it came right down to it, she had made a pig's ear out of the whole thing.

She sighed. It was no use. She could dodge about the issue as much as she liked, but when it came down to basics it was what had happened before she had made such an ignominious retreat that was causing her so much heartache. Even now, hours after the event, she could still feel the imprint of his body against hers, still taste the sensual invasion of his tongue. She had taken a shower earlier, and afterwards she had stood in front of her dressing-table mirror, wondering why she suddenly felt such an awareness of her own sexuality. Paul had never made her feel that way, and until now she had assumed it was something that came from knowing someone else completely; knowing as in the Biblical sense of the word, that was. But it wasn't true. When she had kissed Matthew Putnam—and in spite of her initial resistance that was what she had done—she had felt a kind of sliding abandonment; and the flame that had leapt between them had left no room for second thoughts. She had found herself in the totally unfamiliar position of wanting him to go on, of wanting him to touch her, and caress her, and do all those things she had always stopped Paul from doing. Dear God, with his mouth on hers she had been helpless, at the mercy of every mindless hunger in her body. There had even been a moment when she wouldn't have cared if he'd pushed her down on to the floor and...

She shivered, violently, and immediately Paul was beside her, perching on the arm of her chair and slipping his arm about her shoulders. 'Hey, it looks as if you're getting a cold!' he exclaimed solicitously, giving her a hug. 'That's probably why you've got a headache, too. There's a lot of flu about.'

Samantha looked up at him tensely, wondering if he had any idea what was going through her head at this moment. What would he say, she wondered, if she told him what she was thinking? How would he react to the knowledge that, instead of welcoming his embrace, she was wishing it were another man's arm about her shoulders? That, when she looked at his pale hand, with its fleshy fingers and liberal covering of sun-bleached hair, resting just above her breast, she was comparing it with another man's hand. A hand that was dark-skinned and virtually hairless, with fingers that were long and hard, and possessive, yet which had looked so right against the lace-trimmed material of her blouse...

She felt a sickening wave of self-contempt. God, how could she even think such a thing? She was disgusting; shameless! And completely crazy, she acknowledged harshly. For heaven's sake, a man had virtually forced her to make love with him, and she was sitting here, mooning about what had happened as if what he had done had been perfectly acceptable. Was actually comparing that—that—bastard—with her fiancé; with Paul. If it weren't so squalid, it would be laughable. There was no comparison between Matthew Putnam and Paul. And she deserved a thrashing for even entertaining such an idea.

Nevertheless, she was inordinately grateful when Paul decided to cut the evening short. She didn't look well, he said. She should get to bed; have an early night. He'd see her tomorrow.

But, although Samantha did do as he had suggested, sleep was not something she found it easy to attain. She tossed and turned for hours, alternately too hot or too cold, depending on what direction her thoughts took her. It was useless to pretend that any self-flagellation could control the workings of her mind. She might not want to think about Matthew Putnam, but she didn't seem capable of stopping herself. And when she eventually achieved her objective her unconscious mind was prey to every treacherous emotion she possessed.

The next few days passed without incident. Samantha, who had half expected Matthew to appear at the café again, didn't know whether she was relieved or disappointed. She knew how she ought to feel, but when did life ever imitate ideology? Instead, she lived in a kind of limbo, mid-way between anticipation and apprehension. At the end of each day she was glad that she hadn't had to face her own ambivalence, but that didn't stop her from waking every morning to the same state of awareness. She would be better once that final dinner party was behind her, she decided. With that hanging over her head, how could she get on with the rest of her life?

But, when the night of the dinner party came, the affair passed off without a hitch. It was at the home of a friend of Jennifer Spellman's, and the eight members of the party were very complimentary of Samantha's efforts. So much so that she half wished she had not made such a hasty decision about refusing any future commissions. She could have accepted at least half a dozen more that evening, and she knew they were curious to know why she had decided to give it up.

Driving home later, she had to admit she had been rather foolish. But, deep down, she had secretly expected Matthew to turn up at this dinner party as well, and she had wanted the dubious satisfaction of telling him her decision. It would have been a small satisfaction, it was true, but she hoped it would have shown him what she thought of him and his friends.

It was only now that she realised how unrealistic that had been. She had placed far too much importance on what had been for him just a game. She had accused him of as much, and he hadn't denied it. So how could she have imagined he might want to pursue the connection, particularly after that embarrassing scene in his office? If it was his office. And what did it matter anyway?

She had no answers to give herself. Her mind was in turmoil, and there seemed no escape from the duplicity of her thoughts. Matthew had no intention of seeking her out again. And she should be grateful. Without the tenuous connection her catering had provided, there wasn't the faintest likelihood that their paths might cross.

Which was why she got such a shock when she came out of the café the following Monday evening and found him waiting for her. At long last the weather had changed, and the sun was still quite warm on her shoulders as she secured the front door. It made her wish she hadn't bothered to pull on the chunky thigh-length sweater over her working clothes. But she was meeting Paul after she'd been to the wholesaler's, and she expected it would be cooler later.

She hardly noticed the man leaning against the wall between the café and the newsagent's next door. People were often hanging about when she left the café. There was a bus-stop further along the High Street, and with the car park opposite it was a popular meeting place. It was only when he straightened and came towards her that she permitted him a passing glance. Then her lips parted helplessly as the breath left her lungs.

'Hello,' he said, one hand pushed deep into the pocket of a navy blue cord jacket, and the other gripping the portfolio she had dropped in his office a week ago.

Samantha struggled to find her voice. It surfaced at last, but her answering, 'Hello,' held none of the aggression she had been nurturing towards him. She tried again, this time with more success. 'What do you want?'

Matthew shrugged. 'I came to see you, obviously.' He lifted the portfolio. 'And to return this, of course.'

'You took your time.' Samantha was ungracious, but she couldn't help it. She held out her hand. 'Thanks.'

'My pleasure.' He glanced round. 'Are you on your own?'

Samantha held up her head. 'Why shouldn't I be?'

'The girl—what was it she said she called her-self——?'

'Do you mean Debbie?'

'Yes. That's right. Debbie. Isn't she with you?'

'Obviously not.' Samantha stiffened. 'She goes early to catch her bus.' She hesitated. 'Why? What do you want with Debbie?'

A lazy smile deepened the lines that fanned out from his eyes. 'Jealous?' he queried, with stomach-wrenching accuracy, and Samantha swung abruptly away. He was not going to make a fool of her a second time, she thought, despising herself for even giving him the chance. Whatever he was doing here, she wanted no part of it.

'Hey, Sam——'

But his protest went unheeded as she stood at the kerb, waiting for a gap in the traffic so that she could cross. She couldn't wait to put the width of the street between them, and it was just her luck that the traffic lights had changed against her.

'Sam,' he said, coming after her, and taking hold of her arm. 'We have to talk.'

'No, we don't.' She tried to shake him off without success, and her jaw jutted frustratedly. 'You know, it did cross my mind that you might have come to apologise, but you didn't, did you?'

'Apologise?' Clearly, the idea had never even oc-curred to him. 'Well—OK. If that's what you want.' He grimaced. 'I apologise.'

Samantha seethed. 'You don't mean that!' she ex-claimed. 'You're only saying it to pacify me!'

'Whatever it takes,' he agreed infuriatingly. And then his eyes dropped to her mouth. 'Don't go.'

Samamtha's breathing felt suddenly constricted. 'I—I have to,' she stammered, but he only applied a little more pressure to her arm, and drew her back until her shoulder nudged his chest. His jacket was unbuttoned, and the heat of his body was palpable through the thin cotton shirt he was wearing.

'No, you don't,' he said, his warm breath lifting the hairs on her forehead. 'Come on, Sam. I've thought about little else but you for the past six days. Don't tell me you haven't thought about me—just a little, hmm?'

Samantha caught her breath. 'Will you let me go?'

'Will you not run away if I do?'

She caught her lower lip between her teeth, then she nodded her head, and to her relief he released her. It enabled her to widen the gap between them, and she inhaled several times before saying, 'You shouldn't have come here. You're wasting your time!'

'I know.' His lips twitched. 'You don't do ethnic food!'

Samantha gasped. 'Can't you ever be serious?'

His eyes darkened. 'I'd like to be.'

'Oh, God!' She dragged her eyes away from his, and looked about her. That wasn't what she had meant, and he knew it. 'Mr Putnam——'

'Matt.'

'Mr Putnam!' She shook her head. 'What do you want from me?'

'Let's go somewhere, and I'll tell you.'

'No!' She was scandalised. 'This—this has got to stop.'

'Has it?'

'Yes.' She took a steadying breath, and looked at him again. 'I don't want to talk to you.'

'I don't believe that.'

Samantha made a helpless sound. This was going on too long. Cars were passing them all the time, and any one of them could be Paul's, or someone else's who knew her. And who was she going to say was talking to her?

'Don't you have any moral feelings at all?' she demanded, and he made an indifferent movement of his shoulders.

'About what?'

'About the fact that I'm engaged to be married!' she retorted hotly. 'Oh, I realise things are done differently in your world, but in mine, if a girl is engaged to be married to one man, she doesn't play around with another!'

His brows descended. 'And what makes you think things are done differently where I come from?'

'Because they are.' Samantha hesitated. 'I—I saw you.'

'Saw me?' He looked confused. 'Saw me—what?'

'With—with that woman. Miss Mainwaring. I saw you together.'

'Yes?' He still didn't appear to understand. 'And what did you see?'

Samantha felt the colour invade her cheeks. 'That doesn't matter.'

'I think it does.'

'Oh, for heaven's sake!' Samantha's hands clenched round the portfolio. 'I have no intention of satisfying some perversive streak in your nature. Let's just say, you weren't exactly strangers to one another.'

'No, we weren't. We aren't.' Matthew expelled his breath rather heavily. 'At one time, Melissa thought she was going to marry me. Does that make it easier for you?'

'Oh!' Samantha knew a sudden weakness in the pit of her stomach. 'I—see.'

'Do you? I doubt it.' His tone was ironic now, as he closed the space between them, and looked down at her. 'Look—I need a drink. Come with me.'

Samantha bit her lip. 'I don't drink and drive.'

'A lemonade, then.'

That was said with rather less tolerance. He was losing patience. She could see it in the faint lines of tension that bracketed his mouth. She had only to wait long enough and he would get tired of humouring her. He would realise she meant what she said. She wasn't like Melissa Mainwaring. She had principles. But—oh, God!—how smug she sounded.

'Sam, please!'

The rough appeal in his voice raked her already crumbling defences. She wanted to tell him to go; to do the right thing; to prove to herself, if no one else, that everything was still the same as before. Only it wasn't. It couldn't be. No matter how she tried to deny it, things had changed. *She* had changed.

The truth was, unprincipled or not, she wanted to accept his invitation. And she knew that if she refused he would never ask her again. This was her last chance. And what was one drink, after all? It wasn't as if it meant anything. As he had said the last time he came to the café, he wasn't asking her to go to bed with him!

'I—all right,' she said, regretting the words as soon as they were uttered. It suddenly seemed quite unpardonable to accept a drink from a man who had proved to be so dishonest. Had she forgotten the way he had tricked her into going to his office? And what about his behaviour while she was there?

'OK.' His response to her acceptance was obviously relieved. She guessed he wasn't used to rejection, in any form. 'The car's parked just round the corner. In—Pilgrim Street, is that right?'

'The car?' Samantha blinked. 'I thought you just invited me for a drink.'

'I did.'

'Well?'

He pushed his hands back into his pockets. 'You think we should go into one of these pubs in the High Street?' He grimaced. 'If that's what you want.'

It wasn't. Samantha pressed her lips together. The pubs around the Market Square did not have a particularly salubrious reputation. It would be just her luck to be seen coming out of one of them with Matthew Putnam. Damned on two counts, instead of just one.

'I suppose you know somewhere better,' she challenged, deciding to let him think he would have to persuade her, but he merely fell into step beside her, and shook his head.

'It's immaterial to me,' he replied, and she gazed at him frustratedly. 'You choose,' he added. 'You know better than me.'

Samantha suppressed a groan. She should have known. A man like Matthew Putnam was unlikely to fall for her little schemes. He was far too experienced for that.

'We'll go somewhere else,' she muttered in an undertone, and he glanced sideways at her.

'Come again.'

She knew he had heard her the first time, but she had to repeat herself, and Matthew's mouth twisted in a most infuriating way.

Pilgrim Street was log-jammed, not least because of the black Porsche that was parked half on the pavement and half on double yellow lines. It was causing the traffic turning out of Pilgrim Street into the High Street to cross into the incoming lane, and at rush hour the hold-up was totally unforgivable.

'Who would park——?' Samantha was beginning disgustedly, when Matthew left her to walk round the car and unlock it. 'I should have known,' she muttered grimly, as the driver trapped behind the Porsche raised his hand in an explicit signal. Then, when Matthew pushed open the passenger door from inside, she hurriedly took her seat. She just hoped no one had recognised her. It was going to be hard enough to explain.

The Porsche moved off at the first break in the traffic, and Samantha, who was still smarting from the insulting gesture she had had to suffer, gave a resentful snort. What was she doing here? she asked herself disbelievingly. Risking everything she cared about for a crazy impulse.

'It's a cliché, I know,' remarked Matthew, evidently misunderstanding her reaction, 'but it's not mine. It's Rob's. My—a friend's. He likes obvious status symbols. I don't.'

Samantha noticed her skirt had ridden up almost to her thighs, in the hasty scramble into the car, and endeavoured to inch it down. 'Don't tell me—you drive a Robin Reliant,' she retorted, in no mood to be friendly. And then felt a curl of raw awareness in her stomach when he gave a husky laugh.

'Not exactly,' he replied, glancing sideways at her, and she knew he had observed her awkward manoeuvrings. 'Driving in London is pretty hopeless, anyway. As no doubt you know in your business.'

'It's not my business,' said Samantha shortly, giving up any attempt to be circumspect, and tugging forcefully at her hemline. 'Not any more. I've given up working for other people.'

'Why?'

Matthew was negotiating the roadworks in Falls Way as he spoke, but that didn't stop him from giving her a curious look. It was her opportunity to tell him exactly what part he'd played in her decision, but for some reason she chose not to. Why should she give him the satisfaction of knowing he was responsible? she argued. It really was nothing to do with him. It was her fault for being so naïve.

'Because—because the only time I see my fiancé is in the evenings, and it was taking up too much time,' she said at last. 'Um—where are we going? I can't be too long, you know.'

Matthew's mouth turned down. 'Because you're meeting your fiancé, I suppose.'

'As a matter of fact, yes.'

He nodded. 'Will this do, then?' he asked, indicating the swinging sign of a pub on the outskirts of the town, his tone considerably cooler. 'The Black Raven! That sounds appropriate.'

Samantha didn't answer him, and Matthew swung the sleek sports car into the car park and brought it to a restrained halt. 'OK,' he said, thrusting open his door and swinging his long legs out of the vehicle. 'Let's hope they serve their Scotch in generous measures.'

Samantha struggled out with as little dignity as she'd got in. But she didn't want him coming round to help her. 'You shouldn't drink——'

'—and drive, I know,' he finished for her tersely. 'Don't worry, *mou kardhia*. My constitution is quite used to it.'

Samantha frowned as he locked the door. 'Moo—moo, what?' she echoed, having heard nothing after that rather musical address.

'*Mou kardhia*,' he repeated, making the second half of the first word sound like *e*. 'It's Greek,' he added flatly. He nodded towards the entrance. 'Shall we go in?'

Samantha blinked, but when he started towards the open door she hurried after him. 'Greek,' she said, a little breathlessly. 'Do you speak Greek?' She shook her head. 'How—clever of you.'

'Not really. My mother's Greek,' he informed her carelessly. And then, pausing in the narrow hallway of the hotel, 'Bar or lounge? It's up to you.'

Samantha left the decision to him, and then wished she hadn't when they ended up in a dark booth in a corner of the smoky bar. Exactly the sort of place she had imagined he would choose, she thought irritably, as he took the seat opposite. The only difference was that his knees brushed hers, instead of his thigh, but she quickly moved her legs to avoid that situation.

She had asked for a mineral water, and, although Matthew had given her a wry look when she did so, that was what he set in front of her. For himself, he had a foaming glass of the local brew, and Samantha couldn't help her look of surprise when he set the glass on the table.

'So I took your advice,' he remarked, after she had shifted out of his way. 'Is this what your fiancé drinks? Real ale?'

Samantha didn't particularly want to be reminded about Paul at this moment, and her shoulders stiffened. 'Yes, as a matter of fact,' she retorted, resenting the disparaging way he said it. 'But I'm sure you're not interested in what Paul drinks.'

'On the contrary.' He took a mouthful of the beer and wiped the back of his hand across his mouth. 'I'm interested in everything about you. Including your fiancé.'

'Have you no shame?'

The words burst from her, and he expelled a resigned breath. 'Apparently not. Where you're concerned,' he appended ruefully. 'Does that damn me in your eyes?'

Samantha chose not to answer that and, after a moment, he said gently, 'Tell me about you; about what you like to do. Whose idea was it to open the café?' He paused. 'Paul's?'

'Yes, as a matter of fact.' Samantha pressed her lips together. 'Paul—supports me a lot. In—in everything.'

'Except when it interferes with his time with you.'

'What do you mean?'

'He forced you to give up the outside catering, didn't he?' Matthew reminded her mildly, and she guessed he had used those words deliberately. 'Which is a pity, because I—had a commission for you.'

She was tempted to tell him that he had had more to do with her giving up the catering than Paul had, but that would have been playing into his hands once again. So, instead, she said, 'Another one?' managing to sound almost as disparaging as he had sounded earlier.

'Hmm.'

Matthew looked into his drink, stroking one long finger down the condensation on his glass. In spite of herself, it reminded her of those same fingers sliding down the quivering column of her throat. She experienced almost the same sensation, and when he lifted his heavy lids and intercepted her gaze she suspected he was thinking of it, too.

'What's he like?' he asked huskily, and for a moment she was too mesmerised to speak.

'I—I beg—your——'

'Paul,' he prompted, cradling the glass between his palms. 'Does he make you happy? In bed, I mean,' he added incredibly. 'Because I have to tell you, I don't think he does.'

'You know nothing about——'

'If I didn't know better, I'd say you were totally inexperienced,' he went on, as if she hadn't said anything. 'He must be a rank amateur, that's all I can say.'

'I don't think you'd better say anything else,' hissed Samantha, clutching her glass. 'Not unless you want me to throw this over you.'

Matthew shrugged. 'So what are you doing here with me?'

Samantha gasped. That he should ask her *that*! When he had practically *kidnapped* her outside the café! Forget the fact that she had agreed to come with him of her own accord. It was his fault she was here, and that was that.

'I think you'd better take me back to town,' she declared unsteadily, but when she would have slid out of the booth his thigh was in the way.

'Don't do this,' he implored wearily. 'Not again.' He captured her trembling hands. 'All right. That was unforgivable. I apologise. Now, will you cool down?'

'No.' Her eyes sparkled resentfully. 'I should have known better than to expect any kind of respect from you! You just enjoy tormenting me, don't you?'

His eyes darkened. 'There are things we'd both enjoy a hell of a lot more,' he told her shortly. And then, before she could comprehend what he was doing, he had levered his lean frame out of his side of the booth and into hers. His arm went along the back of her seat, and it took all her will-power to resist the urge to try and melt into the woodwork. 'Let's both stop playing games, shall we?' he murmured, his free hand turning her face to his. His thumb brushed sensually across her parted lips. 'Do you have any idea what I want to do at this moment?'

Samantha breathed unevenly. There didn't seem to be enough air in the booth, and every time she tried to fill her lungs she was intensely conscious of her full breasts straining at the lacy confines of her bra. She rather thought he was aware of it, too, and there was a frankly sensual curve to his mouth as he watched her agitation.

'Do you?' he prompted again, and she moved her head in a helpless sideways gesture.

'I've got to go,' she said instead, glancing half apprehensively towards the bar, but the bartender was busy, and no one was paying any attention to them.

'No, you don't,' he contradicted her gently, bending his head and touching the sensitive hollow beneath her ear with his tongue. 'Be honest: you want to stay.' He

took the lobe of her ear between his teeth and bit it.
'You just feel guilty, that's all.'

'Yes, I do.' She latched on to that statement like a
drowning woman. 'I shouldn't be here. I shouldn't have
come here. I want you to take me back.'

Matthew sighed, his hand falling away on to her lap.
It was where her two hands were clasped together, but
she didn't allow him to take hold of them again. Instead,
she gripped the banquette on either side of her, cooling
her hot palms, and digging her nails into the coarse cloth.

She was aware of him watching her; she was aware of
the strong hand lying weightily against her knees. She
was also aware that she was exuding moisture from every
pore of her body, and that between her legs a pulse was
beating wildly.

'I'll take you back,' he said at last, and she wondered
why that news didn't give her the relief it should. 'But
I think you should listen to what I have to say first,' he
added, turning his hand over and testing its strength
against her taut thigh. 'It's my grandfather's birthday
at the end of this month. On Easter Saturday, actually.
My mother is giving a party for him, and I suggested
that you might be willing to help her.'

Samantha's breath caught in her throat. 'Your—your
grandfather?' she got out, in a high, unnatural voice,
and Matthew inclined his head.

'Hmm,' he said, flexing his fingers against her leg. He
looked down as his knuckles brushed the hem of her
short black skirt, but instead of withdrawing his hand
he slid it back and forth against the ribbed mesh of her
black tights. 'I guess we're talking about fifty people,
or thereabouts.' His eyes sought hers. 'A family get-
together. What do you think?'

Samantha swallowed, a convulsive movement of her
throat that owed more to the sensitised state of her body
than to any sense of consternation at the numbers. 'I—
couldn't cater for fifty people,' she protested weakly, but
his lazy smile sent a shaft of pure, unadulterated hunger
through her shaking body.

'No one's asking you to,' he murmured, taking advantage of her parted lips and tracing their softness with his tongue. 'She just needs someone to help her, that's all,' he went on, bestowing a light kiss at the corner of her mouth. 'I told her you'd be the ideal person.'

Samantha shivered. 'You—you said—your mother was Greek,' she stammered, torn between the desire to destroy this intimacy once and for all, and the aching wish that he would kiss her properly, and put her out of her misery. 'Wh-where do she and—and your grandfather—live?'

'In Greece, of course,' he declared, shattering her hopes and reaching for his drink. 'Well? Will you do it?'

CHAPTER SIX

MATTHEW came up out of the ocean, shaking water from every limb. At this hour of the morning the sea was icy cold and refreshing, still harbouring the cool temperatures of winter, and not yet tempered by the already strengthening sun.

He swept his hair back with a careless hand, and squeezed moisture from where it clung to the back of his neck. The cold drops ran down over his muscled shoulders and disappeared into the waistband of the shorts he had worn to sleep in, and he shivered. But it felt good to be alive, and a lazy hand confirmed that the thickening at his midriff had been checked. Since he had cut down on his drinking and started exercising again, his health had improved considerably, and he could face each morning without the recurring hangover he had grown to accept.

And he owed at least part of it to Samantha, he reflected ruefully, feeling his body stir as it always did when he thought of her. But, in the thin shorts, his reaction was unwelcome, particularly as he could see his grandfather sitting on the terrace waiting for him. The old man always rose at six. He had forgotten about that. It was his mother he had been thinking of when he'd kept his shorts on for swimming. But his grandfather had arrived the night before, and now Matthew was glad he had decided to show some respect.

He had left a towel lying on the sand, and now he picked it up and took a moment to dry his head and shoulders. Then, knotting it loosely about his waist, he crossed the fine sand to the steps that led up to the terrace.

'Papa,' he addressed the old man politely, and Aristotle Apollonius inclined his grey head in a look that mingled slight displeasure with reluctant pride.

'Matthew,' he accorded, gesturing to the cushioned chair at the other side of the lacquered wrought-iron table. 'You did not use to be such an early riser.'

'No.' Matthew acknowledged the faint censure in his grandfather's tone, and although he would have preferred to go straight into the villa for his shower he humoured him and sat down. 'The water's very inviting.'

His grandfather had spoken in Greek, and, although Matthew knew the old man could speak English as well as he could, he responded in the same language. He had no wish to get into an argument over his rejection of his mother's culture in favour of his father's. Not when there was already a rift between them big enough to double the Marianas Trench.

'Are you sure it is not the imminent arrival of this young woman—what did you say her name was? Max-Maxell?'

'Maxwell,' corrected Matthew patiently, knowing that a man who could recite the tonnage of a hundred oil tankers at a stroke was unlikely to be daunted by one surname. 'Her name's Samantha Maxwell. I believe my mother told you that several days ago.'

'She may have done.' Aristotle was dismissive. 'But I cannot be expected to remember the name of every female you sleep with.'

Matthew's mouth compressed. 'Did my mother tell you I was sleeping with her?' he enquired pleasantly, and his grandfather shifted somewhat uncomfortably.

'I do not know,' he responded, adjusting the collar of his white linen jacket. 'She may have done. As I say, I do not always remember.'

Matthew gave him an old-fashioned look. 'Really? I doubt if you'd like your competitors to hear that,' he remarked, leaning forward, legs apart, his forearms along his thighs. 'Are you getting old, Papa?'

'Yes, I am.' The old man's eyes flashed with sudden anger. 'And what do you care? My one and only grandson? I have to have a birthday before you can find the time to see me!'

'That's not true.' Matthew breathed out on a sigh. 'I came to see you—three months ago. In Athens.'

'Did you? Did you?' Aristotle's lips twisted. 'As I recall it, you were drunk at least three-quarters of the time you were there. And you slept the rest!'

'Yes, well——' Matthew felt a momentary sense of guilt. 'That was different.'

'How was it different?' The old man sneered. 'You were drunk because some little tart refused to spread her legs for you! Your mother told me. She had sympathy for you. I did not.'

Matthew's jaw tightened. 'Did I ask for your sympathy?' he demanded, as, just for a moment, the familiar sense of bereavement he had felt at Melissa's betrayal gripped him.

'No.' His grandfather expelled the word with raw frustration. 'But that doesn't mean I forgive you. Or that I'll feel any different this time, when the Maxwell girl realises she's wasting her time.'

Matthew suppressed a sudden urge to lash out at the old man and lay back in his chair, determinedly crossing one ankle across his knee. 'That won't happen,' he declared flatly, watching as sunspots appeared on the blue, blue waters of the small bay. 'And, just for your information, I haven't slept with her. Yet.'

'But you intend to.'

Matthew's mouth twisted. 'Yes. I intend to.'

His grandfather grimaced, taking a Cellophane-covered cigar out of his breast pocket, and peeling the wrapper. He trimmed it with a gold clipper and felt about in his pockets for some matches. 'Who is she anyway?' he snapped, discovering a book of matches, with the logo of an exclusive Athens nightclub on the flap, and striking one irritably. 'Caroline says she's a waitress.' He puffed at the cigar. 'Cannot you find enough women of your own class, without getting involved with a *waitress*?'

'I didn't realise you were a snob, Papa,' Matthew countered evenly, though he was finding it increasingly difficult to keep his temper. 'And, as it happens, she's not a waitress. As my mother knows, and as I'm sure she's told you, Sam runs a small café. And—until recently—she did some outside catering, too. I'd have thought you'd admire initiative. You've always told me that that was how you made your fortune. And speaking of class——'

'That will do, Matthew.' His mother's voice overrode what he had been about to say, and, although he was tempted to ignore her, his grandfather's heaving chest deterred him. 'Apollo, you know what the doctor said about smoking,' Caroline added, whisking the cigar out of her father's hand and grinding it beneath the heel of her painted sandals. 'Now, why can't I leave you two alone for more than five minutes without finding you at each other's throats?'

'Hardly that,' remarked Matthew quietly, getting to his feet, and loosening the knot of the slipping towel. He slotted it about his shoulders. 'I need a shower. If you'll both excuse me, I'll go and wash the salt from this debauched body of mine.'

'Oh, Matthew!' His mother caught his bare arm as he passed. 'You're not—you're not planning on doing anything silly, are you, darling?'

'Silly?' Matthew looked puzzled. 'Like what?'

'Like—leaving, for example.'

'With his new mistress arriving later this morning, I should hardly think so,' put in her father drily. He pulled out another cigar. 'Let the boy go, Caroline. He and I understand one another. Which is more than you and I ever did.'

Matthew left his mother protesting that her father was going the right way to kill himself by ignoring his doctor's orders, and crossed the marble tiles into the wide entrance hall of the villa. Vine-hung, trellised walls gave this area of the house a natural airiness, and, although at the height of summer an efficient air-conditioning system came into operation, much of the building's coolness was owed to Minoan design. That ancient civilisation had believed in a through-flow of air in their homes, and many of the buildings on Delphus still imitated these fundamental principles.

Not that the rest of his grandfather's villa could be said to resemble any ancient precepts, Matthew mused as he walked along an arched corridor to his own suite of rooms. Beneath his bare feet, the mosaic of Italian marble was strewn with soft Bokhara rugs, and the walls beside him had been decorated by a master hand. Expertly etched murals, in jewel-bright colours, reflected the duality of his grandfather's history. His father, Matthew's great-grandfather, had had his origins in the deserts of North Africa, and although the old man didn't like to be reminded of his Arab antecedents he couldn't deny his love of Moorish architecture.

And there was plenty of room here for him to indulge in whatever style of architecture took his fancy, thought Matthew, pushing open the heavy-panelled door into his sitting-room. Built in the days when his grandfather had hoped to have a large family, it sprawled over more than an acre, with halls and reception-rooms of mammoth proportions. The twenty or so guest suites had all been designed to take advantage of the villa's surroundings, and, stepping out into flower-filled courtyards, you were immediately assailed by the absolute perfection of the view. From its position on a rocky promontory the villa was surrounded on three sides by the sparkling waters of the Aegean, and, for all his ambivalence about coming here, Matthew accepted there was nowhere more uniquely placed.

That he didn't come as often as he should was a source of both bitterness and frustration to his grandfather. But then, Matthew conceded with a trace of self-mockery, he had always been something of a disappointment to the old man. Who else, born into a shipping dynasty, would have chosen to ignore all the benefits his grandfather's wealth could give him, and start his own company? Who else would have gone against the strength of his grandfather's will, and clung to the admittedly weaker link of his father's heritage?

The trouble was, he had never been able to explain his reasons to the old man. Aristotle—*Apollo*—whatever he cared to call himself, had never had the time to listen to his grandson's opinions. Well, not when he had needed to voice them, anyway, Matthew amended now, stepping out of his wet shorts, and padding into the Byzantine luxury of the bathroom.

Growing up in his grandfather's house in Athens, a house necessarily protected from the outside world, he had longed to escape; to be like the children who played beyond the electrified gates that kept him a prisoner. Going to school in England had been a revelation, for, no matter how his grandfather might resent the system his father had chosen for him, the boarding school in Hertfordshire had been far from the old man's influence. That was when Matthew had started to rebel. That was when he had started to fight the stifling control of his mother's family. He didn't want the responsibilities his grandfather would have put on him. He didn't want to live in a world where bodyguards were an accepted part of life and every move he made was reported on. He wanted freedom, and choices. He wanted to be Matthew Putnam; not Matthew Apollonius.

Of course, it hadn't been easy. There had been threats from his grandfather, and tears from his mother. But he had done it. He had made a life for himself, forged his own destiny—if only temporarily, he allowed with a certain irony. He knew that, sooner or later, fate would catch up with him. He was his grandfather's heir. Victor's presence was a constant reminder. And, while he might succeed in eluding his responsibilities for a while longer, much of his future was tied up in bills of lading at Piraeus.

He sighed, tilting his face up to the hot spray of water that cascaded from a decidedly modern faucet. Its pummelling force put feeling back into his shoulders, which had become chilled during his conversation with his grandfather. *Conversation*? He pulled a wry face. Confrontation, more like.

But, for all that, bringing Samantha here was undoubtedly an unwise move. Not only as far as his grandfather's blood-pressure was concerned, but also because of his own reasons for doing so. Frankly, he wasn't too sure why he had done it. It had certainly not been his intention when he'd intercepted her outside the café. But circumstances had contrived to force his hand, and although he despised the impulse that had caused him to make such a suggestion it was done now, and he had to live with it.

Nevertheless, that didn't stop him from feeling a heel. He had invited her here under false pretences; and, even if some despicable core of his anatomy welcomed the knowledge, he couldn't excuse his own behaviour.

After all, he knew his mother would never allow an outsider to interfere with her plans for the birthday celebrations. Besides, the arrangements had been completed weeks ago, with every detail honed to perfection. Apart from anything else, there was an army of servants at the villa, capable of feeding the five thousand, let alone a paltry fifty guests. It was only Samantha's lack of experience that had allowed him to pull such a stunt. But then, she still had no idea who he really was.

His lips tightened. If he had a shred of decency in him, he would tell her the truth right away, instead of letting her go on believing she had some purpose here beyond the plans he had for her. He should send her back where she had come from, no better or worse than when she left. Back to her fiancé, and her steady, boring existence.

But he knew he wouldn't do it. She was sensitive, and naïve—and incredibly innocent—and he was about to ruin her life. He was using her to expunge his frustration over Melissa, but for the first time in weeks he felt alive again. She had done that for him. And it wasn't as if she was indifferent to him. God, he had known that night in the pub that she was vulnerable. All that defensive indignation! It had all been an act. If she hadn't wanted to see him again, he wouldn't have forced her. But it had taken so little persuasion to change her mind...

With an impatient hand he switched the temperature control to cold. He felt hot now, hot and ridiculously excited, considering it was more than fifteen years since a contemporary of his mother's had taught him how to please a woman. And, incidentally, how to please himself, too, he recalled, turning off the tap, and tugging a thick bathsheet from the rack. It was years since he had remembered that initiation, but since then several women had benefited from the experience. And Samantha...

He frowned. What time was it? he wondered. He had taken his watch off before he went for his swim, and now he wrapped the towel about him and went into his bedroom.

It was lying amid the tumbled sheets of the enormous bed, which occupied a bare quarter of the floor-space in the huge, high-ceilinged apartment. A tapestry quilt in shades of green and gold was lying in a heap on the floor, and he heaved it back on to the bed before picking up the timepiece. It was still early, he saw. Barely seven o'clock. Samantha wouldn't be arriving for another five hours, at least. Always supposing she didn't get cold feet at the last minute and let the plane go without her, he brooded tersely. But no. She wouldn't do that. She had said she would come, and she would. She trusted him.

Samantha didn't know what she had expected to happen when she landed in Greece, but being met by a complete stranger had definitely not figured in her plans.

When Matthew had sent her a return ticket to Athens, with the flight number and time of departure clearly indicated, she had naturally assumed he intended to meet her at the airport himself. Beyond telling her that Delphus, the place where his mother and grandfather lived, was some distance from Athens, he had given no details of how she was supposed to get there. Which was why she had expected he was going to meet her. Surely he must know how nervous she was.

But instead she had been met by an admittedly trustworthy-looking individual in a pilot's uniform, who introduced himself as Spiro Niarchos. He had explained, somewhat confusingly, that he worked for the Apollonius Corporation, and that he had been sent to escort her to her destination.

Samantha had had little choice but to go with him. Even if, at that time, her interpretation of his uniform had run along the lines of its being that of a chauffeur. But, instead of a limousine, he had escorted her to a gleaming blue and silver helicopter, with the logo of the Apollonius Corporation emblazoned on its side.

Now, some distance out over the blue-green waters of what she had guessed was the Aegean, her earlier doubts and fears had congealed into a tight knot of apprehension inside her. Where were they really going? she wondered. And would his mother and his grandfather really be there when they arrived? And if they weren't, what was she going to do about it? She had agreed to come, knowing full well that Matthew Putnam wanted more than her professional services.

Dear God!

She closed her eyes for a moment as the enormity of what she had done washed over her. It was no use telling herself that so far as Paul and her parents were concerned this was just another assignment, when she knew it wasn't. Just because she had managed to persuade them that this was an opportunity she couldn't turn down didn't alter the fact of her duplicity. She had told lies; invented excuses; even used her friendship with Jennifer Spellman to justify what she was doing. And why? Because she was *mad*, that was why. Mad to even think that a man like Matthew Putnam really cared anything about her. And yet...

She opened her eyes again on a scene of breathtaking loveliness. It wasn't like flying in an aeroplane, which reduced everything to matchbox proportions. From the windows of the helicopter she could see even the smallest island, and yachts and other sailing craft, cruising these land-locked waters.

So, she acknowledged tensely, Matthew's family must live on one of these islands. Remembering what she knew of Greek geography, she guessed his grandfather must be either a fisherman or a farmer. Probably the former, she decided thoughtfully, running her tongue over her lower lip. Unless the island was bigger than she expected—and, as she'd never heard of it, that didn't seem likely—there didn't seem a lot of room for cultivation. The smaller islands they were passing over were rocky outcrops in the main, with just a few sheep, and a handful of fig or olive trees providing shade. Not the kind of place to hold a party for fifty people, she would have thought. But then, she didn't really know what kind of party it was going to be.

She sighed uneasily. The conviction that she was making a terrible mistake by coming here was growing stronger by the minute. What did she know of Greek people? What did she know of Greek food? She had read somewhere that the Greeks were very hospitable. But the article had been concerned with tourism, not with a single Englishwoman venturing into the unknown.

She glanced sideways at the pilot and noticed that his uniform bore the Apollonius Corporation logo, too. What did it all mean? The name was vaguely familiar to her, and she thought she remembered hearing it used in connection with shipping. But why would a helicopter belonging to a shipping company be transporting her to Delphus? Unless, Matthew's company, J.P. Software, was part of the Apollonius Corporation, too.

The more she thought about it, the more logical it sounded. It explained so much, not least the helicopter, and Matthew's apparent thoughtlessness at not meeting her in Athens. And she should be feeling grateful that she was not having to spend several hours on an inter-island ferry. Judging by the distance they had flown, it would have probably taken the rest of the day by sea. Even so...

She pressed surreptitious hands against her churning stomach. The fact remained, she was still taking an enormous risk by coming here. She knew nothing of Matthew's family, and hardly more about himself. Could she really pretend his motives were honourable, when he'd virtually admitted they weren't? And what did she want anyway? Her future was in Northfleet, with Paul.

Desperate to escape the downward spiral on which her thoughts were taking her, Samantha turned to look at the pilot again. She was sitting beside him, in the front of the aircraft, and because the engines were noisy she had to speak to him by means of the microphone that was attached to the helmet he had given her to wear.

'Are we nearly there?' she asked, hoping his English didn't just stretch to the formal greeting and necessary instructions he had issued earlier.

'Almost,' he conceded, polite but unforthcoming, and although she sensed his reticence she persevered.

'Does—er—does Mr Putnam often use the helicopter?'

It was a stupid question, and she hoped he didn't think she was trying to find out if he had brought any other young women to the island. Besides which, Matthew wasn't exactly using the helicopter, was he? She didn't honestly know if he ever had.

The pilot's expression as he looked at her mirrored her own uncertainty, and she was convinced he was wondering what Matthew saw in her. But then, almost indifferently, it seemed, he shrugged his shoulders, and returned his attention to flying the aircraft.

'It is—at his disposal, whenever he wishes it,' he said, after a lengthy hesitation, and Samantha, who had decided he was not going to answer her, caught her breath. 'But, as he lives in England,' Spiro Niarchos continued slowly, 'I am employed most frequently by his mother.'

Samantha gulped. '*His mother*!'

'*Ne*. Kyria Putnam.' He paused, and then added, politely, 'You have met *Mrs* Putnam, have you not?'

'No. No, I haven't.'

Samantha answered almost absently, her mind racing with the possibilities his casual words had created. Who was Matthew's mother, if she used a helicopter to get around in? And why hadn't he warned her that this was no ordinary family?

It was her own fault, she thought miserably. She should have insisted on some answers before agreeing to this trip. But, although she had suspected that anyone who gave a party for fifty people had to be fairly well off, she had never imagined anything like this.

The truth was, she had been so wrapped up with her own guilt at deceiving Paul that everything else had assumed a lesser importance. The only people who had figured strongly in her thoughts were herself and Matthew, and it wasn't until Spiro Niarchos had spoken of Matthew's mother that she had realised how naïve she had been.

What was she doing here? she asked herself again. What gave her the right to play fast and loose with her relationship with Paul, which had lasted more than six years? If she had wanted a taste of excitement—and she could think of no other excuse for what she was doing—she should have chosen someone in her own league. Not allowed herself to get entangled with a man whose background became more intimidating by the minute.

'We will be landing in less than fifteen minutes,' Spiro told her a little while later, and Samantha curled her nails into her damp palms. What would he do, she wondered, if she asked him to turn round, and fly her back to Athens? Probably refuse, she decided glumly. And it didn't matter anyway. She didn't have the nerve to suggest it.

They were flying diagonally into the sun now, and the light on the water was dazzling. Below the helicopter she could see the swell that ran before the bow of a gleaming schooner, and as they swept in lower she saw a man on water-skis, zigzagging in the wake of a launch.

She stared, but the man wasn't Matthew, even if he did have the same dark skin. He was older, too. Probably in his late forties, or early fifties, with a stocky, well-fed physique that spoke of too many liquid lunches. A relative, perhaps, she guessed tautly, having to abandon her theory that Matthew's grandfather might be a fisherman. She drew her lower lip between her teeth, and bit down, hard. It served her right for telling lies, she thought unhappily. Nothing good ever came from trying to cheat fate.

The island was beneath them now, and in spite of her misgivings Samantha gazed down at it intently. It wasn't large, but it was bigger than she had expected, with lush green slopes tapering down to the shimmering waters of the Aegean. At the northern end of the island a cluster of white-painted buildings hugged a narrow inlet, which was apparently the only means of access by sea. Samantha glimpsed several fishing boats moored in the harbour, and the bell-tower of a church, before the helicopter swept her south again, towards a broad, jutting peninsula.

There was a house on the peninsula; or perhaps it was a hotel, she speculated nervously, no longer sure of anything in the present situation. It was painted white, too, a brilliant, blistering white that made her eyes ache, with turrets and arches, giving it the look of a medieval palace. Whatever it was, it seemed to spread in all directions, with flower-filled courtyards, tennis courts, and vine-hung terraces, above acres of coarse brown sand.

It was evidently their destination, and her stomach clenched in sudden panic as Spiro lowered the helicopter on to a custom-build pad maybe a quarter of a mile from the house. If he was aware of her strained reaction to their arrival he was polite enough not to mention it, and in any case Samantha was immediately diverted by the sight of a man lounging on a stone wall, just yards from where the aircraft landed.

It was Matthew. She recognised him instantly, and she didn't know whether she felt angry or relieved. In all honesty, she didn't know how she felt, and although she had to get out of the helicopter her legs felt ridiculously weak.

She suspected it was seeing him again. She hadn't laid eyes on him since the evening when he had persuaded her to come here, and although she had spoken to him once on the phone it wasn't the same. And he wasn't the same either, she fretted, as he pushed himself up from the pile of stones, and strolled, barefoot, towards the helicopter. In frayed denim shorts and nothing else, with the sun beating down on his exposed head and shoulders, he looked little like the man she remembered. Seeing him now, like this, she could quite believe he wasn't wholly English. Indeed, he looked totally alien, and only the lazy smile that tugged at the corners of his mouth betrayed his identity.

Perhaps she was wrong, she thought desperately. Perhaps, even now, she was making a mistake. It was always possible that his mother worked at the house—*hotel*—behind them. After all, he didn't look anything like the wealthy playboy she had seen water-skiing...

'Hi, Spiro!' Matthew had reached the helicopter now, and was jerking open the door at her side. His gaze flicked swiftly over her tense face, and then he returned his attention to the pilot. 'No problem?'

'No. No problem.'

Spiro responded with obvious warmth, and Samantha, covertly observing the exchange of looks between them, knew her worst fears were being realised. For, in spite of Spiro's cordiality, there was a definite note of respect in his voice. The kind of respect he might have for his employer, she determined anxiously. Oh, lord, why hadn't Matthew warned her?

'Good!' Matthew's gaze moved back to her stiff form. 'Sam,' he added, in a low voice. 'Do you need any help?'

Not from you!

The words trembled unspoken between them, and Samantha knew he was as conscious of her hostility as she was. That was why he hadn't wasted any time in lengthy greetings. He must know as well as she did that she didn't want to get out at all.

But she couldn't stay in the helicopter indefinitely. Spiro was apparently waiting to take off again, and she was obliged to make a move. Taking off the helmet, she placed it carefully on the console, and then, uncaring of how she looked, she swung her legs out of the aircraft.

She narrowly missed winding Matthew by her unexpected action, but his fingers grasped her elbow when she dropped the few inches to the concrete apron

'I can manage,' she snapped as soon as she had re-gained her balance, and Matthew merely raised his eye-brows before turning to help Spiro with her luggage.

She had only brought one suitcase and a canvas flight bag, and Matthew hefted them easily. *'Tha idhothoume avrio,'* he nodded, after denying he needed Spiro's help, and then, switching to English, he said, 'Let's go. Unless you want to be blown away by the propellers.'

Samantha pressed her lips together, but the logic of his argument was undeniable. The landing pad was situated just a few yards from the beach. The air was still quivering with dust from the helicopter's landing, and when it took off again...

Besides which, she had no desire to stay outside in this hot sun. She was already feeling uncomfortably warm in her jacket, and the fine woollen trousers, which had seemed so suitable in England, were now clinging damply to her legs.

The propellers began to pick up speed behind her, and she hurried the few feet to where Matthew was waiting, watching the aircraft take off. She concentrated on the helicopter in an effort to distract her gaze from Matthew's muscled torso, but she was overpoweringly conscious of him standing there beside her. It was the first time she had seen him without his city clothes—practically without any clothes at all, she amended tensely—and she was sharply aware of the width of his chest, and the hair-roughened muscles of his thighs. He looked dark—and dangerous, she conceded uneasily. And unnervingly like a stranger; someone she'd never seen before...

CHAPTER SEVEN

SAMANTHA stood at the open french doors, gazing out at the ocean. The scent of mimosa hung in the still afternoon air, and the scarlet petals of geraniums tumbled from a dozen tubs strewn about the courtyard. In the centre of the courtyard, a stone nymph spilled water from an urn she was holding into the marble basin at her feet. It meant Samantha could always hear the cooling sound of running water, and she already knew the fountain was spread with lilies at its base.

Beyond the courtyard a walled garden gave on to a flagged terrace. And, beyond the terrace, steps led down to a sandy beach. From her position by the folding glass doors Samantha had a spectacular view of blue-green waters creaming along the shoreline, with the occasional glimpse of snow-white sails, nudging the horizon.

It was all quite breathtaking, and unbelievably beautiful. And certainly nothing like she had expected. Oh, she had been prepared for the light and colour of Greece, particularly after an English winter, but the unashamed luxury of Matthew's grandfather's house had left her feeling numb and confused.

She glanced round at her suitcase lying on the carved chest at the foot of the bed. Even her luggage looked lost in these surroundings. And as out of place as she was, she acknowledged with a sigh. She should never have come here. She should never have succumbed to Matthew's sensual persuasion. How could someone who lived in this place ever require her assistance? It simply wasn't credible. It had all been just a lie.

And yet, she admitted, sliding a weary hand through her hair, she had known from the beginning that helping Matthew's mother organise his grandfather's birthday party had never been the whole reason for her trip. So why was she feeling so depressed now? Just because the circumstances were vastly different from what she had expected, why did she feel so empty, as if something precious had been taken away from her?

She sighed, and, moving away from the windows, she surveyed the cream and rose splendour of her surroundings. When she had first been shown into these rooms she had been convinced someone had made a mistake. The richly furnished sitting-room, with its soft velvet sofas and carved cabinets, could not be for her. Any more than could the huge bed, in the room adjoining, with its exotically hanging draperies, or the lavishly equipped bathroom, sporting a step-in pool deep enough to swim in. These were not the apartments of someone who had come here under false pretences. And it was certainly not the kind of accommodation she had had in mind when she had agreed to come.

Which was really what was wrong, she acknowledged dully. Until she had seen this place, she had been labouring under the not unnatural illusion that, despite Matthew's involvement with Melissa Mainwaring, he was not so different from herself. It was difficult to make sense of what she had been thinking, but she knew that, deep down, she had entertained some notion that she and Matthew might——

She drew a breath. Might what? she asked herself bitterly. Might become friends? *Lovers*? Might fall in love?

The naïveté of such thoughts appalled her now. No one who lived in a place like this could conceivably care about someone like her. Whatever he had brought her here for—and she knew now that helping his mother with anything was out of the question—it was not because he had any serious intentions towards her. He found her a diversion, and quite amusing, but apart from going to bed with her there was nothing else he wanted.

It was almost feudal really, she brooded, flicking the strap of the nightgown that was hanging half-in, half-out of the case. She had been brought here to keep Matthew amused. No expense spared—so long as she didn't get ideas above her station.

If only she had had the chance to talk to Matthew before Spiro Niarchos took off for Athens. If only she had had the chance to talk to Matthew, period. But she hadn't. No sooner had the helicopter lifted off than a smiling maid servant had appeared to escort her to her room. And, although Matthew had brought her suitcases into the house, another servant, a man this time, had relieved him of that duty too.

He must have known how she was feeling, but he made no attempt to accompany her. Instead, it had been left to the maid to show her to her suite. And, although she might have expected him to join her for a late lunch, a tray of food had been waiting for her when she emerged from the bathroom.

She supposed it was possible that he had thought she might be tired. After all, it had been very early when she'd left Northfleet, and she might have wanted to have a rest. But Samantha was too strung-up to rest, too apprehensive to sleep. Beautiful as this place undoubtedly was, she couldn't relax here.

And he must know it, she fretted, as resentment took the place of consternation. That was why he was keeping out of her way. He must know she couldn't stay here, meeting his family, and joining his grandfather's guests as if she were one of them. She wasn't. She could never be. It was just another of his games, and she had been foolish enough to fall for it.

Of course, she conceded tightly, glancing down at the chainstore-bought cotton trousers and vest-top she had changed into for coolness, he might have no intention of introducing her to his family. Just because she had been given a luxurious place to stay was no guarantee that she was to be treated like all the other guests. This might be as much of the villa as she was intended to see. Her own sitting-room; her own private courtyard! Why should she assume she'd be invited to join the family?

She glanced down at her watch. It was four o'clock, she saw unhappily, taking a choked breath. If she hadn't thought someone might see her, she'd have gone for a walk on the beach. Anything to get away from this gilded cage, and the disturbing images it created.

Of course, she could always finish her unpacking, she thought bitterly, realising that, whatever happened, she wasn't going to find it easy to get away from here before the party was over. But the party wasn't until tomorrow night, and there were an awful lot of hours between.

She heard a sound from the sitting-room next door, and her mouth went dry. But when no one called her name she expelled an uneven breath. No doubt someone had come to take away the untouched tray, she thought despairingly. But she hadn't been able to eat a thing, not with God knew what hanging over her head.

'Feeling better?'

The softly spoken enquiry startled her, and Samantha swung round almost guiltily. Not that she had anything to be guilty of, she assured herself grimly. Not with these people, at least. And when she saw Matthew standing in the arched doorway to the sitting-room her most immediate feelings were those of frustration.

All the same, she was instantly receptive to his dark sexuality, which was only enhanced by the narrow-fitting chinos he was wearing. They accentuated the powerful length of his legs, moulding his thighs, and stretching taut across his sex. Samantha looked once, and then away, forcing herself to concentrate on a point somewhere to the left of his right ear.

And, 'No,' she said, in answer to his question. 'I should never have come here.'

'Why?' Matthew moved further into the room, glancing round at the icon-hung walls, and digging the toe of his expensive loafers into the thick carpet. 'Don't you like it?'

Samantha made a face. 'No,' she said, not altogether truthfully. 'I don't like it.'

'But why?' Matthew pushed a hand through his hair, and allowed it to rest at the back of his neck. The action parted the lapels of his shirt, a hand-embroidered item that Samantha guessed must have cost a small fortune, and compressed the longer hair at the back of his head against his nape. 'Aren't you comfortable?'

Samantha made a strangled sound. 'Comfortable?' she echoed. 'I suppose it depends what you mean by comfortable, doesn't it?'

Matthew's dark eyes came to rest on her agitated features. 'I don't understand.' He frowned. 'Has someone said something to you?'

'No.' Samantha wrapped her arms across her body, and pressed her palms against her elbows. 'No,' she repeated, turning away from his disturbing presence, and moving towards the open doors again. 'I haven't spoken to anyone. I don't speak Greek, do I?'

She sensed him crossing the width of the room to stand beside her, but she held her ground, even if the urge to widen the gap again was strong inside her. They had to have this out, she thought tensely. Even if the idea of arguing with him here was somewhat reckless.

'And that's what's wrong?' he asked, his attractively hoarse voice only inches from her ear. He ran two fingers down her flushed cheek. 'You think it's important that you don't speak the language?'

'Oh, stop it!' Samantha could bear it no longer. Dashing his hand away from her face, she smeared her fingers over the spot. 'Of course that's not what's the matter, and you know it. For heaven's sake, what do you think I am? Don't you think I have any feelings? Oh—probably not. I'm only a—a *waitress*, after all!'

'Hey!' His hand on her shoulder was warm and possessive. It sent a wave of longing surging through her body that she couldn't even begin to deny. 'Don't be angry because I didn't tell you the whole truth——'

'The *whole* truth!' She didn't let him finish, but whirled away from him, grasping the still-warm frame of the french door, and gazing at him with wild, impassioned eyes. 'The whole truth! I doubt if anything you've said to me bears the slightest resemblance to the truth!'

Matthew exhaled slowly. 'You don't like this place,' he said mildly. 'Well, I have to admit, it is a little over the top——'

'I don't care about this place!' Samantha fairly yelled at him, and then, aware that her voice was probably audible from other parts of the villa, she toned it down. 'Stop pretending you don't know what I'm talking about. You let me think you worked for a computer company——'

'I do.'

'—when all the time——' His words suddenly diverted her. 'What do you mean, you do?'

'I mean I do work for a computer software company.'

Samantha looked suspicious. 'But you don't have to.'

'Oh, I do. If the company fails, I'll lose all my money.'

'All your money!' Samantha's expression was cynical. 'And I'm expected to believe that?'

'It's true.'

She shook her head. 'So who owns this place?'

'My grandfather.'

'And what does your grandfather do?'

'What does he——' Matthew broke off abruptly, and lifted his shoulders. 'You don't know,' he murmured, after a moment. And then, 'No. How could you?' He made a rueful sound. 'Well, he—he——'

It was the first time she had seen Matthew at a loss for words, and suddenly it all made sense. 'Apollonius!' she exclaimed. 'It was on the helicopter. The Apollonius Corporation! Of course. Your grandfather must be— what was the name?—Aristotle? Yes, that's right. Aristotle Apollonius. My God!' She paled. 'Am I right? Is that who your grandfather is? Aristotle Apollonius!'

Matthew's expression was enough, and she clung to the wooden frame now for support. All the time she had been here, fretting over Matthew's reasons for deceiving her like this, she had never once given a moment's thought to his grandfather's identity. But now she had, and the revelation was mortifying.

'So now you know,' he said, and there was a curiously flat note to his voice. 'Does it make a difference?'

'Does it make a difference?' Samantha gasped. 'Of course it makes a difference!' She quivered. 'How could you even imagine it wouldn't?'

'No.' Matthew shrugged. 'I suppose you're right.'

'You suppose I'm right.' She kept repeating everything he said, but she couldn't seem to help herself. 'Good lord, don't you understand? I came here because I thought—oh, never mind what I thought. I came here believing you were just—just an ordinary person. Not so different from me. A little better off, perhaps. But nothing outrageous. And now—now I find that you're— Aristotle Apollonius's grandson! You're probably going to own this place one day. And—and everything else!'

Matthew's face was sombre. 'And that matters to you?'

Samantha blinked. 'Of course it matters to me. What do you take me for?'

'What do *I* take *you* for?' Now it was Matthew's turn to play mimic. 'I'm afraid I don't understand.'

'Don't you?' Samantha's lips twisted. 'Well, let me put it in words of one syllable for you. I am not your whore! I am not for sale! You can't buy me like you can buy anything else you want, Kyria Putnam!'

'*Kirie*. It's *kirie*,' Matthew corrected automatically, but his eyes were dark and wary. 'Sam——'

'Don't speak to me!' she choked, and now, because this whole interview had taken so much out of her, she was near to tears. 'Just—just find a way to get me out of here. Tonight. Tomorrow. As soon as possible.'

Matthew shook his head. 'You want to leave?'

He seemed astounded at the notion, and she wondered if she was going mad, and that she hadn't said any of the things she thought she just had. 'Yes,' she told him unsteadily. 'I want to leave. What did you expect? That finding out who you really were might persuade me to forgive you?'

Matthew gazed at her half disbelievingly. 'Let me get this straight,' he said, and she closed her eyes for a moment, wondering how much more she could take. 'You're not—impressed by this place.'

'I'm not impressed by *you*!' retorted Samantha, glaring at him. 'Of course I'm impressed by the house. Who wouldn't be? It's—it's beautiful! But it's not the house we're talking about, is it? It's you. And—and the lies you've told to get me here!'

Matthew looked bemused now. 'You're angry,' he said wonderingly, and Samantha wondered what she had to do to prove it decisively to him. 'God,' he added, with more assurance. 'You really are angry.'

'Of course I'm angry!' she exclaimed, her brows drawing together in sudden confusion when an unexpected smile tipped the corners of his mouth. She clenched her fists. 'I'm glad you think it's funny.'

'I don't think it's funny,' he replied abruptly, sobering. But the smile still lurked in the corners of his eyes, and she didn't altogether believe him. He moved his shoulders in a negligent gesture, and moved closer. 'You never fail to surprise me, Sam. That's what I like about you.'

Samantha stiffened. The change in his tone was unmistakable, and when he put out his hand, and captured one of hers, she was hardly surprised at his audacity.

'Is—is that supposed to placate me?' she asked, realising that the only way she could defeat the emotions he aroused inside her was by hanging on to her anger. 'I want to go home. And—and if you won't arrange it, I'll call Paul, and ask him to get me out of here.'

Matthew's mouth flattened. 'Will you?' he said, turning her hand over, in spite of her resistance, and carrying it to his lips. He pressed a kiss on to her palm, and then traced its contours with his tongue. 'And what if I tell you there's no way you can get off this island without my grandfather's permission? The harbour's too small to handle the ferry, and there isn't enough room for a plane to land.'

Samantha's nostrils flared. 'I don't believe you.'

'It's true.' Matthew looked at her through his lashes. 'Would I lie?'

'Yes,' she snapped, snatching her hand away from him She shook her head. 'Oh—you have no shame, do

you? You don't care what happens to me, so long as
you get what you want!'

'Forgive me, but I thought it was what you wanted,
too,' Matthew ventured, with soft insistence. His eyes
drifted down to her mouth. 'And so far as that's concerned, nothing's changed.'

'You're crazy!' It was like knocking her head against
a brick wall. 'Haven't you listened to anything I've said?'

'Yes, I've listened.' His eyes dropped to the toes of
his loafers. 'You resent the fact that I haven't been entirely honest with you about my background.' He lifted
his shoulders in a dismissing gesture, and Samantha, who
had been diverted by his apparent submission, suddenly
found herself cornered, with the wall of windows on one
side, and his arm on the other. 'So—I'm sorry.'

'*Sorry*?'

It was little more than a squeak, with the draught of
his breathing shifting the moist hair on her forehead.
He was too close, too disturbing, not touching her
physically yet, but surrounding her with his warm male
presence. Everything about him spelled temptation, and
danger, and she knew if she had any sense she'd fight
him tooth and nail.

The trouble was that her emotions got in the way of
common sense. After living for twenty-four years believing herself capable of handling any situation, *any
man*, she was discovering a part of herself she couldn't
control. Although she knew he had lied to her before,
and would probably lie to her again, he aroused feelings
she'd hardly begun to understand, and even without
touching her he could turn her bones to water.

'Yes, sorry,' he repeated now, sliding his hand into
her hair, and cradling her scalp against his palm. He
bent and licked her upper lip with his tongue. 'You're
not going to spoil our weekend together just because I
wasn't entirely honest about the party?'

Samantha's heart was hammering in her chest. She
felt hot, and excited, but frightened as well. Frightened
of what he was doing to her, frightened of what she was
getting into. Something inside her was telling her that if

she let Matthew make love to her there would be no
turning back. It was an irrevocable step, and one she
would probably live to regret. And yet...

'I—don't know——'

Her words were weak, helpless. *Fool*! *Fool*! The inner
warning voice sounded so loud in her ears, she was
amazed Matthew couldn't hear it. But evidently he
couldn't, because his other hand moved to trap her face,
and his thumb brushed sensuously over the lower lip.

'Please,' he said, and the husky tenor of his voice was
incredibly persuasive. 'Please.' He lowered his head, and
covered her mouth with his. 'Please me,' he begged,
against her lips, and his tongue slipped into her mouth.

His arms went round her, his hands sliding down the
curve of her spine to her hips. He pulled her against
him, against the lean male strength of his body, and between the muscular power of his legs. He held her firmly,
inescapably, inflaming her with his heat. Every inch of
her body was sensitised by his nearness, and the urgency
of his caresses left her no room to think.

He kissed her many times, over and over, possessing
her mouth, bruising her mouth, inspiring a burning need
that wouldn't be denied. Time lost all meaning as he
plundered the vulnerable sweetness of her lips, and
although Samantha had begun by resisting his invasion
her senses were soon spinning out of reach.

That was when she began to kiss him back, when instincts she had barely grazed with Paul began to take
control. She wanted to touch him as he was touching
her. She wanted to feel the delight of his skin against
hers. Her hands slid up to his neck, and she coiled her
fingers in the silky smooth hair at his nape. Then her
hands invaded his collar, and she spread her palms
against the brown flesh of his shoulders.

'Sam, Sam,' he whispered raggedly, tipping one strap
of the vest off her shoulder, and running his teeth across
the narrow bones he found there. Then, with a slightly
unsteady finger, he traced a line from just below her jaw
to the dusky hollow between her breasts. 'So responsive,' he muttered, as her swollen nipples surged

against his shirt. And, with an impatient gesture, he tore open his shirt, and brought her even closer. 'I wanted to see you like this. You have such a beautiful body.'

'M-me?' she stammered, gazing up at him, and he deliberately cupped her breast, and crushed the taut bud against his palm.

'You,' he said, averting his eyes. 'Look—have you ever seen anything more beautiful than this?'

She had to look, even though the idea of admiring her own body was as alien to her as the wicked shamelessness of her responses. And, as she watched, he tugged the vest off her shoulders, and allowed his exploring fingers to slide over both naked breasts.

'No bra?' he teased, and her face flamed intolerably.

'I—I didn't bring a strapless one with me,' she protested, but he wasn't listening to her excuses. Instead, he had bent his head towards her and took one exposed nipple into his mouth, suckling on it insistently before transferring his attention to the other.

Samantha's knees almost gave way, and there was an ache in the pit of her stomach. But it wasn't an unpleasant ache. It was an expanding sensation of weakness that spread right through her abdomen, and down into the quivering muscles of her thighs. And with it came a sense of guilt for what she was doing. How could she allow Matthew to caress her in this way, when she had always denied Paul such intimacies?

But coherent thought ceased when he found her mouth again. With his tongue stroking hers, and the unmistakable evidence of his own arousal pressing against her stomach, she felt her senses swimming. Matthew had backed her against the wall, holding her there with his body, so that his hands were free to slide sensuously over her hips and her waist, to the moist underside of her breasts. His thumbs brushed the nipples, still wet and aching from the roughness of his abrasion, and then moved on to her ears, and the sensitive skin just beneath.

'I want you,' he said, against her neck. 'I want to bury myself inside you, and make love to you until you're senseless.'

'Do you?'

It was all she could say, and even that was barely audible. She had never been in such a state before. Never acted this way; never felt this way; never known what it was like to lose control. With the blood drumming in her ears, and all her pre-conceived ideas of her own needs shot to pieces, she was dazed and submissive.

'Yes,' he breathed, his hands cupping her bottom, and bringing her into intimate contact with his swollen manhood. His breath escaped him in a slightly unsteady rush. 'God! You make me feel like a sex-hungry adolescent!'

'Do I?'

Her response was no less unintelligent than before, but with Matthew's lips covering her uptilted face with dozens of hot, eager kisses, and his fingers gripping the backs of her thighs, she was incapable of rational thought. She was drowning; melting in the heat of his arousal; and the only reality was in the demanding pressure of his mouth.

But then, when her scattered senses were crying out for him to take her to the bed, and finish what he had started, he gently, but firmly, pulled away from her. While she gazed at him with uncomprehending eyes, he ran a possessive finger from the waistband of her cotton trousers to the cleft between her legs. But, although his expression was decidedly sensual, his withdrawal was unequivocal.

'You do,' he said, and it took her a moment to realise he was answering her. 'However, even adolescents have to show some restraint.' His lips twisted, and although she sensed it took an effort he turned away from her. 'We're expected to join the family for afternoon tea. A habit my mother acquired when she was married to my father.'

Samantha let her breath out on a gasp, and, hearing her, Matthew paused. Half turning towards her, he took in the wanton picture she made, still resting against the wall of glass, and for a moment he impaled her with his stare.

'Get dressed,' he said tautly, and although Samantha's hands automatically groped for the vest that was balled about her waist her eyes registered the blatant proof that he was still as incapable of controlling his body as she was.

'I—don't know what I'm supposed to wear,' she protested, drawing the crumpled vest against her breasts, and he closed his eyes for a moment, as if he was in pain.

'Right,' he said, after a moment, tugging at the material that was compressing his groin. 'I'll see to it.' And without even a backward glance he walked away from her.

CHAPTER EIGHT

MATTHEW was on his second Scotch when Samantha appeared. Despite his mother's disapproval, he had eschewed tea in favour of something more fortifying, but he was still stunned by his reaction when Samantha walked out on to the terrace.

She looked stunning. He had to admit it. In the knee-length silk shorts and matching halter he had rifled from his mother's wardrobe, she had acquired a surface sophistication that was at once unexpected and appealing. The outfit was mainly turquoise in colour, with exotic streaks of green and blue that shone iridescently when they caught the rays of the dying sun. Combined with her honey-coloured hair and pale skin, the clothes accentuated a latent sensuality, and with gold rings hanging from her ears she was disturbingly unfamiliar.

Yet, when she caught his gaze, he saw at once the uncertainty in her eyes. She might look sophisticated, but she wasn't, and he knew the almost overwhelming urge to stake his possession.

But the maid who had escorted Samantha from her room was intercepted by his mother, and it was Caroline who took narrow-eyed stock of her unwanted house guest. His mother, who had so many clothes she wouldn't recognise them all, was probably wondering how someone in Samantha's position could afford a designer playsuit, Matthew reflected drily, but he returned Caroline's stare with innocent enquiry when she cast an accusing glance in his direction.

There were perhaps thirty people in various stages of relaxation on the terrace. Although his grandfather had had no other children after Matthew's mother, his own siblings had been far more prolific. In consequence, any family gathering was bound to be extensive, with great-

118

aunts and uncles, all eager to enjoy the famous Apollonius hospitality.

Which meant Matthew had to be patient while his mother introduced their guest to the other members of his family. Of course, he could have intervened, and exposed his interest, but he didn't. In spite of his initial reaction to her appearance, he refused to admit his attraction towards her was anything more than a novelty. All the same, he couldn't deny the sense of irritation he felt when one or other of his cousins appeared captivated by her modest smile and lissom figure. He hadn't brought her here to be ogled by his Greek relations, he thought resentfully. He hadn't lent her his mother's clothes so that some other man—most notably his second cousin, Alex—would find her quite so unmistakably to his taste.

But, because he had determined not to display his preference, he was obliged to stay on the sidelines nursing his grievances. And it wasn't until his grandfather came to join him by the drinks trolley that he became aware his attitude had not gone unnoticed.

'So that is the famous Miss Maxwell,' remarked Aristotle Apollonius drily, in his own tongue. 'I must say, she is not what I expected.'

Matthew's brows arched, but that was the only sign he gave that his grandfather's words interested him. 'Really?' he responded politely, picking up the decanter of fine malt whisky and pouring another generous measure into his glass. He glanced at the old man. 'Do you want to join me?'

'In abusing my liver and addling my brain? I don't think so.' Aristotle shook his head disparagingly. 'I shall have one small ouzo before the evening meal. Aside from that, I prefer to keep my wits about me.'

Matthew acknowledged the subtle reproof with a sardonic smile. 'As you say, Papa,' he essayed, adding more ice to his glass, and raising it to his lips. He took a mouthful, and deliberately savoured its texture. 'At your age it's important to preserve your health.'

'And at yours, boy, and at yours,' retorted the old man harshly, his temperament less capable of control than his grandson's. 'For pity's sake, Matthew, why do you persist in provoking me? Do you want to see me dead?'

Matthew's mouth tightened. 'Don't exaggerate, Papa. How I choose to mess up my life is my concern, not yours.'

'I disagree.' The old man squared his shoulders, annoyed as always that Matthew's height gave him the advantage. 'You know what is expected of you. You know that both your mother and myself want to see you married; settled. The whole future of this family rests with you, Matthew. Yet you persist in making gestures which you know will give us pain.'

Matthew kept his temper with a supreme effort. 'And what would you have me do, Papa?' he enquired silkily, watching Samantha as she responded laughingly to something one of his uncles had said. For someone who didn't speak their language, she appeared to be having great success in making herself understood. The knowledge both vexed and aggravated him, and his mood was not improved by his grandfather's persistent recital of an old refrain.

'You should have married Melissa Mainwaring when you had the chance,' declared Aristotle shortly. 'You purported to love her. God knows, you have taken her rejection badly enough! This is why you are standing here, drowning your sorrows in alcohol, is it not? Instead of dancing attendance on that young woman your mother is showing so much interest in.'

Matthew's fingers clenched around his glass. He resented his grandfather's interference in his affairs. It was always the same. Whenever he came here, the old man always treated him as if he were still a boy. But, although he lifted the glass to his lips again, he put it down without drinking. Not because of the truth of what his grandfather had said, but rather because he knew the old man couldn't have been more wrong.

His lips compressed as he realised it was days since he had thought of Melissa with any sense of anguish. The raw bitterness he had lived with since she told him they were through was gone. Oh, he still felt aggrieved and resentful. But that was just his pride reasserting itself.

'What did you say she did for a living?' Aristotle was asking now, and Matthew forced himself to answer the old man civilly.

'Sam?' he queried, watching her progress towards him with increased awareness, and his grandfather sighed.

'Who else? I do not remember Miss Mainwaring having an occupation.'

'No.' Matthew was finding it difficult to concentrate on what his grandfather was saying, and absorb the freedom his contemptuous words had given him. 'No. Melissa enjoys being a lady of leisure. That's why she's marrying Ivanov. He's wealthy enough to give it to her.'

'And you were not?' Aristotle was sceptical.

'I didn't say that. But I don't respond well to coercion,' replied Matthew smoothly.

'And Miss—Maxwell? She does not coerce you?'

'No.'

'So, what does she expect of you?'

'Nothing.' Matthew was abrupt. 'She expects nothing.'

'I find that hard to believe.' His grandfather fixed the young woman in question with a frowning stare. 'Tell me about this—café: is it in need of capital or what?'

'I thought you couldn't remember what she did for a living.' Matthew scowled now. 'But no. So far as I am aware, the café presents no financial problems.'

Aristotle tilted his head. 'So why is she here?'

'Because I invited her,' retorted Matthew. He made another move towards his glass, and then, as if resenting the impulse that had driven him to seek its balm, he thrust his hands into the pockets of his trousers. 'Do you want to meet her?'

'Do you need an excuse to remove her from your mother's protection?' suggested the old man shrewdly, and Matthew gave him a fulminating glare.

'What is that supposed to mean?'

'Why—only that you have been watching her for the past fifteen minutes with undisguised impatience,' responded his grandfather mildly. 'If I did not know better, I would say you were jealous.'

Matthew's jaw clamped. 'But you do know better,' he said, between his teeth. 'And if I appear concerned, perhaps it's because my mother isn't usually known for her benevolence towards outsiders.'

'Hmm.' His grandfather conceded the point. 'And this girl means something to you?'

Matthew stiffened. 'Not in the way you mean, old man,' he answered, disliking his own unguarded reaction to the idea. Just for a moment, his senses had leapt, and then a brooding sense of foreboding swept over him. However, he brushed such thoughts aside in his eagerness to forestall his grandfather. He decided it was easier to foster the belief that he was still fretting over Melissa's departure than to admit Samantha had any—albeit transient—hold on his affections. 'She intrigues me because she's so independent,' he said, adopting a determinedly careless tone. 'And Melissa deserves a little taste of her own medicine.'

'So—you are using this young woman to effect some—revenge?' Aristotle sounded appalled, and Matthew sighed.

'Not entirely,' he admitted, unable to maintain that, even to himself. 'But, our association is—purely—sexual.' His mouth tightened again as a spasm of pure physical need scorched through him. And, to divert his grandfather's attention from any further introspection, he added, 'I need a woman, Papa. Surely you haven't forgotten how that feels?'

'No.' Aristotle emitted a rueful sound. 'No, I have not forgotten the demands of the flesh. But beware of imitations, Matthew. There is an old proverb that says the man who lights the fire is not immune from being burned.'

Matthew offered a faint smile, but he made no comment. In all honesty, it was taking all his powers of restraint to remain where he was. For, although

Samantha's introduction to the other members of his family was now complete, his mother was making sure she didn't interrupt his conversation with his grandfather.

It angered, and infuriated him. And he was damn sure his grandfather was aware of it. Had they concocted this between them? he wondered with a rare flash of self-persecution. My God! He was getting neurotic! The sooner he got what he wanted from Samantha and sent her packing, the better it would be for all of them.

And, to expedite this decision, he took a deep breath, and said, 'If you'll excuse me, Papa,' before striding purposefully towards his objective. He no longer cared that he was showing his hand. It mattered little to him what his relatives, distant or otherwise, might think of his behaviour. Threading his way between chairs and lounges, and gaily striped couches, he made his way towards Samantha without deviating, the words he exchanged in passing barely civil in their brevity.

She saw him coming. In spite of the fact that she was having tea with his uncle Henry, she seemed to sense his relentless approach. Of course, his mother noticed it, too, but she was far more adept at hiding her feelings. And Henry, who was once again playing truant from Aunt Celia's many illnesses, was the obvious choice of companion, as he was English, too.

And it was Henry who greeted his nephew with his usual aplomb. 'Getting your usual lecture from the old man, Matt?' he asked, after the usual courtesies had been exchanged, and Caroline Putnam gave him a glowering look.

'No doubt Apollo was only saying how delighted he was that Matthew's here,' she retorted, as her son placed a proprietorial hand on Samantha's shoulder.

'And the rest,' jeered Henry irrepressibly. 'Anyone who likes to be called Apollo has to have a fairly high opinion of themselves. And we all know what the old man expects of his grandson.'

'I notice you don't turn down his invitations!' exclaimed Caroline hotly, torn between her desire to defend her father and the knowledge that by excluding Matthew and Samantha from the conversation she was running the risk of losing her advantage. 'Matt——' She caught his arm as he would have turned away. 'Aren't you going to introduce Samantha to your grandfather?'

'Later,' said Matthew flatly, in no mood to have another run-in with Aristotle. He glanced round, and saw to his relief that his grandfather had been joined by several other members of the family. 'He's busy right now,' he added, feeling Samantha's resistance as he endeavoured to guide her away. 'You don't mind if we go for a walk, do you? I'd like to show Samantha the caves.'

'Oh, well——' Caroline was evidently casting about in her mind for some reason why he ought not to leave the party, but Matthew was not prepared to humour her either.

'*Herete*,' he said, using the Greek farewell deliberately. And before his mother could say anything else he urged Samantha across the terrace.

'You might have asked me if I wanted to go for a walk,' she hissed, as they reached the shallow steps that led down to the beach. 'I may be here because you brought me, but I do have feelings, you know.'

'I know.' Matthew offered his hand as she descended the steps and scowled when she refused it. 'But we couldn't have had a private conversation with my mother around. What did you think of her, by the way? What did she say to you?'

Samantha's expression was not encouraging. He could tell she was uneasy at being removed from the comparative security of being with other people, and he guessed she had had second thoughts about what had happened earlier that afternoon.

'Your—your mother was very nice,' she replied now, taking off her shoes, and carrying them suspended from one hand. 'She asked me how long I'd known you.'

Matthew glanced sideways at her. 'And what did you say?'

'I said, not long,' she replied shortly, turning aside from his dogged trek along the beach, and heading for the water. She was evidently aware that by doing so she remained within sight of the terrace, and Matthew stifled his impatience as he kicked off his shoes and joined her.

She was already paddling in the shallows, gasping when a wave more aggressive than the others splashed foam about her calves. She looked up when he joined her, but her eyes were dark and wary. It was obvious she wasn't happy, and he was irritated by his concern.

'So what else did she say?' he persisted, treading into the shallows, and she gave him a shocked stare.

'You're getting your trousers wet!' she exclaimed, pointing at the water lapping round his ankles, but Matthew only moved nearer.

'I'll take them off, if you like,' he said, feeling a certain malicious satisfaction when her face bloomed with colour. 'Come on, Sam. Don't shut me out. I thought we agreed to call a truce for this weekend.'

The tip of her tongue appeared, and Matthew wondered how such a simple gesture could affect him so. 'I—I don't remember anything about a truce,' she said, looking down at the specks of water that dappled her shorts. 'You didn't even tell me what I was supposed to do after I got changed.'

Matthew frowned. 'Didn't Rosita wait for you?'

'The maid?' Samantha shrugged. 'Yes, I suppose so. But you must have known how I'd feel, meeting all these people! And—and instead of being there, you let your mother——'

'My mother got to you before I could,' he retorted, taking a wind-blown strand of her hair between his thumb and forefinger, and smoothing it tensely. 'Sam, believe me, I wanted to be with you. But sometimes it's better to let events take their course.'

She looked up. 'Was your grandfather talking about me?'

Matthew hesitated. 'Among other things.'

'He doesn't like you bringing me here, does he?' Her lips twisted. 'I don't think your mother's too overjoyed about it either.'

'Why?' Matthew stepped nearer, so that the rippling waves had only a narrow channel between their feet. 'If she said anything to upset you——'

'She didn't.' Samantha broke in before he could voice the fury he was feeling. 'I—just got the impression that— well, that she was warning me off, that's all. She implied I shouldn't take you too seriously.'

'Did she?' In spite of the fact that only a short time before he had been telling himself much the same thing, Matthew felt a wave of raw resentment sweep over him. How dared his mother presume on their relationship? And what the hell did she know of his feelings, when they only saw one another perhaps a dozen times a year?

'It doesn't matter.' Samantha put up a hand and removed her hair from his fingers, before turning away. 'Oh, look—isn't that a pretty shell? When I was young I used to collect shells, and make them into bracelets.'

Matthew exhaled heavily. 'And did you tell her how we met?' he persisted, moving up behind her, and sliding his arms around her waist. To hell with the fact that anyone who chose could watch them from the terrace. He needed to touch her, and the warmth of her slim hips was heaven against his tortured body.

'Matt!' Her protest was half-hearted, but she, much more than he, was conscious of their audience. 'Your mother can see us,' she added, as he brushed her hair aside, and kissed the soft skin at the nape of her neck. 'Oh—please, Matt! You can't do this. What will your grandfather think of us?'

'He'll think I'm a very lucky man,' muttered Matthew huskily, turning, so that she was hidden by his lean frame. Then his fingers spread possessively over the burgeoning fullness of her breasts. 'Mmm, baby, can you feel what you do to me?'

'You mustn't!'

Her denial was breathless, and automatic, but for all her words she was leaning into him, yielding against his arousal that swelled unmistakably against her rounded bottom. Like him, she was responding to the flame of

pure desire that swept between them, and his words were
barely audible against the hollow of her ear.

'Come and see the caves,' he breathed, twisting her
round in his arms, and gazing down into her wide,
anxious eyes. 'At least no one will see us there.'

Samantha swallowed. Matthew watched the nervous
contraction of her throat, and was amazed at the proprietorial feeling he felt towards her. She belonged to
him, he thought irrationally; not her fiancé, Paul,
whoever he might be. He'd decide when he'd let her go.
And it might not be as soon as he'd thought.

'I—all right,' she gave in huskily, and for a moment
Matthew was tempted to kiss her there, in full view of
anyone who cared to look. But discretion—and the
awareness of his own ungovernable impulses, so far as
she was concerned—persuaded him to be patient, and,
turning her beneath the arch of his arm, he drew her
more familiarly along the shoreline.

The caves stretched for some distance around the curve
of the headland. A labyrinthine warren of caverns and
tunnels, they had once been the haunt of pirates and
thieves. In the early part of the nineteenth century, they
had also been used as shelter, by the peasants fleeing
from the Sultan's men. It was said that thousands of
men and women had been shipped to Constantinople,
and sold into slavery.

Happily, nowadays, the only occupants were crabs and
seabirds. The smooth, sandy floors were strewn with
seaweed, not kegs of rum, and the arched roofs only
echoed to the sound of the ocean.

Matthew's intention, of taking Samantha into his arms
the minute they were out of sight of prying eyes, was
diverted by her reaction to the caves. She was enchanted
by the realisation that there were several entrances to the
caverns, and her delight at discovering they could walk
under the headland, and emerge on to another beach
that had no other means of access, was infectious. He
found himself sharing her search for shells, and admiring the veined bones of marble that pushed through
the cliff-face He even shared her laughter when a hermit-

crab appeared from behind a rock, and threatened to
nip her toes.

She was unaffected, and amusing, and Matthew
couldn't help responding to her natural charm. It wasn't
just that he wanted to make love to her. Though he did,
more and more, he reflected ruefully. It was simply that
she was marvellous fun to be with, and he found himself
in the unexpected position of wanting her all to himself.

The knowledge didn't please him. He was allowing
the demands of his libido to influence his reasoning, he
thought irritably. He wanted to have sex with her, that
was all. Once he had satisfied his physical needs, the
other characteristics about her that he admired would
all fall into perspective.

But what if they didn't? a small voice argued. What
if, by making love to her, he only opened the gates to a
deeper involvement? After his relationship with Melissa,
how could he even contemplate the traumas of another
affair?

He couldn't, he decided abruptly. This whole situation was getting dangerously out of hand. His mother
and grandfather were right. He shouldn't have brought
Samantha here.

He glanced at his watch. It was after five. The gathering on the terrace would have broken up by now,
everyone retiring to their own apartments, to rest for a
while before changing for dinner. It was a very leisurely
life they led here on Delphus. There was far too much
time to dwell on other things.

His jaw tightened as he turned to look at Samantha.
She was squatting down by a rock-pool, chasing a tiny
nautilus shell with her finger. The position she had
adopted drew his attention to the provocative curve of
hip and thigh, and the dipping of her neckline exposed
the creamy-soft roundness of one perfect breast.

His hands clenched. What he wanted to do at that
moment was tumble her on to the sand and kiss her
senseless. But instead he looked away, and said in a voice
that couldn't help but reveal his tension, 'Shall we go?'

'Go?' Samantha came to her feet in one fluid motion, and her eyes were an unknowing mirror to the confusion of her thoughts. 'I—why, yes.' She glanced around her. 'Can we come here again?'

'If you like.' Matthew was offhand, but he couldn't help it, and, pushing his hands into his pockets, he walked back the way they had come.

She followed him, but he sensed she was as disturbed as he was by the sudden darkening of his mood. It was crazy, he told himself angrily. His emotions weren't involved here; only his senses. So why was he acting like a moron, when she was his for the taking?

He was relieved to see that the terrace was practically deserted when they reached it. Only a handful of servants were bustling about, clearing the remains of the tea-party, and stacking the chairs for the night. They smiled politely at Matthew, but he guessed his and Samantha's prolonged absence had been commented upon. He had probably been judged, and found guilty, of every sin in the book, he reflected bitterly. Greeks respected their women; they didn't take advantage of them.

'Do you know the way to your rooms?' Matthew asked as they entered the wide entrance hall that was flooded now with the golden light of early evening. He was already contemplating the prospect of the decanter of Scotch his grandfather kept in the library with some desperation, and his heart thudded heavily when Samantha shook her head.

'I'm sorry, no.'

She looked—anxious; hurt! Those eyes, that he had once pictured dark with passion, possessed a troubled expression. He wasn't totally convinced of it, but he suspected she was on the verge of tears. Dear God! he thought despairingly. What was he going to do?

Keeping his hands securely in his pockets, he managed a casual, 'OK.'

But her, 'I'll ask one of the maids to direct me,' stung him to the core.

'Don't be silly,' he retorted, setting off along the corridor to their right. 'Come on. I'll show you how to find your way. Then—then when it's dinnertime, you won't need anyone's assistance.'

Samantha sighed. He heard the soft expellation of her breath behind him, but he didn't look back. And presently she fell into step beside him, probably aware that, by dragging her heels, she was only prolonging the situation.

It was shadowy in the long corridors, the lamps that cast their illumination by night not yet reaching their full potential. Instead, the brass-shaded lanterns cast pools of shadow over the rug-strewn floors, and Matthew hoped fervently that Samantha wouldn't lose her footing. He didn't know what he might do if he had to touch her. Every inch of his skin was sensitised to every move she made.

But Samantha didn't slip, and they reached her door without incident. Set in an angle of the corridor, its grilled panels had never appeared so welcome, and Matthew managed a grim smile as he indicated that they had arrived.

'Dinner's not until nine o'clock,' he said, keeping the vision of his grandfather's decanter firmly in his sights. 'If you have any difficulties in finding your way, just pick up the phone.'

Samantha nodded. She hadn't bothered putting her shoes on again since they re-entered the house, and in consequence the difference in their height was more pronounced. But, when she tilted her head and looked up at him, she had no problem in meeting his gaze.

'Is something wrong?' she asked softly, and Matthew's breathing stilled.

'I'm afraid I——'

He wasn't sure what he had been about to say, but in any case he wasn't allowed to continue. 'Did I do something wrong?' she queried, putting out her hand and touching his taut chest. Her fingers brushed the fine dark hair exposed by the opening of his shirt, and he shuddered. 'You know what I'm talking about. You've hardly said a word for the last half-hour.'

Matthew sucked in a laboured breath. 'You're imagining things.'

'No, I'm not.' Amazingly, she seemed prepared to stand and argue with him. Her face, pale in the artificial light, took on a shuttered look. 'I think you're having second thoughts about bringing me here——'

'No!' Matthew's hard-won restraint faltered, but he made a valiant effort to keep his head. 'No, I—just think we both need a breathing space, that's all. I've been doing some—thinking, and I guess what I'm saying is—that——'

'—you wish you hadn't brought me here!' she finished tensely, and, stepping round his astounded frame, she marched into her apartment.

Matthew saw the door closing behind her, swung by the aggressive sweep of her arm, and somehow his foot prevented it from slamming. 'For pity's sake, Sam!' he exclaimed, striding after her, and it was not until he had caught her arm, and jerked her round to face him, that he realised how reckless he had been.

She was crying. The tears he had suspected earlier were now a reality, overspilling her eyes in the aftermath of their encounter. Salty streaks smeared her cheeks, and she smudged them away with the back of her hand, as she struggled to meet his angry gaze.

'Oh, God!'

The oath he muttered was as much a prayer for his own deliverance as a protest at her vulnerability. But it was impossible for him to look at her without touching her, and when he pulled her into his arms he felt only relief.

'I'm sorry,' he muttered harshly, chasing her tears with his tongue, before finding the parted softness of her mouth. 'I never meant to hurt you, and what I've done has hurt us both.'

The sound she made could have been a protest, but her hands were gripping the hair at the back of his neck, and she was reaching up eagerly towards him. So much so that Matthew's tongue brushed the dewy softness at the back of her throat, and her eyes closed against the passion she saw in his.

She felt so good in his arms, he thought unsteadily, her shoulders warm from the unaccustomed rays of the sun. Her skin felt like satin, and when he insinuated one hand into the waistband of her shorts he was amazed at the sense of power it gave him.

He wanted her! Lord, how he wanted her! He had never felt such a need to be a part of a woman before, and the hunger she inspired in him made a nonsense of his resistance. What was the point of sending her away? He knew that if he did sooner or later he'd go after her. He wouldn't rest until she was his, and to hell with the consequences.

She was kissing him back now, her tongue seeking his in an eager parody of his possession. Her body was leaning into his, and the unmistakable scent of her arousal rocked his senses. Whatever kind of relationship she had with her fiancé, he was convinced she had never responded like this before. It was crazy, but for all her eagerness to taste his mouth there was an immaturity in the way she went about it. Instinct alone seemed to be responsible for the wilful urgency of her lips, and although she must have some experience there was a guileless naïveté in the way she let him take the lead.

The curve of her bottom was like the softest silk beneath his hand. His fingers cupped it, squeezed it, used it to urge her even nearer, revelling in the expectation of that soft skin against his own.

Eagerness was making him reckless. He hardly remembered that while he had been escorting her to her room he had been steeling himself against her. His earlier plans of spending the evening in a sensual anticipation of the night ahead; of watching her across the supper table, and teasing his senses with thoughts of her eventual acquiescence, had all been discarded. The idea of savouring her submission, of picturing her slim body, pale against his crisp sheets, had become too dangerous to contemplate. Yet, suddenly, even those images seemed too distant to withstand.

He wanted her now; this minute. Holding her like this, feeling her yielding body responding to the urgency of his, made even his pre-conceived seduction superfluous. Far from tempting her, she was tempting him, driving him to distraction with her bewitching innocence.

His hand groped for the door behind him, and he slammed it shut. Then, keeping his mouth on hers, he urged her back, towards the bed. The swagged edge of the counterpane halted their progress, and Samantha sat down rather suddenly, jerked out of her bemusement by the coolness against her legs.

Realising it might not be wise to give himself time to rekindle any doubts about what he was doing, Matthew dropped on to his haunches in front of her. He moved between her splayed knees, and cupped her face in his hands, parting her lips with his thumbs, and slipping his tongue between.

'Matt...'

His name on her lips was dazed and questioning, but there was no trace of resistance in the word. On the contrary, as his fingers moved to stroke down the column of her throat, she shifted against him, brushing his hand with her breasts as a whispering sigh rippled over her.

Matthew found he was trembling. The gentle hands that probed his shoulders were unknowingly sensuous, and his whole body yearned for their delicate caress. He could feel his muscles stirring, growing and expanding, and the ache between his thighs was becoming unbearable.

He found the ends of the cords that kept the halter in place, and tugged decisively. The two sides parted, and the silk fell away. Her breasts were just as beautiful as he remembered, and he pressed his face between them, reaching behind her again to unfasten the ties at her waist.

The halter was tossed on to the floor beside him, and her eyes met his half nervously as his hands slid from her waist to cradle the undersides of her breasts. The rose-tipped crests semed to surge towards him, and she quivered when his teeth closed around one sensitised peak.

He suckled greedily, causing a flood of feeling to torment his groin. He had never experienced such a sensation of excitement; never felt such a rush of adrenalin, spreading through his veins like wildfire. His heart was thumping; the blood was pounding in his head. Every nerve and sinew was demanding satisfaction.

Cool it, Matt, he chided himself, drawing back for a moment and looking down at the floor, trying to calm his rioting senses. But the sight of his own aroused body was unavoidable, and the palpable nearness of hers made a nonsense of his efforts. It was impossible to behave rationally in his present state of upheaval. His brain felt as if it was on fire, and his physical needs were paramount.

His hand moved down, one finger drawing a line from the waistband of her shorts, over her flat stomach, to the heated junction of her legs. She jumped when he pressed his thumb against her, and he felt the throbbing pulse beneath the silk. He couldn't wait to strip the shorts from her. He wanted to touch her without the barrier of anything between.

And yet there was a tantalising delight in prolonging his own torture. He knew that what was going to happen between them would be good, and he wanted her to enjoy it as much as he would. That was why he drew one of her hands to his body, sucking in his breath when her slender fingers traced the turgid outline of his flesh.

She was trembing now, and if he hadn't known better he'd have said she was half afraid of what was happening. But she didn't draw back. In fact, she seemed disarmingly eager to learn anything he had to teach her. And, when her fingers went to release his zip, he decided she still had a lot to learn.

He moved then, tumbling her back on to the bed, and coming down on it beside her. With one hand, he tore open his shirt, so that when he bent over her her breasts were flattened against the hair-roughened skin of his chest, and with the other he cushioned her head, bringing her mouth to his.

It was so good to feel her beneath him, so good to find the button of her shorts and ease them down over her hips. She was wearing lacy briefs beneath, but they were soon disposed of. And then his fingers found the damp sweetness they had been seeking.

'God, Sam,' he muttered, releasing the button of his trousers and jerking open his zip. He almost groaned at the relief he felt when his swollen flesh spilled into his hand. Dear God, he thought incredulously, this had never happened to him before, not even with Melissa. He was as horny as a schoolboy on his first date.

She was shifting beneath him now, and although when his mouth found hers and his tongue plunged deeply into her mouth she responded avidly he sensed her uncertainty. And why not? he asked himself, with a brief spurt of conscience. It was obvious she had never been unfaithful to her boyfriend before. Indeed, if she hadn't been so adamant about her relationship with her fiancé, he might even have suspected she had never done this before.

But he didn't want to think about that. She was too deliciously desirable, and responsive. Her lips, bruised now from his kisses, were a constant delight, and the ripeness of her breasts simply begged for his attention.

His gaze drifted down to her hips and her flat stomach. The curly mound of her womanhood was soft and irresistible, and he slid his fingers into the cleft that was wet with wanting him. Even though he longed to taste her, he knew he dared not risk that right now. His own urgent body demanded release, and he had to content himself with stroking the hot little nub that pulsed against his thumb.

She jerked beneath his touch, and the whimpering sounds she emitted drove him crazy. He wanted her to make those sounds when he was inside her, and, sliding his hand along her thigh, he parted it from the other. With his tongue tracing the column of her throat, he moved between her legs, and guided himself into that dark moist passage, and when she bucked against him his flagging control gave way.

He entered her swiftly, more swiftly than he had intended, and even when he encountered that unbelievable—but unmistakable—barrier, he couldn't draw back. For the first time in his life, his own needs got the better of him, and, even though he struggled to resist, the marvellous tightness of her muscles defeated him.

He climaxed almost immediately, spilling most of his seed inside her. For, although he dragged himself away from that spiralling ecstasy, the effort had exhausted him, and he slumped heavily beside her . . .

CHAPTER NINE

SAMANTHA stared up at the ceiling. Even in the lamp-light the delicate plasterwork was clearly visible. The flowing style, which gave each leaf and flower such vitality, must have taken a craftsman months to create. Leaves and flowers that had no colour, she reflected tautly. Like everything else at the villa, they weren't exactly what they seemed.

She sighed. She supposed she ought to be feeling bad at this moment. Or guilty, at least, for behaving as she had. If Paul could see her now, he would never forgive her. So why did she just feel empty, and incapable of grief?

She wished Matthew would go. He was still motionless beside her, one arm raised, and his head turned away from her. He was probably still nursing his outrage at finding she was still a virgin. Judging by the oath he had uttered seconds before he had slumped beside her, he was unlikely to forgive her. Join the queue, she thought indifferently. She would probably never forgive herself.

She supposed she was still numb from the experience. Certainly, it had been nothing like what she had expected. It had been more painful, for one thing. But then, remembering the rampant power of Matthew's body, she ought not to have been surprised. No wonder women were afraid of men forcing themselves upon them. Matthew hadn't done that, but he had hurt her. The blood still caked her thighs with its sticky, cloying scent.

What was harder to understand were the feelings that had swept through her body like a forest fire, and now seemed no more substantial than a mirage. What had happened to them? Why did they seem so unreal? Her

137

ignorance had to be the key; that, and a hopeless sense of inadequacy.

She didn't blame Matthew. The responsibility was all hers. She had gone into this with her eyes open. It was her fault it had turned out the way it had.

He stirred then, and, unable to prevent herself, she stiffened. If he touched her, she would scream, she thought unsteadily. For God's sake, why didn't he just go? How much longer was this to go on?

But Matthew didn't go. Nor did he touch her; not initially, anyway. He merely rolled his head on his arm so that he was looking at her, and she stared at the ceiling with greater concentration.

'Am I supposed to say I'm sorry?' he asked softly, expelling his breath on a low sigh. 'I am. But not for the reason you think. I haven't done this since I was in school.'

In spite of herself, that got her attention. Unable to resist, she turned to look at him, her narrowed eyes mirroring her arrant disbelief. 'Really?'

'Yes, really.' Matthew's eyes were dark and intent. 'I'm usually in control. This time I wasn't. As I say, I'm sorry. I'll make sure it doesn't happen again.'

'Again?' Samantha gasped. 'You surely can't imagine this might happen again?' His shamelessness disturbed her, and she hurriedly looked away. 'I'm not blaming you, but—it was a mistake. I knew it before I came here, and this has only proved the point.'

'Why?' Matthew shifted, so that his weight was supported on one elbow, and he was looking down at her. 'Because you'd never been with a man before?' He ran lazy fingers into his hair, and, seeing the movement out of the corner of her eye, Samantha knew a moment's panic. 'You should have told me. I hurt you, I know. But,' he shrugged, 'it had to happen some time.'

'You would say that, wouldn't you?' Samantha had to catch herself back from saying something quite vituperative about this experience. For a moment a wave of some emotion she refused to recognise swept over her. And she despised herself for being more conscious of his nakedness than her own. 'Well—as I say, I'm not blaming you. I knew what I was doing. I just—didn't think it through.'

The trace of a smile tugged at the corners of Matthew's lips. 'No one thinks this sort of thing through, sweetheart,' he told her gently, and she clenched her fists against the casual endearment. 'And forgive me, I don't believe you did know what you were doing. If it's any consolation, nor did I.'

Samantha refused to be cajoled. Pulling her lower lip between her teeth, she said, 'I think you'd better go. It's getting late. Your—your mother will be wondering where you are.'

Matthew shrugged, his shoulders brown and muscular in the subdued light. 'That's not a consequence that troubles me greatly,' he remarked, his eyes drifting down over her taut body. 'I just wish I'd locked that door. There are some things no one else should see.'

Samantha's head jerked around. 'You don't think——'

'Relax.' His hand came to touch her now, and she hardly noticed the light caress. She was too shocked at the idea that anyone else might see her humiliation. She could just imagine the gossip that would cause.

'Stay there,' he said after a moment, seeming to find it difficult to withdraw his hand from the smooth curve of her arm. But at least he didn't touch her breasts, which were already hardening against her will. Dear God, she thought, as feeling flooded back into her bones, she couldn't want him again; not after what had happened before.

Matthew slid off the bed, and although she wished she could look anywhere else but at him, her eyes followed his unashamed progress to her bathroom. He disappeared inside, and presently she heard water running. For heaven's sake, she wondered, was he taking a shower? Of course! He'd want to clean all trace of their lovemaking from him.

She sat up and looked down at herself, finding no pleasure in the sight. If only there were another

bathroom. she thought. If only she could cleanse herself
before he came back Crazy though the thoughts were,
she doubted anyone would want to touch her at the
moment. Which should have been a source of relief—
but wasn't.

Matthew seemed to take forever, and she was on the
point of deciding she could at least put on her dressing-
gown when he came back. But he hadn't had a shower.
His hair was dry, and there was no lingering smell of
soap clinging to his body. On the contrary, his skin was
still glistening with sweat, and when he came towards
the bed she saw he was fully aroused.

'Come on,' he said, and before she could ascertain his
intentions he had scooped her up into his arms.

Shock soon gave way to comprehension, when he
carried her into the bathroom. Instead of the shower she
had thought he was taking, Matthew had filled the
enormous tub, and now he paused on the marble rim,
looking down into the gently steaming water. Then, just
when she thought he was going to lower her into the tub
and leave her to her ablutions, he stepped down into the
pool by means of the shallow steps cut into the side, and
deposited her on the ledge that encircled it below the
waterline.

The water was neither hot nor cold, and Samantha
felt the instant relief of its soothing balm, pine-scented
and luxurious, against her sore body. She realised she
really could have swum in its depths, but it was far more
sybaritic just to let its heat relax her.

'Good, hmm?' Matthew murmured, and Samantha,
who had been too bemused by her surroundings to notice
that he was still there, caught her breath.

His presence both shocked and disturbed her. Shocked,
because she had never taken a bath with a man before;
and disturbed, because she was aware that her attraction
towards him had by no means been abated by what had
happened.

'I—very good,' she answered him now, suddenly aware
of her breasts, clearly outlined beneath the water that
lapped about her shoulders And of the abandoned way

she was lounging, also visible to his appraising gaze.
'Um—thank you.'

Dammit, why didn't he go? she wondered frantically.
He must know how embarrassing this was for her. She
couldn't believe, with his vast experience, he didn't know
exactly how she was feeling.

But instead of getting out of the tub he reached for
an ivory tablet of soap that was set on a dish to one side
of the bath, and applied its softness to the sponge he
was squeezing in his other hand. Then, to Samantha's
astonishment—and mortification—he began to lather her
arms and shoulders.

'I—don't,' she protested, as the sponge made a circle
round her breast, and Matthew's lips tilted at her obvious distress.

'Why not?' he asked, ignoring her in any case. 'I'll
be very thorough, I assure you.'

'Because—because you can't,' Samantha gasped, her
voice rising dramatically as the sponge moved lower.
'Matt—please! You're embarrassing me.'

Matthew's hand stilled. 'Don't be silly,' he said,
leaning towards her and circling her lips with his tongue.
'Just pretend I'm your body-slave.' He drew back and
grinned. 'I am, anyway.' The sponge slid along her thigh.
'Come on. I won't hurt you. I promise.'

'Oh, Matt!' To her dismay, she felt the stirring heat
of the same emotions that had betrayed her once already.
It couldn't be true, she told herself. After the fiasco of
what had happened, how could she even contemplate
making love with him without horror?

'Oh, baby,' he countered softly, drawing her off the
ledge and into his arms. 'God, Sam, what are you doing
to me?'

What was she doing to him? Samantha could have
laughed at the incongruity of it all. What was he doing
to her, more like? With the water soothing her aching
limbs, the idea of making love again was no longer so
painful, and all thoughts of right and wrong fled.

Matthew lifted her out of the bath with the utmost
tenderness, wrapping her in a huge silky towel that en-

cased her like a cocoon. Then, uncaring of his own wetness, he laid her on the bed and finished his task.

However, by the time he had attended to her breasts, punctuating the towel's soft abrasion with sensuous kisses, and caressed the calf and instep of each long, shapely leg, she was weak and clinging to him. She no longer cared that his throbbing arousal might hurt her yet again. She just wanted him inside her, hot and fulfilling.

And he was hot: hot, and fulfilling, and marvellously real. There was no pain, just an aching fullness as he stretched her taut muscles, and slid into her sheath. His mouth bruised hers as he withdrew part-way, only to thrust himself inside her again, and a growing sense of anticipation flowered in her stomach.

Instinct took over. She was hardly aware of what she was doing. With Matthew's tongue taking possession of her mouth, mimicking the hard possession of his body, and his hands cupping her bottom to bring her even nearer, she wrapped her legs around his waist, and let him take her. The plunging heat as he drove himself into her was like a mounting wave of pleasure, the slickness of his body welding them together. She moaned out loud as the fiery heat of their lovemaking reached a crescendo, and then a splintering delight engulfed her, sending her spinning over the brink...

Samantha dressed for supper with shaking hands. Although she knew Matthew would be there to support her, she would have given everything she possessed just to avoid joining the rest of his family for the evening meal. She was convinced they would know exactly what had happened between that too-obvious walk along the beach, and supper. She was sure they would see Matthew's mark upon her. And, although the only bruises she had were hidden by the long skirt of her Laura Ashley print, she felt so different that she couldn't believe she didn't look different, too.

But different didn't mean like him, she reminded herself tensely. In spite of what had happened—in spite of the fact that he had turned her world upside-down in the space of a few hours—Samantha knew that nothing had really changed. She was still the owner of the Honey Pot Café, and Matthew was still Aristotle Apollonius's grandson.

Still? She questioned her use of the adverb. Matthew wasn't 'still' anything. Until today, she hadn't even realised he owned J.P. Software International. J.P.? She frowned. P for Putnam, no doubt. If only she had been more astute. She might have put two and two together before it was too late.

But it was too late, she acknowledged. Much too late. Whatever happened in the future, today had been a crucial turning point in her life. It was the day she had learned now naïve she had been to believe she had control of her life. It was the day she had learned that, whatever happened now, she would have to tell Paul she couldn't marry him.

She looked down at her bare finger. Even though she had only been wearing her engagement ring for a few weeks, she missed its narrow band. It had represented so many things to her—home, security, normality! The common-sense values she had always lived by. Now she realised what a momentous thing she had done when she had taken it off on the plane. She had done more than remove a ring, she thought ominously. She had shed the beliefs of a lifetime.

She drew an uneven breath. So what now? she wondered tautly. Where did she go from here? The common sense that had deserted her when Matthew touched her had now returned with a vengeance. All right, for a few hours he had shown her heaven. But, although she didn't have his experience, she was sensible enough to realise that what he had shared with her he had probably shared with someone else. More than one someone, probably. She had to accept that, no matter how painful that possibility might be.

So where did that leave her? What could she expect from this relationship? At the most, a few weeks of Matthew's time. A brief, if sexually satisfying, affair, with no commitment from either of them? Or would she

become another Melissa, using any ruse to see him, even
if it meant using another man? For she had the uneasy
feeling that Matthew's strange appearance at Melissa's
engagement party was less of a coincidence than he had
admitted. He had said Melissa had expected to marry
him! At least Samantha had had no such expectation.

She sighed, and took another look at her appearance.
The dress was fine, but she wasn't. She didn't belong
here. No matter that only an hour ago she had held
Matthew, shuddering in her arms. No matter that, in
spite of everything, she was very much afraid she had
fallen in love with him. She was only prolonging the
agony. He didn't love her. He *wanted* her, that was all.
She doubted he had ever really loved anybody. Love—
and marriage—were not part of his agenda. They didn't
fit in with his plans for the future. So how could she,
when her ambitions would always be so different from
his?

Half of her wished there were some way she could
leave without seeing Matthew again. The prospect of the
weekend ahead filled her with alarm. No matter how
strong her resolve might be—to break this alliance before
it broke her—the longer they were together, the harder
it was going to be. She didn't want to get used to being
with him. She didn't want him to break her heart.

But the other half, the emotional half of her being,
saw the next two days quite differently. Forty-eight hours
was a long time, she told herself optimistically. Matthew
might even fall in love with her. And, as she couldn't
get away, why shouldn't she take what the gods had offered, and be grateful?

Fat chance! she thought, pragmatism overwhelming
her illusions. Get real, Sam, she ordered bitterly,
dragging a brush savagely through her hair. This was
life, not some fancy daydream! And anyway, did she
really want to marry a man who saw no shame in seducing another man's fiancée?

She threw down the brush, and turned away from the
mirror. It didn't help to see her own culpability in her
eyes. Matthew would not have made love to her if she

hadn't accepted his invitation. The only person responsible for messing up her life was herself.

The knock at the door brought an abrupt end to her unhappy introspection. And, although moments before she had been torn with indecision, she didn't hesitate before going to answer it. There was nothing she could do, she insisted, when the low insidious voice of reason still protested. When she got back to England, she would tell Matthew she couldn't see him again. But, until then, she was helpless.

She had locked the door on his departure an hour ago, the defensive action a small sop to her conscience. Which was probably why he hadn't just walked in, she acknowledged drily. After what had happened between them, she couldn't imagine Matthew showing any reticence.

But, when she opened the door, it wasn't Matthew who was standing outside. It was his mother. And Samantha gazed at her blankly, but with a growing sense of dread.

'Samantha.' Caroline Putnam—or did she still call herself Apollonius? Samantha wondered wildly—smiled disarmingly. 'May I come in?'

'I—of course.' What else could she say? Samantha stepped back automatically. 'Um—is something wrong?'

It was a foolish question. Something was obviously wrong, or Matthew's mother wouldn't be here. Images of herself and Matthew in various stages of undress flashed guiltily before Samantha's eyes. Dear God, she hadn't seen them, had she? Samantha fretted. The door hadn't been locked then. Matthew had remarked upon it.

The older woman said nothing until Samantha had closed the door behind her. Then, linking her hands together at her waist, she paused in the middle of the floor.

'I'm afraid I've got some bad news,' she said, and for an awful moment Samantha was afraid that something dreadful had happened to Matthew. She clasped her hands, and pressed them to her throat, feeling absurdly as if she was choking. But his mother's next words removed that fear, and replaced it with another. 'I have to tell you, on his behalf, that Matthew's had to return to London.'

'To London!'

Samantha blinked, and Caroline Putnam nodded. 'Yes. I'm afraid there's been something of an emergency. Melissa—that is, the girl we all hope Matthew will eventually marry—has been involved in—in an accident. Naturally, as soon as he heard, he made arrangements to fly back to England to be with her.'

A mixture of feelings swept over Samantha at that moment. Dismay; disbelief; indignation. How could Matthew have gone back to London and left her here, whatever the emergency? He must know how she would feel. How could he do this to her?

'I'm sure this must have come as a shock to you,' Caroline was saying now, and Samantha knew she had to hide her real feelings. There was no way she was going to let Matthew—or his mother—know how humiliated they had made her feel. She had to pretend her reaction was one of inconvenience.

'Oh, dear,' she said, turning aside so that she could surreptitiously dry her damp palms on her skirt. 'What a nuisance!'

'Yes.' But Matthew's mother was not as gullible as all that. 'He's hurt you, hasn't he? I was afraid he would.'

'No!' Samantha's response was more defensive than she would have liked, but the other woman's words had stung. She didn't want anybody feeling sorry for her. 'I—our relationship was never serious, Mrs Putnam. If Matthew told you that it was, then he was exaggerating.'

'Well—no. No, he didn't.' Samantha winced. She had never expected he had. 'But I know, from personal experience, you understand, that my son can be totally insensitive.'

There wasn't a lot Samantha could say to that. 'I agree' sprang most readily to mind, but that would have sounded too much like the resentment she was desperate to hide.

'Anyway, I—just wanted to warn you,' Caroline continued after a moment. 'And—naturally you're welcome to stay for the rest of the weekend, if that's what you'd like to do.'

That was her cue, Samantha realised bitterly. No one, least of all Matthew's mother, really wanted her to stay for the rest of the weekend. This wasn't just a social gathering; it was a family party. And now that Matthew had gone, she had no legitimate reason to remain.

'Um—that's very kind of you,' she said now, watching the wary expression on the older woman's face. Was Caroline really afraid she might call her bluff, and accept her invitation? For a malicious moment Samantha was tempted to hesitate, just to get her own back. But she didn't. 'However, I think I'd rather go, if you don't mind.'

Caroline's relief was almost palpable. 'Of course I don't mind,' she said. 'But I'm afraid you won't be able to leave until tomorrow morning. I'll arrange for Niarchos to come and pick you up. Would nine-thirty be all right? Or perhaps a little later?'

'Nine-thirty would be fine,' replied Samantha firmly, and Caroline smiled.

'Good. I'll have my secretary check out the times of flights to England. I'm sure that won't be a problem. There are several flights in and out of Athens every day.'

'Fine.'

Samantha adopted what she hoped was an equally determined smile, and waited for Caroline to leave. She had done what she came for with obvious success. So why was she waiting? What more did she have to say?

'Er—about supper——'

Samantha stiffened. 'Yes?'

'I—we'll—quite understand if you'd rather have it here, in your room,' Matthew's mother ventured smoothly, and, although until that moment that was exactly what Samantha had wished, the older woman's insensitivity struck a nerve.

'Oh, I don't think so,' she responded now, realising exactly what Matthew's family would think if she didn't appear. Poor cow, they'd titter, only it would sound somewhat different in their language. Too embarrassed to show her face, now that Matthew's deserted her! 'I'd like to join you, if you have no objections. It's such a lovely evening. It seems a shame to waste it.'

Which was why Samantha found herself sitting on the terrace wall some time later, gazing somewhat tearfully at the moon. It was all very well pretending a brashness she didn't feel, but she wasn't as thick-skinned as Caroline imagined. It had taken an enormous amount of courage to walk into a crowded room earlier that evening and behave as if she had a right to be there. Oh, she had been introduced to many of the other guests that afternoon, and one of them, at least—Matthew's cousin, Alex—had made no secret of his willingness to take Matthew's place. But, without the man who had brought her here, she felt very much the outsider, and that was why, after the meal, she'd escaped outdoors.

She wondered what Matthew was doing at this moment. She wondered what emergency had necessitated his presence. Had Prince Georgio had an accident, perhaps? Or had Melissa simply broken her engagement? Whichever it was, and whatever Matthew had said, his family still expected him to be the one to marry her. So what was he doing with her? Samantha sniffed. Was it all a game to him, or was he trying to make Melissa jealous?

She shook her head, and tried to take pleasure in her surroundings. It was a beautiful evening. By moonlight the water looked dark and mysterious, and the sky was a silver-studded arc of blackness overhead. From indoors, the plaintive sound of bouzouki music stirred her senses. There was a breeze, too; quite a cool breeze, that brought the scent of Havana tobacco drifting to her nostrils. It should have been a night for love, but instead Matthew was far away in London, comforting a woman who was engaged to someone else . . .

'You do not find the view to your liking, Miss Maxwell?'

The gruff, accented voice came out of the darkness, somewhere to her right, and Samantha started violently. She had been unaware that she was not alone on the terrace. She had believed everyone was inside, indulging in the impromptu dances Greek music always seemed to inspire. They were rehearsing for tomorrow evening, when a group of musicians had been hired for the occasion. Samantha had heard all about it from Henry Putnam before Caroline's scrutiny—and her own despair—had driven her to seek this quiet sanctuary.

Now, she turned her head and saw the glowing tip of a cigar. And, as her eyes adjusted to the shadows, she saw it was Matthew's grandfather, sitting watching her, framed by a fan-backed cane chair.

She had met him earlier. Caroline had performed the introduction—if introduction was the right word for the perfunctory presentation she had made. It had been a reluctant duty at best, and she had made sure Samantha was not allowed to stay around and make any embarrassing comments. Matthew's mother had taken her off on the pretext of wanting to introduce her to someone else, and so far as Samantha was aware he had forgotten her. But apparently not.

'I'm sorry,' she said now, sliding down off the wall, and showing every indication of leaving. 'I didn't realise I was intruding.'

'You are not.' The old man frowned. 'Please.' He pointed to another chair, set at right angles to his own. 'Join me.'

Samantha hesitated. 'It's very kind of you, but—really—I was just going in.'

'Were you?' He sounded disconcertingly like Matthew. 'You looked quite at home before I spoke to you. A little sad perhaps, but in no particular hurry to seek the isolation of your apartments.'

Samantha allowed a breath to escape her. 'I—don't think we have anything to say to one another, Mr Apollonius,' she said quietly. 'And –I have packing to do. I'm leaving in the morning.'

'Yes. So Caroline tells me.' He paused. 'This is your decision?'

'Yes.' Samantha nodded.

'Does my grandson know?'

Samantha suppressed the retort that sprang to her lips. 'Perhaps,' she said, smoothing her hands over her skirt. 'It doesn't really matter. He's not here any more, and I should never have come.'

'So why did you?'

Matthew's grandfather raised his cigar to his lips, and regarded her intently. It was not an unexpected question, and yet Samantha was unprepared for it. It was reasonable enough that he should want to know. But she had the feeling he already knew the answer.

'Because—because Matt—Matthew—invited me,' she replied, glancing over her shoulder, towards the lights of the villa. 'I'm sorry if you think it was an imposition. But—I didn't know anything about—about your grandson, until I saw this place.'

The old man's eyes narrowed, but whether it was with scepticism, or simply the effects of the cigar smoke, Samantha couldn't be sure. 'What do you mean?' he asked. 'What did you not know?'

'Oh, really——' Samantha didn't want to get into this, particularly as she was fairly sure he wouldn't believe her. 'I made a mistake, that's all,' she offered, shrugging. 'And, contrary to your suggestion, I love the view.'

Aristotle's mouth compressed. 'You did not know Matthew was my grandson?' he persisted, and Samantha sighed.

'No.'

'You knew his name?'

'Putnam. Yes, I knew his name.'

'And the company he owns?'

'I didn't know he owned it, but yes. I knew about J.P. Software!'

The old man studied her taut face. 'That was said with some feeling. Do I take it you have had some dealings with J.P. Software? Is that how you met my grandson?'

'No.' Samantha shook her head. 'No.'

'Then tell me.' The old man gestured to the chair again. 'And sit down.'

Samantha's fists clenched, but, short of defying him, there was little she could do. So, with obvious misgivings, she came and took the chair beside him, moving it a few inches away from his, before subsiding on to the cushioned seat.

'Good.' Aristotle regarded her submission with evident satisfaction. 'Now I do not have to keep tilting my head to look at you. And, at my age, it is very pleasant to have the company of a beautiful woman.'

Samantha's features felt stiff. He didn't have to do this, she thought. He didn't have to say these things to get her to tell him how Matthew brought her here. It wasn't a secret, after all. Caroline probably knew all about it.

'So,' he prompted. 'Tell me how you met my grandson.'

Samantha bent her head. 'It's a long story.'

'We have all night.'

Samantha gave him a half-rueful look. 'I'm sure you know already.'

'No. No, I do not. He told me you ran a small café, that is all. I am curious to hear how he introduced himself.'

That again! Samantha's mouth flattened. What he really wanted to hear was how she could pretend not to know who he was, when his grandfather was so famous. Perhaps he thought Matthew would have told her. If he did, he knew his grandson as little as she did.

'There was a party,' she said slowly. 'I did the catering, and—Matt was there. End of story.'

'Beginning of story,' Aristotle corrected her, puffing on his cigar. 'I assume my grandson asked to see you again.'

'Not then, no.' Samantha took a wary breath. 'Look, I was—*I am*—engaged to someone else. I told Matt I couldn't see him. But—he wouldn't take no for an answer.'

'That sounds like my grandson,' remarked the old man drily. 'And ultimately, it seems, he had his way.'

In more ways than one, thought Samantha, though she didn't voice it. 'You could say that,' she agreed, pleating her skirt with trembling fingers. 'He got— someone else—to offer me a catering assignment at J.P. Software. Then, when I got there, I found out it was him.'

Aristotle frowned. 'Someone else? Who?'

'I don't know.' Samantha lifted her shoulders. 'Someone called—Burgess! If that was his real name.'

'Ah. Victor.'

'You know him?' Samantha couldn't hide her curiosity.

'Yes.' The old man inclined his head. 'Victor Burgess is my grandson's valet, for want of a better word. He refused to have a bodyguard, so Victor was installed.'

'A bodyguard!' Samantha stared at him. 'Why does Matt need a bodyguard?'

'He is my grandson,' said Aristotle simply. 'I regret that there are too many unscrupulous men around who would stop at nothing to get their hands on my family.'

'Kidnapping?' Samantha was appalled.

'Kidnapping; extortion; murder! The list is endless, Miss Maxwell. And Matthew is so independent. That is why he formed his own company. To prove he doesn't need me or my money.'

Samantha caught her breath. 'Oh, I'm sure that isn't true...'

'Are you?' The old man's lips twisted. 'But how well do you know my grandson?' He paused. 'Not very well, I'm afraid. *Dhen pirazi*, one day he will have to take my place.'

Samantha watched as he crushed the remains of his cigar in a crystal ashtray. For a moment she actually felt sorry for him. In spite of everything, she was sure he loved his grandson. There was a certain wistfulness in his words that betrayed it.

'I'd better go,' she murmured, shifting to the edge of her chair, but his outstretched hand detained her.

'You said you were—betrothed,' he ventured, the old-fashioned word sounding almost musical on his lips. 'So, why did you come away with Matthew?'

'Because I was a fool,' replied Samantha, shaking off his hand and getting to her feet. 'Don't worry, Mr Apollonius. I shan't be seeing your grandson again.'

CHAPTER TEN

'WHERE is she?'

Matthew strode angrily across his mother's bedroom and came to loom over her, his hands gripping the vanity unit on either side of her shrinking figure. She could feel the aggression pulsing from him, and his reflected image in the mirror in front of her was dark and threatening. She found it hard to keep his face in focus, and for the first time in her life Caroline felt intimidated.

'Where do you think?' she exclaimed now, making a brave effort to continue with her make-up. But the hand holding the mascara brush slipped, and a streak of charcoal smeared her cheek. 'Damn!' she muttered. 'Matthew, will you get away from me?'

'When you tell me what you said to her,' retorted her son grimly, as she dabbed ineffectually at the mascara with a tissue. 'You knew I was coming back. I said I'd be here for Apollo's party, and I am. So what the hell did you say to send her back to England? I told you to explain.' He straightened. 'God! I should have known better than to trust you! I should have spoken to her myself.'

Caroline quivered as he moved away from her. 'I understood you'd tried to speak to her yourself,' she retorted, flinching when his savage gaze impaled her once again. 'Well—you said she wouldn't open the door,' she protested.

'I said the door was locked,' Matthew declared inflexibly. 'I did not say she wouldn't open it. She must have been in the bathroom or something, and couldn't hear me.' His eyes darkened. 'And you were so eager for me to go.'

'I was worried about Melissa,' replied his mother defensively. 'And you must have been, too, or you wouldn't have gone rushing off like that.'

'Yes—well, we both know what a fiasco that was, don't we?' he stated scornfully. 'Just tell me, did you have anything to do with it, by any chance?'

'Matthew!'

She gazed at him indignantly, but Matthew gazed back without remorse. 'It's not beyond your capabilities,' he retorted, pushing his hands back into the pockets of his dark trousers, and pacing nerve-rackingly about the room. 'You're the one who's always agitating for me to get married and settle down. Did you really think Melissa's pathetic attempt to get attention would succeed, when all her other efforts didn't?'

His mother winced. 'That's a cruel and heartless thing to say, Matthew!'

'But true, nevertheless,' he essayed coldly. 'Half a dozen paracetamol tablets hardly warrants the time and trouble the doctors and nurses took over her. And let's get it in perspective, shall we? Ivanov had found out she'd been sleeping with someone else. Not me,' he added hastily, before Caroline could even consider it. 'Melissa's a hot little body. She always was. And apparently Ivanov doesn't keep her—happy—in that area.' His lips twisted. 'Her words were rather less polite, but suffice it to say she thinks certain parts of his anatomy are as frozen as the steppes he comes from.'

'I don't wish to hear that.' Caroline reached for a jar of moisturiser, and unscrewed the cap with slightly unsteady fingers. 'I can't believe Melissa could be so foolish!'

'No.' Matthew conceded the point without rancour. 'But then, we all do foolish things when our emotions are involved.'

His mother's head jerked up. 'You mean you regret not marrying her when you had the chance?'

'No.' Matthew was adamant, and his expression had darkened again. 'I mean *you* did a foolish thing when you sent Sam back to England. Did you really think it

would make any difference? Out of sight, out of mind—
is that what you thought?'

Caroline's nostrils flared. 'You mean you intend seeing
that young woman again?'

'Yes.' Matthew paused behind her again, and his eyes
were disturbingly intent. 'And don't call her "that young
woman". Her name's Sam—Samantha. I suggest you
get used to it.'

His mother's cheeks gained a little colour, but this
time she didn't back down. 'Well, I can't stop you, of
course,' she said tersely, smoothing cream over the offending smear of mascara. 'But you might be interested
to hear I didn't *send* Miss Maxwell back to England. She
left of her own accord. It was all her idea.'

'I don't believe you.'

Her son's response was almost instantaneous, but for
the first time since he had stormed into her room
Caroline sensed a faint hesitation. Dear God, she
thought, her hands stilling automatically as the amazing
idea occurred to her. Matthew wasn't sure of her. He
actually had some doubts.

She blinked, and wiped her fingers on a cotton-wool
ball. Of all the scenarios she had entertained during the
past twenty-four hours, the idea that that ordinary young
woman might not be besotted with her son had never
even occurred to her. Oh, it was true she had offered to
leave without much prompting. But Caroline knew she
had been instrumental in promoting that decision. She
hadn't given her a whole lot of choice. But she wondered now if she could have been mistaken. What if the
girl hadn't been as upset as she'd thought? She had made
a show of not caring, but Caroline had discounted that.
She had assumed it was just an act, put on to protect
her sensibilities. But what if it hadn't been? What if her
son was besotted by that girl?

It didn't bear thinking about. He was just on the re-
bound, she told herself. Matthew was still infatuated with
Melissa.

But if that was so, and Melissa's engagement to Prince
Georgio had foundered, why was he here? Melissa still

wanted him; that was obvious. It was why she had asked for him as she was being whisked away to the hospital to have her stomach pumped, or something equally ghastly. And it had seemed such an opportune coincidence: that Matthew should have been with that girl, when Melissa's attempted suicide was reported. Caroline couldn't have asked for anything more guaranteed to cause a rift between them. And, just when everything seemed to be going right, it was turning out all wrong.

She sighed. She might not always have approved of Melissa—and she had certainly resented the disastrous effect the break-up of their relationship had had on her son—but Melissa was good-looking, and personable, and she would make Matthew a tolerable wife. If only her son had ever wanted to get married. But he hadn't.

She supposed she couldn't entirely blame him. Her own ambivalent attitude towards the married state, and his uncle's vicissitudes aside, Matthew was not exactly surrounded by examples of nuptial bliss. His best friend had been married and divorced twice, and his Greek relations tended to use marriage to perpetuate a dynasty. Even her father had not been above taking a mistress when, after Caroline was born, her own mother had proved so disappointingly unproductive. Her son had grown up seeing a succession of other women pass through his grandfather's house, and she could hardly complain if he rebelled against their hypocrisy. Besides, he knew that getting married would mean an end to his individual lifestyle. If he had a wife, he wouldn't be able to deny his identity any longer.

Caroline passed a rather bemused hand across her cheek. It couldn't be true. She was over-reacting. Just because Matthew had shown her a side of his personality she had hitherto not encountered, she was anticipating problems that didn't exist. He was annoyed because she had upset his plans for the weekend, that was all. Well, for heaven's sake, he could do without a woman for one night!

'I said I don't believe you,' he grated now, and she became aware that he was still standing, glowering at her in the mirror. She hoped he couldn't read her mind. The thoughts she had been having were not for publication.

'Well, it's true,' she replied, after a moment, not finding it particularly easy to pick up the threads of their conversation. 'She insisted on leaving first thing this morning.' She crossed her fingers, and then continued firmly, 'I think she'd have left last night, if I hadn't persuaded her otherwise.'

Matthew's mouth compressed. 'Shit!' he muttered succinctly, and in spite of her aversion to his language Caroline's most immediate reaction was one of alarm.

'Really, Matt!' she exclaimed, in a desperate attempt to salvage something from this situation. She adopted a determinedly amused tone. 'You'd think you were in love with the girl!'

Samantha's father came to the café on Monday lunchtime. It wasn't unusual to see him there, but it was unusual for him to leave his table vacant. Instead of sitting down, Mr Maxwell smiled at Debbie, and then walked around behind the display cases to where his daughter was busy preparing sandwiches.

'Sam,' he said, distracting her attention from the chutney she was spooning from a jar. 'Can I have a word?'

'Dad!' Samantha didn't know whether to be anxious or relieved. It was so unexpected of him to make the café a place for them to talk in, and although she thought she could guess what he wanted she wished she'd had more notice of his intention.

'Can we talk?' he repeated, and Samantha glanced around at Debbie, who was hovering by the till.

'I—suppose so,' she said, the look she cast her assistant indicative of her feelings. 'We'll go into the office,' she added, wiping her hands on a tissue. 'Take over, will you, Deb? I'll be as quick as I can.'

Debbie nodded, clearly intrigued by Mr Maxwell's visit, and Samantha led the way into the tiny office, not without some misgivings. It was obvious Debbie would want to know what was going on. Mr Maxwell had never interfered with the running of the café before. She was bound to think it was something serious.

'Your mother asked me to talk to you,' declared Samantha's father, without preamble, as soon as the door was wedged closed behind them. 'She's worried sick over this business with Paul. You can't seriously intend breaking your engagement. Why, you and he have been inseparable since you were in your teens.'

Samantha sighed. 'The engagement's broken, Dad. I spoke to Paul last night. And as for us being inseparable: perhaps that's what was wrong with our relationship. We've been so close to each other, we've never had the chance to see anyone else.'

Mr Maxwell breathed out heavily. 'Sam——' He spread his hands in a helpless gesture. 'Sam, you can't do this. Not just on a whim.'

'It's not a whim, Dad. I mean what I say. It's not fair to Paul to carry on. I don't love him. I don't think I ever did. Not in the proper way, anyway.'

'The proper way!' her father mimicked impatiently. 'What is the "proper" way? I doubt if you know. I know I don't. It's mixing with these well-to-do people, isn't it? They've unsettled you. Given you ideas about making money and getting rich quick!'

'That's not true!' Samantha was indignant. 'I've got no plans, beyond continuing to run the café as I've always done. I've told you I'm not going to accept any more commissions. What more can I say?'

Mr Maxwell grimaced. 'Then what's wrong with Paul all of a sudden? You told your mother there was no one else. Is that true?'

Samantha caught her breath. 'Yes. Yes, it's true,' she declared forcefully. 'I just don't want to get married. Is there anything wrong with that?'

'Yes, there is.' Her father regarded her frustratedly. 'You know your mother's been looking forward to organising the wedding. Why, she's even made a provisional guest list, and talked about what she and I could get you. We thought a couple of thousand pounds towards your mortgage wouldn't come amiss. And what

with Paul being an estate agent and all, he's bound to
have an insight into what kind of property you should
buy.'

Samantha drew a breath. 'No, Dad.'

'What do you mean, no? Of course, he will——'

'I mean, no. I'm not going to marry Paul,' said
Samantha flatly. 'I'm sorry if you're disappointed, and
I'm sorry if Mum was looking forward to being the
mother of the bride, but this time I've got to do what *I*
think is best. Not you.'

'This time?' Mr Maxwell frowned. 'Are you saying
we've interfered in your life before?'

'Oh, Dad!' Samantha groaned. 'I know that anything
you've done for me has been with my best interests at
heart. But, believe me, marrying Paul would be a
mistake. I know that now. So can't you be thankful I
found out, before I had to face a messy divorce?'

Her father stared at her. 'You said you know that *now*.
Why now? Something must have happened to make you
change your mind.'

Samantha wanted to scream, but she didn't. Instead,
she pushed her hands into her apron pockets, and faced
her father bravely. 'All right,' she said, hearing the catch
in her voice, and doing her best to disguise it. 'I had an
affair.' She let that news sink in, and then she added
briskly, 'But it's over now. I shan't be seeing him again.'

'But you told your mother——'

'I lied.' Samantha held up her hand. 'Or, at least, I
didn't tell her the whole truth. There is no one else.' She
paused, and then added uncomfortably, 'There was—
but there isn't now.'

Her father looked stunned. 'An affair!' he echoed
weakly. 'Oh, Sam!'

'It's not the end of the world!' exclaimed Samantha
tersely, her own nerves dangerously near to breaking-
point. 'As I say, it's over now, and no harm done.' At
least, she hoped not. Matthew had probably assumed
she was on the Pill. Until he discovered she hadn't been
with a man, of course. But, by then, it was too late.

'But an affair,' protested her father helplessly, and Samantha realised how naïve he was in this day and age. It was partly her fault, she supposed. Her relationship with Paul had shielded her from the common demands of her generation, and they had all become a little smug because of it. But life wasn't like that, and she should have realised her bland existence could only survive in limbo.

'I'm sorry, Dad,' she apologised now, feeling a little guilty for springing it on him this way. 'I didn't want to hurt you.'

'No.' Mr Maxwell shook his head. 'No, I suppose you didn't.' He paused. 'Have you told Paul?'

'Not yet.' Samantha shrugged. 'He—still thinks he can get me to change my mind. I don't think he'll be so eager when I tell him what I've done.'

'Oh, Sam!' Her father sighed. 'You've shocked me, you really have. I never would have thought it of you.'

'No.' Samantha conceded the point. 'If it's any consolation, nor would I.'

Which didn't augur well for the rest of the day. Mr Maxwell left without even having his usual sandwich, and Samantha spent the remainder of the lunch period in a state of weary aggravation. She felt like a child again, who'd just received a dressing-down from the school head. She was twenty-four years old, and had been running her own business for over two years, and she still felt as crushed as a teenager. For heaven's sake, she argued silently, what she'd done was no big deal. Not really. Most of her friends had had affairs before they'd left college.

But they weren't engaged, she admitted ruefully, and if she'd been so desperate to spread her wings, why couldn't she have done it with someone else, someone she could at least respect? Matthew Putnam was the pits. He was a cheat and a liar, and he hadn't a grain of decency in his body. He had thought nothing about seducing her and then rushing off to see Melissa. She hoped the other woman gave him hell. He deserved it for what he'd done to her.

Or did he? Samantha sighed. The truth was, she didn't like herself any better. What bugged her most was the fact that, if Matthew hadn't walked out as he had, she'd most probably have agreed to continue the affair until he got tired of her. It was so humiliating. She'd been so sure he still wanted her, particularly after those unforgettable hours in her bed. When his mother had told her he had left to go back to London to be with Melissa, she had been completely devastated. It had even crossed her mind that Mrs Putnam might be making the whole thing up, and that was why she had deliberately joined the rest of the family for supper. But it had been true. The looks—sometimes sympathetic, sometimes malicious—that had been cast in her direction as she ate had convinced her of that. And Matthew's grandfather had only confirmed her suspicions. She didn't know Matthew at all.

At least it had brought her to her senses, she reflected later that afternoon, after Debbie had gone to get her bus. Given the fact that Matthew was not to be relied on, wasn't it better to realise it now, rather than spend weeks—months even—pursuing a goal that didn't exist? He had hurt her, it was true, but she'd get over it. And she hadn't had time to feel his loss.

She was about to leave the café to go home when someone rattled the door. 'We're closed,' she called, collecting her bag and keys from the office, and threading her way between the tables. She adjusted the blind and opened the door. 'I'm sorry, we——'

Her voice trailed away into silence. Mondays were usually busy days, and it wasn't unusual for customers to try and get served after hours. She had assumed it was one of the small-holders from the market, wanting a cup of tea and a toasted teacake before driving home. But it wasn't. It was Matthew. And, for all her much-vaunted practicality, her knees wobbled.

'Can I come in?' he asked, his eyes resting disturbingly on her mouth, and Samantha let out her breath in a rush. He was the last person she had expected to see, and it took longer than she had expected to pull her wits together.

'I—no,' she denied, after a moment, though his leather-clad frame successfully blocked her exit. 'I was just leaving,' she added, as if it was relevant. 'Please will you get out of my way?'

Matthew didn't move, except to raise one arm and rest it against the wooden frame. From that position of dominance, he looked down at her half impatiently, and she wished she hadn't opened the door and given him the advantage.

'I have to talk to you, Sam,' he said, and, although she was sure this was all just another move in the game to him, there was no trace of humour in his eyes. On the contrary, they were red-rimmed, and brooding, and painfully intent. They roamed over her face and figure with a thoroughness she would have found insolent from anyone else. But she was in such a nervous state that she didn't have time to object to his appraisal.

'I don't think we have anything to talk about,' she said tersely, desperate for some way to get him off her doorstep. 'Look, we've had this conversation before, and nothing's changed. You and I—we just don't have anything in common. I was a fool to let you talk me into going to Delphus, and now I'd like to forget all about it.'

'That's not true, and you know it.' Matthew's voice was harsh. He glanced up and down the High Street, as if gauging whether their altercation was attracting any attention. Then, without giving her notice of his intentions, he removed his arm from the door frame and used it to propel her back into the empty café. And, with his shoulders against the glass panels, the door closed heavily behind him. 'Now,' he said, unzipping his jerkin to reveal an open-necked shirt of dark green silk, 'let's drop the "I don't know what you're doing here" routine, shall we? We have some unfinished business. I want to know why you walked out on me.'

'Why *I* walked out on *you*!' Samantha caught her breath, but his audacity gave her the spurt she needed.

'Forgive me, but I was under the impression that you had walked out on me! How is Miss Mainwaring, by the way? All the better for seeing you, no doubt.'

Matthew's lips tightened. 'All right. I deserved that, I suppose. I did leave without seeing you, but my mother explained, didn't she? Melissa's mother was fairly frantic on the phone, and I guess she believed it was more serious than it was. Sufficiently so that I didn't ask questions. I just grabbed a ride with Spiro, and took the next plane back to London.'

Samantha managed not to show any emotion at this evidence of his continuing involvement with Melissa. Indeed, with every word he spoke she was growing colder and colder. His arrogance appalled her. What kind of a woman did he think she was?

'It doesn't matter,' she said now, still finding it difficult to meet his gaze without flinching. She checked the clasp of her handbag, and tucked it under her arm with businesslike firmness. Anything to avoid looking at the brown column of his throat emerging from the open neck of his shirt. Or remembering how smooth his skin had felt beneath her hands, with its light but silky pelt of fine dark hair.

'Don't say that.' Matthew made a sound that was suspiciously like a moan, and straightened away from the door. 'Sam, you have to believe me when I tell you, I'd never have gone if I'd known then what I know now. They said she'd tried to commit suicide. They said she'd been rushed to the hospital, and that she was presently undergoing treatment. What was I supposed to think? My God, they made it sound as if it was all my fault!'

'And was it?' Samantha's question was automatic.

'No.' Matthew raked restless fingers through his hair. 'Sam—Melissa and I—that's history. I don't care if I never see her again.'

That brought her head up, but the heat radiating from Matthew's eyes made her look away again. It also brought a little bloom of colour blossoming in her neck, and she put a nervous hand to her throat.

'I—I'm not really interested,' she declared at last, concentrating on the fact that there was a menu missing from the table in the window. 'How you choose to treat your ex-girlfriends is entirely up to you. I've told you how I feel. I wish you'd go away, and let me get on with my life.'

'Like hell!' With the oath still issuing from his tongue, he closed the space between them, his hands descending on her shoulders with unmistakable intent. 'You want me,' he muttered unsteadily, forcing her chin up with his thumbs, so that he could see her face. 'No. Don't look away from me. We want each other, Sam. You know it as well as I do. God, baby, did you honestly think I'd let you go?'

Samantha shivered. It was the moment of truth, and she was no more ready for it now than she had ever been. The grip of his hands, the heat of his skin, the heady scent of the soap he used, which mingled with the sharper odour of his body, all combined to seduce her reason. She had never dreamed he might come after her; never imagined that, having sent her back to London, he might want to see her again. The memory of his love-making came back to torment her, and an actual physical ache for the pleasure he had taught her was sapping her resistance.

But it was only lust, she warned herself repeatedly. He wanted her; the undisguised arousal of his body showed her that. But that was all. As she had assured herself many times on the flight back from Athens, he had never pretended otherwise. Apart from anything else, she didn't fit into his world. With Matthew, there could be no lasting commitment.

So, though it took every ounce of will-power she possessed, Samantha forced herself to remain passive in his arms. She didn't attempt to fight him. She knew from past experience that that would do no good. When it came to brute strength, Matthew would always have the upper hand. And she had no desire to cause a conflagration that might consume them both.

'Damn you!' Matthew cupped her face in his strong hands and gazed down at her with dark frustrated eyes. 'Damn you,' he muttered again. 'Don't do this to me, Sam. You know how I feel about you. I would have come sooner, only I'd promised the old man I'd stay for his birthday party. I haven't slept a wink since I left Delphus on Friday night.'

Samantha steeled herself. Matthew in any mood was attractive. Matthew in this mood was well-nigh irresistible.

'I—can't help that,' she got out jerkily. 'You—you should have stayed with Melissa. I'm sure she'd have been only too happy——'

'Will you shut the hell up about Melissa?' he snarled menacingly. 'I don't give a damn about Melissa!'

'That's not what your mother said.'

The words were unwise, and impulsive. She knew that as soon as they were uttered, but it was too late then. His brows descended, and his thumbs dug almost painfully into her cheekbones. 'My mother?' he echoed. 'What—exactly—did my mother tell you?'

Samantha's shoulders made an involuntary gesture. 'She—she just said that you—that she—hoped—you'd eventually marry Melissa——'

'My God!'

'—and that—that—was what the rest of the family hoped as well.'

'*Beautiful*!' On Matthew's lips it was an oath. 'And you believed her?'

Samantha shrugged. 'I've told you, I—it's nothing to do with me.' She paused, and then went on doggedly, 'I've had time to think, and I realise now that it was probably the best thing that could happen. We're from two different worlds, Matt. It was never going to work, and you know it.'

'You don't mean that.'

'I do.' Samantha gathered strength from the look of uncertainty on his face. 'There was never going to be any future for our relationship. I was just a novelty. I belonged to someone else, and you couldn't bear to think I might prefer Paul to you.'

Matthew's mouth flattened. 'You didn't sleep with Paul.'

'No.' Samantha held up her head. 'Because he had too much respect for me as a person——'

'Respect be damned,' retorted Matthew harshly. 'You didn't sleep with him because he didn't make you feel the way I do. Don't trivialise what we had together. It was good——'

'It wasn't real,' she protested, but his continued nearness was wearing her down.

'That's not true.' Matthew's hands left her face to shape her throat, and then moved down, over the quivering sides of her breasts, to the slender swell of her hips. He watched her as his hands explored her body, and it was the hardest thing Samantha had ever done to stand still in his grasp. 'It was so real, it was the best thing that ever happened to me,' he told her huskily. 'I want you in my life, Sam. You're warm, and passionate, and endlessly desirable. I want you to come and live with me. I've only got an apartment at the moment, but if you'd rather we lived in a house then we'll buy one. All things are possible, because I love you. If you care for me at all, for God's sake don't turn me down.'

Samantha trembled. She couldn't believe it. Matthew had said he loved her. He had actually said he loved her. Dear God, what was she supposed to do now?

And, as if the bemused expression that had crossed her face at his words had given him some encouragement, he bent his head and caressed her ear with his tongue. 'Don't look so surprised,' he whispered with wry humour, his hands on her hips urging her against his heavy arousal. 'You don't imagine I enjoy living in a constant state of frustration, do you?'

Samantha couldn't speak. Her cheek was pressed against the soft leather of his jerkin and the skin of his throat was only inches from her lips. She could see the shadow of his chest hair under his silk shirt, and knew it arrowed down to the virile pubescence that cradled his manhood. She already knew how that felt against her softness. In fact, it was frightening to realise how familiar she was with his lean body, and how vivid were the memories his words conjured up.

'I—can't,' she got out at last, fighting for her own salvation, and Matthew let out a strangled cry.

'Why can't you?' he demanded, drawing back to rest his forehead against hers. 'You want me. I know you do. And—you may even learn to love me one day. So long as we're together, I'm prepared to take the chance.'

'Well, I'm not.' In spite of the fact that his mouth was only inches from her own, and the temptation to taste it was almost unbearable, she had to keep her head. 'Is—is this what you told Melissa?' she asked, her hands firm against his jacket. 'Before she realised you had no intention of marrying her?'

'Oh, God!' Matthew groaned. 'I thought I told you to forget about Melissa. My relationship with her was never like this, believe me. I may have thought I loved her once, but now I know differently.' He gave a grim laugh. 'Do I ever!'

Samantha swallowed. 'So what are you saying?' She was sure she already knew the answer, but she had to know. 'Is this—a proposal?'

'A proposal!'

In the seconds before Matthew could avert his gaze, she saw the stunned expression in his eyes, and her heart faltered. She had known it all along, of course. Nothing could have been further from the truth. Matthew didn't want a wife—particularly not someone like her. He wanted something entirely different.

But, even as she wrenched herself away from him, he was recovering his confidence. 'Sam,' he began, the beguiling softness of his voice belying the insensitivity of his words, 'don't you think one engagement is enough for the time being?'

'You——'

Words escaped her, and before she could summon up the right ones to get him out of there the door behind them opened, and Paul Webster stepped into the café.

'Sam,' he said, eyebrows raised, his voice cool and suspicious. He looked at Matthew, then back at Samantha. 'Is something wrong?'

Samantha felt an insane desire to laugh. Of all the people to walk into the café, it had to be Paul. Of course, she'd known the night before, when she gave him back his ring, that he hadn't believed she really meant it. But, even so, she hadn't expected him to turn up here today. It was just as if last night had never happened, and she didn't know whether to be glad or sorry.

Matthew's eyes had narrowed as he surveyed the other man's appearance, and Samantha guessed he wasn't pleased. The fact that she hadn't had time to tell him yet that she had broken her engagement now seemed like rough justice. Was he wondering how she was going to handle it? Was he worried that she might tell Paul that he had seduced her?

But no. With bitter logic she knew that Matthew was unlikely to worry about anything. And she was fooling herself if she believed either of them would risk life and limb for her honour. Matthew had no honour, and Paul had no excuse.

'No,' she said at last, realising it was up to her to make whatever amends she could of this situation. There was no point in inflaming tempers with emotive words. For Paul's sake—and for her own self-respect—she had to get rid of Matthew. 'Mr—er—Putnam was just leaving.' Her hostile gaze dared him to deny it. She walked past Paul and opened the door. 'Thank you for your offer,' she added coldly. 'But I don't accept that kind of assignment.'

CHAPTER ELEVEN

MATTHEW strode into his office in the Purcell building, only to halt abruptly at the sight of the man reclining in the chair behind his desk. 'Papa!' he exclaimed, hiding his irritation behind a mask of politeness. He advanced more slowly into the room. 'I didn't know you were in London.'

'No, I know.' For once his grandfather spoke in English. 'I asked your mother not to tell you I was coming.'

'Really?' Matthew's dark brows arched interrogatively. 'Any reason why?'

'Yes. I wanted to be sure you would not invent some non-existent reason for being out of the country when I arrived,' replied Aristotle mildly. His dark eyes, so like his grandson's, glittered with malicious satisfaction. 'I also wanted to see for myself that your mother was not exaggerating.'

Matthew's features stiffened. 'My mother?'

'You did not think she would not share her worries about you with me?' enquired the old man, with rather more animation. '*Thee mou*, Matthew, it is six months since my birthday! Six months since you told me you never wanted to see the Mainwaring woman again!'

'So?' Matthew shrugged.

'So, why does Caroline tell me you are never out of the office these days?' He glanced at the thick gold watch on his wrist. 'Are you aware it is already after nine o'clock in the evening? What are you trying to do, *aghori mou*? Work yourself to death?'

Matthew's mouth flattened. 'Don't be ridiculous!'

'What is ridiculous?' The old man jerked forward angrily. 'Have you looked in a mirror lately? You look—*ill*!'

'No, I don't.' Matthew heaved a sigh, and flung himself into the chair across the desk from his grandfather. 'I'm tired, that's all.'

'Tired!'

'It's true.' Matthew crossed one ankle across his knee, and rested his hand on his thigh. 'I can tell you what I've been doing, if you like. Only you generally say you have no interest in J.P. Software.'

'I don't.'

'There you are, then.' Matthew lifted his shoulders. 'You won't want to hear how I've been rewriting a program for translating English into a foreign language and vice versa. And not just any language, I might add. I've been experimenting with——'

'*Arketa*!' The old man silenced him with an angry gesture. 'You are right. I do not wish to hear how successful you have been in thwarting my efforts to ensure the corporation's future. I am sure that if you had your way you would have me sell off its assets, and put thousands of people out of work. But I cannot do that, and it angers me that you care so little for my feelings.'

'That's not true.' The words were mumbled, but they were audible just the same. 'Of course I care about your feelings, Papa. And, whatever you think, I do know my responsibilities. But—I'm not a boy. I can take care of myself.'

'Can you?' His grandfather didn't sound any more convinced, but there was concern, not irritation, in his voice now. 'Matthew, your mother is worried about you. And frankly, having seen you for myself, so am I. She says you do not eat enough, and you have obviously lost weight. Must I take it that you are drinking again?' He gestured towards his grandson's appearance. '*Thee mou*, this is not just the result of overwork!'

Matthew tipped his head back on his shoulders. 'Leave it, Papa. I'm all right, really. And I'm not drinking— well, not to excess anyway. But we all need a little stimulation sometimes. Even you.'

His grandfather shook his head. 'That woman has a lot to answer for,' he snapped bitterly.

'What woman?' Matthew's head tipped forward again, his eyes dark and wary.

'Why—the Mainwaring woman, naturally,' complained his grandfather irritably. 'What I do not understand is, why do you not marry her and have done with it? You know that was why she got engaged to Ivanov. And you told me yourself she was never in any danger of taking her own life. It was just her way of trying to get you back. And she is still in London. Caroline tells me so. Why, only the other day your mother met her at some charity function or other. She may be a fool, but she obviously cares about you——'

'Papa!' Matthew's harsh words overrode his grandfather's monologue. 'How many times must I tell you, I don't care that—— ' he snapped his fingers impatiently '—for Melissa's feelings? I know why she put on that act about taking those tablets. I'd made sure she knew about—well, about me taking someone else to Delphus, but she thought she just had to pull my strings and I'd come running. But it didn't work. Oh, I'm not denying I went to see her. How could I do anything else, when I didn't know at that time how serious it might be? But there was never any chance of us resuming our relationship. Believe it, old man, whatever I saw in Melissa is well and truly dead!'

'Then, why——?'

'Why what?' Matthew turned flat, emotionless eyes on him. 'For pity's sake, Papa, don't you and my mother have anything better to do?'

The old man's brows drew together, a bushy grey line above features that were not unlike his grandson's. He stared at Matthew, as if trying to see into his mind, and then uttered a disbelieving snort when his grandson looked away.

'Of course!' he exclaimed, smacking his forehead with the heel of his hand as if punishing himself for not thinking of it sooner. 'I am a fool! I saw it for myself, and I let you persuade me otherwise. It is her, is it not? The other one. The—*kopela* who runs the café!'

'Oh, for God's sake!' Matthew's foot hit the floor with a thud, and he thrust himself up from his chair. 'Why do you do this, Papa? Why can't you accept the fact that it's been a long hard slog, getting this program running? I've worked long hours; I admit it. And I've missed the odd meal here and there; I admit that, too. But I'm not unique. Other people work just as hard. Just because I've lost a little weight, you've let my mother browbeat you into coming here to play the heavy father. Well, it's not necessary. I don't need anyone to hold my hand!'

Aristotle was not intimidated. 'And this is why there are no women in your life?' he enquired mildly. 'Hard work requires celibacy?'

'Maybe.' Matthew fought his way past his indignation, and managed a faint smile. 'Maybe it does,' he repeated, leaving the desk to walk across to the windows. Outside, the lights of the city provided a glittering display, throwing his reflection back at him through the darkened glass. He thrust his hands into his trouser pockets and wished the old man would go. He didn't need anyone else telling him he was losing weight. Loss of weight he could cope with. What he was afraid of was that he was losing his mind.

'So—your association with Miss Maxwell was unproductive?' came his grandfather's voice behind him, and Matthew's hands balled into tight fists.

'It depends what you mean by unproductive,' he responded shortly, as memories of Samantha's soft skin beneath his hands returned to torment him. Desperate to dispel the images that were always more painful after dark, he spoke with rather less caution. 'But if you mean did I make any lasting impression on her life, then perhaps you should ask her husband!'

'Her husband?' Aristotle's slightly stooped figure joined his reflection in the window. 'She was not married when you brought her to Delphus.'

Matthew glanced sideways at him. 'What if she was? Why should you care? As I recall, you've brought a number of married women there yourself.'

'That is beside the point.' The old man sounded tired suddenly. 'The women I knew were older; sophisticated; they knew what they were doing. The Maxwell girl was young, and—I believed—innocent.'

Matthew stared at him. 'How do you know that? You didn't even speak to her.'

'You are wrong.' His grandfather held up his hand. 'That night—the night you went back to England to see Melissa—we talked on the terrace. She was unhappy. I could tell. I suspected it was because your mother had been less than tactful.'

'Hmm.' Matthew remembered the conversation he had had with his mother, after talking to Samantha at the café. Caroline had taken the brunt of his frustration. But even she had had no idea of exactly how desperate he'd felt.

'You did not speak to her yourself, before you left for London?' the old man pressed now, and although since then he hadn't spoken of his feelings to anyone Matthew found himself shaking his head.

'No. She'd locked her door. I couldn't make her hear.'

'And Spiro was waiting to leave, of course.'

Matthew nodded. 'Of course.'

'But you saw her when you got back to England, after that weekend?'

Matthew hesitated. 'Briefly. For about fifteen minutes, to be exact.'

His grandfather frowned, and Matthew guessed he was having to re-think his argument. 'You did not apologise?'

Matthew sighed. 'Of course I apologised!' he exclaimed. And then, because the temptation to confide his real feelings to someone else was just too much, he added wearily, 'I screwed up. I told her how I felt about her, and asked her to come and live with me. She turned me down.'

Aristotle sucked in a breath. 'You asked her to marry you?'

'Not marry, no.' Matthew's tone was flat. 'In any case, she was engaged to someone else.'

'Ah, yes.' His grandfather nodded. 'But the engagement could have been broken, could it not?'

'Maybe.' Matthew heaved a sigh. 'Maybe I didn't want to get married. Maybe I was afraid you'd try and stop us. Maybe I just saw marriage as giving in to what you and my mother expected of me. And, let's face it, my experience of marriage hasn't been good.'

'Because of me,' said his grandfather shrewdly. 'All those women you talked about. I guess you think I should have had more respect for your grandmother.'

'Well, shouldn't you?' suggested Matthew drily, and the old man laughed.

'Perhaps. But your grandmother was not like Miss Maxwell. She did not marry me because she cared about me. Ariadne married me because it was what her father wanted. Because he wished to join his company with mine.' He grimaced. 'That was the start of the Apollonius Corporation, do you know that? Skiathos Ferries and Apollo Shipping! How far we have come since then.'

Matthew shrugged. 'Indeed.'

'So——' His grandfather paused. 'Miss Maxwell is now Mrs——'

'Webster,' supplied Matthew bleakly. 'Her fiancé's name was Paul Webster. I had Victor check him out.'

'Really?' The old man looked reluctantly impressed. 'And the marriage took place—when?'

Matthew turned away. 'June, July. I don't know. Does it matter?'

'It does, if that is what is eating you up inside,' replied his grandfather impatiently. 'Do you mean to tell me you do not even know if they are married? For shame, Matthew! I thought I had taught you better than that.'

Matthew walked to his desk. 'You seem to forget she didn't want me, Papa. That afternoon, when I went to see her, I knew it. As soon as her fiancé turned up, she couldn't wait to get rid of me.'

'Well——' The old man turned to look at him, obviously searching for a reason. 'As you say, they were still engaged.'

Matthew's expression was eloquent of his feelings. 'Nice try, old man, but it won't run. Sam had her chance, but she didn't take it. She'd had her bite of the apple, and she didn't like the taste.'

The wind whistled round a corner of the house, and something blew over on the paved patio her father had had laid the previous year. It was a little unnerving, hearing inanimate objects falling about like live creatures, but the doors and windows were locked, and the storm had been predicted.

Samantha shivered. Perhaps she should have taken her mother's advice and gone with them to Tenerife. Right now, she could have been sitting in a bar, drinking sangria, with nothing more to worry about than what bathing suit she was going to wear to sunbathe in the next day. But the summer flu she had contracted in July had lingered on into September, and she dared not close the café again, and risk losing the rest of her customers.

Not that anyone would really care, she reflected unhappily. Now that she had competition in the High Street, it was getting harder and harder to hang on to her clientele. And the truth was, her heart wasn't in it any more. Since she had been so ill, she had lost interest in everything.

No, that wasn't precisely true, she corrected herself, reaching for the *TV Times* and scanning the evening's programmes. Actually, she had had no interest in anything since that afternoon Matthew had come to the café. She blinked back the tears that seemed to come so readily to her eyes these days. She should never have sent him away.

It was impossible to read the programme times in her present state, and, tossing the magazine aside, she plucked another chocolate from the open box beside her. An orange cream, she saw dispassionately, biting into its soft centre without really tasting it. She had bought the chocolates that afternoon in the hope that they would cheer her up. But it wasn't much fun eating them alone.

She looked around the cosy sitting-room, and tried to count her blessings. She had a good home, a good family and, aside from a maudlin tendency to feel sorry for herself, she was all right. The café would pick up again once she found another assistant. She shook her head. Imagine Debbie getting married like that! Still, it was probably the best thing for the baby.

Her eyes filled with tears again, and she dashed them away with an impatient hand. She ought to consider herself lucky, she chided. That could have happened to her. And what would she have done with a baby? What would her father have thought then?

She sniffed. She was remembering how she had felt in those weeks before she'd known for certain that she wasn't pregnant. For a brief spell she had actually hoped she was expecting Matthew's baby. It would have been something of him to cherish. Someone who needed her love.

A bang, louder than the rest, startled her out of her reverie. And then the doorbell rang, echoing round the quiet house with loud insistence. Samantha looked at the clock. It was half-past nine. Who on earth would call so late in the evening? Her nerves tingled apprehensively. Who knew she was here alone?

Paul!

Her breath escaped in a rush, and she got up unwillingly from the couch. Only Paul knew the rest of the family was away on holiday. Only Paul was likely to call so late. And, although she had heard he was seeing someone else, she wouldn't put it past her father to have asked him to look in on her. Mr Maxwell still held out the hope that his daughter might change her mind. It didn't seem to occur to him that Paul's new girlfriend was unlikely to appreciate his interference.

It was dark in the hall, and Samantha was suddenly reluctant to turn on the light. What if it wasn't Paul? she fretted. How many times had women been warned about the dangers of opening their doors after dark? She could be in line to be the first victim of the Northfleet strangler! Murderers had to start somewhere, didn't they?

The doorbell didn't ring again, and she leaned uncertainly against the wall. Perhaps whoever it was had gone away. It could have been someone delivering circulars. But the letterbox didn't provide any clues.

She sighed, and straightened. This was ridiculous, she thought grimly. She wouldn't relax until she'd opened that door and made sure there was no one outside. It could be a thief, of course, checking to see if anyone was at home. At least if she opened the door she'd prove there was.

She unlocked the door without giving herself any more time to change her mind. Then, inching it open, she peered out. The wind swept into her face, bringing a scattering of leaves into the hallway. But, although the front gate was swinging back and forth, the caller seemed to have vanished.

And then she heard a groan from somewhere near the ground, and she let out a startled cry. A man was propped on the doorstep, his shoulders hunched, his body curled in on himself, as if he was in pain. Her initial reaction was to slam the door and call the police. But there was something about his appearance that was achingly familiar.

Dear God! Her throat went dry, and instead of slamming the door she squatted down on her haunches beside him. His head was lolling, and it was an easy matter to turn his face to the light. 'Matt!' she breathed, wondering with a sense of alarm if she was hallucinating. How could he be here, sitting on her doorstep? He didn't even know where she lived.

But it was him. Dark eyes, which seemed somehow glazed, lifted to her face. 'Sam,' he said, and she could have sworn he sounded relieved. 'Hell, Sam, isn't this the damnedest thing? I seem to have lost the use of my legs.'

Samantha stared at him helplessly. She couldn't believe he was here. It was like the answer to her dreams, and she wanted to take him in her arms. But once again common sense came to her rescue.

'Are—are you ill?' she asked, curling her nails into her palms, to prevent herself from touching him, and Matthew grimaced.

'No,' he replied. 'I don't think so.' He uttered a short laugh. 'Give me a hand up, will you? This is what comes of drinking Scotch on an empty stomach.'

Samantha blinked. 'You mean—you're drunk?' She scrambled to her feet, contempt for herself, and resentment at his habitual indifference to anyone's feelings but his own, contorting her face. The pathetic dreams she had had about him crumbled about her feet! She couldn't imagine why he was here, but it wouldn't do her any good.

'No, I'm not drunk,' Matthew muttered now, and, grabbing hold of the door frame, he hauled himself up. 'I guess I should have eaten something before I left the office.' He frowned, and pushed back his overlong hair with a weary hand. 'I can't remember when I last had any food.'

Samantha didn't know whether she believed him, but she took a step back and looked at him more thoroughly. He didn't look drunk, she conceded, seeing no evidence of that state in his tired eyes. He looked pale, and exhausted, and he had definitely lost weight. But now that he was on his feet he looked more sinned against than sinning.

It reminded her that she was hardly dressed for callers either. Her baggy dungarees, worn over an old sweater, and the woolly slippers on her feet, were hardly flattering. In addition to which, it was weeks since she had done anything but run a brush through her hair. In consequence, it now hung straight and unstyled, way past her shoulders.

'How—how did you get here?' she questioned, unable to bring herself to ask why he was here, and Matthew turned and gestured towards the road.

'In that,' he said, indicating an unremarkable black saloon parked at the kerb. 'And before you ask, I didn't take a drink until I passed your local. I guess I chose the wrong kind of Dutch courage.'

Samantha clutched the door. 'Dutch courage?' she echoed disbelievingly. 'Why would you need Dutch courage?'

'Why do you think?' retorted Matthew wearily, propping himself against the door. 'Can I come in? I need to talk to you.'

Samantha didn't move. 'How—how did you know where I lived?'

Matthew sighed. 'I looked you up in the phone book.'

'Our number's not in the phone book.'

'Oh, for Pete's sake!' Matthew's red-rimmed eyes bored into hers. 'OK. I had someone find out, right? Now—can I come in? Or do I have to ask your father?'

Samantha licked her lips. 'My father's not here.'

Matthew's eyes flickered. 'But this is his house,' he probed warily, and she nodded. 'So,' he seemed to breathe a little more easily after that, 'let's find somewhere less public to talk.'

Samantha swallowed. 'What about?'

Matthew sighed again. 'You and me.'

'You and me?' Samantha stepped back almost involuntarily, and he took advantage of her momentary lapse to step inside. Supporting himself, with his back against the coat-rack, he closed the door. Then, as if he couldn't help himself, he closed his eyes, groping for a handhold to prevent another collapse.

'I'm sorry,' he muttered, opening his eyes again, and in spite of her misgivings Samantha found herself offering him her shoulder to lean on. With some difficulty, she managed to get him along the hall and into the sitting-room, then watched with anxious eyes as he lowered himself on to the sofa.

He looked much worse in the brighter light of the sitting-room. His eyes were haggard, and his face was drained of all colour. He lay back against the cushions as if it was days since he had had any rest. And, although she told herself it was nothing to do with her, she couldn't prevent the wave of compassion that swept over her.

'Are your parents out?' he asked, making an evident effort to hide his weakness, and Samantha decided that there was no point in telling lies.

'They're not here,' she said. 'They're on holiday in Tenerife. They only left this morning.'

Matthew hauled himself upright. 'For how long? I mean—how long have they gone for?'

Samantha hesitated, and then mentally berated herself. What could he do? He was practically an invalid.

'Two weeks,' she answered now, hovering by the door. 'Um—do you want a sandwich or something? If you haven't eaten since lunchtime——'

'I haven't eaten since God knows when,' retorted Matthew harshly, pushing himself to the edge of the sofa, almost as if he intended getting up again. 'Sam——' He paused. 'Sam, are you still going to marry Webster? I have to know. I have to know where I stand. I don't know how much more of this I can take.'

Samantha quivered. 'How—how much more of what?'

'This!' He looked up at her impatiently, and then forced himself into a standing position. 'God, Sam, answer the question! Are you still engaged to Webster or not?'

She came forward then, her concern for his welfare outweighing her doubts about him being there. 'Sit down,' she said, putting her hands on his forearms. 'Sit down before you fall down! Look—I'll get you a sandwich, then we can talk——'

'Like hell!' he muttered savagely, and when she tried to urge him back on to the sofa he used her strength against her. He sank down but he took her with him, tumbling her on to his lap, and capturing her face in his hand. 'Tell me,' he demanded, and his eyes glittered with a sense of purpose she wouldn't have believed he possessed. 'You know that I'm in love with you. Can't you at least put me out of my misery?'

Samantha gazed at him. His warm breath, only slightly flavoured with whisky, was fanning her temple, and he smelt of soap, and cigarette smoke, and the sharp autumn air. It was months since she'd seen him, yet she felt she

knew every pore of his features, and her hands itched
to smooth the long unruly hair back from his forehead.

'No,' she said at last, realising there was nowhere to
run any more. 'I—broke my engagement to Paul months
ago. Right—right after that night I spent on the island.'

'You didn't!' Matthew grasped her face between hands
that even she could feel were trembling. 'Sam, do you
mean to tell me you weren't engaged to Webster that day
I came to the café?'

She nodded.

He shook his head. 'But why? Did——' He broke off,
and then continued doggedly, 'Was I responsible? Oh,
God, what I'm trying to say is, did I destroy your life?'

Samantha clutched the lapels of his jacket, the need
to get nearer to him overwhelming any lingering doubts.
'Only—only when you went away,' she got out huskily,
gazing up at him with tear-wet eyes, and a dawning comprehension filled his gaze.

'Why—why didn't you tell me?' he demanded,
smoothing back her hair with agitated fingers. 'Oh, God,
Sam, I thought that was what you wanted.'

'I—I was afraid,' she admitted, putting up her hands
now and cupping his face. 'I loved you, and I was afraid.'
There was no point in denying it any longer. He could
have his revenge, if he wanted. She wouldn't stop him.
So long as they were together, her life would have some
meaning again.

'Oh, Sam!'

Matthew's groan was uttered against her mouth, and
his arms slid convulsively around her. With a tenderness
he had never shown before, he wrapped her in his protection, cradling her against him as if he'd never let her
go.

It was some minutes before they spoke again, minutes
of warmth, and passion, and heart-stopping sweetness.
Matthew couldn't seem to get enough of her, and kisses
that had begun so gently soon became an urgent duel of
tongues.

But at last he dragged himself away, and rested his
forehead against hers. 'You're not going to send me away

again, are you?' he demanded huskily. 'I mean, I know I've made mistakes, but I think I've got a chance now to put things right.'

Samantha was shaking, but she managed to move her head from side to side. She realised it wouldn't be easy convincing her parents that what she was doing was right. But she had proved she couldn't live without Matthew, so whatever happened she would have to live with him.

'OK,' he said, and she could tell he was near the end of his strength. 'We'll get married, as soon as I can get a licence.'

'Married?'

The astonishment in her voice caused him to gaze at her a little anxiously, but then her weight, and his own weakness, caused him to slump sideways on to the sofa.

'Yes, married,' he said, his arms falling away from her. 'Sam, don't argue, *please*! Not till I've had some sleep.'

It was the sound of the shower that alerted her to the fact that Matthew was awake. She hadn't heard him come upstairs, but then the wind had been buffeting the house all night, and she had grown used to hearing unusual creaks and groans.

She hadn't slept much. Her mind had been too active. Besides, just the thought that Matthew was asleep on the sofa downstairs was enough to keep her adrenalin running. She kept having to pinch herself to make sure it wasn't just a dream. But when she'd tiptoed downstairs in the early hours, and draped a blanket over him, his pale, well-loved features were incredibly real.

She glanced at the clock. It was just after six, which was why it was still fairly dark outside. She wondered if Matthew had seen the sandwich and the flask of coffee she had left for him. Well, at least he had had the strength to climb the stairs, she thought. And there was something very reassuring in listening to him taking a shower.

She had tried not to think about what he had said before exhaustion conquered him. He had asked her to marry him, and she should have been overjoyed. But his proposal reminded her of who he was, and what was

expected of him. And even though she loved him she
doubted it would be enough.

The landing creaked outside her door, and for a
moment she stopped breathing. But when the door remained unopened she slid out of bed, and went to see
what he was doing.

He was just coming out of her parents' room. He was
naked, except for the towel he had slung about his waist,
and his wet hair clung damply to his neck. 'What are
you doing?' she asked in an undertone, and then realised
how unnecessary it was for her to whisper. But there was
something delightfully wicked about their being here
alone together, in her parents' house, and when he turned
to face her her knees felt distinctly weak.

'I was looking for you,' he said simply, and she could
see in the light that streamed out of the bathroom how
much less exhausted he looked. He crossed the landing,
and gave her modest lawn nightdress an appraising look.
'Let's go to bed,' he added thickly. 'It's still the middle
of the night.'

Hours later, Samantha awakened to find Matthew was
already awake, watching her. In spite of all the intimacies they had shared she was still incapable of meeting
his lazy gaze without blushing, and he deliberately turned
the covers back so that he could kiss one creamy breast.

'I love you,' he breathed, his tongue dampening the
taut nipple. 'Did I tell you that already?'

'Sev-several times,' she said unsteadily, her hand
closing round his nape and holding him against her. 'Oh,
Matt—I'm glad you came last night.'

'Hmm, so am I,' he agreed, moving so that she could
feel his arousal against her. 'So—when are you going to
make an honest man of me?'

'Oh, Matt!' She shifted then, not turning away from
him exactly, but putting an inch of the narrow mattress
between them. 'You—you don't *have* to marry me. I'm
not making any conditions. Not this time.'

'I am.' Matthew followed her, only this time he imprisoned her beneath the muscled strength of his body.
'Do you think I'm going to take a chance on you walking

out on me again? Oh, no. You're going to be Mrs Matthew Putnam. I want everyone to know exactly who you are.'

Samantha caught her lower lip between her teeth. 'Including your family.'

'*Especially* my family,' agreed Matthew forcefully. He bent to bestow a lingering kiss at the corner of her mouth.

'So your children know who their father is?' suggested Samantha softly, and Matthew groaned.

'You know,' he said, 'it did cross my mind that I might have made you pregnant.' His thumb brushed over her lips. 'You weren't on the Pill, were you?' And at her denial, 'Believe it or not, I actually hoped I had. I'd have done anything to get you back.'

Samantha frowned. 'But you didn't come back.'

'No.' Matthew stroked her shoulder. 'Not after I'd made sure you were still seeing Webster. The only thing I didn't know was that you hadn't married him. But—thanks to my grandfather—I eventually got up the courage to find out.'

'What do you mean? How did you know I was still seeing Paul?'

Matthew's cheeks gained a little colour. 'How do you think?'

'You had me followed?' Samantha gasped.

'Well——' He was unrepentant. 'At first I couldn't believe you'd go through with your engagement. But—when the reports came in——'

'Paul wouldn't take no for an answer. I—I told him about you——'

'Did you?' Matthew's mouth quirked.

'—but he still kept coming to the house.' She paused. 'Not any longer, though. He's got another girlfriend now.'

'Has he?' Matthew hesitated. 'And how do you feel about that?'

'Pleased. Relieved.' Samantha shifted a little restlessly beneath him. 'Matt, I can't breathe.'

'Good,' he said, somewhat smugly, but he moved so that his thigh was resting between hers. 'Ah, God! Is that the time? I have an appointment for lunch at half-past twelve.'

Samantha looked up at him. 'Are you going?' she asked, a little anxiously, and his smile gave his gaunt features a disturbing attraction.

'Not without you,' he told her gently. 'It's very convenient, actually. I'm having lunch with my mother at the Savoy.'

'Oh!'

Samantha's mouth drew in, and Matthew laughed softly at her obvious dismay. 'It's time she met the future Mrs Putnam,' he said firmly. 'Don't worry. She knows when she's beaten.'

'What do you mean?'

'I mean my grandfather told her yesterday, in no uncertain terms, that she had ruined my life. He said if she hadn't interfered, and sent you back to England, we would probably have been married by now.'

Samantha gasped. 'I don't believe you.'

'It's true.' Matthew grinned. 'Would I lie?'

'You have done, on occasion,' she told him severely, and he shrugged.

'Only to get what I wanted,' he replied irrepressibly. 'And I've wanted you since the first moment I saw you.'

'But——' Samantha made one last attempt to be serious. 'I don't know whether I want to be like your mother. Being—being rich doesn't seem to have made her happy, does it?'

'I don't want you to be like my mother either,' retorted Matthew fervently. 'Which is why I've persuaded my grandfather to make her the nominal head of the Apollonius Corporation when he retires. You and I are going to live in London, and I'm going to go on running J.P. Software. By the time Caroline gets tired of giving orders, you and I will be putting our grandchildren to bed.' He smiled. 'Now—will you marry me?'

And as Samantha agreed she knew that heaven was within her grasp...

SNOWFIRE

PROLOGUE

HE WAS standing in the dining-room, by the window, gazing out at the rain that had been falling solidly ever since they left the church. Olivia guessed he must be thinking it was an omen. After weeks and weeks of dry weather, it had to be the day of the funeral that it changed.

She halted in the doorway, realising he was not yet aware of her presence, and dreading the moment when she would have to say goodbye. If only she were older, she thought. If only Sally had considered before blithely making Philip her son's guardian. But who would have expected Sally and Keith to die before either of them was thirty-five? And Philip was Sally's brother. He was obviously the natural choice.

Even so...

Olivia caught her lower lip between her teeth as she stared at the boy's drooping figure. Today had been more of a strain for him than for anyone, and his bent head and hunched shoulders spoke of a misery he could no longer hide. He had done well, she thought, handling himself through the tortuous rites of the burial with a dignity and self-possession enviable in a much older man. But now, believing himself unobserved, he had given way to his real feelings, and Olivia's heart went out to him as she recognised his grief.

'Conor.'

His name was barely audible across the silent room, but he heard her. He turned then, dashing his hand over his face as he did so, struggling to resume the defensive posture that had kept his tears at bay.

'Oh—hi, Aunt 'Livia,' he said, forcing a smile that was determinedly bright. 'I was just watching the rain.

The garden's waterlogged. Mum's——' He broke off abruptly as the mention of his mother's name disconcerted him, and then continued with an obvious effort, 'Mum's dahlias are really taking a hammering.'

'Are they?'

Olivia came to stand beside him, noticing almost inconsequentially that he had grown another couple of inches in the last twelve months. He was almost as tall as she was now, and at five feet seven inches—nine in her heels—she was considered above average height.

But now she feigned an interest in the flowers Sally had planted in the borders. The rain-soaked garden showed little of the colour it had flaunted earlier in the summer. The last time Olivia was here they had all had tea on the lawn...

She glanced at the boy beside her, more concerned about him than about his mother's flowers. What was he really thinking? she wondered. Was he wishing he had gone with his parents on that fated day trip to Paris? He looked so pale and drawn, his sandy hair, which always seemed to need cutting, straggling over the collar of his dark suit.

If only they had made her his guardian, she thought helplessly. At fifteen, a boy needed to know who he was; he needed roots. Everything he knew and loved was here in Paget. He knew no one in the United States. He hadn't even been to Florida for a holiday.

'Do I have to go?'

The low, impassioned words were uncannily like an echo of her own thoughts, and Olivia wondered if he could read her mind. Certainly her association with the Brennans had always been a close one, and only in the last couple of years, since she had gone to live and work in London, had their friendship suffered because of the separation.

Of course, it was his mother with whom Olivia had had the most in common, she acknowledged. She had been ten when Keith and Sally Brennan had moved into the big old house next to her grandmother's cottage. And, from the beginning, she had been a welcome visitor there. Naturally the fact that the Brennans had also had a baby son had been a great attraction, but as Olivia grew older it was Sally who had shared all the hopes and fears of her teenage years.

Olivia had hardly known her own parents. They had been involved in a car accident when she was little more than a baby herself, and although her mother had lingered on in the hospital for several weeks after the crash there had never been any real hope of her recovering consciousness. In consequence, Olivia's paternal grandmother had taken her to live with her and, although Mrs Holland had done her best, she had been too used to living alone to have much patience with a lively toddler.

That was why Olivia felt such an enormous sense of empathy with Conor now. She had known him since he was two years old. She had watched him grow from a mischievous schoolboy into a confident teenager. She had combed his hair and scrubbed his knees, and sometimes told him off. And lately she had teased him about his girlfriends: the procession of budding Madonnas who hung around outside his gate. He was the closest thing to a nephew she was ever likely to have, and she was going to miss him badly.

'I—think so,' she answered now, finding it difficult to say the words with his anxious eyes upon her. She struggled to sound optimistic. 'Look at it this way—it'll be a fresh start. And—where your Uncle Philip lives sounds really beautiful. Imagine being able to swim all the year round!'

'I don't want to go.' Conor's response was desperate. 'I want to stay here. Why can't I stay here? This house is mine now, isn't it?'

'Well, yes, but——'

'There you are, then.'

'Conor, you can't stay here alone!' It wasn't as if her grandmother still lived next door. Last year Mrs Holland had had a stroke, and she had been moved into a retirement home. The cottage had been sold, and Sally had said they hardly knew the new occupants.

'Why can't I?' he demanded now. 'I've stayed here on my own before.'

'Not for weeks you haven't,' replied Olivia flatly, finding it impossible to sustain his cornered gaze. 'Conor, you're only fifteen——'

'Sixteen,' he interrupted her swiftly. 'I'll be sixteen in three months.'

'No, Conor.'

'Then why can't I come and live with you?' he demanded, seizing on the idea. 'I wouldn't get in your way, honestly. I could get a job——'

'Conor...' She sighed. 'Conor, you have to finish your education. It's what your parents would have wanted.'

'In Florida!' His lips twisted.

'Yes.' Olivia knew she had to be firm.

Conor sniffed. 'I see.'

'Oh, don't say it like that.' She couldn't bear his defeated stare. 'If there was anything I could do——'

'—you'd do it. I know.' But Conor sounded horribly cynical. 'I'm sorry. I should have realised. You're going to be a hotshot lady lawyer! The last thing you need is a raw kid hanging around your apartment, cramping your style, when you bring clients home——'

'Conor, I don't have an apartment, and you know it,' she protested weakly. 'I have a room in a house that I share with three other women. It's just a bed-sit, really. And there's no way you could live there.'

'Well, why can't you get something bigger? Something we could share? I'd help with the rent——'

'No, Conor.' Olivia squashed that idea once and for all. 'I'm not your guardian,' she explained gently. 'Your Uncle Philip is. Even...even if it were possible—which it's not,' she put in hurriedly, 'he wouldn't allow you to stay with me.'

'And aren't you glad?' Conor's expression changed to one of bitterness. He swung away from her, thrusting aggressive hands into his trouser pockets, rounding his shoulders against an unforgiving fate. 'I bet you can't wait to get in your car and drive away from all this, can you?' he exclaimed scornfully. 'It's not your problem, so why get involved? I don't know what you came here for. You can't help, so why didn't you stay away?'

'Oh, Conor!'

Olivia's composure broke at last, and, as if her grief was all that was needed to drive a wedge through his crumbling defiance, he turned back to her. For a few tense moments he just stared at her, and she saw the glitter of tears on lashes several shades darker than his hair. Then, with a muffled groan, he flung himself into her arms.

He was shaking. She could feel it. And his thin, boyish frame seemed even bonier than she remembered. One of the neighbours had told her he hadn't eaten a thing since he had learned that the plane carrying his mother and father to Paris had exploded over the Channel. He had borne it all bravely, but inside it was eating him up.

'I'm sorry, I'm sorry,' he muttered at last, dragging himself away from her. He rubbed the back of his hand across his cheek, looking at her rather shamefacedly. 'I've wet the collar of your blouse.'

'It doesn't matter.' Olivia wished the dampness she could feel against her neck was all she had to worry about. 'I just wish there was something I could do. Your mother was my best friend. I don't want to let you down.'

Conor's lashes drooped to veil eyes that were presently a watery shade of green. He had long lashes for a boy, and they did a successful job of hiding his feelings. Dear God, why had this had to happen? The Brennans had been such a close family. They had come to live in Paget when Keith, who was a physiotherapist, got an appointment at the hospital in nearby Dymchurch. Sally, meanwhile, had been content doing social work and looking after her garden, and Conor had been the centre of their universe . . .

'What time are you leaving?' he enquired abruptly, and she guessed what it must have cost him to ask that question. But he knew, as well as she did, that it would take her some time to drive back to London. And now that the nights were drawing in again . . .

'Um—pretty soon,' Olivia answered now, putting out her hand to brush a thread of lint from his jacket, and then withdrawing it again as he flinched away from her touch. She linked her hands together instead in an effort to control her own anguish, and glanced behind her. 'I— you will write and let me know your address, won't you? You know where I live, and I'm looking forward to hearing all about Port Douglas.'

Conor shrugged. 'If you like.'

There was a flatness to his tone now, an indifference, and inwardly Olivia groaned. It was foolish, she knew, but the thought of leaving him, of not seeing him again for God knew how long, was tearing her apart, and she realised she had to get away before she gave in and said something she would regret. He couldn't stay with her. There was no way she could support herself *and* a boy of his age. And it was no use toying with the idea of abandoning her legal training, getting a job down here, and offering to live with him, in this house, as a kind of guardian-cum-housekeeper. Philip Cox would never allow it. And, in any case, the house was probably going to be sold to pay for Conor's education.

Biting her lip, she took a steadying breath. 'So,' she said, striving for control, 'you're going to be all right?'

Conor's mouth twisted. 'Of course.'

Olivia hesitated. 'You do—understand?'

Conor shrugged. 'Does it matter?'

'Of course it matters.' Just for a moment Olivia lost her hard-won detachment, and a little of her own frustration showed in her voice. 'I want you to be happy, Conor. And you will be. Believe me!'

"Of course it matters," that for a moment Olivia lost her hard-won detachment, and a little of her own time truths showed in her voice. "I want you to be happy, Conor. And you will be. Believe me—"

CHAPTER ONE

THE small hotel, part of a row of wood-faced Tudor-type dwellings, many of which owed their origins to the days when the Cinque Ports provided ships to fight the Spanish Armada, stood at the end of the quay. Of course, the old buildings had been much renovated and repaired since Elizabethan times, but the Ship Inn's low doorways and timbered ceilings were too attractive to tourists to be replaced, however inconvenient they might be.

Not that Paget attracted as many visitors as Romney, or Hythe, or Dymchurch. It was too small, for one thing, and, for another, the salt-marshes were not suitable for children to play on. But, as a fishing village that hadn't altered drastically since the sixteenth century, it was one of a kind, and many visitors, Americans particularly, came to take photographs of its ancient buildings and cobbled streets.

But at this time of the year there were few tourists stalwart enough to brave the east wind that came in over the marshes. The first weeks of February had been wild and blustery, and only that morning there had been a sprinkling of snow over the fishing boats lying idle in their stocks. Storm warnings had been out all along the coast, and the few fishermen willing to venture out into the choppy waters had been driven back again by the gales.

Standing at her bedroom window, her head stooped to accommodate the low lintel, Olivia felt no sense of regret at the inclement weather. On the contrary, it suited her very well that she did not have to put on a sociable face when she went down to the tiny dining-room for breakfast. She hadn't come to Paget for familiarity or company. She didn't want to talk to anybody, beyond the common courtesies politeness demanded. Because he hadn't recognised her name, the landlord had assumed she was a stranger here, and it had suited her to foster that belief. As far as Tom Drake was concerned, she was one of 'them crazy Londoners', she was sure. Who else would choose to come to Paget while winter still gripped it in its icy grasp? Who else would book a room for an unspecified period when it was obvious from her appearance that she would have benefited from a spell in the sun?

Of course, the fact that she looked thin and pale and tended to drag her left leg might have given the staff other ideas, Olivia acknowledged. After all, this was hardly the sort of place to come for a rest cure. Perhaps they thought she had some awful terminal illness and had come to Paget to die. It was impossible to speculate what they might think, but in the week that had elapsed since she came here they had respected her privacy and left her alone.

And Olivia was grateful. In fact, for the first time in more than a year she actually felt as if she was beginning to relax. Her leg was still painful, particularly if she walked further than the doctors had recommended. But her appetite was improving a little, and she didn't always need barbiturates to sleep.

Her lips curled slightly as she accorded that thread of optimism the contempt it deserved. Imagine needing drugs to enjoy a night's rest, she thought bitterly. She was thirty-four, and she felt at least twenty years older!

But her low state of fitness was not entirely unwarranted, she defended herself. The shock of learning that Stephen had been unfaithful had barely been blunted when the accident happened, and weeks spent in a hospital bed had served to exacerbate her sense of betrayal. If she'd been able to carry on with her work, lose herself in its legal intricacies, she might have weathered the storm fairly well. It wasn't as if her marriage to Stephen had been ideal from the outset. It hadn't, and it had taken her only a short time to acknowledge that she had allowed her biological clock to induce her into a situation that was primarily the result of pressure. Pressure from her friends, pressure from her peers, but also pressure within herself at the knowledge that she was twenty-nine, single, and facing a lonely future. In consequence, she had allowed herself to be persuaded that any marriage was better than no marriage at all, and it wasn't until the deed was done that she had realised how wrong she was.

She couldn't altogether blame Stephen. Like herself, he had been approaching an early middle age without a permanent companion, and, if some of his habits had been a little annoying, and his lovemaking less than earth-moving, she had determined to make the best of it. No doubt there were things she did that annoyed him, too, and if her grandmother had taught her anything, it was that life was seldom the way one wanted it to be.

But, predictably enough, she supposed, it was Stephen who tired of the marriage first. And, equally predictably, she was the last to find out. Perhaps if her job had not been so demanding, if she had not spent so many evenings visiting clients or preparing briefs, she would have noticed sooner what was going on. But Stephen's job in wholesaling meant that he was often away overnight, and it wasn't until a well-meaning friend had asked if she had enjoyed her mid-week break in Bath that she had been curious enough to examine their credit-card statements more closely. What she had found was that Stephen often occupied a double room on his nights away, and that, while this was not so incriminating in itself, another receipt, showing dinner for two at a bistro in Brighton, was. Olivia knew that Stephen had purportedly gone to Brighton to attend a delegates' conference, and the presentation dinner that followed it had supposedly been a dead bore.

When she confronted him with her suspicions, he had tried to deny it. For all the inadequacies of their marriage, he had still wanted to maintain the status quo. It had suited him to have a wife who wouldn't divorce him hovering in the background. It gave him an excuse not to get too involved, and he'd enjoyed the thrill of forbidden fruit.

For Olivia, however, the idea of continuing such an alliance was abhorrent to her. She wanted out. She had learned her lesson, and she wanted her freedom, and Stephen's pleas to give him another chance only filled her with disgust.

Nevertheless, although she moved out of the apartment they had shared in Kensington, Stephen had continued to hound her. Even though she employed a solicitor in another partnership to represent her, Stephen insisted he would fight the petition in court. And Olivia knew, better than anyone, how messy such divorces could be. And how ironic that she should be caught in such a situation which could only be damaging to her career.

In the years since she had become an articled solicitor she had gained a small reputation for competent representation. She still worked for the large partnership with whom she had trained, but her obvious abilities had not gone unnoticed. There was talk of a junior partnership, if she wanted it, or the possibility of branching out on her own. Neither option would benefit from adverse publicity of any kind, and Olivia knew Stephen would do anything to embarrass her. He was bitter and resentful, and, incredibly, he blamed her for their estrangement. He was not going to let her go easily, and his threats were a constant headache.

Which was probably why the accident had happened, she acknowledged now, even though she had never blamed Stephen for any of it. She had already been sleeping badly, and the extra hours at work she had been putting in, in an effort to keep other thoughts at bay, had taken their toll. She shouldn't have been driving. She should have taken a taxi to the station, and caught a train to Basingstoke. But she hadn't. She had driven—

straight into one of the concrete pillars supporting a bridge over the M3. Or at least, that was what they had told her. She didn't remember anything after leaving the office.

Of course, Stephen had been sorry then. He had come to see her in the hospital, when she was still strung up to so many machines that she must have looked like a marionette. She could have her divorce now, he'd said. He wouldn't oppose it. He'd contact her solicitor straight away, and get the thing in motion. It wasn't until later that she'd wondered at his speed.

By then, by the time she was lucid enough to understand that she was lucky to be alive, she had had other problems to contend with. Not least the news that, although her skull was evidently thicker than it had a right to be, and her wounds would heal, and her broken limbs would mend, her left leg had suffered multiple fractures, and it was unlikely she would ever run again.

She remembered she'd tried to joke about not being able to run before, but, as time went on, she realised what they had been trying to tell her. Her left leg had been crushed, badly crushed, and, although all the skills of modern surgery had been brought to bear, the tendons had been damaged quite beyond repair.

Physiotherapy had helped a lot. That and her determination to walk again. When she first left the hospital she had had to get around on crutches, and for weeks she had struggled to and from the clinic in an ambulance. But gradually she had been able to put the crutches aside and manage with a walking-stick, even taking up her job again, although that had been rather harder. Her leg ached if she had to stand for any length of time, and the stress of both the accident and the divorce had taken a toll on her defences. Eventually, she had had to accept that if she wasn't careful she was going to have a complete nervous breakdown, and the senior partner at Hallidays had suggested she take a holiday.

Olivia knew he had had something different in mind from the east coast of southern England. The West Indies, perhaps, or South America. Somewhere where the sun was hot and life was lived at a slower pace. Somewhere she could relax, and restore the tattered remnants of her existence.

Of course, her colleagues didn't know the whole story. They had assumed that Stephen's defection had precipitated this crisis. But the truth was that the weeks of inactivity had given Olivia time to re-evaluate her life, and, despite a sense of frustration at her weakness, she was no longer sure of what she wanted.

For so long her career had been the yardstick by which she had measured her success. She had wanted to become a lawyer, and she had succeeded. She had wanted to be offered a partnership, and that, too, was within her grasp. So why did it all seem so empty, somehow? What had happened to the ambition that had sustained her for so long?

She had tried to tell herself that it was the old biological thing again. That, however pointless her marriage to Stephen had become, it had still been her best chance to fulfil herself as a woman. If she had had a baby, would things have been different? They had never taken any precautions, but it had evidently been not to be. Maybe she couldn't have children. Maybe that was why she felt so empty now. Or was it, as Conor had said once, that she had got hard in her old age? But then, he had wanted to hurt her, and undoubtedly he had succeeded.

Conor...

Leaving the window, Olivia crossed to the dressing-table and seated herself on the padded stool in front of the mirror. As she examined her pale features without pleasure, she wondered where he was, and what he was doing now. It must be—what?—nine years since she'd seen him. In fact she had only seen him that one time since he had gone to live in the United States.

She grimaced. It was not a visit she remembered with any affection. At seventeen and a half, Conor had changed totally from the sensitive boy she had known. He had been loud, and cocky, and objectionable, full of his own importance and brimming with conceit. He had been in London with a group of students from the college he attended in Port Douglas, and he had arrived at the house she still shared one night, already the worse for drink.

To Olivia, who was used to the Conor she knew from the letters he had occasionally sent her, he was almost a stranger, bragging about the life he led back in Florida, impressing her with the parties he went to, the car he drove. He was arrogant and brash, decrying the room she had furnished with such care, and disparaging her lifestyle compared to his. He had said she was a fool to spend all her time working, that he was glad he'd got out of England when he had. And when Olivia had defended herself by taking a stiff-necked stance, he had accused her of getting hard in her old age.

Oh, yes. Olivia traced the curve of one eyebrow with a rueful finger. That visit had not been repeated. Indeed, it had taken her quite some time to get over it, and when there were no more letters she wasn't really surprised. Who'd have thought it? she mused. That two years should have made such a difference. But then, he *had* been young, she conceded, as she had done numerous times before. Perhaps it had been his way of dealing with the situation. There was no doubt that losing both his parents had been quite a blow.

Still, in spite of the lapse in communication, she did continue to think about him sometimes. Particularly times like this, when she was feeling rather low. Which was probably why she had chosen to come to Paget, even though, since her grandmother's death five years ago, she had no connection with the place. She hadn't wanted to go anywhere hot and noisy. She supposed what she'd really wanted to do was return to her roots.

A final grimace at her appearance, and she was ready to go downstairs. The trouble with very dark hair, particularly the unruly variety, was that it accentuated any trace of pallor in her face, she thought ruefully. Since the accident it had grown so long that she was obliged to confine it in a knot at her nape, and even then it contrived to escape every hairpin. She looked like a witch, she decided, all wild hair and black-ringed eyes. It was a reminder—if any reminder was needed—of why she had always kept her hair short in the past.

She left the walking-stick propped by the door. Slowly but surely, she was managing to do without it for a little longer every day. Eventually, she told herself, only the slight dragging of her foot and the ugly scars that would never completely disappear would be all that remained of her trauma. And in three weeks she'd possess her decree absolute, and Stephen would no longer play any part in her future.

Poor Stephen, she thought, with an unwarranted sense of pity. He hadn't been able to wait to dissociate himself from any responsibility for what had happened to her. He had got quite a shock when he saw her in the hospital. He must have been afraid he was going to be tethered to an invalid for the rest of his life.

Men! She shook her head regretfully as she closed her door behind her. Her experience of the opposite sex was that a woman should not rely on them. Olivia determined that, whatever she decided to do, she would not be taken in again. She was free—or she would be in three weeks—over twenty-one, and independent. What did she need a man for?

Since she was the only guest staying at the inn right now, Mrs Drake always made a fuss of her after she'd negotiated the narrow, twisting stairs that led down to the lower floor. Seating her at the much-coveted table in the leaded window embrasure, the publican's plump wife rattled through a series of questions about how she was, whether she'd slept well, had she everything she needed, and, finally, what did she fancy for breakfast this morning?

As she only ever had coffee and toast, that question was really academic, but, as always, Olivia answered her, adding a polite enquiry as to her and Mr Drake's health.

'Oh, we're in the pink, as they say, Mrs Perry,' Mrs Drake assured her, as she usually did. 'But it's a raw morning, that it is. Tom thinks we'll have more snow before nightfall.'

'Do you think so?' Olivia glanced out at the chilly scene beyond the windows. There were few people about, and those who were had their collars up against the wind as they hurried along the flagged quayside.

'So he says,' agreed Mrs Drake, raising her pencilled eyebrows. 'Now, you're sure you wouldn't like a bit of bacon and an egg? A bit of dry toast doesn't seem to have much sustenance in it. Not at this time of the year.'

Her speculative gaze swept critically over her guest's slim figure, and, in spite of the bulkiness of her sweater, Olivia knew she had been assessed and found wanting. Mrs Drake wouldn't say so, of course. Olivia's attitude had not encouraged familiarity. Nevertheless, she was aware that they were curious about her. But for once her disability had provided a useful barrier.

'Just toast, please,' she insisted now, accompanying her refusal with a smile. And Mrs Drake stifled her opposition, taking her dismissal with good heart.

The daily newspaper Olivia had reluctantly ordered when she checked in was lying beside her plate, and although she wasn't much concerned with the politics that had made the headlines she felt obliged to pick it up. There was no television in her room here, even though Mr Drake had said he could arrange for one if she wanted it, and, despite the fact that she had politely declined his offer, it did seem rather childish to cut herself off completely.

She flicked idly through the inner pages, scanning the gossip columns with assumed interest. But the activities of the latest hot property in the pop world seemed aimless, and her eyes drifted back to the Drakes' cat, washing its paws on a pile of nets across the way.

A man strode past the window, hands thrust into the pockets of a leather jacket, his collar tipped against the weather. He was a fairly tall man, solidly, though not stockily built, with fairish hair and skin that was browner that it should have been in this chilly part of the world.

The landlord emerged from the inn as he was walking past, and the two exchanged the time of day. It was a brief encounter, not least because Tom Drake was in his shirt-sleeves, and Olivia guessed the state of the weather had been mentioned. But, as the man lifted a hand to rake back his sandy hair before continuing on his way, she was struck by his resemblance to Conor Brennan. It was a fleeting glimpse, of course, and she guessed there must be dozens of men around who might be said to resemble the youth she remembered. Even so, it was an amazing coincidence, coming as it had on the heels of the thoughts she had had earlier.

Which was probably why she had imagined the resemblance, she conceded to herself now, as Mrs Drake returned with her toast and coffee. She was tempted to ask the woman who Mr Drake had been speaking to, but to do that would invite exactly the kind of questions she was hoping to avoid. It would mean admitting some connection with the village, for why else would she be interested in one of its inhabitants unless there was some reason why she might know him?

In any case, she didn't know the man. It had just been a momentary aberration. If Conor had come back to this country for any reason, surely he would at least have tried to get in touch with her? He might not have her address, but he still knew where she worked.

Her appetite had been negligible since the accident, and this morning was no exception. But the pot of coffee was very welcome, and she managed to swallow half a slice of toast. Then, leaving the warm fire that was

burning in the dining-room, she went back up to her
room. She had decided to go for a walk. So long as she
wrapped up warmly, she would enjoy the exercise.

But today she didn't walk around the harbour and out
on to the breakwater as she usually did. Nor did she
venture across the salt marshes, which, even in winter,
provided a veritable haven for birds. Instead, she decided to test her leg by walking inland, up Paget's cobbled
streets to where houses clustered on the hillside. It was
further than she had ventured before, but it was time
she took a look at her grandmother's old cottage, she
told herself. She refused to admit what her real intentions were. But anyway, what was wrong with being
curious about who was living in the Brennans' house
these days? she argued. It was years since it had been
sold to pay for Conor's education.

Her thigh was aching by the time she reached Gull
Rise. And the irregular row of Victorian dwellings looked
much the same as she remembered them. They were
mostly cottages—some terraced, like her grandmother's, and others independently spaced. The house
the Brennans used to occupy was bigger than the rest,
but Olivia remembered Sally saying they had got it fairly
cheaply, because it had needed so much doing to it. The
young couple had spent their first few years at Gull Rise
renovating the place, and by the time Conor was in his
teens it was a home to be proud of.

It still was, Olivia saw poignantly, her eyes flickering
over her old home and settling on the house next door.
She felt an unfamiliar ache in her throat. Someone had
cared enough about it to keep the exterior bright and
shining, she noticed. The woodwork was newly painted,
and the drive was clear of weeds.

She halted a few yards from the house, on the opposite side of the road. With the collar of her cashmere
coat pulled high about her ears, and her gloved hand
shielding her face, she didn't think anyone would recognise her. Besides, most of her grandmother's old

neighbours had either died or moved away, and the gauntness of her own features would deceive any but her closest friends.

There was a car parked in the drive, she saw—a small Peugeot, with current licence plates. And, even as she watched, a young woman came out of the house and unlocked the car, before pausing, as if someone had attracted her attention. Her blonde head tipped expectantly towards the door of the house, which she had left ajar, and, leaving her keys in the car, she sauntered back.

Her actions spurred Olivia to life. For heaven's sake, she chivvied herself irritably, was she reduced to spying on other people for entertainment? The house was lived in, and evidently by someone who cared. She had satisfied her curiosity, and that was all she needed to know.

But, as she turned away, a man appeared in the doorway across the street. A tall man, with light hair, wearing a black leather jacket. Seen face on, his resemblance to Conor was even more striking, and with a sense of alarm she realised it was him.

But, it couldn't be, her brain insisted, refusing to accept the evidence of her eyes. Conor didn't live in England, he lived in America. There was no way he could have bought this house and settled down here. It was too much of a coincidence. Too incredible to be true.

And yet she lingered, aware that her injured leg was cramping beneath her. Dear God, how was she going to find the strength to walk back to the harbour? she fretted. If she didn't move soon, she was going to collapse on the spot.

But the truth was that the sense of panic she was feeling was as much psychological as physical. Whoever the man was—and the young woman was kissing him now, running a possessive hand down his cheek, and saying something that brought a grin to his lean face—he wouldn't appreciate the thought that she had been prying into his affairs. If it was Conor, he evidently had no need of her assistance.

But it hurt that he should come back to England without even letting her know. She had been his surrogate aunt, for heaven's sake. His parents had been her close friends. And she had known Conor since he was two years old! That should have meant something to the boy he had been.

Of course, he wasn't a boy any more, she acknowledged ruefully. He was a man, and an extremely attractive one at that. Even from a distance, she could see he looked bigger and stronger than his father had ever been. And the young woman, with her silky blonde hair and long, unscarred legs, evidently thought so, too.

Olivia's lips tightened. Who was she? Who were *they*? If it was Conor, was this his wife? And why should it mean so much to her? He obviously didn't desire her approval.

Sucking in her breath as a sharp, stabbing pain shot up her thigh, she made a determined effort to extinguish her curiosity. It was nothing to do with her, she told herself grimly, endeavouring to put one foot in front of the other. She could look in the phone book when she got back to the inn. In fact, she wished she had just done that in the first place. Then she could have made up her mind to ring, or not to ring, without any knowledge of his status.

Tears sprang to her eyes as the wind swept a sudden gust of sleet into her face. Oh, great, she thought bitterly, as the frozen flakes stung her cheeks. This was all she needed: soaking to the skin!

Afterwards, she was never sure how it happened—whether her leg had simply given out on her, or her foot had slipped on a thread of ice. But, whatever the cause, she found herself falling, hitting the pavement heavily, and scraping her gloved palms.

It was so humiliating. She had never considered herself a particularly graceful creature, but she had never been as clumsy as she was now. Landing on her bottom, she felt a jarring sensation all up her spine, but she knew she should be grateful she hadn't fallen on her leg.

Blinking back the hot tears that never seemed far away these days, she was making an ungainly effort to get to her feet when strong hands gripped her arms. 'Steady,' said a husky male voice, holding her where she was without much effort. 'Take it easy, ma'am. You've had quite a shock.'

CHAPTER TWO

HE WAS beside her, not yet able to see her face, and Olivia wished the ground would just open up and swallow her. If she had had any doubts about his identity before, the soft southern drawl had dispelled them. There couldn't be another man who looked like Conor in Paget, not with the same transatlantic accent.

'I'm—fine,' she muttered shortly, shaking off his hands, and keeping her face averted. She was aware that the other woman had come to join them. She had heard the hurried tap of her heels, with the impatient, 'Is she all right?' enquiry, which put Olivia squarely into the category of being a nuisance.

'She says she is,' replied Conor, ignoring the young woman's tone and squatting down on his heels. Even though she couldn't see them, Olivia was aware of his eyes appraising her bent head. 'Are you?'

Olivia sighed. And, with a sense of resignation, she accepted there was no way she was going to be able to avoid the inevitable. Much against her better judgement, she lifted her head, and Conor sucked in his breath with an audible gulp.

'Aunt 'Livia!' he exclaimed, and Olivia thought how typical it was that he should make her feel even older than she did already.

'Hello, Conor,' she responded, taking advantage of his stunned expression to clamber stiffly to her feet. Using the fence of a nearby garden for support, she endeavoured to hide the throbbing pain in her femur, and was inordinately glad she was wearing trousers to hide her leg's wasted appearance. 'I didn't know you were back in England.'

'No.'

26

Conor seemed to be having some difficulty in adjusting to her appearance, and Olivia lifted a nervous hand to her hair, wondering if she looked as distraught as she felt. It had obviously been a shock for him, seeing her like this, and she guessed he was dismayed at how she'd aged.

'Conor...' The young woman touched his arm as he got dazedly to his feet, and he looked at her almost without recognition. 'Conor,' she said again, 'I didn't know you had relatives in England. Is this your mother's sister or something?'

'No!' The denial he made was vehement, and she widened her big blue eyes in faint alarm.

'But you called——'

'—her Aunt 'Livia. I know,' agreed Conor shortly. He looked at Olivia as if he still couldn't believe his eyes, and then added, half impatiently, 'It was a token form of address, that's all.'

'Then, who is——?'

'I lived next door to Conor and his parents, many years ago,' said Olivia stiffly, glancing down at her coat, and noticing that it had suffered somewhat from the impact. Much like herself, she thought frustratedly. She tested her weight on her injured leg and drew back instantly. Oh, God, it wasn't going to stand her walking on it.

'Oh, I see.' The girl was evidently losing interest in the affair. She jogged Conor's arm, and gestured back across the street. 'Con, I've really got to be going. I told Marie I'd be in at eleven.'

Conor dragged his thoughts back to the present with obvious difficulty. 'Then go,' he said, the indifference in his voice audible to anyone's ears. The relief Olivia had felt when he had been obliged to look away from her was tempered by his evident irritation, and the younger woman's lips tightened with resentment.

'Well, aren't you coming?' she exclaimed. 'I thought you had an appointment at the clinic.'

'I do.' Conor's expression hardened, and for a moment Olivia was reminded of the boy he had once been. But then her brain made the connection between the girl's words and his response, and she wondered with sudden concern why he should be attending a clinic.

The young woman looked at Olivia without liking. 'Aren't you going to introduce us first?' she protested, and Olivia knew that wasn't what she wanted at all. It was just another attempt to extricate Conor from the situation, without leaving him alone with her. Though why she should feel the need to do so, Olivia couldn't imagine.

If only she could leave, she thought. If only she could make some casual excuse for being there, and saunter off along Gull Rise. But every minute she delayed accentuated her growing weakness. She was going to have to get a taxi. Even if it meant knocking on a stranger's door.

'Sharon Holmes; Olivia—Perry,' Conor said now, after a moment's hesitation, and it took a second for Olivia to register that he had used her married name. But before she could wonder how he had found out that she had been married, he had bent, and was running exploring hands over her injured leg.

'Don't do that!' Olivia's horrified objection almost drowned out Sharon's angry, 'Con!' Both women reacted unfavourably to his outrageous interference, and Olivia shuddered visibly when his hands massaged her calf.

Conor straightened without haste. 'You were standing there like a stork,' he said, his eyes going directly to Olivia's wavering gaze. 'I thought you must have hurt your leg when you fell, but it's more than that, isn't it? I guess you'd better come inside while I make a proper examination.'

Olivia gasped. 'I beg your pardon?'

'I said——'

'I heard what you said,' she retorted, wrapping the folds of the mud-stained cashmere coat closer about her slim figure. 'But I don't want you to give me an examination. You—can call me a taxi, if you like. I admit I don't think I'm up to walking back to my hotel. But that's all, thank you. Just a cab.'

Conor glanced at Sharon, who was staring at him with undisguised irritation, but he chose not to obey the warning in her gaze. 'I'll give you a lift back to where you're staying after you've told me what happened,' he retorted briefly. 'Now, can you walk across to the house or shall I carry you?'

Olivia wished she could tell him what to do with his assistance, but she couldn't. The truth was that she felt as if she were rooted to the spot. The very idea of putting any weight at all on her injured leg was anathema to her. If only she had brought her walking-stick, instead of pretending she didn't need it.

'Like that, is it?'

Conor had evidently read her uncertainty correctly, and, without giving her the opportunity to voice any further protest, he bent and plucked her off the pavement. Then, with the girl, Sharon, fluttering ineffectually at his side, he strode purposefully across the road.

Argument was useless, Olivia decided helplessly, as the welcome relief of being off her feet entirely brought more tears to her eyes. Even the hard strength of his arm beneath her knee was preferable to the agony of continually supporting herself on one leg. He must be strong, she thought, to carry her so effortlessly. He had picked her up as if she were a doll, and he wasn't even breaking sweat.

'Con, what are you going to do?'

Sharon overtook him as he started up the drive, taking little backward running steps in an effort to attract his attention. Olivia, obliged to rest her arm around Conor's neck for support, felt embarrassed at being the cause of her frustration. But what could she do, except promise herself to keep out of their way in future?

'I'm going to give Liv a drink, and then I'm going to take her back to her hotel,' he replied shortly, waiting for her to step aside so that he could mount the steps to the door. 'I thought you were going to work,' he added, as she followed them into the house. 'A few moments ago you were desperate to be gone.'

A few minutes ago she hadn't expected her husband to bring a strange woman into the house, reflected Olivia drily, knowing exactly how Sharon was feeling. But for her to try and excuse herself would bestow the situation with an intimacy it didn't deserve. Besides, Conor had called her *Aunt* 'Livia when he first saw her. Surely Sharon could see she had no competition here?

'Well, are you going to the clinic?'

Sharon's voice had taken on a resentful note now, and this time Olivia felt she had to say something.

'The clinic?' she echoed, as Conor lowered her onto a sofa in the comfortable drawing-room. 'Um—if you have an appointment, oughtn't you to keep it? I mean, if you need treatment——'

'He doesn't need treatment. He's a doctor,' declared Sharon scathingly, drawing another impatient look from her husband. 'Con, I'm only trying to find out what's going on. D'you want to phone David?'

'I want you to go to work,' said Conor, in a low, controlled voice, and Olivia could feel Sharon's hostility clear across the room. 'If it's necessary to phone Marshall, I'll do it.'

'Oh . . .' Sharon's mouth tightened. 'Well, if you're sure.'

Conor didn't say anything then. He just looked at her. But Olivia had the feeling that the message he was emitting was loud enough. Sharon evidently thought so too, because, after only a slight hesitation, she offered a brief word of farewell and departed. The sound of the outer door slamming was a flagrant indication of her feelings, however, and Olivia made a conspicuous effort to avoid Conor's knowing gaze.

It wasn't difficult. Her surroundings were so familiar that it was easy to find another outlet for her thoughts. Incredible as it seemed, little had changed in the eleven years since she was here last. The room had been re-decorated, of course, and the sofa, on which she was reclining so unwillingly, had been re-covered. But the tall cabinets that had contained Sally's collection of Waterford crystal were still there, along with the writing-desk in the window where Keith used to keep the accounts. Even the ornaments adorning the Victorian mantel were pieces Conor's parents had collected on their frequent trips to the Continent. They used to spend their summers camping in the south of France, she remembered. She had even gone with them a couple of times, when Conor was six or seven years old.

'I'll get the coffee,' he said now, as if realising she needed a few minutes to relax. 'I won't be long. I was making a pot before—well, before I saw you.'

Olivia didn't have time to think of a response before he had left the room. In any case, she was still stunned by the fact that the house had evidently not been sold, after all. Her grandmother had never mentioned it before she died, and Olivia had never thought to ask. But then, after moving into the nursing home, Mrs Holland had lost touch with many of her friends. She hadn't even attended Sally's and Keith's funeral.

Taking a deep breath, Olivia used her hands to ease herself to the edge of the sofa. Then, with some trepidation, she lowered her feet to the floor. Her leg still hurt, but the pain was bearable now. An indication that she was improving, she thought wryly. If only it had improved earlier, before she had got herself into this predicament.

'What are you doing?'

Conor's impatient voice arrested her appraisal of her condition. Not that it mattered really. There was no way she could leave here without his co-operation. Even if she insisted on taking a taxi, she would have to use his phone.

Now Conor came into the room carrying a tray bearing two beakers, a cream jug, and a pot of coffee. Hooking a low end-table with his foot, he positioned it near the sofa, then set down his burden before subsiding on to the seat beside her.

His weight brought a resulting depression in the cushions, and Olivia had to grasp the arm of the sofa closest to her to prevent herself from sliding towards him. It was a timely reminder—if any were needed—that Conor was no longer the skinny youth he used to be. Without his jacket, which he had apparently shed somewhere between here and the kitchen, his upper torso was broad and muscular beneath the knitted shirt he was wearing. She couldn't help noticing his legs, too, as she shuffled uneasily towards her end of the sofa. Spread as they were, to allow him easy access to the coffee, one powerful thigh was barely inches from the hand with which she was supporting herself. She knew a momentary urge to spread her fingers over his thigh, but happily that madness was only fleeting. It was just so amazing to remember him as a child and compare that image with the man he was now.

'Cream?' he asked abruptly, and Olivia blinked.

'Oh—no. Just black,' she said hurriedly. Maybe the strongly flavoured brew would help to normalise the situation. Just at the moment, she had a decided feeling of light-headedness.

'So,' he said, after handing her the beaker of coffee, 'd'you want to tell me what you're doing here?'

Olivia cradled her cup between her palms, and cast him a sideways glance. He wasn't looking at her at the moment, and she was grateful. It gave her an opportunity to study his features without fear of apprehension, and she needed that. Dear God, she thought, her gaze moving almost greedily over lean cheekbones, a strong jaw, and a wide, thin-lipped mouth—she had not dreamed he could be so familiar to her, not after all these years. But he was. Older, of course, and harsher; but essentially the same. She wondered how long he had been in England. Not too long, she guessed, judging by his tan. And those sun streaks in his sandy hair; he hadn't acquired them in this northern climate.

Conor finished pouring his own coffee, and Olivia quickly looked away. Concentrating her attention on the fireplace, she noticed the ashes lying in the grate. Although the house was centrally heated, someone had had a fire the night before. The image of Conor and his wife sharing this sofa in front of the open fire, even perhaps making love by firelight, flashed into her mind. It brought an uneasy prickling to her skin, and she angrily thrust it away. It was because she still thought of this as Sally's and Keith's house, she told herself grimly. And of Conor as a boy, when he was obviously a man.

'Well?' he prompted, and she was aware of him turning to look at her now. It made her glad she still had her coat wrapped about her. The honey-coloured cashmere hid a multitude of sins.

'Well,' she countered, turning his way, but not quite meeting his eyes. 'Small world, isn't it? Who'd have thought you'd come back to Paget?'

'Why shouldn't I?' Conor was curt. 'It's my home.'

'Yes, well—I didn't realise the house hadn't been sold until now.' She cast a determinedly casual look around the room. 'It's amazing. Everything looks the same.'

Conor's mouth compressed. 'Are you saying that when you came up here you didn't know it was my house?'

His tone was vaguely accusing, and Olivia's head swung back to him with some haste. 'Of course,' she exclaimed, meeting his green gaze half indignantly. She felt the warm colour surge into her throat at his cool appraisal. 'I—I just wanted to—to look around.'

'For old times' sake?'

'Yes.' The colour had reached her cheeks now, but she refused to look away. 'After all, you didn't tell me you'd come back to England. How was I supposed to know?'

Conor put down his cup. 'Point taken,' he conceded, lounging back against the cushions and propping one booted ankle across one twill-covered knee. 'I guess I didn't think you'd be interested. You haven't exactly kept me up to date with your affairs.'

Olivia dragged her gaze away and looked down into her cup. She was aware that her heart was beating far faster than it should have been, and, in spite of the cold day outside, she was sweating. She should have taken off her coat, she thought, though all she did was draw it more closely about her. She needed its comforting folds to disguise her trepidation.

'So,' she said, feeling obliged to make some comment, 'you're a doctor now.'

'Don't make it sound so unlikely.' Conor inclined his head. 'I told you what I wanted to do, when I came to see you in London. Actually, I'm still in training. I've decided I want to specialise in psychological disorders, so for the last six months I've been working at the drug rehabilitation unit in Witterthorpe.'

'I see.' Olivia was impressed. 'Did—er—did you do the rest of your training in England?'

'No.' Conor reached for his coffee again and took a drink. 'Uncle Philip had a heart condition. He died soon after I started medical school. I stayed on in the States until I'd finished at med. school, because that was what Aunt Elizabeth wanted. She'd been good to me, and I guess I owed her that much. When I came here, I began the extra training you need to get a full British qualification.'

Olivia absorbed this with a pang. So Philip Cox had died, too. Just another aspect of Conor's life that she had known nothing about. But she could understand that Elizabeth Cox would have found comfort in her nephew.

Philip had only fathered daughters, which was probably why Sally had left Conor in his care.

Her coffee was almost finished, and, surreptitiously testing her foot against the floor, Olivia decided she was strong enough to stand. But, when she replaced her cup on the tray and inched forward on the sofa, Conor's hand closed about her sleeve.

'We've talked about me,' he said, 'but you still haven't told me what you're doing in Paget. You mentioned that you're staying in the village. Would that be at Tom Drake's place? I had a word with him this morning, but he didn't mention he had a visitor.'

'Why would he?' Olivia moved her arm so that he was forced to release her. 'He doesn't remember me. My married name means nothing to him.'

'Ah, yes. Your married name.' Conor lowered his foot to the floor, and leant forward, his arms along his thighs. 'You're a married lady, aren't you? Is your husband with you? Am I going to get to meet him?'

'No.'

Suddenly, Olivia had no desire to tell Conor about the divorce. His intimation that they might see one another again unsettled her, and, for some reason she didn't choose to recognise, she didn't want his sympathy. So long as he believed she was still married, he couldn't get too close to her. Though why the idea of his getting close to her should disturb her so, she couldn't imagine.

'No?' Conor's eyes were uncomfortably intent. 'Why? You ashamed of me or something?'

'Don't be silly.' Olivia licked her dry lips. 'He's not here, that's all. He—I'm just taking a short holiday. On my own.'

'Recuperating,' suggested Conor quietly, and she hesitated only a moment before allowing a taut nod. 'So what happened?' he persisted. 'D'you want to talk about it?'

'So you can psychoanalyse me?' she taunted, needing to make light of what was threatening to become a seriously heavy development. 'No, thanks. I crashed my car, that's all. It's a common enough story. Nothing exciting, I'm afraid——'

'When?'

'When what?'

'When did you crash your car?' Conor was unnervingly direct.

'Oh...' Olivia shrugged. 'A little while ago. Eight or nine months, I think.' She took a steadying breath. 'Look, I must be going, I've got some phone calls to make.'

Conor didn't move. 'And that was when you smashed up your leg? Eight or nine months ago?'

'Well, I didn't do it by falling over,' she retorted, still trying to lighten the mood. 'Conor, it's been lovely seeing you again, and I'm sorry if I upset your wife——'

'My wife?' At last something she said had distracted him. He raked back his sun-bleached hair with a restless hand. 'Sharon's not my wife!'

'Oh!' Once again, Olivia could feel the heat flooding up under her skin. 'Well, your—er—girlfriend, then,' she muttered, getting determinedly to her feet. She swayed rather unsteadily on one leg, as she gauged the distance between the couch and the door. 'Please explain that I don't make a habit of this. I'd hate her to think I was spying on you!'

'Spying on us?'

Conor came to his feet with a lithe movement, successfully reminding her of his superior height and build. It hardly seemed possible that he had once cried on her shoulder, she thought. These days, he was almost a head taller than she was.

'Well, you know what I mean,' she mumbled now, wishing she had chosen a less emotive word to describe her position. 'I really was curious to see this house again. And the cottage, too, of course. It was just my luck that I slipped and fell at the wrong moment.'

'Or mine,' remarked Conor softly, looking down at her, and she wondered how he could imbue those words with such a measure of intimacy.

Heavens, he was good, she thought ridiculously, unable to sustain his warm, disturbing gaze a moment longer. It probably amused him to see how he could disconcert her. A delayed payment for the way she had bossed him about in his youth.

'Look—I've got to go,' she said, wishing he would get out of her way so that she had an unobstructed passage to the door. She didn't want him to carry her again. She didn't want him touching her.

'OK.' As if sensing her frustration, he moved aside, and Olivia limped heavily across the room. Her leg would support her now, just, but she was conscious of his eyes upon her. He was probably gauging the possible seriousness of her injury, she thought crossly. He was a doctor, after all. He would know how restricted her movements were.

'I'll get the car,' he said, as she reached the doorway, and Olivia had no choice but to let him do it.

'What about your appointment?' she protested, realising she should have asked to use the phone as soon as she got here. She could have had the coffee while she waited for a cab.

'Let me worry about that,' he replied, brushing past her to collect his jacket from the banister in the hallway, and she clutched the door frame at her back in an unconsciously defensive gesture.

Conor's car had been in the garage, which explained why Olivia had only seen Sharon's Peugeot in the drive. Conor reversed his mud-smeared Audi round to the front of the house where Olivia was waiting, and she was glad she had been able to negotiate the steps without him watching her.

'I can manage,' she insisted, when he would have got out to help her into the front of the car, and Conor sank back into his seat.

'It's no sin to need assistance,' he remarked drily, as she eased her leg into a more comfortable position, and she wondered why she felt so absurdly sensitive with him. If she wasn't careful, she was going to arouse his suspicions as to why that should be so, and she couldn't even explain it to herself.

She always felt a certain sense of trepidation when she got into a car these days. It wasn't that she hadn't driven since the accident. On the contrary, she had insisted on replacing the car she had wrecked with a new one almost immediately. An automatic, of course, which for some time lay idle in the garage. But lately she had gained in confidence, and only the fear of the car breaking down had deterred her from attempting the drive to Paget.

Conor drove well: fairly fast, but not uncomfortably so, and any lingering fears left her. He traversed the narrow streets and intersections with an ease that spoke of long familiarity, and she guessed he knew the place better than she did these days. And obviously, he was used to driving in this country. She realised she had been in danger of thinking him a stranger to Paget.

They arrived at the Ship Inn, in what seemed an inordinately short space of time, and Olivia's fingers tightened round her handbag. 'Well—thank you,' she murmured politely, glancing up at the wooded façade of the building. 'I appreci——'

'When can I see you again?'

Conor's husky enquiry cut into her careful words of gratitude, and when she turned her head she found he had turned at right angles to the wheel, his arm along the back of the seat behind her.

Olivia gave a nervous laugh. 'Oh, I don't think——'

'Why not?' His expression flattened. 'As we haven't seen one another for God knows how many years, don't you think we ought to at least share a meal, for old times' sake?'

Olivia swallowed. 'You don't want to have a meal with me!' she protested.

'Why not?' he repeated.

'Well . . . I was—your mother's friend, not yours. You don't have to feel any obligation towards me.'

Conor slumped lower in his seat. 'Who said anything about an obligation?'

'Even so——'

'Even so nothing. OK. You were like my aunt, right? If it pleases you to remember the relationship like that, then no problem. How about me taking my favourite "aunt" to dinner? Like tonight, maybe. If you've not got anything else on.'

'I can't tonight.'

The words just sprang from her tongue, the refusal as necessary to her as her independence had been earlier. But there was no way she was going to put herself through any more torment today—physical or otherwise.

'Tomorrow, then,' he said, without hesitation, and, to her dismay, his fingers began plucking at the scarf she wore about her shoulders. He had nice hands, she noticed unwillingly, long-fingered and capable, and brown, like the rest of him. Or the part of him she could see, she amended shortly, uncomfortably aware of where her thoughts were taking her. *God*! She shivered. What was the matter with her?

'I—don't know,' she muttered, wishing she had the strength to be more decisive. But the truth was that, in spite of everything, she wasn't totally convinced she didn't want to see him again. After all, she defended herself, he was Sally's son. Surely, it was what *she* would have wanted—for them to be friends. But it was the ambivalence of her feelings that troubled her. That, and the sure knowledge that nothing was as simple as it seemed.

Conor toyed with the patterned scarf between his fingers. 'Tomorrow,' he said, the warmth of his breath moistening her ear. 'I'll pick you up at seven o'clock. What do you say?'

'I . . .' Olivia opened her mouth to make some further protest, and then closed it again. His face was much

nearer now, and although his eyes were averted she had
an unhindered view of his long lashes. They were sun-
bleached these days, she noticed, like his hair, but just
as vulnerable as she remembered them. 'Oh—all right,'
she gave in weakly, knowing herself for a fool, and when
he lifted his head she was sure of it. There was nothing
vulnerable in his gaze at all. His face was quite ex-
pressionless. Whatever she thought she had seen in his
expression was just wishful thinking.

But then he smiled. 'Great,' he said, withdrawing his
arm from the back of the seat, and thrusting open his
door. Then, before she had a chance to forestall him,
he had circled the car and opened her door, offering her
his hand to help her out.

'I can manage,' she exclaimed, frustration giving way
to irritation, as annoyance at her weakness overwhelmed
her. She shouldn't have allowed any of this to happen,
she thought angrily, aware that the frown that drew her
dark brows together did nothing for her appearance. But
she had had a chance to end this association here and
now, and she had blown it. Now she was committed to
a whole evening in the company of a man she hardly
knew.

CHAPTER THREE

THE next day and a half dragged.

It wasn't, Olivia assured herself, that she was looking forward to the evening ahead with pleasure. On the contrary, every time she thought about it she was struck anew with how unnecessary it seemed. It wasn't as if they had anything in common these days, she thought frustratedly. The Conor of today bore no resemblance to the helpless youth he'd been.

No, what she really wanted to do was get it over with. They would have dinner—possibly here at the inn—and share a stilted exchange of news. She would tell him some of the more amusing cases she had dealt with—carefully omitting any reference to her marriage—and he would talk about his job at the rehabilitation unit, and perhaps explain the differences between treatment here and in the United States.

All incredibly polite—and incredibly boring, she thought fretfully, particularly for someone whose taste in women obviously ran to the more glamorous specimens of her species. Like Sharon Holmes, for example, she acknowledged, irritated that she could remember the girl's name so clearly.

And when, the following evening, she seated herself in front of her dressing-table mirror to apply her make-up, it was Sharon's face that persisted in filling her mind. Why was it that blondes always seemed to hog the limelight? she wondered. Was it that blonde hair usually went with a peaches-and-cream complexion, so different from her own pale features?

Whatever the reason, she wasn't here to compete with Conor's girlfriend, she thought crossly. Her only desire was that he shouldn't be ashamed of her. And if that meant wearing a dress instead of trousers, and trying to tame her curly hair into a more sophisticated style, so be it. She owed it to herself to do the best she could.

The folds of the satin wrap she had put on after her bath parted as she leant towards the mirror. The cleavage it exposed was not as generous as it had once been, and she had never been over-endowed in that department. Now, the lacy bra she was wearing was hardly necessary. She had only put it on to satisfy a need.

Clutching the lapels together again, Olivia viewed her appearance without encouragement. There wasn't much she could do with dark eyes that seemed to fill her face, or improve about bone structure that was definitely angular. She supposed she could disguise the hollows in her cheeks with a cream foundation, and use a cherry lipstick to give colour to her mouth. Thank God her lashes were long and thick and didn't need mascara. She had never been particularly expert when it came to using cosmetics.

With the make-up applied, and her black hair coiled into a rather precarious knot on top of her head, she pronounced herself satisfied. Well, she would have to be, wouldn't she? she thought grimly, pulling the only dress she had brought with her out of the wardrobe. She looked older than she was, but what of it? At least she wasn't afraid of her maturity. People would probably think she was Conor's mother. Dear God, why had she let herself in for this?

The dress was a warm Laura Ashley print, in shades of russet, green and brown. Its main attraction to Olivia was that it had a high neck and long sleeves, and the hem was only a few inches off her ankles. With opaque black tights to complete her cover, Olivia was reasonably satisfied with the result. Low-heeled shoes were not unattractive on someone of her height and slenderness, and she was glad that the days of precarious heels were a thing of the past.

It was a few minutes to seven when she looked at her watch, and she wondered what she ought to do. She supposed she should go downstairs and wait for him, but ought she to take her coat with her? She had spent a good half-hour that morning brushing the dried mud stains off it. But if she took it with her, would Conor see that as an indication that she expected him to take her out?

It was a problem. The last thing she wanted was for him to feel obliged to take her to some expensive restaurant. The food at the Ship was good and wholesome, if a little lacking in imagination, but it suited her. Yet if she appeared without her coat and she needed it it would mean another trip upstairs to collect it. Something she would much rather not have to do at present.

She was still prevaricating when the phone rang. It startled her, as much because she guessed who it would be as from any shock at the sound. But the thought that it might be Conor ringing to say he couldn't make it made her move quickly to answer it. Perhaps he'd had an emergency. Doctors were notoriously unreliable.

Picking up the receiver, she put it to her ear. 'Hello?'

'Liv?' Conor's voice was unmistakable. 'You ready?'

As I'll ever be, thought Olivia drily, but she answered in the affirmative.

'Good. D'you want me to come up and fetch you, or will you come down? I thought we might have a drink in the bar before we go.'

Before we go! Olivia grimaced. So, they were dining somewhere else, after all. 'I'll come down,' she said crisply, not wanting another exhibition of his high-handedness. He had insisted on seeing her up to her room the day before, and embarrassed her horribly. Only her frozen expression had deterred Mrs Drake from making some comment when she served her supper that evening, and the idea of having a drink with him now, in the bar, was not appealing. Perhaps she could persuade him that they'd be better off drinking somewhere else. If she could forestall him, before he ordered himself a drink . . .

'OK.'

Conor accepted her decision without argument, and Olivia hurriedly collected her coat and handbag. The sooner she got downstairs, the better, she thought. If she knew Tom Drake, Conor was unlikely to be left on his own for long.

Thankfully her leg was much better this evening. She hadn't ventured out of the inn since the previous morning, and the prolonged rest had done it good. Happily, the weather had remained cold and windy, with snow flurries, so she had not had to explain her reasons for missing her usual walk.

The low-ceilinged stairway came down into the narrow reception hall of the inn. There was a small kiosk, which opened off the Drakes' living quarters, where guests went to check-in, or collect their mail. There were doors to the tiny dining-room, and to the smoke-room and bar, the latter commandeered by locals at this time of the year. And as Olivia couldn't see Conor hanging about the hallway, she guessed he had joined them. After all, he was a local, she reflected, her spirits sinking at the thought.

Deciding that if she put her coat on she would at least look as if she was waiting to leave, Olivia slid her arms into the sleeves. Then, as there was no one about, she checked her wavy image in the smoked glass of a lantern. Oh, well, she thought wearily, she might as well get it over with.

But, when she entered the bar, she couldn't immediately see Conor. It was already fairly busy, probably due to the fact that most people were coming out early to avoid the icy roads later. But, although there were several people standing at the bar, he wasn't one of them, and it wasn't until he spoke her name that she turned her head and saw them.

Yes, *them*, she saw incredulously, as her eyes took in the fact that Conor was not alone. But it wasn't Tom Drake, who was sipping a glass of white wine, and shifting his weight from one foot to the other, beside Conor. It was Sharon Holmes, wide-eyed and sultry-lipped, wearing a short-jacketed scarlet suit that exposed most of her shapely legs.

Olivia could not have been more taken aback. In spite of what she had seen the day before, and their obvious familiarity with one another, she had never considered that Conor might bring his girlfriend tonight. It had been foolish, she saw with hindsight, to imagine his invitation had meant anything more than a token homage to duty. She had been his mother's friend, she had been around for most of his early life, and he felt sorry for her. She had embarrassed all of them by appearing out of the blue like that, so he had offered her dinner as a means of absolving his responsibility. He didn't really want to spend the evening in her company. In fact, he was just as reluctant as she was. How could she have thought otherwise?

Now he left his companion to come and greet her, but although she attempted to proffer a nervous hand he ignored it, and brushed his lips against her cheek. The odour of the shaving foam he had used invaded her nostrils, along with the distinctly masculine scent of his body, and she caught her breath. But she bore the salutation valiantly, and even managed a smile when he drew back.

'How's the leg this evening?' he asked softly, his words for her ears only, and she said, 'Better, thank you,' in a stiff tone that couldn't help but reveal her feelings. But what else could he expect? she thought tensely. She was still recovering from shock.

He looked even more attractive this evening, though his clothes were not as formal as she had expected. Probably because she was too accustomed to dining with older men, she reflected ruefully. After all, even Stephen had been almost ten years older than she was. None the less, Conor's button-down collar—worn without a tie, she noticed—and black corded trousers were decidedly casual. The fine wool jacket he was wearing with them was a sort of dusty green, and matched neither his shirt nor his trousers. Yet, for all that, the clothes suited him, accentuating still more the differences between them.

Now, as if afraid she was missing something, Sharon joined them, and Olivia felt as dowdy as a sparrow with two gorgeous birds of paradise. No, not a sparrow, a starling, she corrected drily. Sparrows were small and compact, not long-legged and ungainly.

'Hello, Mrs Perry,' she said, once again relegating Olivia to an older generation. 'Isn't it cold? I bet you wish you'd chosen the Caribbean for your holiday.'

Olivia's smile felt glued to her mouth. 'Oh—yes,' she murmured, wondering exactly what Conor had told Sharon about her. He had evidently mentioned that she was married. She just hoped he hadn't said too much about the crash.

'Let me get you a drink,' suggested Conor swiftly. 'You two can find somewhere to sit down.'

'I'm quite capable of standing,' said Olivia, well aware that they hadn't been occupying one of the wooden tables when she came in. She gave Conor a resentful look, and then looked away again. 'I'll have a gin and tonic, thank you. No ice.'

Conor inclined his head, and although he didn't say anything she sensed his indignation. Well, she thought defensively, she wasn't an *old* lady. Not as old as he was implying, anyway. He might mean well, but she didn't like it. Not when she already felt like the ripest gooseberry in the basket.

'Shall we sit down?' asked Sharon, after Conor had departed to get her drink, and Olivia sighed. Oh, what the hell? she thought; perhaps she was being foolish in refusing the opportunity to take her weight off her leg. She'd already had one experience of what could happen

when she acted recklessly. Her present predicament was
a direct result.

So, 'If you like,' she agreed offhandedly, and followed the girl to a table in the corner.

Sharon set her drink on the table in front of her, and
then looked thoughtfully at her companion. 'Conor says
you're a lawyer,' she remarked. 'That's not how you got
to know Mrs Brennan, is it?'

Mrs Brennan! For a moment, Olivia didn't understand who she was talking about. Her thoughts had been
so wrapped up with Conor and this awful situation that
it took several seconds for comprehension to dawn.

'Oh—you mean Sally,' she said hurriedly, and Sharon
gave a nod. 'No—I—as I believe I told you, my grandmother used to live next door. At number seventeen Gull
Rise, I mean. I lived with her after my own parents died.
That's how I met—all the Brennans.'

'I see.' Sharon studied her consideringly. 'So you've
known Conor a long time.'

'A—fairly long time,' conceded Olivia reluctantly,
realising that Conor had apparently been less lo-
quacious than she'd thought. She endeavoured to change
the subject. 'Do—er—do you work with Conor, Miss
Holmes?'

'Heavens, call me Sharon!' She uttered a girlish laugh.
'Miss Holmes makes me sound so *old*!' She let the implications of this sink in, and then added carelessly, 'No,
my friend and I run a boutique in Ashford. I don't think
Conor likes career-minded women.'

Or intelligent ones either, thought Olivia maliciously,
meeting the other woman's eyes, and glimpsing avidity
in their depths.

'Oh—present company excepted, of course,' Sharon
added, clapping a rueful hand over her mouth. 'But
you're different, Mrs Perry. You're—well, you're sort
of——'

'—older?' suggested Olivia pleasantly, deciding there
was no point in antagonising Sharon needlessly. It wasn't

Sharon's fault she was here, after all. It wasn't Sharon's fault that Olivia had mistaken Conor's motives.

'Well, yes,' the girl was continuing now, and then rushed on, as though Olivia was a confidante, 'You wouldn't believe what Conor has to put up with, working with so many women. Women doctors, that is. The women patients get a fix on him, of course, but that's different. They're sort of dependent, aren't they? But some of those women medics are man-hungry!' She rolled her eyes. 'I don't know what causes it. I suppose hospitals have always been known for stuff like that. Life and death! It sort of brings you close to nature. Regular hotbeds of intrigue, aren't they?' she added, with a giggle. 'If you'll excuse the pun!'

Olivia shook her head. She had the feeling Sharon watched too many soap operas. 'Did—er—did Conor tell you that?' she enquired mildly, and the girl reached determinedly for her glass.

'Not in so many words,' she admitted, but her eyes were moving past Olivia, her lips parting to allow her tongue free access to her upper lip. 'Here's Con,' she added, somewhat unnecessarily, and Olivia's lips tightened. The girl's expression was as hungry as any man-hunter's at that moment, and she wondered if Sharon was really as ingenuous as her words would have her believe.

'One gin and tonic, as requested,' Conor announced, setting a glass containing a measure of gin in front of her. He delivered himself of the small bottle of tonic water to go with it, and then took the stool beside Sharon. He had got himself a drink, too, Olivia noticed. Orange juice, by the look of it, and her eyebrows lifted almost involuntarily. 'I'm driving,' he said, reading her expression all too easily. 'Cheers!' He lifted his glass towards her.

'Cheers,' Olivia echoed, adding a splash of tonic to the gin, and taking a generous mouthful. Perhaps she should have chosen something more innocuous, she re-

flected, aware that she was probably going to need to
keep her wits about her this evening. But right then she
needed the boost that only alcohol could give her.

'I've been telling Mrs Perry about the clinic,' said
Sharon, not altogether truthfully, and Olivia guessed she
was warning her against making some unwary comment.
'You wouldn't believe what people will do to get money
to support their drug habit.' She smiled artlessly into
Conor's eyes. 'Con's ever so patient with them. I some-
times think I should become one of his addicts myself.
I might get more attention that way.'

Olivia didn't know where to look. Instead of returning Sharon's gaze, Conor had turned his eyes on
her, and she wondered if he knew how uncomfortable
she felt. But, of course, he must do, she thought bitterly,
remembering how effortlessly he had read her thoughts
before. He was probably enjoying this. Waiting to see
how she would react to the situation.

But, to her surprise, it was Conor who saved her embarrassment. 'I'd guess Liv has to deal with enough drug-
related offences, without wanting to spend the evening
talking about them,' he remarked evenly. 'And call her
Olivia, will you? She's not my mother!'

'Oh, thanks!'

Olivia's mollification was short-lived, as Conor's
mouth curled into a most infuriating smile. The pig! He
was enjoying this, she thought angrily, glaring at him.
But one thing was certain. She was not going to pander
to his ego.

'My pleasure,' he responded silkily, and Sharon put
her glass back on the table with a decided snap.

'I've told—Olivia—about the boutique,' she intervened, obviously not enthusiastic about using the other
woman's Christian name, but unwilling to be ignored.
'She might like to call in some time. We sell clothes to—
to everyone.'

Including older women, appended Olivia drily, but at
least Sharon's words had attracted Conor's attention.

'I'm sure Liv appreciates the offer, but I doubt she'll take you up on it,' he said. 'It's quite a trek to Ashford, and Liv doesn't drive.'

'Yes, I do.' Despite her misgivings, Olivia couldn't let him get away with that. 'I admit I haven't brought the car with me. But I do have one. In spite of everything,' she finished, a trifle smugly.

Conor's gaze was interrogative now. 'You've had approval from your doctor?'

'Yes.' Olivia took another swig of gin, resenting his implication.

'And it's an automatic, I presume?'

'Yes,' she said again. 'Really, Conor, I'm not an invalid! However disappointing that may be!'

It was an unforgivable thing to say, and she regretted it almost at once. Looking away towards the bar, where Tom Drake was leaning on the counter, chatting with one of his cronies, she wondered if she could just make some excuse and join them. Anything would be better than spending the evening fending off Sharon's spite and Conor's sympathy.

An uneasy silence had fallen now, and she was almost relieved when Sharon said, 'Oughtn't we to be leaving? You did say you'd booked the table for eight, didn't you, Con? And if the roads are slippy...'

'What? Oh—yes, I guess so.' Conor swallowed the remainder of the orange juice in his glass, and set it back on the table. He paused, and then said quietly, 'Are you ready, Liv? You can leave the rest of your drink, if you want to. We'll have some wine when we get to the Roundhouse.'

The Roundhouse. Olivia absorbed the name he had used without recognition. But, contrarily, she chose to empty the contents of her glass before rising, meeting his gaze with a defiant one of her own, because she didn't have an alternative.

If Sharon was aware of the undercurrent between them as they drove the three miles to the restaurant, she chose not to acknowledge it. Instead, she kept up an incessant chatter about the girl she worked with at the boutique, and other friends Conor seemed to know. And, as Olivia was ensconced in the back of the car, and didn't know any of these people anyway, her isolation was complete.

The Roundhouse turned out to be a converted windmill, whose stark white-painted façade belied the colourful warmth within. A mirror-backed bar adjoined the circular restaurant, and there was a comfortable air of bustle, and the delightful smell of good food.

Sharon hadn't brought an overcoat with her, but Conor suggested Olivia might like to leave hers in the cloakroom. It would be easier than having it draped over her chair all evening, and she was glad of the opportunity to escape for a few moments.

There were two women already in the cloakroom, chatting to the attendant, but Olivia was aware that their eyes were drawn to her as she limped across the floor. She was beginning to realise how frustrating it could be to be disabled. She wished people would just ignore her, or treat her like everyone else. She didn't want their sympathy. She didn't need it.

The face that looked back at her from the mirror was no more appealing. She should never have worn the cherry lipstick, she thought. It looked too bright and garish, and the speed with which she had downed the gin and tonic had brought an unnatural blush of colour to her cheeks. It wouldn't surprise her if Sharon thought she was having hot flushes, she brooded cynically. It would be all one with the way the girl was treating her. And she wasn't improving matters by acting like a shrew.

The truth was that she had got out of the habit of being in company, she admitted. Since the accident, she had tended to avoid social gatherings. Which was one of the reasons why returning to work had not been such a good idea. She seemed to have lost the ability to communicate with people. She needed a breathing space. A time for her mind to mend, as well as her body.

To her relief, the two women departed before she was ready to hand over her coat. And then, delivering it to the attendant, she discovered she had made another error of judgement. They hadn't been gossiping about her at all.

'Isn't it awful,' the attendant sighed, 'losing a child so young? I expect you heard that lady say her daughter had just died of leukaemia, didn't you? Only thirteen, she was. Poor woman. How do you get over something like that?'

Olivia made some suitable rejoinder, and emerged from the cloakroom feeling duly chastened. When she saw Conor and Sharon waiting for her by the bar she determined to be more positive. It wasn't their fault she wasn't enjoying the evening, she told herself. She was far too sensitive about herself, and they were bearing the brunt. She had to stop looking for trouble, and stop being so touchy.

'I've got you a glass of white wine,' Conor said now, handing it to her, and Olivia squashed the unworthy thought that he was treating her like Sharon. All the same, she couldn't help wondering if he doubted her ability to hold her liquor. Did he imagine she must have been tipsy to have made that insulting remark earlier?

With her mind about to hop on to the old tack, she remembered what she had promised herself as she came to join them. Conor had bought her a drink, that was all. She ought to be grateful. Besides, the wine was nice, and probably much better for her.

'Our table's almost ready,' said Sharon, checking one of the gold studs she wore in her ear with a scarlet-tipped finger. 'The food here's really special. You ought to try the watercress mousse. It practically melts in your mouth.'

'I may do that.' Olivia was pleased to hear her voice sounded reasonably friendly as she responded to Sharon's suggestion. 'Do you come here often? I suppose it's fairly handy.'

'Sometimes. If we don't feel like making a meal,' responded Sharon cosily, giving Conor an intimate smile. 'But we don't mind staying in, do we, Con? We don't need a lot of entertaining. We can entertain ourselves.'

'I'm sure you can.'

Olivia buried her nose in her glass and wished for the waiter to come and save her from herself. But dear God, did the girl have to be so obvious? They lived together. Conor had as good as said as much. So what of it? It didn't mean anything to her.

To her relief, her prayers were answered, the dark-coated *maître d'* arrived at that moment to escort them to their table near the window. In the polite process of choosing where each of them was going to sit, Olivia was able to relax, and she was happy to use the excuse of studying the menu to avoid any further eye-contact with Conor.

But when their orders had been taken there was nothing to prevent him from looking directly at her, and she wondered if it had been such a good idea to avoid the seat next to his. And, in an effort to try and restore the conversation to a more casual footing, she determinedly asked him how his aunt was, and whether she still lived in Florida.

'Still in the same house,' agreed Conor, lounging indolently in his chair. 'We're a consistent family. We like familiarity. And my aunt has a lot of friends in Port Douglas.'

'I'm sure.' Olivia ignored the reproof, and persevered, 'I suppose your cousins are married now. Do they live in Port Douglas, too?'

'One of them does,' Conor conceded evenly. 'The other lives in California. But they come home fairly regularly. It's a big house. There's lots of room.'

'And I suppose you go home fairly regularly, too,' Olivia ventured, feeling a little more confident, but when she lifted her head Conor's expression was less than encouraging.

'Paget is my home,' he declared, his eyes as cool as ice-floes. 'Why else d'you think I wanted to keep the house?'

'Well...' Olivia shrugged. 'I thought—after living in the United States for so many years——'

'Only nine years, Liv. I've been back in England for quite some time. I was a resident at a hospital in London, before I came back to Paget.'

Olivia licked her dry lips. 'Oh! I didn't know.'

'How could you? You were too busy with your own life.' Conor almost made it sound like a criticism. 'So, tell us,' he continued, 'what does your husband do for a living?'

Olivia hesitated. Knowing what she did about Conor, there was no earthly reason why she should choose to keep her divorce a secret any longer. But the idea of confessing her inability to sustain a relationship to Sharon brought an unwelcome tightness to her throat.

'He—I—a sales manager,' she got out jerkily, immediately ashamed of her dishonesty. 'He—works for an electrical manufacturer,' she added, when it became apparent that something more was needed. 'Food processors, blenders, that sort of stuff.'

'Ooh, I bet you have all the latest gadgets in your kitchen,' exclaimed Sharon, half enviously, and Olivia felt even worse.

'Not necessarily,' she mumbled, and once again she was saved from further embarrassment by the arrival of the wine waiter. The discussion that ensued erased any further need to elaborate, and happily Sharon seemed to prefer talking about her own affairs to anyone else's.

The food lived up to Sharon's prediction, and although Olivia found it difficult to do it justice she couldn't deny that the delicate mousse and juicy steak were every bit as delicious as she could wish. But, even though Sharon monopolised Conor's attention for most of the meal, her appetite was practically non-existent. In consequence, she drank rather more of the fine claret Conor had ordered than perhaps she should have done, and when they rose from the table her unsteadiness wasn't wholly the result of her injury.

As though sensing her uncertainty, Conor moved round the table to put his hand beneath her elbow, and although Olivia cast him an indignant look she couldn't deny she needed his support. Just till she got her balance, she told herself, as his strong fingers bit into her arm. He probably resented having to do this just as much as she did.

'Go get Olivia's coat, Sharon,' Conor ordered, as soon as they reached the foyer, and although it obviously wasn't a popular request the girl didn't argue.

'I could have got it myself,' protested Olivia, after the young woman had departed clutching the redemption ticket. She endeavoured to move away from him. 'Thank you. I can manage now.'

'Can you?' Conor didn't look convinced.

'Yes.' Olivia jerked her arm out of his grasp and backed away. 'I wish you'd stop behaving as if I shouldn't be out without a keeper!'

'Stop exaggerating, Liv!' Conor's mouth compressed. 'All I did was hold your arm.'

'Because you thought I was in danger of showing you up!' retorted Olivia hotly. 'Well, don't worry, Conor. I won't let it happen again.'

'No?'

'No.' Olivia glanced swiftly around to make sure their conversation was not being overheard, and then added grimly, 'I'm sure you'll be as glad when this evening is over as I will. It was kind of you to invite me, but I think you'll agree it was a mistake!'

Conor's face darkened, but Sharon's return prevented him from making a reply. Which was just as well, thought Olivia ruefully, as the doorman helped her to put her coat on. Judging from his expression, it would not have been anything good.

The journey back to the Ship was accomplished without incident. Even Sharon had little to say, beyond commenting on how full she felt. She was looking forward to going to bed, she added. She felt *so* sleepy. But not too sleepy, Olivia hazarded, with a cynical twist to her lips.

However, when they arrived at the inn, Conor turned off the car's engine. 'I won't be long,' Olivia heard him say to Sharon, as she was levering herself out on to the pavement, and she caught her breath. Dear heaven, she thought, surely he wasn't going to insist on seeing her up to her room tonight? Not with his girlfriend waiting, and the car in danger of losing its heat.

She was standing beside the car when he came round to join her, and although their last words had hardly been cordial she strove for a friendly tone.

'Thank you—both of you—for the evening,' she murmured, aware that Sharon had lowered her window to hear what was said. 'It's been lovely——'

'I'm glad to hear it,' responded Conor, and she wondered if only she could hear the irony in his voice. Ignoring her resistance, he turned her forcefully towards the building. 'Let's go, hmm? It's bloody cold out here.'

Olivia glared at him, but he had her at a disadvantage, and he knew it. So, instead of fighting him, she cast a helpless smile in Sharon's direction. 'Goodnight,' she called, with rather more warmth than she had shown the girl thus far. 'I won't keep him.'

Fortunately the lobby was empty, though there was plenty of noise coming from the bar, and Olivia was able to wrench her arm from Conor's grasp. 'Don't do this to me,' she warned, but he followed her up the stairs anyway, and by the time she reached her door she was panting from exertion.

'All right,' she said, backing up against the door as he loomed over her, his shadow elongated by the light from the stairs. 'Now will you leave? You've done everything you possibly can to humiliate me. So please, just—go away.'

'How?'

'How what?' Olivia was confused.

'How have I humiliated you?' asked Conor, propping his shoulder against the wall beside her. 'What did I do?'

'What did you . . . ?' Olivia broke off and gripped the handle of the door behind her, wishing she could just slip inside without further argument. 'Look—I really don't want to talk about it. Can't we just say goodnight? I—just want to go to bed.'

Conor frowned, then he put out his hand and lifted a tendril of dark hair that had fallen beside her ear. 'Are you mad because I brought Sharon?' he asked softly, and Olivia was so shocked she was sure she must have misheard him.

'I—beg your——'

'I thought it might make things easier for you,' he added, as she turned horrified eyes in his direction. 'You seemed so nervous of me yesterday morning, and I guess I was a little nervous myself. I've thought about how I'd feel seeing you again after so long, and I was so afraid of screwing up!'

Conor? Afraid? Olivia couldn't believe it. 'Oh, really,' she began, but he wouldn't let her continue.

'I mean it,' he said, his hand dropping to the belt that rode low on his hips. 'Hear me out. Please.'

Olivia shrugged. 'All right.' She was purposely not looking at him, but she couldn't help watching those strong supple fingers easing their way under the taut leather. She was suddenly aware that she was wondering how they would feel touching her. And, although she stifled the thought instantly, its memory remained.

'I know I always say the wrong thing,' he muttered now, and she was aware of his eyes moving over her face. 'Hell, don't I?' he added. 'Tell me about it. And I know your opinion of me is coloured by the way I behaved that time I came to see you in London, but I can't do anything about that. Honestly, Liv, you don't know how much I've regretted mouthing off as I did. I was just a stupid idiot, and if I hurt your feelings, then believe me, I'm sorry.'

Olivia took a deep breath. 'Conor, it really doesn't matter that much——'

'Yes, it does.' As if he couldn't help himself, his fingers moved to straighten the lapel of her coat. 'Liv, I wanted us to start afresh. I wanted us to be friends.'

Olivia lifted her shoulders. 'We are friends——'

'Are we?'

'Yes.' Olivia was beginning to feel the strain of standing in one position for too long, but it wasn't just her physical discomfort that made her add swiftly, 'Honestly, Conor, I've forgotten all about that time in London.' It was a lie, but he was not to know that. 'Heavens, it was years ago. Now, don't you think you ought to go? I'm sure Sharon must be getting very impatient——'

'So, you'll let me see you again?'

'What?' Olivia caught her breath. 'Oh, I—I don't think so.'

'Why not?' He looked down into her anxious brown eyes, and, before she could stop him, he had cupped her face in his hand. 'If we're friends,' he reminded her roughly. His eyes darkened, and as his fingers moved against her flesh she could feel their hard pressure clear down to her toes. 'Hot damn, I wish you weren't married,' he groaned suddenly, and, bending his head, he brushed her parted lips with his mouth.

CHAPTER FOUR

AT TWO o'clock the next morning, Olivia got up to take a sleeping pill. Staring at her reflection in the mirror above the wash-basin in the bathroom, she tried to get what had happened into perspective. But she couldn't. She was too tired—and too confused—to make any sense of it at all.

Why had Conor kissed her? As she fished one of the capsules out of the bottle, she acknowledged that that was the real reason she was finding it so difficult to sleep. His action had taken her completely by surprise, and while she was sure she was exaggerating its importance, the fact remained that he had kissed her mouth.

Filling a glass with water, she chided herself for allowing him to disconcert her like this. Heavens, she thought, as she tossed the capsule to the back of her throat and swallowed it with a gulp of the ice-cold water, it wasn't as if it was anything out of the ordinary. Men and women kissed all the time. In the circles she moved in, it was an accepted form of salutation between the sexes.

But it was the way he had kissed her that troubled her most. She was almost convinced she had felt his tongue probing her lips. God! She had been as shocked as a virgin on her first date. And when he'd made that crack about wishing she was single she'd felt as guilty as any cheating wife.

Her stomach heaved as the water churned up the mixture of gin and wine she had drunk earlier. The alcohol was probably responsible for her feeling so overstimulated, she reflected. Her body was tired, but her brain wasn't getting the message.

She crawled back into bed, and tried to tuck her freezing toes into the hem of her nightshirt. She was so cold, in spite of the thick quilt that covered her. Sharon wouldn't have that problem. Not with Conor's muscled body coiled around her...

Dammit!

Olivia shifted crossly on to her other side. Where had that thought come from? For heaven's sake, she wasn't jealous of the girl, was she? Just because Conor had kissed her, surely she wasn't allowing herself to think she had some claim to his affections? Dear lord, he was only a boy! Thinking of him as anything else was—was ridiculous!

But he wasn't a boy, a small voice reminded her drily. He was a man, in every sense of the word, and an attractive one at that. No wonder Sharon had said those women at the clinic hung on his every word. It would be incredibly easy to be seduced by his lazy eyes and smiling mouth.

But not for her, she chided herself fiercely. She wasn't like those other women. She was just someone who had known his mother, and because of that he felt a certain closeness to her. But it wasn't the kind of closeness he had with Sharon. It had no—sexual—connotation.

She pressed her hand to her throat. Just thinking about him with Sharon brought an unpleasant tightness to her breasts, and she was aware of them peaking against the soft cotton. The abrasion was unwelcome, and she ran her hand half impatiently down her body, trying to soothe her perverse flesh. But her arousal stemmed from another part of her body, and she rolled on to her stomach to try and subdue its craving.

All the same, the knowledge that she could feel like this, with so little provocation, was alarming. In spite of the fact that it was almost two years since she and Stephen had shared a bed, she had never before felt she was missing anything. On the contrary, she had grown used to regarding herself as a dispassionate woman. That

was why she was so good at her job. And, although she
had never objected to Stephen's lovemaking, she had felt
no great eagerness for it either.

Which was why what was happening to her now was
so disturbing. It was like shedding a layer of skin, and
finding a stranger underneath. She didn't recognise
herself, and she wasn't sure she wanted to. It was safer
to stay immune from the hungers of the flesh.

Nevertheless, when she awakened the next morning it
was to discover that the problem hadn't gone away. Not
that that was so surprising really. She had spent what
was left of the night in a haze of heat and sweat, and
sexual frustration. But one thing was certain: she had
to get herself under control before she saw Conor again.
She would hate him to find out that his careless kiss had
caused such an emotional furore inside her.

A cool shower worked wonders, and by the time she
had pulled on a pair of dark green leggings and a thigh-
length sweater and brushed her unruly hair into a severe
knot she was almost convinced she had been exaggerating. The mind was a funny thing, she thought, following Mrs Drake's ample form across the tiny dining-
room later. It was open to suggestion—even self-deceit.

'Oh—there was a phone call for you earlier,' Mrs
Drake exclaimed, after Olivia was seated. She pulled an
apologetic face. 'I almost forgot. It was young Dr
Brennan.'

'Was it?' Olivia could feel the familiar warmth enveloping her. What price self-deception now?

'Yes.' Mrs Drake folded her hands across her midriff.
''Course, Tom put the call through to your room, but
you didn't answer. I said to him, I did, you must be in
the shower. Can't hear that phone ringing when the water's running, and that's a fact.'

'I see.' Olivia was grateful for the warning. 'Um—did
he leave a message?'

'Only that he'd ring again later,' declared Mrs Drake
ruefully. 'Sounded real disappointed, he did. Have—er—
have you two known one another long?'

Olivia looked down at her place mat, with its black
and white lithograph of the Romney, Hythe and
Dymchurch railway. This was what she had been afraid
of, of course. So far, she had managed to maintain her
anonymity, but Conor's intervention had given her in-
quisitive landlady an opening.

'Quite long,' she replied at last, pretending to be
interested in the morning newspaper. She glanced up as
Mrs Drake still stood there, miming surprise. 'Just toast
and coffee, as usual, please.'

It was hardly polite, and in other circumstances she
would never have been so abrupt, but Mrs Drake was
far too garrulous to confide in. However, she had bar-
gained without taking the other woman's persistence into
consideration. 'Had dinner with him and young Sharon
last night, didn't you?' she declared, flicking a speck of
dust from the table with the hem of her apron. 'Nice
girl, Sharon. Her mother and me went to school together.
Connie Simmons, as was. Family lived over towards
Witterthorpe. Her mother's an auxiliary at the clinic
where Dr Brennan works.'

'Really?'

The coolness of Olivia's tone was in direct opposition
to the turmoil of her thoughts. Somehow, she hadn't
thought of Sharon as having a family living locally. She
had assumed they'd met while Conor was working in
London. She hadn't imagined their relationship was so
short-lived.

'Yes—well . . .'

Mrs Drake shrugged, and, evidently deciding her guest
was unlikely to be any more forthcoming, she ambled
away. But, when she was alone, Olivia put the newspaper aside, and gazed unseeingly out of the window.
Of course, she could be wrong. Conor could have known
Sharon since they were at school, too. She wondered how

long they had been living together. And how serious the affair was.

Deciding she was becoming far too interested in Conor and his concerns, after breakfast Olivia collected her coat from her room and left the inn. She didn't tell the Drakes where she was going. And if Conor rang again they would have to tell him she still wasn't answering her phone. But right now, she needed some fresh air. A leisurely stroll across the marsh sounded very appealing.

The path took her over the sand-dunes, where clumps of tussocky grass held out against the encroaching sea, and out across the salt marshes, where sandpipers and herring gulls scavenged for food. It was a crisp morning—bright, but cold—and, beyond the break-water, the channel lay as still as a mill-pond. But, in spite of the lack of wind, the air was chilling, and even with her gloved hands tucked securely into her pockets Olivia could feel its bite.

But her leg felt much better, and she was relieved. Despite her restless night, a couple of days without any undue exertion had restored its fragile strength. Oh, she still had a bruise or two here and there, to add to her other scars. But nothing incapacitating, as she had first imagined.

She returned to the inn at lunchtime feeling considerably more optimistic. She had managed to pass the whole morning without thinking about Conor, or worrying what she was going to do about him. She had determinedly emptied her mind of all her personal problems, and even the prospect of returning to London didn't give her the sinking feeling it usually did.

'Did you have a nice walk, Mrs Perry?' Mrs Drake called from the reception kiosk as Olivia headed for the stairs, and she turned back good-naturedly.

'Very nice, thank you,' she replied, taking off her glove to push an unruly strand of hair out of her eyes. Then, deciding there was no point in resenting the woman's curiosity, she added, 'I went as far as the lighthouse. It was exhilarating.'

'Yes.' Mrs Drake smiled. 'You like your walks, don't you, Mrs Perry? Oh—before I forget, you had another call while you were out.' And, as Olivia stiffened, she fished a scrap of paper off the desk and held it out to her. 'I think it was your husband. Anyway——' she watched avidly as it was read '—he's left you a number where you can reach him.'

Olivia caught her lower lip between her teeth. Sure enough, the number was familiar to her. It was the number of Stephen's mobile phone. The one he never went anywhere without. As if she would ever forget it, she thought bitterly. But how had he known where to find her?

'Would you like me to dial the number for you?' suggested Mrs Drake hopefully, and Olivia guessed she was dying to know what was going on. After all, she had been staying at the inn over a week now, and so far she had had no contact with her husband.

'I'll ring him later,' Olivia murmured now, stuffing the scrap of paper into her pocket. And then, before she could stop herself, 'Um—that's all, is it? There weren't any other calls?'

'Dr Brennan didn't ring again, if that's what you mean,' declared Mrs Drake immediately, and Olivia thought how conspicuous she was, being the only guest. 'I expect he's busy with his patients. A queer lot some of them are, risking their health with heroin and suchlike. Can't see any sense in it myself. What's the point of injecting yourself with drugs to get some passing thrill, when most times they're too zonked out to enjoy it?'

Olivia gave a rueful smile. 'I really don't know,' she said, deciding there was no advantage to be gained in arguing the point. To hear the finer details of human need and social deprivation was not what Mrs Drake wanted from her. Besides, Olivia had no desire to get into a discussion where the particulars of her personal involvement became an issue.

She had started for the stairs again, when Mrs Drake called her back. 'Will you be wanting lunch, Mrs Perry?' she asked expectantly, and Olivia's breath escaped on a sigh.

'I—yes. Yes, in about fifteen minutes,' she agreed, grasping the gnarled banister with a determined hand.

'That'll give you time to make your call,' observed her landlady irrepressibly. 'It's steak and kidney pudding. Just what you need on a day like this.'

Olivia managed a smile, and then set off up the stairs, before Mrs Drake could think of anything else. It was ironic, really, but they had had more conversation in the last few hours than they had had in the whole of the past week. Olivia hoped it wasn't going to become a habit. She was too private a person these days to enjoy talking about herself.

Of course, she thought, as she shed her coat in her bedroom, Conor knew plenty about her now, and if he told Sharon, and Sharon told her mother... But no. Olivia refused to consider what might happen in that eventuality. If things became too awkward, she could always go somewhere else.

Still, sitting down to a plate of steaming steak and kidney pudding some time later, she hoped it wouldn't come to that. Until she had taken that ill-advised sojourn into the past, she had been enjoying her stay at the inn. Even if she had been born somewhere else, Paget was where she had her roots. She mustn't allow her unwelcome awareness of Conor to influence her actions.

In any case, at the moment, she decided she was more concerned with why Stephen should be trying to get in touch with her. It was months since she had seen him, months since they had had any communication, except via their respective solicitors. She hoped there was no hiccup over the finalising of their divorce. She wanted it to be done with. She wanted to be free.

The newspaper she had left by her plate at breakfast-time was still there, and she propped it against the salt and pepper shakers as she dipped her fork into the rich concoction of meat and vegetables on her plate. It tasted as delicious as it looked, and, in spite of her anxieties about Stephen, she was hungry. With the local news for company, she ate more enthusiastically than usual, only lifting her head when a shadow fell across the table.

She had expected it to be Mrs Drake, and she was getting ready to compliment her on the pudding, when she realised the intruder was not female. Leather brogues, a beige suit whose trousers needed pressing, and a flapping trench coat all added up to a masculine presence, and, for all she hoped it wasn't so, she wasn't really surprised when her eyes travelled up to her husband's triumphant face.

'May I join you?' he asked, already pulling out a chair, and seating himself opposite. 'Long time no see.'

'What are you doing here, Stephen?'

Olivia could barely keep the indignation out of her voice. She was already imagining what Mrs Drake would make of this, and the thought of her asking if he was staying the night, and having to explain that they didn't share a room any more, filled her with dismay. So much for keeping her affairs private, she reflected impatiently. What did he think he was doing?

'Don't sound so pleased to see me. I might get a swelled head,' he remarked now, easing his trench coat off his shoulders, and picking up the menu card. 'What's the food like here? What you're eating smells good.' He looked across at her, and his eyes moved speculatively over her face, noting the becoming colour her walk had given her, and approving the brightness of her eyes. 'I must say, it seems to be agreeing with you. You look good, Ollie, really good.'

'Don't call me Ollie,' she said, between her teeth. 'And how did you know where I was? I didn't even tell Mr Halliday my address.'

Stephen tapped his nose with a smug finger, and Olivia knew a growing sense of resentment that he should think he had the right to come here and disrupt her holiday. All right, so Paget wasn't everybody's idea of a relaxing location. That didn't alter the fact that she had chosen it because she wanted to be alone.

Mrs Drake's appearance was inevitable. Viewing her two guests with evident satisfaction, she made her way purposefully to their table, her face beaming. 'Will the gentleman be wanting lunch, too, Mrs Perry?' she asked, her eyes missing nothing of Stephen's appearance. 'This wouldn't be the gentleman that phoned earlier, would it? Oh—pleased to meet you, Mr Perry. I'm Mrs Drake.'

Olivia sat there, helpless, letting Stephen introduce himself with a feeling almost of disbelief. This couldn't be happening, she thought incredulously. She and Stephen had nothing more to say to one another. Their marriage was over. How dared he come here now and disrupt her privacy?

But, watching him practise his charm on Mrs Drake, she knew Stephen was completely indifferent to her feelings. He always had been. She should have divorced him long ago. She had only been fooling herself by imagining she could have ever made it work.

She couldn't even imagine what she had ever seen in him, these days. Of course, he was older than when she had married him—they both were—but the preceding years had not been exactly kind to Stephen. His hair was getting quite thin on top, and the belly, which spoke of too many liquid lunches, was beginning to bulge above his waistband. He looked what he was: a middle-aged travelling salesman, who had spent too many years on the road.

When Mrs Drake departed to get him a helping of the steak and kidney pudding, Olivia could hold back no longer. 'I don't know what you've come here for, Stephen,' she said, 'but, whatever it is, you're wasting your time. I'd like you to leave. As soon as possible.

Before Mrs Drake comes back would suit me very well. Don't worry about paying for your food. I'd consider it a privilege.'

'Oh, Ollie!' The reproachful diminutive grated on her nerves. 'What a way to treat your husband!'

'You're not my husband,' retorted Olivia, glad they were the only occupants of the dining-room. 'Stephen,' she sighed, 'don't you think this is rather silly? The last time I saw you—in the hospital, wasn't it?—you couldn't wait to exempt yourself from any responsibility for me.'

Stephen's face suffused with colour. 'That's not true, Ollie. You wanted the divorce, not me. And—and when you were at death's door, so to speak, I wanted to do anything I could to aid your recovery.'

Olivia's mouth compressed. 'Oh, really?'

'Yes, really.' Stephen seemed to gain confidence from affirming this belief. Indeed, she realised, he had a positive flair for self-deception. 'I would have cared for you, if that were what you'd wanted. But the doctors said your condition was critical, and I did what I could to relieve it.'

'Oh, Stephen!' The disgust was evident in Olivia's voice. 'Stop deluding yourself. You were shocked out of your mind when you saw my injuries. And an invalid wife was the last thing you wanted. Be honest for a change. It suited you to pull the plug.'

'Well, you're not an invalid now, are you?' he exclaimed, and Olivia blinked. 'As a matter of fact, you've never looked better. Losing weight obviously suits you. If you didn't wear your hair tugged back like that, you'd look a proper stunner.'

'Stephen!'

'Well, I've always thought you were a good-looking woman,' he replied defensively. 'I wouldn't have married you if I hadn't been attracted to you. No, I—regret what happened to us. We were a good couple. And old man Darcy always liked you.'

'Did he?' Olivia didn't know how she kept her temper, but she did. 'However,' she continued thinly, 'the opinion your boss has—or had—of me isn't an issue here——'

'But it is.' Stephen broke into her words, to lean across the table. 'It is an issue, Ollie. He—well, he's not at all happy about the divorce. He likes his salesmen to be married. He says it keeps their minds on the business, if you see what I mean.'

Olivia's breath gurgled in her throat. 'As you did, you mean?' she exclaimed chokingly, realising she could actually laugh at what had happened now. The whole affair seemed ludicrous in retrospect, and Stephen's part in it no more than he deserved.

'That wasn't funny,' he declared now, his rather full face mirroring his indignation. 'Just because I made a mistake——'

'*A* mistake?' broke in Olivia scornfully. 'Don't you mean a whole handful of them? Come on, Stephen. I may have been gullible once, but not any longer.'

Mrs Drake's reappearance with his lunch was an untimely interruption as far as Olivia was concerned. She had hoped, rather futilely, she realised, that she might have persuaded him to leave before the landlady returned. It also gave him a breathing space, and that irritated her, too. There was no way he could convince her that his motives for being here were anything more than selfish. And if he thought he had a chance of persuading her to think again at this late date he was more stupid than he looked.

Besides, why would he want to? She didn't believe that rubbish about Harry Darcy objecting to the divorce any more than she believed that Stephen was still attracted to her. It was possible that the company preferred its executives to be family men, but no one in this day and age was likely to balk if a marriage wasn't working. Least of all Harry Darcy, who had been married twice himself.

'Will—er—will your husband be staying overnight?' enquired Mrs Drake chattily, setting the meal and the pint of lager Stephen had ordered on the table in front of him.

'No...'

'Yes.'

They answered simultaneously, and, although Olivia had intended to go on and explain that Stephen would be leaving after lunch, his response left her speechless.

'Oh, then I'll have Dory change the sheets,' declared the landlady happily. 'It'll do Mrs Perry good to have some company, sir. Not much to do in Paget at this time of the year. But I expect you know that, seeing as how you and your wife have friends in the area.'

Now it was Stephen's turn to look confused, but Olivia had no intention of enlightening him. She was too infuriated by his audacity to care what he thought. 'No, don't bother changing the sheets, Mrs Drake,' she replied harshly, finding her voice. 'We don't sleep together. We don't even share the same room!'

'Oh...' The woman was taken aback. 'Is that right?' She looked to Stephen, as if for confirmation, and Olivia wondered how she kept herself from screaming.

'Yes, that's right, Mrs Drake,' she insisted, glaring at Stephen so threateningly that it would have taken a stronger man than him to defy her wrath. 'If Mr Perry is staying—and I don't think he's made up his mind yet—I'm afraid you'll have to find him alternative accommodation.'

Stephen's mouth briefly took a sullen slant, and he took a hefty swallow of the lager. Then, wiping his mouth on the back of his hand, he tore his eyes away from Olivia's angry face, and looked up at the landlady with a winning smile. 'I'm afraid my wife's right, Mrs Drake,' he said ruefully, and Olivia's nails dug into her palms at his reproachful grimace. 'We don't share a room these days. After the accident, her leg was in such a bad way that the doctors advised me not to take any chances. I might have bumped it, you see. And I didn't want to hurt her. Unfortunately,' he went on, ignoring Olivia's horrified expression, 'she's got used to sleeping alone. I am hoping to get her to change her mind, but for the time being...'

He allowed the sentence to tail away, and Mrs Drake looked just as sympathetic as he had intended. But Olivia's feelings about this were nothing compared to her fury at his mention of the accident, and it was no surprise when the landlady seized her chance.

'There, now,' she said, turning to her other guest. 'I said to Tom, I did, "Mrs Perry's got some sort of problem with her leg." And now you say you've had an accident. Well, I can't say I didn't suspect as much.'

Olivia pressed her lips together. Then, realising Mrs Drake's imagination was likely to run riot if she refused to answer, she said stiffly, 'I was involved in a car crash, that's all. Nothing too dramatic, I can assure you.'

'All the same...' Mrs Drake shook her head. 'No wonder you looked so peaky when you got here. Mind you, you're looking a lot better this morning. I said to Tom a few minutes ago, "Mrs Perry's got some colour in her cheeks again."'

'Exactly what I've been saying myself,' remarked Stephen smugly, and Olivia wondered why she didn't just tell the landlady about the divorce, and be done with it. But to do so now would mean she would have to admit she had been lying earlier. Oh, why hadn't she refused to speak to him, instead of making herself a liar by omission?

'Yes, well, I dare say seeing you again has helped,' Mrs Drake declared, looking approvingly at Olivia's almost empty plate. 'I see you enjoyed your lunch, Mrs Perry. Now, can I get you anything else before I go?'

'Nothing.' If the woman thought she was less than gracious, Olivia couldn't help it. She just wanted her to go so she could tell Stephen exactly what she thought of him. How dared he put her in this invidious position?

But when Mrs Drake had gone, it was Stephen who broke the silence. 'Looks like you're stuck with me,' he said, forking a huge amount of food into his mouth. 'I gather you haven't told anyone here that we're getting a divorce. Well, that suits me just fine——'

'Stephen!' Olivia's voice had risen several octaves, and it was with an immense effort that she toned it down again. 'What are you doing here? What do you want from me? You can't seriously imagine that I would take you back!'

Stephen shovelled another wedge of pudding into his mouth, and then regarded her as he chewed. 'I could say we're not divorced yet, Ollie,' he remarked, as soon as his mouth had emptied sufficiently for him to speak. 'If I was to tell your solicitor that you and I had had a reconciliation——'

'But we haven't. And we won't,' retorted Olivia, getting awkwardly to her feet. 'Don't threaten me, Stephen. Just at this moment, you've got more to lose than I have.'

'Oh, Ollie!' Putting down his fork, Stephen's expression underwent a complete change. Instead of aggression, his face took on a look of weary contrition, and, before she could avoid it, his hand had clutched her sweater. 'Must we have a slanging match? We loved one another once. Can you honestly say that that's all over?'

'Yes.' Olivia was unmoved. 'Stephen, if you care anything for me at all, you'll finish your lunch and then get out of here. I don't want to see you; I don't want to talk to you. And if you want to stop me hating you, you'll forget you ever came here.'

Stephen expelled his breath heavily. 'I can't do that, Ollie.'

Olivia dragged her sweater out of his grasp. 'Then I will!' she stated grimly, and started for the door.

'I can still *say* we had a reconciliation,' Stephen's voice called after her. 'It might not do any good, but are you willing to take that chance?'

Olivia halted. 'You bastard,' she exclaimed, turning back.

'No, I'm just desperate,' replied Stephen, glancing at her over his shoulder. 'Look, if you'll come back and sit down, I'll tell you what's happened.'

'I don't care what's happened.' Olivia was desperate, too.

'Not even if I tell you that if you just help me this one time I won't do anything to jeopardise the divorce?'

Olivia's shoulders sagged. She had seen enough messy divorces to know that judges were not always objective if a defendant was convincing enough.

'Why should I believe you?' she asked, hating herself for even listening to him.

'I don't see that you have a lot of choice,' he retorted, and, as if he knew he had said enough, he turned back to his lunch.

CHAPTER FIVE

WHEN Conor hadn't rung again by seven o'clock that evening, Olivia decided to ring him.

It wasn't the wisest thing to do. She knew that. Stephen's arrival hadn't made her feelings for Conor any easier to understand, but at least her ex-husband's presence did provide what she was doing with a little justification. She needed someone to talk to, and there wasn't anybody else.

Not that she intended to discuss Stephen with Conor, she reflected dourly. Although he was now occupying the room across the hall from her own, she was determined to ignore the fact. No, she needed someone to talk to who wasn't Stephen, and who didn't know Stephen. Someone who wouldn't tell her she was crazy for allowing him to stay at the inn.

She sighed. She was a fool for allowing him to do so, nevertheless. She knew that, too. She didn't owe Stephen a thing, and his present predicament was no more than he deserved. His story—that Karen Darcy had pursued him both at and after the Christmas party, and not the other way around—was hardly credible, but, either way, if Harry Darcy found out, the result was likely to be the same. Stephen's boss was known to be insanely jealous of his young wife, and any suspicion that one of his employees might be involved with her could cause untold repercussions. To say that Stephen would immediately find himself without a job was the least of it. Olivia knew Harry Darcy, and her opinion was that he would not be content with simply sacking the culprit. In his own world, Harry was a powerful man, and the possibilities of how he might take his revenge were endless.

Which was the prime reason she had agreed to help Stephen, Olivia realised now. In spite of his threats, she felt sorry for him, and she had no wish to play any part in his downfall. If, by pretending she and Stephen were still on friendly terms, if, by saying, should she be asked, that he had spent a particular evening with her, and not with Karen, she could divert Harry's wrath, she would do it. She didn't like it. But she liked the thought of the possible consequences of not doing so even less.

Now, after pressing the button to obtain an outside line, she dialled the number she had found in the local directory. It had been listed under Conor's name only, with no mention of Sharon or his medical status.

Listening to it ring, Olivia contemplated what she would say if Sharon answered. She ought to have something prepared, something more than just an urgent need to hear a friendly voice. Sharon already thought she was a nuisance. How would she regard an unsolicited phone call?

Well, it wasn't entirely unsolicited, Olivia defended herself swiftly. Conor had rung her that morning. She was only returning his call. Yes, she decided, that was how she would phrase it, if Sharon answered. She had waited until the evening to ring, because she had assumed Conor would be spending the day at the clinic.

All the same, her palm was slick as it gripped the phone, and when, after three rings, the call was connected, she almost rang off. But, as she hesitated, there was a click, and Conor's recorded voice came on the line to inform her that he was unavailable at that moment. The message went on to say she should leave her name and number, and the time of her call, and he'd get back to her.

Dammit! Olivia sighed in frustration. She hated talking to a machine. And what she hated even more was the thought that Sharon might be the one to listen to her message. She was tempted not to leave one.

The recorded voice had finished and the bleep advising her to say her piece had sounded. If she was going to answer, now was the time to do it. Or did she want Conor to think there was some pervert on the line?

Expelling her breath rather quickly, she hurried into speech. 'Conor, um—this is Olivia——'

'Liv!' Conor's instant response had her sucking in her breath again in sharp surprise. 'Live, are you still there? Sorry about this, but I was in the shower. I heard the phone ringing, but it took me a couple of minutes to grab a towel.'

'Oh.'

Olivia couldn't think of anything else to say at that moment, and he went on, 'I was going to ring you later. Didn't you get my message this morning?'

'Well—yes.' Olivia realised how pathetic she must sound, admitting she had been too eager to speak to him to wait for his call. 'It was just that——' she sought desperately for an excuse '—well, that I'm going to have dinner, and I didn't want you to ring when—when I wasn't here.'

'You're having dinner *now*?' Conor sounded impatient. 'Liv, it's only seven o'clock!'

'I know that.' Olivia could hear the impatience in her tone now, but it was just a defence against the disbelief she could hear in his. 'Anyway, I—I just wanted to take the opportunity to thank you again for taking pity on me last night. It was good of you and—and Sharon— to let me share your evening. I'm sure I cramped your style, and I want you to know I appreciate the trouble you——'

'What trouble?' Conor cut into her pitiable monologue to voice his own frustration, and Olivia wondered fleetingly if Sharon was listening to what they were saying. 'For Christ's sake, Liv, stop talking as if what I did was an act of charity or something. I wanted to spend the evening with you, for God's sake! I was hoping you'd let me do the same tonight.'

Olivia swallowed. 'Tonight?' she echoed faintly.

'Yes, tonight.' He sighed. 'Look, I suppose I should have rung earlier, but things have been pretty hectic today. We had an emergency at the clinic, and I didn't get away until after six. Then, when I got home, I went straight into the shower. But my intention was to get dressed and come down to see you. I guess I thought you'd find it harder to turn me down if we were face to face.'

Olivia's tongue circled her dry lips. 'I see.' But she didn't really. Was he asking her to spend another evening with himself and Sharon?

'I thought you might be agreeable to me fetching you back here,' he appended, adding to her confusion. His voice took on a persuasive note. 'We could have a pizza out of the freezer, or I have been known to produce a fairly decent omelette. What d'you say?'

Olivia shook her head. 'I—don't know——'

'What don't you know?' Conor sounded impatient again. 'Damn, I knew I should have come to see you myself.' He paused. 'Look, give me five minutes to put on some clothes, and I'll come down to the harbour. I won't be long, and you can tell me what you want to do over a half of lager——'

'No!'

'Liv——'

'I mean . . .' Olivia decided that anything was better than spending the evening dodging her ex-husband. 'I—I will have dinner with you. But I'll meet you outside in—in twenty minutes?'

'Make that fifteen,' amended Conor roughly, and, without giving her a chance to argue, he rang off.

Of course, as soon as he had done so, Olivia's doubts returned. It was all very well wanting to evade Stephen's company, but was spending another evening with Conor a sensible alternative? After what had happened the night before, she ought to be avoiding anything that might aggravate her awareness of him, and what would Mrs

Drake think if she found out that Mrs Perry was going out without her husband?

Deciding it was too late now to be having such thoughts, Olivia surveyed the clothes she had brought with her with critical eyes. She couldn't wear the same dress she had worn the night before, and if they were eating at home something more casual was obviously called for. The trouble was that clothes had not figured high on her agenda when she decided she needed to get away. In consequence, she had filled her suitcase with the first warm items that had come to hand, and she realised now how limited she was.

The ski pants she had worn the morning she walked up to Gull Rise seemed the most attractive. Black, and narrow-fitting, they clung to her slim hips like a second skin. But at least she had no unsightly bulges, she thought wryly. Even if she knew she could have done with a few more pounds of flesh on her bones.

Another chunky sweater completed the outfit: a creamy Aran knit, whose wide neckline tended to slip off her shoulder. It was just as well she didn't need to wear a bra, she thought. She certainly hadn't thought to pack a strapless one.

Sitting at the dressing-table a few moments later, trying to find some more attractive way to do her hair, a wave of self-disgust swept over her. What was she doing? she asked herself, dragging the coarse curls back into their usual knot. Conor already knew what she looked like. There was no point in trying to look younger than she was. Sharon would know immediately what she was doing, and did she really want to lose the slight advantage that being older gave her?

She was putting on her coat when someone knocked at her door. Conor? she wondered, her heart racing, but when she called, 'Yes?' it wasn't Conor's voice that answered.

'Ollie!' Stephen's irritating abbreviation of her name came clearly through the panels, and she was inordinately glad she had locked the door earlier. 'Ollie, are you ready? I thought we might go down and have a drink before dinner.'

Olivia caught her breath. Just like that, she mused incredulously. He really thought they could behave as if nothing had happened. A drink; dinner. My God, she wouldn't be surprised if he was considering asking her to spend the night with him! Why not? she reflected cynically. Sleeping with a woman didn't mean that much to Stephen. He had done it often enough, goodness knows!

'I...' Her hands tortured the lapels of her coat, as she fought back the urge to tell him what he could do with his invitation. 'Well——' she licked her lips '—I'm not ready yet, Stephen. Why—why don't you just go ahead? I'll—see you later.' And so she would. Though perhaps later than Stephen imagined.

'OK.' Clearly the prospect of another pint of Tom Drake's lager was attractive enough to save any argument. 'I'll be in the bar.'

'Fine.'

Olivia was amazed he couldn't hear the sound of her heart beating. It seemed to be pounding in her chest. But, happily, her ex-husband had no reason to assume that she meant anything other than his interpretation of her words, and she heard the creak of the banister as he started down the stairs.

Only then did she expel her breath on a long sigh. Dear lord, she breathed, and she had left London to avoid any more stress! Now she had the problem of getting out of the inn without either Stephen or the Drakes observing her departure.

In the event, it was easier than she had anticipated. There were already several customers, as well as Stephen, in the bar, and at this hour of the evening Mrs Drake was, as usual, busy in the kitchen. The inn supplied a modest selection of bar meals, as well as those that were served in the dining-room, and, although many of them were of the instant variety, Mrs Drake liked to supervise

their preparation. No doubt she was preparing something special to celebration her husband's arrival, reflected Olivia ruefully. Well, Stephen would enjoy it
anyway. She just hoped he didn't see her absence as an
excuse to pump the landlady about her possible
whereabouts.

It was raining outside, but at least it wasn't as cold as
it had been the previous evening. Nevertheless, Olivia
hoped she wouldn't have to wait long before Conor got
there. Even with her coat collar tipped high about her
ears, she felt a drop of dampness invading her neck.

When a car skidded to a halt beside her, she drew
back in some alarm. But then, recognising the muddy
Audi, she stepped forward again, barely avoiding the
passenger door, which was thrust open savagely from
inside.

'What the hell are you doing, standing in the rain?'
snarled Conor, as she got awkwardly into the seat beside
him. 'God, when you said you'd meet me outside, I
didn't realise you meant it literally!'

Olivia sucked in her breath. 'I don't think there's any
need to be so rude, Conor. I'm here, aren't I? You didn't
have to wait for me, as I've had to do for you. You said
fifteen minutes. You should have stuck to the twenty as
I suggested.'

Conor's face was grim as he slammed the car into gear
and took off again as aggressively as he had arrived.
'Don't patronise me, Liv,' he retorted, as she hastily
groped for the seatbelt. 'What's the matter? Having
second thoughts?'

Olivia gasped. She'd had just about enough of being
made to feel as if she had something to be guilty about,
first with Stephen, and now with Conor. 'It seems to me
that you're the one having second thoughts,' she returned coldly. 'But don't worry about it. You can always
take me back.'

'Don't talk rubbish!' In the subdued light from the dashboard, she saw his face take on an exasperated expression. 'Just because I was concerned about you!'

'Oh!' Olivia jammed the safety clip into place. 'Is that what it was? You could have fooled me.'

Conor gave her a fulminating look. 'Will you stop trying to turn this into something it's not? I was annoyed, that's all. Did you have to make your reluctance to be seen with me so obvious?'

Olivia shook her head. 'That—that's stupid!'

'Is it?' Conor arched one brow. 'So why did you want to meet me outside?'

'I—had my reasons.'

'What reasons?'

Olivia sighed. 'Look, does it matter? You'll just have to believe me when I say it had nothing to do with— with who you are. It's not as if the Drakes don't know we know one another. Heavens, Mrs Drake was telling me how she went to school with Sharon's mother.'

'Really?' Conor's brows descended. 'I got the impression you kept yourself pretty much to yourself. I wouldn't have thought you were the type to enjoy a heart-to-heart with old Eva!'

'Old Eva? Oh, you mean Mrs Drake.' Olivia stiffened her shoulders. 'Well, that's what we old women do, didn't you know? Gossip about the past!'

'You're not an old woman,' replied Conor irritably. 'God, what are you trying to do here, Liv? Ruin the evening before it's begun?'

'I think you did that already,' she retorted heatedly, and the expletive he uttered successfully silenced her for the remainder of the journey.

Consequently, when they turned into the gates of Conor's house, Olivia was already searching for reasons why she shouldn't stay long. Perhaps she could pretend her leg was hurting her, she considered. It was a sufficiently ambiguous statement not to require too much elaboration. Indeed, she wondered now why she hadn't just used it as an excuse earlier. She could always have asked Mrs Drake to serve her dinner in her room, thus saving herself from Stephen's company, too.

The car had stopped, she realised suddenly, and while she had been musing over what she might have done Conor had got out and come round to open her door. 'Come on,' he said. 'If *you* don't mind getting soaked, *I* do.'

It was hardly gracious, but she allowed him to take her gloved hand and help her to her feet. After all, if she wanted to foster the belief that her leg was giving her trouble, it wouldn't do to be too independent.

'Thank you,' she said politely, as he leant forward to slam the door behind her, and his lean tanned features softened into a rueful grin.

'I'm sorry,' he said huskily, rubbing the knuckles of one hand down her cheek. 'I guess you think I'm a bastard, mmm?'

Olivia's throat constricted. 'I—I—*no*! No, of course not.' It was an effort to keep her tone impersonal. 'Don't be silly, Conor.'

His hand fell away. 'If you persist in treating me like a schoolboy, I may be forced to prove you wrong,' he answered, turning away to climb the steps and insert his key in the lock. He glanced back. 'Are you coming, or do you need some help?'

'I can do it.'

Olivia used the iron handrail to mount the steps behind him, surprised that Sharon hadn't come out to see what was taking them so long. There were lights on in the house, and because the curtains were not yet drawn she could see into the elegant drawing-room. Someone had lit a fire, and it was burning cosily in the grate. It gave the room such a familiar look that she wouldn't have been surprised to see Conor's parents sitting on the sofa. For a moment, the thought of how things might have been filled her with regret. No wonder Conor had wanted to keep the house. It must be filled with memories.

Conor thrust the door open, and the light from inside spilled on to Olivia's pale face. 'Now, what is it?' he demanded, glimpsing something of the sadness she was feeling, and Olivia shook her head.

'I was just thinking about your mother and father,' she admitted unwillingly, following him into the hall. 'I understand now why you wanted to keep the house.'

'Do you?'

Conor's response was vaguely enigmatic, and Olivia turned to close the door. Then, tugging off her gloves, she thrust them into her pockets, before tackling the buttons on her coat. But every minute she expected Sharon to come bursting out to meet them, eager to demonstrate her authority as mistress of the house. Even if it was in name only, thought Olivia, rather maliciously. Though she knew that, if Sharon had her way, that would only be a matter of time.

She was easing the coat off her shoulders when Conor seemed to remember his manners, and came to help her. His cool fingers brushed the nape of her neck as he did so, and she shivered. It was too easy to imagine how those hard fingers would feel touching her with more than just accidental intent, and she drew an uneven breath as he hung the coat on the old-fashioned umbrella stand.

'Go ahead,' he said, as she waited uncertainly for him to finish. 'You know the way.'

'Into the drawing-room?' she ventured, unwilling, in spite of everything, to steal Sharon's thunder.

'Sure.' Conor was removing the leather jacket he had worn to fetch her, revealing a black shirt and black jeans. He came up behind her, and the heat from his body was palpably real. 'What are you waiting for?'

'I—um...' Olivia moved hurriedly away from him. 'Wh—where's Sharon?'

'Sharon?' Conor's astonishment was not feigned. 'Did I give you any reason to think she would be here?'

'Er—no.' Olivia stepped somewhat nervously into the drawing-room. 'But—well, where is she? She hasn't gone out for the evening because she knew I was coming, has she?'

Conor gave her an old-fashioned look. 'Why do I get the feeling we're talking at cross purposes here?' he asked wryly. 'Let me get this straight—Sharon told you she lived here, right?'

Olivia gripped the back of a Regency-striped arm-chair. 'No-o.'

'Did I?'

She shook her head. 'No.'

'OK.' He inclined his head and started across the room to where a tray of drinks was residing on a low bookcase. 'I'm glad we've cleared that up. So—what are you going to have to drink? I've got scotch and sherry, and sherry and scotch.' He grimaced. 'I was going to buy a bottle of gin, when I came down to the pub. But—well, it didn't work out that way, did it?'

Olivia caught her lower lip between her teeth. 'Sharon doesn't live here?' she asked, still not quite able to believe it, and Conor unscrewed the cap of the sherry and filled two glasses.

'No,' he replied patiently, and, lifting both glasses, he carried them towards her. 'Here. I'm assuming you're not opposed to an appetiser.' He handed one of the glasses to her, and she wondered if he noticed her scramble to grasp the stem to avoid his fingers. 'Cheers.'

'Cheers,' she echoed faintly, taking a sip of the dry sack. 'Mmm—this is nice.'

'Is it?' Conor's mouth compressed. 'So, what made you think Sharon lived here?' he probed. 'Did Mrs Drake tell you that?'

'No.' Olivia shifted a little uncomfortably. 'I—I've obviously made a mistake.'

'In coming here?' enquired Conor drily. He gestured towards the sofa. 'Why don't we sit down? Then you can tell me all about it. Right now, I get the feeling that one wrong word from me and you'll be dashing to phone a cab!'

'That's silly.' Olivia expelled her breath rather unevenly.

'So?' Conor bent to switch on another lamp. 'I don't bite, you know. Well,' he grinned, as he straightened, 'only occasionally.'

Clutching her glass, Olivia circled the armchair, and went to perch on the end of the sofa. She would have preferred to sit in the armchair, but she had already aroused his amusement, and she had no wish to make a complete laughing-stock of herself. Besides, it was warmer on the sofa.

She had stretched out her toes toward the blaze, when Conor came to sit beside her. Unlike her, he didn't balance on the edge of the seat, but dropped heavily on to the cushions, his long black-clad legs only inches from hers.

'Comfortable, isn't it?' he remarked, crossing his feet at the ankle. 'You've no idea how often I longed to experience a real winter again, when I was living in Florida.'

Olivia relaxed a little. 'Don't they have winters in Florida?'

Conor tipped his head back against the cushions. 'Oh, yeah,' he said cynically, 'they have winters. Maybe once in ten, twenty years the temperature drops below freezing, and all the growers panic in case it kills the fruit trees. I believe they even had snow, once. But I didn't see it. Where we lived, on the Gulf coast, it rarely drops below sixty. That's Fahrenheit, of course.'

Olivia was impressed. 'I'd say there are quite a few people who'd envy you, living in a semi-tropical climate like that,' she said. She took another sip of her sherry. 'I almost envy you myself.'

'So why didn't you go somewhere warm to recuperate?' Conor's eyes were intent. 'Instead of coming here.'

'Oh...' Olivia shrugged. 'I didn't want to go where there were lots of people. I wanted some peace and quiet. And you have to admit, Paget has that.'

'But without your husband,' murmured Conor quietly, and she was glad she could blame the fire for her hot face.

'Stephen has a job to do,' she replied obliquely, wondering how long it would be before he found out that her ex-husband had spent a night at the inn. 'Um—tell me about your job at the clinic. Is it like a hospital? Are the people sick, or what?'

'Oh, yes. They're sick.' Conor let himself be diverted, and to her relief his gaze turned to the fire. 'But it's not really like a hospital. More like a prison, I guess.'

'Go on.'

Olivia was intrigued, and Conor good-naturedly explained a little about its purpose. 'We deal with a lot of habitual offenders. The kind you've probably defended in court. Addicts who, for one reason or another, can't—or won't—kick the habit.'

'Young people?'

'Addicts tend to be young,' remarked Conor drily. 'Not a lot of them make it into old age.'

'But—I mean—juvenile offenders.'

'No. Mostly they're late teens or twenties. But I'm talking about real people here. Young men and women from all walks of life. Not just the pimps and the pushers.'

'And you counsel them?'

Conor pulled a face. 'Well, we try to. David Marshall—he's the guy who runs the place—he's working on the theory that people have to *want* to be cured before it happens.'

'So what causes young people to turn to drugs? Curiosity? Peer pressure?'

'It's not as simple as that. The theory that kids take to drugs because their friends are doing it doesn't really hold up. If that were true, or if it only worked that way, all young people would be potential addicts. But they're not.' He paused. 'That's not to say that most young people aren't exposed to drugs at some time in their life. They are. The widespread use of heroin and cocaine is a very real problem. Teachers find needles behind the bike sheds these days, as they used to find condoms years ago.' He gave a rueful grin. 'Unfortunately, these days they find both.'

Olivia's lips twitched. 'So what's your theory?'

'It's a lot of things. I think television has a lot to answer for.'

'The violence, you mean?'

'Not in this case, no.' Conor shook his head. 'Oh, I'm sure the amount of violence we all see on television has some bearing on the way we live our lives. There's no doubt that it's a powerful force for change. And kids are brainwashed to the extent that when they see real pictures of dead bodies it doesn't mean anything. I read a report once about some teenagers being shown a video that was shot in Vietnam. The pictures were horrific, really gruesome, but they didn't turn a hair. It was the guy teaching them who threw his guts up in the john.'

'What did you mean, then?'

'Oh—aspirations, I guess.' Conor spoke flatly. 'Television makes people feel inadequate. Particularly young people. They see people living in glossy houses, driving glossy cars and living glossy lives, while they can't even get a job. What do you think that does to them?'

'But they're not *real* people,' exclaimed Olivia, and Conor gave her a narrow-eyed stare.

'But they are,' he declared softly. 'To some of the kids I deal with, they're just as real as the old lady who got mugged in her armchair, or the napalm victims in Vietnam.'

Olivia swallowed. 'So what can we do?'

'Is that a rhetorical question, or do you mean what can *I* do?'

Olivia looked rueful. 'Both, I suppose.'

'Well...' Conor slid the fingers of one hand through his hair until they came to rest at the back of his neck. 'I guess I have to try and convince them that there's more to life than what they see on television.'

'And do you succeed?'

'Who knows?' Conor's hand dropped to his chest, drawing her unwilling attention to the fine pale hair nestling in the opened V of his shirt. 'We seem to. But it's not possible to keep track of what happens to all of them after they leave the clinic.'

Olivia nodded. 'And what kind of treatment do they get?'

'After we've got them off the hard drugs, you mean?' He shrugged. 'Well, in addition to the counselling, there's therapy; sometimes psychotherapy, although that doesn't work for everyone.'

'So what do you do then?'

Conor's lips twisted. 'Hey, that's enough about what I do.' He surveyed her with wry amusement, and then lifted his hand to squeeze the back of her neck. 'I don't want to spend the whole evening talking about me.'

Olivia quivered. His fingers were absurdly intimate, and although she had expected him to let go of her again he didn't. He just sat looking at her with that disturbingly sensual green gaze, and she was helpless against the insidious emotions he aroused inside her.

CHAPTER SIX

'OH—I'M not very interesting,' she denied now, and the jerky movement she made had the neckline of the sweater sliding off one soft shoulder.

'I disagree.' Conor's eyes darkened as they fastened on that vulnerable exposure of flesh, and his hand slid from her nape to her shoulder. 'It's like silk,' he said, almost to himself, his eyes dropping to follow the caressing movement of his brown fingers against her pale skin. 'But you're too thin. What have you been doing to yourself?'

'I—I thought thin was supposed to be fashionable,' Olivia protested lightly, and, gathering her scattered senses, she got abruptly to her feet. 'Um—what was that you said about an omelette? I'm hungry.'

She wasn't, of course, and she was sure Conor knew it. But he swallowed the remainder of the sherry in his glass, and obediently stood up. 'You can choose,' he said, matching his tone to hers. 'I found some ribs in the freezer, as well as the pizza. Come and see.'

She let him lead the way into the kitchen, which was at the back of the house. The dark oak units and terracotta tiles had been Sally's pride and joy, and Olivia had lost count of the number of meals the four of them had eaten at the stripped-pine table.

It was dark, and when Conor switched on the lights they illuminated the pile of unwashed dishes in the sink. 'Unfortunately, Mum didn't see any need for a dishwasher,' he remarked, steering her away from them. 'Just ignore the mess. I'll clear up later.'

'I'll do them,' declared Olivia firmly, grateful to have something uncontroversial to do. 'Shall I make the omelettes, too?'

'No.' Conor gave her an aggrieved look. 'I'm not one of those guys who can't even boil an egg. I've had to look after myself for quite some time now, and, as you can see, I haven't starved.'

'That's the truth,' murmured Olivia barely audibly, but he heard her.

'So?' he challenged. 'Is there something wrong with the way I look?'

'No, of course not.' Olivia was glad she could busy herself running water into the sink. But she couldn't help thinking that Conor would probably be shocked if he knew what she had been thinking about his lean, muscled frame. His touching her might have been quite innocent, but her thoughts at this moment were definitely not. And it disturbed her.

'How about if we have a pizza omelette?' he suggested, opening the freezer door, and Olivia lifted her head to see him watching her reflection in the darkened glass of the window.

'A pizza omelette?' she echoed faintly. 'Can you have such a thing?'

'Hey, when I was in med. school, I ate anything going,' he responded, grinning. 'But OK. Maybe a pizza omelette isn't such a good idea. How about pizza *and* omelette, with a little green salad to satisfy the health nuts?'

Olivia laughed. She couldn't help herself. And, as she did so, she realised how long it was since she had had so much fun. Even with her hands plunged in soapy water, and a pile of dishes waiting to be dried beside her, she was enjoying herself. Being with Conor was like being young again. She had forgotten what it was like to be foolish and carefree.

'That sounds good,' said Conor, suddenly behind her, his reflection looming above her in the now misty glass. His hands descended on her shoulders for a moment, before sliding down her arms and away. 'You should laugh more often. I like it.'

Somehow, Olivia managed to get the remainder of the dishes washed and dried, and by the time she had done so the pizza was hissing in the microwave, and the omelettes were bubbling in the pan.

They ate, as Olivia remembered them doing so many times before, at the kitchen table. Conor had half-heartedly offered to lay the table in the dining-room, but Olivia had been adamant.

'It's nicer in here,' she said. 'Cosier.' And then looked away from his lazy gaze, with a feeling almost of panic. She was enjoying this too much, she thought unsteadily. Just because Sharon wasn't here, that didn't mean she didn't exist.

Nevertheless, she ate the food Conor had prepared with more enthusiasm than she had felt for years. The pizza, oozing with cheese, made a remarkably delicious accompaniment to the omelettes, and the crisp salad was served with a yoghurt dressing that was tart and refreshing. There was even warm French bread and butter, had she wanted it, but although she enjoyed watching Conor munching through its golden crust she couldn't manage anything else.

'Good?' he enquired, when they were both reduced to sipping glasses of the smooth hock he had supplied with the food, and Olivia nodded.

'Very good,' she agreed, stroking the film of condensation that had settled on her glass. 'I feel pleasantly full, and——'

'—mellow,' put in Conor softly, pushing back his chair, and getting up. 'Let's go and finish the wine in the other room.'

'But what about clearing up?' protested Olivia, looking up at him, and his lips twisted.

'Not right now,' he stated, coming round the table to draw back her chair. 'Come on. It's happy hour.'

Conor drew the curtains across the drawing-room windows, immediately reducing the dimensions of the room to the lamplit area by the fire. Then, after waiting until Olivia had seated herself on the sofa again, he tossed another log on the glowing coals and resumed his place beside her.

'OK,' he said quietly, 'are you going to tell me why you thought I lived with Sharon?' He sighed. 'And sit back, can't you? I want to look at you, not your back!'

Olivia could have told him that that was exactly why she was sitting perched on the edge of the cushions, but she didn't. Easing her hips a little way further on to the seat, she gave an uncertain shrug. 'I thought I did. Tell you why I thought you lived with Sharon, I mean.'

'No.' To her alarm, Conor's hand descended on her shoulder again, but all he did was urge her against the cushions at her back. 'You said you'd made a mistake. I'm curious to know why.'

'Oh, come on.' Thankfully, he had released her as soon as he achieved his objective, and she realised her best option was to attack his argument. 'That morning, when I walked up here, well—you're not going to tell me she hadn't spent the night here——'

Conor arched a quizzical brow. 'Why not?'

'Why not?' Olivia hadn't thought he would contradict her. 'Well, because—because——'

'As a matter of fact, she'd called in on her way to work,' he essayed flatly. And then, meeting Olivia's disbelieving gaze, he added, 'I'm not saying she hasn't slept here. She has. I'm not a saint, Liv. I need sexual satisfaction, just like anyone else.' His eyes darkened. 'As you do.'

That was a little close to the bone, and Olivia hurriedly transferred her attention back to her wine. 'Even so——'

'Even so—what?' Conor leaned forward so that he could look into her face. 'Sharon was acting as if she owned me, is that what you're trying to say?'

Olivia stifled the gulp of panic that was rising in her throat. 'It—it's nothing to do with me.'

'Isn't it?' Conor's voice was incredibly soft. 'You're not interested in what I do with Sharon, is that right?'

'Conor.' Olivia moistened her dry lips, and somehow managed to meet his probing gaze. 'Don't you think this is a rather pointless conversation? You have your life to lead. And—and I have mine. Did—er—did I tell you I'd been offered a partnership with—with Hallidays?'

'It doesn't surprise me.' Conor shrugged. 'You always were ambitious.'

Olivia was taken aback. 'Do you think so?'

'I know so.' Conor's voice was dry as he leant forward to put his empty glass on the coffee-table.

'How?'

He lounged back beside her. 'You don't have any family, do you?'

'Children, you mean?'

'What else?'

Olivia tried to gather her composure. 'Isn't that a rather sexist remark?'

'All remarks are sexist, I guess.'

'No, you know what I mean.'

'Why? Because it challenges your femininity?'

Olivia straightened her spine. 'How do you know I haven't tried to have children?'

'Have you?'

Olivia gasped. 'That's my business.' She used the excuse of putting down her glass to evade his enquiring stare. Then, running a nervous hand over the knot at her nape, she took a surreptitious look at her watch. 'Heavens, is that the time?'

'It's only nine-thirty,' he remarked mildly. And, before she could say anything more, his hand curled around her neck, under her hair. 'You're not going yet.'

She'd never expected him to restrain her; not like that: so proprietorially, so *possessively*. As if he thought he had the right to keep her there against her will, she thought unsteadily. His hard fingers moved sinuously against her flesh, and her heart palpitated wildly. Dear

God, what was he doing? And why was she letting him do it?

'Conor!' Her protest was strangled, but then, putting on her coolest, most authoritative voice, she added, 'Don't do that!'

'Don't do what?' he asked softly, moving closer, and if she had had any doubts that she was over-reacting they were quickly dispelled. His warm, wine-scented breath caressed her cheek. 'Oh, Liv,' he breathed, 'you have no idea what I want to do.'

Common sense wasn't working. 'Conor,' she exclaimed again, and this time she tried to lighten her tone. 'Conor, I think you're teasing me. Now, come on. Let me go.'

But that didn't work either. Instead, she felt the pins that held her hair in place being deliberately withdrawn, and, although she put up her hands to stop him, presently the unruly cloud of dark hair tumbled about her shoulders.

'Mmm. That's better,' he said, ignoring her astounded expression, and, taking a handful of hair, he threaded it through his fingers. 'I've been wanting to do this ever since you got here.'

'And now you have,' said Olivia tautly, letting him see how angry he had made her. 'Conor, I don't know what you think you're doing, but I think this has gone far enough. Now, I suggest you call me a cab——'

'It hasn't,' he cut in huskily, still smoothing her hair between his fingers, and her dark brows drew together.

'What are you talking——?'

'Gone far enough,' he appended huskily, drawing the neckline of her sweater aside, and touching her shoulder with his tongue. 'I haven't gone nearly far enough.'

Olivia jerked her shoulder away from his mouth. 'Conor, what on earth do you think I am?'

His eyes lifted to hers. 'I think you're a beautiful woman,' he replied simply, and she gasped.

'I think you've taken leave of your senses,' she retorted, grimly hanging on to her sanity. 'Conor, you're not a boy any more!'

'Would you let me do this if I were?'

'No!' Olivia felt as if she was getting into deeper and deeper water. 'Conor, I'm married!' she declared, using her erstwhile status as a final attempt to deter him, and then shrank back in alarm when his hand came to cup her face.

'D'you think I don't know that?' he demanded, his thumb and forefinger digging into her cheeks. His eyes moved almost hungrily over her shocked features for a moment, and then softened.

'Anyway, what's wrong with me wanting to kiss you? You never used to object before.'

Olivia's senses felt scrambled. 'You—you know what's wrong,' she got out jerkily. 'As—as I said, you're not a boy now. And—and I don't appreciate being put in this position.'

'What position?' His thumb brushed her mouth, and, almost against her will, her lips parted against that sensuous abrasion. The pad of his thumb probed inside her mouth, scraping the tender flesh inside her lower lip, and smearing its wetness against her chin. 'How many positions do you know?'

Olivia caught her breath. 'Conor...' she began again, but, before she could voice her faltering indignation, his lips took the place of his thumb.

Pure, unadulterated panic gripped her now. As his warm mouth brushed lightly over hers, and the hand that had been holding her face in place slid caressingly to her throat, the recklessness of what she was doing swept over her. But she wasn't afraid of Conor. It wasn't fear of him that was turning her limbs to water. It was the clear and certain knowledge that she wanted him to kiss her just as much as he wanted to do it.

'Sweet,' he muttered roughly, his mouth settling more firmly over hers, and the hot invasion of his tongue was like a shaft of electricity jolting through her. It plunged deeply into her mouth, filling her with the feel and the taste of him, seductive, and velvety, and achingly real.

Olivia moaned in protest, but it was a puny thing at best, and the hands that had balled against his flat midriff opened like the petals of a flower against his chest. But they didn't keep him away from her. On the contrary; when she felt the thudding beat of his heart beneath her hands, she shuddered uncontrollably, and she clutched handfuls of his shirt with fingers that were damp and greedy. God, she trembled, with her last coherent thought, what was he doing to her?

Her head sank into the cushions behind her, and Conor's fingers slid along her hot cheek, holding her a prisoner beneath his hungry mouth. And that mouth strayed from her lips to her eyes, closing her lids with feathery light kisses, so that her world was reduced to one of touching, and feeling, and shattering sensation. He kissed the curve of her cheekbones, the dark arch of her eyebrows. His tongue explored the unexpectedly sensitive cavern of her ear, and his teeth fastened on her earlobe, though the pain was not unpleasurable. On the contrary, Olivia was discovering that hitherto unknown areas of her face and neck were incredibly responsive to his touch, and each new invasion caused the tight pain of awareness to stir deep inside her.

The blood was pounding in her head, but it was thick and turgid, battling through her veins in an effort to bring oxygen to her swimming senses. She felt as if she were drowning in emotion, and, totally against her will, her hands groped for his neck. Her fingers tangled in the silky hair at his nape, and she clung to him helplessly, caught in a spell that was older than time itself.

Conor's breathing had quickened, too, and when he sought her lips again there was urgency as well as pulsing passion in the demanding pressure of his mouth. She felt his hand invade the neckline of her sweater, smoothing the fine bones of her shoulders, before attempting to reach her throbbing breasts. But the neckline wasn't loose enough for that, and his hand slid down to find the button-hard nipples, taut beneath the rough wool of the sweater. He rolled the sensitive little peak against his palm, and Olivia couldn't suppress the gulp of anguish she felt at the harsh abrasion. And, as if sensing her discomfort, Conor's hand moved down to the hem of her sweater, slipping beneath the wool to find the soft flesh beneath. His hands caressed her slim waist, one finger probing the buttoned fastening of her trousers, before moving up again to take possession of one swollen breast.

'Better?' he breathed against her mouth, and she felt herself nodding, mindlessly. In her present state of responsiveness, he could have stripped the clothes from her and she wouldn't have objected. She was completely caught up in the things he was doing to her body, and the fact that he was becoming as sexually aroused in the process as she was didn't really register.

She had slipped lower on the sofa, and Conor was lying half over her now. When he moved to wedge one leg between hers, her legs splayed automatically. It made it easier to accommodate the disturbing ache she could feel between her legs, and when he rubbed his thigh against that throbbing juncture she made a convulsive little sound of pleasure, and moved against him.

'God, Liv!' he choked, and it was the words he spoke that made her aware that he was trembling. Made her aware, too, of the thrusting pressure of his manhood, throbbing against her thigh, threatening to split the zip of his trousers. 'Let me make love with you.'

And, although the blinding instincts of desire urged her to go on, to reach down and open his zip, and let him do what he wanted, the cool breath of reality was rearing its ugly head. What was she doing? she asked herself in dismay. How had she allowed such a situation to develop?

The awareness of her own complicity caused a wave of embarrassment to envelop her. Dear lord, she thought, it wasn't as if she were a naïve girl, unaware of what happened when a woman allowed a man to kiss her, and caress her, and touch her naked breasts. Indeed, she doubted anyone was that naïve these days. And particularly not a woman who had been married and divorced, and whose husband had proved so susceptible to the temptations of the flesh. Dammit, there were no excuses for what she was doing, even if, for a short time, he had caused her to abandon her identity. And that had never happened before.

She shifted beneath him then, pushing his leg away from that most sensitive part of her anatomy, and struggling to ease herself up against the cushions. God, had she really let *Conor* do this to her? She must have drunk more wine that she'd realised. There could be no other reason for her behaviour.

'Hey—Liv!' Conor's reaction to her withdrawal was not unexpectedly impatient. 'Don't do that,' he protested, when she put both hands against his chin and tried to push him away. 'What are you trying to do? Break my neck?'

Olivia fought back a sob. 'Let me up, Conor,' she exclaimed, not answering him. 'For God's sake, let go of me!'

'What's wrong?' Resisting her efforts to force him away from her, Conor looked down at her with anxious eyes. 'Did I hurt you or something? Talk to me, dammit. What did I do?'

Olivia caught her breath. 'What didn't you do?' she cried, bringing a look of dawning comprehension to those sea-green eyes. 'Conor, get off me! I want to get up.'

Conor's long lashes veiled his eyes. He could still see her, but she didn't find it so easy to read his expression any more. 'Don't you think you're over-reacting?' he suggested softly, but there was a thread of exasperation in his voice now, and she told herself she was glad.

'Possibly,' she responded, wishing she had more experience in these matters. She had the feeling she was handling this badly, but she didn't know what else to do. 'Look,' she added, 'as I'm quite a lot older than you are, you'll just have to take my word that this was a mistake. Trust me. It was.'

Conor watched her tugging her sweater down over her hips, and then said evenly, 'Not that much older,' and she realised it was going to be even harder than she'd thought.

'I was your mother's friend,' she pointed out tensely, aware that her body was not responding to the dictates of her brain. 'How—how do you think she would feel, if she could see us now?'

Conor shrugged. Clearly that consequence didn't bother him. 'You're not old enough to be my mother,' was all he said. And then, huskily, 'I got the distinct impression that you didn't exactly object to what I was doing.'

'Well, you were wrong!' Olivia swallowed on the lie, and resumed her efforts to shift him. 'I was a fool to come here. I should have stuck to my original intention, and refused your invitation.'

Conor's mouth thinned. 'That was your original intention? To turn me down?'

'Yes.' That, at least, was true.

'Why?'

'Why?' Olivia took an uneven breath. 'I just told you why.'

'No. You've just spun me a tale about your being too old for me.' One brow arched. 'That's bullshit!'

'Conor, I mean it——'

'So do I.' And, avoiding her fluttering hands, he pushed his fingers into the coarse tangle of black curls that framed her flushed face. Then, bending his head, he brushed her quivering mouth with his, and a helpless shiver of anticipation enveloped her. 'You have no idea how long I've wanted to have you like this,' he told her roughly. 'God, I used to fantasise about how you'd look—how you'd feel.' His lips twisted. 'So don't expect me to react favourably when you tell me this is all a mistake. Don't expect me to believe it either.'

'Even if it's true?'

'I don't believe you.' Conor was infuriatingly complacent. 'And before you hit me with the fact that you're married, and that I shouldn't be lusting after a married woman, I want to say I don't think much of a man who abandons his responsibilities so readily, who lets his wife spend weeks alone on a remote part of the east coast, without even taking the trouble to come and see if she's all right.'

Olivia stiffened. 'How do you know he hasn't?'

'Because Tom Drake told me you hadn't had any visitors since you got here,' he retorted flatly. 'Believe it or not, but last night he said he was glad I was showing you some attention. He and Eva had been feeling sorry for you——'

Any weakening Olivia might have been feeling towards him vanished. 'How dare you?' she demanded, somehow finding the strength to propel him away from her, and lurching to her feet. 'How dare you?' she said again, clutching back her hair with one hand, and fumbling for the pins that had got caught in her sweater with the other. 'Did you honestly think that telling me you'd been gossiping about me with the landlord would make me feel better? My God! What do you think I am? Are you saying that because I'm disabled you feel some misguided sort of responsibility for me?'

'No!' Conor scowled. 'Hell, Liv...' He got up now, and against her will she noticed that his shirt was half open down his chest. Had she done that? she wondered, half disgustedly, even while her eyes fed greedily on the muscled flesh it exposed. 'I have not been *gossiping* about you with anyone. What Tom Drake said, he said with the best of intentions. God, if you ask me, the Drakes care more about what happens to you than your husband does.'

'But I didn't ask you, did I? And I see now what all this is about,' she added painfully. 'You felt sorry for me, too. Tell me something, does Sharon know you've been spending this evening consoling this poor abandoned female?'

'God!' Conor swore now. 'Haven't you listened to a word I've said? I've told you how I feel about you being here, and Sharon doesn't come into it.' He reached for her arm. 'Goddammit, you know it! This is just you and me!'

'And—Stephen,' put in Olivia recklessly, evading his outstretched hand. She held up her head. 'I forgot to tell you. He arrived this afternoon. He's waiting for me back at the inn.'

Conor's expression ran the whole gamut of emotion from raw frustration to disbelief. 'You're lying.'

'Why would I lie?' she retorted, though there was a tremor in her voice all the same. 'That's why I didn't want you to come into the pub. If you don't believe me, ring Tom Drake. I'm sure he'd be only too pleased to confirm it.'

CHAPTER SEVEN

To Olivia's relief, she didn't see Stephen again until breakfast.

Conor had let her phone for a taxi to bring her back to the hotel, and she had managed to hurry upstairs to her room without anyone noticing her. And she had made sure her light was out before Stephen came up to bed. She was half convinced he had stopped outside her door, but, to her relief, he hadn't attempted to disturb her.

Not that she'd have opened the door anyway, she assured herself tautly. The evening had been quite disastrous enough, without her ex-husband adding his contribution to it. Indeed, she couldn't even remember feeling as shattered as she had done when she arrived back at the inn. And, although she had crawled straight into bed, it was hours before she had got to sleep.

The trouble was that, as soon as she closed her eyes, the events of the evening had replayed themselves endlessly behind her lids, and, no matter how she tried, she couldn't displace the image of Conor's face as she had last seen him.

God, would she ever forget how he had looked when she told him Stephen was waiting for her at the inn? He had tried to deny it, of course, but the fact was she wouldn't have said it, if it couldn't be proved, and he knew it. The bleakness that had descended on his features when he realised she wasn't lying had been positively frightening. And, watching him, what she had desperately wanted to do was retract her words and comfort him. Only the knowledge that it was probably the kindest way to let him down had kept her silent. After all, when she left Paget, she would never see him

again. Aside from the fact that she would probably be
a cripple for the rest of her life, she was too old for him.
He needed someone young, and vital. Like Sharon, she
admitted, somewhat ruefully. Someone who could take
what he had to give, without expecting anything in
return. And something told her—in that regard—she had
more to lose than he had...

In consequence, although she would have liked to ask
if she could have breakfast in her room, she squared her
shoulders and went down to the dining-room. If she
wanted to convince the Drakes—and indirectly Conor—
that she and Stephen were still on good terms, she had
to behave as normally as possible. But that didn't stop
her wondering whether she wouldn't be wiser to leave
right away. Stephen knew where she was now, she reminded herself defensively, and, although she didn't
think she was ready to go back to town yet, an alternative
base might be a good idea. She had the uneasy feeling
it would take her a little time to reconcile herself to the
feelings Conor had so effortlessly aroused.

Stephen was already sitting at the window table—
reading her newspaper, she saw indignantly—when she
went downstairs, and it was not without some misgivings that she made her way towards him. Unwillingly,
her mind was already making comparisons between his
puffy eyes and balding head and Conor's masculine
beauty, and she acknowledged it was probably rough
justice, when he remarked, scathingly, 'God, what did
you do with yourself last night? You look grim!'

'Thanks.' Snatching her newspaper out of his hand,
she seated herself opposite, and buried her face in its
pages. She refused to give in to the childish desire to tell
him she had been thinking the same—about him—and
it was left to Stephen to try and make amends.

'Well, you do look pale,' he muttered. 'You don't look
as if you've been to bed at all. Is that leg still giving you
problems?'

'No.'

Olivia resented having to tell him anything, and, as if losing patience, Stephen reached across the table and squashed the paper down until he could see her face. 'So, where did you go last night?' he demanded. 'I waited over an hour for you to show up, and by the time I got my supper it was cold! I suppose you thought it was funny, making a fool of me like that in front of the Drakes!'

Olivia extracted the newspaper from his grasp and meticulously straightened the pages. 'I didn't give it a lot of thought,' she admitted honestly. 'And I don't think I have to give you a résumé of my movements, Stephen. I went out. Where I went is my affair.'

Stephen scowled. 'I suppose you were with that doctor and his girlfriend again, weren't you?' he asked, startling her. 'Oh, yes,' he added, with a mocking smile, 'I've heard all about *Dr* Brennan. The Drakes didn't know how you knew him, of course. I think they thought you'd met him in London, but I put them straight on that account.' He sneered. 'They were so surprised to hear that you used to live here.'

Olivia was coldly furious. 'You told them I used to live in Paget?'

'Yeah.' Stephen lounged back in his chair, enjoying his triumph. 'Why not? It's not a secret, is it?'

'You had no right...' began Olivia hotly, and then, realising she was just playing into his hands, she bit off her words.

But Stephen was not prepared to leave it there. 'Oh, yes,' he reminisced, 'they were very interested to hear that you were old Mrs Holland's granddaughter. Impressed, too, when I told them you were a lady lawyer. I'd say you were quite a rarity around here. I doubt if Paget's produced too many lady lawyers.'

Olivia's teeth ground together, and she dug her nails into her palms to prevent herself from wrapping them around Stephen's smug neck. In the space of an evening, he had destroyed all her hard-won anonymity. And as for Conor...

'Yes.' Stephen wouldn't leave it alone. 'You have to admit I've got a good memory. I mean, when the Drakes started talking about *Dr* Brennan, I didn't immediately catch on. But then, I remembered you telling me—soon after we were married, I think it was—about this family who used to live next door to your grandmother. I remembered their name was Brennan, and how the parents were killed, and the son went to live in the United States.' He shrugged modestly. 'Well, as soon as Mrs Drake mentioned that the good doctor had lived in the States before coming back to Paget, I soon put two and two together. Clever, hmm?'

'Masterly,' conceded Olivia contemptuously. 'And while you were telling the Drakes all about my affairs, did you happen to add that you're the low-down ratfink who's been jerking off his boss's wife?'

Stephen's expression was almost comical. He lurched forward in his chair, casting a ludicrously apprehensive look over his shoulder, before snarling angrily, 'Watch your mouth, can't you? For Pete's sake, Harry may have sent someone down here to spy on me, for all I know. It's not as if it was difficult to find out where you were staying. All I did was bribe the caretaker of your apartment building to give me the address you'd left in case of emergencies. Hell, this was an emergency. And Harry could do the same.'

Olivia shook her head. 'So?' she countered, annoyed that Mr Parkinson should have taken Stephen's money. 'Why should I care what happens to you? Maybe Harry would do us both a favour if he shut your mouth for good!'

Stephen blanched. 'You don't mean that, Ollie.'

'Don't I?' Right then, Olivia wasn't too sure. She regarded him without sympathy for a moment, and then added curiously, 'You don't honestly think he would— well, do something criminal, do you?'

'Who knows?' Stephen expelled an unsteady breath. 'If he was mad enough.' He shook his head. 'Oh, I don't know. Maybe he wouldn't go as far as—wiping me out, or anything dramatic like that. But he would make me pay, one way or another.'

'Oh, Stephen——'

'Well, it's true, Ollie. And you know what a low pain threshold I have. I can't bear being hurt; physically hurt, that is. Hell, I faint at the sight of blood! After I'd visited you in hospital that time, when you were all strung up to those IVs and things, I went out and threw up. Literally threw up, and if Darcy's minders get hold of me——'

'Oh, shut up!'

Olivia didn't want to listen to any more. She didn't want to feel responsible. But, much as she despised him, she couldn't stand by and see him beaten up by hooligans. Not that she really believed it would come to that. But, just in case...

Mrs Drake's appearance, to take their orders for breakfast, was as timely as the day before. 'So there you are, Mrs Perry,' she exclaimed. She smiled at Stephen. 'Your husband was quite worried about you last night. Disappearing like that without telling us,' she chided. 'And me making one of my special chicken casseroles for you both.'

'Really?' Olivia folded the newspaper into a neat oblong, and laid it by her plate. 'Well, I'm afraid—Mr Perry—is getting rather absent-minded. I did tell him I had a supper engagement. He must have forgotten to pass it on.'

'Is that right?' Mrs Drake turned to Stephen now, and Olivia was amused to hear him trying to wriggle out of the situation.

'I believe she did say something about going out,' he muttered, red-faced, 'but I thought it was tonight.' He gave Olivia a glowering look. 'Still, no harm done, eh?'

Mrs Drake didn't look as convinced of the veracity of that statement as he seemed to be, but she knew better than to argue with her guests. Instead, she flipped open her notebook and took their orders for breakfast, and, if there was a certain tightness around her mouth as she did so, Olivia was grateful that it averted any discussion of her identity.

When they were alone again, however, Stephen lost no time in voicing his complaints. 'Making me the scapegoat!' he muttered, his mouth a sullen line. 'Why couldn't you have got me an invitation from this bloke Brennan? We could have made up a foursome. I bet that's what the Drakes think.'

'I don't care what the Drakes think,' retorted Olivia shortly, picking up her newspaper again. 'I suggest you think about what time you're leaving. Immediately after breakfast would seem appropriate to me.'

'Oh, would it?' Stephen sounded belligerent at first, but then his shoulders hunched. 'Yes, well—I suppose I will have to go,' he muttered. 'I've got an appointment in Eastbourne at half-past three.'

Olivia looked down at her place mat, not wanting him to see the relief in her eyes. But once Stephen was gone, she intended to make her own arrangements, and this time no one would know her destination.

She was gazing out of the window, wondering if escaping the sight of Stephen ploughing his way through bacon, eggs, sausage and fried potatoes was worth giving up her second cup of coffee for, when someone entered the tiny dining-room. As before, when Stephen himself had interrupted her meal, Olivia expected it to be Mrs Drake. But it wasn't. To her dismay, it was Conor who was crossing the room towards them.

Her sudden intake of breath was clearly audible, and Stephen looked up from his plate. 'Burnt your mouth?' he scoffed, around a mouthful of toast. 'Serves you right. You should eat something, Ollie. Heaven knows, it's not as if you don't need it!'

Olivia looked away from his greasy lips, lifting her head to Conor's dark-skinned face. Oh, God, she thought despairingly, what was he doing, coming here? And why did just the sight of him sing like music in her soul?

Her expression, guarded though it was, alerted Stephen to the fact that they were no longer alone. 'What...?' he began irritably, glancing round. And then, as the other man came to stand beside their table, he put down his knife and fork, and wiped his face with a nervous hand. 'What do you want?'

It came to Olivia in a flash that Stephen was actually alarmed. He was sweating profusely, and his fair skin was red and blotchy. The contrast between his hot agitation and Conor's calm self-possession could not have been more pronounced, and she was sorely tempted to let him stew. It was obvious he thought Conor must work for Harry Darcy, and if she had had any doubts that he had been exaggerating his fears they were quickly extinguished.

'I said, what do you——?' Stephen was beginning again, shoving back his chair and getting unsteadily to his feet, but, before Olivia could speak, Conor took the initiative.

'I'm Conor Brennan,' he said coolly, offering his hand. 'A friend of—your wife's. And you must be Stephen.'

It was only then that Olivia remembered what she had told Conor. Here she was, enjoying Stephen's discomfort, and any minute he was going to tell the other man that they were divorced. She sighed. Oh, why had Conor come here? A phone call would have been enough to ensure that she wasn't lying about Stephen's visit.

Stephen had stopped blustering, and he shook the other man's hand almost automatically. But his eyes were definitely suspicious. 'You're—*Dr* Brennan,' he exclaimed, his eyes flicking back and forth between Conor and Olivia. 'You're the family friend she had dinner with last night?'

'That's right.' Conor thrust both hands into the pockets of his black leather jacket. He was all in black again today—black jacket, black trousers, his black shirt buttoned to the collar. But no tie, she noticed almost illogically. Yet, she thought, he looked so much better than Stephen in his business suit.

'I understand you've just arrived from London,' Conor continued politely. 'Are you staying long?'

Stephen frowned, and Olivia guessed he was wondering how much she had told Conor about their situation. Not nearly enough, she thought uneasily, not really wanting Stephen to know she had lied about their relationship.

'Stephen's leaving this morning,' she put in hurriedly, glad she was sitting down when she said it. When Conor turned those clear green eyes on her, her legs felt distinctly wobbly. And it had nothing to do with the accident.

'Really?' Conor's expression was unreadable. He turned back to Stephen. 'Just a flying visit, then?'

Stephen hesitated a moment, and then resumed his seat. 'In a manner of speaking,' he said, looking thoughtfully at his ex-wife. He put a forkful of fried potato into his mouth, and his eyes narrowed speculatively. 'I had to come and see how my—wife—was faring, didn't I? It was good of you to look after her, Brennan. Ollie's had a hard time of it lately, and there aren't many young chaps, like yourself, willing to spend an evening cheering up an old friend of their mother's.'

Olivia's face flamed. She couldn't help it. And resentment that Stephen should talk about her as if she were some decrepit old crock brought her to the point of revealing exactly how unaltruistic Conor's motives had been.

But, once again, it was Conor who saved her from herself. 'It's my pleasure,' he said smoothly, and Olivia wondered if she was only imagining the thread of steel in his voice. 'And I don't regard Liv as just a friend of my mother's. We grew up together.'

'Oh, come on.' Stephen had recovered himself now, and his smile was openly disparaging. 'That's carrying chivalry a bit far, don't you think? Ollie's years older than you are.'

Conor's features hardened. 'Well, no one could accuse you of an excess of chivalry, could they?' he retorted, and, although the words were undeniably offensive, they were delivered in such an even tone that Stephen was clearly unsure how to take them.

His uncertainty was transparent in the suspicious face he turned up to the other man, but apparently discretion got the better part of valour. 'Yeah, well—there's no point in avoiding the facts,' he muttered, evidently deciding that in any physical contest between them he'd come out the loser. 'Say it how it is—that's been my motto in life. And I haven't done too badly, all things considered.'

Conor's contempt was almost tangible. 'You think not?' he remarked, with a wintry smile. 'Then I'm sure you'll appreciate my reasons for saying that, as far as I can see, you don't give a shit about anyone but yourself!'

Stephen's jaw sagged, and Olivia was treated to a sickening view of half-masticated food. But that was a minor misfortune compared to the reaction Conor's words had evoked. There was no way Stephen could ignore the insult this time, and her heart sank convulsively as he struggled to find his feet.

'Just who do you think you're talking to?' he demanded incredulously. 'Look——' he wiped his face on his napkin and threw it down on the table '—I don't know what lies Ollie's been telling you, son, but take it from me—you don't know what the hell you're talking about.'

'Don't I?'

Conor hadn't even taken his hands out of his pockets. He just stood there, eye to eye with the other man, a vaguely insolent smirk on his lean features, and Olivia wanted to die. What did he think he was doing? she fretted anxiously. Her ex-husband might be a coward, if the odds were stacked against him, but he might not be able to resist taking a pot-shot at such an unguarded target.

'Aw, hell!' Stephen snorted. 'What are you trying to do? Pick a fight with me?' He spread his hands. 'Why? What's Ollie to you?'

'That's enough!' Almost overbalancing her chair, Olivia rose and pushed herself between them. 'It's barely nine o'clock in the morning, do you realise that? You haven't even got the excuse that you've been drinking. How do you think Mrs Drake will react, if she comes back and finds you two brawling?'

'Well, it's not my fault,' retorted Stephen, and, although she knew Conor had only been defending what he thought were her rights, Olivia had to agree with him. 'You'd better get your—*boy*friend to apologise,' he added balefully, and she was relieved to hear that he was willing to back down.

'In a pig's eye,' remarked Conor distinctly, and Olivia's stomach hollowed. 'I meant every word I said.'

Stephen gazed at him disbelievingly, and Olivia had to admit she shared a little of his incredulity. What was Conor trying to do? she wondered anxiously. Force the other man to attack him?

There was a moment when she thought he had driven Stephen too far, but evidently her ex-husband was not prepared to risk physical violence. 'I think you'd better go,' he said, and she guessed he was hoping Conor would take his victory with good grace. 'I'm going to do us both a favour and forget this ever happened. And if you want to continue working in this country, I suggest you do the same.'

Conor's mouth twisted, and Olivia just knew he wasn't going to let it go at that. 'Oh?' he said scornfully. 'Why?'

Stephen lifted his chin. 'I should have thought that was obvious. The British Medical Association don't take kindly to their practitioners behaving like hooligans, threatening decent, law-abiding citizens.'

Conor lifted his shoulders, indicating his hands were still in his pockets. 'Am I threatening you?' He shrugged. 'I can't help it if you don't like your own medicine—if you'll forgive the pun.'

Stephen looked at Olivia now, and she could see the anger and resentment he was trying so hard to disguise. 'What the hell have you been telling him?' he demanded, and she guessed that if they had been alone his words would have been much stronger. 'For God's sake, I wasn't responsible for the accident. If you'd spent less time in the office, and more with me, you wouldn't be in this mess!'

Olivia put an involuntary hand to her throat. She didn't know whether she was dismayed or relieved that he had so obviously misunderstood Conor's motives. But before she could make any response, Conor's hands came to grip her upper arms, and, although at first she was afraid he was going to remove the barrier she represented, he spun her round to face him.

'Get your coat, Liv,' he said, his eyes glittering with some unidentifiable emotion. 'Go on. I'll wait outside in the car.'

'My—coat?' Olivia was confused.

'Yes. I'm taking you out,' he said, his gaze flicking briefly to Stephen, as if daring him to challenge his statement. 'Don't worry. I won't touch him while you're gone.'

'The hell you won't!' snarled Stephen belligerently, but Olivia knew he wouldn't do anything now. He'd had his chance, and ducked it. Nevertheless, he was determined to have the last word. 'Well, well, well,' he sneered. 'So that's the way it is.'

'Shut your mouth, Perry.' Conor kept his tone polite, but there was no mistaking the underlying note of menace. He looked at Olivia. 'Well, what are you waiting for?'

Olivia shook her head. 'I don't think——'

'So, don't,' cut in Conor flatly, turning her round and pointing her towards the door. 'Or do you want me to get it for you?'

'No...' Olivia glanced between the two men. 'No, I'll do it,' she said, somewhat unwillingly. But the situation wasn't of her choosing. What price her eager plans to leave now?

As if sensing her unwillingness to leave them alone, Conor followed her out into the hallway. 'Don't be long,' he said, striding towards the outer door. And, in spite of her misgivings, Olivia found herself going obediently up the stairs.

She was renewing her lipstick with a slightly unsteady hand when the bedroom door opened and Stephen stepped into the room. He stood there, watching her outlining her lips with the red gloss, his expression mirroring his resentment. And, although she knew she ought to object, she couldn't think of a thing to say.

'So, how long has this been going on?' he demanded at last, and the sheer effrontery of his question brought her quickly to her feet.

'There's nothing going on,' she said, putting the cap back on the lipstick and reaching for her hairbrush. 'Get out of my room, Stephen. We have nothing to say to one another.'

'I disagree.' Stephen made an aggressive move, but then, as if realising that wasn't the way to get her attention, he tucked his hands into his trouser pockets and rocked back on his heels. 'In a hurry, aren't you?' he sneered. 'I would be, too, if I had someone young enough to be my daughter panting after me!'

Olivia ground her teeth. 'You're disgusting!'

'Am I?' Stephen's lips curled. 'I wondered why you came to this God-forsaken place. Now I know, don't I?'

'Will you get out of here?' Olivia could hear her voice rising and struggled to hold it down. 'Don't judge everyone by your own standards. Conor and I are friends. Friends, that's all. A man and woman can be friends, although I doubt that's something you know anything about.'

Yet, even as she said the words, Olivia knew herself for the hypocrite she was. How could she dismiss what had happened last night as a 'friendly' encounter? If she hadn't come to her senses when she did, heaven alone knew what might have happened.

Which was why her tone was less than confrontational when she added, 'Just for the record, I didn't know Conor had come back to live in Paget when I came here. I thought the Brennans' house had been sold years ago.' She held up her head. 'But it hadn't.'

'And you just happened to run into him?' suggested Stephen sceptically, and she nodded.

'Yes.'

Stephen was silent for so long that she was sure he was trying to read her mind. But it wasn't really a lie, she told herself defensively. Though not quite the truth either, she conceded with a sigh.

'All right.' To her relief, Stephen seemed to accept her explanation. 'So what's going on?'

'Going on?'

'Yes, going on.' Stephen dipped his head in the direction of the front of the inn. 'You can't seriously pretend you don't know what he's after.'

'Stephen, please!'

'Well, it's the truth.' Stephen scowled. 'And you're a fool if you think he's serious about you. Hell, I don't want to hurt you, Ollie, but take a look at yourself. You're a woman, approaching middle age, to whom fate hasn't exactly been kind. Oh, you've got nice hair, and nice eyes, and you used to have nice legs before——'

'Yes, thank you.'

Olivia cut him off before he could go any further. But there was a tremor in her voice as she did so, and she despised herself for allowing anything he said to upset her. Whatever else, his comments were not unbiased, and she hated the thought that he might detect her weakness.

'Well——' Stephen shrugged now '—all I'm saying is that you're not someone he'd get seriously involved with. I mean—he's young, and even I can see that he'd attract the birds. But you're not a bird, Ollie. You're someone he's known since he was a kid, and he feels sorry for you. Maybe he does think you've had a rough time. He may have some justification for thinking I walked out on you just when you needed me most. But, hell—I didn't know how things were going to turn out. I never wanted this divorce, remember? I hope you told him that.'

Olivia moistened her lips. 'I think you'd better go.'

'OK.' To her relief, he didn't argue. 'But think about what I've said, Ollie. You're an intelligent woman. You know it makes sense.'

'Stephen——'

'All right, all right.' He sauntered towards the door. 'So—I'll be seeing you, right?'

Not if I see you first, muttered Olivia under her breath, and then felt the hot sting of tears behind her eyes. Damn him, she thought painfully, crossing the room and slamming the door behind him. Why did he have to be right?

CHAPTER EIGHT

ONLY the thought that Conor might get tired of waiting and come looking for her forced Olivia to collect her coat and go downstairs. But she had no intention of going out with him, she told herself severely, as she checked the knot of hair at her nape. She would just tell him she had a headache—*more lies!*—and get rid of him.

The Audi was parked at the front entrance, with Conor at the wheel. When she emerged from the inn, he thrust open the door from inside, as he had done the night before. 'Get in.'

'No.' Olivia hung back. 'I—er—I've just come to tell you I've got a headache. I'm going to take a couple of capsules and rest for a while on the bed.'

Conor's mouth compressed. 'I said, get in,' he repeated, and she could tell he didn't believe a word. 'Or do you want me to get out and force you into the car?'

Olivia stood back. 'You wouldn't dare.'

Conor said nothing more. He just thrust open his door, and, rather than scuttle back inside like a frightened rabbit, Olivia said, 'Oh, all right,' and scrambled into the seat beside him.

But, if she'd thought that Conor might give her a few minutes to think of another excuse, she was wrong. As soon as she was inside the car and the door closed, he took off at speed, the rear of the car fish-tailing briefly, before maintaining its grip on the icy road.

'Are you crazy?' she exclaimed, groping for her seatbelt, and he immediately eased his foot off the accelerator.

'Sorry,' he muttered ruefully. 'I guess that was a bit thoughtless. Did I drive too fast last night? Was that why you wouldn't let me bring you home?'

'You know why I got a taxi back last night,' retorted Olivia shortly, and Conor lifted one shoulder.

'Oh, sure. I'd been drinking,' he conceded calmly. 'And you didn't want me to lose my licence, right?'

Olivia only glared at him, not prepared to go any further with that particular argument. 'Why did you come to the inn this morning?' she demanded. 'You knew Stephen would be there. What did you hope to prove?'

'That you're not happy with him?' suggested Conor, less flippantly. 'I know. You're mad at me. But, dammit, I didn't start it.'

Olivia's expression didn't change. 'You are joking.'

'No.' Conor's hands tightened on the wheel. 'Hell, Liv, how could you marry that moron?'

'Stephen's not a moron.' Hardly aware of why she was doing so, Olivia found herself defending him. 'He's just—unthinking sometimes.'

'He's a creep!' muttered Conor, without compassion. 'When he said what he did about the accident, I wanted to stuff my fist down his throat.'

'Yes.' Olivia swallowed. 'Yes, I think he—we—all—knew that.' She licked her dry lips. 'But—he's right, you know. It's not your problem.'

Conor glanced her way. 'And if I choose to make it my problem?'

'You can't.'

'Why can't I?'

Olivia shook her head. 'You had no right to speak to Stephen as you did. My God, you were deliberately trying to provoke him. And he's right, you know. The BMA would view your behaviour very unsympathetically.'

'To hell with the BMA,' responded Conor succinctly. 'And as far as your husband is concerned, I consider I acted with remarkable restraint, in the circumstances.'

'Well, I don't.' Olivia frowned, and then added with some reluctance, ''What circumstances?''

Conor glanced her way. 'Last night,' he said evenly.

Olivia turned her head towards the window. 'Where are you taking me?' she asked, refusing to consider what he might mean by that. Besides, while she had been caught up in their conversation, Conor had driven out of the village. They were on the coast road now, heading towards Witterthorpe, with Pagwell Priory looming out of the mist.

'Liv...' Conor removed one hand from the wheel, and covered both of hers, which were curled tightly in her lap. 'Liv,' he repeated softly, 'don't shut me out. I need to know how you feel about that—about Stephen.'

His fingers brushed her thigh, her muscles taut beneath the velvet Lycra of her leggings. She had an insane urge to part her legs and crush his hand between them. God, she wanted him to touch her there, just as he had done the night before. What on earth was the matter with her? She'd never felt like this before.

'Talk to me, dammit. I have a right to know.'

Conor's words broke the feeling of self-absorption that had been gripping her. Abruptly, she pushed his hand away, and pressed her legs together. 'You have no rights where I'm concerned,' she retorted. 'None at all. Now— are you going to tell me where we're going, or is this another silly game?'

Conor's jaw compressed. 'I have to call at the clinic,' he said, and Olivia's lips parted.

'The rehabilitation clinic in Witterthorpe?' she exclaimed, and Conor inclined his head.

'Unless you know of another,' he remarked sardonically, looking at her mouth. 'Don't worry. I won't keep you long. I just have to check on the patient who delayed me last night.'

Olivia felt his gaze as if it were something tangible, and for a moment she couldn't say anything. But then, in spite of her unwillingness to get involved in his life, curiosity got the better of her. 'The emergency?' she ventured, as he looked back at the road. 'What happened? Can you tell me about it?'

'I could.' Conor spoke carelessly. 'But you probably wouldn't be interested.'

Olivia sighed. 'Why not?'

Conor gave her an old-fashioned look. 'Come on. You've spent the last fifteen minutes showing me that you're not interested in anything about me, that you care about your husband, and that I'm just wasting my time trying to get through to you. Well, OK. If that's the way you want it, there's not a lot I can do about it. I may not like it, and, whatever you say, last night you did want me just as much as I wanted you. But—you are married, and I guess I have to respect that.'

Olivia's chin scrubbed the collar of her blouse. She had worn a blouse this morning, a cream blouse with a round collar, together with a long honey-brown cardigan that skimmed the tops of her thighs. Over this, she was presently wearing her cashmere coat—unbuttoned and gaping open, it was true, but very warm just the same.

Which was why she suddenly felt hot all over, she decided unsteadily, smoothing her damp palms over her knees. It wasn't what Conor had said, or the empty feeling she had experienced when she had realised he was backing off. It was just the warmth of her clothes, and the heat of the car, and the undeniable nearness of his body.

'Right?' he asked now, glancing her way again, and she nodded rather vigorously.

'Oh—right,' she echoed sturdily, transferring her attention to the window again. This was what she wanted, wasn't it? And why shouldn't she use Stephen to achieve her ends? He hadn't hesitated in doing the same.

The clinic was situated on the outskirts of the small market town. It had originally been the gynaecological unit of the Witterthorpe General Hospital, Conor told her, but when a new obstetric wing had been built the older building had been utilised as a rehabilitation centre.

'The facilities aren't exactly custom-made,' he added, parking the Audi in one of the staff bays. 'You'd better come in. You can wait in my office.'

Olivia understood what he meant as soon as she entered the building. In spite of the freshly painted walls and bright tubular furniture in the waiting-room, the long, draughty corridors and lofty ceilings were distinctly Victorian in appearance. She guessed it must cost a fortune just to heat this place, and at this hour of the morning the radiators were not winning the battle. As well as feeling chilly, there was also a distinctive smell of antiseptic in the air, and the memories it evoked were not welcome.

Conor regarded her wrinkled nose with thin-lipped resignation, however. 'Perhaps you'd better wait in the car,' he said, and she knew he hadn't connected her expression with the prolonged spell she had spent in a hospital just like this.

'It's all right,' she said, ignoring her queasy stomach, and tipping up the collar of her coat. 'Which way is your office? I hope you've got a heater.'

The receptionist greeted Conor warmly, but her eyes lingered longer on his companion. Olivia realised she was probably being assessed as a prospective patient. She doubted the manicured blonde behind the desk would mistake her for anything else.

The corridor had been carpeted, no doubt to help dispel the atmosphere of a hospital ward, and Conor walked more quickly than Olivia. It meant that he had to stop and wait for her to catch up, and she automatically quickened her step, to escape his probing eyes.

'Shit,' he said, as she reached him. 'You must think I'm a thoughtless bastard! That's why you looked so sick when we came in. I should have realised a place like this would bring back memories you'd rather forget.'

Olivia tucked her hands deeply into her pockets, as two women and a man emerged from a room further along on the right. 'I can live with it,' she said lightly, and hoped that Conor wouldn't feel the need to introduce her to his colleagues.

'But can I?' he responded obliquely, reaching naturally for her arm, and drawing her aside. 'Anyway, it's not much further now. And, yes, I do have an electric heater.'

To her relief, the three members of staff—whose only means of identification were the plastic-covered name tags, showing their picture, that they wore on their lapels—didn't have time for a prolonged conversation. The talk was all of some youth, who had apparently nearly killed himself the day before. It seemed he had taken an overdose of a substance known as 'crack', and Olivia, who knew exactly how dangerous a drug it was, wondered what it was doing here, in an establishment dedicated to its destruction.

Nevertheless, in spite of the seriousness of the topic, Olivia found herself watching Conor almost compulsively. Here, among his peers, she was seeing him in a different light, and she knew an undeserved sense of pride in his achievement. He spoke to the others so confidently, his manner relaxed, his knowledge undeniable. The two women were obviously older than he was, and yet they seemed to defer to his opinion. It made Olivia realise that age was not necessarily synonymous with ability—or with intelligence either, she reflected ruefully, thinking of Stephen.

She did wonder who they thought she was, and she guessed they were curious, too, in spite of everything. Particularly the women. Were these two of the 'man-hunters' Sharon had spoken about? Olivia speculated drily. Somehow she doubted it. She suspected that most women enjoyed the company of an attractive man. And just because these women were doctors they weren't immune from the condition. Sharon had just been warning her off—not in the most subtle way imaginable.

In any event, Conor excused himself before any lapse in the conversation could leave room for unwanted questions. With polite smiles all round, the two groups separated, and Olivia was relieved when they reached a door bearing the legend, *C. Brennan, M.D.*

She touched the nameplate as she passed, running her fingers over the letters almost wonderingly. Sally and Keith would have been so pleased, she thought, feeling almost tearful for a moment. But then she met Conor's inscrutable gaze, and she hastily disguised her emotions.

His office—or was it a consulting room? she wondered—was infinitely more inviting than the corridor outside. The walls here were hung with posters, and the carpet underfoot was plum-coloured and attractive. There was a desk, but there was also a couch and two armchairs, forming a kind of conversation piece in one corner. And there was a rubber plant, and a winter-flowering poinsettia, all adding to the impression of a secular apartment.

'This is nice,' she said, looking round, as he riffled through the papers—messages?—on his desk. She gestured towards the plants. 'Did—er—did Sharon get these for you?'

Conor was standing behind his desk, but now he looked up with a trace of impatience. 'What? Oh, no. The rubber plant was already here when I arrived, and Aunt Elizabeth sent me the poinsettia at Christmas. To remind me of home,' he added drily. 'She still regards Florida as my home.'

Olivia couldn't help herself. 'Do *you*?'

'No.' Conor's eyes were hard. 'I've told you,' he said tersely. 'Paget is my home.' He straightened the papers he had been scanning and came round the desk again. 'Now I've got to go. You'll be all right here. I'll have one of the nurses bring you some coffee.'

Olivia hesitated. 'I—couldn't help overhearing what you were saying just now.' She nodded her head towards the corridor outside. 'Is that right? One of your patients took an overdose?'

Conor's mouth twisted. 'I guess so.'

'But——' Olivia lifted her shoulders '—how could that happen?'

Conor shrugged. 'Someone supplied the stuff,' he said carelessly. 'It happens.'

'Someone on the staff?'

'Could be.'

Olivia shook her head. 'How could they?'

'Try money,' remarked Conor, taking his own identity tag out of his pocket, and making for the door. 'I won't be long.'

Olivia found herself going after him. 'There's no—danger—is there?' she ventured, suddenly reluctant to let him go, and Conor's eyes softened.

'Not to me,' he assured her gently, putting out his hand and looping an errant strand of hair behind her ear. 'You'll wait for me, hmm?'

Olivia pulled a wry face. 'Do I have a choice?'

'Well, you could call a cab,' he remarked flatly, and she wondered why that hadn't occurred to her. 'But you won't,' he appended, holding her gaze. 'You're going to give us both the pleasure of letting me drive you home.'

Of course, after he had left her, she thought of all the things she should have said to him. Not least, a reminder that his behaviour was hardly fair to Stephen. If they had still been married, how would she have reacted then? It was disturbing to discover she was ambivalent about her answer.

But it was difficult to feel any obligation towards Stephen, real or imaginary, she defended herself. His actions had hardly been honourable, and her only real loyalty was to Sally's memory. But it was becoming equally difficult to keep that in mind, even if she suspected Conor's attraction to her was rooted in the past.

She had turned on the electric fan to supplement the heat coming from the radiator, and was sitting at Conor's desk flicking idly through a copy of the *Lancet* when the door opened. She thought perhaps there had been a knock first, albeit a perfunctory one, but, before she

could answer, the door had opened and a woman came
into the room.

She was a middle-aged woman—in her late forties,
Olivia estimated—with permed blonde hair, liberally
streaked with grey. She was wearing a white overall, unbuttoned at the neck to reveal the lacy jabot of a hot
pink blouse, and rather unsuitable high heels. She was
also carrying a polystyrene cup of coffee, which she set
down on the desk rather heavily, causing some to splash
over Conor's papers.

Olivia snatched a tissue from her pocket to mop up
the steaming liquid, but, even as she did so, she was
struck by the woman's familiarity. She bore a striking
resemblance to someone she had seen recently, and only
as comprehension dawned did the possible reasons for
the woman's vaguely hostile stare become apparent. Mrs
Drake had told her that Sharon's mother worked at the
clinic. And this woman was simply an older version of
her daughter.

'Thank you,' she said now, feeling awkward for no
reason, and wondered whether she ought to mention the
resemblance. But, before she could make up her mind,
Mrs Holmes forestalled her.

'Milk, but no sugar,' she said, indicating the slightly
murky-looking liquid in the cup. 'We don't keep those
sachets of sugar on the premises, for obvious reasons.
But I believe Conor keeps a supply of sugar in his drawer,
if you want some.'

'No.' Olivia dropped the damp tissue into the waste
bin and held up her hand. 'No, this is fine,' she assured
her. 'I don't take sugar.'

'No, I thought not,' observed the other woman, with
all her daughter's discretion. 'Still, not many people do
nowadays. It's like smoking. It's going out of fashion.'

Olivia was tempted to say that fashion had little to do
with the decline in smoking, but she had no wish to get
into an argument with the woman. Besides, everyone
was entitled to their own opinion.

'You're Mrs Perry, aren't you?' the woman continued now. 'Sharon's told me all about you. Oh—I'm Sharon's mother, by the way. Mrs Holmes.'

Olivia's lips twitched a little at the form the introduction had taken. But then, guessing that the woman was probably waiting for her to taste the coffee, she wrapped her cold hands around the warm cup. The insulation kept the hot coffee from burning her fingers as she brought it to her lips, and she took a tentative mouthful, before adding, 'Mmm, that's good.'

Mrs Holmes folded her arms across her midriff. 'Sharon says you're here on holiday,' she remarked, and Olivia realised her hopes of being left alone had been premature. So far as Sharon's mother was concerned, her daughter's relationship with Conor gave her the right to interrogate his friends. 'Funny place to come for a holiday, isn't it? I mean—at this time of the year.'

Olivia took another sip of the coffee. It wasn't as good as she had implied, and it tasted of powdered milk. But it did give her a few moments to think of a response, and Mrs Holmes seemed to wilt in the vacuum.

'Well,' Olivia said at last, 'I used to live in Paget, you see. And—it seemed as good a place as any to relax.'

Mrs Holmes sniffed. 'I can think of better places,' she muttered. Then, changing tack, 'I suppose it's nice for you, seeing Conor again. I imagine you've seen quite a change in him. He was just a boy when you saw him last, wasn't he?'

Olivia pressed her lips together. 'Something like that,' she conceded after a moment, beginning to resent this questioning. For heaven's sake, had Mrs Holmes appointed herself Conor's keeper?

'Of course, we're all very fond of him here,' the woman went on, her voice starting to grate on Olivia's nerves. 'Professor Marshall—he's the chief administrator—he speaks very highly of Conor's abilities. He's hoping he'll stay here. He's got a real—a real—oh, you know! With the patients?'

'Rapport?'

'Yes, that's it.' The woman nodded. 'A real rapport with them. They talk to him, when they won't talk to anyone else. I think it's because he's so close to them in age. It makes a difference, you know. Don't you agree?'

'Oh—sure.'

Olivia could hear the edge in her voice, but she couldn't help it. And, anyway, Mrs Holmes wasn't listening to her.

'Yes,' she went on, cupping her elbow with one hand and resting her chin on the heel of the other, 'you forget sometimes how young he is. Oh, but he's had Sharon's dad and me in stitches a dozen times, talking about his student days.' She laughed reminiscently, and Olivia wanted to slap her. 'Those interns! It's a wonder any of their patients survived!'

Olivia finished her coffee with a convulsive swallow, and allowed the empty cup to join the tissue in the waste bin. It seemed a shame to soil the bin, which, until she had used it, had been pristine. Perhaps she should ask Mrs Holmes to empty it, she thought maliciously, and then chided herself for permitting such a thought.

But the picture of family domesticity the woman was painting rankled. She could tell herself it was a deliberate attempt to show Conor's relationship with Sharon in another light, but she still felt annoyed. Why bother? she wondered irritably. Did they really think she was some kind of threat?

'Anyway,' Mrs Holmes continued smugly, 'I suppose I'd better be getting on. It's been nice talking to you, Mrs Perry, but I really shouldn't waste any more time.'

Another dig? Olivia's smile was thin. Who asked you to? she wanted to say childishly. She'd just as soon have missed out on this enlightening experience.

'Did Conor bring you here?' the woman probed, as she did a kind of sideways *chassé* to the door, and Olivia wondered, for the first time, what Conor had told her. How had he conveyed the news that he had brought a

visitor to the clinic? And what excuse had he given for
bringing her here in the first place?

But, 'Yes,' she responded now, not prepared to pre-
varicate. 'He—um—had a patient he wanted to see.'

'Oh—Stuart Henley, yes.' To Olivia's dismay, Mrs
Holmes lingered. 'The silly fool nearly killed himself in-
haling a mixture of crack and baking powder. Do you
know, his heart stopped beating! If it hadn't been for
Conor, he'd be dead or brain-damaged or something.'

Olivia found her breath catching the back of her
throat. 'But—he's all right now?' she murmured tensely,
sure she shouldn't be asking Mrs Holmes the question,
but unable to prevent herself just the same.

'He's still alive,' agreed Sharon's mother, with the air
of someone who'd played a crucial part in his survival.
'These kids! They don't have any sense. Thank heavens
my Sharon's never got involved in anything like that.'

'Mmm.'

Olivia couldn't argue with her there, and, to her relief,
Mrs Holmes reached for the handle of the door.

'I'd better go,' she said once again. 'I've got work to
do.'

Olivia managed a thin smile. 'I'm sure.'

'You—er—you'll have to get Conor to bring you over
to tea one day,' she continued, as she swung the door
open. 'I'll tell our Sharon to fix it up, shall I? It'll give
you a bit of company, won't it? And I'm sure Sharon's
dad would like to meet an old friend of Conor's parents.'

CHAPTER NINE

OLIVIA was standing staring out of the window when Conor came back. She had been sitting down; she supposed she should still be sitting down. But Sharon's mother had made her so mad that she couldn't wait to get out of there.

She knew she was a fool, letting the other woman get under her skin, but that final dig about Conor's parents had been the last straw. Good God, she was not that old! If Sally and Keith had still been alive they'd have been forty-six and forty-eight respectively. She was thirty-four! Eight years older than Conor, it was true, but not their contemporary.

She was attempting to admire the clumps of daffodils growing wild beside the footpath, when Conor came into the room. Unlike Mrs Holmes, he hadn't knocked, but the face she turned towards him was still vaguely apprehensive.

And he knew instantly that something had happened. 'What is it?' he asked, with some resignation, closing the door with his shoulders, and slipping the pen he had been holding back into his pocket. 'Didn't anyone bring you any coffee?'

Olivia's mouth thinned. 'Oh, yes,' she said, slipping her hands back into their pockets and propping her hips against the sill. 'A Mrs Holmes attended to it.' Her wintry smile was ironic. 'I think she wanted to check me out.'

'Oh, God!' Conor swore. 'How did she find out you were here?'

'Who knows?' Olivia was dismissive. 'Are you ready to leave? Because if not——'

'I'm ready. I'm ready.' Conor pushed himself away from the door, and glanced half impatiently about the room. 'I gather she came back to collect the tray.'

'What tray?' Olivia propelled herself up from the window-sill. 'You don't need a tray for a disposable cup.'

Conor exhaled almost wearily. 'Connie must have been desperate,' he remarked, walking across to his desk. He pulled a folder out of a drawer, and, sorting through the papers on the desk, he stuffed some of them into it. His hands encountered the damp pages Olivia had tried so hard to sponge dry, and he gave her a wry look. 'What did she do? Throw it at you?'

Olivia had to smile. 'Something like that,' she admitted ruefully, moving over to join him. 'Is anything spoiled?'

'No.' Conor was laconic. 'But, believe it or not, I did ask one of the nurses to make the coffee. Real coffee, not that machine crap.'

'It doesn't matter.' Olivia shrugged. 'So—how is he?'

Conor widened his eyes. 'How do you know it's a he?'

Olivia grinned. 'I even know his name. Your Mrs Holmes is very chatty.'

'She's not *my* Mrs Holmes.'

'Well, *your* Sharon's mother, then,' declared Olivia equably. 'Once she'd assured herself I wasn't a threat to your relationship, she became quite friendly.'

Conor's mouth turned down. 'Did she?'

'Hmm.' Olivia found it was quite enjoyable to turn the tables on him for a change. 'She's even invited me over to their house for tea. She says she'll get Sharon to fix it up with you.'

Conor's mouth compressed. 'I don't think so.'

'Oh?' Olivia feigned disappointment. 'Why not?'

'Because I don't expect to be seeing Sharon again,' he told her shortly, and she was still absorbing this statement when his arm looped about her shoulders, dragging her towards him. 'I'd stop inviting trouble, if I were you,' he added, his hot breath moistening her ear. 'That is, unless you're prepared to take the consequences.'

Olivia pulled away from him at once, and he let her. But she had no illusions that, had he not wished to let her go, she wouldn't have succeeded. As it was, she was red-faced and eager to change the subject, and her, 'You—you didn't say how the boy is?' was a desperate attempt to rescue her composure.

Conor picked up the folder from the desk. 'He's off the respirator and he's stable,' he replied, much to her relief. But it was mostly relief that he hadn't pursued his earlier statement, rather than concern for someone she didn't know.

'And—did you find out where he got the stuff?' she persisted, and Conor gave her a look that said he knew exactly what she was doing.

But, humouring her, he explained that his patients had visitors, that this wasn't a prison, and that, although security measures were taken, sometimes the system broke down.

'We may never find out where he got it from,' he declared, and when he moved she hastened awkwardly towards the door. 'So let's go and get ourselves some decent coffee.' His smile was faintly malicious. 'And perhaps I should hear some more about this—friendship—you've struck up with Sharon's mother.'

Olivia had forgotten how cold it actually was until she got outside, and then she was quite glad to tuck herself into Conor's car. If his obvious amusement at her discomfort irritated her at all, she was not prepared to pursue it, and she had settled comfortably in her seat when he got in beside her.

'Am I forgiven?'

His first words startled her, and she turned her head to look at him in some surprise. 'For what?'

Conor flicked the key in the ignition, and put the Audi into gear. 'Well, not for teasing you about Connie,' he remarked, releasing the hand-brake, and reversing out of the parking bay. 'I meant——' he glanced her way '—for upsetting your husband.'

'Oh.' Olivia's fingers linked convulsively. 'I—perhaps you should ask Stephen.'

'I don't want to ask Stephen,' retorted Conor tersely, accelerating to the gates of the clinic, and turning out on to the main road. 'Perhaps I should have phrased that differently.' He paused. 'I'm not sorry for what I said. I meant every word. But—dammit—it's obvious your marriage is having problems as it is, and I guess I and my big mouth will only have added to them.'

Olivia glanced his way. 'Why—why do you think my marriage is having problems?' she asked sharply.

'Call it intuition.' Conor was sardonic. 'Hell, Liv, I have had some experience in these situations.'

'I bet you have.'

Her tone was bitter, and he uttered an angry expletive. 'Not from a personal standpoint,' he retorted harshly. 'But I have counselled enough adults to know what goes on.'

Olivia shrugged. 'So what am I supposed to forgive you for?'

'I don't know.' Conor was resentful. 'You twist my words so much, I don't know what the hell I mean.'

'Then perhaps we shouldn't talk about it,' she said, turning her attention back to the scene outside the car's windows. 'Oh, look—it's starting to snow.'

'We have to talk about it,' stated Conor grimly, and she was glad the icy roads meant he had to keep his hands on the wheel. 'If you and Stephen aren't having problems, why did you agree to have supper with me last night?'

Olivia sighed. 'All right. I suppose I should have told you sooner——'

'That's not what I meant, and you know it.' Conor was savage. 'Dammit, Liv, stop treating me like an idiot. If you're not happy, you've got to do something about it.'

'Why?'

She deliberately kept her face turned away from him, but she heard his harsh intake of breath. 'Because of us,' he responded, and she could feel his eyes boring into her back. 'Because if there's any chance of you divorcing him, I want to know about it.'

Olivia expelled her breath as quickly as he had sucked his in. 'Really?' she exclaimed, striving for a mocking tone. Steeling herself, she turned and looked at him. 'Why? Are you going to offer to counsel us?'

'Liv!' Conor's expression was ominous. 'Don't do this. You know what I'm talking about. I don't have to explain. God—you have to know how I feel about you. I've been trying to tell you since I was sixteen years old——'

'No!' Olivia tried to stop him. 'Conor, stop this! I don't find it at all amusing!'

'And you think I do?' he countered, swinging the car too violently round a corner, and having to hang on to the wheel until it righted itself again. 'Hell, Liv, I can't remember a time when you haven't played a part in my life. OK, I had some growing up to do, I accept that. And I also accept that when I came to London to see you, I played it all wrong. But God—I didn't have my head straight in those days. I thought I knew it all, but I didn't.'

'Oh, Conor——'

'No, hear me out, Liv. I was a fool, I know that. I got involved in things you don't want to know about. But that's all over now. I'm all grown-up. I'm a man, Liv, and I know what I want.'

'Not—me——'

'Why not you?' His eyes darkened as they rested briefly on her mouth. 'I don't believe you don't feel something for me.'

'Well, I do, of course——'

'You do?'

'—but not—not in that way,' she protested, anxious to convince herself as well as him. 'Conor, whatever happens between Stephen and me, it isn't your concern.'

'Isn't it?'

'No.' Olivia was adamant.

'Because I'm too young?'

Olivia sighed. 'Yes.'

'You're crazy!'

'No, I'm not.' She took a steadying breath. 'I don't know why I'm saying this, but, apart from anything else, I'm sure it hasn't missed your notice that—that I'm crippled!'

Conor gave her a bitter look. 'That's Stephen's excuse, not mine.'

'Oh, Conor!' Her head was aching with the effort of sustaining this argument. 'Just—just take me home,' she mumbled, digging her chin into the collar of her coat, and thereafter there was silence in the car.

The snow was falling more heavily now, she noticed, tipping her head back against the upholstery. It was congealing on the windscreen, forcing the wipers to work twice as hard to clear it, settling in fluffy flakes on the roadside, covering everything in a cloak of white. It was pretty, she supposed, struggling to think of anything but Conor, and the things he had been saying. It would be all too easy to give in to his persistence, all too easy to let him have his way.

But, although she was prepared to accept that he was attracted to her, she didn't believe the part he said she had played in his life. In the nine years since she'd last seen him, she doubted he'd even given her a second thought. Maybe at Christmas, and birthdays, she reflected sadly. But that was all. Then, three days ago, fate had taken a hand. She had stepped into his path, and he was flattered because he thought she'd sought him out. And maybe he was a little bored with Sharon, too, she appended, despising herself for the comfort that thought brought her. He had been looking for a diversion, and she had provided it.

It wasn't until Conor turned the car into the drive of the house on Gull Rise that Olivia realised where they were. With the snowstorm obliterating all but the most immediate surroundings of the car, she had hardly been aware that they were back in Paget. But when he braked and brought the car to a halt, she sat up in some confusion.

'This isn't the inn,' she exclaimed rather foolishly, and Conor turned to look at her with wry eyes.

'No,' he conceded, studying her unguarded face for a heart-stopping moment. Then, turning away, he thrust open his door. 'As I said, we're going to have ourselves some decent coffee.'

'They serve coffee at the Ship,' Olivia pointed out swiftly, as he walked round the car, but if he could hear her he chose to ignore her words.

'Come on,' he said, yanking open her door, his hair already flecked with snow. 'It's cold out here.'

The house, conversely, was beautifully warm, and Olivia had to admit, as Conor helped her remove her coat, that it was much nicer here than at the inn. Indeed, if it weren't for her unwelcome awareness of him, she knew she would have enjoyed familiarising herself with the old place again. As it was, she couldn't resist admiring the carpeted curve of the staircase, or running a finger over the polished mahogany of the banister as she followed Conor along the hall.

She halted in the kitchen doorway, arrested by the sight of him filling the coffee-maker with water, spooning coffee grains into a filter. He worked with an easy economy of effort, obviously well used to making his own coffee, and not at all perturbed by her interested appraisal.

Then, when the machine had been switched on, he turned and rested his hips against the drainer, his hands cupping the Formica at either side of him. 'Are you hungry?' he asked, and, realising she was staring at the spot where his shirt entered his trousers, Olivia hastily removed her gaze and shook her head.

'No. But if you——'

'I'm fine.'

His tone was clipped, and, deciding it was up to her to show him she intended to keep their association on a friendly basis, she spread her hands in an encompassing gesture. 'So,' she ventured lightly, 'who looks after this place for you? I can't believe you do all the housework yourself.'

'No.' Conor hesitated a moment, as if considering whether to answer her at all. And then he said carelessly, 'One of the local women comes in twice a week.'

'Ah.' Olivia hid her relief that it wasn't Sharon after all. 'Well, she does a wonderful job!'

'Doesn't she?' Conor was sardonic. 'Do you want a guided tour?'

'I—why, no. No, of course not.' Olivia gathered her briefly scattered composure. 'I should think I know my way around here almost as well as you do.'

'Oh, yes.' Conor removed his hands from the work-surface, and folded his arms. 'I forgot. You used to tuck me in, didn't you? How could I forget that?'

Olivia took a steadying breath. 'Please, Conor——'

'Please what?' His eyes glittered. 'Please don't say anything to embarrass you? Please don't talk about things that you'd rather ignore? Like how much you're wanting me to touch you at this moment?'

'That's not true!' Olivia was appalled that he could read something into her actions that simply wasn't there. 'If you're going to start that again, then I think I'd better go.'

'Start what again?' he asked, harshly. 'Making you look at yourself as you really are, and not as you'd like to be?'

'No.' Olivia straightened her spine, putting almost all her weight on her undamaged leg. 'I've told you how I feel about you, Conor. I'm fond of you—of course I am. How could I not be after—after——'

'—all these years?' he supplied contemptuously, and with a helpless gesture she turned back into the hall.

'If you say so,' she replied wearily, and with an angry oath he came after her.

'All right,' he said, thrusting his balled fists into his jacket pockets, and she guessed how much it had cost him to give in to her. 'All right, I won't say anything else to upset you. So—where do you want it?'

Olivia's hand sought her lips. 'What?'

'The coffee,' declared Conor, a rueful twist to his mouth. 'What else?'

Olivia expelled her breath in a rush. 'Oh.' She licked her lips. 'Well—in the kitchen, I suppose. But——' she glanced round '—would you mind if I used your bathroom first?'

'Help yourself.' Conor's tone was dry. 'I guess I don't have to tell you where it is.'

'No.' Olivia shook her head, but, although Conor went back into the kitchen to check on the coffee, all the way upstairs images of him as a baby, splashing his way through a hundred noisy bath-times, filled her head.

Of course, Conor's present bathroom bore only a passing resemblance to the one Olivia remembered. The old porcelain tub had been removed, and in its place there was a perspex-walled shower cubicle, and a modern corner bath. It had been tiled, too, and on the glass shelf above the wide hand-basin a razor and blades had taken the place of the old rubber duck Olivia remembered.

There was a damp towel, too, lying on the floor, where Conor must have dropped it and, unable to help herself, Olivia bent and picked it up. The faint aroma of the soap he had used still clung to the cloth, and with a feeling of despair she buried her face in its clammy folds.

'Liv!'

Conor's voice brought her to an unwelcome awareness of what she was doing, and she flung the towel aside almost convulsively. God, she was going out of her mind, she thought, with a tremor of self-disgust. Was she really reduced to seeking comfort from a *towel*?

'Liv!' Conor's voice was much nearer now, and she realised that by not answering him she had achieved what she had been trying to avoid: his awareness of her as a vulnerable human being. 'Liv—are you OK?'

He sounded as if he was just outside the door, and she gazed at her flushed face with frustrated eyes. If only she had brought some cosmetics with her. As it was, there was no way she could disguise the fact that she had been crying.

'Liv——'

'Yes, I'm all right.' In spite of her efforts, her voice was higher than it should be. 'I—I'll be down in a minute.'

'Well—if you're sure.'

'I'm sure.' Olivia stood on the other side of the door, praying he wouldn't ask what she was doing. She cleared her throat, and managed a lower tone. 'I'm sorry for taking so long.'

There was a silence that was almost audibly ana-lytical, and then Conor said, 'No problem,' in a flat, unemotional tone, and she heard him move away to-wards the stairs.

She waited several minutes until she was sure he had had time to reach the kitchen, and then opened the door. As she had expected, the landing was deserted, and, moving silently across it, she opened the door into what had once been Sally and Keith's bedroom. She guessed it was most probably the room Conor used now, and, while the connotations of that reality caused a fluttery feeling in her stomach, her need was greater than her fears.

Besides, she consoled herself, her motives were innocent enough. Well, mostly, she conceded, as her eyes moved hungrily over the familiar appointments of the apartment. But it had occurred to her that if Sharon had *stayed*—she stumbled over the word—at the house, she might have left a lipstick behind her. Not that the idea of using anything of Sharon's was particularly appealing to her, but she was desperate.

However, as she walked across the soft oatmeal carpet, it wasn't Sharon's presence that invaded her senses. In fact, there was no evidence that Sharon had ever been in the room. It was Conor's clothes that were strewn haphazardly about the place, and Conor's towelling bathrobe draped over the rail at the foot of the unmade bed.

Her eyes flicked quickly away from the bed, but the temptation to touch his clothes was almost irresistible. Still, she overcame it, and approached the solid oak dressing-table. If Sharon had left any personal belongings behind, surely this was where they would be, and, ignoring the censure she knew she would see in her reflection, she jerked the top drawer open.

'Looking for something, Liv?'

Conor's quiet enquiry almost scared the life out of her, and she dropped the box of cuff-links she had been holding, feeling like a thief caught rifling the premises. The tiny gold and silver items spilled all over the floor, and Olivia wanted to die of embarrassment.

'I...' She dragged her eyes away from the scattered pieces and looked helplessly at him. But the need to justify herself was uppermost. 'I—wasn't being nosy.'

'Did I say you were?' Conor had been standing with his arms folded, his shoulder propped against the frame of the door, but now he straightened and came into the room. 'Not that I've got anything to hide.'

Olivia sighed, and, remembering why she had wanted something to disguise her appearance, she felt a sense of resignation. She could only hope that he would attribute her swollen eyes and bare lips to the ignominy of her position.

'I—was—just looking for a—comb,' she improvised swiftly, realising she *couldn't* admit to searching for something of Sharon's. 'I'm sorry.'

Conor glanced at the dressing-table. 'Isn't my comb good enough?' he asked drily, and, following his gaze, Olivia saw the silver-backed brushes and comb she had overlooked earlier.

Allowing her breath to escape from lungs that felt decidedly inadequate at this moment, she moved her shoulders in a helpless gesture. 'I . . . didn't notice them,' she mumbled lamely, averting her gaze, and Conor's hand came to lift her chin.

'Why don't you ever admit the truth, Liv?' he demanded, his thumb brushing across her stiff lips. 'You wanted to see for yourself that I wasn't lying when I said Sharon didn't live with me.'

'*No*!' His words were sufficiently outrageous to give Olivia the strength to jerk her chin from his grasp. 'You flatter yourself, Conor Brennan!' she snapped, and, grasping the corner of the dressing-table, she levered herself down on to the floor, and began gathering the scattered cuff-links together.

It wasn't the most elegant thing she had ever done. As yet, she couldn't bear her weight on her injured knee, and consequently she had to sit on the floor, with one leg tucked under her, and the other stretched out. It also meant she had to shuffle across the floor on her bottom when those nearest to her had all been collected into a small pile.

'Liv!' Conor's use of her name was exasperated, and he squatted on his haunches beside her, successfully preventing her from reaching the last few pieces. 'Liv, leave them! I'll pick them up later.'

'I can do it,' she exclaimed, aware that several tendrils of hair had come loose from the knot she had secured earlier, and were now falling into her eyes. She pushed them back with a frustrated hand as she attempted to edge past him, but the dressing-table stool was in the way, and she got herself wedged. 'Will you move?'

'Liv, listen to me...' he began, but she was no longer totally in control of her actions. She was desperate to prove she was not the helpless creature he seemed to think her, and when he reached out to grasp her hand she forcibly pushed him away.

Unfortunately, Conor was caught off balance. Squatting as he was, his weight was not evenly distributed, and when she pushed him he tried to save himself by grabbing the rail at the foot of the bed. He missed, his hand only encountering the folds of his bathrobe and bringing it down on top of him. Then, as Olivia watched with horrified eyes, he toppled back on to the floor, his head striking one of the solid black castors with a sickening thud.

'Oh, God!' Abandoning her search for the cuff-links, Olivia scrambled towards him, and for once she never even felt the protesting pain in her leg. 'Conor!' she cried, when she saw that his eyes were closed, and, reaching awkwardly across him, she fumbled for the pulse beneath his ear.

It was still there—fast and erratic, it was true, but reassuringly strong. What she would have done if it hadn't been, she didn't care to speculate. All that mattered was that he was still alive, and her hand trembled as it brushed his cheek and the bronze tips of his absurdly long lashes.

'Oh, Conor,' she breathed, and, unable to help herself, she bent her head and touched her lips to the slightly parted contours of his mouth.

CHAPTER TEN

CONOR'S response was unexpected, and instantaneous. His tongue came to meet her lips, and she found her mouth clinging to his. Almost compulsively, her fingers slid into the silky length of his hair, and the kiss deepened to a breath-robbing assault.

His eyes opened as she was drawing back, a belated sense of the impropriety of what she was doing causing her to try and rescue her composure, but his expression was frankly sensual.

'Don't go,' he said, and she felt his hand at the back of her neck. 'I may be in need of more mouth-to-mouth resuscitation.'

Olivia pressed her lips together, trying to summon some resentment towards him for frightening her like that, but she was so relieved he was all right that she could only shake her head. 'You—you're impossible,' she said unsteadily, becoming aware that he had removed his jacket while she had been using the bathroom, and he grinned.

'Whatever it takes,' he said huskily, and, drawing her mouth back to his, he rolled over until she was lying flat on her back. 'Just don't—tell me you don't want me now.'

Olivia groaned. 'But I—I'm such a mess,' she stammered, while his mouth, moving over the silken curve of her cheek, denied her protest.

'You're crazy,' he told her, threading his hands through her hair, and scattering her hairpins as she had scattered his cuff-links a few minutes ago. His thumbs smoothed the dark shadows her tears had painted beneath her eyes. 'Is that why you were crying?'

She moved her head helplessly from side to side. 'We—
we shouldn't do this——'

'But we're going to,' he essayed a little roughly. His
eyes lowered to where his fingers were tracing the neckline
of her blouse. 'This is for us. No one else.'

Olivia's resistance was faltering. Everywhere he
touched, her skin felt sensitised, and when he unbuttoned the first few buttons of her blouse and delicately
stroked the tops of her breasts a wave of uncontrollable
longing swept over her. Her nipples hardened beneath
their lacy covering, and she knew he had noticed her
reaction when his tongue circled his lips in undisguised
anticipation.

Her eyes drooped beneath the hunger she could see in
his. What if she disappointed him? she thought raggedly.
What did she know of making love, other than the rather
unsatisfactory coupling she and Stephen had indulged
in? What if this turned out to be a terrible mistake? How
would she live with herself if it all went wrong...?

'Look at me,' Conor said, interrupting her anxious
introspection, and when her lids flickered upwards she
saw he had torn open the buttons of his own shirt and
dragged it out of his trousers. 'Help me,' he added, and
almost automatically her hands moved to ease the shirt
off his shoulders.

But, after he had discarded it on to the floor, her hands
lingered on his chest, and on the fine pelt of honey-
coloured hair that arrowed so enticingly down to his
navel. It felt so clean—so *good*—that she wanted to bury
her face in its downy softness, and she knew Stephen
had never made her feel so aware of her own weakness.

Conor was unbuttoning the rest of her blouse now,
and his fingers made short work of the front fastening
on her bra. Experience, she supposed, as a fleeting surge
of uncontrolled jealousy swept over her, but then he bent
his head to her breasts and all negative emotion was cast
aside.

She caught her breath as he licked the sensitive peak of one breast, and when his teeth fastened round the nipple and tugged, ever so gently, her heart nearly exploded.

'Beautiful,' he breathed, his hand running possessively down her body to her thigh, before returning to ease both her blouse and the chunky cardigan from her shoulders. 'But now, I want to see you naked.'

Olivia stiffened. Until then, she had been so wrapped up in what he was doing to her body that she hadn't given a thought to how she would feel about him seeing her totally nude. It was all very well—if a little exaggerated—for him to say she was beautiful, when his attention was concentrated on the slender curve of her torso. But how would he feel—how would *she* feel— when he peeled off her leggings, and...?

But she couldn't go any further. 'I—can't,' she got out miserably, suddenly aware of the texture of the carpet at her back, the incongruity of making love on the floor when there was a perfectly good bed just a few feet away. 'You don't understand...'

Conor's eyes were so dark a green that she felt as if she were drowning in their shaded depths. 'What don't I understand precisely?' he asked, one leg wedged between her knees, and a finger lightly probing the waistband of her leggings. The timbre of his voice lowered. 'Do you really think I don't know what you're afraid of?'

Olivia moved her head. 'You don't know what I look like,' she insisted, and Conor sighed.

'Then let's see, shall we?' he suggested evenly, and, ignoring her outraged hands, he dragged the leggings down over her hips.

The fact that her silk knickers were tugged away along with the leggings didn't immediately register. She was so shocked at the high-handed way he had acted that she could only lie there with her eyes closed, as a wave of hot embarrassment swept over her. Only it wasn't just embarrassment, she acknowledged painfully. It was shame, and humiliation, and downright anger. How could he have done such a thing? Without even the protection of a sheet to hide her blushes?

And then, like a balm to her mortified flesh, she felt his mouth moving on her thigh. His lips were following the line of the ugly scar that seared from her groin to her knee, she realised incredulously. He was kissing her, soothing her quivering limb with sensuous caresses that burned their way into her consciousness, and left her weak and helpless.

Her eyes opened, shifting quickly from the high ceiling to the amazing sight of Conor's bent head. The snowstorm was over, and the clear light from a white world filled the room with brilliance. It silvered Conor's hair, showing up the darkness of the strands the snow had dampened earlier, and as he sensed her gaze and lifted his head a silky wave fell against his temple.

Olivia moved then, her hand lifting to touch his hair before sliding to the nape of his neck. But Conor captured her fingers in passing, drawing her palm against his mouth. Then, with his eyes still on her, he allowed his tongue to caress her palm, causing the drenching heat of excitement to pool between her legs.

Olivia was shaking with emotion when he knelt and lifted her into his arms. Then, lowering his mouth to hers, he got to his feet, and walked the short distance to the bed.

The sheets were cool, but oh, so soft against her bare shoulders, and he only paused long enough to strip off his trousers before sliding on to the bed beside her.

'Better?' he breathed huskily, spreading her hair out on the pillow, and burying his face in its dusky tangle, and she could only nod bemusedly. But the world had narrowed to this room, this bed, and this man, and for the first time in their association she was prepared to let him have his way.

His tongue slid into her mouth, filling her with the taste and the feel of him, hot and wet, and devastatingly real. Against her breasts, the hair-roughened skin of his chest was unbearably erotic. When he rolled to one side to explore her hips and her navel and the sensitive inner curve of her thigh, she looked down and saw the glistening shaft of his manhood rearing from its nest of darker blond hair.

Her nails dug into her palms as the emotions the mere sight of his arousal evoked inside her threatened to overwhelm her, and then, unable to stop herself, she uncurled her fingers and let them seek their own destiny. The hot velvety skin swelled beneath her touch, and with a groan that was half pain, half ecstasy, Conor slid over her.

'Don't—don't do that,' he implored her brokenly, and then, seeing her instinctive withdrawal, he drew her hand back to his body. 'All right, do it,' he conceded. 'Just don't expect my control to be limitless.'

Olivia licked her lips. 'What control?' she asked, relaxing, and Conor's mouth cut off the soft smile of understanding that tugged at her lips.

Her head swam as his weight pressed her into the mattress, and her legs parted to admit his probing hand. His fingers slid between the moist curls, seeking the slick cleft that was already throbbing in anticipation, and when he stroked the sensitive nub of her femininity she could barely suppress the urge to thrust herself against him.

'Good,' he whispered, the unsteadiness of his voice revealing his own dwindling self-control, and, instead of answering, she wound her arms around his neck.

It was all an exquisite agony, a soul-wrenching torture that demanded its own fulfilment. She had never felt this way with Stephen, never felt this way before, and the need for him to invade her body was becoming an unbearable torment.

She found herself moving against him, rotating her hips, inviting his participation, showing him without words exactly how she felt. Her mouth was swollen, bruised by the hungry possession of his mouth, but it was another possession entirely that she wanted now.

And Conor had driven himself beyond the point of rationality. With movements that were motivated purely by instinct, he guided himself to the very threshold of her womanhood and then, with an aching need that Olivia's body echoed, he buried himself in her yielding flesh.

'Oh, God,' he groaned, as her muscles expanded to admit him and then closed tightly about him. 'God, Liv—I'm going to make a mess of this.'

'Sh-sh,' she whispered, content for the moment just to enjoy the sensation of him stretching her and filling her in a way she had never experienced before. Acting purely on impulse, she lifted her legs to facilitate his moving even deeper inside her, and a moan of frustration broke from him.

'Aw—hell!' he swore, and, feeling the sudden hot flood of his release, Olivia guessed what had happened.

'It's all right,' she breathed, hanging on to his shoulders when he would have dragged himself away. 'I don't mind, honestly.' And, in spite of her own unrequited needs, it was true. She had wanted to please him and she had. And that was what mattered.

'I mind,' he muttered, some minutes later, when the shuddering spasm of his climax had left his body. He levered himself up on to his elbows, placed at either side of her head. 'I wanted this to be perfect. Instead of which, I lost control like a demented schoolboy!'

'Well, you were,' she said softly, smoothing the damp hair back from his forehead with teasing hands, and he frowned.

'I was what?'

'Demented,' she told him gently, and, guessing he thought she had meant something else, she added, 'But nothing like a schoolboy.'

'And I didn't wear anything,' he declared, turning his lips against her fingers. 'After all the advice I've given my patients on the need to use a condom, and when you touched me I couldn't wait long enough to put one on.'

Olivia took a quivering breath. 'Do you wish you had?' she asked, and Conor gave her a rueful look.

'No,' he said huskily, lowering his forehead until it was resting against hers. 'It's you I'm concerned about, not me.'

'Well, don't be,' she whispered, guessing he would assume she was using some other form of protection. She stroked his mouth with her finger. 'Did I—did you—was it all right?'

His expression was tender. 'You are joking?'

Olivia caught her lower lip between her teeth. 'I just thought——'

'Liv, I've wanted you here, in my bed, for longer than I can remember. And since that morning you practically collapsed on my doorstep I've thought of nothing else but you.' He used his thumbs to massage her temples, as his lips and his tongue caressed her willing mouth. 'How do you think it feels to know I'm a part of you? I could live forever and never top the magic of this moment.'

'Oh, Conor...'

Her breathless cry was against his lips, and her arms closed convulsively around his neck. She was very much afraid she would never know such happiness again, and the prospect of him leaving her made every second precious.

The growing awareness of his arousal caused her hold on him to falter. She hadn't known a man could become aroused again so quickly, and Conor's eyes, as she pressed him away from her, were faintly rueful.

'Yes,' he said softly, taking one of her quivering hands and drawing it down to where their bodies were joined. 'Did you honestly think it was over? God, Liv, we could stay here all day and night as well and I'd still want more.'

Olivia's eyes were wide and luminous. 'You—you don't have to say that,' she protested, and Conor's lips twisted.

'Oh, yes, I do,' he averred huskily, pushing her back against the pillows, and the possession of his mouth left her no room for doubts.

And nothing had prepared her for the way she would feel when Conor began to move inside her. The sensations she felt when his powerful body slid in and out of hers filled her with a spiralling kind of torment. They taught her that what she and Stephen had shared had had no force, no substance, and how could she hope to assuage a hunger that had never been slaked?

But as Conor cupped her buttocks so that he could penetrate to the very core of her being, the flame he had ignited began to engulf her. His urgent body thrust ever more forcefully into hers, and every straining muscle brought an answering response that was purely physical. Her mind might be torturing her with her lack of experience, but her body knew exactly what it wanted.

Hardly aware of what she was doing, she clutched Conor's neck, her nails digging into his flesh, and she dragged his mouth back to hers. Now, her tongue invaded his mouth, sucking his lips, crushing herself against him, so that from breast to thigh there were fused together by the sweat of their bodies.

'God, Liv,' he groaned, ramming himself into her, and the raging fire in her blood melted the final restraints inside her. With a choking sob, she reached the precipice and plunged eagerly over the edge, spilling out into a space so incredibly beautiful that she could feel the hot tears of gratitude running helplessly down her cheeks. Seconds later, Conor joined her, the rushing warmth of his seed sending her into another involuntary convulsion, so that it was some time before either of them was capable of coherent thought...

Predictably, it was Conor who eventually broke their embrace. Realising he was probably crushing her beneath the weight of his powerful body, he rolled with evident reluctance on to his back, shielding his eyes from the glare outside with a lazy arm.

Then, expelling his breath on a contented sigh, he rolled on to his side. Propping himself on one elbow, he looked down at her, and it said something for Olivia's state of mind that she didn't immediately rush to drag the covers over her.

'I love you,' he said, his green eyes dark and intent. 'And I want you to divorce Stephen, and marry me.'

Olivia blinked, and then, when his hand came to rub the treacherous tears from her cheeks, she struggled to summon all the objections that had been so obvious in her before he robbed her of all intelligent thought.

But lying there, looking up into his soulful gaze, it was difficult to think of anything but the singular delight it would be if he were to make love to her again. Having once tasted heaven, she could quite see why someone would want to taste it again, though in Conor's case her involvement was probably not essential.

'Are you listening to me?' he demanded now, his hand drifting down over her throat, lingering momentarily at the helpless arousal of her breast, before continuing on to the cluster of dark curls that guarded her womanhood. He bent his head to touch her there, and then, his voice thickening, he added, 'Don't tell me you still love him, because I don't believe you.'

Olivia felt her legs parting under that deliberate stimulation, and it was a distinct effort to press them together. But, in doing so, she trapped his fingers, and she reached down to remove his hand with scarcely concealed anguish.

'No,' she said, groping for the sheet that was crumpled beneath them. His weight was on it, and she tugged ineffectually. 'Please!'

'Please, what?' he said, half annoyed by her obvious efforts to dislodge him, and Olivia rolled on to her side away from him.

'I—I have to go,' she said, and with an impatient oath Conor dragged the sheet out from underneath him, and tossed it over her.

'If you're so desperate to hide yourself—here,' he said, shifting on to his back again. 'But for God's sake, Liv, stop kidding yourself that what's just happened is going to go away.'

'It has to,' she said, in a muffled voice, knowing she should get off the bed, but incapable right then of doing so. 'Conor, I—I'm not saying that—that I don't care for you——'

'Oh, thanks!'

'—but you and me—we're no good together.'

Conor swore. 'Don't be stupid!' His hand reached for her shoulder, turning her on to her back again. He rolled to face her, his eyes dark with a mixture of both passion and anger. 'After what we've just shared, you can still say——'

'It's not enough,' insisted Olivia painfully, the words she was trying to say tearing her apart. 'Conor, what we just had was—was sex; plain and simple. Not something on which to build a lifetime's commitment; not when there are so many other reasons why we'd fail.'

Conor scowled. 'Tell me, then. Tell me these reasons. I've told you I care about you, and I'm pretty sure you care about me. That's not sex talking, Liv. That's love!'

The urge to give in, to tell him she agreed with him, that she'd do anything he wanted, as long as they could stay together, was almost unbearable. How could she turn him away? How could she deny what they had undeniably had? Was anything worse than the trauma of never seeing him again? For if she left him now, that was what it meant. She couldn't do it any other way.

But the habits of a lifetime were hard to break, and she was simply not able to justify that kind of weakness, even to herself. She had to end it now, before his persistence and her own need undermined her reason. At least she had known how it could be with someone you loved. Some women went through their whole lives without experiencing perfection.

'I'm—too old for you,' she began, knowing what he would say, and prepared for it this time. 'Conor, you're young, you're ambitious, you've got your whole life in front of you. I would only hold you back. You know it, and I know it. Besides, I—still have a husband.' She crossed her fingers on the lie. 'And he's not likely to divorce me if he thinks that you're involved.'

'Then I'll wait,' said Conor flatly. 'Sooner or later, he's got to give in.'

'No——'

'Yes.' He closed his eyes against the denial he could see in her face. 'Liv, I don't care how long it takes. I've waited eleven years already.'

Olivia let her breath out rather unevenly. 'So you say.'

'So I know.' His eyes flicked open. 'What do I have to do to make you believe me? What's five years more or less in a lifetime?'

'It's the difference between me being thirty-four and nearly forty,' retorted Olivia harshly. 'Conor, when you get married, you'll want children. I don't even know if I can have any. I—I haven't had any luck so far. And—and before you ask, I—might have done.'

Conor's expression was grim. 'And if I say that I don't care whether or not you can perpetuate the Brennan dynasty?'

Olivia sighed. 'I care,' she said steadily. 'And—and your mother would care, if she were still alive.'

Conor stared at her for another heart-stopping moment, and she had the feeling that if he touched her now her defences would crumble like the pathetic things they were. But then an expression of bitterness filled his face, and without another word he got up from the bed.

He paused when he reached the bedroom door, however, turning back to look at her, heartbreakingly appealing in his naked masculinity. 'My mother would never have stopped us, you know,' he said, his eyes dark with pain. 'But if that's the only excuse you've got to offer, then I guess I did get the wrong message.'

Olivia closed her eyes against the subtle accusation of his words, and when she opened them again he was gone. A few moments later, she heard the sound of water running, and as she dragged herself off the bed she guessed he was taking a shower.

She wanted to go to him even then. She knew the bathroom door wouldn't be locked, that he would be hoping, even now, that she would change her mind. All she had to do was open the door, step into the shower cubicle with him, and let the future take care of itself. She could do it. She wasn't married, even if he still thought she was. She had nothing to be ashamed of.

But it was the fear of his ultimate rejection that made her turn aside from such temptation. The fear that she would last no longer than Sharon, or any of the other women he had known since he left England ten years ago. And, strangely enough, she knew he could hurt her far more than Stephen had ever done. And she had had too much pain already.

Besides, she argued, she had her career to consider. She wasn't like Sharon. She had never allowed any man to come between her and the people she had been trained to defend. In that, she conceded, Stephen had been right. She had had too little time for him. So why should it be any different with Conor? She wasn't the emotional type.

Only she was. *She was.* Standing there, staring at her reflection in the long cheval-mirror, she acknowledged that what had been wrong with her marriage to Stephen was that she simply hadn't loved him enough. But, until now, she had had nothing to measure it against. Now she had. Crazy as it sounded, she was falling *in love* with Conor.

But she couldn't. As her fingers probed the bruises his lovemaking had left on her body, she knew she had to start thinking with her mind again, instead of her senses. It would be too easy to give in to the insidious attraction he had for her, too easy to forget that she already had one failed marriage behind her, and that she had sworn when she divorced Stephen that she would never get herself into that situation again.

Of course, that was before she had met Conor again, she admitted, before she had realised that the love she had had for him when they were children could mature into something infinitely more powerful. Which was just another reason why she couldn't let it go on. If she had been younger, fitter, maybe they would have stood a chance. As it was, she would be fooling herself if she thought this relationship could bring her anything but more heartache. And of a much more devastating kind...

She suddenly realised that the water had stopped running, and, aware that Conor would come back at any second, she hurriedly scrambled into her clothes. She was buttoning her blouse when he came back into the room, and she averted her eyes as he crossed the room to take clean underwear from the dressing-table drawer.

'You could have had a shower, too,' he observed, and she was shaken by the absence of feeling in his voice. It was as if their relationship had never progressed beyond the point of bare civility, and she turned to look at him with unguarded eyes.

But then, realising she was in danger of revealing exactly what his attitude meant to her, she groped for her cardigan. 'I—I'll have one later,' she stammered, fumbling her arms into sleeves that were turned inside out. She moved to the window. 'Um—at least it's stopped snowing.'

'Has it?' Conor's tone hadn't changed, but the contempt in his face was shrivelling. 'You know, I hadn't noticed.'

Olivia bit her lower lip. 'I—don't be like this,' she implored, and for a moment she glimpsed the anguish he was trying so hard to conceal.

'I thought this was what you wanted,' he replied, and her nails dug into her palms as he pulled a navy polo shirt over his head. It was probably the last time she would share such an intimacy with him, and her heart ached at the futility of what she was doing.

But, 'Yes. Yes, it is,' she mumbled, and, even though it was tearing her to pieces, she met his accusing gaze with calm determination. She limped heavily to the door. 'Will you take me home?'

CHAPTER ELEVEN

THREE months later, on a perfect day in late spring, Olivia stood beside Stephen's widowed mother, as his coffin was lowered into the ground. The older woman was crying, stifling her sobs in the handkerchief she had pressed to her face. And, although Olivia was less affected by her surroundings, she, too, could feel the tightness of grief gripping her throat.

But it was all so unbelievable, she thought. That Stephen should actually be dead! That they should be burying a man who would have only been forty-five on his next birthday. It seemed so unfair.

Not that his death had been the act of revenge she had at first imagined. When Mrs Perry had rung in tears, begging her to come and comfort her, Olivia had instantly thought of Harry Darcy, and Stephen's fears when he had come to the inn in Paget. In spite of the pain even thinking of those days evoked in her, she had briefly wondered if Harry had found out about Stephen's affair with his wife, and carried out his threat.

But, to her considerable relief, she had discovered that that was not the case. Although it had evidently been difficult for his mother to admit, she had eventually confessed that Stephen had breathed his last in another woman's arms. A married woman, it was true, but not Karen Darcy. Her son had died, as he had lived, without giving any thought to the consequences of his actions.

Which was why it was left to Olivia to make all the arrangements for his funeral. Mrs Perry was too distressed to do it for herself, and, until her sister arrived from Manchester, Olivia had borne the whole burden of her tears and recriminations.

155

She hadn't blamed Olivia, exactly. But she had made it known that she considered Olivia was responsible for the divorce. No *reasonable* woman expected a man to be totally faithful, she said. Which had made Olivia wonder about the kind of life Mrs Perry had led with Stephen's father. Like his son, Mr Perry had died of a heart attack in middle age.

In any event, by the day of the funeral Olivia was quite relieved to hand over the reins to Mrs Perry's sister. She had been glad to help, but it had become something of a strain. Her own life was not without its complications, but it was not something she could confide in Stephen's mother.

Harry Darcy approached her as they were leaving the cemetery. As Stephen's employer, he had naturally attended the service, and his swarthy features were kind and sympathetic.

'Well, Olivia,' he said, 'this is a tragedy. Particularly as Steve had told me that you and he might be getting back together again. What can I say?'

Olivia's gaze flickered over the face of the willowy blonde clinging to Harry's sleeve. Karen Darcy looked nervous. And why not? thought Olivia drily. Stephen was dead, but Olivia wasn't, and she must know he had confided in his ex-wife. And, for all his faults, Stephen had paid a high price for his indiscretions. Why should Karen escape scot-free?

But, with a mental shrug of her shoulders, Olivia accepted Harry's condolences without controversy. She neither confirmed nor denied the comment he had made about their relationship, but that didn't matter. And after all, there was nothing to be gained by hurting Karen now. She only hoped the younger woman had learned her lesson.

Though, as she watched them walk away together, Olivia somehow doubted it. Now that the burden of guilt had been lifted from her shoulders, there was a definite spring in Karen's step.

Lucky Karen, thought Olivia later that afternoon, as she said goodbye to Mrs Perry and her sister, and got behind the wheel of her small saloon to drive home. If only her own problems could be dealt with so carelessly. If only she had someone to solve them for her.

And it had seemed simple enough when she left Paget. By putting the best part of a hundred miles between her and Conor, she had proved she had the strength to do it. And, with her work, and the friends who hadn't deserted her after the divorce, she had been determined to forget all about him.

Of course, the events of that snowy morning had altered her plans. The idea of continuing her holiday had been quickly cast aside. All she had wanted to do was go to ground, preferably in familiar surroundings. Even the thought that Stephen might pester her if she went back home had seemed infinitely preferable to risking seeing Conor again.

Looking back now, she realised what she had really been doing was running from herself. Her fears of seeing Conor, the urgency she had felt to immerse herself in familiar things, had been her way of blinding herself to the truth. When she had boarded the train to London, the relief she'd felt had been just an illusion. And, like all illusions, it had eventually evaporated.

The dreams had come first, invading her sleep with images, not of herself and Conor, but of Conor with some other woman. Sometimes it was Sharon, and those images were bad enough. But, later, it was someone else, someone Olivia didn't know, and they were the worst of all.

So, she slept badly, and awakened drained of all energy. Her cosy apartment, which had previously been such a welcome haven, began to stifle her. Insidiously, the pain had surfaced, subconsciously at first, and then sharply real. It made a nonsense of the unhappiness she had felt over Stephen's deception. Her need for Conor was like a living disease, feeding on her flesh.

She started going out then, trailing round the shops for hours, desperate for diversion. She even joined a health club, and spent long hours exhausting herself in the swimming-pool. Her leg strengthened, and, because her appetite improved, she put on a little weight. But while her body mended, her brain corroded, and she knew something had to be done to retain her sanity.

She went back to the office the following week. Mr Halliday was endearingly pleased to see her, even if he did wonder whether she ought not to have given herself a little more time before returning to work. But her apparent eagerness, and the air of confidence she managed to convey, convinced him she knew what she was doing. And, to her relief, she discovered that at that level she could still function fairly normally.

And, gradually, the madness had subsided. She was even able to question her feeling of devastation when Conor hadn't so much as picked up a phone to assure himself that she'd got home safely. And he might have done. Once he'd got over his pique. It wasn't as if she'd been wiped off the face of the earth. His protestations of undying love must have melted along with the snow.

That the manner of her leaving had not been entirely unselfish was something she preferred not to dwell on. That Conor might have had some justification for his anger was best set aside. If her own fears of rejection had worked against her, she chose not to recognise the fact. And even when something happened to mitigate the pain, she refused to consider the consequences.

Stephen's death had come at a time when she was trying not to think about the future. And, selfish as it sounded, it had given her a breathing space. For a time, someone else's needs had taken precedence, and she had submerged her own problems in theirs. But it was over now. She had to get on with her own life.

Letting herself into her apartment, she looked about her with rueful eyes. For the past seventy-two hours she had been at Mrs Perry's beck and call, and her neglect of this place showed. There were crumbs on the floor, and dishes in the sink, and her bed hadn't been made in days. She had come home to sleep and little else. Even the light on the answerphone was blinking.

Well, it would have to wait, she decided. Everything would have to wait. She needed a shower and something to eat, not necessarily in that order.

Fifteen minutes later she came out of the bathroom with a towel tucked sarong-wise under her arms. She had washed her hair, too, and she paused in front of the dressing-table to towel it dry. As she did so, the sarong slipped away, and she was left with the disturbing reflection of her own naked body.

Her hands stilled, and, lowering her arms to her sides, she stared at herself with troubled eyes. Was it visible yet? she wondered. She turned sideways. Yes, barely. Just the slightest thickening at her waist giving her condition away.

Swallowing, she bent and lifted the bath towel again. Then, wrapping it tightly about her, she turned away from the mirror. Sooner or later, she was going to have to make a decision, she realised tensely. No matter how unattractive the prospect might be, the choice had to be made.

Beyond her windows, the trees in the park were burgeoning with new life, and she stood for several minutes staring at them before her growling stomach drove her into the kitchen. She was burgeoning with new life, too, she thought ruefully, as she prepared herself a peanut butter sandwich. And, whatever happened, it was a cause for rejoicing, not regret.

Carrying her sandwich back into the living-room, she perched on the arm of her sofa and pressed the rewind button on the answerphone. It was the dilemma of how—*or if*—she should tell Conor that was causing her so much heart-searching, and as she munched on her sandwich she had to acknowledge she was no closer to a decision now than she had been before Stephen's untimely death.

The trouble was, she had no way of knowing how he might react to the news that he was going to be a father. If, as she expected, he had got over his infatuation for her, he would certainly not welcome such daunting news. Oh, she was sure he wouldn't abjure his responsibilities. He was an honourable man, and he would respect her wishes. But did she really want to tie him to her, on any terms? And particularly like this, the oldest trick in the book.

In all honesty, it would be easier to keep it from him, and she guessed that after learning that Stephen had spent the night at the inn in Paget her friends would assume the child was his. She could handle it that way if she wanted.

But, deep inside her, she had a powerful need to tell Conor the truth. That was the real dilemma. She wanted him to know she was having his baby. She wanted him to share in the wonder.

What wonder? she thought now, crossly, as the rewind button clicked off, and the first recorded message was replayed. Taking another mouthful of her sandwich, she listened as a colleague from work informed her that one of her clients, presently on bail, had absconded. The man was believed to have fled to Ireland, but Olivia couldn't summon any real irritation at the news. Ever since she had discovered she was pregnant, her focus had altered completely, and she had to force herself to consider the case with some degree of subjectivity.

The next voice was not immediately familiar to her, and, switching off the machine, she went to get herself a can of juice from the fridge. She couldn't drink coffee any more without feeling nauseous, and it was this as much as anything that had first alerted her to her condition. She had never actually suffered from morning sickness. But the scent of freshly brewed coffee was definitely taboo.

She carried the can back into the living-room, and resumed her position beside the phone. Depressing the button on the recorder, she re-started the next message, tackling the ring-pull on the can as she did so. Unfortunately, the can must have been shaken, because the juice fizzed out all over the towel, and she was muttering to herself as she went to get some paper towels from the kitchen when the identity of her caller hit her. It was Mrs Drake, calling from Paget. And, although Conor's name hadn't been mentioned, Olivia abandoned the can and hurried back to re-wind the tape.

'Mrs Perry? Mrs Perry, are you there?' Olivia caught her upper lip between her teeth as her erstwhile landlady's voice betrayed her uncertainty. Then, 'Oh, it's one of those awful machines,' she said, and for a few seconds there was silence. But, eventually, she overcame her reticence and went on, 'Mrs Perry, this is Eva Drake calling. From the Ship. That's the Ship Inn, in Paget,' she added, bringing a faint smile to Olivia's strained face. 'You remember?' You stayed with us a few months ago.'

How could she forget? Olivia contained her impatience, and the woman continued, 'I'm calling about a personal matter, Mrs Perry. I hope you won't think I'm poking my nose in where it's not wanted, but after I'd spoken to Connie, well...'

She broke off again, and Olivia wanted to scream. If she wasn't careful, the woman was going to run out of tape. And she had the feeling Mrs Drake wouldn't ring again.

'You remember Connie, don't you, Mrs Perry? She said she met you one day at the clinic. Connie Holmes, that is. Sharon's mother.'

Yes, yes, go on, Olivia implored silently, and to her relief she did. ·

'Of course, I didn't tell Connie I might ring you, Mrs Perry. Even now, I'm not sure I'm doing the right thing. But your husband did say you'd known the family for a long time. And when I heard about poor Dr Brennan——'

Conor! What about Conor?

'—I thought maybe you'd want to know.'

To know what?

Olivia was almost beside herself with frustration now. Hurry up, Mrs Drake, she begged. What's happened to Conor?

'It seems there was an—accident at the clinic,' the woman faltered, the doubt in her voice growing stronger. Olivia was half afraid she was going to ring off without finishing the call. 'Course, you may know this already, but when Connie said Sharon had lost patience with him, and that he was letting nobody into that house to help him, I had to do something. That's my nature, Mrs Perry. I like to help people.'

Thank God for that, thought Olivia weakly, wishing she had felt more charitably towards her while she was there. But there was still so much she hadn't explained.

'Anyway,' Mrs Drake was saying now, and it was obvious she was preparing to hang up, 'I've done my duty. If—if Dr Brennan had some family, it would be different. But he doesn't. He's got nobody, Mrs Perry. And—I just thought that you—well, you'll know what I mean,' she finished, and the line went dead.

An hour and a half later, Olivia was driving along the M20 heading for Folkestone. It was already seven o'clock, and she would have been further had it not been for the rush-hour traffic in London. Her apartment was fairly central, and getting out of the city on a Friday evening was never easy. Apart from the usual log-jam of cars that used the motorways every evening, there were the weekend trippers, heading for coast and country with a total disregard for serious travellers. To drive in London at all you had to have nerves of steel, and Olivia thought it said much for her concern for Conor that she hadn't flinched at joining the queues.

But the awful memories of her accident were now behind her, thank goodness. These past months of physical activity had helped enormously. She still dragged her left leg a little, particularly if she was tired, but even the scars were fading now that she was gaining weight.

It was ironic, really, she thought. She had been going through one of the most traumatic periods of her life, and she had put weight on. Thank heavens for small mercies, she mused, running a possessive hand over the slight swelling beneath her waistband. This baby had saved her life. Perhaps it would save Conor's, too.

But such thoughts were futile. She had no real idea what was wrong with Conor. Mrs Drake had said there had been an accident at the clinic, but that could mean anything. And had the fact that Sharon had rejected him had anything to do with it?

Her brain buzzed with possibilities, and for once she wished she had a car-phone. She had tried to ring Mrs Drake for more details before she left the apartment, but the line was engaged. And she had been so desperate to get on her way that she had given up trying.

At least she wasn't feeling sleepy. The shower she'd had earlier had refreshed her, and hearing what Mrs Drake had had to say had proved a powerful stimulant. Now, responding to the urgency building inside her, she pressed her foot harder on the accelerator.

But luck was with her. She cruised past the turn-offs for Maidstone and Ashford without even dropping below seventy. It was only when she left the motorway that she was compelled to lower her speed, and she managed to contain her impatience all the way to Paget.

Thankfully, it was still light as she drove along the coast road. And, glancing at the sun sinking in the west, she reflected what an eventful day it had proved. First Stephen's funeral, and that pathetic little encounter with the Darcys; then her own ambivalence over telling Conor about the baby, Mrs Drake's message, and the anxiety that had sent her dashing here—and it wasn't over yet.

She hesitated when she reached the harbour, wondering if she ought to speak to Mrs Drake before driving up to Conor's house. But the car park at the inn was

full, and the prospect of going into the pub and encountering so many curious eyes deterred her. She would
thank Mrs Drake for her call—but later. Probably when
she returned to request a room for the night, she considered ruefully. Until she had spoken to Conor, she had
no idea how he would react to seeing her again.

She seemed to reach Gull Rise very quickly, and she
realised that now she was here she was no longer so convinced of the wisdom of what she was doing. Indeed, it
seemed almost presumptuous to believe that she might
succeed where others had failed. After all, Conor had
nothing to thank her for, and he could quite legitimately
refuse to speak to her.

She brought the car to a halt in front of the house.
Although the drive was empty, she didn't have the nerve
to park there, and she sat for several moments just
looking up at the windows. The curtains in Conor's
bedroom were drawn, and she wondered if that meant
he had already retired for the night. Perhaps they hadn't
been opened, she mused, remembering the state of her
own bedroom. If what Mrs Drake had said was true, it
seemed unlikely that he would regard making his bed as
a high priority.

She gnawed on her lower lip, mentally rehearsing how
she was going to explain her arrival. 'Oh, hello, Conor!
Long time no see!' No, that was no good. She frowned.
'Hi! I was in the neighbourhood, and I just thought I'd
look you up!' That was no good either. All right, then.
'Hello, Conor. Guess what? You're going to be a father!'
God, no!

She sighed. So what was she going to say? How could
she explain her appearance without involving Mrs Drake?
He would never believe she had been actually pondering
the advisability of coming here of her own free will. It
was too convenient. Too coincidental.

If she'd been secretly hoping that Conor might see the
car and come to investigate, she was disappointed. Even
though it was a good five minutes since she had turned

off the engine, the house remained as anonymous as ever. In fact, if Mrs Drake hadn't said that he was holed up in the house, she'd have assumed he was away. Thank heavens for Mrs Drake, she thought uneasily, not at all sure she really meant it. What if Conor sent her away? What would she do then?

Pushing open her door, she put such thoughts to the back of her mind. They were defeatist, and negative. She was not going to consider what might, or might not, happen. Not until she had spoken to Conor and gauged his mood.

She shut the car and locked it, aware that she was taking her time, delaying the moment when she had to walk up the drive and ring the bell. But eventually she had to approach the door, and as she mounted the steps she thought how much easier they were for her to climb now. Three months had made an enormous difference. Not least in her feelings about herself.

There was no sound when she pressed the button, but it was a large house, and she couldn't remember whether she used to be able to hear the bell or not. However, after several abortive attempts, she resorted to knocking, bruising her knuckles against the panels without achieving any more success.

'Damn,' she said aloud, glancing around. Could Conor really not hear her? Or wasn't he answering the door to anyone?

She could see into the drawing-room through the wide bay, but there was no sign of life. In fact, the room had a definite air of neglect, and the anxiety that had tormented her all the way from London increased its grip. Where was Conor? Why didn't he answer the door?

The last resort was shouting through the letter-box, and, hoping that the one or two tenants still working in their gardens wouldn't come to investigate, she did just that. But, although she called his name and identified herself, the result was the same. The house remained unnervingly silent, and her anxiety gave way to an ominous feeling of foreboding.

She sighed. What now? She had to do something. She had to get into the house. But the idea of seeking official assistance to achieve her ends was simply not practical. It wasn't as if she was a relative or anything. The police would probably tell her to go away and mind her own business.

But she couldn't do that. In spite of a growing conviction that Conor wouldn't want to see her, she couldn't go away without assuring herself that he was all right. If only she knew what had happened. If only she knew the sequence of events. The only person who might be able to tell her was Sharon herself, and she didn't even know where she lived.

Of course, Mrs Drake would know Sharon's address. Mrs Drake probably knew more than she had said. But Mrs Drake wasn't here. And if there was nothing wrong Conor wouldn't thank her for being a scaremonger.

So, she had to find some way of getting into the house herself. She could always break a window, she mused recklessly, while the practical side of her nature threw up its hands at her audacity. But not at the front, she appended. Besides, these windows were too big.

A footpath ran between the wall of the house and the garage, and, walking along it, Olivia found herself in the back garden. There was a crumbling post, covered in honeysuckle, clinging to the rear wall of the garage, and she remembered that in Sally's day there had been a latticed gate here to keep the infant Conor from straying out on to the road. The gate was gone now, but the garden was amazingly familiar, and she paused for a moment as a whole host of memories surged over her. But then the reason she was here swept them away, and she turned her attention to the back of the house.

And, as she did so, another memory surfaced. Years ago, long before the Brennans had taken possession of the house, there had been a coke boiler in the cellar. In those days, the fuel had been delivered in sacks, and tipped, by means of a trapdoor, into the cellar. Of course, the boiler had been defunct before the Brennans moved in, and Keith had cleaned out the cellar, and used it for storage purposes. But the trapdoor must still be there.

And it was. Hidden beneath a trough of flowering shrubs, it was securely padlocked, as always, but surely offering her best chance of getting into the house. She knew the cellar. She and Conor had played there. And the door into the house had never been locked.

Breaking the padlock presented the most immediate problem, but a rummage among a pile of plant pots and canes turned up a metal tube, which looked as if it had once been part of the bicycle Conor used to ride. No wonder thieves had such a cosy time of it, she reflected, as the padlock broke at the third attempt. A little local knowledge, and the rest was easy.

The trapdoor was stiff, but it opened, and Olivia found herself gazing down at an old step-ladder, which someone had left propped against the trapdoor. 'Bingo,' she breathed, getting to her feet and starting down it. She didn't want to give herself time to have second thoughts.

The cellar was still a store-room. Olivia was glad of the light from the open trapdoor, as she stumbled over old rolled-up carpets and abandoned suitcases. Keith's wine-rack was still there, though the bottles she could see were of a more modern vintage. And there was Sally's old sewing-machine, and the tailor's dummy, which briefly gave her quite a shock.

But at last she was standing at the foot of the steps that led up into the house. The last hurdle, she thought, regarding the door at the top of the steps with some uncertainty. It was such a heavy door. What if it was locked?

At first when she turned the handle, she thought it was. It didn't open at the first attempt, and her heart sank. But, as anxiety gave way to frustration, her frenzied tugging bore fruit. It was just stiff through lack of use, and with a concerted effort she brought it swinging back against her. It nearly flattened her against the wall, but she managed to save herself, inching her way around the door and into the hall of the house.

So far so good. Closing the door behind her, Olivia rubbed her slightly grubby palms down the seams of her jeans. Now all she had to do was find Conor. If he was here...

The air felt musty, as if it was too long since anyone had opened a window. And there was a curious smell, too. She couldn't immediately identify it, but it was sweet and cloying. She frowned. Dear God, what had been going on here?

The kitchen and dining-room were as deserted as the drawing-room. There weren't even any dirty dishes in the sink, she noticed. Only a cup on the drainer, bearing dregs of what appeared to be coffee. So, Conor had to be upstairs. In bed? Remembering the closed bedroom curtains, she knew a moment's hesitation. What made her think he would be any more pleased to see her than Sharon? Particularly as she had virtually broken in. What price her legal training now?

But she had to see him. She had to know if his feelings for her had changed. If they had, then she would have to live with it. But she had to hear it from his lips. And if, by some miracle, they hadn't...

She went no further. Instead, she started up the stairs, aware that she had no real idea what she would find. It occurred to her that what she had smelt could be co-caine. She had only ever smelled marijuana before, but it had a sweet smell, too.

A board creaked as she stepped on to the landing, but, although she froze for a second, it aroused no re-action. The landing was as silent as the rooms downstairs had been, and she felt her nails digging into her palms as she made her way to Conor's bedroom door. It wasn't completely closed, just pushed to, and with her tongue trapped between her teeth she widened it until her head could fit into the opening.

And then she sucked in a gulp of air. Conor was there, sure enough, stretched out flat on the bed, with only a sheet to cover his nakedness. But the relief she felt at finding him was instantly forgotten when she saw the capsules scattered over the top of the bedside unit. Some had even spilled on to the carpet, along with the now empty glass of water he must have used to swallow them.

Oh, lord!

The air left her lungs in a panic-stricken rush, and, abandoning any doubts about how she came to be here, she hurried to the bed. 'Conor,' she cried, grasping his shoulder and shaking him urgently. 'Conor, wake up!'

His skin felt cold to the touch, and for one awful moment she thought she was too late. Was that sweet smell, which was so much stronger here, the smell of death? The taste of the peanut butter sandwiches she had eaten before leaving home rose sickeningly into her throat. But she couldn't afford to be ill now, she chided, as, to her relief, his flesh warmed beneath her hand. If Conor was unconscious, he must have taken an overdose. No one knew the strength of the drugs he was using better than he did. It couldn't have been a mistake.

Then, just as the realisation that she should get him off the bed and on to his feet and call an ambulance brought a frantic return of sanity, she saw the blood on the sheet. How she could have missed it earlier, she didn't know. There was enough of it, for God's sake! But her whole attention had been focused on the drugs. Now, the staining that skirted his waist brought a wave of dizziness sweeping over her, and this time she couldn't hold back. She had identified the smell and it terrified her. With a muffled cry, she ran for the bathroom, reaching the toilet basin just in time.

She was still kneeling there, trying to find the strength to get to her feet again, when a hand descended on her shoulder. 'Liv?' Conor's voice said disbelievingly. 'God, Liv, what are you doing here?'

CHAPTER TWELVE

OLIVIA scrambled to her feet, unable for a moment to say anything. The shock of seeing him awake, and on his feet, was too much for her, and she could only cling to the toilet cistern, praying it wasn't just a dream.

Conor appeared real enough, though much paler than she remembered, his untidy hair and unshaven chin adding to his air of debilitation. But he had dragged a navy silk dressing-gown over his nakedness, and, had she not seen the blood on the sheet, she might have been persuaded that there was nothing wrong with him that a shower and a decent night's sleep wouldn't cure.

'Liv,' he repeated now, his confusion giving way to guarded weariness. 'How the hell did you get in?'

Olivia shook her head, and then wished she hadn't when the room revolved around her. She waited a moment for the giddiness to pass, and then moved determinedly towards the sink. 'Can—can I just rinse my face and hands?' she asked, hoping he wouldn't try to deter her. It was bad enough that he had caught her throwing up in his bathroom. She didn't think she could cope with an argument just yet.

However, Conor obediently stepped aside, and, turning her back on him, she hurriedly sluiced her face and hands, and cleaned her teeth with her finger. Then, feeling much better, she straightened and reached for a towel.

'Did—did I—that is, were you asleep?' she ventured nervously, slipping the towel back on to the rail, suddenly aware of how presumptuous she had been.

Conor's eyes were narrowed and unreadable. 'Obviously,' he said at last, stepping back so that she could precede him out of the room. 'Now, how much longer are we going to continue this, before you tell me what in hell is going on?'

Olivia drew a steadying breath, and paused on the landing, not sure which direction to take. The obvious choice was to go back into Conor's bedroom, but she no longer had the temerity to believe that she would be welcome there. So instead she turned towards the stairs.

He followed her down, and, remembering the blood she had seen on the sheet, Olivia found herself biting her lower lip. She wanted to ask what it was, what had happened, but she didn't have the nerve. She was already having to face the fact that Conor didn't want her here, any more than he had wanted anyone else. Was he going to escort her off the premises, without even giving her a chance to tell him why she'd come?

But, when they reached the lower floor, he said, 'The kitchen,' and, breathing a little more easily, Olivia walked along the hall. But she was aware of him behind her, watching her every move.

It was getting dark, she noticed, a fact that was endorsed when Conor switched on the track of spotlights. They immediately darkened the windows, and cast shadows on to his hollow cheeks, accentuating his pallor and the unforgiving twist of his lips.

'Sit down,' he said, but she preferred to stand, and with a careless shrug he hooked out a chair and dropped into it. A stab of pain crossed his face as he did so, betraying that unseen injury, but his expression warned against her offering sympathy. 'Well?' he prompted, as she pushed her anxious hands into her pockets, and leaned against one of the dark oak units. 'Go on. I'm listening.'

Olivia drew a breath. 'I did ring the bell,' she began, rather lamely. 'And—and knocked. But I couldn't make you hear.'

'How do you know?'

His question confused her, and she gazed at him uncertainly. 'How do you know what?'

'How do you know I didn't hear you?'

'Oh.' Encountering his cool, enigmatic gaze, Olivia was half prepared to accept that he had heard her after all. But she couldn't let that deter her. 'Well, I can't be sure, of course——'

'No, you can't.'

'—but you were—asleep—when I came into the bedroom.'

'Was I?'

'Oh, Conor!' Her helpless cry seemed to affect him. His cheeks drew in, and a muscle jerked with spasmodic insistence. But he obviously had no intention of making this easy for her, and she was forced to continue. 'Anyway,' she went on, 'I was—worried about you.' And, responding to his scornful expression, 'I was! After—after what...' She bit back Mrs Drake's name, and proceeded awkwardly, 'I—wanted to see you.'

'Why?'

'Why?' She lifted her shoulders as a convincing answer escaped her. 'Why do you think?'

Conor lay back in his chair, and, although she was sure he would have preferred her not to see it, he couldn't disguise the wince of pain that brought a sudden starkness to his pale features. Almost involuntarily, his hand moved to protect his midriff, and her mouth dried at the thought that he might have more than one injury. But his cold face forbade any mention of the fact, and she was forced to watch his efforts to cover his reaction in silence.

'I—think—someone—contacted you,' he said at last, and, aware of what it had cost him to speak normally, Olivia wondered how she had ever found the courage to leave him. She wanted to put her arms around him so badly that it was a physical effort not to do so, but she was so afraid that he would reject her. 'Who was it?' he went on. 'Sharon? Aunt Elizabeth?' He frowned, resting his elbow on the edge of the table, and dropping his head against his hand. 'There is no one else.'

Olivia hesitated. And then, realising they couldn't go on unless they were completely honest with one another, she said, 'It was Mrs Drake, actually,' and he groaned.

'I knew it,' he muttered. 'I knew you wouldn't have come here of your own free will!'

'That's not true!' Olivia was defensive.

'No?' Conor sounded weary now. 'Don't tell me—you were packing your bag to come down here when you got the message.'

'No. I was at Stephen's funeral, actually,' replied Olivia quietly, and this time she was sure she had his full attention.

'Say what?'

'I said——'

'Dammit, I heard what you said,' he exclaimed, lifting his head. He ran a hand that shook slightly through the unruly tangle of his hair. 'But—how? Did he have an accident?'

Olivia shrugged. 'It was a heart attack,' she said simply. 'According to his doctor, there was a weakness. It could have happened any time.'

'Shit!' Conor closed his eyes for a moment, and when he opened them again his face was paler than before. 'And I guess I contributed to the attack, didn't I? He must have guessed there was something going on between us.'

'No!' Olivia's renunciation was vehement. 'He'd been warned not to overdo things, but Stephen never would listen to anyone's advice.'

Conor blinked. 'Isn't that pretty callous? Even for you?'

Olivia noticed the qualification, but now was not the time to take him up on it. How callous she had been in leaving him only time would tell, but for now she had to concentrate on other matters.

'You don't understand,' she began, pushing herself away from the unit, but Conor wouldn't let her finish.

'Your husband's just died, for God's sake!' he muttered savagely. 'For pity's sake, Liv, you've just buried him today!'

Olivia expelled the air in her lungs in a long sigh. 'He wasn't my husband,' she said, linking her fingers together. 'Our divorce became final just after I got back to London.'

Conor came up out of his chair with a baleful oath. 'What?'

'It's true.' Olivia was nervous of the look on his face, but she had to go on. 'I—I asked Stephen for a divorce before I had the accident,' she blurted. 'He—he had been seeing other women, and when I found out...' She licked her lips. 'He didn't agree at first. But... when I was in the hospital, he—changed his mind.'

Conor was supporting himself against the edge of the table. 'But—he came here,' he said harshly. 'He spent the night at the inn. Mrs Drake told me.'

'I know.' Olivia gazed at him despairingly. 'But she could have also told you that we had separate rooms. You see, Stephen was in some trouble over—over his boss's wife, and he needed an alibi.'

A pulse was beating in Conor's temple. She could see it, hammering away under the skin. It was the only evidence she had that his reaction to what she was saying was not all negative. Surely that erratic little vibration wasn't wholly motivated by anger? Why should he react so violently if it meant nothing to him?

'So, you were lying,' he said now, and her heart sank at his words. 'God, Liv, was it so hard to tell me you didn't want to get involved?'

'It wasn't like that!' Olivia took a couple of steps towards him, and then halted uncertainly. 'Conor, you know my—marriage—wasn't a problem with us.'

'Wasn't it?' There was accusation in his eyes, and she gave an inward groan at the seeming impossibility of her task.

'No,' she insisted now. Then, unable to sustain the implacability of his gaze, she bent her head. 'Don't pretend you believed everything I said.'

Conor swore. 'I don't know what I believe any more,' he stated unevenly. 'Are you telling me you've changed your mind?'

Olivia swallowed and lifted her head. 'And if I am?'

Conor stared at her for a long, disbelieving minute, and then he swung away, making for the window, gripping the sink below it with white-knuckled hands. He looked out of the window for so long that what little confidence Olivia had had evaporated, and by the time he turned his head to look at her again she was visibly shaking.

'Why did you come here, Liv?' he asked, and, of all the things she had thought he might say, this was the least expected.

'I—I've told you,' she said, wishing she had something to hold on to. 'I wanted to see you.'

Conor's lips twisted. 'Yes. But would you have come if some do-gooding individual hadn't chosen to tell you I was a mess?'

'Yes——'

'Yes?' He didn't sound convinced. 'Liv, that little scene upstairs said more about you than you know. God knows what tale Mrs Drake had spun you, but when you came into the bedroom you thought I was unconscious!'

Olivia hesitated. 'Maybe.'

'There's no "maybe" about it,' he exclaimed, angrily. 'Because you couldn't get a reply, you thought I'd taken an overdose, didn't you? And that really scared you. So much so that you were puking up your guts when I walked into the bathroom.'

'All right.' Olivia saw no point in denying it. 'I did get a shock when I saw you. There were capsules all over the bedside cabinet, and blood on the sheet——'

'Dried blood,' he cut in sharply.

'—and I—I panicked.'

Conor turned to face her. 'There was no need. I dropped the bottle as I was taking a couple of pain-killers, that's all. If I'd known I was expecting a visitor, I'd have picked them up.'

Olivia took a breath. 'What about the blood?'

'I cut myself,' he replied dismissively.

'And the accident?'

'What accident?'

'The accident at the clinic,' she persisted. 'Mrs Drake said——'

'Mrs Drake should learn to mind her own business,' he retorted. 'I had a—a run-in with an irate visitor, that was all. It was something and nothing. Certainly not serious enough to bring you haring down from London.'

'That wasn't why...' began Olivia swiftly, and then made an impatient gesture. What was the point? He wasn't going to believe her, whatever she said.

Conor left the sink and came back to rest his palms on the table. She suspected it was because, whatever he said, he needed some support. But his next words sent all other thoughts out of her head.

'Tell me,' he said, dispassionately, 'what would you have done if I had been unconscious? I'd like to know.'

'What would I...?' Olivia gasped. 'I'd have called an ambulance, of course.'

'Would you?' He looked at her through the veil of his lashes. 'Even though it would have meant getting involved?'

Olivia caught her breath. 'What do you mean?'

'Well...' Conor straightened with an evident effort. 'You have left me before. And you didn't care then whether I lived or died.'

'My God!' Olivia was horrified. 'Of course I cared. I've always...' She bit back the shaming admission, but the look in his eyes forced her to go on. 'Do you hate me that much?'

'I don't hate you at all,' he told her succinctly, his voice breaking on the words. 'And believe me, I've tried!'

'Oh, Conor!'

Unable to hold back any longer, Olivia gave in to the sexual tension that had been building inside her. She couldn't wait to hear if he was going to reject her. If he did, then so be it, but for this moment in time she had to feel his arms about her. Moving too quickly for him to evade her, she circled the table until there was barely a hand's-breadth between them. Then, reaching up, she cupped his face in her hands, and brought his unwary mouth to hers.

He sucked in his breath as she pressed herself against him, but when she would have drawn back again his hands went swiftly to her waist, and held her where she was. 'Not now,' he breathed, against her lips, and when his tongue slid into her mouth her legs felt too weak to disobey him.

She clung to him desperately, to the solid warmth of bone and muscle she had dreamed for so long of holding. His heart was thudding against his ribs, his skin smooth and male beneath her hands. He was impatient and ungentle, but so familiar, and she felt her senses swimming beneath his urgent assault.

He kissed her many times—hard, angry kisses at first, which gradually gave way to the sensuality of passion. He wanted to hurt her, as she had hurt him, but he seemed to realise as his kisses gentled that he was only hurting himself.

'I should kill you for what you've done to me,' he muttered, when his lips sought the scented curve of her neck. His fingers stroked the vulnerable skin and tightened perceptibly. 'Do you know you nearly killed me when you walked out like that?'

'I have some idea,' she confessed unsteadily. 'I haven't exactly found it easy myself. I'm still not sure it's the best thing for both of us. But when I heard about the accident I couldn't keep away.'

He drew back briefly to look down at her. 'You'd better be sure now,' he said roughly, cupping her face in his hand. 'Because, whatever it takes, I'm not going to let you go this time.'

'I—don't want you to,' she assured him huskily, turning her lips against his fingers. 'That's what I came to tell you. Only, as usual, I made a mess of it.'

Conor's lips twisted. 'Am I supposed to believe that?'

'Yes.' Olivia's response was defensive at first, but then, glimpsing the mockery in his eyes, she grabbed his arms and shook him. 'It's not funny,' she said fiercely. 'I love you, you big idiot!'

Conor's response was to utter a muffled moan and slump heavily against her. His weight pinned her against the fridge-freezer behind her, and for a moment she thought he was still teasing. But his eyes were closed, and there was a thin film of sweat on his forehead, and when she tried to push him away from her he didn't resist.

'Conor!' she exclaimed, horror-stricken, convinced he had now passed out. But, as her brain struggled to cope with this disaster, he put a hand on the unit and pushed himself away from her: weaker, paler, but unmistakably alert.

'Sorry about that,' he muttered ruefully, groping for the table behind him, and sinking down on to its rim. 'I guess the relief was just too much for me. It won't happen again.'

'No, it won't,' said Olivia, more forcefully than she felt. She wasn't deceived by his attempt to dismiss what had happened as relief. Propelling herself towards him, she took advantage of his weakness to part the lapels of his dressing-gown, catching her breath, aghast, at the ugly gash that scarred his midriff.

'Hey, do you mind?' he protested mildly, as the gown threatened to open completely. 'I don't mind you seeing me naked, but not in front of the neighbours, please!'

But Olivia wasn't listening to this attempt to distract her. She was gazing at the wound, which her playfulness had caused to weep a little, and she felt like weeping herself for the pain she must have caused him.

'This is why they were so concerned about you at the clinic, isn't it?' she exclaimed, gazing at him with worried eyes. 'Oh, Conor—love—why haven't you had it properly attended to? You're a doc——'

'Say that again,' broke in Conor irrepressibly, catching her wrists, and pulling her between his legs. 'That bit where you called me "love". I like it.'

But Olivia wouldn't let him get away with it, even though she couldn't prevent herself from responding to the tender kiss he bestowed at the corner of her mouth. 'You know how easily infection can set in,' she persisted, touching the bruised flesh around the gash with delicate fingers. 'Have you had any antibiotics?'

'I'll be OK,' Conor told her gently. 'Now that you're here, I'll do anything you want.' His thumbs brushed the sensitive inner curve of her wrists, before he bent to kiss them. 'I didn't much care what happened to me before.'

'Oh, Conor,' she exclaimed, smoothing back the hair from his damp forehead with a shaking hand. 'If only I'd known.'

'I thought you did know,' he replied gravely. 'What do you think I meant when I told you I loved you?'

Olivia couldn't allow herself to think of that now. 'How—how did it happen?' she asked instead, releasing herself from Conor's grasp, and moving to the sink. 'You said something about a visitor,' she added, concentrating on turning on the taps. 'Um—do you still keep the first-aid box in this top cupboard?'

Conor sighed, but he nodded, and, standing on tiptoe, Olivia brought down the small first-aid chest, which had been kept in that cupboard when Conor was a baby. 'Always keep medicines out of the reach of children,' Sally had used to say, and Olivia remembered feeling very grown-up because Sally had let her get the box down.

She didn't feel grown-up now. She felt ignorant and inexperienced, and totally incapable of dealing with such a dangerous-looking injury. She was sure he needed hospital treatment, but he was unlikely to agree to that. So she would have to think positively, and do the best she could.

Sorting through the plastic tapes and bandages, she soon realised that most, if not all of these things had been in the box since Sally's day. A bottle of camomile lotion, which she had once used to cool Conor's spots when he had chicken-pox, was crusted and sedimentary, and the tubes of antiseptic had all split with age. She wouldn't have used the iodine she found to corrode metal, let alone to treat human tissue. Even the surgical scissors were rusting in their case.

'This is useless!' she exclaimed, lifting her head and looking at him, and she realised he had only let her waste her time because it had given him room to recover.

'Stop fussing,' he said, his eyes dark and disturbing. 'I'll survive. Now, why don't we go upstairs and finish what we started?'

Olivia sighed. 'Conor——'

'All right, all right. I'll put some alcohol on it,' he exclaimed, pushing himself up from the table, and swaying on his feet. 'If you look in that drawer, you'll find some new plasters. That's all I've been using, and it's worked so far.'

'Has it?' Olivia gave him a dubious glance, before crossing the room and opening the drawer he had indicated. She came back to where he was standing, and pushing him back on to the table. 'Now, are you going to tell me what happened?'

Conor scowled. 'If I must.'

'You must,' she assured him unsteadily, drawing the sides of his robe apart again to reveal the purpling flesh. 'Um...' She swallowed. 'Where—where do you keep the alcohol? Oh—I remember. In the drawing-room, isn't it?'

'There's a bottle of scotch in that cupboard behind you,' Conor conceded, but as she would have turned to get it he grasped her hand. 'You don't have to do this, you know. I can do it myself.'

'I—I want to,' she said, and Conor muttered an oath as he briefly pulled her into his arms.

'But afterwards,' he told her hoarsely, and there was no question what he promised...

An hour later, Olivia was sitting, cross-legged, on the bed in the spare room, watching Conor as he slept. Asleep, he looked so young and vulnerable, and her heart ached at all the time she'd wasted. Life wasn't about certainties, she thought, with the insight that being in love had brought her. At best, it could only be an imponderable. There was no way she could be sure that Conor wouldn't hurt her, but because they loved each other they had a better chance than most.

And she could so easily have lost everything, she thought shakily, unable to prevent herself from stroking the silky hair that shadowed his rib-cage. The man Conor had surprised, selling cocaine to one of his patients in the men's lavatories at the clinic, could so easily have destroyed their future. As it was, the knife had he drawn had gouged an ugly furrow in Conor's midriff, before Conor had dashed it from his grasp. Even then, it was only the fact that one of the other doctors had come into the men's room that had stopped him from finishing the job. Conor had been losing blood rapidly, and it was arguable how long he could have held out against such a desperate assailant.

Not that Conor had said as much. On the contrary, he had insisted on making light of it, even when the alcohol Olivia had used to cleanse the wound must have been tearing him apart. It had taken all her will and determination to dress the wound afterwards, but she had known she had to do it. And Conor had assured her it wasn't life-threatening.

Nevertheless, she intended to make sure he looked after himself from now on. There was no way she was going to risk losing what she had found. The future, which had once seemed so bleak, was now full of promise. The day that had started so badly had ended so well.

'What are you thinking about?'

Conor's drowsy voice interrupted her reverie, and, for the first time, she didn't rush to cover herself when he looked at her. In the lamplight, her pale skin had a pearly lustre, and Conor was not immune to the nearness of her flesh.

Pushing himself up on his elbows, he regarded her with evident satisfaction, brushing the tumbling darkness of her hair aside, and trailing one finger from her throat to the rosy tip of her breast. Her breasts were still tingling from the eager attention of his mouth, and they responded to his caresses with a totally shameless ease.

'Mmm—come here,' he said, and beneath the thin sheet that covered him from the waist she could see the unmistakable hardening of his arousal. It was still a source of amazement—and delight—to her that she could do this to him, and, although she was tempted to give in to him again, there were things she had to say.

'Not yet,' she murmured, slipping off the bed and wrapping his discarded dressing-gown about her. 'We— we have to talk.'

'Why?' Conor's eyes were wary now, and, had she been more sure of herself, she'd have recognised his anxiety. As it was, she was still troubled by her own sense of inadequacy, and she had no idea how he would react to the things she had to tell him.

'Because we do,' she replied now, lifting her hands to free her hair from the collar of the dressing-gown. As she did so, the robe parted again, and she hurriedly gathered it together, over the swelling mound of her stomach.

Conor didn't notice. He was too intent on her words, and, pushing himself up against the pillows, he linked his hands behind his head. 'All right,' he said, completely unaware of the provocation of the growth of golden hair in his armpits. It was ridiculous, she thought, but there was something so sensual about Conor's body hair. It made her want to go to him, and bury her face in the musky smell of him, and, in spite of her determined practicality, it showed.

And Conor recognised it at once. His own anxiety melted beneath the yearning look in her eyes, and, throwing back the covers, he went after her.

She turned away from his too-appealing beauty, but all he did was slide his arms around her waist from behind, drawing her back against him. 'Be careful,' she said, ever conscious of the dressing on his midriff, but he only made a dismissing sound and buried his face in the hollow of her neck.

'Come back to bed,' he said. 'We can talk there.' His hands parted the robe and slid inside, over the throbbing fullness of her breasts. 'You know you want to. And we can talk in the morning.'

Olivia drew a trembling breath, and for a moment she gave in and yielded against him. But then the importance of what she had to tell him forced her to stiffen, and Conor said an oath, and turned her round to face him.

'OK,' he said. 'What is it? You're not going to tell me this isn't real, I hope?' His face was strained, and she suddenly realised what he was afraid of. In spite of all she had said, he still had doubts about her motives for being here.

Shaking her head, she lifted her hands to his face. 'I love you,' she said. 'I guess I've always loved you. But I was afraid to tell you. I was afraid of being hurt.'

Conor's smile was rueful. 'So you hurt me instead.'

'I hurt us both,' she admitted huskily. 'You see, I was sure that what you felt for me was just infatuation. That if I went away you'd realise that truth.'

'Oh, Liv!' He grasped one of her hands and brought it to his mouth. 'You should have known it wasn't infatuation. God,' he groaned, 'I'd been crazy about you since I was a teenager. Only you always seemed so—remote, after you went to live in London. Then, when Mum and Dad died, it was like a living hell for a while. I'd lost everything I loved—everyone I loved, including you. No.' His smile was gentle. 'Most especially you. No wonder I went to pieces. That's why I owe Aunt Elizabeth so much. She and Uncle Philip stuck with me, even when I let them down.'

Olivia frowned. 'What do you mean?'

'I mean, I got involved in the drug scene myself,' said Conor heavily. 'Oh, not cocaine or heroin. But I smoked pot, and that day I got up the courage to come see you in London I was really high. The first and last time I used drugs to give me confidence,' he added grimly. 'I knew I'd blown any chance of making it with you after that, and, believe me, that was a powerful deterrent.'

'Oh, love!'

She reached up to kiss him, and for a few moments there was silence in the room. But then, reluctantly, he lifted his head.

'Anyway,' he went on slowly, 'I kicked the habit after that. I worked hard, and I graduated from med. school, and then I told Aunt Elizabeth that I wanted to come and work in London. I knew I wanted to see you again, and I guess I was hoping it still might work out. But,' he shrugged, 'when I checked out your old address, the landlady there told me you'd left to get married.' He shook his head. 'That was a pretty bad day.'

Olivia was amazed. 'I never knew.'

'No. How could you? I didn't have the guts to come and say hi. Not when I knew how much I was hurting. I didn't want to hear how happy you were with somebody else.'

Olivia sighed. 'So—you came back here?'

'Eventually.' He grimaced. 'It dawned on me that you might have children by now, and I didn't want to know about them either. Then when you turned up, practically on my doorstep, I couldn't believe it. God, it was like a sign. I thought, somebody up there likes me after all.'

Olivia grimaced. 'I was so embarrassed that morning.'

'I wasn't. I was on cloud nine.' He grinned. 'Until I met Stephen, that is. Then, all I wanted to do was break his neck.'

'Poor Stephen.'

'Yes, poor Stephen.' Conor acknowledged the truth of her words. 'This must have been quite a day for you. And then driving down here tonight.'

Olivia's lips twitched. 'I wanted to.'

'Yes.' Conor bent to kiss her. 'I'm so glad you did.' He frowned. 'But that reminds me, how did you get in?'

'Through the cellar,' she admitted ruefully. 'I'm afraid I broke the padlock. Will you forgive me?'

'I'll forgive you anything,' he told her huskily. 'After these weeks of going around like a zombie, all I want to do is show you how much I love you, and marry you as soon as possible. Now, is that clear enough for you, or would you like it in writing?'

Olivia shook her head. 'And if I were to tell you...'

She broke off, her courage giving out on her at the last minute, and Conor scowled. 'If you were to tell me what?' he demanded. 'Liv, for pity's sake. What is it now?'

For an answer, she took his hand and brought it to the slight mound of her stomach. 'I'm—pregnant,' she said, watching anxiously for his reaction, and Conor's jaw sagged as he felt the unmistakable swelling.

'Pregnant?' he said, in a shaken voice. 'But you said— you and Stephen——'

Olivia gasped. 'Conor!' she exclaimed. 'This has nothing to do with Stephen! I—it's yours! I mean—ours! Yours and mine.'

Conor blinked. 'But I thought——'

'I know what you thought. I'd said that Stephen and I had never had a child. And we haven't. But it just obviously wasn't meant to be. Whereas this——'

Conor swallowed. 'So when you said you'd been thinking of coming to see me, this—this was why?'

Olivia felt a momentary chill, but she nodded.

Conor absorbed this for a moment, and then he said flatly, 'How long have you know about it?'

Olivia lifted her shoulders. 'A month, six weeks.' She gazed helplessly at him. 'Why? Aren't you—aren't you pleased?'

Conor turned away from her. 'Whether I'm pleased or not doesn't have a lot to do with it, does it?' he muttered, raking back his hair in that gesture she was coming to know so well. 'My God! So that's why you're prepared to marry me now. To get a name for your baby.'

'Conor!' Olivia stared at his back disbelievingly, and for a sickening moment she felt as if everything she had had had been torn away from her. She had been afraid it might happen, of course. That was one of the reasons why she had been so nervous about telling him in the first place.

But he was like her, she realised suddenly, as the force of her convictions gave her back her strength. He was so afraid now of being hurt, and it was up to her to prove to him that those desperate days were over.

'I—could get an abortion, if that's what you want,' she offered softly, as he riffled in his wardrobe and pulled on a pair of drawstring trousers, and he turned to her incredulously.

'What did you say?'

'I said—it's not too late for me to have an abortion,' she replied evenly, playing with the cord of his robe. 'Well,' she added, as his face contorted with emotion, 'if that's what it takes to make you believe I love you, and not what you can give me, so be it.' She took a step towards him, and then finished breathlessly, 'I don't care any more if we never have a baby. It's you I want, Conor. Do I have to put it in writing, too?'

He didn't hesitate then. His need for her was too great, and with a groan of anguish he pulled her into his arms.

'Do you mean it?' he choked, cupping her face in his hands and staring down at her as if he'd read the answer in her soul. 'You want me with or without this baby?'

'How can you doubt it?' she whispered brokenly. 'I never want us to be parted again.'

Conor stared at her. 'You mean it.'

'You'd better believe it,' she assured him unsteadily, hardly able to believe herself that everything was going to be all right. 'Darling, you have a very poor opinion of me if you think I'd risk another disastrous marriage, just to give your child a name. That's why I was afraid to come and tell you. I didn't want you to marry me just because you felt responsible.'

'Oh, Liv, how could you think that?'

'You did,' she reminded him softly. 'Which reminds me, you haven't told me how you feel.'

'Me?' Conor was bemused. 'It seems like a dream.' He shook his head. 'If you're happy, I'm happy.' And then, 'But do you mind? About giving up your work, I mean?'

'I'm—ecstatic,' she told him honestly. 'As far as my work is concerned, I think I deserve a break. About five years' break, at least,' she dimpled becomingly. 'Or longer, depending on the size of our family.'

'Liv——'

'But now I think we should get some sleep,' she said firmly. 'It's going to be morning soon. And you need some rest.'

Conor grinned. 'Oh, it's a long time until morning,' he assured her huskily. 'But I like the way you said *we* should get some sleep. At last I've got you where you belong: in my bed!'

TIDEWATER
SEDUCTION

CHAPTER ONE

IT COULDN'T be him: it shouldn't be him; but it was. Striding towards her, across the terrace where she was having breakfast, giving every indication he had expected to find her there.

Joanna glanced, half guiltily, about her, wondering even then if she was making a mistake. Maybe he had seen someone else—some other guest. But no. She was breakfasting late, and the hotel coffee shop was almost empty, most of the other guests all too eager to acquire that all-important tan. She was the only person sitting in her corner of the terrace, her olive skin as brown now as it was ever going to get.

Uncle Charles, her father's brother, used to say, teasingly, that she was the changeling in their otherwise so-English family. With her dark skin and silky black hair, she was nothing like her blonde and brown-haired parents. She had to be a throw-back to some scandalous liaison in the family's history. But until her marriage to Cole Macallister she hadn't found it a problem. Of course, that marriage, and the much-publicised divorce that had followed, had rather shaken her confidence. But, in recent months, she had managed to put the past behind her. Until this moment, she acknowledged tensely, experiencing an almost overwhelming urge to run, kicking and screaming, from a confrontation she had never thought to have to face.

Happily, she succeeded in controlling that compulsion, however, and by the time he stopped beside her table she had even contrived a faintly ironic smile. What the hell! She had nothing to be ashamed of, she assured herself tautly, crossing one long leg over the other in an

5

unconsciously defensive gesture. She had just as much right to be here as he had.

'Hello, Jo.'

His greeting was scarcely original, and she gained assurance from his diffidence. 'Cole,' she returned coolly, toying with the handle of her coffee-cup. 'How are you?'

'Fine.'

And he looked it, she conceded reluctantly. Even though he had never been a conventionally handsome man, the harsh planes and angles of his lean features possessed a much more potent attraction. A latent sexuality radiated from eyes as blue as amethysts, fringed by short thick lashes, several shades darker than his hair. There were rugged hollows beneath his arching cheek-bones, and she knew his nose had been broken in his youth. But his mouth was what drew her gaze, thin, and hard, and masculine, yet infinitely sensual, and gentler than when she'd last seen it.

But the silvery blond hair was the same, she noticed, chiding the treacherous emotions that still found beauty in his face. Longer than was fashionable, it brushed the open collar of his chambray shirt, the fine strands up-turned against his neck. He was not a man you could ever ignore, thought Joanna uneasily, though God knew she had done her best to do so for the past three years.

'May I join you?'

The question was unexpected, and for a moment Joanna knew the mouth-drying sense of panic she had experienced when she first saw him coming towards her. No, she wanted to say harshly. No, you can't. I don't want you to. I don't want to talk to you. I don't want you spoiling my affection for these islands by your presence.

But, of course, she didn't say any of those things. Although she knew she was probably being incredibly stupid, she was far too—polite—to behave so childishly, so *obviously*.

So, instead, 'Why not?' she murmured, moving her glass of orange juice aside, and relocating the cooling pot of coffee. 'Be my guest.'

'Thanks.'

With the inherent grace that had always seemed so unusual in a man of his size, Cole pulled out one of the vinyl-cushioned plastic chairs, and, turning its back to the table, straddled it. His bony knee, clad in cream cotton trousers, brushed the side of her bare thigh as he positioned himself, and it was all Joanna could do not to flinch away from even that slight contact. But Cole seemed not to notice any withdrawal on her part, as he draped his arms along the back of the chair, and cast a casual eye over the palm-shaded stretch of sand only a few yards away.

'Beautiful, isn't it?' he observed, and Joanna disciplined herself to make the obvious rejoinder.

'Beautiful,' she agreed, looking towards the ocean, creaming on to the crushed coral, beyond the coloured umbrellas, and oil-slick bodies. Although it wasn't the Caribbean, the waters cradling the sun-rich islands of the Bahamas were every bit as warm and inviting, their blue-green depths a magnet for yachtsmen and underwater explorers alike. 'I've always loved it.'

'Yes.' Cole's mouth compressed. 'Your family have a villa here, don't they?'

His brows, distinctly darker than the ash-pale subtlety of his hair, drew together speculatively, but before he could voice the question his words had provoked Joanna forestalled him.

'Not any more,' she stated swiftly, avoiding his enquiring gaze. 'In any case, it's not important. And I'm sure it has nothing to do with why you're here.'

'No.' Cole agreed with her. 'But you are.'

Joanna stared at him. 'You knew I was here?'

'Obviously.'

'No, not obviously.' She felt her nails digging into her palms, and determinedly relaxed herself. 'I assumed you must be here on holiday. That—that this meeting was accidental.'

'Hardly.' Cole regarded her dispassionately. 'That would be quite a coincidence, wouldn't it?'

Joanna took a steadying breath. 'Then I think you'd better leave. Or I will.'

She wanted to get to her feet. She wanted to walk away from the table, and pretend this had never happened. Perhaps, if she pinched herself hard enough, she might wake up. Oh, what she would give to find out this was all a dream—or a nightmare!

But she had run away from Cole once before, and she was damned if she'd do it again. He couldn't hurt her now. Not any more. And she would just be playing into his hands, if she allowed him to see he had upset her.

So, with admirable restraint, she helped herself to a croissant, from the napkin-lined basket in front of her, and picked up her knife to butter it.

Cole watched her. She was aware of his gaze, though she didn't acknowledge it. He had always had the ability to make her aware of him, even when she least wanted it. There was a brooding intensity to his appraisal that pierced any façade of indifference she might raise against him. Even now, buttering her croissant, with hands that only by a supreme effort on her part remained steady, she could feel his eyes upon her. What was he thinking? she wondered. What did he want? And how had he known where she was?

'Prickly, aren't you?' he said at last, and Joanna fought back the angry defence that sprang to her lips.

'I'm—curious,' she admitted, proud of the lack of aggression in her tone. 'How did you know I was here?'

'Grace told me,' he replied, mentioning his aunt's name without inflexion. 'You must know we keep in touch. And just because she's English, you shouldn't automatically assume she'll take your side.'

Joanna swallowed hard. Grace, she thought grimly. She should have guessed. Blood was thicker than water, and the Macallisters—even estranged ones—evidently believed that stronger than most.

'Don't think badly of her,' Cole said now, as Joanna stared down at the croissant. 'She didn't have a lot of choice. Not in the circumstances.'

But Joanna wasn't listening to him. Damn Grace, she was thinking, abandoning the untouched roll in favour of another cup of coffee. She knew, better than anyone, that for the past three years Joanna had done her utmost to forget Cole, and what he had done to her life. How could Grace have told him she was here, taking the first holiday she had had in twenty solid months of hard slog? This was supposed to be her reward to herself for finishing ahead of time. The paintings for the exhibition were completed. She hadn't even brought her materials with her. She had intended to have a complete break. And now——

'Where's—Sammy-Jean?' she demanded, looking beyond him, as if expecting the other woman to appear. 'You did marry her, didn't you?' She forced a mocking lilt into her voice, as she added, 'Sammy-Jean Macallister! Oh, yes, that sounds so much better than Joanna Macallister ever did.'

Cole's lips tightened. 'You won't get an argument from me,' he retorted, but she realised to her amazement—and delight—that, for once, she had got under his skin. A faint trace of colour ran up beneath his tan, and the hands resting on the chair-back balled into fists.

But then, exercising the same kind of control Joanna had used earlier, he expelled his breath. 'I didn't come here to talk about Sam,' he said tautly, meeting her gaze. 'My father's dying.'

Joanna gulped. She couldn't help it. Ryan Macallister had always appeared invincible to her. It scarcely seemed credible that he was mortal, like the rest of them.

Even so, he had never been any friend of hers, and her dark brows rose without sympathy. 'Is that supposed to mean something to me?'

Cole regarded her grimly. 'He wants to see you.'

'To see me?' Joanna's voice came out several degrees higher than normal, but Cole only nodded.

'That's what I said.'

Joanna caught her breath. 'You can't be serious.'

'Why not?'

'Why not?' She made a sound of disbelief. 'Why— he doesn't even *like* me!'

Cole's eyes dropped. 'Maybe he does,' he said, picking up the spoon that was lying beside the unused place-setting in front of him. 'Maybe he doesn't.' He spun the spoon between his fingers. 'In any case, he says he wants to see you, and that's all there is to it.'

'You wish!' Joanna stared at him incredulously. 'If you think I'm going to give up my holiday to go and see an old man who never even gave me the time of day, if he could help it, you're very much mistaken!'

Cole looked up, and the blue eyes were as cold as steel between narrowed lids. 'Are you really that hard?' he asked, his lips curling contemptuously. 'God, Ma said you wouldn't come, but I didn't believe her.'

'Believe it,' said Joanna flatly, pressing her hands down on the table and getting to her feet. 'I wish I could say it's been a pleasure, Cole, but lying was never my strong point!'

'Like hell!'

Cole had kicked the chair out from under him, and was up on his feet to confront her, before she could make good her escape. And, even though she stood a good five feet nine inches in her ankle boots, she was no match for his six feet plus. Add to that broad shoulders, a flat stomach, and long muscular legs, and she could see no means of retreat. Short of causing a scene, of course, and Joanna didn't want to do that, when this was only the second morning of her holiday.

'Isn't this rather ridiculous, Cole?' she asked, looking up at him rather tensely. 'What do you hope to achieve? You can't force me to go with you.'

'Can't I?'

Cole's response was predictable enough, but it lacked conviction, and Joanna realised that, for all his belligerence, he was unsure of his ground. It gave her a feeling of triumph just watching him—a rippling sensation of pleasure she hadn't felt before.

'I think you'd better get out of my way,' she said, not afraid to meet his gaze. 'What can you do to me—that you haven't already done?'

'Son of a——'

Cole bit off the expletive, but not before Joanna had glimpsed the raw frustration in his eyes. It was the first time she ever remembered him being at a loss for words, and there was a tantalising enjoyment in watching him squirm.

'So, if you'll excuse me——'

Brushing his chest with just the tips of her fingers, Joanna edged around him—and he let her. It was rather like baiting a tiger, she thought, the fluttering excitement in her throat threatening to choke her. It was so intoxicating that she felt quite high, and she could hardly contain herself as she deliberately sauntered across the terrace and into the hotel.

She knew his eyes followed her. She could feel them, boring into her back, as she swayed provocatively between the tables. And she was glad he would see nothing to betray the emotional trauma he had once wrought in her life. Her figure was as slim now as it had ever been, due as much to hard work as careful dieting. Her legs were long, and shown to some advantage in the frayed Bermudas she was wearing with a buttoned vest. Even her hair had the shiny patina of good health, longer now than she used to wear it, and caught at her nape in a silver barrette.

Of course, she came down to earth again as quickly as she had gone up. As soon as she was inside the glass screens, which had been folded back to allow free access between the indoor and outdoor sections of the restaurant, the sense of exhilaration she had felt while she was with Cole quickly abated. Besides, once the desire to thwart his plans had been accomplished, she was troubled by an annoying twinge of conscience. Whatever Cole thought, she was not as hard as he imagined. And, although it was true that Ryan Macallister had never accepted her as Cole's wife, he was an old man, and dying, if Cole was to be believed.

She paused in the lobby of the hotel, not sure now of what she wanted to do. She had been intending to get a book from her room and spend the morning sitting in the sun, but her confrontation with her ex-husband had left her disturbed and restless.

She needed her swimsuit anyway, so, forcing thoughts of Cole aside, she took the lift up to her room. She was on the fourth floor, just one below the penthouse suites. She had a large room, that was part-sitting-room, part-bedroom, with a wide balcony overlooking the Atlantic. All the rooms had balconies, but they were made private by the solid walls that divided them.

As she stripped off her vest and shorts and put on a scarlet *maillot*, Joanna couldn't help wondering where Cole was staying. She guessed he must have flown down from Charleston yesterday evening, and it was infinitely possible that he was staying at this hotel. But he had probably just booked in for one night. He had no doubt expected to persuade her to fly back with him later today.

She sighed, regarding her reflection in the long closet mirrors, without really noticing how well the strapless swimsuit looked. Perhaps she should just sunbathe on her balcony this morning, she was thinking. She didn't think Cole would know her actual room number, and even if he did he was unlikely to come looking for her.

Then she frowned. No, she told herself firmly. She was not going to run away from this. She had proved she could challenge Cole and get away with it. Why shouldn't she do so again, if it was necessary? It didn't matter what he said, or what he thought of her. She was a free woman. She could do what she liked.

In any case, she added, in a less than radical afterthought, Cole was unlikely to hang around, once he realised she meant what she said. It was early May, after all. A busy time of the year for him. And if his father was seriously ill——

But Joanna refused to think about it. She would not allow herself to feel guilty about a man who had always hated her, and her beliefs. Dear God, he had even destroyed his own son in his efforts to get what he wanted!

The phone rang as she was pulling an outsize T-shirt over her head. The baggy cotton garment barely skimmed her thighs, but its shoulders would keep her cool if the sun got too hot. It served the dual purpose of covering her swimsuit and providing protection, and she liked it better than some custom-made jacket.

When the phone rang, she hastily jammed her arms into the sleeves, and tugged it down around her. Then, halfway to answer the call, she halted. What if it was Cole? She was not sure she was ready yet for another altercation. She needed time to build her defences. She wasn't sure she was as immune to his censure as she thought.

But the realisation that it was more likely to be her mother, calling to make sure everything was OK, forced her to think again. Neither of her parents had been particularly keen on her taking this holiday alone, not to mention travelling so far from her home in London. In spite of her abortive marriage to Cole—or perhaps because of it—they had become increasingly protective, and, although she had phoned them on her arrival two days ago, they probably wanted an update on her movements.

Even so, there was a definite edge to her tone as she picked up the receiver, and the woman's voice that greeted her revealed a similar tension.

'Jo? Jo, darling, is that you? Oh, God, you sound so clear. Are you really thousands of miles away?'

Joanna's relief was almost palpable, and, running her tongue over her dry lips, she smoothed one damp palm down the seam of her T-shirt. But with the relief came a kindling of resentment towards her caller, and her voice was only slightly warmer as she answered, 'Yes. Yes, Grace, it's me. A sitting duck, as you expected.'

'Oh, Jo!' Grace sounded anxious now. 'I know what you must be thinking, but try to understand my position. Ryan is my brother-in-law, after all. When—when Cole asked where you were, I had to tell him.'

Joanna absorbed this in silence. Although she still resented the fact that Grace had betrayed her whereabouts, without even clearing it with her first, she wasn't unmindful of Grace's family responsibilities. Oh, it was easy enough to dismiss them by reminding herself that Grace's marriage to Ryan Macallister's brother had been no more successful than her own, but the truth was Grace was more dependent on the Macallisters than she was. Grace and Luke Macallister had two sons, Evan and Luke Junior. If she wanted to continue seeing her sons on a regular basis, she couldn't afford to offend the man who could deny her that privilege.

'Jo? Jo, are you still there?'

Grace's worried tones brought Joanna's attention back to the phone. It was her own fault really, she thought. As soon as her marriage to Cole broke up, she should have found herself another agent. But she had known Grace for almost ten years. Grace had recognised her talent long before the water-colours she produced became popular. Heavens, it was through Grace that she had met Cole—though the virtues of that particular introduction had long since been debased. Nevertheless, she was fond of Grace, she owed her a lot, and it wasn't fair to expect her to jeopardise her relationship with her own flesh and blood.

'Yes, I'm still here, Grace,' Joanna answered now, expelling her breath on a long sigh. 'OK, I forgive you. I suppose you didn't have a lot of choice. But, dammit, you should have warned me! I couldn't believe it when I saw Cole across the terrace.'

Grace made a sound of surprise. 'You've seen Cole?'

Joanna frowned. 'Of course.' She paused. 'What did you expect?'

'Oh—I don't know.' Grace sounded doubtful. 'When he phoned, I got the impression he didn't want to leave Tidewater at this particular time.'

Joanna shrugged. 'Well, he must have changed his mind.'

Grace hesitated. 'And are you going back with him?'

'No.'

'No?' Grace sounded dismayed. 'But Jo, Ryan's dying!'

'So?' Joanna refused to allow the other woman to influence her.

'He has cancer,' Grace persisted. 'According to Cole, the doctors give him a few weeks at most. Jo, he is Cole's father. Can't you find it in your heart to feel some compassion? I know you and he have had your differences, but——'

'Differences!' Joanna almost spat the word. 'Grace, that man and I did not have *differences*! We were totally opposed to one another in every way. Ryan Macallister doesn't deserve anyone's compassion. He's a twisted, evil man!'

Grace sighed. 'You really hate him, don't you?'

'Wouldn't you? *Don't* you?'

'Not hate, no.' Grace was tentative. 'Oh, I know what you're going to say. If Ryan hadn't made such a big thing of my wanting some independence, Luke would never have found the guts, strength—call it what you will—to make that ultimatum. But Jo, it was Luke who made me choose between staying at Tidewater, and vegetating, or making a life for myself. Ryan might have fashioned the bullets, my dear, but Luke fired them.'

'Yes, but——'

'Hear me out, Jo. I want you to know I haven't regretted what I did. Not really. Oh, I miss the boys, of course, but it's not as if they were babies when I left. And I've had a good life here. Running the gallery, becoming Ray's partner. He and I have more in common than Luke and I ever did. Luke was different. He was exciting. And I don't deny that Ray and I—well, we don't have the same kind of relationship. Ours is more—intellectual, if you know what I mean. But I'm not bitter. I have everything I need. I can afford to feel pity.'

'Well, I can't.'

Joanna pressed her lips together, and Grace breathed deeply. 'No,' she conceded, after a moment. 'No, I see that. I suppose I'd forgotten how much you love Cole——'

'*Loved*!' Joanna amended harshly. 'You'd forgotten how much I loved Cole. Not any more. That love died when they killed Nathan. Or did you forget about him, too?'

There was silence for a while, and when Grace spoke again there was regret in her voice. 'No,' she said softly. 'No, of course I haven't forgotten Nathan. I'm sorry, Jo. Naturally you must do what you think best.'

Conversely, Joanna felt guilty now. Oh, not about Ryan Macallister, she consoled herself, but perhaps she had been hard on Grace.

'It doesn't matter,' she said, forcing her mind on to other things. 'Um—how are the arrangements for the exhibition going? Do you think it's going to attract enough interest?'

'Are you kidding?' Grace responded eagerly, evidently as anxious as Joanna to turn their conversation on to a business footing. 'I've already had acceptances to the opening from all the most important critics, and even Howard Jennings has agreed to make an appearance.'

'Oh, good.'

Joanna tried to summon some enthusiasm for the news that the editor and presenter of a monthly television arts programme was apparently interested enough to attend, but somehow the importance of the exhibition had been blurred. In spite of all she had said, the image of Cole's father, sick and dying of that most pernicious of diseases, would not go away, and she was inordinately grateful when Grace said she would have to go, and rang off.

But, if she had hoped that by severing the connection with Grace she could sever all thoughts of the Macallisters, she was mistaken. Memories of Cole, and his father, and Tidewater just kept on coming back, and it was with an angry sense of resentment that she snatched up the bag containing her book, sun-screen, and dark glasses, and left the room.

CHAPTER TWO

THE sun was soothing. It was hard to think of anything with its rays beating against her closed eyelids, and bringing a film of perspiration to her supine body. It was hot beside the pool, hotter than on the beach, where there was at least a breeze off the water to temper the humidity. But Joanna welcomed the numbing effects of the heat, and the mindless lethargy it engendered.

Her hands uncurled against the cream towel she had spread over the slatted sun-bed, and she arched one leg in an unknowingly provocative pose. Oh, yes, she decided contentedly, this was definitely the life! She refused to think about anything, except what she was going to have for lunch.

She had chosen a chair in a secluded corner of the pool deck. It wasn't that she was unsociable. It was just that she had no wish to appear in need of company. She knew perfectly well that a woman alone often attracted unwelcome attention from the opposite sex, and indulging in any kind of holiday flirtation was not what she had come here for. At home, she did accept an occasional invitation to dinner, or the theatre, but that was different. On the whole, her escorts knew that she was not interested in any serious commitment, and if any of them showed they would prefer a more intimate relationship they were quickly discarded. She liked men, but at a distance. She was polite, and friendly, but nothing more. She had been hurt badly once, and she had no intention of repeating the experience.

Consequently, she was not a little irritated when someone came to occupy the chair next to hers. Through half-closed lids, she glimpsed the cuffs of dark blue

18

swimming-shorts, and brown, muscular legs that curved beneath the cuffs into tight masculine buttocks.

Damn, she thought, closing her eyes again, and pretending she was unaware of him. There were at least fifty other sun-beds set at different angles around the pool. And surely among them were other single women, who would be flattered to receive his attention. Why couldn't he have chosen one of them? She wanted to relax, not spend her time fending off passes.

The seductive stroke of a cool finger along her arm brought her eyes open with a start. The light, sensitive touch was unwillingly sensual, but she was too angry to admit its effect. What cheek! she thought furiously, pushing herself up. Was it too much to expect that she should be left alone?

Jerking down her sunglasses, which she had been wearing as a kind of surrogate head-band, she turned her incensed gaze on the man beside her. And then her jaw sagged disbelievingly. It wasn't some pool-side Romeo who was resting on the chair beside hers. It was Cole!

'Hi,' he said non-committally. 'I'm pleased to see you don't encourage boarders.'

Joanna's anger floundered. 'What are you doing here, Cole?' she exclaimed. 'I thought you'd be on the next flight back to South Carolina.'

'Hmm. I guess you did.' Cole stretched his long legs comfortably, and laced his hands beneath his head. 'Well, as you can see, I'm still here.'

'I won't change my mind, you know.'

Joanna's response was half peevish, and she wished she hadn't felt the need to defend herself, when Cole merely shifted to a more restful position.

'I haven't asked you to, have I?' he countered, looking up at her through the sun-bleached tips of his lashes. 'Relax, Jo. It's much too hot to fuel all that adrenalin.'

Joanna pressed her lips together mutinously, trying to regain her composure. Now that she was assured that no one was trying to proposition her, she ought to be able to rekindle her sense of well-being.

But, of course, she couldn't. Although she determinedly lay down again, the feeling of tranquillity had left her. She felt on edge, and agitated, and far too aware of the man on the sun-bed beside her.

His arm was only inches from hers, she observed covertly, tautly muscled, and displaying the tiny tattoo of a venomous bushmaster, which he had had etched when he was just a boy, and for which, he had told her, his father had soundly beaten him. The muscle flexed, as she watched it, tightening and hardening, before relaxing once again. The skin that covered the rest of his arm was brown and smooth and flawless, almost hairless, and lightly sheened with sweat.

Without any volition on her part, her body responded to the sensual appeal of his. The sight of his bare chest, with its flat nipples, and light dusting of hair, disturbed her. She found her eyes following the provocative arrowing of hair that disappeared beneath the elasticated waistband of his shorts. His restless movements had inched the waistband of the shorts down below his navel, and his pelvis made a cradle of his sex.

God! She tore her eyes away, and stared blindly across the pool. What was the matter with her? she chided, as her hands coiled into tight fists. It wasn't as if Cole's naked body was any novelty to her. She had lived with him for more than two years, for heaven's sake! She had seen him in every pose and attitude, in every state of undress. He had a beautiful lean body—a perfect specimen of American manhood. It was a pity the contents didn't live up to the wrapping!

'Do you want a drink?'

She was so tied up with her thoughts that Cole's first question didn't register. 'I—beg your pardon?'

'I said—do you want a drink?' he repeated, propping himself up on his elbow, drawing up one leg, and half turning towards her. 'There's a waitress making a tour of the deck, taking orders. I thought you might like something long and cold and refreshing.'

'Oh——' Joanna swallowed, and explored her dry lips with her tongue. 'Well, yes. I think I will have some lemonade. But I'll get my own. You don't have to bother.'

'It's no bother,' Cole assured her, swinging his feet to the ground. He moved swiftly, so that by the time the bikini-clad waitress reached them he was standing up, and Joanna saw to her chagrin that his southern courtesy did not go unnoticed.

'You didn't have to stand up,' she muttered irritably, as he resumed his seat, and Cole's mouth tilted.

'No, I know,' he agreed, brushing an insect from his thigh with a lazy hand. 'But it costs nothing to be polite.'

'Would you have stood up if it had been a man?' she persisted, and Cole's lips parted to reveal a row of even white teeth.

'I guess,' he said, his eyes leaving hers to move insolently over her body. 'What's the matter, Jo? Something eating you?'

Joanna shifted uneasily beneath his taunting gaze, and she was aware that she was still aroused from her thoughts earlier. Her own nipples were as taut as buttons, and she tugged surreptitiously at the front of her swimsuit to hide their provocative display.

Unable to think of an answer sharp enough to puncture his mocking self-confidence, she turned her head, and pretended to watch the antics of two young people in the pool. They were teenagers, she guessed, holidaying together for the first time, and from the way the girl draped herself around her companion they were not ignorant of each other's bodies. There was an intimacy between them that spoke of long nights exploring the intricacies of love. She and Cole had once explored those same intricacies, she remembered. During those long southern nights, before things started to go wrong...

The waitress returned with two tall glasses of lemonade, liberally spiked with ice. Cole took one for himself, and held the other out towards Joanna, and although she was loath to take anything from him it would have been childish to refuse. So, sitting up, cross-legged, she took the perspex tumbler from him, drinking from it thirstily, before tipping her head back on her shoulders, and luxuriating in the intense heat.

Cole was still sitting sideways on the sun-bed, legs spread, bare feet resting on the tiled surface of the pool-deck. It meant she was constantly aware of his eyes upon her but, despite her irritation, she supposed his presence was deterring any unwelcome attention.

'You look good,' he said suddenly, and her eyes jerked towards his before she could prevent them.

'Thank you,' she returned, striving for a careless tone as she took herself in hand again. 'So do you. Sammy-Jean's evidently doing something right.'

Cole's expression hardened for a moment, but then he returned to the attack. 'You always were a beautiful woman,' he murmured. 'And, if anything, you look better now than you did when we got married.'

'Then I must be doing something right, too,' declared Joanna shortly, impatient at the wave of colour that swept into her neck at his words. 'Living in London isn't all bad, whatever you think. Our climate may not be as good as yours, but it has its compensations.'

Cole's brows arched for a moment, and then he looked down at his drink, resting in hands hanging loosely between his thighs. 'I guess it does,' he conceded at last. 'I'm sure Grace would agree with you.'

'I'm sure she would.' Joanna nodded. But she didn't like this conversation. It wasn't what Cole was saying that troubled her exactly. But the tone he was using did. He was so polite. His lazy southern drawl scraped across her nerves, like a nail over raw silk, and every time he looked at her she grew more and more tense.

'Um—how—how's your mother?' she asked, hoping to divert the conversation away from herself, and Cole lifted his head.

'Ma's OK.' His eyes skimmed her mouth, and although she had just drunk about a quarter of a pint of lemonade Joanna's lips felt parched. 'She's getting older, like the rest of us. But she still works just as hard as ever.'

'And—and Ben and Joe?' Joanna felt compelled to keep him talking about his family. 'And the twins? I bet Charley can swim now, can't she? Did they start high school yet? Oh, yes, of course, they must have done.'

Cole regarded her between narrowed lids. 'Are you really that interested?' he queried, his brooding gaze bringing a deepening of colour in her cheeks. 'Sure, Ben and Joe are fine. Joe's married now, and his wife's expecting their first baby. Charley and Donna started high school last year, and Sandy's going to join them come fall.' He paused. 'I guess that about covers it, wouldn't you say?'

Joanna bent her head, the weight of her hair sliding over one shoulder to expose the vulnerable curve of her neck. 'I was just being—polite, that's all,' she said, half defensively. 'I—like your brothers and sisters. And, I used to think that they liked me.'

'They did.' Cole shook the ice around in his empty tumbler. 'Charley often used to talk about the time you and she got stuck out on Palmer's Island. If you hadn't swum back to get help, you might both have been swept away.'

'Oh——' Joanna made a deprecating gesture. 'You'd already discovered we were missing. When the boat was washed on to the bank, you'd have guessed where we were.'

'Maybe not soon enough,' he insisted, and Joanna felt a remembered sense of apprehension. She could still recall how scared she had been in the water, fighting her way against the current, feeling her arms getting weaker by the minute. She had been unable to stand, when she hauled herself out of the river. If Cole and his brothers hadn't been searching for them, it might still have been too late. The flooding torrent of the Tidewater River had left Palmer's Island under several feet of water for hours. No one could have survived its fury, least of all ten-year-old Charley, who couldn't even swim.

Joanna grimaced now, unwilling to think of that near-tragedy, and Cole stretched out his hand towards her. She thought for one heart-stopping moment that he was going to touch her, and she instinctively drew back against the chair. But, although his lips flattened for a moment, revealing his awareness of her reaction, all he did was lift the empty tumbler out of her hand.

'I'll get rid of these,' he said, dropping one inside the other, and while she tried to recover her self-possession he sauntered across the deck to dump the tumblers.

By the time she heard the depression of his chair's plastic slats, she was once again reclining on her towel, on her stomach this time, with her eyes closed, and her face turned deliberately away from him. Surely he would get the message, she thought tensely. She didn't want to have to spell it out for him again. He was wasting his time if he thought he could get her to change her mind. They had a saying in the south, about catching more bees with honey than with vinegar, but if that was Cole's intention it wasn't going to work. He was an attractive man, sure, and, even though she had more reason than most to regret the fact, she wouldn't have been a woman if she hadn't found him easy to look at. But that was all. She wasn't attracted to him. Not any more.

'You're going to get burned,' his lazy voice observed, revealing his skin was thicker than even she had thought, and Joanna clamped her jaws together.

'No, I'm not,' she retorted, through her teeth. 'My skin's too dark, remember?'

'It's also used to a colder climate,' Cole replied, and she heard him get up from his chair again.

God! Joanna lay completely still for a moment, and then, unable to withstand the suspense a moment longer, she rolled over on to her back—just as Cole was lowering his weight on to the side of her slatted mattress. It was just by a swift removal of her arm that she avoided being sat on, and her eyes sparkled indignantly at his uninvited presumption.

'What the hell do you——?' she was beginning, when Cole showed her the tube of sun-screening cream in his hand.

'This is yours, isn't it?' he asked, and she guessed he had rifled it from her bag. 'Turn over,' he added, unscrewing the cap and squeezing a curl of its contents into his palm. 'There's no point in torturing yourself just to spite me.'

Joanna pressed her lips together and stared up at him, resentment oozing from every pore. The last thing she wanted was his help, in anything. And she certainly didn't want him touching her. But once again he had her at a disadvantage, caught between the desire to show her real feelings, and the knowledge that by doing so she would be handing him all the cards.

So, instead of snatching the cream out of his hand and hurling it into the pool, she forced a tight smile and obediently rolled over again. Let him do his worst, she thought, stifling her angry reaction against the towel. After all, although her skin didn't tan, it did burn sometimes, and she could do without that aggravation as well.

Cole's hands were amazingly cool against her hot flesh. Of course, he had just been handling the tumblers containing the ice, she reminded herself grimly, as his long fingers slid across her shoulders, and his thumbs found the nubby column of her spine. She found it was important to keep a sense of proportion, as his probing hands found every inch of exposed skin. She was relieved she wasn't wearing a bikini. At least the modest *maillot* left her some dignity.

But not a lot, she had to concede, as the sinuous brush of his fingers began to lull her into a false sense of security. It would be so easy, she thought, to go with the flow; to allow her flesh to respond to the sensuous touch of his; to admit she was enjoying his expert ministrations. Because of the limitations of the sun-bed, his leg was wedged beside her hip, and although the swimsuit protected the upper half of her pelvis his hair-roughened thigh was against the exposed curve of her bottom. It meant that every stroke of his hands on her shoulders brought a corresponding increase of pressure against her hip, and the images that evoked were all sexual . . .

'I—think that will do,' she declared firmly, arching her back away from his fingers, and getting up on to her knees. 'I'm not planning to stay out here that much longer.'

'No?' With a resigned shrug of his shoulders, Cole moved obediently back to his own chair. 'What are you planning to do, then?'

Joanna didn't look at him. 'I think that's my business, don't you?'

'I guess.' Cole screwed the top back on the tube of sun-cream and dropped it carelessly into her bag. 'Only askin', lady.'

'And I'm telling you, it's none of your business,' said Joanna shortly. 'In any case, don't you have a plane to catch, or something?'

'Not until tomorrow,' Cole replied, wiping his greasy hands over his knees. 'Sorry.'

'I should have guessed.' Joanna's impatient gaze darted over him. 'You obviously came prepared.'

'You mean these?' Cole hooked a thumb into the waistband of his shorts. 'I bought them this morning in the shop, here in the hotel. Along with a couple of pairs of underpants, and a fresh shirt.'

Joanna's lips pursed. 'Really.'

'Yes, really.' Cole inclined his head 'It wasn't my intention to stay away from Tidewater any longer than I had to.'

Joanna dropped her sunglasses down on to her nose again. She had pushed them up into her hair, while she had been lying on her stomach. But now she felt the need for them again, and the doubtful protection they provided.

'I guess this is a good place to paint, huh?' Cole murmured, gazing narrow-eyed towards the ocean. 'Grace told me you've got an exhibition coming up.'

'Oh—yes.' Joanna wondered what else Grace had told him. 'The—er—the opening's a couple of weeks after I get back.'

'A couple of weeks?' His eyes flickered. 'Maybe I should buy a ticket. Get myself an investment for the future.'

'You're not serious!'

Joanna's reaction was unguarded, and he turned to look at her with mild enquiry. 'Why not?' he countered. 'I can tell everyone it was painted by my ex-wife. Should add a lick of glamour to the price, if I ever want to sell it.'

'That's sick!'

'Is it? Why? Just 'cause maybe I wan' somethin' to 'member you by?'

'Don't talk like that!'

Cole's brows arched. 'Like what?'

'Like you didn't know better,' retorted Joanna crossly. 'Oh—do what you like. I can't stop you.'

His shoulders hunched, and when he spoke again his voice was low and husky. 'You could have dinner with me tonight.'

'Have dinner with you?' Joanna was taken aback.

'Sure. Why not?'

'Well——' Joanna floundered. 'I—can't.'

'You having dinner with someone else?'

'No.'

The response was automatic. But she could hardly say she was, when if he walked into the restaurant he would find her eating alone. Too late she realised she could have gone out to eat, or ordered room service, but she had answered without thinking. In any case, she didn't see why she had to make an excuse. It wasn't as if she wanted to have dinner with him.

'You afraid to eat with me?' he suggested slyly, and her resentment flared anew.

'No,' she denied tautly. 'Why would I be? But I don't think your father, or Sammy-Jean, would approve of our socialising, do you?'

'And that's why you're refusing? Because you don't want to offend my father?'

'No!' Joanna tore the dark glasses off her nose, and stared at him frustratedly. 'Cole, why are you doing this? You know you don't really want to have dinner with me at all.'

'Don't I?' His deep blue eyes ranged disturbingly over her flushed face. 'Maybe I do. For old times' sake. What do you say?'

Joanna's hands clenched around the stems of her glasses. Of course, she did know why he was doing this, she told herself. Cole was nothing if not tenacious, and he had evidently got it into his head that sooner or later she would crack. The small talk, the lemonade, and the massage were all intended to soften her up, to make her more receptive, when he mentioned his father's illness again. He had even bitten the bullet and asked about the exhibition. That must have really galled him. Her work had always been a source of conflict in the past.

Her lips twisted. So how far was he prepared to go, to gain his own ends? If she agreed to have dinner with him, what then? He could hardly talk about something as serious as cancer over the red snapper. So, when did he intend to make his next move? And how?

An imp of vengeance stirred inside her. It might be amusing to find out. In spite of the casual way he had handled the conversation this morning, she hadn't forgotten his reaction when she turned the tables on him. So long as she was on the defensive, he had nothing to fear. But if she decided to play a different game...

Could she do it? That was what she had to ask herself. She hadn't to forget that people who played with fire sometimes got burned. But she was over Cole, completely and irrevocably. Her body might still respond to the sexuality of his, but her mind was not involved. And how she chose to behave was no one's business but her own.

Taking a deep breath, she came to a decision. 'All right,' she said, sliding the dark glasses back into place. 'For old times' sake. Why not?'

Protected by the glasses, she caught the fleeting trace of surprise that crossed his face at her words. Evidently, he had expected it to be harder to get her to change her mind. None the less, he recovered himself with admirable efficiency, and his lazy smile tugged the corners of his mouth upwards.

'OK,' he said, making no objection when she began to gather her belongings together with the obvious intention of leaving. 'I'll meet you in the lobby of the hotel at seven o'clock, right?'

'Right.'

Joanna forced a matching smile. But her expression was distinctly cat-like, as she negligently made her departure.

CHAPTER THREE

JOANNA decided to skip lunch, and go into town. She had intended to get a snack from the poolside bar, but the prospect that she might run into Cole again before the evening decided her against it.

Besides, she hadn't been into Nassau since her arrival. The international airport on New Providence was situated at the north-western end of the island, and the Coral Beach Hotel was on the coast that lay between the airport and the town of Nassau. The previous day she had spent recovering from her jet lag, and basking in her new-found freedom. But today she felt too strung-up by the thought of the evening ahead to relax any-where. She needed action, and distraction, and the chance to spend some of the dollars she had brought with her.

After taking a shower to remove the combined effects of the heat and the protective cream Cole had applied, Joanna dressed in the shorts and soft boots she had worn earlier. But instead of the vest she donned a loose-fitting T-shirt. No point in risking sunburn, she told herself sardonically. Not when she wanted to look her best that evening.

She took a taxi from the hotel into town. The gar-rulous Bahamian driver dropped her in Bay Street, and she spent a pleasant couple of hours browsing through the shops and the Straw Market. She bought herself a length of vividly patterned cotton, to wear sarong-wise around the pool, and a chunky handful of bracelets, sculpted from shells, that clattered attractively every time she moved her wrist. She also treated herself to a new swimsuit, a bikini this time, patterned with the many exotic flowers of the islands.

30

Before going back to the hotel, she bought herself a can of Coke, and strolled down to the harbour to drink it. A huge cruise liner was tied up at Prince George's Wharf, and she sat for a while on the sea-wall, watching the activity around the ship.

Passengers came and went, stores were taken on board, members of the crew took time out to stretch their legs on dry land, and local youths on bicycles milled about the quay. If she had had her sketch pad with her, Joanna knew, she would not have been able to resist trying to capture the scene on paper. There was so much colour and excitement, and when she eventually left the harbour the images were still buzzing inside her head.

Perhaps she ought to buy herself a sketch pad, she thought, strolling up into Rawson Square. She had no doubt she would be able to get what she wanted along Bay Street. Although it wasn't pretentious, it was one of the most comprehensive shopping streets in the world.

But then she shook her head and hailed a taxi to take her back to the hotel. This was supposed to be a holiday, she chided herself. Just because Cole had come, upsetting her carefully arranged schedule, and reminding her that she had once used her work as a means of escape, was no reason to go rushing for the charcoal. She could handle Cole now. She had proved it earlier. And this evening he would realise she was no longer the vulnerable girl he had married and divorced.

Selecting what to wear that evening was rather more difficult than she had expected. While she wanted to look provocative, she did not want to appear tacky. Sexy clothes were all very well, but it was all too easy to go over the top. Luckily, she had gone shopping before she left England, so her choice was not limited. But whether it should be a mini cocktail dress, or a slinky trouser suit, was not an easy decision to make.

She eventually chose to wear a dress. A silk-satin sheath in shades of green and purple that complimented her dark colouring, and brought out the tawny highlights in her eyes. It was short, barely reaching mid-thigh, and the on-the-shoulder, off-the-shoulder neckline exposed the creamy beauty of her skin. She wore no bra or tights, only a lacy brief, for modesty's sake. It made her look—interesting, she decided. Thank God the extra inches she had acquired after the divorce, when eating and drinking had seemed her only consolations, had all been coaxed away by careful dieting. These days, the energy she gave to her work burned off any unwanted calories. And attending a weekly work-out class kept her body lean and supple.

She left her dark hair loose, securing it away from her face on one side with combs. Although it was silky straight, it was thick and shining, and swung smoothly against her shoulders. Like the rest of her, it was sleek and healthy, and she spared a moment's unwilling consideration for the man who'd sent Cole here.

If the thought of how what she was planning to do might affect Sammy-Jean disturbed her, she dismissed it. Sammy-Jean had shown no qualms about seducing her husband, so wouldn't it be ironic now if she could return the compliment? Not that she wanted Cole back again, she assured herself. But taking him away from Sammy-Jean did have a certain malicious appeal.

She needed very little make-up. Her lashes were naturally dark, and only a little dusky eyeshadow was needed to add mystery to the depths of her eyes. A trace of blusher over her cheekbones gave a little colour to her face, and a shiny amber lip-salve enhanced the sensitive fullness of her mouth.

When she viewed her reflection in the mirror, before going downstairs, she was reasonably content with her appearance. She looked young, and sexy, but tantalisingly remote.

The lobby of the Coral Beach Hotel was an atrium, arching to a high, glass-vaulted ceiling. The several floors of rooms curved round the central area, which served as both reception and shopping mall. Tall plants and flowering shrubs filled every available space, with a stone-carved fountain providing a focal point.

As Joanna came down the staircase from the mezzanine, she could see Cole waiting by the fountain. She had chosen to get out of the lift at the floor above ground level, so that she might observe him before he saw her. It was a careful ploy, born of her desire to control every aspect of the evening they were to spend together. Besides, it gave her the opportunity to compose her entrance. Streaming out of the lift, with a throng of other passengers, right where he was standing, was not what she had in mind.

As she had hoped, he saw her before she reached the bottom of the stairs. His searching gaze alighted on her slender figure, as she negotiated the last three steps, and although she affected not to have seen him she was instantly aware of his sharp reaction. He didn't come to meet her, but his eyes followed every move she made. Much the way the snake he had tattooed on his shoulder watched its victim, she mused fancifully. But that was not a comparison she wanted to make.

He was wearing a jacket, she noticed, a concession to the fact that it was evening. He certainly didn't need it, even in the air-conditioned lobby of the hotel. Bahamian nights were deliciously warm and inviting. But the more exclusive restaurants insisted on this small formality, so evidently they were dining somewhere expensive.

And God, didn't he look good! she acknowledged objectively. So good, in fact, that for a moment she doubted her ability to pull this off. But then the reluctant admiration she saw in his eyes restored her confidence. Even if he had deserted her bed for Sammy-Jean's, he was not indifferent to her. Though she guessed he would hate to admit it.

'Hi,' she said, as she closed the space between them. 'I hope I haven't kept you waiting.'

Cole shrugged, his broad shoulders moving sinuously beneath the beige twill of his jacket. 'I had nothing better to do,' he said, his eyes flickering swiftly over the tantalising curve of her breasts, exposed by the dipping neckline of the dress. Then, looking beyond her, he added, 'I didn't realise there were guest rooms on the mezzanine.'

Joanna's dark brows arched enquiringly. 'Does it matter?'

'You walked down from the mezzanine,' Cole reminded her sardonically. 'Funny. I got the impression you were staying on one of the higher floors.'

Joanna hid a smile. Evidently, Cole had made it his business to find out exactly where she was staying, but she had been prepared for his question, and her lips tilted charmingly.

'I made a mistake,' she lied ruefully. 'The lift stopped and I got out.' She grimaced. 'Silly me!'

'Hmm.'

Cole's grunt of assent was hardly sympathetic, but Joanna had achieved what she wanted to achieve, and she could afford to be generous. 'Does it matter?' she exclaimed, looking up at him disarmingly. 'I'm here now. So—where are we eating?'

Cole's mouth flattened. 'I thought we might eat at the Commodore Club. They have an excellent restaurant, and you might like to visit the casino later.'

Joanna nodded. 'Sounds good to me.' She tucked her leather bag against her side, and slid her fingers round his arm. 'Shall we go?'

The muscles of his upper arm were taut beneath her grip. She sensed he would like to release himself, and she wondered how he had expected her to behave. It was obvious he was confused by her apparent willingness to co-operate, and he was wary of her appearance, and the provocation it presented.

A row of taxis waited on the forecourt of the hotel, and a black-suited major-domo summoned one at Cole's request. Joanna climbed into the back of the cab unaided, smoothing down her tight skirt as she scrambled across the seat. She had noticed before that no one bothered to walk round the cabs, and get in at the opposite side. And Cole was no exception as he followed her inside.

But she noticed he kept his distance during the fifteen-minute ride to the Commodore Club. His dark-clad thigh—had he bought a whole wardrobe at the hotel shop?—rested on the worn leather upholstery, several inches away from hers. And, because the majority of taxis Joanna had seen were old American limousines, there was plenty of room.

Getting out of the taxi, he was obliged to offer her his hand. Whatever else he might be, Cole considered himself a gentleman. One of the South Carolina 'good ole boys', thought Joanna cynically. Just like his father, and his father before him.

Even so, putting her hand into Cole's was a disturbing experience. His hand was cool and firm, with calluses at the base of his fingers. And when those fingers curled around hers she was hard-pressed not to hold on.

But, even if she'd wanted to, Cole had to pay the fare. After helping her out, under the striped canopy of the club, he bent to speak to their driver. Then, returning his wallet to his hip pocket, he straightened, urging her into the foyer, with his hand in the small of her back.

It saved touching her skin, Joanna thought ruefully, as they stepped on to the escalator which would take them up to the bar and restaurant. She wondered what he was thinking. Somehow, she sensed she was not going to have it all her own way.

'Do you want a drink before we eat?' Cole asked, as they crossed the carpeted upper floor, and Joanna tilted her head.

'Mmm,' she said. 'Something long and cool, with a bite to it. What would you recommend?'

Cole's eyes glinted. 'I'm sure I'll think of something,' he said, guiding her towards an empty table. 'I seem to remember you had quite a fancy for mint-juleps. You used to down quite a few of them, while Pa and I were out in the fields.'

Joanna's lips tightened for a moment, as the memories his words evoked came back to haunt her. But when she looked at him none of her anguish showed in her face. You shouldn't have said that, Cole, she thought malevolently. I'm going to make you pay for every little dig you make!

'So I did,' she warbled now, and no one listening to her would have imagined the offence she had felt at his words. Bastard, she said silently, while her eyes sparkled with mirth. 'I was a pain, wasn't I? No wonder you preferred Sammy-Jean to me.'

It was Cole's turn to look bitter now, but the arrival of the waiter to take their order prevented him from venting his spleen. Besides, she guessed he couldn't be entirely sure exactly how she had meant it, and although he might suspect her motives he really had no proof.

'Bourbon and branch,' he said sourly, 'and something *sweet* for the lady. What do you suggest?'

'How about pineapple rum?' asked the waiter cheerfully. 'Pineapple rum, coconut rum, and pineapple juice, shaken over ice. Delicious!'

'It sounds it,' put in Joanna smoothly, crossing her legs, and running spread fingers over her knee. She smiled at the man. 'Cold, but hot. Exactly what I need.'

The waiter's eyes danced. 'Yes, sir,' he said, swinging on his heel, and walking back to the bar. 'A Valentine's Special, man,' he ordered from the bar-keep. 'And make it real cold!'

Cole's eyes were far from friendly when he looked at Joanna again. 'Just what the hell do you think you're doing?' he demanded, his tone hard and explosive. 'Do you want everyone to think you're using?'

'Using?' Joanna's eyes widened innocently. 'Using what?'

'You know!' retorted Cole savagely. 'Hell, maybe you are. What would I know about it?'

Joanna's humour evaporated. 'I don't use—or shoot up—or mainline—or any of the other ways people take drugs,' she declared scornfully. 'I was having fun, that's all. *Fun*! Or have you forgotten the meaning of the word?'

Cole's mouth compressed. 'You weren't just having fun,' he argued. 'God, you were coming on to the man!'

Joanna's brief spurt of anger died. 'What's the matter, Cole?' she asked mockingly. 'You jealous?'

Their drinks came before Cole could make any response, but his brooding expression was eloquent of his feelings. Oh, this *was* fun, thought Joanna, a little breathlessly. Why had she never realised it was far more exciting to be bad?

The pineapple rum was delicious. It came complete with an assortment of tropical fruits, with a long curling straw to enable her to avoid the tiny striped umbrella. The umbrella bore the logo of the Commodore Club, and she was tempted to keep it as a souvenir of the evening.

'Have you and Sammy-Jean had any family yet?' she queried after a moment, risking Cole's displeasure yet again. She knew perfectly well that had Cole become a father she would have heard about it. Grace would surely have told her. But why should she avoid a subject that was clearly so exploitable?

Cole regarded her over the rim of his glass. 'No,' he said, and she could tell by his tone that he was not unaware of her intentions. 'But it's not for want of trying, if that's what you're implying.'

Joanna looked down into her drink. Her hands had tightened around the stem, and, noticing her white knuckles, she forced herself to relax. If she wasn't careful, the glass would break, and Cole would imagine he had scored a victory. What did it matter to her how many times Cole made love with Sammy-Jean? Sammy-Jean was his wife now, and she, Joanna, didn't give a damn!

'Something wrong?' Cole's blue eyes were smugly intent, and Joanna expelled her breath on a rueful sigh.

'No,' she said, deliberately wistful. 'I was just remembering how good you were in bed.'

'Good God!' Cole's jaw hardened. 'You don't give up, do you?' He swallowed the remainder of his drink

in one violent gulp, and gestured for the waiter to bring
him another. 'What do you want from me, Jo? *Blood*?'

Joanna knew a fleeting sense of conscience, but then
the waiter arrived to replace Cole's glass, and she consoled herself by taking another mouthful of her own
drink. But her lips around the pink straw were unconsciously provocative, and Cole uttered an imprecation as
he lifted his bourbon to his mouth.

'You folks dinin'?' enquired the waiter, and at Cole's
curt nod he flourished two enormous menus from under
his arm. 'Take your time,' he added, his knowing gaze
taking in the situation at a glance. 'I'll be back later to
take your order.'

Propping her menu on the table in front of her, Joanna
continued to enjoy her drink as she studied its contents.
There was a vast array of dishes to choose from, with
imported American steaks and locally caught seafood
providing the main selections. There was fried chicken,
too, prepared with the familiar 'peas 'n' rice', which was
a national passion.

'What do you want?' asked Cole, after a few minutes,
his tone cool and unfriendly, and Joanna felt a trace of
regret.

'The grouper, I think,' she answered, mentioning the
name of the most popular fish in the area. 'And melon,
to begin with. I'm not very hungry.'

Cole acknowledged her choice with a brief inclination
of his head, and the waiter, who had evidently been
keeping an interested eye on their table, came to take
their order.

Cole ordered the grouper, too, but with a salad starter.
'And bring the lady another of those,' he said, as Joanna
set down her empty glass. 'And I'll have another
bourbon.'

Joanna arched her brows, half in protest, but the
waiter was already sauntering away between the tables.
Besides, the drink had been delicious, she conceded. And
fairly innocuous, too, judging by the clearness of her
head.

There was silence between them for a while. Joanna could have broken it with some other audacious comment, but she realised she was in danger of alienating Cole completely, and that hadn't been her intention at all.

So, instead of sniping at him, she pretended an interest in their fellow guests, thanking the waiter for her drink when it came, without any further attempt to provoke her companion.

And, as she had half expected, Cole was eventually forced to say something. She guessed he was not unaware that their lack of communication had been noticed by the people at the next table, and as he had been the one to cause their isolation he chose to be the one to end it.

'Do you see much of Grace?' he asked, in a voice that would have cracked ice, and Joanna turned her gaze from a bowl of exotic plants to look at him.

'That depends,' she said, moistening her lips with the tip of her tongue.

'On what?'

The question was wrung from him, and Joanna smiled. 'On whether I'm working or not,' she declared smoothly. 'Grace is my agent. She's only interested in when I'm going to finish my next painting.'

'I'm sure that's not true.' Cole's tone had lost some of its chilliness. 'Grace always liked you. She considers you a friend.'

'Mmm.' Joanna stirred her drink with the straw. 'Well, let's say things have been a little strained between Grace and me, since we—broke up.'

Cole frowned. 'I don't believe it. Hell, I'd have thought you and she had a deal in common.'

'Would you?' Joanna looked at him through her lashes. 'You should know Grace won't have a word said against your father.'

Cole's mouth thinned. 'Unlike you, huh?'

'I don't have two sons whose livelihood is dependent on someone else's goodwill,' she countered lightly. 'Your father can't hurt me, Cole, and that must be a real source of aggravation to him.'

'I doubt if he cares that much, one way or the other,' retorted Cole bitterly. 'But you always had to face him down, didn't you? You'd never admit that sometimes he just might be right!'

'Like when he accused Nathan of sleeping with your wife?' she enquired tautly, and then, seeing the dark, tormented, expression her words had provoked, she quickly regressed. 'Forget I said that. It doesn't matter. He did us both a favour, didn't he? Oh—here's the waiter. Our table must be ready.'

CHAPTER FOUR

A FOUR-PIECE West Indian band was playing in the grill room, and Joanna was glad that the music negated any real obligation to talk while they were eating. Not that she ate a lot. The melon slid down smoothly enough, but the fish, which was served with a bouquet of vegetables, was rather more difficult to swallow. Instead, she turned to the wine Cole had ordered to accompany the meal, drinking several glasses of the chilled Californian Riesling.

There was a small dance-floor beyond the tables, where those guests who had finished their meal indulged in a little after-dinner exertion. Joanna spent most of her time watching them, uncaring for once if Cole was looking at her. With her elbow propped on the edge of the table and her chin cupped in one slender hand, she was unaware of the dreamy expression that crossed her face as she watched the swaying couples. For a while, she was completely oblivious of her surroundings, and it took a definite effort to concentrate again when the waiter came to ask if they wanted a dessert.

'Just coffee,' said Cole, without consulting her, and Joanna pulled an indignant face.

'I might have liked a dessert,' she pouted, and although she suspected he was only acting Cole's face softened.

'Coffee first, like back home,' he insisted wryly. 'I don't want to have to carry you out of here.'

'Would you do that?' she asked huskily, a feeling of heat sweeping over her, and although it wasn't all that easy to focus on his lean face she thought his eyes darkened at her words.

'If I have to,' he answered. 'Why? How do you feel?'

'Muzzy,' she admitted, emitting a rueful little laugh. 'Maybe I do need that coffee, after all.'

'You always were a cheap drunk,' he said, but for once there was no malice in his tone, and Joanna knew an overwhelming urge to make him as aware of her as she was of him.

Concentrating hard, she stretched out her hand and ran her fingers over his thigh. He jerked back automatically, but not before she had felt the instinctive tautening of muscle under her touch. From his groin to his knee, his leg stiffened defensively, and his lazy humour disappeared beneath a scowl of irritation.

But when he would have pushed her hand away, she thwarted him with an appealing smile. 'Dance with me,' she invited, turning her hand into his, and letting her thumb drift against his palm. 'Please, Cole. To show you're not mad at me. For old times' sake, as you said.'

He wanted to refuse. The evidence of that was clear in his face. And he resented her for using his words against him. But something—the memory of why he had come here, perhaps, or a desire to prove he was in control of his own destiny, who knew?—made him hesitate long enough for her to draw him to his feet.

'I don't dance,' he said, then, his voice clipped and harsh, 'I think we should get out of here. You need some fresh air.'

'Do I?'

Joanna swayed, most convincingly, which wasn't too surprising considering the wine had made her feel decidedly unsteady on her feet. But she could handle it, she told herself, not prepared to lose the advantage now.

'Yes, you do,' he muttered, as she continued to cling to his fingers. 'Jo, what do you think you're doing? This isn't the way to the exit.'

'I'll leave after we've danced,' declared Joanna firmly, tugging him after her. 'We used to dance before. Don't you remember?'

'That wasn't dancing,' snapped Cole, but Joanna's behaviour was attracting attention, and she could see he didn't like it.

'Whatever,' she murmured, reaching the square of polished tiles, and turning into his arms. 'Don't be a spoil-sport, darling. Don't you want to dance with me?'

Cole scowled, but there was no turning back. Besides, the face she turned up to his was innocent of all deceit, the amber eyes pleading with him to give in.

And he did. With a grim tightening of his lips, he gripped her waist, and held her away from him. Then, fixing his gaze on some distant point above her head, he began to move rather awkwardly in time to the music.

Joanna caught her lower lip between her teeth, as a smile tugged at the corners of her mouth. Oh, lord, she gulped, trying to contain her mirth, she had forgotten what a hopeless dancer Cole was. He had never mastered any step, beyond the square dances he had learned in school, and only her guidance had made him half decent on a dance-floor.

But not like this, she conceded drily, with at least six inches between them. She didn't want to remember the other occasions when they had danced together, but she couldn't help it. Then, the steps they used hadn't been important. They had moved to the rhythm of their bodies—just like when they were making love...

She shivered, and the feathering of her flesh reminded her of where she was, and what she was doing. The dance-floor was getting crowded, and when a careless elbow nudged her in the ribs her determination hardened. She could have withstood the painful jab quite easily, but she chose not to. With a startled cry, she launched herself against him, successfully dislodging his hands, and clutching his lapels.

'God!'

Cole's reaction was just as violent as she had anticipated, but when he would have drawn back again her hands slid up to his neck.

'Sorry,' she breathed, her breath wafting sweetly across his cheek, and a nerve jerked spasmodically at his jawline.

'What in hell do you think you're doing?' he demanded, his hands reaching up to grab her forearms, with the obvious intention of hauling them down from his shoulders. 'Damn you, keep still!'

'I'm just dancing,' she protested innocently, rotating her hips against his. 'Don't be so touchy! You need all the help you can get.'

'I did warn you,' he grated, and with a little sigh Joanna allowed him to pull her arms down to her sides.

But she didn't move away from him. And, although Cole would clearly have preferred to leave the dance-floor, they were trapped within the circle of the other dancers.

'Is this so bad?' she asked, looking up at him with wide tawny eyes, and she saw the glittering awareness enter his. He might not want to admit it, but his reasons for keeping her at a distance were not because he didn't like dancing with her. And when his gaze dropped to the appealing curve of her soft mouth Joanna felt her own senses sharpen.

'We're leaving,' said Cole abruptly, taking her upper arm between his forefinger and thumb, and pushing her determinedly through the swaying press of people. His nails bit into her flesh as he steered her back to their table. 'Get your bag. I'll pay the bill.'

'But what about our coffee?' she argued, looking longingly at the breakfast-size cups of the aromatic brew waiting on the table, but Cole was unrepentant.

'You can get some coffee back at the hotel,' he stated bleakly, and summoned the startled waiter who had served them.

Outside, Joanna did feel slightly unsteady in the night air. But Cole's expression forbade any attempt to use his arm for support, and when the taxi came she collapsed gratefully into the back.

Cole gave the driver his instructions, and then joined her on the back seat. But his mouth was scornful in the half-light. 'You really are smashed, aren't you?' he declared, shaking his head. 'My God! And I thought we might have a serious conversation.'

Joanna turned her head towards him, her dark hair falling sensuously over one shoulder. 'What about?' she asked silkily, sweeping it back again. 'The fact that you still want me?'

Cole swore, and turned his head away. 'You wish,' he snarled, clenching his fists. 'God, why did I ever agree to this pointless exercise?'

'Because Daddy asked you to,' retorted Joanna shortly. 'And you always do everything Daddy says, don't you? You're Daddy's blue-eyed boy. Even if it means sacrificing other people in the process!'

Cole's jaw clamped. 'Shut up!'

'Why?' Joanna felt fairly safe in baiting him, with the comfortingly broad shoulders of the Bahamian taxi driver firmly in view. 'You don't like to hear the truth, Cole. In fact, you don't hear anything but what Daddy says. I'm surprised you ever learned how to have sex with a woman! Or was Daddy in on that, too——?'

Cole moved then, covering the space between them in one swift lunge. His hand closed about her throat, cutting off her words with unexpected violence, and his eyes glittered dangerously in the twilight world of the cab.

'Shut up,' he commanded again. 'Shut the hell up!' And then, as her eyes fought with his, and terror gripped her stomach, he uttered a muffled oath and brought his mouth down on hers.

As kisses went, it wasn't pleasant. With Cole's hand practically cutting off the air to her windpipe, Joanna could hardly have been expected to enjoy it. On top of that, despite the lightness of his hair, and the fact that he had probably shaved before coming out, Cole's chin was abrasively male. And as his mouth ground against her teeth, all Joanna could think of was how abused she was going to look when he let go of her.

But something happened when he kissed her. Although his original intention had been to hurt and humiliate her, that melding of their mouths seduced his reason. A groan of anguish rumbled in his throat, and he tore his mouth from hers, only to return again with an urgent imprecation.

And when he did so, his fingers relaxed, releasing her throat from his throttling grasp. Instead of bruising her flesh, they became achingly gentle, smoothing the tortured skin with a sensuous caress.

Now, Joanna felt as if her breathing had been suspended. Her chest rose and fell with the tumult of her emotions, but she didn't seem to be getting any oxygen into her lungs. Indeed, there didn't seem to be enough oxygen in the car, and her senses swam dizzily beneath his searching touch.

Cole's kiss became hungry, and fiercely demanding. His tongue forced its way into her mouth, and she let it have its way. That hot, wet invader was disturbingly familiar, and her tongue twined around it, helpless to resist. There was nothing gentle about him now, but his demands inspired a matching need. Her legs splayed, her head dipped low against the squabs, and when his hand slid inside the neckline of her dress and touched her breasts she felt her arousal, clear down to her thighs.

The cab, braking outside the brilliantly lit foyer of the Coral Bay Hotel, brought Cole, belatedly, to his senses. With a groan of anguish he pushed himself up and away from her, but not before the smirking taxi driver had glimpsed what had been going on.

Joanna struggled up with rather less energy. She was still bemused by the upheaval of her senses, and it was difficult to think coherently, when her body was dewy with perspiration. Her hair was mussed about her shoulders, and even in the semi-gloom of the cab she guessed her swollen lips had not gone unremarked. And even Cole made a point of buttoning his jacket as he got out of the car.

She knew why, thought Joanna tensely, stumbling out after him. Standing on the floodlit forecourt, she wet her bruised lips with a soothing tongue. Cole had been as aroused as she was. She had felt the heavy heat of his manhood against her stomach, its throbbing tumescence straining at the zip of his trousers. Known, too, that Cole's self-control had been slipping. He had wanted her; she knew it. And if they hadn't been interrupted...

'Let's get inside.'

Cole's hand at her elbow, and his harsh impersonal tone brought her swiftly back to earth. With a gesture that was barely civil, he escorted her inside the hotel. Then, after accompanying her to the bank of elevators, he inclined his head and released her.

But, when he would have walked away, Joanna caught his arm. 'Where are you going?'

Cole's eyes flickered over her flushed face, which still bore the signs of his assault, but there was no compassion in his gaze. 'I need a drink,' he replied, removing her hand from his sleeve. 'Go to bed. You're a mess!'

Joanna winced at his callous choice of words, but she didn't let him see he had hurt her. 'And if I am?' she taunted. 'Whose fault is that? What's the matter, Cole? Don't you like seeing the proof of your weakness?'

'Damn you,' he said, but she guessed his choice of epithet was for other ears than her own. If they had been alone, he would not have been so polite. She could think of other—four-letter—words he had used with less provocation. 'I don't want to see you again,' he added, his mouth curling contemptuously. 'I'll be leaving in the morning. If you have any sense, you'll stay out of my way till then.'

Joanna held up her head. 'All right,' she said. 'If that's what you want.' And afterwards she bitterly regretted the need to thwart him that had taken over her already battered ego. 'But don't you think you ought to tell me what time we're leaving? I've got to pack and pay my bill. And I'd like to phone Grace, and my parents, just to let them know what I'm doing.'

In her room, some time later, Joanna was still appalled at the predicament her impulsive tongue had got her into. My God, she thought, as if she couldn't just have been grateful that Cole was leaving, without achieving what he had come here to do! He had already been as mad as hell. She knew that. He would have liked nothing better than to slam his fist into her face for the crazy way he had acted in the taxi. But no. Just because he had chosen to vent some of his spleen on her, she had retaliated in the most asinine way imaginable. She had actually agreed to do the very thing she had sworn she would never do: go back to Tidewater.

She was so stupid, she groaned now, flinging off the satin sheath, and marching into the bathroom. She had got her way, and she had fluffed it. She had completely screwed up. Instead of waving Cole a mocking farewell, she had agreed to go with him. She couldn't back out now without losing all her credibility.

And, although Cole had been incensed by her announcement tonight, that had only been his knee-jerk reaction. Sooner or later, he was going to realise exactly what it meant. He had got his own way, without any further effort on his part.

A cold shower later, Joanna was still in no state to try and get some sleep. Besides, she supposed she ought to make some attempt at her packing. Although Cole had refused to discuss his travel arrangements with her, a swift call to the hotel concierge had elicited the information that the Charleston flight left at eleven-thirty the next morning. That meant leaving for the airport soon after nine, which would leave her very little time for organising her affairs. Of course, what the concierge had not been able to tell her was whether there were any seats available on the flight. The airline offices were closed for the night, so that would have to wait. But, one way or another, she was committed to making the effort. And if the flight was full, there would be others.

Groaning, she flopped down on to the side of her bed, hitching up the towel, which was her only covering. She needed to talk to somebody, she thought unhappily. Preferably, someone who wouldn't tell her she was all kinds of an idiot for getting herself into this mess. There only was one person: Grace.

Picking up the phone, she dialled for an outside line, and when the dial tone came through she punched in Grace's London number. It seemed to ring forever, and she was on the point of replacing the receiver when Grace picked up the phone.

'Yes?' she said, and there was a lazily peeved edge to her voice. 'Who's there?'

'Me. Jo. Joanna,' she responded uncharitably. 'Where were you?'

'Try bed,' retorted Grace shortly. And then, 'Jo, do you have any idea what time it is here?'

'Oh, lord!' Joanna pushed back her damp hair with a guilty hand. 'Oh, hell, Grace, I'm sorry. I never thought——'

'Obviously.' But Grace's impatience was giving way to anxiety now. 'So, what is it? What's wrong?'

'Oh, Grace!' Joanna sighed. 'Look, it's not that important. I'll talk to you tomorrow——'

'Don't you dare!' Grace said something in a muffled aside—to Ray, Joanna suspected, feeling even worse—and then continued forcefully, 'Come on, Jo. Spit it out. It's Cole, isn't it? What's happened? Has he been threatening you?'

If only, thought Joanna ruefully, flinging herself back on the bed. His threats she could deal with. It was his frustration she found so appealing.

'No,' she replied now, examining the fingernails of one hand, in an effort to sustain normality. 'No, he hasn't been threatening me, Grace.' She paused, and then added painfully, 'I've said I'll go with him.'

'To Tidewater?'

Grace was evidently astounded, and Joanna couldn't blame her after what she had said. But, 'Yes,' she agreed, finding it no easier to cope with now than she had earlier. 'So tell me how I can get out of it, without looking a complete idiot.'

'But, Jo, you said——'

'I know what I said, Grace. But—well, Cole made me mad, and I just said the first thing that came into my head.'

'That you'd go to Tidewater?'

'Yes.'

'But why?'

It was obvious that Grace couldn't comprehend her reasoning, and without any explanation of the facts Joanna could understand her bewilderment. But how could she tell Grace what had happened in the taxi? How could she explain what Cole had done? In retrospect, it all seemed slightly incredible anyway, even to her.

'He—said something,' she mumbled now, half wishing she had never made this call. But she hadn't known that Ray Marsden would still be there. From what Grace had told her in the past, she had assumed their relationship was still fairly perfunctory. But, if Ray was sleeping at the gallery...

'Something rather important, by the sound of it,' Grace put in drily, when Joanna said nothing more. 'I take it you've not had second thoughts?'

'About his father?' Joanna's lips tightened. 'No.'

'I see.' Grace sounded troubled. And then, to her companion, 'Tea? Oh, yes, darling, that would be lovely.'

Joanna pushed herself up again. 'I'd better go——'

'You'd better not.' Grace snorted. 'OK. Ray's gone to get us some tea, bless him. So, why don't you tell me what this is really all about?'

Joanna caught her breath. 'I've told you——'

'That you're going back with Cole? Yes, I know. But what did he say, for God's sake? And why would anything he said persuade you? You seemed so—adamant!'

'I was. I *am*.' Joanna hunched her shoulders. 'Oh— well, if you must know, he—he made a pass at me.' A *pass*? Liar!

'He made a pass at you?' Grace was clearly flabbergasted. 'When? Where?'

Joanna licked her dry lips. 'He—took me out for dinner.'

'Last night?'

'Well, tonight, actually,' murmured Joanna ruefully. 'It's only eleven o'clock here.'

'Of course.' Grace gave a resigned sigh. 'So where is he now?'

'Where is he?' Joanna frowned. 'What do you mean, where is he? He's in his room, I suppose. Probably fast asleep by now.'

'Hmm.' Grace hesitated. 'Well, I hope you haven't done anything stupid!'

Joanna blinked. 'Anything stupid?' she echoed. 'Don't you call agreeing to go back to Tidewater stupid?'

'You know what I mean, Jo.'

'No, I'm afraid I don't.' Joanna was totally confused. 'Are we talking at cross purposes here?'

Grace groaned. 'Jo, what I'm asking is, are you still taking the pill?'

'The pill?' For a beat, Grace's meaning was lost to her. 'What pill?'

'*The* pill,' exclaimed Grace, not without some impatience. 'For pity's sake, Jo, you know what kind of pill I'm talking about.'

'Oh!' Joanna felt the hot colour run up her face, and was glad no one else could see it. '*That* pill.' She swallowed. 'Well, no, of course not.'

'*Jo!*'

Joanna gasped. 'I haven't had sex with him, Grace!' She shook her head. 'What do you take me for?'

'Well, thank heavens for that.' Grace sounded distinctly relieved. 'When you said——'

'When I said Cole made a pass at me, I didn't mean we'd been to bed together.' Joanna was indignant.

'So why are you so upset?'

'I should have thought that was obvious.'

'Because you've said you'll go with him?'

'That's right.'

'Was that before or after he made a pass at you?'

'After, of course.'

'Why, of course?' Grace sounded sardonic. 'Jo, if you were upset because Cole—well, because of what he did—why on earth did you tell him you'd go with him?'

'Because it made him mad!' retorted Joanna crossly. 'He—resented the fact that he still—well, that I could still——'

'I get the picture.' Grace's tone was dry. 'Well, love, I don't see how you can back out now. Not unless you want Cole to think you're afraid of him. But, please—be careful. I don't think you realise how vulnerable you are.'

CHAPTER FIVE

JOANNA had heard Charleston compared to an eighteenth-century Venice, and from the air that description seemed even more apt. With its old but elegant houses, painted white and gleaming in the sun, it had an indomitable air. As it stood on a peninsula, with the sea never far from its back door, it was not surprising that its real heyday had been in the latter years of the eighteenth century, when the great sailing fleets from Europe had followed the trade winds to the Caribbean. Twentieth-century Charleston was rather less successful, but its jumbled streets and ante-bellum colonialism were preserved here as nowhere else.

Not that Joanna knew the city very well. In the early days of their marriage, Cole had shown her the tourists' view of Charleston, and the military academy, and the curved esplanade, known as the Battery, were fairly familiar to her. But Tidewater Plantation was some distance from the city, and the small town of Beaumaris was their main supplier.

None the less, it had given her her first taste of South Carolina, and she could still remember the heat and the humidity, and the rain, which had come in a bone-chilling deluge. But she hadn't cared in those days. She was in love with Cole, and she would have lived in the heart of a volcano, if he had asked her to.

How foolish she had been, she thought now, turning her head to look at her antagonist, lounging carelessly in the seat beside her. How naïve! In those days life had seemed so simple, so uncomplicated. She had actually believed in happy-ever-after. But that was before she had met Cole's family, and realised that, so far as they were concerned, Cole had made a terrible mistake. In mar-

53

rying her, of course, she appended harshly. Macallisters did not marry outsiders, particularly not women, who had too much to say for themselves.

Joanna sighed. She hadn't considered she was particularly opinionated before she went to live in Tidewater County. Nor especially revolutionary either, until Ryan Macallister put her straight. Macallisters didn't mix with the poorer families of the district. They didn't set up maternity clinics, or treat the plantation workers as social equals. Not openly, anyway. The fact that Ryan Macallister promulgated one policy, and practised another, was what had brought Joanna into open conflict with her father-in-law. And signalled the end of her marriage, she acknowledged bitterly. That...and Nathan's death...

But she didn't want to think about Nathan now. The pain of that tragedy, and the ugly lies that had caused it, didn't hurt her any more. Not a lot, anyway. Time had laid its healing balm over those old wounds, and she would be unwise to test its resistance. It was enough that Cole had proved he was not immune to the past, and it was going to be amusing showing his father exactly how futile his schemes had been.

Or would it? Joanna chewed unhappily at her lower lip. She was not naturally a vindictive woman, and the unwilling memory of why she was here brought its own uncertainty. How could she stand up to a man who was already dying? What crueller retribution could there be? And she still had to find out why he should want to see her. As far as she was aware, they had nothing more to say to one another.

The stewardess's warning, to take note of the 'Fasten Seatbelts' sign, and to extinguish all cigarettes, reminded her of the imminence of their arrival. Checking that her seatbelt was securely in place, Joanna's eyes briefly locked with Cole's. But she could read nothing from his expression and, in any case, he looked away. As he had done since this morning, when they had shared a cab to the airport on New Providence. He had made it blatantly obvious that he had decided to remove himself mentally, if not physically, from any contact between them, and, for the time being, Joanna was prepared to let him.

That they were travelling together at all was another matter. Joanna had felt justifiably furious when she woke up that morning, and found the plane reservation that had been pushed under her door. She had not slept particularly well, and, snatching up the folder, she had discovered, to her chagrin, that the booking had been made the previous day. It was galling to think that, even after all she had said, Cole had been so sure of her compliance. As soon as she accepted his dinner invitation, he must have thought it was a foregone conclusion. The only comfort she had was that the evening had not gone exactly as he had planned. He might have got his own way, but at what cost to his self-esteem?

An hour later, Joanna was already feeling the effects of the pre-summer heat in this semi-tropical corner of the United States. Cole's brother, Ben, had met them at the airport. After a rather awkward greeting, he had loaded Cole's flight bag and her own suitcases into the back of the solid four-by-four estate car, before taking the wheel for the drive to Tidewater. He had been polite, but hardly friendly, and as Cole had been eager to hear about their father they had immediately excluded her from their easy communication.

Not that she cared, thought Joanna, not altogether honestly. Just because she and Ben had once been friends was no reason to feel slighted now. It was obvious that he would take his brothers—and his father's—word before her own. And she had no doubt her name had figured in some bitter conversations.

But, for now, she contained her feelings, and fanned herself with a languid hand. Although she was almost sure the vehicle possessed an air-conditioning system, Ben was driving along the coastal highway with all the windows open. In consequence, the moist air was causing her shirt and cotton cut-offs to cling to her damp body, and it was enough to try and find a comfortable position. Nevertheless, she viewed the back of Cole's head with some resentment. He was on his own ground here, and the heat didn't bother him a scrap.

Yet, for all her frustration, Joanna couldn't deny the attraction of the area. Humid it might be, but it was also lush, and colourful, and extremely beautiful. The coastal region was a mass of lakes and waterways, where salt marshes melted into acres of sand dunes, and houses were built high for coolness. At this time of the year, gardens were alight with crimson and pink azaleas, blooming amid jasmine and roses, waxy white camellias and flowering dogwood. Wistaria overhung walls and porches, and wide verandas sported terracotta tubs, and cane furniture. This was the low country, and life moved at a less hectic pace than in the city.

Deciding she wasn't prepared to be ignored for the whole journey, Joanna unfastened another button on her shirt, and determinedly leaned forward. Resting her arms along the backs of the seats in front, she expelled a sigh that just happened to waft close to Cole's ear, and forced a smile.

'So—how are you, Ben?' she enquired, ignoring Cole's sudden intake of breath. 'Got your own place yet?'

'Um——' Ben cast a worried look in Cole's direction, before shaking his head. 'N-no. Not yet. Too much to do around Tidewater.'

Joanna's lips flattened. 'But I thought you wanted a place of your own,' she persisted, and Cole turned his head to give her a dark look. 'Well, he did,' she added, responding to that grim warning. 'How old are you now, Ben? Twenty-five? Twenty-six?'

'He's twenty-four,' stated her ex-husband shortly. 'Two years younger than you, as I'm sure you know very well.'

'You remembered!' Joanna's brows arched with teasing intent. 'That makes you thirty, doesn't it?' She tugged the neckline of the shirt away from her moist throat. 'My, aren't we getting old?'

Cole didn't dignify her remark with a reply. He merely swung round in his seat again, leaving Joanna to search wildly for something else to say. But she had no intention of letting him intimidate her, verbally or otherwise, and when her elbow brushed his neck she was more than satisfied by his sharp withdrawal.

'Cole tells me Joe's married now,' she inserted, into a conversation about the current state of land erosion. She had addressed her question to Ben again, and, once more, he looked at his older brother before replying.

''S right,' he muttered, clearly not enjoying being pig-in-the-middle, but Joanna couldn't afford to consider anyone's feelings but her own.

'And he still lives at home?' she prompted. 'It's just as well it's a big house. With three families living in it.'

Now Ben glanced at her. '*Three* families?'

Joanna nodded. 'Well, as Cole and Joe both have wives——'

'Cole doesn't——' he began impulsively, and then he broke off, his fair skin suffused with colour. 'That is——' He swallowed convulsively, his Adam's apple protruding through his taut skin, and he gave his brother a sidelong look. 'Didn't Cole tell you?'

'Obviously not.' Cole spoke before Joanna could say anything else to embarrass him. He looked at her now, but his blue eyes were as cold as glaciers. 'Sammy-Jean left Tidewater some time ago,' he told her bleakly. 'She lives in California, as far as I know. Does that satisfy you?'

It didn't, but Joanna was too surprised to say anything at that moment. No, more than that, she admitted. She was shocked. Astounded. After all, Sammy-Jean had been Ryan Macallister's choice of a wife for his eldest son. And Joanna knew the other woman had been after Cole ever since they were in high school together. She had made no secret of it. She had been crazy about him. And crazy for him. So what had gone wrong?

With her mind already probing the implications of this announcement, the obvious question sprang to her lips. 'Are—are you divorced?'

Cole's exhalation of breath was savage. 'Yes,' he said curtly. 'Now can we leave it? It's no concern of yours.'

Wasn't it? Joanna wondered. Would she have come here at all, if she had known Sammy-Jean wasn't going to be around to protect her? She wasn't prepared to consider at this moment why she should think she needed any protection. Suffice it to say that Grace's final words suddenly had a deeper meaning.

'Does—does Grace know?'

She had to ask, and Cole uttered an aggravated oath. 'I said we wouldn't talk about it.'

'No, but——'

'God!' He raked angry fingers against his scalp. 'What does it matter?' And then, after allowing himself a minute to calm down, he added, 'Of course she knows. Why wouldn't she? It's not a secret, for God's sake.'

'Then why didn't she tell me?' demanded Joanna, and then wished she hadn't, when sardonic eyes were turned in her direction.

'Who knows?' taunted Cole, enjoying her discomfort. 'Perhaps she was afraid you might come rushing back to comfort me.'

Joanna's hands clenched on the leather back of the wide seats, but, although her initial reaction was to retaliate in kind, this time she thought before she spoke. 'Perhaps I would at that,' she murmured, aware that Ben's head had swung round at her words. He was obviously bewildered by the sudden switch in emphasis, and he showed it. 'Did you need comforting?'

'Not by you,' declared Cole rudely, salvaging what he could from the wreckage. 'When I need a woman, I can always pay for one.'

'Just like your daddy,' retorted Joanna, stung in spite of herself.

Flinging herself back in the seat then, she tried to ignore the sudden pain his words had brought her. It was all very well trading insults with him, but for all her determination her skin was not as thick as his. She scowled sourly out of the window. Bastard, she thought, finding some relief in calling him names, even if he couldn't hear. Jerk! Creep! How could she have allowed herself to get into this situation?

They passed the exit for Beaumaris, and the sign that read 'You are now entering Tidewater County', but Joanna hardly noticed. She was too wrapped up in feelings of bitterness and frustration, and it wasn't until they turned between the gates of Tidewater Plantation that a sense of panic gripped her stomach. They were here, she gagged. They were really here. Tidewater! Where she had sworn she would never set foot again.

She tried to calm herself. Arriving at the house in a state of wild emotion would get her nowhere. She needed every bit of self-confidence she possessed to face Cole's family. Not to mention a stiff back and a strong will, she added grimly. No one was going to make a fool of her again.

They approached the house through an avenue of live oaks liberally hung with Spanish moss. The creeper gave the trees an eerie, ghostlike appearance, particularly at night, when dampness rose from the river to cloak the house in a drifting grey mist. At other times, with the moon shining through the swaying tendrils, it could be quite romantic, and Joanna found herself remembering the first night she had spent here, when Cole had taken her to see the river, and they had made love on a bed of wild thyme...

She expelled a harsh breath, and hauled herself up in the seat. Now was not the time to start remembering things like that, she chided herself grimly. She had been incredibly foolish in those days. She had actually believed that love could conquer all. How stupid could you get?

Forcing herself to look around, Joanna cast a detached eye over the lush paddocks that lay beyond the white fence that edged the driveway. Glossy-coated mares, and their foals, cropped acres of green, green grass, and the breeze that invaded the windows of the car came straight from the salt marshes. She knew it was possible to see the ocean from the first-floor balcony of the house, and with the river lapping not too far from its doors you were never far from the sight and sound of water.

But, although Tidewater had not yet succumbed to the lure of turning itself into a tourist attraction, as so many other plantations had done, it no longer relied on its cultivation of rice and indigo to keep it solvent. Nowadays, many of the rice fields had been drained, and given over to the raising of cattle, and thoroughbred horses lived in stables that had once quartered its immigrant work-force.

Not that Joanna had taken any part in the running of the estate. As Cole's wife, she had been entitled to live in the house, and eat at the table, but anything more than that had been denied to her. Ryan Macallister and his sons ran the plantation, and his wife ran the house. And Margaret Macallister had wanted no help from anyone, least of all a girl her son had married against their wishes.

A shiver feathered along Joanna's spine. Now that she was here, so many memories came flooding back to her. How could she have forgotten the many humiliations she had suffered at Cole's mother's hands—the petty slights and ignominies that Cole had known nothing about?

She caught her lower lip between her teeth as she remembered. She had come from a normal, loving family, a family that had welcomed Cole into their midst with no real reservations. Even though it had meant Joanna leaving her home, and her country, to go and live in some distant corner of the New World, her parents had accepted it. They had accepted that she loved Cole, and he loved her, and that she knew what she was doing. They had granted her the privilege of believing her old enough to make her own decisions, and although they were going to miss her terribly they had been generous in their support.

Not so Cole's family. From the beginning, Joanna had been left in no doubt as to their disapproval of the marriage, and, although in those early days Cole had defended her against any overt criticism, when he wasn't there she was vulnerable. The truth was, she had never encountered that kind of antagonism before, and Margaret Macallister had lost no opportunity to belittle her in front of her husband.

It still hurt. Tamping down the choking sense of indignation that rose in her throat, Joanna forced herself to remember that this time it was going to be different. She hadn't wanted to come here; they had sent for her. And she was an independent woman now, not a lovesick girl, with no experience of life.

She could just imagine how her mother would react, when she found out where her daughter had gone. That was why she had prevailed on Grace to ring her parents and tell them what she was doing. She had known that, if she had spoken to her mother, Mrs Seton would have done her utmost to get her to change her mind. And, for all her determination, Joanna had not been sufficiently confident of her own ability to withstand such an onslaught.

Now, as they approached the house, Joanna began to wonder if it wouldn't have been more sensible to get her mother's opinion. Maybe she was making a terrible mistake.

But the sound of barking dogs and the slowing of the estate car made such misgivings immaterial. A bend in the drive had revealed the house, standing squarely against a backdrop of oak and pine trees. Its white-painted walls and verandas stretched majestically towards a sky splashed with the colours of early evening, and Joanna's nerves prickled in anticipation. Grills, lattices, louvred shutters; it had all the elegance of a bygone era. And, although the original plantation house had long since fallen into decay, this outward facsimile, built between the two great wars, was every bit as imposing as its antecedent.

Joanna stiffened. Just seeing the house, and the handful of foxhounds that rushed excitedly to meet the car, brought an unwelcome feeling of *déjà vu*. Only it had been old Moses, one of the grooms, who had met her and Cole on that first occasion. A warning of the opposition they had had to face.

The big Buick came to a halt, and Cole had his door open almost before the wheels had stopped turning. Ordering the hounds away, he turned to open Joanna's door, just as a tall, well-built woman emerged from the house.

Joanna's stomach hollowed. Margaret—Maggie—Macallister hadn't changed. She was still as formidable as ever, her broad-shouldered figure clad in one of the floral prints she favoured, and her long grey hair wound in a plaited coronet around her head.

'Cole,' she said, in a voice that was half accusing, half relieved, 'thank God you're home!'

'Why?' Leaving Joanna's door ajar, Cole sprang up the flight of steps to where his mother was waiting on the veranda. 'Nothing's happened, has it? Pa's not——'

'No, no. He's the same.' Gripping her eldest son by the shoulders, Maggie Macallister looked at him with tears glistening in her eyes. 'I was just—so worried. When you didn't come back yesterday——?'

She didn't finish the sentence, but Joanna, climbing reluctantly out of the car, thought its meaning was unmistakable. Cole's mother was reminding him of his responsibilities, and using the opportunity to show her exactly what to expect.

'I'm sorry.' Cole allowed his mother to pull him into an eager embrace, and Joanna, hauling out a heavy suitcase and her flight bag, couldn't help but glimpse the look of triumph Maggie Macallister cast in her direction. You might have seduced him away from his

family once, that look seemed to say, but, as you can
see, it won't happen again.

Won't it? thought Joanna grimly, tugging at the second
suitcase. We'll see, you old harridan! We'll see who has
the last laugh!

'Here—I'll do that.'

Joanna was so intent on giving back stare for stare
that she had been unaware of Ben coming round the
vehicle to help her.

'Let me,' he insisted, lifting the second case effortlessly on to the crushed-shell forecourt, and Joanna gave
him a winning smile that was all the warmer because of
its audience.

'Thanks,' she said, deliberately tipping her head to
one side, and looking him over. 'I'd forgotten you were
so strong.' She touched his biceps with teasing fingers.
'Solid muscle!'

'And no brains,' said Cole abruptly, pulling himself
out of his mother's arms, and coming back down the
steps to where Ben was red-facedly trying to handle all
the luggage. He gave Joanna a chilling look, and took
one of the cases from Ben. 'Come on. I'll show you
your room.'

But not without meeting Ma, brooded Joanna unwillingly, following him up the steps. No one was allowed to do anything around here without Ma's
permission. And right now Maggie Macallister was
watching their exchange with grim-eyed disapproval.

Joanna started to pluck her shirt away from her body
as she followed Cole up to where his mother was waiting,
but then she changed her mind. What did she care if
Maggie Macallister thought she was brazen, because the
damp material was clinging to her taut breasts? They
were nice breasts—and Ben had evidently thought so,
too—judging by the way his eyes had nearly popped out
of his head.

Even so, it took an enormous amount of courage to
face the woman who had helped to destroy her marriage. For all her resolution, it wasn't easy to forget the

last time she had stood on this veranda. Or dismiss the pain and anguish that she would always associate with her departure.

Nevertheless, there was a difference. As Joanna mounted the last stair and came up beside Cole, she realised what it was. Whereas before she had been eager—fool that she was—to make a good impression, now she didn't have to. It didn't matter to her what Cole's mother thought, and although she didn't actually voice the words she saw the dawning comprehension in Maggie Macallister's eyes.

There was an awkward moment, while the two women appeared to size one another up. And then, when it became apparent that her erstwhile daughter-in-law was not going to be the first to speak, Cole's mother cracked a frosty smile.

'Joanna,' she said, regarding the younger woman's appearance with undisguised disdain. 'You look hot.'

'Oh, I am.' Joanna expelled her breath in an upward draught. 'I can't wait to strip off these tight trousers.'

Maggie's mouth compressed. 'I'm sure,' she murmured, exchanging a speaking look with Cole. 'If you wait a moment, I'll get Sally to show you to your room.'

'Oh, but...' Joanna pretended a confusion she certainly wasn't feeling. 'Cole said he'd show me where I'm to sleep.' Her look was all wide-eyed innocence. 'Isn't that right, honey?'

It was hard to decide who was the most incensed by her remark, but Cole recovered first. 'That's right,' he said tersely, picking up her cases again, and making for the open doorway. 'We don't want there to be any mistake, do we?'

'Hell, no.' Before Maggie could make any endorsing statement, Joanna pulled a rueful face. 'I might find myself sharing a bathroom with you, sugar.'

'Unlikely,' the older woman assured her coldly, having no choice but to follow them into the house. 'I don't think any of us is likely to forget the past, Joanna. Least of all Cole.'

Joanna's jaw compressed, but, try as she might, she couldn't think of any flip comment to make. And while she was in that state of uncertainty Cole's elbow nudged her in the back.

'Let's go,' he said, jerking his head towards the forked staircase that led up to a galleried landing. 'Before I'm tempted to put a foot in that big mouth of yours.'

CHAPTER SIX

JOANNA lingered in the shower, resting her slim back against the cold tiled wall, and allowing the pummelling spray to do its worst. But it was so good to feel cool again, and she was loath to step out into the moist evening air.

Beyond her windows, the velvety darkness was alive with the whirrings and rustlings of the night. Huge moths beat their wings against her blinds, and she'd already had to dispose of a family of termites that had taken up residence on her veranda. She'd forgotten how many minor drawbacks there were to living at Tidewater, and her city sensibilities needed to be redefined.

But she had wanted to call for help when she found a cockroach in the shower-stall. She hated the ugly insects, with their hard shells, that crunched if you stood on them. Nevertheless, she had dealt with it herself. After the harsh words she and Cole had exchanged, she doubted he would have been willing to accommodate her. And, although she could have summoned one of the servants to attend to it, she was unwilling to show any softness in this house.

Besides, she wasn't usually so squeamish. It was just that it had been a long day, and these small difficulties were wearing away her defences. She needed time to adjust—to adapt to her situation, and restore her equilibrium. But, if Cole had his way, she wasn't going to get it. In fifteen minutes, she was expected to go downstairs and join the family for the evening meal.

Pushing herself away from the wall, she reached out and turned off the taps. Then, sweeping the curtain aside, she stepped out on to the marble-tiled floor. A huge white bathsheet encased her from her neck to her ankles, and, draping it securely about her, she padded through to the bedroom.

Viewing her appearance in the gilt-edged pier-glass, she felt a sense of resignation. Her haunted expression was not what she wanted to see, and the stark whiteness of the towel accentuated the dark rings around her eyes. She looked—defeated, she thought impatiently. Young, and vulnerable, and—defeated. And all because she was hot, and tired, and desperate to see a friendly face.

The knock that came at her door at that moment was badly timed. At the sound, all her defences sprang into active life, and with her hackles up, and her hands clenched tightly in the folds of the towel, she determined not to answer it.

But when the door-handle rattled she tensed in dismay. There had been no key to lock the door, and although she had wedged the back of the chair beneath the handle before she went for her shower she doubted it would be sufficient deterrent to so determined a visitor.

Then she heard someone say her name, and her misgivings fled. The voice was unmistakably feminine, and when the word was repeated in hushed, urgent tones she flew across the room to remove the chair.

She practically flung open the door, and the girl, who had been inclined towards the panels outside, almost fell into the room. 'Jo,' she said again, her face flushed with anxious colour. 'Oh, Jo, I can't believe it!'

'Charley!' Securing the towel beneath her breasts, Joanna withstood the onslaught as Cole's fifteen-year-old sister launched herself at her. 'Gosh, Charley, it's good to see you.'

'You, too.' Charley hugged her with all the strength of her sturdy young frame, and then drew back to gaze at Joanna with unconcealed delight. 'How long are you staying?'

'I—I'm not sure.' Joanna realised that that was something she hadn't given a lot of thought to. 'A few days, maybe.' She blinked back an errant tear. 'So—how are you? And Donna? And Sandy? I guess he must be twelve now, is that right? Heavens, aren't you growing up!'

'We're OK.' Charley gave a careless shrug of her shoulders. She brushed back the thick braid, which was several shades darker than Cole's hair, and grimaced. 'Donna's still Donna, and Sandy still follows Cole around, like he always did.'

Joanna nodded. Donna was Charley's twin, but the two sisters had never been really close. Meanwhile Sandy—Alexander—was the youngest member of the family.

'I guess you know about Pa,' Charley continued now, as Joanna cast a doubtful glance up and down the corridor outside before closing the door. The girl sauntered across the room, evidently dressed for supper, in her white linen tunic, ankle socks, and patent shoes, and picked up Joanna's hairbrush from the dressing-table. 'He's pretty sick.'

'Yes.' Joanna's mouth dried, and she hitched the towel a little tighter. 'I'm—sorry.'

'Why should you be?' Charley swung round to face her. 'It isn't as if you ever liked him.'

Joanna moistened her lips. 'No,' she conceded evenly. 'He's—not an easy man to like.'

'Tell me about it.' Charley raised her eyes towards the ceiling in a gesture that was surprisingly adult for someone of her age. 'You know he's already told me I've *got* to go to college!'

'Well . . .' Joanna lifted her shoulders. 'That doesn't seem too unreasonable——'

'Not to you, maybe.' Charley tossed her head. 'Jo, I don't want to go to college. Donna's the academic one, not me. I'd just as soon stay here and help Ma.'

Joanna shook her head. 'You may change your mind. I mean, it's a few years yet——'

'I won't.' Charley scowled. 'You don't understand, Jo. I—I—want to get married.'

'Married?' Joanna was astounded, and showed it, and Charley hurried on.

'Yes, married,' she said, clasping her hands together and facing Joanna with a stubborn light in her eyes. 'Next year. When I'm sixteen.'

Joanna caught her lower lip between her teeth. 'You've got someone in mind, I gather.'

'Of course.' Charley looked scornful. 'You remember Billy Fenton, don't you? His mother used to visit the clinic. You helped her——'

'I remember Billy Fenton,' Joanna interrupted quickly, her spirits plummeting. The Fentons were a poor white family who occupied a one-roomed shack on the edge of the estate. Boulevard—*Bull*—Fenton used to be employed in the stables, until his craving for liquor and his employer's patience collided. Ryan Macallister had thrown him out, indifferent to the burdens Bull's being without a job would put on his entire family.

Not that people had blamed Cole's father for what he'd done. It was a well-known fact that Bull was bone idle; that he beat his wife and kids, and that he had set up a whiskey still, somewhere back in the woods. Of course, the police had never found any evidence to convict him with, but the rumours persisted, and so did Bull's drunkenness.

But it was Bull's wife, Susan, Joanna had felt sorry for. Although the girl had been little more than her own age, she had already had seven babies, three of whom had been stillborn. She was a little mouse of a creature, afraid of her brutal husband, yet without the will to leave him. All Joanna had been able to do was give her the means to prevent the yearly pregnancies, and gradually, over a period of months, she had seen the woman regaining her self-respect.

Billy had been her oldest child, and thankfully nothing like his father. Joanna guessed he must be sixteen or seventeen now, and probably quite a hero to someone like Charley. But Charley would probably never have noticed him if she hadn't helped Joanna at the clinic during her school holidays. And, while it was unfair to judge Billy because of his background, Joanna knew there was no way Charley's family would countenance such a liaison.

'Why are you looking like that?' the girl demanded now, evidently sensing something from Joanna's silence that Joanna herself had hoped to conceal. 'You think I'm too young, don't you? Well, I'm not. And no one's going to send me away to college, if I don't want to go.'

Joanna breathed a little more freely. In her concern about Billy's suitability, Charley's age hadn't even come into it. But now she seized on the girl's words with some relief.

'I think it's too soon to be thinking about next year,' she replied carefully. 'Heavens, you could change your mind next week.'

'I won't.' Charley sounded very definite. 'So—will you talk to Cole about it? He never listens to me, but I know he'll listen to you.'

'Cole!' Joanna almost laughed. 'Charley, Cole's hardly likely to listen to anything I have to say.'

'He might.' Charley hunched her shoulders. 'And—and if Pa's dying, Cole's going to be the one to make the decisions around here, isn't he?'

Joanna expelled her breath heavily. 'I—look, Charley, we can't talk now. I've got to get my hair dried, and get dressed for supper. Let—er—let me think about it, OK? Now, off you go. Before your mother starts wondering where you are.'

'All right.' Charley bestowed an impulsive kiss on her cheek, and skipped across to the door. 'I'm so glad you're back, Jo. I just know things are going to work out. You'll see.'

Joanna wished she could feel as optimistic, as she hurriedly dried her hair, and pulled on silk leggings and an over-size shirt that barely skimmed the tops of her thighs. The leggings and shirt were cream, and she slotted the ends of a chunky black belt together, and allowed it to rest loosely on her hips. Glossy hooped earrings swung against her neck, and she let her hair loose, a fall of black silk that framed her delicately arched cheek-bones, and dipped into the exposed hollow of her throat.

Of course, she was late. Even without Charley's appearance, she would have been hard-pressed to make it downstairs at the appropriate time. As it was, she had the dubious pleasure of being the last to appear, and although she hadn't intended to make an entrance it turned out that way.

The whole family was waiting for her in the library. Even though it was more than three years since she'd left Tidewater, Joanna had known exactly where she would find them. Even the slightly musty smell of the books was the same. And nine pairs of eyes acknowledged her appearance, mostly alike in their expressions of disapproval.

'I'm sorry,' she said, walking into the room with an air of confidence she was far from feeling. 'I hope I haven't kept you waiting long.'

And it was as she was bestowing an appeasing smile on the room in general that she realised one of the pairs of eyes that had monitored her arrival was Ryan Macallister's. Unlike his son, he wasn't standing, which was why Joanna hadn't noticed him at once. He was seated in a wing-back chair, beside the flower-filled fireplace, and even a passing glance was enough for her to realise that Cole had not been exaggerating when he said his father was very ill. Skeletally thin, Ryan seemed to have shrivelled to a shadow of his former self, and in spite of the heat in the room, which the turning fans only moved around, he was wrapped in a Paisley shawl, with a blanket over his knees.

Joanna was temporarily nonplussed. She didn't know what to say to him. It was obvious something was expected of her, but for a moment she felt incapable of speech. Her eyes flickered uncertainly over the other members of the family. Joe, the brother closest to Cole in age, was there, and she assumed the rather sharp-faced woman at his side must be his wife. Certainly, the woman was regarding her with undisguised hostility—

much like her mother-in-law, thought Joanna drily. Of course, Charley's was a friendly face, and even Ben's lips moved in silent approbation. But Donna was too much like her mother to offer any support, and Sandy was too young to count. As for Cole..

Joanna's gaze turned from his guarded face to Maggie's. Cole's mother was openly contemptuous, but whether that was for her, or for what she was wearing, she couldn't be sure. It was obvious she didn't conform to the standards set by Maggie and her daughters: crisp shirtwaists and white stockings had never been a part of her wardrobe.

Joanna drew a steadying breath, and, realising it was up to her to show all of them that she could not be intimidated, she approached the old man's chair. 'Mr Macallister,' she said, and her cool English voice rang out loud and clear. She had never progressed beyond calling him *Mr* Macallister, and she saw no reason to change that now. 'How are you?'

Ryan Macallister's mouth compressed. 'How do I look?' he enquired harshly, and Joanna realised he had lost none of his irascibility.

She hesitated. 'Not good,' she said at last, to the concerted sound of several indrawn breaths. 'But I'm sure you already know that.'

Ryan's eyes narrowed. They had once been as blue as his son's, but now they were an indeterminate shade of grey. 'Pretty sure of yourself, aren't you?' he muttered, bony fingers kneading the empty glass in his hand. 'Hope I didn't make a mistake bringing you back here. I don't want any trouble. Not from you, or anyone else.'

Joanna felt an insane desire to laugh. *He* didn't want any trouble. Dear God, surely he didn't think she did!

'Why did you ask me to come here, Mr Macallister?' she enquired politely, but Cole's father was not prepared to make it that easy for her.

'You'll find out,' he said gruffly, and then, holding out his empty glass to Cole, he muttered, 'Get me another drink, will you? And whatever she wants.'

'Ryan!' As her son moved to do his father's bidding, Maggie took an involuntary step forward. 'Ryan, you know what the doctor said.'

'Don't I just?' The old man gave her a scornful look. 'What's the matter, Maggie? You heard what Joanna said. I don't look good. And I sure as hell don't feel good. So why would I restrict myself to one drink, when two, or even three, make me feel so much better?'

Maggie's thin lips tightened, and the look she cast in Joanna's direction was baleful. But, thankfully, Joanna was able to give her attention to choosing a drink, and if Cole's expression was no less forbidding, at least he kept his opinion to himself.

'Just fruit juice, please,' she said, deciding that in this company it would be wise to keep her wits about her, and only the faint drawing together of Cole's brows indicated his reaction to it.

Then, as if at some silent signal from their father, the other members of the family clustered round her. Joe unbent sufficiently to deposit a swift kiss on her cheek, before introducing his wife, Alicia, and even Donna fingered the smooth, satiny fabric of her shirt, and expressed a wish that she had one like it.

'You're too fat,' remarked Charley, who had never had any tact, and Donna's resentful eyes turned on her twin.

'Jo used to be fat, too,' she retorted, and Joanna thought how typical it was that she should be made the brunt of their argument.

'That was because she drank too much,' countered Charley, uncaring of Joanna's feelings. 'Pa said so.'

'Pa said a lot of things,' said Ben, in a low voice, stepping between the two sisters. 'That doesn't mean it was true. Now, why don't you two stop embarrassing Jo, and go and help Lacey?'

'Lacey doesn't need any help,' said Charley, but she gave Joanna a rueful smile as she did so. 'Sorry. I didn't mean you used to be really fat. Just—just——'

'Overweight?' suggested Joanna drily, and Charley gave a vigorous nod.

'Clear off,' ordered Ben, not at all appeased by his sister's attempt at an apology, and the twins mooched away, still continuing their argument. 'So,' he added, when they were alone, 'is it as bad as you expected?'

Joanna allowed herself a wry smile. 'Worse?' she suggested lightly, and then shook her head. 'No. Not worse. Different.'

'Because of Pa,' murmured Ben, moving so that he was between her and his father, and Joanna nodded.

'It's funny,' she said, only just realising that it was true. 'He doesn't scare me any more. Why's that, do you suppose?'

'Because he's ill?'

'No.' Joanna frowned. 'At least, I don't think so. He's still as belligerent as ever, and it's obvious he still has all of you running round after him.'

'Except Cole,' said Ben softly, and Joanna looked up at him in surprise.

'What do you mean?'

'You'll find out.' Ben shrugged. 'Cole's changed. He's not the same as he used to be.'

Joanna glanced towards her ex-husband, who was presently making his way towards them, a tall glass of fruit cordial in his hand. 'He seems the same to me,' she muttered, in an undertone, and Ben raised his eyebrows meaningfully as Cole joined them.

'One fruit juice,' he said, handing Joanna the glass, before giving his brother a studied look 'Did I interrupt something?'

'Heck, no.' Ben coloured a little now, and Joanna's feeling towards him warmed, at this indication of his youth. 'We were just discussing Pa, that's all.'

Cole turned his head to where Joe and Alicia were standing over his father's chair, and then pulled a wry face. 'He seems more animated tonight than I've seen him in a while.' His cool gaze moved to Joanna. 'Perhaps we have you to thank for that.'

'Oh, heaven forbid that you should have to thank me for anything,' Joanna responded mockingly. She tasted her drink, and then put out her tongue to lick the last drop of mango juice from her lips. 'Hmm, this is delightful! I'm glad you made it, Cole. I'm sure your mother wishes it was hemlock!'

'You can't blame my mother for not trusting you,' declared Cole, in a low, harsh tone, and Ben, evidently feeling surplus to requirements, went to stop Sandy from tormenting the twins. 'You didn't exactly make things easy for her.'

'It wasn't my fault that your father's duplicity came home to roost,' responded Joanna shortly, and then, forcing herself not to get involved in another argument with him, she added, 'Is Sarah still living in Beaumaris, by the way? I'd like to see her while I'm here.'

'That's not a good idea,' said Cole, staring at some point over her head. 'I doubt if that was why my father brought you here.'

'I doubt if it was,' agreed Joanna pleasantly. 'But, nevertheless, I intend to see her. With or without your approval.'

Cole's eyes were dark with anger when they dropped to hers again. 'Don't,' he said savagely. 'You'll only cause her more pain. Nathan's dead, and there's nothing any of us can do about it.'

'And aren't you glad?' she retorted, suddenly finding the fruit juice too sweet for her taste. She set down her glass, and looked round for Ben. 'Excuse me; I need some fresh air.'

'Wait!'

Cole's hand around her upper arm arrested her, and even through the material of her shirt she could sense the frustration in those fingers.

'Yes?' She tilted her face up to his, and, although only seconds before she had been goading him with memories of his dead brother, suddenly the air between them fairly crackled with electricity.

'Please,' he said, and she sensed how hard it was for him to plead with her. Her stomach hollowed at the look of stark anguish in his face, and for a moment she would have promised him anything. 'Stay away from Sarah,' he added thickly. 'Stay away, or—or I'll——'

He broke off abruptly, but Joanna had stiffened. 'Or what, Cole?' she taunted, her weakness coagulating into a hard core of resentment inside her. 'You can't threaten me. If I want to see Sarah, I will. Why shouldn't I? We have a lot in common. We both trusted men who betrayed us.' And, lifting his fingers from her sleeve, she walked swiftly away.

'*Jo*!'

His violent use of her name fell on deaf ears, and his mother, who had been watching their altercation with evident misgivings, now came after Joanna.

'Is something wrong?' she demanded, reaching the louvred doors just ahead of her quarry. 'What has Cole been saying?'

Joanna's look of disbelief was not feigned. 'I beg your pardon?'

'I said——'

'I know what you said.' Joanna looked about her with some frustration. 'But I don't think it's any of your business, do you?'

'He doesn't want you back, you know.' Maggie's thin lower lip curled. 'He may have agreed to bring you here, because his daddy asked him to. But it wasn't his idea.'

Joanna caught her breath 'Thanks for the vote of confidence.'

'Don't get sassy with me, girl!'

'I'm not.' Joanna felt a little of her tension dissolve. Overt hostility she could deal with. It was the other kind that gnawed away at your composure. 'Don't worry, Maggie. I don't want your precious son.' She paused, and then a little imp of mischief made her add, softly, 'Not on a permanent basis, anyway.'

Cole's mother's face turned crimson. 'You—you——'

'*Ciao*,' murmured Joanna silkily, and, deciding to quit while she was ahead, she sauntered away.

CHAPTER SEVEN

JOANNA slept surprisingly well. She hadn't expected to. Not after the rather nerve-racking evening she had spent. But perhaps it was the fact that she hadn't slept much the night before. Whatever the reason, she lost consciousness as soon as her head touched the pillow, and it wasn't until one of the maids opened her curtains that she realised it was morning.

'Morning, miss—*ma'am*,' fumbled the girl, whom Joanna didn't recognise at all. Evidently she had been employed since Joanna left Tidewater, and her uncertain expression mirrored her inexperience.

'Miss will do,' said Joanna lazily, levering herself up on her pillows, as the delicious scent of coffee drifted to her nostrils. 'What's your name?'

'Rebecca, miss,' answered the girl, coming forward to lift the breakfast tray from the bedside cabinet. She set the legs at either side of Joanna's recumbent form, and fussed about, tidying the cutlery, which had slipped as she moved the tray.

'That's OK. Honestly.' Joanna held up a deterring hand. She looked down at the tray. 'Hmm. This looks wonderful.'

'Juice, eggs, and ham, toast and coffee,' declared Rebecca, blushing in confusion. 'Anything else I can get you, Miz Macallister?'

'It's Seton,' said Joanna drily. 'I'm Joanna Seton. I used to be Macallister, but not any more.'

'I understand.' Rebecca coloured again. 'You care for some pancakes, to go with your eggs?'

'Oh, no.' Joanna smiled, and shook her head. 'No, thanks. I doubt if I can manage all this.'

Rebecca hesitated. 'Well, if you're sure——'

'I'm sure,' declared Joanna, stifling a yawn. 'Um— what time is it?'

'Well,' Rebecca reflected, 'Miz Macallister said to bring up your tray at ten o'clock. I guess it must be a quarter after that now.'

'After *ten*!' Joanna was appalled. She never normally slept so late, and she could just imagine what Cole's mother would be thinking. Maggie had called her a lazy slut, in the not-too-distant past. And lying in bed till ten o'clock was as good as justifying the accusation.

But it wasn't true. It had never been true. If Joanna had stayed in bed in the past, it was because there had been nothing to get up for. Maggie wouldn't let her do anything; not a thing. And even her will to paint had been stifled in the closed atmosphere of Tidewater.

'Ain't nothing spoiling, miss,' Rebecca added, a little disturbed at Joanna's shocked reaction. 'Mr Macallister—he don't get up much before noon these days, and the boys—they're long gone.'

'The *boys*,' echoed Joanna ruefully, flopping back against her pillows, and Rebecca leapt forward to steady the tray.

'All 'cept Sandy,' she agreed, straightening up again. 'The young 'uns, they're all off to school. That Charley—she didn't wanna go. Said you and she had things to talk about. But Miz Macallister made her go, just the same.'

She would, thought Joanna broodingly, but she didn't say so. Besides, Charley's problems would have to wait. Right now, she was more concerned with finding out why Ryan Macallister had brought her here.

'I better go.' Rebecca seemed to think Joanna's silence was an indication that she had been gossiping too much, and it took quite an effort to assure her that this wasn't so.

'Thanks again,' Joanna offered, as the maid hurried towards the door. 'It's been nice meeting you. I hope we get to talk again.'

'Oh——' It was worth it to see Rebecca's cheeks bloom. 'Yes, I do, too,' she appended, and, with a little conspiratorial smile, she let herself out of the room.

After she was gone, Joanna wriggled up into a sitting position, and lifted the tray to one side of the huge, colonial four-poster. Then, sliding her feet to the floor, she stood up.

There was an expanse of cream shag carpet between where she was standing and the window, and she crossed it swiftly. The bedroom at her apartment in St John's Wood would have fitted a couple of times into this huge room. Apart from the bed, there were an assortment of heavy chests and cabinets, an antique *chaise-longue*, as well as the free-standing mirror Joanna had used the night before. There was also a walk-in closet, with fitted robes, a vanity unit and a long, velvet-padded bench to sit on.

Everything at Tidewater was larger than life, she thought wryly, drawing the louvred shutters aside and stepping out on to her balcony. Including its inhabitants, she conceded, with a certain tightening in her stomach.

It had been fairly warm in her bedroom, in spite of the shutters, but outside the heat was almost palpable already. It soon bathed her in a cloak of perspiration, and even the cotton nightshirt she was wearing clung damply to her skin. And this wasn't even the hottest it could get, she remembered, realising she would once have regarded this as only temperate. Yet, for all that, there was something decidedly sensual about such an abundance of nature's bounty, and the scents from the gardens below were positively intoxicating.

But it was the distant line of the ocean that caught her eyes. A breeze, both warm and salty, ruffled the loose tendrils that curled at her temple, and she put her hand against the back of her neck to lift the weight of hair away from her skin.

And that was when she saw Cole. He had evidently been out with the horses, and was presently unsaddling a huge blood bay in the paddock nearest to the house. He had seen her, too. As he straightened from loosening the girth, he looked straight at her balcony, and even from a distance she could sense his anger and his hostility.

But he looked good, she thought ruefully, her nerves prickling in unwilling anticipation. In tight jeans, leathers, and a shirt open halfway down his chest, he visibly breathed sexuality, and the heat that enveloped her at that moment had nothing to do with the climate. His hair, darkened by his exertions, lay damply against his head, and some uncontrollable part of her longed to run her fingers into the silvery gold strands clinging to his nape.

With oxygen suddenly becoming a scarce commodity, Joanna dragged a gulp of air into her lungs. Then, because she sensed his unwillingness to be caught looking at her balcony, she raised a hand in mocking acknowledgement. He might not want her here, but, whatever compulsion she possessed, he was not unaware of it. And, before he could do anything to rob her of that conviction, she turned and walked back into the room behind her.

Nevertheless, her own hands were not quite steady as she poured herself a cup of the coffee Rebecca had brought her. She perched on the edge of the bed to drink it, realising she wasn't used to this kind of sexual gamesmanship, and, while she was determined to keep the pressure on Cole, it was decidedly wearing on the nerves.

The eggs and ham were congealing on the plate, but she knew she couldn't face anything as substantial as a fried breakfast at this time. She was wondering if she could wrap them up in a paper napkin, and surreptitiously feed them to the dogs, when common sense reasserted itself. She didn't *have* to eat the meal, for heaven's sake. Just because, at one time, she would have done anything to avoid a confrontation with Cole's mother, she was allowing herself to be seduced by her surroundings. Now she could do exactly as she liked, and if Maggie had any comment to make about wasting food, so what?

Nevertheless, she knew she had to eat something. This was not the time to start starving herself. She would need all her wits about her in the next few hours, and a slice of toast and some orange juice sounded very palatable.

As it turned out, she couldn't resist eating two slices of toast spread with the chunky marmalade that was made from oranges grown on Tidewater land. Then, realising she was only delaying the inevitable, she went for her shower.

Half an hour later, she was ready to go downstairs. White shorts, and a scarlet vest, which emphasised the rounded curve of her breasts, seemed suitably provocative, and she had threaded her silky hair into a single plait that bobbed against her bare shoulder. She pushed her feet into rope-soled espadrilles, and then, with a final glance at the length of leg she was exposing, she threw herself a rueful grin, and picked up the tray.

Her suite of rooms was situated at the south-western corner of the house. A white-panelled corridor led to the galleried landing that overlooked the hall below, and she traversed it swiftly, pausing only once to absorb the once familiar configuration of the building. The rooms she and Cole used to occupy were in the opposite wing, and she guessed Maggie was responsible for her present situation. Or it might have been Cole, she conceded, guessing he probably occupied the other suite. The main apartments were all in the other half of the house, which was infinitely cooler than where Joanna was sleeping. Dear Maggie, she mused sardonically, starting down the stairs, always doing everything in her power to make her feel unwelcome.

The lower floor was cooler. It had been designed to allow for a free flow of air from front to back, and because the ceilings were high and wide it was possible to feel the benefit of the constantly turning fans. It reminded her that Cole had wanted to install an air-conditioning system, when she came to live at Tidewater But his father had declared that what had been good enough for his father was good enough for him, and. in any case. it was an unnecessary expense.

Par for the course, she thought drily. glancing back up the stairs, and then did a double-take when she saw the subject of her musings gazing down at her from the upper floor.

'What you doing with that tray, girl?' Ryan Macallister demanded, and although his voice didn't carry the same authority it had once done, he startled her.

'The tray?' Joanna echoed, a little blankly. And then, quickly gathering her composure, 'I'm taking it to the kitchen.' She forced a polite smile. 'Ought you to be out of bed?'

Although Cole's father was clinging to the rails of the gallery with obvious necessity, his bony features took on an indignant scowl. 'I'm not dead yet,' he grated. 'Put that tray down, and get yourself up here. I want to talk to you.'

Joanna pressed her lips together, but she refused to be intimidated. 'After I've taken the tray to the kitchen,' she declared pleasantly. 'I won't be long——'

'Unless you want me to take a dive down these stairs, you'd better forget about the blasted tray and get your butt up here,' snapped Ryan harshly, and although Joanna wasn't totally convinced of his sincerity her conscience wouldn't let her take that risk.

With a helpless shrug of her shoulders, she deposited the tray on the iron-bound chest that stood in the lee of the stairs, and ran back up. She had guessed that Cole's father was hardly likely to ask her for help unless he had to, and certainly the fingers that grasped her arm for support felt suitably desperate.

'God-damned disease!' he muttered, causing her to stagger a little, as he transferred all his weight from the banister to her shoulder, and she realised he had not been joking about falling down the stairs. It really was an effort for him to get around at all.

'Take it easy,' she offered, as they made an unsteady progress back to his bedroom, and Ryan gave an obscene exclamation.

'Who're you to tell me to take it easy?' he exhorted breathlessly. 'Do you know what it's like to feel like a feeble-minded geriatric? Judas Priest, I'd be better off dead!'

'I don't think your family would agree with you,' murmured Joanna evenly, easing open his bedroom door with her hip, and helping him to cross the shagged carpet, and Ryan snorted.

'But you would, wouldn't you?' He took a laboured breath and heaved himself on to the side of the bed. 'You would, wouldn't you, girl? 'Cos you'd know I'd feel the same, if it was you.'

Joanna stepped back. He didn't need her help now. He was perfectly capable of ringing the bell beside the bed if he needed any further assistance. And, quite honestly, all she wanted to do was put as much distance between them as the limitations of Tidewater would allow.

But when she moved towards the door his voice stopped her. 'Where're you going?'

Joanna steeled herself and turned. 'I think you should rest, Mr Macallister.'

'Do you?' He made a sound of contempt. 'Just because I hurt your feelings, you're going to walk out on me, right?'

'Right.'

'Wrong.' He eased himself back against his pillows. 'We have to talk, and I don't know how much time I've got.' He grimaced. 'Humour me.'

'Why should I?'

'Good question——' But he broke off to give a hacking cough, and Joanna's resistance foundered.

'Look,' she said, 'I'll come back. I promise. When you're feeling—stronger.'

'Huh.' He wiped his mouth on the back of his hand. 'I guess this is as strong as I'm going to get. Besides, what do you care? Seeing me like this must be the sweetest kind of revenge——'

'No!'

'No?'

'No.' Joanna swallowed 'Hard as it may be for you to believe, I do have some compassion.'

'Ah.' The old man's lips curled with evident satisfaction. 'I hoped you'd say that.'

'You did?' Joanna blinked. 'Why?'

'Because I want my son back,' declared Ryan abruptly. 'And you're the only one who can do that for me.'

'Your son?' Joanna felt totally confused. 'What son are you talking about?'

'Don't play games with me, girl.' Her answer was obviously not the one he had anticipated. 'You know which son I mean. Cole, of course. I want you to tell him I wasn't to blame for his brother's—accident!'

Joanna caught her breath. 'Nathan,' she said, through dry lips. 'That's what all this is about: Nathan!'

'*No!*' Ryan's voice was savage, and if he could have reached her she was sure he would have slapped his hand across her mouth to silence her. 'I've told you what it's about,' he grated. 'Cole. I want Cole to treat me like a father again. I want him to give me his respect. Dammit, the boy's my son! He owes me that much.'

Joanna couldn't take this in. 'But I thought——'

'I don't care what you thought.' Ryan sucked in a gurgling breath. 'Just listen to me.' The air whistled in his lungs as he sought to calm himself. 'You did this. You turned him away from me. You and your prissy liberal ideas. Teaching people to want things they can't have. I won't forgive you for what you did. I'll never forgive you. But I need your help, dammit, and you're going to give it to me!'

The air outside was doubly sweet after the cloying atmosphere of the sickroom. Stepping down from the shaded columns of the veranda, Joanna crossed the neatly cut turf to the paddock. Resting her hands on the white-painted rail, she took several deep breaths of the moist-scented air. Then, she sagged against the fence. She felt drained, both emotionally and physically, and the elegant house behind her was a prison from which she had made only a temporary escape. She was trapped, and she knew it.

But of all the reasons why Ryan Macallister should have wanted to see her, surely his request was the least expected. To ask her to speak to Cole on his behalf! To persuade Cole that his father had not been responsible for what happened to Nathan; that he had played no part in his death!

Joanna shivered in spite of the sun burning down on her bare shoulders, and closed her eyes. When Cole had told her his father wanted to see her, she hadn't given it a lot of thought. She had been too intent on making Cole's task as difficult as possible, and, as she had no intention of coming here, any curiosity she might have felt would have seemed a sign of weakness. Of course, when she had been so reckless as to change her mind, she had wondered then, but never in her wildest dreams could she have predicted Ryan's reasoning. Because she possessed an immutable core of compassion inside her, she had naturally assumed Cole's father must be the same. She had actually entertained the notion that he wanted to beg her forgiveness for what she had suffered at his and Maggie's hands.

She opened her eyes again, as a low moan escaped her lips. God! How wrong could you be? Ryan Macallister didn't have a compassionate muscle in his body. He was all unforgiving bone!

A lanky-legged colt, evidently used to being spoiled, came to nuzzle at her white-knuckled hands, and Joanna gave him a rueful smile.

'I'm afraid you're out of luck,' she said, displaying her empty palms. 'You and me both.'

'Feeling sorry for yourself?' enquired a drawling voice, and, turning her head, Joanna saw her ex-husband strolling across the grass towards her. For the past few moments, she had forgotten she had seen Cole in the paddock earlier, and now it took a distinct effort to face his undisguised hostility.

'I guess you'd like to think so,' she retorted, avoiding his gaze. She gestured towards the colt. 'What's his name?'

Cole halted at the other side of the fence, pulling an apple out of his pocket to give to the mare, who had come to see what her offspring was doing. 'He doesn't have a name yet,' he replied, his lean fingers easily breaking off a corner of the apple to give to the colt. 'Henry calls him Beau, for obvious reasons.'

'Hmm.' Joanna stretched out her hand and stroked the colt's dusky head. 'He is beautiful, isn't he?' And then, reacting to the name Cole had used, she looked up. 'Henry's still here?'

'Why wouldn't he be?' asked Cole shortly. 'He works here.'

'Yes, but——'

'Have you seen my father yet?'

Cole cut into her words with a taut enquiry, and although she would have preferred to pursue her line of thought, rather than his, the question was too urgent to be ignored.

'I—yes,' she said brittlely, deciding to be honest. 'That's why I'm here. I needed to get some fresh air.'

Cole's brows, which were several shades darker than his hair, descended in a glowering look. 'Must you always be so offensive?' he demanded, putting his hand on the top bar, and vaulting over the railing. 'The man's dying, for God's sake. Can't you show him some respect?'

'As you do?'

The words sprang, unguardedly, from her tongue, and she was hardly surprised when Cole reacted to them. 'What the hell do you mean?' he muttered, glaring at her with angry eyes, and Joanna's heart skipped a beat as he thrust his face close to hers.

'Why, what do you think I mean, darlin'?' she taunted, realising this was her only means of defence. She lifted her hand and let her knuckles slide down his cheek, which was roughened by a fine stubbling of silvery-blond beard. 'I was only teasing, wasn't I? Everyone knows, you're Daddy's blue-eyed boy!'

Cole's hand clamped about her wrist, dragging it down to his side. 'You can't wait to cause trouble, can you?' he snarled, and although his grasp was painful the burning frustration in his eyes wasn't.

'Careful, darlin',' she murmured, her slim fingers reaching out to stroke the taut muscle of his thigh, exposed by the tight-fitting denim. 'Your mother might be watching, and we wouldn't want her to think we can't get along.'

CHAPTER EIGHT

JOANNA ate lunch with Maggie and Ben. Cole didn't come to the table, and Ben told her that Joe and Alicia had built their own house on the property, and spent most of their time there. The three younger members of the family were at school, of course, and the conversation during the meal was decidedly strained. But at least Ryan Macallister didn't join them, for which she was grateful. She needed time to decide what she was going to do, before confronting him again.

After lunch, she learned that Cole had gone into Beaumaris. Maggie took great delight in informing her that he wouldn't be back until that evening. Joanna managed not to show any emotion to his mother, but she was annoyed just the same. If she'd known he was leaving, she'd have found some way to get him to take her with him. But probably he had known that, too, she acknowledged, which was why he hadn't mentioned it.

So, unwilling to risk another encounter with Ryan Macallister, Joanna spent the afternoon in her room. It did cross her mind that she could go down to the stables, and renew her acquaintance with Henry, but she was loath to open that particular can of worms today. Instead, she kicked off her espadrilles, and stretched out on the bed. Perhaps she'd feel better after a nap.

But she didn't go to sleep. Her brain was too active to allow her to relax. Even though the events of the morning had taken their toll, her mind kept re-running the reasons that had brought her here. She'd thought she'd put the past behind her. She'd thought she was immune to anything the Macallisters could to to her. But coming back to Tidewater, meeting Cole's family again, had acted like a catalyst on her emotions. She might be tougher than she used to be, but she wasn't out of danger.

How strange it was, she thought, that one small incident could change your whole life. She certainly hadn't expected a faulty fuel pump to be her stepping-stone to fame and fortune. And yet that was exactly how it had happened.

As the youngest child of older parents, born when the offspring closest to her in age was already ten years old, Joanna had lived a fairly solitary existence until she went to school. She had become used to entertaining herself, and her aptitude for drawing did not go unnoticed. But, although her parents were proud of her artistic skills, they did not consider them a viable occupation. Joanna was encouraged to work hard at her academic studies, and even though she insisted on leaving school at eighteen, to give her more time to study her art, she spent her days in the merchant bank, which her father's family had founded.

When the tutor at the night class she attended suggested putting a couple of her paintings on exhibition at the local library, Joanna had never expected anyone to be interested. But Grace, who had been driving back from an exhibition in Sussex, developed a fault with her car in Guildford High Street, and while it was being mended she wandered into the little gallery.

Of course, Joanna's success didn't happen overnight. But Grace had sufficient faith in her to offer her the chance to show her work in the West End gallery she managed. Just one painting, at first, and, when that sold fairly quickly, another, until by the time Joanna was twenty-one she was able to give up the bank, and devote herself to her art.

In the meantime, she and Grace had become close friends. In spite of the difference in their ages, they had a lot in common, and after Joanna found herself a flat in London Grace became her agent as well. And, naturally, they shared confidences. Grace heard all about Joanna's lonely childhood, and Joanna learned that

Grace had once been married to an American, and that she had two teenage sons living in South Carolina.

Which was why, when the tall American strolled into the gallery one day, when Joanna was alone, and asked where Grace was, she gave him a rather cool reception. She had guessed he must be some relation of Grace's ex-husband—in spite of her antipathy towards him, she had not been able to deny the attraction of his lazy southern voice—but, as he was too old to be either of Grace's sons, she had assumed Grace wouldn't be too pleased to see him.

However, as with so many things about Cole, she thought ruefully, she had been wrong. When Grace returned, fortunately only a few minutes later, she had greeted him with real affection, and it had been obvious that, whatever relationship she had with her ex-husband, his nephew was a great favourite of hers.

And, because Grace had been so insistent that they should become friends, Joanna had unwillingly accepted the invitation to join them for dinner that evening. Ray Marsden had joined them, too. To make up a foursome, Grace had said, although subsequent events had led Joanna to make a different interpretation of that arrangement. In any event, they had all enjoyed one of Grace's home-cooked meals, served in the tiny apartment she occupied above the gallery. And afterwards Cole had taken her home.

Looking back now, Joanna recognised that, despite her initial misgivings about him, she had probably fallen in love with Cole that very evening. He had been so attractive, so amusing—and so downright sexy—that she hadn't stood a chance. Although he was only four years older than she, he was aeons older in experience, and while common sense warned her to be careful her leaping senses had left her little room for compromise.

Naturally, he had known better than to rush her. There had been no furtive grapplings in the hall outside her apartment, no abortive attempts to invade her space without her involvement. That first evening, he had es-

corted her home without even attempting to kiss her
goodnight. He had been polite, and courteous, and she
had been the one left with a disturbing sense of loss.
Indeed, she had half wondered if she had only imagined
the lingering looks he had cast in her direction during
the course of the evening. Perhaps he wasn't attracted
to her, after all. Perhaps it had just been good old-
fashioned southern gallantry.

There had been no reason for her to go to the gallery
the following day, but, after spending a wasted morning
at her easel, she decided to go for a walk. It was early
summer, and the rhododendrons were out in the park.
A good enough reason, she thought, for her to cast a
critical eye over them.

She stayed out for a couple of hours. She was loath
to go back to face a blank sheet of sketching paper. She
knew exactly where she wanted to be, but she wasn't
confident enough to go for it. Instead, she bought French
bread and cream cakes. She'd decided to console herself
with starch.

But when she got back to her apartment she found
she had a visitor. Cole was sitting on the low wall that
skirted the garden of the Victorian conversion. In tight-
fitting jeans that clung to his long legs, and a black T-
shirt, he looked lean, and tanned, and muscular, his
brown hands resting on the wall at either side of his lazy,
lounging frame.

The colour raced to Joanna's face, but she couldn't
help it. She had been thinking about him all day, and
every image she'd had had been accurate. He was just
as attractive as she remembered, and her artist's eye
lingered lovingly on his broad shoulders and rippling
muscles. The belt that secured his jeans rested low on
his narrow hips, the silver buckle drawing her eyes like
a magnet. Seduced them, too, to the worn cloth of his
fly, and the sun-bleached denim that cupped his sex.

But she knew, if she was honest, it was not his male
beauty, as a subject for her easel, that caused the blood
to race madly through her veins at that moment. For

the first time in her life, she knew what it was like to actually *want* a man. She wanted to look at him, and touch him, and for him to touch her. But she hadn't the faintest notion of how to bring that about.

In an age when behaving promiscuously was the rule rather than the exception, Joanna was still a virgin. Oh, she had had boyfriends. She was young and, in her eyes, moderately attractive, and she had never had any lack of admirers. But, perhaps as a result of being born to older parents, she had acquired their values, rather than those of her own generation. In consequence, she had always regarded sex as a fairly overrated occupation. Certainly, none of the young men she had dated had inspired any great desire to experiment in that way. Which was why her instantaneous attraction to Cole was so astonishing to her. Astonishing, and disturbing. She wasn't entirely sure she wanted that kind of complication in her life.

'Hi,' he said, getting up at her approach, and taking the bag of groceries from her. 'Let me help you with that.'

Joanna's tongue made a hasty circuit of her upper lip. 'Have—have you been waiting long?' she asked—as if she'd been expecting him, she chided herself irritably. 'Um—I've been shopping.'

The banality of her response made her cringe, but she couldn't help it. She didn't know what else to say. If only she had put on a dress before she went out, she fretted. Her purple dungarees were splashed with paint.

'I guess I should have called first.' Cole removed any sense of embarrassment with his easy charm. 'But I didn't know your last name, and I didn't care to ask Aunt Grace.' He gave a rueful grin. 'She might not have approved of my seeing you again.'

Joanna blinked. 'Oh?' She lifted her slim shoulders, and the shoulder-strap of her dungarees fell off one shoulder. 'Why not?'

Cole's mouth flattened. 'She might think I wasn't to be trusted,' he conceded softly, putting out his hand and restoring the strap to its proper position. His fingers lingered against her shoulder and, although she was wearing a cotton shirt under the dungarees, his touch seared her flesh. 'She's very fond of you.'

'And—and I'm very fond of her,' stammered Joanna, shifting so that his hand fell harmlessly away. 'She—she's been very good to me.'

'The way I see it, you've been pretty good to her, too,' responded Cole. 'Without the commission she's taken from your work, she wouldn't have been able to buy into the gallery. Marsden's no fool. He saw the advantages of tying Grace into that partnership.'

Joanna moved her head. 'I'm sure you're exaggerating.'

'I don't think so.' Cole regarded her steadily for a few disturbing moments, and then glanced behind him. 'Are you going to invite me in?'

'What? Oh!' Joanna realised she was being unforgivably rude. Whatever she felt about him, he had taken the trouble to come here, and he had been holding her shopping bag for the past few minutes. 'I—of course.' She fumbled for her keys. 'It's up several flights of stairs, I'm afraid.'

'Tell me about it.' Cole was sardonic. 'You folks don't go much for elevators, do you?'

Joanna unlocked the outer door, and smiled. 'The gallery?' she suggested, and Cole nodded.

'You got it,' he agreed. 'No wonder Grace keeps her figure. I'd be a physical wreck if I had to climb those stairs every day.'

Joanna led the way up the first flight of stairs. 'I doubt it,' she murmured, giving him a surreptitious glance, and Cole's eyes narrowed appraisingly.

'Do you?' He shifted the shopping bag to his other arm. 'But you don't know anything about me—yet.'

'I—I don't think you're likely to be—to be worn out by a few stairs,' she insisted, as they started up the second flight.

'Is that so?' Cole's tone of enquiry brought her eyes to him again, and she missed a step, and had to grab for the banister.

'Y-yes,' she answered, feeling a complete fool. And thereafter she concentrated on what she was doing until they reached her floor.

Joanna's apartment was on the third floor of the old building. Originally used as the servants' quarters, in the days when the house had been lived in by only one family, the rooms had been small and airless, with tiny windows set up high in the walls. But a far-sighted developer had knocked down walls, heightened ceilings, and installed wide picture windows that gave a magnificent view of the surrounding area. He had also had the foresight to enlarge an existing skylight, and nowadays that room was used as Joanna's studio.

Now, Joanna unlocked the door, and led Cole into a rather untidy living-room. When she was working, she tended not to notice her surroundings, but now, looking at the room through his eyes, she wished she had concentrated on her housework, instead of mooching about in the park.

It was basically a two-bedroomed apartment, with the kitchen adjoining the living-room, and her bedroom, bathroom, and the studio opening from the hall that led off the living-room. There was no dining-room, as such, and she was sure it was much smaller than any apartment Cole was used to—except perhaps Grace's. But it hadn't been cheap, and she was proud of it. It was a symbol of her success, and as such she loved the independence it signified.

While she was fretting over the wilted carnations, drooping in their vase, and the papers strewn across the couch, Cole had leaned against the door to close it, and walked across the room to admire the view.

'Impressive,' he said, both arms wrapped around the supermarket bag, and, remembering her manners, Joanna went to take it from him. 'Just show me where you want it,' he intoned huskily, and, aware of the *double entendre*, she turned jerkily towards the kitchen.

'Here,' she said, gesturing towards the least cluttered work-top, and Cole deposited the bag where she had indicated. But when he gave the kitchen an equally interested inspection, she added, hurriedly, 'I'm sorry the place is such a mess. I—er—I wasn't expecting visitors.'

Cole's eyes danced. 'You only clean the place when you're expecting company, is that right?'

Joanna flushed. 'No,' she said defensively. 'It's not usually like this.'

'No sweat.' Cole shrugged his broad shoulders, and tucked his thumbs into the low belt that circled his hips. 'I didn't come to see the apartment anyway.'

Joanna stiffened a spine that weakened every time he looked at her in quite that way. 'If—if you'd like to go and sit down, I'll make some coffee,' she declared, in her most repressive tone, but Cole made no move to do as she had requested.

'How about we get a beer, and sit down together?' he suggested, and Joanna's stomach hollowed alarmingly.

'I'm afraid I—don't have any beer,' she offered apologetically. 'Just—just Coke.'

'Coke's fine,' Cole assured her, nodding towards the fridge-freezer. 'In there?'

Joanna nodded, watching helplessly as he swung open the fridge door, and took two cans of Coke from the shelf. Illuminated by the light inside, his face was disturbingly sensual, and she wondered at her own ability to handle the situation. But when the door closed, and the light went out, her mother's training asserted itself again. 'The—er—the glasses are in here,' she murmured, opening one of the wall cupboards.

But Cole only gave her a lazy glance. 'Tastes better out of a can,' he assured her. Handing her one of the ice-cold containers, he tore the tab off his and raised the can to his lips. The brown column of his throat rippled as he swallowed the liquid, and Joanna couldn't help watching him, her eyes as wide and startled as those of a mesmerised rabbit.

Then, gathering her scattered senses, she dragged her gaze away. For heaven's sake, she chided herself, he was only a man! But it was hard to concentrate on anything and her attention slipped again, so that the tab came off unevenly, and snagged the pad of her thumb.

Cole had started to walk into the living-room, with the can still raised to his lips, when he heard her muffled exclamation. Glancing round, he saw at once what had happened, and, slamming down his drink, he came to take her hand.

'How the hell did you do that?' he exclaimed, but his tone was indulgent. Taking the injured finger into his mouth, he licked the blood away. 'What a pity it wasn't your lip. Then I'd have had an excuse to do this.' And, lowering his head, he brushed her mouth with his tongue.

Joanna's legs wobbled. He was fast, she thought, trying to keep a hold on her senses. He hadn't been in the apartment fifteen minutes, and already he had kissed her. Or was that really kissing? It hadn't happened to her before, so she didn't really know.

'You OK?' he asked, and she realised he was watching her fairly closely. Close enough to glimpse the uncertainty in her eyes, she thought. Close enough to realise she was getting out of her depth.

'I'm—fine,' she got out hurriedly, her tone tense and clipped. 'I think I'd better get a plaster. I don't want to get blood everywhere.'

'A plaster?' Cole looked puzzled for a moment, and then his face cleared. 'Oh, you mean a Band-aid.' He nodded. 'Right.'

'Right.' Joanna drew her hand firmly away, breathing a sigh of relief, when he let her. 'Why—er—why don't you go and finish your drink? I won't be a minute.'

Cole didn't move. 'Is something wrong?' he queried, and Joanna, who had started rummaging about in a drawer for the packet of Elastoplast she knew was there somewhere, gave him a guilty look.

'Something wrong?' she echoed, trying to sound surprised. 'No. No. Why would there be?'

'You tell me.'

Joanna shook her head, feeling more and more awkward. 'I don't know what you mean.' She found the box of plasters, and her fingers fastened weakly about it. 'Really—I won't be long.'

Cole regarded her intently for what seemed an inordinate amount of time, and then, moving forward, he took the box from her. 'Let me do it,' he said, and although Joanna wanted to argue it was easier to give in.

Besides, she had to admit later, he had made a neat job of wrapping the plaster round her thumb. It was certainly neater than she could have managed. But, when she opened her mouth to thank him, he forestalled her.

'Tell me something,' he said, holding on to her fingers when she would have withdrawn them again. 'Did I get the wrong signal here?'

Joanna swallowed. 'The wrong signal?'

'Yeah.' Cole smoothed his thumb over the back of her hand. 'Do you want me to go?'

Joanna's jaw sagged, and she moved her shoulders in a helpless gesture. Her skin was prickling with awareness and, somewhere down in her stomach, she could feel a dull pain. 'I—why, no,' she said at last. 'Why should you think that?'

Cole shrugged. 'The way you acted when I touched you,' he replied.

Joanna tried to act casually. 'You're touching me now,' she pointed out lightly, but Cole didn't smile.

'You know what I mean,' he said flatly. 'Is this a turn-off?'

Such words he used! Joanna shook her head. She didn't know how to answer him. She had never met anybody who asked such personal questions before. Her dealings with his sex had been fairly simple up till now. The men she had dated had been the kind of men who let her dictate the pace of their relationships. And, because she had never been emotionally involved before, their encounters had never been in any danger of getting out of hand. But Cole was different. She had known that as soon as she met him. What she hadn't recognised was *how* different. And, in her eagerness to know him better, she had walked into a situation she simply didn't know how to deal with.

'I don't think—we should rush things,' she got out at last, wondering how the abrasive brush of his thumb could cause such havoc inside her. 'We—we hardly know one another.'

'Don't we?' With a little jerk, he brought her unwary body towards him. Then, before she had a chance to protest, he released her fingers and put both his hands on her hips. The weight of those hard hands burned through the thin material of her dungarees, and because, underneath, her hips were bare, they were disturbingly intimate, too. 'So,' he crooned softly, 'let's get to know one another better.'

'Oh, really!' Joanna's hands spread against his shirt-front. It was a puny defence and she knew it, but events were moving far too swiftly. 'I wish you wouldn't do this.'

'Do what?' asked Cole huskily, looking down into the open V of her shirt, and causing a wave of heat to envelop her. 'Say, are you wearing anything under this coverall?'

'You know I am.' Joanna's response wasn't hesitant this time, and Cole's eyes glimmered with undisguised amusement. But, conversely, his humour upset her almost as much as his advances had done, and in a tight, angry tone she added, 'I suppose you think this is very funny!'

Cole's eyes softened. 'Don't be so touchy.' He lifted one hand and stroked it down her cheek. 'Is all your skin as soft as this?'

Joanna's breathing felt constricted. 'Cole——'

'Hmm.' His hand had left her cheek, and had now coiled around her neck. His thumb was rubbing the skin on the underside of her jaw, as if he was testing for an answer to the question he had asked earlier, and his fingers beneath her hair were hard against her nape. It was strange, she thought bemusedly, how his hands were so hard, while hers were so soft. Everything about him was hard and masculine, and she had the craziest urge to lean into him and feel his hardness right down her body...

'Cole, I think—I think we should go into the other room,' she stammered, as the realisation of what was happening to her brought her briefly to her senses. 'I—I could make us something to eat——'

'I've got something to eat,' retorted Cole huskily, bending his head to stroke his tongue from a point just below her ear to the curve of shoulder he was exposing. He tipped off the strap of her dungarees, and slipped his hand into the neckline of her shirt. 'God, you taste good,' he muttered, taking a tender circle of flesh between his teeth and tugging it into his mouth. 'So good...'

Joanna trembled. All the juices in her body seemed to be melting and expanding, rising to the surface of her skin and dissolving her resistance. She knew she was going to have a bruise on her neck later, but there was nothing she could do about it. Her senses were blinding her to everything but the needs he was building inside her, and her eyes closed instinctively, shutting out the world.

He pulled her against him, his hand finding the swollen fullness of her breast. The engorged aureole surged against his palm, and he rubbed its sensitive tip urgently. Then he lowered his head and dragged the aching nipple into his mouth.

Joanna's legs sagged. Like a drowning woman now, she wrapped her arms around him, and pressed her face against his chest. His shirt was half open, and the hair that clustered in the V was rough against her cheek. But the scent of his skin was heavenly, and she opened her mouth wide to taste his fragrance.

Cole moved into her then, imprisoning her against the wall behind her, and jerking her mouth up to his. His hungry tongue surged into her mouth, fierce and possessive, and his jeans-clad thigh was insistent as it eased its way between her legs. His assault was demanding, but sweetly sensual. And nothing had prepared Joanna for her own need to respond.

This couldn't be happening, she told herself in one lucid moment, when the coolness of the air around her thighs warned her that her dungarees were in a heap around her ankles. Cole had flipped the other strap from her shoulder, and the loose-fitting overalls had slipped cleanly down her body. Now his hands were cupping her rounded bottom as he tugged her even closer, and not even the tight-fitting denim could hide his huge arousal.

But what troubled her most was her own willingness to give in to him. The firm pressure of his mouth and the sensuous invasion of his tongue were becoming as important to her as breathing. Innocent she might be, ignorant even, of the many forms of sexuality. But her instincts were all rebellious, and her blood felt as if it was on fire. The touch of his hands against her bare flesh; the musky scent of his body. She could think of nothing more desirable than to feel his naked flesh against hers. And, acting without thinking, she tentatively touched the bulge of his erection.

'Oh, *God*!'

Cole's reaction was—not entirely unexpectedly—violent. When her slim artist's fingers strayed along the straining teeth of his zip, he visibly shuddered. With a burning impatience, he sloughed off his belt and tore open his jeans. Then, he took her down on to the floor in the same instant that his hard manhood surged into her hands.

'God, you're beautiful!' he muttered, cradling her head on one arm, and using the other to peel away her shirt. And, although common sense was telling her she must not let this go any further, the admiration in his eyes was an overpowering temptation.

Besides, her curiosity about him was just as compelling. Probably more so, she admitted, looking down at his magnificent body. It was the first time she had seen a man naked and aroused, and even though he had only bared his sex its rampant power was mesmerising.

Cole's head blocked her view, as he bent to lay a trail of kisses from the tip of one breast to the hollow of her navel. His forefinger hooked into the band of her bikini briefs, tugging them out of his way, and then his mouth concluded its journey in the moist curls that hid her womanhood.

She jerked then, her inexperienced limbs responding to the fever he was creating. Her legs splayed, and then she clamped them tight together. Dear God, she thought disbelievingly, did she want him to think she was cheap? But, in spite of all her misgivings, Cole eased her legs apart again. While his tongue searched the helpless cavern of her mouth, his finger slid inside her, finding the dew-drenched honeycomb, and the sensitive bud of her sex.

Her eyes, which had drifted shut, now opened in alarm, but Cole's expression was sensuous, revealing he was just as involved as she was. And she relaxed as she looked at him, revelling in the knowledge that he found her beautiful. He was beautiful, too; beautiful and sexy. She wanted him to go on touching her, and she shuddered at the needs he was arousing.

'Do it,' he said huskily, and she realised he could read her thoughts as well. 'Here.' He took one of her trembling hands and laid it on him. 'Yes, that's right. You're a natural. Oh, God, Jo, I want you. And I don't think I can wait any longer.'

CHAPTER NINE

'GOD, Jo, you should have told me!'

Cole lay beside her on the cool tiles of the kitchen floor, one arm raised across his eyes, and the other lying by his side. It was funny, Joanna thought, but she could never have imagined she would lose her virginity in such unlikely surroundings. When she had occasionally daydreamed about how it would happen, a bed had always been involved. A bed; and champagne; and a rather fetching négligé.

'It doesn't matter,' she said now, wondering if he regretted it already. For herself, she hardly knew what she was feeling. It had been so much less—and yet so much more—than she had anticipated that she felt almost numb. She was shocked by what had happened, yes; but she was also anxious that it might never happen again.

And she wanted it to happen again, she knew that. Whatever kind of a disappointment it had been for Cole, she had experienced feelings she had not even dreamed were possible. He had invaded the limits of her sexuality, and time and place meant nothing, compared to the sensations that had gripped her.

Even now, she remembered every moment of his possession. The surging heat of his manhood, pressing its way inside her. The momentary withdrawal, when he had felt her inexperience. He had wanted to draw back then, she knew it. But her hands clutching his buttocks, and the undoubted invitation of her expanding muscles, had compelled him to go on. Besides, there was a limit to his endurance, she had guessed that for herself. He had wanted her. He had said so. And the aching fullness of his loins had demanded its own release.

But he had drawn back before his shuddering spasms informed her of his climax. And the mindless race inside her had come abruptly to its end. But, even though the little knowledge she possessed told her that there had to be more, she was inordinately grateful that it had been Cole who had taken her virginity. No other man had ever aroused the feelings inside her that he aroused, and, although she knew she ought to feel some measure of regret for what had happened, she didn't.

And, when he rolled on to his elbow to look down at her with rueful eyes, she felt no embarrassment for her nudity. On the contrary, if nothing else, Cole had taught her that she was beautiful, in his eyes at least, and she moved instinctively, unconsciously inviting his approval.

'It matters,' he said at last, but there was a sensual twist to his mouth as he bent to touch her lips with his. 'God, Jo, I've never done anything like this before.'

'Have you wanted to?' she asked, unknowingly pro-vocative, and he shook his head, the sweat-streaked blond hair brushing her sensitised skin.

'No,' he admitted gruffly, but when her arm curved around his neck he couldn't prevent the kiss from deepening.

This time, Joanna's tongue was the invader, teasing his lips and his tongue, until Cole lost control and drove down deep into her mouth. Joanna was overwhelmed with the need to get closer to him. Half experimentally, she coiled one leg about him, revelling in the way it brought the lower half of his body nearer to hers. Sud-denly, she could feel the rigid thrust of his hips, and the hairy tautness of his thigh riding against hers. But it was the muscles between his legs that strained against her. He was already hard again, she discovered. Hard and hot, and as satin-smooth as velvet against her stomach.

'We shouldn't do this,' he muttered, when her hand stroked possessively over his buttocks, and Joanna found the courage to look up at him.

'Why not?' she breathed. 'Don't you want to?' But her question became unimportant when he crushed her beneath him again. For Cole wasn't immune to the needs of his own body, and the readiness of hers was an irresistible temptation. She was wet with longings he had created, and her tight, resistant muscles closed eagerly about him.

Fever gripped Joanna's body. She was still aroused from their previous coupling, and the emotions she had felt before sprang into fervent life. Like an athlete who had faltered before the final hurdle, her body was eager to redress the balance, and when Cole's rhythm quickened she matched him pace for pace.

And, in so doing, she found her own senses slipping away. A mindless pleasure was encompassing her limbs, melting her bones, drowning her inhibitions. She wasn't aware of making any sound at all, yet she could hear gasps, and moans, and anguished pleas escaping her lips.

'Say it's good,' Cole breathed against her temple, and the voice that answered him sounded nothing like her own. It was soft, and husky, and incredibly sensual, and Cole's satisfaction took him even deeper inside her.

'Yes, yes,' she cried, her nails digging into his shoulders, and the wild excitement that had been building and expanding inside her became unbearably sweet. And then it happened. A pulsing wave of pure pleasure enveloped her, sweeping her up and up, until she was half afraid she was going to lose consciousness, and she didn't want that. She didn't want to lose a moment of such incredible beauty, and when Cole would have drawn back she wrapped her legs around him. The flooding heat as he spilled himself inside her just added to her enjoyment, and this time when his body shook she held him close to her breast.

Of course, afterwards, after Cole had gone, and she was alone, Joanna was appalled at the wanton way she had acted. That she, who had always regarded herself as being totally self-possessed, should have lost control so completely was bad enough. But that she should have done so with a man she had known less than twenty-four hours seemed almost indecent. He would think she had been desperate to lose her virginity, she thought, and for days after that she refused to answer either the telephone or the doorbell, in case it shouldn't be him. She had convinced herself he wouldn't want to contact her again, and she submerged herself in her work to the exclusion of everything else.

Eventually, it was Grace who smoked her out; Grace who informed her that, far from not wanting to see her again, Cole had been practically going out of his head with worry, because he couldn't reach her. And, because he was sure Joanna must blame him for what had happened, he had confided in his aunt, and asked for her assistance.

Later, Joanna had understood what it must have cost him to approach Grace. When she learned more about him, and about his background, she had realised how galling it must have been for Ryan Macallister's son to ask a woman for anything, particularly someone his father both disliked and despised.

But, at the time, she had been too overwhelmed by Cole's interest in her to consider how his family might react to another Englishwoman in their midst. She and Cole had seen one another every day, and their relationship just got better and better. So much so that Cole delayed his return to South Carolina long enough to persuade her to marry him.

Of course, Grace had had misgivings, and she had voiced them. The Macallisters were a very close family, she said. They weren't like Joanna's parents, who had taken to Cole from the start. On top of which, Tidewater was another world, with its own laws, and its own traditions. She hadn't been happy there, and she didn't know if Joanna would be, particularly as Cole was just as possessive as his uncle.

But Joanna hadn't wanted to listen, even though the only arguments she and Cole had were about her work. He resented the time she devoted to it and not to him, and, although she was convinced that once they were married it wouldn't be a problem, it was a complication she had foolishly ignored.

The wedding was planned for the end of June, and Cole had flown home to give his family the news. But when he had flown back again, only a couple of days before the wedding, not one of his family had come with him. 'They couldn't leave the plantation,' he had said, his face reddening. His younger brother and sisters were still in school, and there was simply too much to do, particularly since he was away, too.

And Joanna, not wanting to embarrass him any further, had accepted his excuses. But Grace had had no such reservations. The night before the wedding, she had warned Joanna of what she might have to face at Tidewater, and if she hadn't been fathoms deep in love Joanna might have listened to her. As it was, she convinced herself that Grace was exaggerating, and the weeks immediately following their wedding were the happiest weeks she could remember.

But that had been while they were on honeymoon, she conceded drily. Cole had taken her to Tahiti, and during those exotic days and nights she had had no doubts that nothing and no one could come between them. They had been timeless days, when they had been drunk with each other's possession. Days of sun and happiness, and luscious, languid nights. Then they had returned to Tidewater.

To begin with, Joanna managed to convince herself that they would work it out. Even though his mother made no secret of her disapproval of the marriage, and his father was barely civil, she refused to lose heart. When they left the plantation house, and got a home of their own, she told herself, his parents' attitude wouldn't matter. In the meanwhile, it was up to her to try and make it friendly.

And, although Cole's parents could control his days, she controlled his nights. While the heat and the humidity of midsummer made other people terse and irritable, she and Cole continued to revel in those hot, sleepless nights. He taught her so much about her body, and she was a willing pupil. She learned that even the most unlikely areas could prove wildly erotic, and Cole spent hours tracing nerves and sensitive pulses, and setting them on fire with his tongue. Their lovemaking just got better and better, and she responded to his demands with all the urgency of her youth.

But, ironically enough, it was that very eagerness to prove herself that sowed the seeds of her destruction. In trying to avoid conflict, Joanna only joined the family for meals if Cole was going to be there. She had found her skin was too thin to withstand the barbs and insults his father threw around when he wasn't, and she was too proud to tell Cole what they were doing to her.

Besides, what could she have said? Cole himself admitted she wasn't used to the kind of life they led at Tidewater, and he would be the first to agree that she was much softer than the southern women he was used to. And to complain that his mother regarded any efforts she made to help around the house with contempt would hardly arouse his indignation. He would probably have wondered why she cared, without understanding how important it was for Joanna to find her own space.

Even their own rooms were not sacrosanct. Maggie thought nothing of coming into their bedroom without knocking, except when she knew her son was there. Flowers were rearranged; furniture Joanna had altered was replaced; and even her closet was not free from his mothers' influence. Favourite dresses went missing; shirts she especially liked developed unexplained tears, or lost buttons; and any time she wore anything at all provocative, she was made to feel so cheap that she started buying clothes that didn't show her shape.

Just thinking about it now made Joanna feel physically sick. Gradually, over a period of time, they had caused her to doubt herself, and her own sanity, and once that happened she was on a downward spiral.

But that had come later—after the illness, which had caused the first faint cracks to appear in their relationship. Because of the heat, and because she was neither eating nor sleeping enough, those long passionate nights took their toll. A chill developed quickly into pneumonia, and while she was weak and helpless Cole's parents took their chance.

By the time she was lucid enough to know what was happening, Cole's belongings had been moved into another suite of rooms entirely. His mother had only been thinking of her, he said, when Joanna grew strong enough to offer her objections. There was no way he could have continued to share her room without disturbing her. And they all wanted to do their best, so that she would soon be well again.

It was a reasonable excuse, and one with which Cole evidently agreed, but Joanna was uneasy. She was more uneasy still, when Ryan Macallister set up a business trip for Cole to South America, thus delaying his return to her bed even longer. In other circumstances, Cole assured her, she could have gone with him. But as she had been so ill . . .

The night before he went away, she had tried to talk to him about their future. When were they going to get a home of their own? she pleaded. They'd been married more than three months now, and it was time she started looking after her husband herself.

Cole had avoided a direct answer, she remembered. Now was not the time for her to start worrying about things like that, he said. She needed to get her strength back. Better she leave the housekeeping to his mother for the time being. If he remembered correctly, domestic duties had never been her strong point.

He was away a month, and, although she spoke to him frequently on the telephone, by the time he came back, things had changed. Joanna supposed she had been partly responsible for that change, but how could she have known what her innocent befriending of Nathan Smith would stir up? At the time, she had just been desperate for some stimulating adult conversation.

She sighed. Perhaps she had been naïve, she pondered. It wasn't as if all the Macallisters had been hostile. Ben and Joe had been quite friendly, so long as their father wasn't around; and the twins, especially Charley, had developed quite a crush on their new sister-in-law. And there was Sandy—though he had been too young to really count.

But, perhaps because she was becoming so sensitive to any criticism levelled at her, Joanna never felt entirely relaxed around the house. She had done very little sketching or painting since she left England, so now, once again, she endeavoured to submerge her unhappiness in her work. There was certainly plenty of scope for an artist among the vivid varieties of trees and shrubs about the plantation, and she took to taking her sketch book with her every time she went for a walk.

Although she never ventured too far from the house, she became familiar with the stables, and the paddocks, and the salt marshes beyond. She often curled up beside the river, lulled by the gentle music of the water, or scrambled over the mud-flats at low tide, in search of shells. Although her olive skin never tanned, it grew sun-warmed and healthy, and her hair grew long and wind-tossed, accentuating her gypsy appearance.

And, during this time, it never occurred to her not to be familiar with the workers on the plantation. The grooms around the stables, the hands who exercised the horses, even the maids in the house, all benefited from her friendly disposition. She didn't think it had been a conscious effort to oppose Cole's father and mother. It was just her way. But she never, ever dreamed where her attitude might lead her.

Nathan didn't work on the plantation. Although she didn't know that the morning she surprised him on the river-bank. He had been leaning out over the river, trailing his hand in the water, and at that time it was doubtful which of them had been the most shocked by the encounter.

But when he jumped to his feet, with the evident intention of leaving, Joanna had stopped him. 'What were you doing?' she asked, tucking her sketch pad under her arm, and stepping across the grassy bank towards him. She looked down into the water, but could see nothing of value. 'Did you drop something?'

Nathan shook his head. He was a handsome young man, with dark curly hair, brown skin, and the broad nose and full mouth that spoke of a mixed heritage. Joanna assumed he lived in the shacks that bordered the estate to the west. Many of the workers lived in the shacks at Palmer's Point, and Cole had said that he and his father were planning on re-housing the families. However, after listening to Ryan Macallister's views on his poorer employees, and learning of his contempt for people who had more children than they could afford, Joanna was less convinced. She had the feeling that, whatever Cole said, his father was not as committed as his son.

'So what were you doing?' she asked now, and although the young man would have obviously preferred to avoid answering he stood his ground.

'Tickling fish,' he said, his lean features taking on a rueful expression. 'I wasn't taking many. Only one or two.'

Joanna shook her head. 'You mean—you can actually catch fish that way?' she exclaimed. Then she saw the brace of trout resting on a broad palmetto leaf, and smiled. 'I see you can.'

Nathan expelled his breath on a long sigh. 'You must be Cole's wife,' he said, and she wondered why he looked so rueful when he said it. She didn't flatter herself that she was the reason for his discontent. But his tone was intriguing, and she determined to get to the bottom of it.

So, 'Yes,' she agreed, holding out her hand towards him. 'I'm Joanna Macallister. Who're you?'

His hesitation was only noticeable because she was aware of it. 'Nathan,' he said, after a moment.

'Nathan—Smith.' He shook her hand with some reluctance, and she wondered why. 'But I wish you wouldn't tell anyone you'd seen me here.'

Joanna frowned. 'Because of the fish?' she exclaimed. 'Oh, I'm sure——'

'Because I shouldn't be on the property,' Nathan cut in swiftly. 'I know it's asking a lot, but I'd appreciate it.'

Joanna blinked. 'You don't work for my husband or his father, then?'

'No.'

'But you know them. You knew I was Cole's wife.'

'Everyone knows that,' replied Nathan drily. Then, with a rueful glance about him, 'I think I'd better go.'

Joanna caught her lip between her teeth. 'Not on my account,' she protested. 'I won't tell anyone you were here.' She grimaced, remembering. 'There's no one to tell. Cole's away, and I'm not exactly on the best of terms with his mother and father.'

Nathan hesitated. 'Look, you don't know me. You don't know anything about me.' He pulled a wry face. 'I could be a murderer or a rapist, for all you know.'

Joanna regarded him consideringly. 'You have an honest face,' she said, and then, seeing the faint smile that tilted the corners of his mouth, she added, 'I'm prepared to take the risk, if you are. Why don't you show me what you were doing? Perhaps I could learn to catch fish, too.'

And that was how she and Nathan had become friends, she brooded painfully. A chance meeting, and suddenly she was embroiled in a situation she hadn't even known existed. Would Nathan still be alive, if she hadn't persuaded him to stay? It was entirely possible. But Nathan's life had always been in jeopardy, long before she came on the scene.

Still, in the months that followed, they did become close friends. He was interested in her painting, and encouraged her not to neglect her talent. And she found his knowledge of the area's history both informative and fascinating, and she was not at all surprised to learn that he taught at the Baptist school in Beaumaris.

But, these superficial facts aside, she learned very little about his personal life. He told her he was unmarried, and lived with his widowed mother in Beaumaris, but that was all. He wouldn't talk about the Macallisters, or why a feud should exist between them. He spoke of Cole, and Joe, and Ben, but they were not friends of his. If he had any friends, she never heard about them, and because she was lonely, too, she accepted his isolation quite gratefully.

At this time, her relationship with Cole was deteriorating rapidly. She didn't know why, but since his return from Argentina her husband had become increasingly remote. She knew he resented the fact that she had started sketching again, but it was more than that. And whenever she broached the subject of moving into a home of their own his only answer was that the plantation house was big enough for all of them.

It was certainly big enough for him to continue sleeping in a separate bedroom, she reflected bitterly, remembering the arguments they had about that. Cole's only excuse was that as he got up early in the morning and went to bed much later than she did at night he didn't want to disturb her. But Joanna guessed it was his mother's and father's idea. Another way to keep them apart.

A continuing source of conflict was Joanna's failure to conceive. Cole might occupy a different room, but he still came to her bed several times a week. She suspected it was a weakness he wished he could conquer, and because he could be so mean to her at other times she sometimes fought against his possession. But he always overcame her efforts. The feverish mating of their bodies had lost none of its fervour; it was totally obsessive to both of them, and even Cole couldn't deny the hunger in his blood.

Nevertheless, as the months went by and she didn't get pregnant, Cole became suspicious. Obviously his doubts had been fuelled by the things his parents implied, and she found him one day searching her bedside drawers for contraceptives. Her anger at finding him there was overwhelming, and more than erased any advantage she might have gained because his search had proved unsuccessful. But his parting comment, that she probably hid them somewhere else, was the final straw. That night, she locked her door against him, refusing to answer when he hammered on the panels. She even locked the balcony doors and closed the shutters, preferring the airless atmosphere to the shameful demands of her flesh.

Looking back now, she saw how foolishly she had played into Ryan Macallister's hands. Cole was a proud man. He wouldn't beg her to unlock her door. What had begun as an angry revolt against his lack of faith in her quickly accelerated into a full-blown separation. In a matter of days, she and Cole were acting like strangers around one another. And, before she could pluck up the courage to speak to him, something happened that altered her mind irrevocably.

The past few months might not have been the most happy time in her life, but she had always believed that, because she and Cole still had such a good sexual relationship, sooner or later their problems would be resolved. If she hadn't believed that, she couldn't have continued in the marriage. But Cole still loved her; she was sure of it. And, in time, he would see it her way.

She had been given the use of an old station wagon, mainly, she suspected, because it enabled her to take the younger children to school, when no one else was available. But it did give her a certain amount of freedom, and she and Charley often went into Beaumaris at weekends, to potter about the small stores, and watch the fishing boats coming and going from the harbour. Of all the Macallisters, apart from Cole, she liked Charley best. The little girl had become her shadow since the incident in the spring, when Joanna had played such a crucial part in rescuing her from the island in the river, where they had been picnicking. Their row-boat had come adrift, and Joanna had had to swim to the shore to get help. It had been a near thing, and for a while afterwards she and Cole seemed to get close again. But subsequent events, particularly the incident over the contraceptives, had destroyed their understanding, and when Joanna drove into Beaumaris that Saturday morning she was still mulling over ways to make amends.

And then she saw Cole.

He was parked in the centre of town, right where she usually parked, leaning against the bonnet of the dust-smeared pick-up he invariably drove, laughing with a blonde in a hot pink jump-suit.

Joanna had thought he was exercising the horses with Ben. He had gone out earlier that morning, and that was what his mother had told her, when she had asked where he was. But it was obvious from his dress shirt and well-cut trousers that he had never had any intention of going riding.

'Hell!'

Charley's unguarded exclamation echoed the reaction Joanna was feeling. The girl was flirting with Cole now, finger-walking up his shirt, and arching her body towards him. There was a wealth of confidence and intimacy in her attitude, and Joanna's stomach hollowed at the obvious explanation.

But Charley's behaviour could at least provide her with half an answer. 'Who is she?' she asked stiffly, and Charley stifled a groan.

'Sammy-Jean Butler,' she muttered reluctantly, pursing up her face. 'Damn, what's he doing with *her*?'

Trying not to sound as sick as she felt, Joanna tried to make light of it. 'Who knows?' she said, stepping on the brakes, and turning the station wagon into a spot several yards from where her husband was standing. 'It looks as if they just ran into one another.' She wet her lips. 'Is she an old girlfriend?'

Charley hunched her shoulders. 'I guess.'

'Well, is she, or isn't she?'

Charley sniffed. 'Ma and Pa wanted Cole to marry her one time,' she admitted. 'See, the Butlers' place is next to Tidewater, and Pa and Mr Butler used to talk about how good it would be if Cole and Sammy-Jean…'

Joanna remembered how hard it had been for her to get out of the station wagon after that, to go and speak to her husband. And, when she found the pick-up wasn't there any more, she didn't know whether to be glad or sorry. But it served a bitter purpose. She knew she would never trust Cole again.

CHAPTER TEN

CHARLEY came to find Joanna as soon as she got home from school. Her knock at the bedroom door was reminiscent of other occasions, when the girl had spent more time with her sister-in-law than she did with the other members of her family. But in those days Joanna had sought comfort from her. Now, it was Charley who needed commiseration.

'Donna's a bitch!' she declared, after Joanna had let her into the bedroom and resumed drying her hair in front of the mirror. 'Twins are supposed to support one another, aren't they?' Her jaw jutted. 'She just enjoys causing me aggravation!'

Joanna turned off the drier, and regarded her visitor with sympathetic eyes. 'Cool down,' she said. 'It's too hot to get so riled up over anything. What did Donna do, for heaven's sake? Steal your boyfriend?'

'Worse than that!' exclaimed Charley, flinging herself down on the end of the bed, and staring broodingly at the carpet. 'She's just gone and told Ma that Billy and me are going steady.'

'Oh.' Joanna wrapped the silk dressing-gown she had slipped on after her shower closer about her slim figure. 'I see.'

'Is that all you can say?' cried Charley, her eyes wide and indignant. 'Ma's grounded me for the next month, and she says if I try to see Billy again she'll get Pa to throw him out of Palmer's Point.'

Joanna's mouth tightened. Ryan Macallister was good at that, she thought contemptuously. He was good at destroying people's lives. Look what he'd done to Sarah!

117

'Did you talk with Cole yet?' Charley was asking now, and Joanna put her own grievances aside to answer the girl.

She shook her head. 'Charley, I only arrived yesterday.'

'Did you talk to Pa, then? Did he tell you why he wanted to see you?'

'I've spoken to him, yes.'

'And?'

Joanna sighed. 'Charley, I'd rather not talk about that right now.' She paused, and then added, 'Look, I will tell Cole what's happened. But I can't make any promises.'

Charley pushed herself up from the bed. 'You won't need to *tell* Cole,' she muttered. 'Leave it to Ma to do that. I just hoped you'd had a chance to talk with him before it all came out. Damn, what am I going to do? I love Billy. I can't give him up.'

Joanna moved to put her arm around the girl. 'Don't lose heart,' she said. And then, because she understood only too well how Charley was feeling, she went on, 'As I say, I can't promise anything, but there might be something I can do. Leave it with me. And don't you do anything stupid.'

'I won't.' Charley gazed at her hopefully. 'I saw the way Cole was looking at you last night. He's still stuck on you, isn't he? Gee, no wonder Sammy-Jean never stood a chance.'

'What do you mean?'

Joanna knew she shouldn't have asked the question, but she simply couldn't help it, and Charley smirked. 'Come on,' she said. 'I heard Ben telling you, things haven't been the same around here since you walked out.'

'Oh.' Joanna wondered why she suddenly felt so deflated. 'Well, as I say, I'll do what I can about you and Billy. Now, I think you'd better go. I've got to get ready for dinner.'

Tonight, Joanna decided to wear loose-fitting silk cut-offs that allowed the air to flow freely around her legs. They were tan, and combined attractively with the cream and gold box jacket she chose to wear with them. The jacket had a high neck, with an upstanding Chinese collar, and because of its brevity it occasionally exposed an inch of olive skin around her midriff. Her earrings were gold again, beaten squares of metal that accentuated the slenderness of her neck. And she swept her hair up into a loose knot, allowing several strands of midnight silk to droop beside her ears.

To her surprise, the library was empty when she went down. Of course, she was a little earlier than the night before, and it was possible she was the only person dining at home. Apart from Cole's father, of course, but there was no guarantee that he would join her. In any event, Joanna decided to help herself to a drink. She'd had nothing but tap water since lunchtime, and she felt she needed some stimulant to get her through the evening ahead. Even if she had to spend it alone, she consoled herself grimly. There was something about this place that always put her nerves on edge.

The drinks cabinet had been replenished, after the night before, and her hand hovered over the whiskey for a moment, before moving on to the wine. Better she keep her wits about her, just in case, she thought drily. No one was going to accuse her of over-imbibing these days.

She was raising the glass of wine to her lips when she realised she was no longer alone. While she had been concentrating on not spilling any of the wine over the polished surface of the cabinet, Cole had come to stand in the doorway. With his shoulder propped against the jamb, he was watching her actions with narrowed eyes, and when Joanna became aware of him she felt a moment's regret.

He looked so attractive standing there, his hair damp and still clinging to his head after his shower. The water had darkened its silvery-blond strands, casting an artificial shadow across his face, and, in spite of the fact that he had shaved, a glistening of bristle lay over his jawline. He was wearing navy trousers and a roll-necked cotton sweater in a lighter shade of blue. The heat never seemed to bother him, Joanna reflected, but of course he was used to it. And then, part of the heat she was feeling was self-induced, brought on by the unwilling memory of her thoughts that afternoon.

'All alone?' she enquired, going on the old adage that it was easier to attack than defend. 'Can I get you a drink?' She held up her glass. 'The wine's very good. I can recommend it.'

Cole said nothing, but he straightened from his lounging position and came across the room towards her. However, although her skin prickled, and all her pulses set up a wild tattoo, he didn't touch her. Instead, he lifted the bourbon bottle and poured himself a generous measure over ice, swallowing a mouthful before acknowledging her comments.

He smelt good, too, she noticed, the scent of the soap he had been using drifting to her nostrils. She could even smell the heat of his skin, clean, and faintly musky, and incredibly masculine...

God! She brought herself up there, forcing herself to remember where she was. As the realisation of what she was thinking—and what it was doing to her—swept over her in mindless waves, she saw the yawning pit she was digging for herself. He was her ex-husband, for pity's sake! Not someone of critical importance in her life. And she had come to know his scent as well as her own, so— big deal! She could live with that. She took a breath. She had to.

'We'll be dining alone,' he said, as she struggled to assume a casual demeanour, and she wondered whose idea that was. Not his mother's, she was sure. Maggie would never condone such a suggestion.

'I see,' she murmured, her brows arching inquisitively, and, as if sensing a sarcasm she was far from feeling, Cole went on,

'Yes.' He paused. 'Ma, Sandy and the twins are having supper at Joe's. And—Ben has a date this evening.'

'Really?' Giving herself time to think, Joanna took another sip of wine. 'I thought Charley was grounded.'

Cole frowned. 'Grounded?'

Joanna considered quickly. She had no wish to involve Charley yet. Not until she had had a chance to sound out the situation. 'I—it's not important,' she said. Then, tilting her head, 'Will your father be joining us?'

'Not tonight.' Cole's mouth compressed, and he turned to pour more bourbon into his glass.

'Oh?' Joanna moistened her lips. 'Why not? He's not——'

'Worse?' Cole swung around, cradling his glass between his strong fingers. 'Do you care?'

Joanna endeavoured to remain unmoved. 'I hardly think your mother would be spending the evening at Joe's, if he was in any danger,' she replied smoothly, and Cole assumed an irritated expression.

'No,' he said after a moment. 'No, you're right, of course. He's no worse and no better than he was. But——' the word was heavy with meaning '—he thinks it would be a good idea if we—talked to one another.'

Now Joanna understood. But, 'Talked?' she queried, with just the right amount of confusion in her voice. 'What about?'

Cole's jaw hardened. 'What do you think?'

'I don't know, do I?'

He grunted. 'He wants us to—reconcile——'

'Reconcile!' Now Joanna couldn't keep the disbelief out of her voice. 'You mean, he wants us to get together again?'

'No!' Cole swore. 'Not that. He's ill, but he's not senile!' He expelled his breath on a harsh sigh. 'No, he simply wants us to try and heal our differences; to be— civil—with one another again.'

Joanna stared at him. 'Why?'

'Why?' Cole had obviously thought of this himself, but he didn't have an answer for her. 'I—why do you think? He's sick. Near to death. People who are dying sometimes have these crazy ideas. I guess he wants to— to——'

'Salve his own conscience?' suggested Joanna silkily, and Cole's face suffused with angry colour.

'You would say that, wouldn't you?' he snarled. 'I should have known better than to hope you'd show some compassion.'

Joanna shrugged. 'Maybe you should,' she agreed, putting down her glass. She had suddenly lost all taste for the wine. 'Or perhaps you should learn to have some compassion yourself.'

'What's that supposed to mean?'

Joanna hesitated. 'You haven't asked me why your father wanted to see me.'

Cole's mouth flattened. 'I know why. I've just told you why.'

'No, you haven't.'

He scowled. 'Stop bulling me, Jo. You know damn well how hard this is for me—for both of us. Don't— don't make it any worse by lying about it.'

Joanna felt a moment's indignation, but it passed. 'I'm not lying,' she said. 'Your father doesn't care if we hate each other's guts! My God, he and your mother did what they could to bring that about. Why should he feel any differently now? I'm still the foreigner! The outsider! The unwanted intruder, who spoiled all the plans your daddy had for you!'

'That's history, Jo. Let it go. It's not as if you made any attempt to fit in here. I don't remember you doing much else but moan about this place. You didn't like the way we lived, the way we treated the workers, the lack of health care on the estate.' He shook his head. 'No, all you did was cause trouble.'

'My, oh, my!' Joanna brought her hands together in a slow clap. 'You're learning, Cole. I could almost believe that was your daddy talking.'

'Shut up!'

'No. Why should I?' Joanna was keeping her anger in check by a supreme effort. 'It's the truth. Tell me, when are you Macallisters going to realise this is the twentieth century?'

Cole took a step towards her, but, whatever his intentions had been, the appearance of a maid, to inform them that supper was waiting, forestalled him.

'Right, Sally, we'll be right there,' he muttered, and, swallowing the remainder of the whiskey in his glass, he gestured for Joanna to precede him out of the room. And she did so, uneasily aware of her ex-husband's grim presence behind her.

Supper was served in a high-ceilinged salon, where a pair of revolving fans endeavoured to keep the air circulating. It was where they had all eaten the night before, but this evening only two places were set at the long polished table. Predictably, Cole sat in the chair his father had occupied the night previously, with Joanna at his right hand. It was nearer than she would have liked, but at least they weren't sitting opposite one another. She didn't know how she would have coped with such an unguarded appraisal.

As it was, she endeavoured to concentrate on her food, and her surroundings, to the exclusion of all else. She needed time to consider how she was going to proceed, and it didn't help that Cole had his own preconceived ideas of why she was here. The trouble was, she didn't know what she was going to do. She had forgotten how it was here. Somehow, the heat sapped her powers of reasoning. What had appeared so cut and dried in Nassau no longer seemed so easy.

Looking at him out of the corners of her eyes, as he attacked the chunky fish soup, and quail stuffed with cornbread, she wondered why she didn't just tell Ryan Macallister to do his own dirty work, and get out of there. She didn't want to stay. And it was obvious Cole didn't want her here. She didn't owe his father anything. Nothing good, at least.

'Do you ever see Sarah?' she asked abruptly, knowing it would antagonise him, but reckless none the less. Anything to rid herself of this feeling that she was weakening. She had to remember exactly what he'd done.

Cole put down his fork, and reached for the glass of wine beside his plate. 'Why?' he asked, after rinsing his palate. 'What relevance does that have to this situation?'

Joanna bit her lip. 'I'd like to know if she's all right.'

'She is.'

'And Henry?'

'I've told you. Henry still works in the stables.'

Joanna shook her head. 'How can he?'

'How can't he? He still has to live. He earns enough to keep himself and his mother at Tidewater.'

'Conscience money!'

She was scathing, and a nerve jerked in Cole's cheek. 'May I remind you that Henry worked at Tidewater long before you knew anything about his brother? He likes the work. He's good with horses.'

'There are other places——'

'Not for someone like Henry,' retorted Cole savagely. 'For God's sake, what would you have us do? Deprive him of his chance to have some self-respect? If, as you say, you think it's conscience money, think about how he'd live if he didn't come to Tidewater. In any case, it's what Sarah wants. Now, will you give it a rest?'

Joanna took a steadying breath. 'Why don't you want me to see Sarah?'

Cole closed his eyes for a moment. 'Why do you think?'

'I don't know, do I? I'm asking you.'

Cole hesitated. 'All right. In words of one syllable, she doesn't want to see you.'

Joanna gasped. 'I don't believe you.'

'Nevertheless, it's the truth.'

Joanna shook her head. 'I don't understand.'

'Try. Your presence here can only bring back unhappy memories for her.'

'It does?' Joanna winced. 'Does she—does she hate me?'

'No!' Cole was impatient. 'Sarah doesn't hate anyone.'

'Not even your father?'

'Not even him,' declared Cole flatly. 'You know Sarah. She doesn't have a vindictive bone in her body. Now— why don't you stop thinking everyone's your enemy, and try and enjoy your time here?'

Joanna licked her lips. 'With you, you mean?' she ventured, her pulses suddenly racing, and Cole's expression tightened.

'If that's what it takes,' he said guardedly. 'I brought you here. I guess I have to take my share of the responsibility.'

'Gee, thanks.'

Joanna was sarcastic, but she still couldn't control the quickening rate of her heartbeat. A few days with Cole, she mused, with some nervousness. Was that what she really wanted? What she could handle? And was she going to plead his father's case, or was she going to allow him to go on thinking that all his father wanted was some cosy reconciliation?

Cole had picked up his fork again, but, from the way he was pushing the meat and peas around his plate, food was the last thing on his mind. After a few moments, he threw the fork down again, and wiped his mouth on his napkin.

'Tomorrow,' he said, and she knew the words were being dragged out of him, 'tomorrow, we'll take a ride out to Palmer's Point.' He paused. 'There's something you might like to see.'

'What?' Joanna's eyes were curious.

'You'll find out,' he said, pushing back his chair, and getting up from the table. 'Now, if you'll excuse me, I have work to do.'

'Work?' Joanna looked sceptically towards the inky darkness outside, where fireflies and huge, hairy moths clustered against the window-pane. 'What work?'

'Paperwork,' Cole informed her briefly, nodding to the maid to come and clear. 'Someone has to run Tidewater, now that my father isn't able to do it. Mary-Lou will get you anything else you want. I'll see you in the morning.'

He was walking towards the door when another thought occurred to her. Turning her head, she said, 'Cole!' and, with a perceptible stiffening of his shoulders, he halted in the doorway.

'Yes?'

'What time in the morning?' she asked innocently, twining a strand of silky dark hair about her fingers as she spoke, and Cole's eyes narrowed.

'Seven,' he stated harshly, slapping one hand against the jamb, and, without waiting for any response, he strode out of the room.

Joanna was walking along the upper corridor to her room when she heard a whispering sound behind her. For a moment, it unnerved her. She hadn't heard a door open, or anyone call her name, and because the lamps that lit the landing were few, and inclined to flicker, she knew a moment's panic. The old house was like that. Boards creaked; shutters banged; and just occasionally the electricity failed altogether.

She swung round, half prepared to face whatever demon was pursuing her, and then caught her breath at the sight of Ryan Macallister, following her in his wheelchair.

'Did I scare you?' he asked, in a low voice, and she knew damn well he knew he had. But she refused to give him that satisfaction.

'Is that how you get your kicks these days, Mr Macallister?' she asked, keeping her voice steady and adopting a provocative stance. She tipped her head, and rested one hand on her hip. 'And here I was thinkin' y'all had turned over a new leaf!'

If her words, and the way they were delivered, angered him, he did an admirable job of hiding his feelings. Instead, he wheeled himself closer, so that if she had chosen to stretch out her leg she could have touched the foot-rest. Then, looking up into her guarded features, he demanded, 'Did you do it?'

Joanna took a step back. It was an involuntary movement, an automatic recoil from the avidity of his expression. He didn't frighten her, but he did disturb her, and tonight she was in no state to counter his belligerence.

'Did I do what?' she responded now, guessing that pretending ignorance was the only way to thwart him. 'I had dinner with Cole, if that's what you mean. You should have joined us. The quail was——'

'Goddammit, don't mess with me, girl!' Ryan's voice rose in concert with his fury, and he cast an impatient glance over his shoulder. Then, calming himself with an evident effort, he added harshly, 'You know what I'm talking about. Did you talk to him? Did you tell him what I told you?'

'We've talked.' Joanna thought about prevaricating, but she found she didn't have the energy—or the enthusiasm. 'That's all I can tell you.'

'What about?' Ryan's jaw clamped.

'This and that.' Joanna sighed. 'Now, if you don't mind, I'd like to go into my room. I'm tired.'

'Dammit, I know you and Cole talked about Nathan,' Ryan blustered angrily. 'Hannibal heard you asking about Henry, and Cole saying something about Sarah not blaming anyone for Nathan's death——'

'You had Hannibal spy on us?' broke in Joanna disbelievingly, her disgust at the act tempered by her sympathy for Ryan's elderly valet. Hannibal had been at Tidewater since before Ryan was born, and his loyalty to his employer had never been in doubt.

'Not all the time,' muttered Cole's father irritably, but there was no remorse in the words. 'The old fool's half deaf anyway. But don't you try to bluff me, girl. I always know what's going on in this house.'

'Then you won't need me to tell you, will you?' retorted Joanna shortly, and, thrusting open her door, she slammed into the room.

CHAPTER ELEVEN

JOANNA half thought he might try to follow her, but he didn't. Even though she lay back against the closed panels for several minutes, ready to resist if he should try to force his way inside, there was no further intrusion. Evidently Cole's father had decided he had said enough for one night. He had startled her, and attempted to intimidate her, and finally told her she was being spied on. What else could he do?

When she eventually pushed herself away from the door, her movements were heavy and lethargic. It was all very well putting up a defiant front with the Macallisters, but there was no doubt it drained her emotionally. She had to be constantly alert, constantly on her guard. What a holiday, she reflected ruefully. She'd have had less stress white-water-rafting in the Rockies!

She undressed wearily, and after sluicing her face in the bathroom she crawled into bed. She just wanted to forget all about Cole and his family and go to sleep. Maybe tomorrow things would be clearer. Maybe tomorrow she'd find a reason for being here.

But sleep eluded her. She tossed and turned for hours, and eventually had to get up to go to the bathroom. Peering at her pale face in the mirror above the wash-basin as she rinsed her hands, she bemoaned the fact that she was going to look an absolute hag in the morning—when Cole took her riding to Palmer's Point.

She frowned. Why there? she brooded. The shacks at Palmer's Point had always been a bone of contention between them. And it was hardly a beauty spot, although it did overlook the mouth of the Tidewater River. It was where the Smiths had lived, before Adam died, and Ryan

Macallister found Sarah and her two sons a house in Beaumaris. And it was while Sarah was living at Palmer's Point that Ryan first noticed her.

Nathan's mother had been beautiful when Joanna knew her, and it didn't take much imagination to realise that at eighteen she must have been quite ravishing. With her sloe-dark eyes, and her tall, statuesque figure, she must have presented quite a challenge to the arrogant master of Tidewater.

Sarah and Adam had been married for three years, and their son, Henry, had been two years old, when Ryan first started taking an unnatural interest in the Smiths. Henry was already showing signs of slowness, of not being as bright as the other children who lived in the shacks, and Ryan used the boy's disability as a reason for visiting the family. He arranged for the boy to see a specialist, and insisted on escorting Sarah into Charleston himself. And he paid for the child to attend a special school, so that Henry could have a real chance of leading a normal life.

Of course, his reasons were not philanthropic. Ryan Macallister never did anything for anyone without demanding payment. And, although Sarah knew that what she was doing was wrong, she couldn't help being flattered by the older man's attentions. Besides, she consoled herself with the knowledge that he was helping Henry, and only when she found herself pregnant with the other man's child did the fear of how her husband would react when he found out compel her to confront Ryan with her dilemma.

To Ryan, the answer was simple. She must get rid of the baby. He would give her the money to have an abortion. He knew of a woman in Charleston who would do the deed, with no questions asked.

Sarah refused. She was hurt and anxious, but nothing would persuade her to do away with her baby. She would have the child, she said, and if Adam disowned her, so be it. She would get a job and support both her children. She would survive.

But something happened that made her worries about her pregnancy merely academic. Adam was killed—in a freak accident in the fields. He was run down by a mechanical picker, and in her grief at losing the man she had lived with for more than three years Sarah was once again vulnerable to Ryan's persuasion.

It was fairly easy for him to convince her that she wouldn't be happy, staying in the shack, which must contain so many upsetting memories. Instead, he set her up in a house in Beaumaris—far enough from Tidewater so that when her baby was born no one would associate it with him, and near enough so that he could continue to visit her on a regular basis.

Nathan had told Joanna this, when, heartbroken over Cole's behaviour, she had gone to him for support. Nathan had been the only person she could discuss Cole's unfaithfulness with. And, whether to comfort her, or to expunge some of the bitterness he still possessed, she never knew, but he told her the whole, unhappy story.

Joanna had been shocked, but not as shocked as she might have been before learning of Cole's unfaithfulness. And, in the weeks that followed, he took her to meet his mother, and she learned more. She discovered that Ryan still occasionally visited the house in Acacia Street. She discovered that in all these years Margaret Macallister had remained unaware of Nathan's existence. She learned that her father-in-law lived two distinct lives: one at Tidewater Plantation, and the other with his mistress in Beaumaris.

She didn't blame Sarah. Nathan's mother was one of life's victims. Joanna had no doubt that when Ryan first affected an interest in Henry Sarah had taken his kindness at face value. She must have been flattered that her son had been singled out for attention, and, having seen the shacks at Palmer's Point, Joanna could understand her dilemma.

It was through talking to Sarah that Joanna eventually visited the shacks for herself. Nathan went with her, and, although at first the women were suspicious of her, gradually she won their confidence. To begin with, it was just something to do, somewhere to go when Cole was working or away from the plantation. She took her sketch pad with her, and spent hours producing likenesses of the children for their mothers. She talked to the children, and encouraged them to talk to her. And, in time, their mothers began to trust her, telling her their problems, and asking her advice.

She supposed it had been a gigantic step from there to actually starting the mother and baby clinic, but so many of the women had had children who'd died, and others were weary from so many pregnancies. Health care was expensive, and Joanna, who would have loved a baby of her own, whatever Cole thought to the contrary, was more than eager to help. Some of the older women, who were past child-bearing themselves, but who wanted a better life for their daughters, helped too. A derelict shack was appropriated, and between them they repaired and painted the inside, and hung the posters Joanna had provided. There were scales to weigh the babies, and a creaky old couch, where the mothers were examined. Her biggest coup was in persuading the hospital in Beaumaris to offer the services of a doctor, free of charge, one afternoon a week, to provide the medical skills necessary for the clinic to succeed.

It was ironic, she thought, that, while she was so successful in helping other people, she was so unsuccessful in helping herself. Her marriage had failed. She and Cole seldom spoke to one another any more. Oh, she supposed, if she had been willing to overlook his involvement with Sammy-Jean, they might have been able to work something out. If she had been willing to humble herself, and beg him to come back to her. But she had her pride, and she refused to barter it, even though sometimes the need to touch him was like a raging ache inside her.

And then, one afternoon, Cole came to the clinic and found Nathan helping her. Joanna had known he was aware of the clinic's existence. His father knew about it, and he had sworn he would get the place closed down. He objected to his daughter-in-law being involved, and he had told Cole to deal with it. But, as she and Cole rarely had a conversation these days, nothing had happened, and as the weeks went by she had cautiously begun to hope they were safe.

Cole's appearance had destroyed that hope. She had been convinced he could have no other reason for coming to the clinic than to do his father's bidding. That was why she had jumped recklessly into the attack, accusing him of being his father's lackey, and ordering him off the premises.

In retrospect, she could see it had been the wrong thing to do. She had immediately created a volatile situation, and the row that had ensued had been every bit as violent as she had anticipated. And, when Nathan sprang to her defence, things got really ugly.

Even today, it was hard to understand Cole's fury towards Nathan. Rounding on the younger man, he had delivered one of the most abusive speeches of his entire life. He had accused Nathan of every crime he could think of, finishing with a warning that he should stay away from Macallister women and off Macallister land.

And that was when Joanna had told him. Ignoring Nathan's warning hand on her sleeve, she had informed Cole exactly who Nathan was. His name might be Smith, she said icily, but that wasn't the name of his father. His father's name was Macallister, just like his. In fact, he was speaking to his brother.

Cole had been stunned. Looking back now, she had to admit that, of all the Macallisters, Cole had taken it the hardest. For, of course, he had confronted his father with the accusation, and other ears had heard Ryan's angry outburst. The news had spread like wildfire, and what had just been a rumour became a verified fact.

Maggie Macallister showed little reaction, proving, to Joanna at least, that Cole's mother must have known what was happening all along. But, as long as it wasn't talked about, and Ryan was discreet, she had been prepared to ignore it. After all, Nathan was twenty-one. She must have thought the worst was over.

And it might have been, if Ryan had been prepared to leave it there. After all, it wasn't such an unusual story. Without further scandal to feed on, the story would have been nothing more than a nine-day wonder. But Ryan was angry. He wanted retribution. And, because it was Joanna who had betrayed him, he chose to use her to get his revenge.

The first that Joanna knew about it was when she next went into Beaumaris to see Sarah. Although she knocked at the door of the house in Acacia Street, no one answered, and when she went to the clinic, seeking Nathan, she found the shack had been bulldozed to the ground. And none of the women wanted to talk to her. They were cool, and offhand, avoiding her eyes when she tried to get them to tell her what had happened, calling their children away, as if she was to blame for everything.

She knew it was Ryan Macallister who was behind it. She could imagine the threats he had made not just to these women, but to Sarah as well. Was that why Sarah wasn't answering her door? Was that why Nathan was avoiding her?

She thought about going to the school where Nathan taught, and asking him what he thought she should do, but the trouble was, she felt guilty. After all, if she hadn't betrayed Sarah's confidence, none of this would have happened. It was her fault that it had all gone wrong. Her fault that all her hard-earned efforts were wasted.

She knew there was only one person she could appeal to, and that was Cole. She hadn't spoken to him once since that day at the clinic, but somehow she had to make him see that it wasn't fair to punish others for her mistakes. Nathan was such an honourable man. It wasn't right that he should have to suffer for simply being there. He hadn't asked to be born. He hadn't chosen his parents.

She went to Cole's room that night, long after his parents had gone to bed. She knew it was the only time when she might get to speak to him alone, but her hands were trembling as she tied the cord of the silk wrapper around her. Her appearance didn't please her. Since she and Cole had been living separate lives, she had piled on the weight, and her hips swelled unattractively below the belt of the robe. Her breasts were bigger, too, round and voluptuous, bouncing along beneath the wrapper like two melons in a bag.

But, although she spent several minutes trying to attract Cole's attention, he didn't open the door. And, when she eventually plucked up the courage to step inside, she found the room was empty. The maid had turned down the bed, but it hadn't been occupied.

She was debating whether to go back to her own room, when she heard a sound behind her. Cole had evidently just arrived home, and was standing in the doorway, swaying slightly on his heels.

'Well, well,' he said unpleasantly, 'to what do I owe this honour? Or is it a case of if Mohammed won't come to the mountain, the mountain must come to Mohammed?'

His voice was slightly slurred, as if he had been drinking. But the words he used were deliberate, and Joanna coloured. 'I wanted to talk to you, Cole,' she said, wishing now she had waited till the morning. 'I—but it doesn't matter.'

However, when she would have gone past him, he stepped inside and closed the door. 'Go ahead,' he said. 'I'm listening. You'll sleep better if you spit it out. They say that confession's good for the soul!'

'Confession?'

Joanna was confused, but Cole merely unfastened the remaining buttons on his shirt and pulled it free of his trousers. 'Sure,' he said, tossing his jacket aside and running exploring fingers across his chest. 'You're going to tell me how sorry you are for making a fool of me with Nathan. Tell me about it. I hear he's pretty impressive in that department. Got all the right equipment, if you see what I mean——'

'Shut your filthy mouth!'

Joanna's hand swung towards his cheek with all the force she could muster, but Cole only swayed back on his heels and avoided the worst of the blow. Besides, he was probably anaesthetised against any pain by the amount of alcohol he had swallowed, she thought bitterly. Unlike her.

'Hey, that's what they say,' Cole protested, his lean features showing only a mocking disregard for her anger. 'Don't blame me if he's found someone else!'

Joanna seethed. 'He hasn't found anyone else!' she exclaimed, frustratedly. 'That is, our—our relationship wasn't like that!'

'Oh, come on, Jo! I know what a hot little body you've got. And if you're not cooling it with me...' He shrugged expressively.

Joanna gasped. 'Is that all you can think about? *Sex*?'

Cole's face sobered. 'What else is there?' he asked harshly.

Joanna winced. 'I thought we loved one another——'

'Oh, spare me that!' Cole was scathing. 'You don't love me. You never did. All you love are those bloody paintings of yours! They're your family, aren't they? Your children! When we got married, I thought you'd forget all about that nonsense. I thought you'd be so busy having my babies, you wouldn't have time to think about anything else. But that's not what you had in mind. Children are a nuisance. They'd get in the way of your work. And heaven help anything that interfered with that!'

Joanna stared at him. 'You actually expected me to have children here? In this house?'

'Why not? You never gave my family a chance. You were so busy finding reasons for not living here, you didn't see what you were doing to us!'

'I didn't do anything to *us*! I wasn't the one who moved out of our room. I wasn't the one who went off to South America for weeks at a time, so that when you came back we were like strangers with one another.'

'And whose fault was that?'

'Well, it wasn't mine——'

'Not even when I found out what was going on?'

Joanna blinked. 'What *was* going on?'

'Do I have to spell it out?' Cole thrust his hands into his trouser pockets, and Joanna had to drag her eyes away from the taut cloth. 'We've been married over a year, Jo. Why aren't you pregnant?'

Joanna caught her breath. 'Perhaps you ought to ask yourself that,' she retorted indignantly. 'I takes two to make a baby, you know.'

Cole's eyes darkened. 'You bitch!'

'Oh, yes, I'm a bitch, aren't I? Just because I suggest that good 'ole Cole Macallister mightn't have what it takes——'

'Shut up!'

Cole reached for her then, and, although she tried to avoid his hands, he was less intoxicated than she had thought. His fingers fastened around her throat with bruising intent, and when he hauled her up in front of him her eyes opened wide with apprehension.

'You know what I should do, don't you?' he snarled. 'I should wring your lying little neck!'

'Because you can't take the truth?' Joanna taunted, scared, but defiant too, and Cole groaned.

'What the hell are you trying to do to me?' he demanded, his fingers finding her windpipe and exerting an unsteady pressure. 'God in heaven, you'd try the patience of a saint!'

'And we both know you're no saint, don't we?' whispered Joanna, through dry lips. 'Go on, Cole. Do it! Put us both out of our misery!'

Cole's hands tightened, and for a moment she thought he was going to make good his threat. And then they gentled, smoothing the skin of her throat, and tracing the pulsing veins that had risen, threadlike, to the surface. 'You know what I really want to do with you, don't you?' he muttered, his breath wafting across her face, only lightly tinged with the alcohol he had consumed. His hands slid down, over her quivering shoulders, and found the rampant fullness of her breasts. He squeezed them hard, through the slippery silk of her wrapper. Then he bent his head, and sucked one of the button-hard peaks into his mouth, suckling it through the cloth, and sending a wave of longing surging into her thighs.

She thought she was going to collapse, her knees felt so weak. But, as if sensing this, Cole put his hands beneath her bottom, and lifted her into his arms. Her legs curled automatically about him, and she wound her arms around his neck. The feel of his smooth skin felt so good beneath her hands, and when his tongue probed her lips she met it with her own.

'God, I want you!' He shrugged off his shirt, and his bare chest was unbelievably sensuous against her aching nipples. She wanted to tear off the wrapper, and rub herself against him. As it was, the damp cloth only sensitised her awareness of the masculine beauty of his body.

His tongue invaded her mouth, sliding across her teeth, and caressing the moist inner shell. Its greedy possession imitated the thrusting arousal of his body, and she could feel his swelling hardness rising beneath her hip.

When he carried her to the bed, and came down on top of her, she stopped trying to analyse what was happening. Perhaps he was doing this because he hated her. Perhaps he was using her to assuage his lust for Sammy-Jean. But she didn't care. What he was doing to her was what she wanted him to do to her, and the reasons for his urgency didn't really count. She wanted him—on her, and in her, melding their bodies together, and bringing her to a peak of fulfilment only he could achieve. She wanted to hold his sleek length inside her, the fullness of him stretching not just her muscles, but the limits of her consciousness. And she wanted to feel the liquid heat of his seed, lubricating the dryness of her soul.

And he was hungry for her. Of that, there could be no doubt. To her relief, the silk wrapper was quickly thrown aside, and his teeth tugged painfully at her nipple, as his hands fumbled awkwardly with his buckle. She wanted to help him, but he wouldn't let her. Instead, he dealt with his own belt and zip, while his mouth roamed freely over her flesh.

'Watch me,' he ordered once, when her drifting senses caused her eyes to close. 'Look at me!' And she did, as he nudged her thighs apart, and poised, erect and glistening above her. Then, groaning with satisfaction, he eased himself into her tight sheath, allowing her muscles to close about him with an eagerness she couldn't hide.

It was a frantic loving, a desperate meeting of souls, whose only outward connection was through their bodies. Yet it was a spiritual blending, too, a magical experience, when the pounding desire of possession became an urgent invocation of the sublime.

The end came all too soon. Driven to the heights of passion, it was far too tempting to tumble over the brink. Cole wanted to prolong it. She knew that by the way he tried to pace himself. But with her legs around his waist, and the luscious beauty of her mouth luring him on, the needs she was creating were too powerful to subdue. Besides, the desire to reach that tantalising peak was dragging every ounce of strength from him, and when he felt her wild convulsions he couldn't prevent his own explosion. A shuddering wave of tension swept through him, and then he slumped heavily on top of her.

And it was while they were lying in the sweat-slick aftermath of their lovemaking that Cole's door opened. Until then, Joanna had scarcely been aware that the lamps were still on, or that anyone could come into the room and find them. Besides, it was so late. She had believed everyone was in bed. But it was Cole's father who stood in the doorway, and for a moment she saw that his face was as shocked as her own.

Cole's reactions were slower, more lethargic—even defiant, Joanna admitted now. At his father's hoarse exclamation, he didn't immediately spring up from the bed, as she might have expected. Oh, no. He merely rolled on to his back beside her, and turned hooded eyes in his father's direction. 'What do you want?' he demanded tersely. 'We're trying to get some sleep.'

Now Joanna pushed herself away from the bathroom basin, and walked wearily into the bedroom. And, as she did so, she realised it was the first time she had actually recalled the exact words Cole had used to his father that night. What had come afterwards had been so horrible that she hadn't been able to think. And time, and the desire not to remember, had erased the whole scene from her mind.

For Ryan had come to tell his son that Nathan was dead. He had been pulled out of the river an hour before, and his mother had insisted that Cole's father should be informed. In addition to which, the sheriff wanted him to go down to the morgue right away, to identify the body. Sarah was too distraught to see her son right now, and Ryan had agreed to do it. But he wanted Cole to go with him. He needed his eldest son's support.

And Cole had gone, Joanna remembered, leaving her to pull herself together, and return to her own room in a daze of disbelief. Nathan dead! She couldn't believe it was true. And why had he died in the river? For God's sake, couldn't he swim?

Her mind skimmed over the awful events of the next few days. If she and Cole had ever had a chance of regaining what they had once had, Nathan's death had destroyed it. She couldn't help blaming him for the way he had treated his half-brother. And she positively despised Ryan for his selfishness and blatant lack of feeling.

And then, at the funeral, something even more dreadful happened, something that had Joanna packing her bags, and swearing she would never set foot on Tidewater land again. Sarah, racked with grief, and driven to the edge by her son's untimely demise, had accused Ryan Macallister of causing it. He had hounded her son, she said, ever since he discovered that Joanna and Nathan were friends. He had accused him of seducing his brother's wife, of taking revenge for his own unhappy circumstances by destroying his brother's marriage. And Joanna had encouraged him, Ryan had added. Like took to like, he had sneered, with a scathing reference to Joanna's dark colouring.

Of course, Ryan had denied it. Red-faced and blustering, angry, now, that he had submitted to his son's conviction that they should attend the funeral, he had lashed out at anyone who had argued with him. But Joanna had seen his guilt, and despised him for it. And despised Cole, too, for letting it happen to a man who had been so kind, so gentle, so totally lacking in the arrogance his father had in such abundance.

For months afterwards, long after she had returned to London, and resumed her life there, Joanna tortured herself with thoughts of Nathan on that night. She couldn't believe it had been an accident. She had seen him fishing in the river so many times, and she was sure he would never have drowned unless he hadn't wanted to live. And, of course, she had blamed herself, not only for exposing Ryan and causing him to turn on his son, but also for being the unwitting tool his father had used against him. She could never forgive Ryan. Never. The problem was, did she want to forgive his son?

CHAPTER TWELVE

IT WAS years since Joanna had been on a horse. She had learned to ride as a child, and, when she first went to live at Tidewater, she had occasionally ridden with Cole. But only occasionally. After her illness, and their subsequent estrangement, she had had no heart for such a pursuit. It would have seemed too much like pursuing him, and her pride had balked at the idea.

But, after a sleepless night spent reliving the past, she once again found herself in the saddle. Cole had had a beautiful pearl-grey mare readied for her, and the animal shifted a little nervously as Joanna settled herself on its back. She knew that horses, like other animals, could sense nervousness in humans, but in her case it wasn't fear of riding that upset her stomach. It was her unwilling awareness of the man riding beside her. And the uneasy realisation of how attracted to him she still was.

Not that Cole seemed aware of her. He appeared cool and detached, totally in control of his own destiny. Leather-clad thighs moulded the sides of the huge blood bay he was riding, and his booted feet rested confidently in the stirrups. He was wearing a cream shirt, opened down the front to allow whatever breeze there was to cool his skin, and a broad-brimmed hat tipped forward to shade his eyes.

He looked lean and hard, and intensely male, his relaxed hands resting on the reins, nevertheless exuding an unmistakable sense of power. Sometimes, seeing him like this, feeling what his sexuality was doing to her, Joanna wondered how they had ever drifted apart. But then she remembered Nathan, and Sammy-Jean, and her weakness became a hurtful core of indignation.

'You need a hat,' he informed her, appraising her outfit of pink cotton cut-offs and a loose-fitting man's shirt with some contempt. But what did he expect her to wear, for heaven's sake? she asked herself resentfully. She hadn't known when she flew out to the Bahamas that she would end up riding trail in South Carolina. 'You don't want to get heatstroke, do you?'

Joanna shrugged. 'I wouldn't have thought you'd care,' she countered, realising she mustn't let him guess how he disturbed her, and adopting an appealing smile. But Cole only swung down from the bay, and strode back into the stables.

He emerged a few moments later with a rather worn and spotted stetson, and jammed it on to the pommel in front of her. 'Put it on,' he ordered, grasping the bay's reins and resuming his seat in the saddle. 'It's not pretty, but it should serve the purpose.'

'Why, darlin', are you sayin' that ah'm pretty?' Joanna goaded him, examining the hat with some disdain, and Cole's mouth compressed.

'Do you need me to tell you that?' he retorted, skilfully turning the tables, and Joanna pulled a face at his back, as she reluctantly tried the hat for size.

It was a close fit, and it immediately dislodged the knot she had made of her hair for coolness. The silky strands came tumbling down about her shoulders, and, hearing her gasp of irritation, Cole glanced round.

'Having problems?' he enquired sardonically, and, refusing to give him the satisfaction, Joanna shook her head.

'Nothing I can't handle,' she said, bundling all her hair inside the stetson, and jamming it on her head. 'By the way, where's Henry? Or am I not allowed to say hello to him either?'

Cole managed not to utter the retort that was evidently trembling on his lips, and instead he kicked the bay into motion. 'Henry only works here afternoons,' he said, as Joanna hastily nudged the mare into following him. 'He helps his mother at the guest house mornings.'

Joanna blinked. 'The guest house?' she echoed. 'Sarah works at a guest house?'

'She *runs* a guest house,' Cole corrected her shortly. Ignoring her look of surprise, he cast an expert eye over her handling of the mare. 'You fit for a little cantering?'

Joanna's hands tightened on the reins. 'Anything you like,' she declared absently, still mulling over what he had said about Sarah, but when Cole gave the bay its head she was forced to put her thoughts on hold. She hadn't forgotten how to ride, but she was out of practice, and her thighs jarred uncomfortably as she tried to find the rhythm.

They crossed dew-soaked paddocks, where the scent of the grass rose pungently to her nostrils, into rustling woods, where the sun's rays filtered through the boughs. The mare's hoofs crunched on cones and rotting leaves, and caused a startled jack-rabbit to scoot across their path. Birds sang; bees buzzed around a hive of wild honey; and the moisture rose from the forest floor to soak her perspiring skin.

They emerged into fields that stretched towards other forests of oak and palmetto, rich agricultural land, extending into undulating hills. But, instead of cotton fields as far as the eye could see, Joanna saw acres given over to corn and cattle, and orchards of fruit trees, with the mist rising from them.

Cole reined in the bay to guide the animal between rows of sweet-sprouting sugar cane. Insects buzzed about them, making Joanna glad she had remembered to cover the most sensitive parts of her body, and also giving her a reason for wearing the disgusting hat. She was even glad she was on horseback, when she remembered the spiders that thrived in the cane fields. And every time one of the swaying stalks touched her sleeve she brushed away another imaginary horror.

It wasn't until they came out of the sugar cane that she realised where they were. She had been disorientated by the changes that had been made at Tidewater, and it was with some surprise that she saw they weren't far from where the shacks had been situated. She could hear the river, too, and her nerves tightened with remembered pain. Was Cole so insensitive? she wondered. Didn't he understand that this was the last place she wanted to see?

But Cole was already some distance away from her, the bay trotting across the rough turf that separated Tidewater from the cluster of dwellings at Palmer's Point. He didn't look back, and she had only two choices: either go with him, or go back to the house.

And, because the prospect of returning to the house was even less attractive to her, she urged the mare after him. But resentment built as they cantered down the slope, and she glimpsed the roofs of the buildings below them.

She scarcely noticed the river, as she kicked the mare into a gallop and overtook him. She paid no attention to the mud-flats, where she had once spent so many hours, sketching the many birds that came to feed there. She didn't even smell the salty tang of the ocean, or pause to admire the long white stretch of sand that edged the estuary. All she could think about was her own feelings, which reinforced her hostility towards him for bringing her here.

'Is this supposed to be some kind of sick joke?' she demanded, as she passed him, but Cole didn't answer. And then, as the ground levelled out, she saw the cluster of dwellings immediately ahead of her.

Her astonishment was swift and genuine. The village was still there, just as she remembered. But the shacks had disappeared. In their place stood modern tract housing, mostly one-storey buildings, erected on piles for maximum coolness.

'Some joke, hmm?' murmured Cole, his stirrup nudging her leg, and Joanna gave an involuntary start. She had been staring at the bright borders of stocks and pansies that edged the squares of turf in front of each property, and the evidence of cultivation in the tent-like growth of bean-poles at the back.

'Your father did this?' she exclaimed, finding it difficult to associate the man she knew with what she was seeing in front of her, and Cole shrugged.

'Is that so hard to believe?'

'Frankly, yes.' Joanna shook her head. 'It's incredible!'

Cole expelled a long breath. 'Yeah, well...' He shook the reins and sent the bay walking down the dusty lane between the houses. 'As I said last night, I've got something to show you.'

'And this isn't it?'

Joanna was surprised, but Cole didn't answer her. Their arrival had attracted attention, and a woman had come out on to the veranda of the house opposite and called to him.

'Morning, there, Cole,' she said, resting her elbows on the rail, and smiling down at him. 'Somethin' I can do for you?'

'Morning, Susie,' Cole responded, as relaxed and easy as she was, and Joanna shook her head. It wasn't just the houses that had changed around here, she thought drily. And goodness, wasn't that Susan Fenton, Billy Fenton's mother?

'You remember Joanna, don't you?' Cole was saying now, and Susan turned a friendly smile on the other woman.

'Of course,' she said. 'Hi, there, Mrs Macallister. I heard you were back at Tidewater. Guess you didn't expect anythin' like this.'

'No.' Joanna managed a rueful grimace. 'How are you, Susan? You—er—you look well.'

And she did. Whether it was the fact that Joanna hadn't seen her for some time, she didn't know, but the woman looked fit and healthy, and undeniably pregnant. And much too attractive to be looking at Cole like that, Joanna acknowledged tensely. How well did he know her? Had he, like his father, found diversion here?

'Hey, I'm OK.' Susan propped her hip on the veranda rail, and rested a complacent hand on the swelling mound of her stomach. 'Never been better, as it happens. Since Cole moved us into these fancy houses, we all got no complaints.'

'Since Cole——' Joanna broke off and glanced at her ex-husband. 'Yes, I see.' She schooled her features. 'When's the baby due?'

'In a couple of months.' Susan grinned. 'You sure I can't get you anythin'? Some nice cold lemonade, maybe?'

'No, thanks.' Cole spoke before Joanna could say anything. 'You look after yourself, right? And don't let Jonas wear you out.'

Susan dimpled. 'I won't,' she said. 'See you later, Mrs Macallister. Y'all take care now.'

As they got out of earshot, Joanna nudged her horse nearer to Cole's. 'Jonas?' she said, frowning, and Cole pulled a wry face.

'Jonas Wilson,' he told her evenly. 'Her husband.'

'But I thought——'

'Bull's dead,' Cole intoned, acknowledging the greetings of several other women and children, who had come out on to their verandas to see what was going on. 'You've been away three years, Jo. Things change. People change.'

'Including your father?' she queried, tugging on the mare's reins, as a dusky-skinned little boy ran across her path. 'Hey, isn't that Georgie Davis? But no. It can't be.'

'Try his brother Bobby,' said Cole laconically, leaning across to grasp her bridle. 'I guess we walk from here. I'd hate for you to be the unwitting cause of someone's death.'

Joanna looked at him, but he wasn't looking her way, and, because their actions were being monitored by at least a dozen pairs of eyes, she hastily slid out of the saddle. But the significance of what he had said wasn't lost on her, and she wished he hadn't made such a statement right in the middle of Palmer's Point.

Their progress after that was slow. So many people wanted to stop, and pass the time of day. They were obviously curious about Joanna, but strangely enough she felt an outsider. Even though she knew most of these people, it wasn't the same. She had abandoned them, and Cole had taken her place.

Not that she really minded. She was glad Cole had found his own role at Tidewater. And she was truly delighted that she had played some small part in his enlightenment. She just wished he could have told her, before she ran away...

The direction her thoughts were taking her was suddenly frightening. She couldn't mean what she was thinking. Her relationship with Cole had floundered long before Nathan died. There was still Sammy-Jean, and her own inability to conceive. Besides, she had her work. She didn't want to come back to South Carolina and lose her independence and her identity. But the fact remained that, the longer she stayed here, the harder it was to ignore what they'd once had.

She was so busy trying not to be impressed that when Cole halted outside a larger building than the rest she almost ran into him. 'What do you think?' he asked, and for once his voice was totally devoid of expression.

Joanna frowned, but her attention was caught by the square wooden sign, standing in front of the building. 'The Nathan Smith Clinic,' she read, her breath catching in her throat. 'Oh, God, Cole, did you do this?'

'No.' Cole lifted his shoulders. 'Pa did.' He tied the horses' reins to the rail and went up the steps. 'Come on,' he added flatly. 'I'll show you around. After all, it was your idea originally. No one else cared enough to give a damn.'

The tide was out as they walked the horses along the edge of the water. Joanna had taken off her boots and tied them to the pommel of her saddle, and her toes curled coolly into the damp sand. They had left the estuary and the mud-flats behind, climbing into the dunes to clear the headland, and then dropping down on to the beach again to walk along the shoreline.

Cole hadn't said anything since they left the clinic, and Joanna was finding it difficult to assimilate what she had seen with the man she knew Ryan Macallister to be. He must be pretty desperate to gain Cole's approval, she thought, glancing sideways at the man beside her. She just wished she knew what Cole was thinking, and whether Nathan's death was the only reason he was alienated from his father.

Kicking up a spray of salt water, Joanna tilted her head to look at the sun. Even though it was still early, it burned down hotly on her shoulders—and on her uncovered head. But she refused to wear that hat when she wasn't riding, and she had found some pins and skewered her hair on top of her head.

'What're you thinking?' she asked at last, noticing that the cuffs of her shorts were splashed with sea water. 'I've said I'm impressed. Your father must have had some change of heart.'

'Yeah.' Cole's mouth flattened. 'As soon as he knew his tab was almost up.'

Joanna frowned. 'That's pretty harsh, isn't it?' she murmured. She was no friend of Ryan Macallister's, but she was being compelled to find reasons to be charitable.

Cole slanted a narrow gaze down at her. 'Hey, don't tell me he's getting to you,' he mocked, though there was a dark glint in his eyes. 'Be careful, Jo. You might be tempted to tell me why he wanted you brought here. Or shall I tell you? The old devil's found out he's not immortal, after all.'

Joanna let go of the mare's reins, and stopped at the water's edge, scuffing her toes in the water. 'He wants me to—to intercede with you on his behalf,' she said, deciding she wasn't going to gain anything by keeping silent. 'He says—*Ben* says—you and he don't get on like you used to. Do you want to tell me why?'

'No.'

Cole's response was short and succinct, and Joanna sighed. She was going to get nowhere at this rate, and she still hadn't spoken to him about Charley and Billy Fenton.

And, instead of staying with her, Cole had walked on, his broad shoulders and narrow hips arousing an aching sense of denial. She wanted Cole to care what she thought, what she did, Joanna realised painfully. But, however much she might torment him, ultimately, she would be the loser.

'Damn you, wait!' she exclaimed now, stamping her foot, and then made a sound of frustration as the water splashed up to her thighs. She had forgotten where she was for a moment, and now she was nearly soaked to the skin.

Cole had walked a few yards further on but then either a sense of responsibility or simply curiosity caused him to stop and look back. And, acting purely on impulse, Joanna reached down and unfastened her trousers.

That, at least, aroused some reaction. 'Cut it out,' he snapped, striding back to where she was standing, but Joanna only kicked off the cut-offs, and draped them over the saddle.

'They're wet,' she said, shivering in spite of the heat. For, although she was aware that her briefs were no less modest than the bottom half of her bikini, there was something wholly devastating in watching Cole's eyes flick over them.

'This is South Carolina, not the South of France,' he said through gritted teeth, snatching the cut-offs from the saddle, and thrusting them into her hands. 'They'll dry. Put them on.'

'They'll dry much quicker this way,' declared Joanna, tossing them over the saddle again. Then, before he could stop her, she had skipped away into the creaming surf. 'Let's go swimming, hmm? The water's heavenly!'

'Joanna!'

He said her name slowly, and menacingly, but she refused to be daunted. This might be the last time they were alone together, and, however crazy it might be, she wanted him to have something to remember her by.

'Come on,' she said, deliberately unfastening another button on her shirt, so that he could see the dusky hollow of her cleavage. 'Don't be such a spoil-sport, Cole. Where's your sense of adventure? We used to go skinny-dipping in Tahiti, and you weren't so prudish then!'

Cole didn't hesitate. Completely dumbfounding her, he strode into the waves without even bothering to take his boots off. And, because it was the last thing she had expected, he caught her easily. He grasped her elbow, as she turned to flee, and hauled her back into his arms.

She almost overbalanced him, as she thudded against his hard chest, but he spread his legs and saved them both from being submerged. 'No more games, Jo,' he ordered grimly, dragging her back towards the shore, and she kicked her legs in frustration as he waded out on to the sand.

She had soaked him as well as herself now, and, judging by his expression, he didn't find it at all funny. 'You're crazy, do you know that?' he grated, releasing her to examine his wet thighs. 'For God's sake, what are you trying to prove?'

Joanna stared at him, not really knowing the answer herself. All she knew at this moment was that she still wanted him; that, whatever had happened in the past and whatever might happen in the future, her destiny had brought her there, to this spot, right now.

'Cole,' she said helplessly, and something in her voice seemed to strike a chord inside him. He looked at her then—not as he had looked at her before, but with a weary, tormented expression, and her heart wobbled precariously in her chest.

'Well?' he demanded, and she sniffed to hold back the tears of frustration that prickled behind her eyes.

'I'm sorry,' she whispered, not really knowing what she was apologising for. 'I—I didn't mean to make you mad. Honestly.' She stepped forward and bent to brush the pearls of sea water from the legs of his trousers. 'Here; let me help you——'

'*Don't*!'

His denial was strangled, his hand dashing her wrist aside, and knocking her off balance. She tried to save herself, but she couldn't, and, to her ignominy, she stumbled on to her knees at his feet.

'Oh, *God*!' With a muffled curse, Cole came down on his haunches beside her. 'Did I hurt you?' he muttered, gazing down at her bent head, and Joanna's tongue came to circle her lips, and she raised her face to look at him.

'Only my pride,' she murmured ruefully, as a sand-crab, startled by her invasion of its territory, scuttled away across the sand. She shook her head, and sighed as her hair tumbled down about her shoulders. 'I guess you didn't want my help, hmm? I forgot, I'm not supposed to touch you, am I?'

Cole drew a laboured breath. 'I didn't know you wanted to,' he muttered, and she realised that her fall had taken him off guard. He would never have said such a provocative thing to her in the normal course of events, and her breathing quickened automatically at the possibilities it created.

'Oh—I'm sure you did,' she ventured, her own voice not quite steady, and, straightening her back, she lifted one hand to support herself on his knee. Beneath her damp fingers, she felt the instinctive tightening of his bones, and although she wanted to look she kept her eyes on his.

'This is—most—unwise,' he said, and she realised that his momentary loss of control was being checked. Taking another gulp of air, he firmly removed her hand from his leg, but when he would have released her she held on and brought his fingers to her lips.

She was quite prepared for him to snatch his hand away. Cole was a master at controlling his emotions, and consequently she held it tighter than she might have done.

But, although his features tensed, and she saw a pulse palpitating at his jawline, he let her get away with it, watching as she put out her tongue and licked the tips of his fingers.

However, when she was reckless enough to allow her eyes to drop down his chest and over his flat stomach to the unmistakable rigidity of his groin, his tolerance snapped.

'For pity's sake, Jo,' he muttered hoarsely, and she was quite sure he intended to put an end to it there and then. But, before he could get to his feet, she slung her arms around him, and he lost his balance and fell back on to the sand, with her half-naked body on top of him.

Her own astonishment at her temerity was nothing compared to his. Cole lay flat on the sand, gazing up at her with disbelieving eyes, and for a moment she was too shocked to take advantage of it. But then the dawning anger in his gaze, and the subsiding hardness between his legs, warned her that she was in peril of losing her only chance of redemption. She was only where she was now because she had taken him unawares. Any minute, he was going to remove her by force.

With a helpless sense of need, she ignored his forbidding expression and covered his lips with hers, withstanding his instinctive rejection, and pressing her tongue into his mouth.

There was a heartbeat when she thought she hadn't succeeded, when Cole's hands gripping her shoulders seemed in imminent danger of throwing her aside. She fully expected to end up in a humiliating heap on the sand, with Cole standing above her, scowling his contempt.

But her legs splayed across his abdomen detected the moment when the danger passed, and his body came alive again. Although he might despise himself for it, he couldn't prevent his instinctive response. His hands still grasped her shoulders, but his grip was gentling, and as she continued to possess his mouth his pulsing arousal throbbed against her thigh.

'God,' he groaned, leaving her in no doubt as to his frustration, but one hand was tangling in her silky hair, and the other rolled her over so that now he was on top of her. Then, with his thumb grazing the sensitive skin inside her lower lip, he forced her lips apart, fastening his mouth to their trembling sweetness, and filling the soft moist cavity with his tongue.

Joanna lost all sense of time and place. She wasn't even aware of the sand in her hair, or the gritty feel of its damp granules against her back. She hardly noticed the incoming tide, as it swirled in the rock-pools around them, or the cool salty rivulets that wet her legs from her heels to the bottom of her panties. All she was aware of was Cole—his hands, his lips, his tongue; and the satisfying weight of his body, as he ground his hips against her.

Her shirt was open and so was his, and the fine hair that lightly filmed his chest teased the taut nipples of her breasts. Far from feeling cool, she was on fire, and the burning need of his erection demanded to be filled. He cupped her breasts, suckling on their sweetness as sanity slipped away, and everywhere he touched her aroused an ache that only he could assuage.

CHAPTER THIRTEEN

JOANNA awoke to the sound of the phone ringing, and
for a few mindless moments she wondered who it was.
Once upon a time, she had answered the phone without
thinking, and in that happy state between sleeping and
waking she only resented the sound.

But then, as consciousness took hold of her, and the
full weight of her present situation descended upon her,
she slumped back against her pillows. These days, she
avoided speaking to anyone, and as she knew it was most
probably either Grace or her mother she let the annoying buzz go on.

It stopped, finally, and she stretched a hand out of
bed, and turned the clock on the bedside table towards
her. It was half-past ten, she decided, or was it half-past
eleven? Either way, what did it matter? She'd got nothing
to get out of bed for.

Her eyes drifted round the bedroom without enthusiasm. It was a pleasant room, overlooking the
gardens at the back of the row of houses, and because
the room faced east it caught the morning sun. She remembered how much fun she had had, when she bought
the lease of the apartment, choosing the delicately patterned wallpaper, and hanging it herself. She had chosen
the furniture, too, unaware that when she haunted the
salerooms, and decided on solid Victorian pieces, she
was actually anticipating the kind of furnishings she
would find in her husband's home.

Of course, when she and Cole got married, she had
wanted to sell the apartment, but Grace had persuaded
her against it. 'Property's a good investment,' she had
argued, thinking, but not voicing, her fears for Joanna's
future. 'Keep it,' she said. 'As a nest-egg, if nothing else.'

And Joanna had had cause to be grateful for that shrewd piece of advice.

Not that what had happened three years ago was any comfort to her now, Joanna reflected. She might have listened to Grace then, but she hadn't listened to her more recently. When she had phoned Grace that night from the Bahamas, and told her she was going back to Tidewater, Grace had warned her to be careful. She should have paid attention. She had been vulnerable, after all.

She sighed now and rolled over, burying her face in the pillow, and praying for oblivion. But it didn't come. She was wide awake now and unprotected. She knew from past experience that nothing she could do would close her mind to the painful jabs of rejection.

And yet, remembering that morning on the beach, she wondered if she really wished to change anything. She had known a brief taste of happiness, and surely that was worth something. But if she hadn't let Cole make love to her, she wouldn't be going through this emotional crisis now. And what price his lovemaking, when all he'd wanted was sexual satisfaction?

And that only because she had initiated it, she admitted honestly. If she hadn't thrown herself at him, she might still have saved her pride. As it was, she knew he resented her for seducing his intentions, for making him do something he despised.

But, at the time, she hadn't been thinking about how he might react when his body was sated. And it was certain he hadn't been thinking too rationally either. Hunger; passion; whatever primitive need had been driving him on had temporarily paralysed his reasoning. With the hot sun blazing down, and the white surf breaking around them, he had opened his trousers and buried himself in her eager body, just as he had done that very first time in London. He had taken her, right there on the beach, in plain sight of anyone who cared to look.

Sometimes, she wished they could have drowned at that moment, while she was still able to pretend that Cole cared for her as much as she cared for him. She often wondered what might have happened if Ben hadn't come across them. Might they even have salvaged something from the wreckage of the past?

Whatever, he managed to attract their attention, without undue embarrassment. His strident whistle was sufficient to bring Cole to his senses, and he dragged himself away from her with unflattering speed. But, in one sense, Ben had been too late, Joanna reflected wryly. Too late to prevent Cole from exposing his own weakness.

And he hadn't forgiven her for that. In the hours that followed, when he learned that his father had suffered a stroke and had been rushed into hospital in Beaumaris, he wouldn't allow her to comfort him. Indeed, he would have nothing to do with her, staying close by his mother's side, and acting the dutiful son.

But he was only acting, Joanna had guessed that. Even though she and Cole had drifted apart, she could still feel his sense of betrayal. He hadn't forgiven his father for what had happened to Nathan. There was still that tremendous gulf between them.

And, although all her own senses were screaming for her to leave now, before he could hurt her again, Joanna knew she had to do something. She had given up hoping that any good could come from Ryan's death. It wasn't going to make any difference to her situation. And while she owed the man nothing, and cared little for his sensibilities, she was afraid of what it might do to Cole.

Right now, Cole was sure that what he was doing was right, and as long as his father lay in that semi-conscious state, which some stroke victims achieved, he felt he had nothing to blame himself for. His father was still alive, just, and in the back of his mind there must be the thought that there was still time for a reconciliation. But if Ryan died, that chance would be gone, and Joanna knew, from her own experience with Cole, that the memories of what might have been could tear a soul to shreds.

That was why she approached Cole, the evening before she left Tidewater for the last time. She had decided not to stay any longer. What was the point? Cole ignored her. His mother regarded her as an unwelcome intruder. Even Charley was too upset about her father's illness to spend any time with her, and waiting around for Ryan to die seemed unbearably morbid.

Nevertheless, it took all her courage to go looking for Cole after supper that evening. Meals were taken at irregular times at the moment, and it had been no surprise earlier to find she and Ben were the only ones at the table. Not that Ben was particularly chatty either. She guessed he hadn't forgotten what he had seen several days ago on the beach, and, while he might have sympathy for her, he must know how Cole was treating her.

She found Cole in the library, sitting at his father's desk, going over the stacks of bills that still appeared, whatever the circumstances. The management of the plantation was an ongoing thing, and it simply wasn't possible to abandon these mundane tasks.

Joanna paused in the doorway, checking that almost all the buttons of her full-skirted Indian cotton dress were closed. Patterned in shades of green and black, it was the most conservative item in her wardrobe, and she had worn it deliberately, so that he wouldn't think she had anything provocative in mind.

He didn't look up from the desk, even though she was almost sure he must have heard her footsteps, and she had to clear her throat, and say, 'Cole,' before he chose to acknowledge her presence.

He did look up then, and she flinched at the look of loathing in his eyes. If she had had any doubts about his feelings for her, they were extinguished at that moment. He hated her, and it showed. She wanted to turn right around and leave him.

But she didn't. Determination, conscience, remorse, or simply the need to appeal to him one ...st time, kept her where she was. Cole might hate her, but she loved him, and she couldn't allow his father's death to poison the rest of his life. Not if she could help it.

She moistened her lips. 'Could I talk to you?'

'What about?'

Cole's voice was as chilling as his expression, and Joanna knew a hopeless sense of grief. 'I—just wanted to tell you, I'm leaving tomorrow,' she said, choosing the least controversial thing she could think of, and then caught her breath uneasily, when he lurched abruptly to his feet.

'You're leaving?' If she hadn't been able to see his face, Joanna might have been deceived by his intonation. He actually sounded shocked at the news, and almost disapproving.

'Y-yes,' she added quickly, glancing behind her at the empty hall, before stepping awkwardly into the room. 'I—I can't stay here indefinitely, can I? And you can't pretend you want me to.'

Cole's feature hardened. 'Have I asked you to leave? Has *anyone* asked you to leave?'

'No—but——'

'So this is your decision.'

'If you put it like that.' Joanna lifted her slim shoulders in a dismissive gesture. 'I—I've got to get back to London. The—the exhibition——'

'Oh, yes. The exhibition!' The way Cole repeated her words was harsh with sarcasm. In a disconcerting gesture, he came round the desk and propped himself against the front. 'I'd forgotten what a famous painter we have in our midst. Art before honour, is that what they say?'

'I've never heard it.' Joanna held up her head. 'And it's not like that at all.'

'So how is it?'

Joanna swallowed. 'If—if I was wanted here——'.

'Yes?' Cole's brows ascended. 'If you were wanted— what?'

'I'd stay, of course.'

'On sufferance?'

'No, not on sufferance.' Joanna sighed, growing weary of trying to defend herself to someone who was merely tormenting her. 'I'm not wanted here. You know that, and I know that. It's better if I leave. Before—before——'

'Before my father dies, and you might be called upon to show some sympathy,' finished Cole bleakly, and Joanna's shoulders slumped.

'No,' she said, shaking her head. 'That's not what I meant at all. I just—have no place here any longer. And I think it'll be easier for everyone, if I go back to London.'

Cole's face lost all expression. 'Very well. I'll arrange to have Ben drive you into Charleston tomorrow afternoon.'

'Thank you.'

But as Cole pushed himself up from the desk, and started back to his seat, she lingered. She still hadn't said what she'd come here for, and, although the prospect was even more daunting now, she had to try.

'Is there something else?'

Cole had paused beside his desk, and was looking at her with cold, wary eyes, and she shivered. Had she only imagined that morning on the beach? she wondered. She could see little of that man in this remote, unapproachable stranger. Did nothing ever touch him these days? Not even making love...?

Only it hadn't been love, she reminded herself painfully. It had been sex, pure and simple. She had aroused him, and he had responded. At best, they had used each other.

Now Joanna came forward again, until her hands were within reach of the leather-tooled surface of the desk. But she didn't touch it, even though she would have welcomed its support. Her damp fingers were linked tightly together—an indication, if he had needed it, of just how nervous she was.

'It's about your father,' she began, and, ignoring Cole's grim features, she hurried on, 'Can't you forgive him? Oh, I know I've said some harsh things about him in the past, and I know what he did was wrong, but you have to try and forget it. When—when the truth about Nathan came out, he must have panicked. Of course he was angry. Of course he blamed me for making friends with Nathan, and causing it to happen. Maybe he didn't realise how sensitive Nathan was. No one could have guessed what would happen. No one wanted Nathan to die. It was an accident—a horrible accident! It doesn't serve any purpose to crucify the past!'

Cole stared at her impassively, but there was scorn in his voice, as he exclaimed harshly, 'This was what he wanted, wasn't it? This was what he brought you here for? You were meant to plead his case for him. God, I should have guessed!'

Joanna expelled a breath she'd hardly known she was holding, and wondered if Ryan had really thought her appeal would do any good. Cole wouldn't listen to her. He didn't even like her. How could his father imagine that she would stand a chance?

'I'm right, aren't I?' Cole said now, and her silence was answer enough. 'Well, what a pity he left it too late! I guess Nemesis refused to be cheated.'

Joanna sighed. 'It's not too late,' she burst out desperately. 'Not for you, anyway. Make your peace with him, Cole. For your sake, if not for his. Do it, I beg you. If you don't, you're the one who'll regret it. He won't be around to care.'

The silence that greeted this last remark went unbroken. And, for the life of her, Joanna couldn't think of anything else to say. She'd done what she could. Now it was up to Cole. But, looking at his bleak face, she doubted it had been enough.

She slipped away then, and returned to her room to do her packing. She felt numb—not only because she knew she had lost the only thing that had any real value for her, but also because she had perjured herself for no reason. Cole wouldn't listen to her advice, and how could she blame him? It was difficult to be convincing, when you didn't believe what you were saying.

The next morning, Cole didn't appear at breakfast, and she guessed he was keeping out of the way until she had left. It was obviously easier for him that way, but was it really easier for her? Hadn't she secretly hoped to see him if only to say goodbye?

Maggie came out to the car, as Ben was loading her suitcases. She came round to where Joanna was standing, and, in spite of the fact that she had no reason to resent her any longer, Cole's mother couldn't resist having the final word.

'You're leaving,' she said, and there was a wealth of satisfaction in her words. 'Cole give you your marching orders, did he? I knew he would, sooner or later.'

Joanna swallowed. 'It wasn't like that. I—have to get back to London.'

'Really.' Obviously, Maggie didn't believe her. 'Seems like he can't wait to get shot of you.'

Joanna refused to be provoked. She knew it was what the other woman wanted, and she was determined not to give her that satisfaction as well.

'Well, you're wrong,' she declared pleasantly, wishing Maggie's bulk wasn't preventing her from opening the station-wagon door. 'It was my decision.'

'As it was your decision to try and break up this family, right?' Maggie demanded harshly, giving up all pretence of being civil. 'Cole hasn't forgiven you for that, so don't you forget it!'

Joanna gasped. 'I didn't try to break up your family!'

'Then what would you call it? Believing all those lies about Ryan and that woman! That boy could have been any man's bastard! How do you know he was Ryan's? He didn't even look like him!'

Joanna frowned. 'I didn't even know you'd seen Nathan,' she said, trying to remain calm, and Maggie's plump features reddened.

'Oh, I saw him all right,' she blurted defensively. 'I saw the two of you together lots of times. Down there on the river-bank. I told Cole what you were doing. I told him you couldn't wait to give another man what you were denying your lawful husband!'

Joanna gulped. 'You saw us!' She shook her head. 'Nathan and I were friends!' she protested weakly. 'Just friends!'

'And I bet you think I still believe in the tooth fairy,' Maggie sneered. 'There's no man here gonna believe you didn't let that misbegotten son of a bitch get between your legs, girl! Hell, you were quick enough to believe the worst about Cole's daddy!'

Joanna swayed. For a moment, she was sure she was going to pass out, and a cold sweat broke out on her forehead. Although the day was hot, she felt chilled to the core of her being. Oh, God, she felt so dizzy. She could feel all the blood draining out of her face.

'Hey—don't you go fainting on me, girl!'

Maggie grabbed her arm, and it was a measure of Joanna's weakness that she didn't try to shake her off. 'It's not true,' she whispered, gazing at Cole's mother with wide, accusing eyes. 'I didn't—I wouldn't—I never slept with Nathan. You have to believe me, I've never slept with any man but Cole.'

Maggie bundled her aside, and wrenched open the car door. 'Don't matter none now,' she declared, hustling her into the station wagon, and Joanna realised that Cole's mother didn't believe it herself. She had probably never believed it. But it was a way to poison Cole's mind against her, and she used it. As she would have used anything to destroy their marriage, and everything it represented . . .

CHAPTER FOURTEEN

WHICH was why she felt no will to get out of bed these mornings, Joanna reflected, glancing at the clock without interest. Since she got back to London, she had had no enthusiasm for anything, and her parents weren't the only ones who were anxious about her. Grace was worried, too, particularly as Joanna refused to talk about what had happened at Tidewater. For the first time since they had become friends, there was a barrier between them, and no amount of cajoling on Grace's part could break through the shell she'd erected.

It wasn't that she blamed the other woman for what had happened. Heavens, Grace had warned her about going there, even if she had felt some compassion for Cole's father. But Joanna simply didn't have the heart to tell her what had happened as she was leaving. That was simply too painful to confide to anyone.

And she felt such a fool, too. All these years, she had blamed Cole for using his brother as a scapegoat. She had thought Cole wanted a divorce, and that he had used her friendship with Nathan to achieve his own ends. She had never dreamt his mother might have been lying to him behind her back. No wonder he had reacted so violently, when he found Nathan at the clinic.

And the trouble was, if she permitted thoughts like that to germinate, it put in doubt the whole question of why their marriage had failed. Who knew how long Cole had been fed those lies? Their relationship had been in jeopardy ever since he got back from South America. Might he never have got involved with Sammy-Jean, if he hadn't thought she was having an affair?

It was thoughts like these that she had to keep at bay. And she couldn't do that if she spoke of them to Grace.

163

It had been hard enough remembering what Cole had said to his father the night Nathan died, and realising how easy it had been for her to misinterpret his actions afterwards. But, if she ever allowed Maggie's malicious words to mean anything to her, she might truly lose the will to live altogether.

The phone started to ring again, and Joanna pulled a pillow over her head to drown out the sound. But it didn't go away, not even when she reached out and snatched the receiver off its hook, and buried it beneath the bedcovers. The intrusive, persistent sound went on and on, and she realised it was the visitor's intercom from downstairs.

She contemplated not answering it, but Grace would know she was here. Her curtains were still drawn, for heaven's sake. She wished now she had got up earlier and drawn back the curtains, so that she could at least have pretended to be out. But, even so, Grace was unlikely to believe it. Not since she had refused to attend her own first exhibition.

Pushing herself up, she slid her legs over the side of the bed. But, as she padded wearily towards the door, a wave of nausea hit her. It was so unexpected that she hardly had the time to turn and dash for the bathroom, before she was suddenly and violently sick.

For a few moments, the insistent buzzing from downstairs was drowned out by the heavy thumping of her heart. She leaned over the basin, feeling her stomach churning, and trembling like a jelly. For God's sake, she thought weakly, whatever had she eaten? She couldn't believe the tin of soup she had had for supper the night before was responsible for her feeling so ill.

But, to her relief, the nausea subsided as quickly as it had appeared. By the time she had wiped her face on a towel, and examined her pale features in the mirror, she was feeling almost normal. And the buzzing had stopped, she noted gratefully. Oh, well, if it was Grace, undoubtedly she would come back.

Then, as she turned on the taps in the shower, a shattering thought occurred to her. It was exactly six weeks since she had left Tidewater. Six weeks, and she hadn't had a period in all that time!

Turning off the taps again, and with remarkable calmness, she padded back into the bedroom and pulled her diary out of the bedside drawer. She didn't keep a diary, except as a kind of calendar, and she riffled through the pages, looking for the dates in question.

A few moments later, she dropped the diary back into the drawer, and sank down weakly on to the side of the bed. She was right, she acknowledged, even though the written proof had been incidental. Her body clock was already telling her all she needed to know. She had actually missed her second period, and unless there was something radically wrong with her metabolism—which she doubted—there was every possibility that she was pregnant.

Her breath escaped on a wispy sigh. 'Pregnant!' She said it out loud, as if she needed to hear the word to believe it. She was going to have a baby. After all those barren months, when she had begun to believe she might never get pregnant, the impossible had happened. Cole's baby was already growing inside her.

Then she tried to be rational. She didn't know that for sure, she told herself firmly. Accidents happened. She might just be going through some biological upheaval. It was even possible that her emotional state might have something to do with it.

But, deep inside her, she didn't really believe that. As she ran a tentative hand over her still flat stomach, she felt a growing conviction that the baby was real. She wasn't inventing the way she felt; she hadn't imagined her sickness. That morning, on the beach at Tidewater, Cole had given her more than he could ever have imagined.

Cole...

She licked her dry lips. What was she going to do about Cole? Was she going to tell him, and run the risk of his mother trying to take the baby away from her? But how could she keep it from him? Oh, God! The child was his, too.

And then the doorbell rang. Her doorbell this time. Not the buzzer from downstairs. Evidently Grace had bluffed her way into the building. But how could she talk to her now, when she needed time to consider what she was going to do?

Of course, she didn't have to tell Grace, she acknowledged, getting up from the bed again, and opening the bedroom door. She crossed the hall into the living-room, as the doorbell rang once more, and she grimaced. It wasn't like Grace to be so impatient. She must be really worried this time.

But an innate caution, born of these years of living alone, stopped her from actually opening the door right away. It was always possible that someone else knew she lived alone, and she had no desire to become another statistic on London's list of crimes against women in their own homes.

'Grace?' she called, her hand on the deadlock, ready to release the latch.

'No. It's Cole,' declared a low attractive male voice that she had never expected to hear again. 'Come on, Jo. Open up! I was beginning to think Aunt Grace must be wrong, and you weren't home.'

Joanna slumped against the panels, her fingers falling nervelessly from the bolt. '*Cole*,' she breathed disbelievingly. Dear God, had she conjured him up out of the air? And what was he doing here in London? He couldn't know about the baby. She'd only just discovered that herself!

'Jo, come on.' His voice sounded a little terse now, as if he was afraid she wasn't going to answer, and he was using impatience to hide his uncertainty. 'I'm not going away until I talk to you.'

Joanna took a steadying breath and straightened her spine. 'What about?' she asked, her voice as thin and reedy as her stretched nerves, and, although it was barely audible, she heard the muffled oath he uttered.

'Let me in and I'll tell you,' he stated at last. 'Please, Jo. It's important. I haven't flown all this way just to shout at you through the keyhole.'

Joanna gave a helpless shrug, and looked down at her crumpled nightshirt. 'I—I'm not dressed,' she said, using the only excuse she could think of. But it was a valid one, she thought ruefully. She wouldn't want anyone to see her in this state, least of all *him*.

'God, Jo, I don't care if you're stark naked,' he grated, and she heard his fist thud against the door in frustration. 'This isn't a social visit. I need to talk to you. Now, can you cut the waffle, and open this damn door?'

Joanna's mouth went dry. 'I can't. I'm a mess——'

'I've told you, I don't care what you look like.'

'No, but——'

'*Jo!*'

His use of her name was desperate, and, realising it must be something pretty serious to bring him all this way, Joanna gave in. But she still didn't unlock the door.

'Look,' she called, 'give me a few minutes, will you? I—I'll put something on. Hold on.'

Cole said something else, something not very complimentary, she guessed, but she couldn't help it. He would have to wait until she had had a wash, and changed into something decent. Her pride wouldn't let her face him looking such a hag.

Ten minutes later, with her face washed and her teeth cleaned, and a deliberately chosen georgette tunic, in a becoming shade of apricot, giving warmth to her pale features, Joanna opened the door. Her hair was loose, a dusky fall of silk that swung against her cheek as she stepped back to let him in.

She thought, belatedly, that she should have worn something on her feet. In the ordinary way, Cole towered above her. When she was in her bare feet, he was a force to be reckoned with.

And her instinctive recoil when he stepped into the apartment was as much a reaction to the threat he represented as social politeness. She didn't want him there, not now, not while she was still trying to come to terms with her condition. God, she hadn't even decided what she was going to do about the baby. And she certainly wasn't ready to give him that advantage.

Even so, as he stepped forward and took hold of the door to close it behind his back, she had a moment to study his taut features. Her initial thought that he hadn't changed had to be slightly revised. He had changed. He looked older for one thing. And thinner, too, if she wasn't mistaken. Evidently his father's death—for surely Ryan was dead now, and that was why he was here—had hit him rather harder than he had imagined. She hoped he wasn't blaming himself for what had happened. She hoped he had made his peace with his father, however painful that had proved to be.

She took a nervous breath. It was strange seeing Cole in a suit, for once. It made him look more serious, more severe. The dark grey fabric threw the lightness of his hair into prominence, shadowing his cheekbones, and accentuating the thin line of his mouth. And it also served to make him look more remote, and more unapproachable. This was not the man who had made such desperate love to her on the beach. This was still the stranger who had faced her in his father's study.

But she hadn't looked into his eyes, and, when she did so, her interpretation had to be revised once again. There was an uneasy tension in his gaze, and raw desperation. No, not the unfeeling stranger, she thought unsteadily, but perhaps an approximation.

Nevertheless, his presence disturbed her. No matter how she tried to rationalise her feelings, just looking at him gave her a shivery feeling in the pit of her stomach. She hoped it wasn't physical. She hoped she wasn't going to throw up again while he was here. It would be too embarrassing if she had to go dashing into the bathroom.

And, while he'd never guess the real reason, he might get the wrong impression.

The silence was unnerving, and Joanna was too emotional to cope with it right now. 'I—how are you?' she said, realising how inane that sounded after everything that had gone before, but incapable of thinking of an alternative. 'I—I never expected——'

'Grace said you'd been ill,' he interrupted her abruptly, moving away from the door, so that Joanna felt obliged to back further into the room.

She swallowed. 'Ill?' she said faintly. Was that why he was here? Because Grace had sent for him? 'I—I'm fine, really. I don't know what—what gave her that opinion.'

Cole frowned. 'She said you're not working.'

'Oh, that!' Joanna managed to give a short laugh. 'No—well, I'm not. But I don't think that's any concern of yours.'

Cole's jaw tightened. 'Nevertheless, I am concerned——'

'Well, don't be.' Joanna didn't think she could stand this stilted conversation one minute longer. 'If Grace has taken it upon herself to contact you and blame you, because I'm being lazy, then I'm sorry. You've had a wasted journey. I—I'll work again, when I feel like it.'

'She says you didn't even attend your own exhibition.'

'So what?' Joanna was beginning to resent him and Grace for putting her in this position. It was bad enough feeling as if her life had lost all meaning. The last thing she needed was Cole coming here to offer her some guilty consolation.

'So—she's worried about you,' he said shortly, but she had the feeling that Grace's emotions weren't the whole reason he had come. 'God, Jo, do you have to make this so bloody hard? I really hoped you might be glad to see me.'

Joanna tensed. 'Is that what Grace said?'

'To hell with Grace!' retorted Cole savagely. 'Is that the only reason you can think of why I might be here?'

Comprehension dawned. With an effort, Joanna remembered what she had thought when he first came into the apartment. Of course. He must have come to tell Grace his father was dead. It was the kind of thing he would do. So much more civilised than putting it in a letter.

Now she shook her head. 'I'm sorry.'

Cole closed his eyes for a moment, and then opened them again. 'What are you sorry for now? Not my wasted journey again, I hope.'

'No.' Joanna gave a helpless gesture. 'A-about your father. I—I might not have liked him, but I didn't wish him——'

'Dead?' Cole cut in harshly, and she nodded. 'Well, I'm afraid your condolences are just a tad premature.'

Joanna stared at him. 'You mean——?'

'I mean my father is still very much alive.' Cole loosened the button of his collar and dragged his tie a couple of inches away from his neck, as if he was feeling the heat. 'He's even recovered his powers of speech, although he isn't always intelligible. It rattles him like hell, but he makes himself understood, one way or the other.'

Joanna was astounded. 'Grace never told me.'

'Grace didn't know.' Cole paused. 'Not until an hour ago, anyway. I gather you didn't tell her about his stroke.'

'No.' Joanna was beginning to feel uneasy, and she glanced behind her, as if she was getting bored with the conversation. 'I—I haven't talked to Grace much since I got back. I—I—I've been...'

'Too busy?' suggested Cole sardonically, and Joanna felt the warm colour invade her throat.

'Not—exactly,' she said, holding up her head. 'I—do have a life outside of painting.'

'Do you?'

Cole's tone was vaguely accusing, and Joanna wondered what he had expected her to say. For heaven's sake, he knew, better than anyone, how she had felt when she left Tidewater. It wasn't as if he hadn't known she was leaving. Didn't he remember his chilling rebuttal?

Taking a deep breath, she decided this one-sided attack had gone on long enough. 'Why have you come here, Cole?' she asked. 'I'm sure it wasn't to inform me that your father is back at Tidewater——'

'He's not.' Cole broke into her words with a swift denial.

Joanna frowned. 'He's not what?'

'Back at Tidewater.' He paused. 'I said he wasn't dead. I didn't say he was back home.'

'Does it matter?' Joanna felt totally indifferent to his statement. 'As I say, I don't believe your father's—partial recovery was why you came to see me.'

'It wasn't.' Cole took a step forward, and Joanna felt uneasy again. She wasn't ready for this, she thought unsteadily, wishing Grace had warned her that he was coming. But perhaps she had. She remembered those unanswered phone calls with a bitter sense of regret. 'I came because I thought we needed to talk.'

'What about?'

'How about—us?' ventured Cole, with cool audacity. 'Like maybe we're not finished yet. Despite all the signs to the contrary.'

Joanna's arms flailed. 'Grace did send you here, didn't she?' she exclaimed. 'Oh, I wish she'd——'

'Grace didn't even know I was coming to London,' Cole retorted, grasping a protesting arm, and refusing to let go. 'Listen to me, Jo, I'm the last person Aunt Grace would choose to get in touch with. If she's worried about you—and she is—she wouldn't send for the man who she believes is to blame for it all!'

Joanna stared at him indignantly, but his words did have some merit. Grace might love Cole as a nephew, but she had always been wary of him as Joanna's husband. And, knowing what had happened in the past, she was hardly likely to appeal to him now.

His hard fingers were beginning to bite into the soft flesh of her upper arm, and, as if becoming aware of it,

Cole uttered an oath and released her. But he didn't move away. He stayed where he was. And she was still overwhelmingly aware of him, and the threat he represented.

'Look,' he said, and when he spoke again the husky timbre of his voice scraped insistently across her nerves. 'I didn't come here to argue with you. God knows, we've done enough of that in the past.'

'I suppose that's my fault!'

Joanna's response was swift and indignant, but it was as much a protest against the unwilling awareness he was arousing as a defensive ploy. It was hard to remain detached, when his warm breath was wafting over her forehead, and the male scent of his sweat was filling her nose.

'No,' Cole retorted now. 'It's mine.' And she was still trying to absorb this when he added, with bitter self-recrimination, 'I shouldn't have believed my mother's lies, but, when you're in love with someone, you're vulnerable!'

Joanna's knees went weak. 'I—beg your pardon?' she whispered, groping behind her for the back of a chair, anything that could give her some support. And Cole moved a little nearer.

'I said, I was—I still am—in love with you. Why did you think my father and I were estranged? He knew damn well there was only ever going to be one woman in my life. And he'd driven you away. He and my mother between them.' His blue eyes darkened with emotion, as he added, 'That's why I'm here, Jo. That's the only reason. I knew I had to try and make you believe it.'

Joanna had never fainted in her life, but for once she felt near to it. Cole's face was wavering before her eyes, and she was fairly sure she must have imagined what she thought he just said. Was this what losing consciousness felt like? she wondered, unaware of just how pale she'd become.

'I—don't feel very well,' she said, feeling foolish, and Cole's ejaculation was harsh and self-derisive.

'Goddammit,' he muttered, abandoning any lingering shred of self-control, and swinging her up into his arms. 'I always was a tactless bastard..I'm sorry. I'd forgotten Grace told me you were sick.'

'I'm not sick,' argued Joanna faintly, as Cole carried her across to her settee, and deposited her on it. 'Really, I'm not. I—guess it's just the heat.'

'Or what I said,' said Cole grimly, dropping his jacket on to a chair, and perching on the edge of the sofa beside her. He tugged off his tie, and sent it curling on to the floor. 'I didn't intend to blurt it out like that, but, hell, I had to get your attention!'

Joanna felt better now that she was off her shaky legs, but the hard strength of the thigh beside her hip was still daunting. And now that he was without his jacket she could see the shadow of brown skin beneath his cream silk shirt, and glimpse the sun-bleached hair that arrowed down his chest.

'It doesn't matter,' she said, wishing she dared ask him to repeat what he had blurted out. 'Um—do you think I could have a drink of water?' she added, desperate to find some way of getting a little breathing space. 'I haven't had anything to eat this morning, and I am feeling a bit empty.'

'You haven't had breakfast?' Cole got to his feet and towered over her, and now her eyes were irresistibly drawn to the narrow cut of his trousers. Was it her imagination, or were they tighter than they should have been across his hips? Dear God, she thought unsteadily, she was rapidly losing control.

Shaking her head in answer to his question, she was unutterably relieved when he strode away into the kitchen. In the few moments it would take him to find a glass, and run the tap, she had to calm herself. And there was no way she could do that if she thought about what he'd said.

The sense of unreality had passed by the time Cole came back, carrying a tray. But it must have taken longer than she'd thought, she reflected ruefully, for he'd taken the time to filter some coffee and make some toast. Of course, he knew his way around her kitchen, she conceded. He had lived here for several weeks before their wedding. Oh, those blissful days, she remembered wistfully. Before the coils of Tidewater had strangled their relationship.

Cole hooked a low coffee-table with his foot, and set the tray down beside the sofa. Then, to her consternation, he resumed his earlier position beside her.

'Coffee, and toast,' he said unnecessarily, his eyes disturbingly warm and intent. 'Can you sit up?'

'I'm not an invalid,' said Joanna, her voice sharper than it might have been because she was nervous, and Cole inclined his head.

'If you say so,' he allowed, respecting her obvious wish to be independent. He let her shuffle into a sitting position, and then reached for the jug of coffee. 'Cream, but no sugar. You see, I remembered that, too.'

Joanna wanted to say something flip and casual, anything to dispel the unwilling intimacy of their situation, but the smell of the coffee was turning her stomach.

'I—think I'd prefer a glass of water, after all,' she declared, struggling to contain her nausea. 'I—excuse me, for a moment. I have to go to the bathroom.'

When she came back, the tray had disappeared, and Cole was standing by the window, staring out on to the sun-baked grass in the park across the way. His hands were in his pockets, but there was tension in every muscle of his taut frame. But he had evidently heard her behind him, because he glanced over his shoulder as she hovered in the doorway, and his mouth flattened ruefully, as he said, 'I guess you want me to go.'

Joanna, who had just spent the last few minutes learning how appalling it was trying to be sick on an empty stomach, hesitated long enough for him to assume she did. With a tightening of his lips, Cole bent to lift his jacket from the chair where he had dropped it earlier, but when he turned towards the door desperation made her reckless.

'I—what you said,' she stammered, hoping she might bluff him into some kind of confession, 'did you—did you mean it?'

Cole's brows drew together. 'I've said a lot of things,' he replied wearily. 'And I'm not proud of a lot of them.'

'No.' Joanna sighed, realising she was not going to get round it that way. 'Just now. When I asked you why you'd come here. You said—at least, I thought you said—you still—loved me——'

'I do.'

There was no mistake this time, and Joanna clutched the frame of the door with sweating hands. But Cole wasn't rushing towards her with declarations of his intent. He was simply standing looking at her, with a definite air of defeat.

Wetting her dry lips, she tried again. 'But—when I came to see you, the night before I left Tidewater——'

'I was a bastard, I know.' Cole lifted his shoulders in a heavy gesture. 'I guess I was still despising myself for wanting you. And when you said you were leaving, I tried to hurt you as you were hurting me.'

Joanna caught her breath. 'You succeeded.'

'Yes, I know.'

'Then why——?'

'Why did I change my mind?' Cole's lips twisted. 'I'd like to say it was only because I'd begun to suspect that there had been nothing going on between you and Nathan.'

Joanna stared at him. 'There wasn't!'

'No. Well, as I say, I had begun to have my doubts. God, I even had doubts before you walked out on our marriage. But you didn't want to listen to them then. You were too busy hating me for what happened to Nathan.'

Joanna bent her head. 'We all make mistakes. And I didn't hate you. I—just thought I did.'

'Yeah, well—you were pretty damn convincing.' Cole's shoulders hunched. 'And, goddammit, I should have had faith in you. But when you left, I guess I convinced myself that you must be guilty.'

Joanna swallowed. 'So what did change your mind?'

'Ben.'

'Ben?'

'Yes. He heard what Ma said to you as you were leaving. How she'd seen you with Nathan, and spread those lies about you.'

Joanna stiffened. 'She never said they were lies,' she stated honestly. 'As far as I know, she believed that Nathan and I—that we were——' She broke off unsteadily. 'If Ben told you she admitted making the whole thing up, he wasn't telling the truth either.'

She waited then for Cole's expression to change. She hadn't really believed that their problems could be solved so easily, and learning what had brought him here only reinforced that fact. It had been kind of Ben to tell him, kind of him to lie, if that's what he had done. It proved she had at least one friend at Tidewater. At least one member of Cole's family wanted to make amends.

But Cole's expression didn't change, except perhaps to grow a little gentler. 'I know exactly what she said,' he told her. 'Ben gave me it, word for word. But what you don't know is that I never knew until then who it was feeding me that information. Ma didn't talk to me, Jo. She sent me letters, anonymous letters. They started right after I got back from South America. So far as I knew, Ma didn't even know of Nathan's existence.'

Joanna's jaw sagged. 'But how do you know your mother was sending those letters?'

Cole's face hardened. 'I confronted her with it after you'd left, and she had the nerve to tell me she'd done it for my own good.'

'For your own good?'

'Yes. It turns out Ma knew all about my father's involvement with Sarah, and about Nathan, too. But there was nothing she could do about it, not without incurring my father's wrath, so she kept it all bottled up inside her. Then, when you and Nathan got to know one another, she saw a chance to—to——'

'Kill two birds with one stone,' said Joanna shakily. 'Oh, God, Cole! How could she? What had Nathan ever done to her?'

'He existed,' said Cole simply. 'I didn't realise how badly it had affected her until six weeks ago.'

Joanna felt dazed. 'It's unbelievable.'

'I know.'

'Poor Nathan.'

'Yes, poor Nathan.' Cole's mouth tightened. 'Can you ever forgive me?'

'Forgive you?' Joanna realised she was repeating his words, but she couldn't help it.

'Yes, forgive me,' said Cole harshly. 'If I hadn't been so quick to believe the worst of you, none of this need have happened.'

Joanna hesitated. 'And—and Sammy-Jean?'

'What about Sammy-Jean?'

'You—you married her.'

'Yes, I married her.' Cole's shoulders slumped. 'And I know that condemns me in your eyes, doesn't it? But, when you walked out, three years ago, I didn't care what I did any more. It was what Ma wanted,' he added bitterly. 'And, after what Pa had put her through, I thought she deserved a break.'

Joanna trembled. 'Did you love her?'

'If I'd loved Sammy-Jean, I'd have married her five years ago, instead of you,' he replied quietly.

'Oh, Cole!' Joanna moved her head in a helpless gesture, wishing he would put down his jacket and do something, instead of just standing there, staring at her. 'So—what are you saying?'

'I'd have thought that was obvious,' replied Cole flatly, and there was a look of weary acceptance in his eyes. 'I wanted us to be together again. But—I guess I waited too long to tell you.'

CHAPTER FIFTEEN

COLE was turning away, threading his finger through the tab of his jacket, ready to loop it over his shoulder, when Joanna came to her senses. Abandoning the unnatural detachment with which she had listened to his explanations, she flew across the room, and flung herself into his arms. 'What took you so long?' she choked, burying her hot face against his chest. 'Oh, God, Cole, I've missed you so much!'

His reactions were less dramatic than hers, but far more violent. With a groan of anguish, his arms closed about her, and she felt his muscles trembling as he hugged her tight against him.

'I wanted to come after you right away,' he told her unsteadily, his lips against her ear. 'But there were things to do, things I had to see to. I wanted you to know what I was offering, before you made up your mind.'

Joanna wound her arms about his neck. 'Nothing's more important than our being together,' she whispered unsteadily. 'And—and as long as you love me, that's all that matters.'

'No.' Joanna looked a little anxious at his denial, but Cole pushed his fingers into the silky length of her hair, and held her face up to his. 'No, that's not all that matters,' he told her huskily. 'I thought it was once. I thought where we lived wasn't important. I was so selfish—so *jealous* of your work—I wanted to absorb you into my life so completely, you wouldn't have time for anything else.'

'Cole——'

'No, listen to me,' he implored her. 'I was wrong. I was wrong to expect you to live with my family, and I was wrong to try and stop you from continuing with your career.' His thumb brushed an errant tear from her cheek. 'That won't happen again.'

'Oh, Cole——'

'There's more.' He couldn't resist brushing her soft mouth with his, but when she would have deepened the kiss he drew back. 'If you don't want to go back to Tidewater, we needn't. I'll sell the place if you want, and move to England. It's up to you——'

Joanna gasped. 'You'd *sell* Tidewater? But what about your father and mother?'

'Since Pa had his stroke, I've been given his power of attorney. Besides, Pa will never go back to Tidewater, he knows that. He's been moved to a nursing facility in Charleston, where they can monitor his condition on a day-to-day basis. And Ma? Well, she and Sandy and the twins are staying with Joe and Alicia for the time being. She knew she and I couldn't go on living in the same house, and I guess, eventually, she'll get a place in Beaumaris.'

Joanna stared at him. 'So there's no one living at the house?'

'Only Ben.' Cole grimaced. 'And the staff, of course. Not forgetting Henry.'

'And—that's why you waited this long before you came to see me?'

'Yes.' Cole looked rueful. 'I wanted there to be no more misunderstandings. If—if you agree to marry me again, it'll be on your terms, not mine. I'm not much good at relationships. I always screw up.'

Joanna's lips quivered. 'I wouldn't say that.'

'I would.' Cole drew her even closer, and she revelled in the solid feel of his hard body. 'I've had plenty of time to think, and I don't care about anything so long as we're together. You're all that matters to me. You always were; you always will be.'

Some time later, Cole stepped into the shower cubicle beside her, and Joanna gulped as his damp hands curved possessively about her thighs. Drawing her back against his hips, he took over the task of soaping her breasts and stomach, and Joanna shivered uncontrollably.

They had just spent the last couple of hours renewing their marriage vows in the most satisfying way possible, and it was amazing to feel the stirring heaviness of his arousal against her bottom. 'You're insatiable, do you know that?' she whispered unevenly, as his hands slid down between her legs, and Cole chuckled as he turned her towards him.

'Only where you're concerned,' he assured her huskily. 'Does it bother you?'

'Should it?'

'Only if you're thinking of leaving me again.'

Joanna's smile was gratifying. 'I'm not.'

'Honestly?'

She wound her arms around his neck, and lifted one leg to coil it about him. 'What do you think?'

Cole groaned. 'I think if we don't get out of here pretty soon, I'm going to explode,' he muttered thickly. 'God, Jo, you have no idea what you do to me.'

'I have a pretty good idea,' she giggled softly, as he stepped out of the shower with her in his arms, and grabbed a towel on his way back to the bedroom. 'Hey, you forgot to turn off the taps.'

'To hell with the taps,' retorted Cole tersely, and her laughter died beneath the hungry possession of his mouth.

It was hunger of a different kind that eventually drove Joanna to wriggle away from Cole's sleeping form, and slip her arms into the sleeves of her silk wrapper. For the first time since she got back to England, she felt really hungry, and she was munching her way through a dish of cornflakes when Cole appeared in the kitchen doorway. Unlike her, he didn't have a dressing-gown to wear, and his suit trousers had evidently been pulled on in some haste.

'What's going on?' he asked, eyeing the milky cereal. 'Isn't it a little late for breakfast? I was going to suggest taking you out for lunch.'

'Mmm, that sounds interesting.' Joanna nodded, swallowing another mouthful of the cornflakes. 'When I've finished this I'll get ready.'

'When you've finished that, you won't be hungry,' retorted Cole drily, running an exploring hand over the cloud of fine hair that roughened the brown skin of his chest. 'Don't you have anything else we could eat?'

'Not really.' Joanna was rueful. 'I—I haven't felt much like eating since I got back.'

Cole's eyes darkened at her words, and his mouth took on a decidedly sensual slant. 'I'm sorry, baby,' he said, and it took all Joanna's determination to stop her from getting up and going to him.

'Yes—well, we should talk,' she said, pushing the almost empty dish aside, and Cole frowned.

'I thought we had.'

'Oh—well, yes. We have, of course.' Joanna licked a drop of milk from her lips in unknowing provocation. 'But—there's something else——'

'If it's about Sammy-Jean——'

'It's not.'

'You have to understand, I was sick with jealousy——'

'Cole, it's nothing to do with Sammy-Jean.'

'Charley, then.' Cole moved agitatedly about the kitchen. 'I know what you're going to say, but she's too young to make that kind of a commitment.'

Joanna looked puzzled now. 'What kind of a commitment?'

'With Billy Fenton. You do know about her and Billy Fenton, don't you? She said you did.'

'Oh——' Joanna knew a moment's remorse. 'She told you.'

'No, Ma did,' said Cole flatly. 'And, I have to say, I was probably more inclined to take Charley's side, because of what happened to us.'

'And?' Joanna was nervously aware that she was prolonging the moment when she would have to tell Cole her suspicions about the baby.

'And I've agreed to let her go on seeing him, but she has to go to college. I don't want her doing anything she's going to regret later.'

Joanna looked up at him. 'As you did?'

'Yes. As I did,' said Cole roughly. 'God, Joanna, what is it? What's wrong? There's something, I know——' He broke off. 'I've told you—I'll do anything you say.'

'It's not that.' Joanna hesitated only a moment, and then she got to her feet. 'I don't mind if we live at Tidewater.'

'Are you sure?'

'Yes. I'm sure.' Joanna linked her hands together. 'In fact, I think it's only right that our—our children should be brought up there. It's their heritage. It's where they belong.'

Cole's face cleared. 'Children,' he said wryly. 'You're sure we'll have children, then?'

Joanna nodded. 'I'm sure.'

'Well...' Cole came across the room and pulled her into his arms '...just for the record, whether we do or we don't, I'd like to say, here and now, you'll always be the most important thing in my life. And——' he took a breath '—if you don't want a family, I can live with it.'

Joanna sniffed. 'You still think I was using some kind of contraception, don't you?'

'No.' Cole shook his head. 'Not any more. Not after everything that's happened. But—maybe we weren't meant to have any children. God, we've got so much! Why should we be greedy and want more?'

Joanna sniffed again. 'But if—if we did have a baby, you wouldn't object?'

'Object?' Cole pulled a long face. 'Why would I object? All I'm saying is, so long as I have you——'

'I think I'm pregnant!'

The words just flipped from Joanna's tongue, but she couldn't stand the suspense any longer, and she watched Cole's face change from gentle reassurance to stunned incredulity.

'Say—what?' he got out jerkily, and Joanna cupped his face between her hands, and ran the pads of her thumbs over his roughening jawline.

'I think I'm pregnant,' she said again, trembling in spite of herself. 'I know it's sudden, but that—that's why I was so ill earlier. It's just the usual morning sickness. I'm pretty sure I'm right.'

Cole's stunned expression was giving way to anxious concern now. 'Have—have you seen a doctor?' he asked, his lips turning against her palm, and she shook her head.

'I just—realised myself, this morning,' she admitted unevenly. 'About five minutes before you rang the bell, to be exact.'

Cole stared at her. 'And you let me——' He broke off, his lean face reddening. 'God, Jo, you should have told me.'

'Would that have stopped you?' she teased, reaching up to brush his mouth with her tongue.

'I—maybe,' he muttered, still not capable of coping with the situation. 'Oh, Jo——'

'You're pleased?'

'I'm pleased.' Cole shook his head. 'It must have been——'

'That morning on the beach,' agreed Joanna huskily. 'I'm so glad I made you do it.'

'Made me?' Cole groaned. 'I don't know how I kept my hands off you as long as I did. From the minute I walked across that patio in Nassau, I knew I was lost.'

'Did you?' Joanna was eager for more. 'Tell me.'

'Well...' Cole parted his legs, so that he could hold her more closely against him. 'I didn't want to admit it, but you must have known.'

'No.' Joanna shook her head now.

'Not even that night, in the back of the taxi?' suggested Cole drily. 'Come on, Jo, you knew what happened there. Why'd you think I was so bloody to you afterwards?'

Joanna dimpled. 'I thought that was your usual way— with me.'

Cole laughed too now, softly, and somewhat disbelievingly. 'Oh, Jo, do you have any idea how much I
love you?'

'About as much as I love you, I suppose,' she whispered, but he wouldn't have it.

'At least twice as much as that,' he assured her,
burying his hot face in her neck. 'And to think my
mother almost destroyed us. I'll never forgive her for
that.'

Joanna hugged him close. 'I must admit, I blamed
your father,' she said. 'But, as it happens, he was responsible for bringing us together again, wasn't he?'

'I doubt if that was his intention,' said Cole ruefully.
'Though, who knows? After he realised Sammy-Jean and
I weren't going to make it, he had to abandon his ideas
of expanding Tidewater.'

Joanna drew back to look at him. 'I'm so glad you
and Sammy-Jean didn't have a baby,' she whispered, and
Cole sighed.

'Believe it or not, but I didn't sleep with Sammy-Jean
until after you left Tidewater. And then—well, I guess
you could say it was a kind of defence. When you sued
for divorce——'

Joanna spread her fingers over his lips. 'It doesn't
matter.' She managed a misty smile. 'But you are
pleased—about the baby, I mean?'

'As long as you are,' he told her gently. 'I meant it
about your work. I promise not to stand in your way.'

'Hey——' Joanna allowed a husky chuckle to escape
her. 'I'm no great artist, you know. I enjoy sketching
and painting. It gives me pleasure. And it's a great way
to earn a living. But it's not the most important thing
in my life. It never was.'

'Nevertheless——'

'Nevertheless, nothing. The way I feel right now, I
don't care if I never see another paintbrush. I'm going
to have a baby; *your* baby. Here. Touch me! I want us
to share every minute of this miracle!'

It was another hot day at Tidewater, but Joanna was used to the heat by now. It was two years since she and Cole had got married for the second time, and she no longer wilted every time the temperature climbed into the nineties and above. Besides, she was too busy to notice what was going on with the weather. She was expecting visitors—Grace and Ray Marsden were coming to spend a few days of their belated honeymoon at Tidewater—and with an eighteen-month-old toddler underfoot, and another baby on the way, she had far too much to think about.

But she was looking forward to seeing Grace again. Although her parents had come out for a visit the year before, and she was at last on speaking terms with her mother-in-law, it would be nice to see her old friend and colleague.

She guessed Grace would be agitating about the new series of paintings she was engaged on, but her work was no longer the pivotal part of her life it had once been. Cole, and baby Nathan, had first call on her affections, and she had never felt so fulfilled in her life.

Of course, it hadn't been so easy at first. In those early days, it had been hard to come back to Tidewater as its mistress, and even harder to face those members of Cole's family who had done so much to make their lives intolerable.

But time was an amazing healer, and, although she and his father had never actually become friends, they had achieved a grudging understanding before Ryan died.

Cole's mother had been a different story. Maggie had taken a long time to accept that Joanna was back at Tidewater to stay. But the baby had gone a long way towards effecting a change in her attitude—even if Joanna's and Cole's insistence in calling him Nathan had caused a minor upheaval.

But that was all some time ago now, and, although Joanna knew Maggie had no conscience about what she had done, when it came to choosing between losing a son or gaining a daughter-in-law—even one she didn't like—it was no contest.

It had been a great thrill for Sarah, too, when they named the baby after her son. It hadn't taken Joanna long to realise that, far from not wanting to see Joanna again, Sarah was desperate to talk to someone who had been on such close terms with her son. Of course, Cole had done what he could to make her life easier, and Joanna hadn't been at all surprised to learn that her husband had helped Sarah open her guest house. He had been one of her first visitors, in the weeks before his mother had left Tidewater for good.

For the rest, the twins had never really been involved in their parents' affairs, and Sandy had been too young to understand. Even Joe's wife, Alicia, had unbent sufficiently to offer advice about feeding the baby, and so on. Because her baby had been born a few months before Joanna's, she tended to patronise her younger sister-in-law.

And Joanna let her. It wasn't important, after all. So long as she had Cole, she was content. And making him happy was all she had ever wanted after all.

Cole came in at that moment, and found his wife arranging flowers in the guest bedroom. Her face was flushed, damp strands of night-dark hair were clinging to her cheek, and already the evidence of her five months of pregnancy were beginning to show.

'Hey,' he said, putting his arms around her from behind, and pulling her back against him, 'don't you go overdoing it now. This isn't the first time Grace has visited Tidewater, you know. Remember, she used to live on the plantation.'

'I know.' Joanna had renewed her acquaintance with Grace's ex-husband and her two sons soon after she returned to Tidewater. 'But I want everything to look nice. I wasn't here the last time she came.'

'Well, I want you to take it easy,' declared Cole, turning her round to face him. 'You should be doing nothing more strenuous than sitting at your easel.' His hand caressed the gentle mound of her stomach. 'We don't want Nathan's brother or sister to get upset, do we?'

'Nathan's brother or sister is doing just fine, thank you,' retorted Joanna, covering his hands with her own. 'So—what are you doing back at this time of day? I thought you and Ben were going to Charleston.'

'We did. And—we got the pony for Nathan, just as we promised. Do you want to come and see it? Or haven't you got time?'

Joanna smiled. 'I've always got time for you, darlin',' she teased, and when Cole leant forward to brush her mouth with his lips she deliberately deepened the kiss. 'But—have you got time for me?' she whispered, her fingers moving down to his belt. 'Nathan's taking his nap. So I've got all the time in the world.'

Cole groaned, deep in his throat. 'Jo, how did I survive three whole years without you?'

'I don't know,' she responded huskily. 'But as you've mentioned it, we do have a lot of time to make up...'

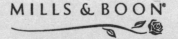

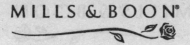

MILLS & BOON®

Next Month's Romances

♡

Each month you can choose from a wide variety of romance with Mills & Boon. Below are the new titles to look out for next month in our two new series Presents and Enchanted.

Presents™

WOMAN TO WED?	Penny Jordan
MISTRESS MATERIAL	Sharon Kendrick
FINN'S TWINS!	Anne McAllister
AFTER HOURS	Sandra Field
MR LOVERMAN	Mary Lyons
SEDUCED	Amanda Browning
THE FATHER OF HER CHILD	Emma Darcy
A GUILTY AFFAIR	Diana Hamilton

Enchanted™

A KISS FOR JULIE	Betty Neels
AN INNOCENT CHARADE	Patricia Wilson
THE RIGHT HUSBAND	Kay Gregory
THE COWBOY WANTS A WIFE!	Susan Fox
PART-TIME WIFE	Jessica Hart
BRIDES FOR BROTHERS	Debbie Macomber
GETTING OVER HARRY	Renee Roszel
THREE LITTLE MIRACLES	Rebecca Winters

Available from WH Smith, John Menzies, Volume One, Forbuoys, Martins, Woolworths, Tesco, Asda, Safeway and other paperback stockists.

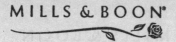

MILLS & BOON®

Medical Romance™

Books for enjoyment this month...

CRISIS FOR CASSANDRA	Abigail Gordon
PRESCRIPTION—ONE HUSBAND	Marion Lennox
WORTH WAITING FOR	Josie Metcalfe
DR RYDER AND SON	Gill Sanderson

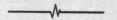

Treats in store!

Watch next month for these absorbing stories...

TRUSTING DR SCOTT	Mary Hawkins
PRESCRIPTION—ONE BRIDE	Marion Lennox
TAKING RISKS	Sharon Kendrick
PERFECT PRESCRIPTION	Carol Wood

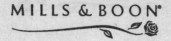

MILLS & BOON®

Mistaken identity brought them together…

MATCHED *by* MISTAKE

This August it's a case of mistaken identity!

We know you'll love these two By Request stories about two couples who fall for each other without knowing exactly who the other is!

And with two talented authors—Penny Jordan and Sally Wentworth—you're guaranteed a compelling read.

Bestselling romances brought back to you by popular demand

Available: September 1996   Price: £4.50

Historical Romance™

Coming next month

EMMA AND THE EARL
Paula Marshall
REGENCY ENGLAND

Miss Emma Lawrence was badly in need of a new job, and
had no choice about accepting the post of governess to
Lady Letitia Hastings, young daughter of Dominic
Hastings, the Earl of Chard. What unkind twist of fate had
brought her to this, working for the man she might have
married when she was the rich Miss Emilia Lincoln?
And—more worrying—would he recognise her? In ten
years they had both changed out of all recognition—but
what had not changed was Emma's abiding love for
Dominic…

SEAFIRE
Sarah Westleigh
REGENCY 1814/15

Having finished school, Miss Miranda Dawson was on her
way to Barbados to join her family. But the uncomfortable
relations between America and England landed her in
trouble when the American ship Seafire attacked. Taken
prisoner of war by the Captain, Adam York, Miranda was
determined not to be cowed, and her defiant attitude
earned the admiration of Adam. But with their two
countries virtually at war, what future did they have?

This month's
irresistible novels from

THE LADY IN THE MIRROR by Judith Arnold

Bachelor Arms

Ex-cop Clint McCreary had come to L.A. from New York for just one reason: to find his runaway teenage sister. Not to have his heart held hostage by Jessie Gale, a lovely luscious blonde who managed a shelter for runaways…

LOOK INTO MY EYES by Glenda Sanders

Secret Fantasies

After the death of her fiancé, Holly Bennett thinks her dreams are shattered, but then she meets mysterious Craig Ford. They share an overwhelming attraction, only Craig can't promise Holly anything, because he has no memories of his previous life. Will his past put an end to their future?

THE LAWMAN by Vicki Lewis Thompson

Urban Cowboys

From the moment sexy Leigh Singleton met cynical cop Joe Gilardini, she knew he was the man for her. His son, Kyle, was an added bonus. But could she help Joe come to terms with his troubled past? And could she convince him she wasn't the criminal he was seeking?

CAUSE FOR CELEBRATION by Gina Wilkins

Overwhelmed by work, Merry James was in no mood for a party. But since theme parties were her livelihood, she was determined to look on the bright side. After the appearance of sexy Grant Bryant, the man she assumed was her temporary secretary, things were certainly looking up. Was a steamy office romance on the cards?

Spoil yourself next month
with these four novels from

TIMELESS LOVE by Judith Arnold
Bachelor Arms

Why did Hope Henley flee in terror from Apartment 1-G—straight into the path of Morgan Delacourt's car? Surviving that experience was one thing…accepting Morgan's generous offer of convalescence at his home was quite another. Suddenly, Hope found herself believing in all sorts of crazy notions…like destined, timeless love with sexy Morgan…

CHARLIE ALL NIGHT by Jennifer Crusie

Dumped by her boyfriend and dropped from prime time, radio producer Allie McGuffey had nowhere to go but up. So she planned to make temporary DJ Charlie Tenniel a household name. But that was the last thing on Charlie's mind. He shunned fame. He just wanted to relax, play good records and make love to Allie—despite her objections!

PRIVATE PASSIONS by JoAnn Ross
Secret Fantasies

By day, Desiree Dupree is an investigative reporter. But at night, she pens sexy, intimate love stories. Lately, mysterious Roman Falconer has been playing a starring role in her fantasies—*and* she's investigating him. Something scary is going on in New Orleans and Roman's novels seem to contain the answers…

A BURNING TOUCH by Patricia Ryan

The nights in Mansfield are hot—an arsonist is terrorizing the town. But that's nothing compared to the heat Detective Jamie Keegan experiences after one look into the lovely eyes of India Cook. She's offered her services as a psychic to the police department, but cynical Jamie doesn't believe a word. What can she do to convince him of her special talents?